ADVENTURES IN GOOD BOOKS

(FOR GRADES 7–12)

- ♦ *Four Famous Adventures*
- *Five American Adventures*
- *Four Adventures in Courage*
- *Four Novels for Adventure*
- *Four Novels for Appreciation*
- *Five World Biographies*
- *Adventures in Fiction*
- *Adventures in Poetry*
- *Four American Novels*
- *Four American Biographies*
- *Four English Novels*
- *Four English Biographies*
- *Five World Plays*
- *Three World Classics*
- *The Idea of Man*

TEACHER'S MANUAL FOR EACH VOLUME

FOUR FAMOUS ADVENTURES

FRANK G. JENNINGS

ERIC W. JOHNSON

EDMUND FULLER, *General Editor*

HARCOURT BRACE JOVANOVICH, INC.

New York Chicago San Francisco Atlanta Dallas

FRANK G. JENNINGS has taught in elementary schools, high schools, and colleges and is now Assistant to the President of the New School. The author of many articles on reading and education, Mr. Jennings is an Editor-at-Large of the *Saturday Review*.

ERIC W. JOHNSON is Vice-Principal of Germantown Friends School, Philadelphia, Pennsylvania. Mr. Johnson is the author of *Improve Your Own Spelling* and *How to Live through Junior High School.*

EDMUND FULLER is a member of the English Department at Kent School, Kent, Connecticut, and has taught at Columbia University. He is also a critic and author of several books, among them *Man in Modern Fiction, A Star Pointed North, Brothers Divided,* and *George Bernard Shaw: Critic of Western Morale.*

Printed in the United States of America

ISBN 0-15-344555-6

Contents

Prefaces and Afterwords by Frank G. Jennings

Study Questions by Eric W. Johnson

FOUR FAMOUS ADVENTURES

The White Company

by A. Conan Doyle

MOST people think of Sir Arthur Conan Doyle as the wonderful creator of the *Adventures of Sherlock Holmes*. These stories are so famous that many people throughout the world belong to a society called the *Baker Street Irregulars*. They meet and read to each other from the Sherlock Holmes stories. They collect anything and everything that is written about the greatest detective of fiction. In fact they often act as if this character were more real than the man who created him.

But, as you will see in *The White Company,* Sir Arthur Conan Doyle could write other kinds of adventure as well. The story takes place in Europe during the Hundred Years' War. This is the time when the awful plague called the *Black Death* had killed every third person in England and even more in Europe. It was a terrible time and yet it was a wonderful time too. The English language was becoming what it is today. People were rediscovering the ancient wisdom of Rome and Greece. They were building the great castles and the greater cathedrals. The Crusades were long over, but they had taught the people of Europe that the world was larger than their little towns and that there were things worth having and doing that they had never dreamed of. All of this was changing the way of life for Englishmen and Frenchmen as well as other Europeans.

There were many companies like the White Company. They got their start in the fourteenth century when Edward III ordered the common people of England to practice using the longbow and to teach their sons to use it properly. The King even made it a crime to "play handball, football, or hockey or any other such idle games." The only proper pastime for an Englishman was archery. This order made every man a soldier. The longbow was the greatest weapon of its time. It brought victory to the English at the great battles of Agincourt, Crécy, and Poitiers. But more important, it accustomed a large number of Englishmen to the soldier's life. The English government came to depend on "private" companies of soldiers as the backbone of its armies in the wars with France. These men were not draftees. Nor were they slaves or serfs. They were professional soldiers with long experience who liked army life. The King would draw up a contract with their leaders at very low pay because both the leaders and their men would gain great booty whenever they won a battle. More than that, these soldiers could count on free lodging, ransom payments (if they captured a wealthy Frenchman), and far more freedom and excitement than they could have found at home.

When the English noblemen and younger sons (who could not claim title to their fathers' lands), together with yeomen, returned from these wars, they brought back not only riches but great tales with which to impress the stay-at-homes. They became objects of envy to their neighbors and probably very good storytellers as well. Sir Arthur Conan Doyle gives us one such tale as they might have told it.

This is a story of an age which will seem far-off and strange to you. In the telling you will find many words and spellings of the time which will be unfamiliar. Many of these words are explained in the footnotes and glossary. Others will be made clear by the material around them. But whether you understand all of them or not, these words will help give you a flavor of the times. You will find yourself in lands which may be foreign, but they will be real.

PUBLISHER'S NOTE: This edition of *The White Company* has been somewhat abridged by John Farrelly because of limitations of space. No important characters or incidents have been omitted.

Chapter 1

HOW THE BLACK SHEEP CAME FORTH FROM THE FOLD

The great bell of Beaulieu was ringing. Far away through the forest might be heard its musical clangor and swell. Peat-cutters on Blackdown and fishers upon the Exe heard the distant throbbing rising and falling upon the sultry summer air. It was a common sound in those parts—as common as the chatter of the jays and the booming of the bittern. Yet the fishers and the peasants raised their heads and looked questions at each other, for the angelus [1] had already gone and vespers [2] was still far off. Why should the great bell of Beaulieu toll when the shadows were neither short nor long?

All round the abbey the monks were trooping in. Under the long green-paved avenues of gnarled oaks and of lichened beeches, the white-robed brothers gathered to the sound. From the vineyard and the vinepress, from the ox-farm, the marl [3] pits and salterns,[4] even from the distant ironworkers of Sowley and the outlying grange of St. Leonard's, they had all turned their steps homewards. It had been no sudden call. A swift messenger had the night before sped round to the outlying dependencies of the abbey and had left the summons for every monk to be back in the cloisters by the third hour after noontide. So urgent a message had not been issued within the memory of old lay brother [5] Atha-

[1] *angelus* (ăn′jĕ·lŭs): a prayer said at morning, noon, and evening, at the sound of the angelus bell. [2] *vespers* (vĕs′pẽrz): a late afternoon or early evening prayer. [3] *marl* (märl): an earthy deposit used for fertilizer. [4] *saltern* (sôl′tẽrn): a place where salt is made. [5] *lay brother:* a monk occupied with domestic or manual labor.

nasius, who had cleaned the abbey knocker since the years after the Battle of Bannockburn.

A stranger who knew nothing either of the abbey or of its immense resources might have gathered from the appearance of the brothers some conception of the varied duties which they were called upon to perform, and of the busy, widespread life which centered in the old monastery. As they swept gravely in by twos and by threes, with bended heads and muttering lips, there were few who did not bear upon them some signs of their daily toil. Here were two with wrists and sleeves all spotted with the ruddy grape juice. There again was a bearded brother with a broad-headed ax and a bundle of faggots upon his shoulders, while beside him walked another with the shears under his arm and the white wool still clinging to his whiter gown. A long, straggling troop bore spades and mattocks, while the two rearmost of all staggered along under a huge basket of fresh-caught carp, for the morrow was Friday, and there were fifty platters to be filled and as many sturdy trenchermen [1] behind them. Of all the throng there was scarce one who was not labor-stained and weary, for Abbot Berghersh was a hard man to himself and to others.

Meanwhile, in the broad and lofty chamber set apart for occasions of import, the Abbot himself was pacing impatiently backwards and forwards, with his long white nervous hands clasped in front of him. His thin, thought-worn features and sunken, haggard cheeks bespoke one who had indeed beaten down that inner foe whom every man must face, but had none the less suffered sorely in the contest. In crushing his passions he had well-nigh crushed himself. Yet, frail as was his person, there gleamed out ever and anon from under his drooping brows a flash of fierce energy, which recalled to men's minds that he came of a fighting stock, and that even now his twin brother, Sir Bartholomew Berghersh, was one of the most famous of those stern warriors who had planted the Cross of St. George before the gates of Paris. With lips compressed and clouded brow, he strode up and down the oaken floor, the very genius and impersonation of asceticism,[2] while the great bell still thundered and clanged above

[1] *trencherman* (trĕn'chẽr·măn): a hearty eater. [2] *asceticism* (ă·sĕt'ĭ-sĭz'm): the belief in self-denial and self-punishment in order to reach a high spiritual state.

his head. At last the uproar died away in three last, measured throbs, and ere [1] their echo had ceased the Abbot struck a small gong which summoned a lay brother to his presence.

"Have the brethren come?" he asked in the Anglo-French dialect used in religious houses.

"They are here," the other answered, with his eyes cast down and his hands crossed upon his chest.

"All?"

"Two and thirty of the seniors and fifteen of the novices,[2] most holy father. Brother Mark of the Spicarium [3] is sore smitten with a fever and could not come. He said that—"

"It boots not what he said. Fever or no, he should have come at my call. His spirit must be chastened, as must that of many more in this abbey. You yourself, brother Francis, have twice raised your voice, so it hath come to my ears, when the reader in the refectory hath been dealing with the lives of God's most blessed saints. What hast thou to say?"

The lay brother stood meek and silent, with his arms still crossed in front of him.

"One thousand aves [4] and as many credos,[5] said standing with arms outstretched before the shrine of the Virgin, may help thee to remember that the Creator hath given us two ears and but one mouth, as a token that there is twice the work for the one as for the other. Where is the master of the novices?"

"He is without, most holy father."

"Send him hither."

The sandaled feet clattered over the wooden floor, and the iron-bound door creaked upon its hinges. In a few moments it opened again to admit a short square monk with a heavy, composed face and an authoritative manner.

"You have sent for me, holy father?"

"Yes, brother Jerome, I wish that this matter be disposed of with as little scandal as may be, and yet it is needful that the example should be a public one." The Abbot spoke in Latin now, as a language which was more fitted by its age and solemnity to convey the thoughts of two high dignitaries of the order.

[1] *ere* (âr): before. [2] *novice* (nŏv′ĭs): one who is training to be a monk. [3] *spicarium:* Latin for "silo," or a storehouse for wheat. [4] *ave* (ä′vē): the Hail Mary prayer. [5] *credo* (krē′dō): the Nicene Creed, sung as a prayer.

"It would, perchance, be best that the novices be not admitted," suggested the master. "This mention of a woman may turn their minds from their pious meditations to worldly and evil thoughts."

"Woman! woman!" groaned the Abbot. "Well has the holy Chrysostom termed them *radix malorum*.[1] From Eve downward, what good hath come from any of them? Who brings the plaint?" [2]

"It is brother Ambrose."

"A holy and devout young man."

"A light and a pattern to every novice."

"Let the matter be brought to an issue, then, according to our old-time monastic habit. Bid the chancellor and the subchancellor lead in the brothers according to age, together with brother John, the accused, and brother Ambrose, the accuser."

"And the novices?"

"Let them bide in the north alley of the cloisters. Stay! Bid the sub-chancellor send out to them Thomas the lector to read unto them from the 'Gesta beati Benedicti.' It may save them from foolish babbling."

The Abbot was left to himself once more, and bent his thin gray face over his illuminated breviary. So he remained while the senior monks filed slowly and sedately into the chamber, seating themselves upon the long oaken benches which lined the wall on either side. At the further end, in two high chairs as large as that of the Abbot, though hardly as elaborately carved, sat the master of the novices and the chancellor, the latter a broad and portly priest, with dark mirthful eyes and a thick outgrowth of crisp black hair all round his tonsured [3] head. Between them stood a lean, white-faced brother who appeared to be ill at ease, shifting his feet from side to side and tapping his chin nervously with the long parchment roll which he held in his hand. The Abbot turned his eager fiery gaze upon the pale-faced monk who faced him.

"This plaint is thine, as I learn, brother Ambrose," said he. "May the holy Benedict, patron of our house, be present this day and aid us in our findings! How many counts are there?"

"Three, most holy father," the brother answered in a low and quavering voice.

[1] *radix malorum:* Latin for "root of all evil." [2] *plaint* (plānt): complaint or accusation. [3] *tonsured* (tŏn′shẽrd): shaved on the top.

"Have you set them forth according to rule?"

"They are here set down, most holy father, upon a piece of sheepskin."

"Let the sheepskin be handed to the chancellor. Bring in brother John and let him hear the plaints which have been urged against him."

At this order a lay brother swung open the door, and two other lay brothers entered leading between them a young novice of the order. He was a man of huge stature, dark-eyed and red-headed, with a peculiar half-humorous, half-defiant expression upon his bold, well-marked features. His cowl was thrown back upon his shoulders, and his gown, unfastened at the top, disclosed a round, sinewy neck, ruddy and corded like the bark of the fir. Thick, muscular arms, covered with a reddish down, protruded from the wide sleeves of his habit, while his white skirt, looped up upon one side, gave a glimpse of a huge knotty leg, scarred and torn with the scratches of brambles. With a bow to the Abbot, which had in it perhaps more pleasantry than reverence, the novice strode across to the carved prie-dieu [1] which had been set apart for him, and stood silent and erect with his hand upon the gold bell which was used in the private orisons [2] of the Abbot's own household. His dark eyes glanced rapidly over the assembly and finally settled with a grim and menacing twinkle upon the face of his accuser.

The chamberlain rose, and having slowly unrolled the parchment scroll, proceeded to read it out in a thick and pompous voice, while a subdued rustle and movement among the brothers bespoke the interest with which they followed the proceedings.

"Charges brought upon the second Thursday after the Feast of the Assumption, in the year of our Lord thirteen hundred and sixty-six, against brother John, formerly known as Hordle John, or John of Hordle, but now a novice in the holy monastic order of the Cistercians. Read upon the same day at the abbey of Beaulieu in the presence of the most reverend Abbot Berghersh and of the assembled order.

"The charges against the said brother John are the following, namely, to wit:

"First, that on the above-mentioned Feast of the Assump-

[1] *prie-dieu* (pre'dyû'): a prayer desk. [2] *orison* (ŏr'ĭ·zŭn): prayer.

tion, small beer having been served to the novices in the proportion of one quart to each four, the said brother John did drain the pot at one draught to the detriment[1] of brother Paul, brother Porphyry, and brother Ambrose, who could scarce eat their none-meat[2] of salted stock-fish on account of their exceeding dryness."

At this solemn indictment the novice raised his hand and twitched his lip, while even the placid senior brothers glanced across at each other and coughed to cover their amusement. The Abbot alone sat gray and unchanged, with a drawn face and a brooding eye.

"Item, that having been told by the master of the novices that he should restrict his food for two days to a single three-pound loaf of bran and beans, for the greater honoring and glorifying of St. Monica, mother of the holy Augustine, he was heard by brother Ambrose and others to say that he wished twenty thousand devils would fly away with the said Monica, mother of the holy Augustine, or any other saint who came between a man and his meat. Item, that upon brother Ambrose reproving him for this blasphemous[3] wish, he did hold the said brother face downwards over the fishpond, for a space during which the said brother was able to repeat a pater[4] and four aves for the better fortifying of his soul against impending death."

There was a buzz and murmur among the white-frocked brethren at this grave charge; but the Abbot held up his long quivering hand. "What then?" said he.

"Item, that between nones and vespers on the feast of James the Less the said brother John was observed upon the Brockenhurst road, near the spot which is known as Hatchett's Pond, in converse with a person of the other sex, being a maiden of the name of Mary Sowley, the daughter of the King's verderer.[5] Item, that after sundry japes and jokes the said brother John did lift up the said Mary Sowley and did take, carry, and convey her across a stream, to the infinite relish of the devil and the exceeding detriment of his own soul, which scandalous and willful falling away was witnessed by three members of our order."

[1] *detriment* (dĕt′rĭ·mĕnt): harm. [2] *none-meat* (nŭn′mēt): afternoon meal. [3] *blasphemous* (blas′fē̇·mŭs): insulting to religious feelings. [4] *pater* (pä′ter): the Lord's prayer. [5] *verderer* (vûr′dẽr·ẽr): official in charge of the King's forest.

A dead silence throughout the room, with a rolling of heads and upturning of eyes, bespoke the pious horror of the community. The Abbot drew his gray brows low over his fiercely questioning eyes.

"Who can vouch for this thing?" he asked.

"That can I," answered the accuser. "So too can brother Porphyry, who was with me, and brother Mark who hath been so much stirred and inwardly troubled by the sight that he now lies in a fever through it."

"And the woman?" asked the Abbot. "Did she not break into lamentation and woe that a brother should so demean [1] himself?"

"Nay, she smiled sweetly upon him and thanked him. I can vouch it and so can brother Porphyry."

"Canst thou?" cried the Abbot, in a high, tempestuous tone. "Canst thou so? Hast forgotten that the five-and-thirtieth rule of the order is that in the presence of a woman the face should be ever averted and the eyes cast down? Hast forgot it, I say? If your eyes were upon your sandals, how came ye to see this smile of which ye prate? A week in your cells, false brethren, a week of rye bread and lentils, with double lauds and double matins,[2] may help ye to remembrance of the laws under which ye live."

At this sudden outflame of wrath the two witnesses sank their faces on to their chests and sat as men crushed. The Abbot turned his angry eyes away from them and bent them upon the accused, who met his searching gaze with a firm and composed face.

"What hast thou to say, brother John, upon these weighty things which are urged against you?"

"Little enough, good father, little enough," said the novice, speaking English with a broad West Saxon drawl. The brothers, who were English to a man, pricked up their ears at the sound of the homely and yet unfamiliar speech; but the Abbot flushed red with anger and struck his hand upon the oaken arm of his chair.

"What talk is this?" he cried. "Is this a tongue to be used within the walls of an old and well-famed monastery? But grace and learning have ever gone hand in hand, and when one is lost it is needless to look for the other."

[1] *demean* (dê·mēn′): behave in a low manner. [2] *lauds and matins* (lôdz; măt′ĭnz): two morning prayers.

"I know not about that," said brother John. "I know only that the words come kindly to my mouth, for it was the speech of my fathers before me. Under your favor, I shall either use it now or hold my peace."

The Abbot patted his foot and nodded his head, as one who passes a point but does not forget it.

"For the matter of the ale," continued brother John, "I had come in hot from the fields and had scarce got the taste of the thing before mine eye lit upon the bottom of the pot. It may be, too, that I spoke somewhat shortly concerning the bran and the beans, the same being poor provender and unfitted for a man of my inches. It is true also that I did lay my hands upon this jack-fool of a brother Ambrose, though, as you can see, I did him little scathe.[1] As regards the maid, too, it is true that I did heft her over the stream, she having on her hosen and shoon, whilst I had but my wooden sandals, which could take no hurt from the water. I should have thought shame upon my manhood, as well as my monkhood, if I had held back my hand from her." He glanced around as he spoke, with the half-amused look which he had worn during the whole proceedings.

"There is no need to go further," said the Abbot. "He has confessed to all. It only remains for me to portion out the punishment which is due to his evil conduct."

He rose, and the two long lines of brothers followed his example, looking sideways with scared faces at the angry prelate.

"John of Hordle," he thundered, "you have shown yourself during the two months of your novitiate [2] unworthy to wear the white garb which is the outer symbol of the spotless spirit. That dress shall therefore be stripped from thee, and thou shalt be cast into the outer world without benefit of clerkship, and without lot or part in the graces and blessings of those who dwell under the care of the blessed Benedict. Thou shalt come back neither to Beaulieu nor to any of the granges of Beaulieu, and thy name shall be struck off the scrolls of the order."

The sentence appeared a terrible one to the older monks, who had become so used to the safe and regular life of the Abbey that they would have been as helpless as children in the outer world. From their pious oasis they looked dreamily out at the

[1] *scathe* (skāth′) or *scath* (skăth): harm. [2] *novitiate* (nō·vĭsh′ĭ·at): period of apprenticeship.

desert of life, a place full of stormings and strivings—comfortless, restless, and overshadowed by evil. The young novice, however, appeared to have other thoughts, for his eyes sparkled and his smile broadened. It needed but that to add fresh fuel to the fiery mood of the prelate.

"So much for thy spiritual punishment," he cried. "But it is to thy grosser feelings that we must turn in such natures as thine, and as thou art no longer under the shield of holy Church there is the less difficulty. Ho there! lay brothers—Francis, Naomi, Joseph—seize him and bind his arms! Drag him forth, and let the foresters and the porters scourge [1] him from the precincts!" [2]

As these three brothers advanced towards him to carry out the Abbot's direction, the smile faded from the novice's face, and he glanced right and left with his fierce brown eyes, like a bull at a baiting. Then, with a sudden deep-chested shout, he tore up the heavy oaken prie-dieu and poised it to strike, taking two steps backward the while, that none might take him at a vantage.

"By the black rood [3] of Waltham!" he roared, "if any knave among you lays a finger end upon the edge of my gown, I will crush his skull like a filbert!" With his thick knotted arms, his thundering voice, and his bristle of red hair, there was something so repellent in the man that the three brothers flew back at the very glare of him; and the two rows of white monks strained away from him like poplars in a tempest. The Abbot only sprang forward with shining eyes; but the chancellor and the master hung upon either arm and wrested him back out of danger's way.

"He is possessed of a devil!" they shouted. "Run, brother Ambrose, brother Joachim! Call Hugh of the Mill, and Woodman Wat, and Raoul with his arbalest [4] and bolts. Tell them that we are in fear of our lives! Run, run! for the love of the Virgin!"

But the novice was a strategist as well as a man of action. Springing forward, he hurled his unwieldy weapon at brother Ambrose, and, as desk and monk clattered on to the floor together, he sprang through the open door and down the winding stair. Sleepy old brother Athanasius, at the porter's [5] cell, had a

[1] *scourge* (skûrj): to whip. [2] *precincts* (prē′sĭngkts): surroundings. [3] *rood* (ro͞od): crucifix or cross. [4] *arbalest* (är′bȧ·lĕst): a steel crossbow. [5] *porter:* gatekeeper.

fleeting vision of twinkling feet and flying skirts; but before he had time to rub his eyes, the recreant [1] had passed the lodge, and was speeding as fast as his sandals could patter along the Lyndhurst Road.

Chapter 2

HOW ALLEYNE EDRICSON CAME OUT INTO THE WORLD

Never had the peaceful atmosphere of the old Cistercian house been so rudely ruffled. Never had there been insurrection so sudden, so short, and so successful. Yet the Abbot Berghersh was a man of too firm a grain to allow one bold outbreak to imperil the settled order of his great household. In a few hot and bitter words, he compared their false brother's exit to the expulsion of our first parents from the garden and more than hinted that unless a reformation occurred, some others of the community might find themselves in the same evil and perilous case. Having thus pointed the moral and reduced his flock to a fitting state of docility, he dismissed them once more to their labors and withdrew himself to his own private chamber, there to seek spiritual aid in the discharge of the duties of his high office.

The Abbot was still on his knees, when a gentle tapping at the door of his cell broke in upon his orisons.

Rising in no very good humor at the interruption, he gave the word to enter; but his look of impatience softened down into a pleasant and paternal smile as his eyes fell upon his visitor.

He was a thin-faced, yellow-haired youth, rather above the middle size, comely and well shapen, with straight, lithe figure and eager, boyish features. His clear, pensive gray eyes and quick, delicate expression spoke of a nature which had unfolded

[1] *recreant* (rĕk′rē·ănt): not faithful to duty.

far from the boisterous joys and sorrows of the world. Yet there was a set of the mouth and a prominence of the chin which relieved him of any trace of effeminacy.[1] Impulsive he might be, enthusiastic, sensitive, with something sympathetic and adaptive in his disposition; but an observer of nature's tokens would have confidently pledged himself that there was native firmness and strength underlying his gentle, monk-bred ways.

The youth was not clad in monastic garb, but in lay attire, though his jerkin,[2] cloak, and hose were all of a somber hue, as befitted one who dwelt in sacred precincts. A broad leather strap hanging from his shoulder supported a scrip, or satchel, such as travelers were wont to carry. In one hand he grasped a thick staff pointed and shod with metal, while in the other he held his coif, or bonnet, which bore in its front a broad pewter medal stamped with the image of Our Lady of Rocamadour.

"Art ready, then, fair son?" said the Abbot. "This is indeed a day of comings and of goings. It is strange that in one twelve hours the abbey should have cast off its foulest weed, and should now lose what we are fain to look upon as our choicest blossom."

"You speak too kindly, father," the youth answered. "If I had my will I should never go forth, but should end my days here in Beaulieu. It hath been my home as far back as my mind can carry me, and it is a sore thing for me to have to leave it."

"Life brings many a cross," said the Abbot gently. "Who is without them? Your going forth is a grief to us as well as to yourself. But there is no help. I had given my foreword and sacred promise to your father, Edric the Franklin,[3] that at the age of twenty you should be sent out into the world to see for yourself how you liked the savor of it. Seat thee upon the settle, Alleyne, for you may need rest ere long."

The youth sat down as directed, but reluctantly and with diffidence. The Abbot stood by the narrow window, and his long black shadow fell slantwise across the rush-strewn floor.

"Twenty years ago," he said, "your father, the Franklin of Minstead, died, leaving to the abbey three hides [4] of rich land in the Hundred [5] of Malwood, and leaving to us also his infant son on condition that we should rear him until he came to man's

[1] *effeminacy* (ĕ·fĕm′ĭ·nȧ·sĭ): softness; similarity to a woman. [2] *jerkin* (jûr′kĭn): jacket. [3] *franklin* (frăngk′lĭn): landowner. [4] *hide:* about 100 acres. [5] *hundred:* a division of a county.

estate. This he did partly because your mother was dead, and partly because your elder brother, now Socman [1] of Minstead, had already given sign of that fierce and rude nature which would make him no fit companion for you. It was his desire and request, however, that you should not remain in the cloisters, but should at a ripe age return into the world."

"But, father," interrupted the young man, "it is surely true that I am already advanced several degrees in clerkship?"

"Yes, fair son, but not so far as to bar you from the garb you now wear or the life which you must now lead. You have been porter?"

"Yes, father."

" Exorcist?" [2]

"Yes, father."

"Reader?"

"Yes, father."

"Acolyte?" [3]

"Yes, father."

"But have sworn no vow of constancy or chastity?" [4]

"No, father."

"Then you are free to follow a worldly life. But let me hear, ere you start, what gifts you take away with you from Beaulieu. Some I already know. There is the playing of the citole and the rebeck. Our choir will be dumb without you. You carve too?"

The youth's pale face flushed with the pride of the skilled workman. "Yes, holy father," he answered. "Thanks to good brother Bartholomew, I carve in wood and in ivory, and can do something also in silver and in bronze. From brother Francis I have learned to paint on vellum, on glass, and on metal, with a knowledge of those pigments and essences which can preserve the color against damp or a biting air. Brother Luke hath given me some skill in damask work, and in the enameling of shrines, tabernacles, diptychs and triptychs. For the rest, I know a little of the making of covers, the cutting of precious stones, and the fashioning of instruments."

[1] *socman* (sŏk′măn): a feudal landholder. [2] *exorcist* (ĕk′sôr·sĭst): one who drives out evil spirits. [3] *acolyte* (ăk′ô·līt): assistant to priest at Mass. [4] *vow of constancy or chastity:* vow to stay in the monastery and not to marry.

"A goodly list, truly," cried the superior with a smile. "What clerk of Cambrig or of Oxenford could say as much? But of thy reading—hast not so much to show there, I fear?"

"No, father, it hath been slight enough. Yet, thanks to our good chancellor, I am not wholly unlettered. I have read Ockham, Bradwardine, and other of the schoolmen, together with the learned Duns Scotus and the book of the holy Aquinas."

"But of the things of this world, what have you gathered from your reading? From this high window you may catch a glimpse over the wooded point and the smoke of Bucklershard, of the mouth of the Exe, and the shining sea. Now, I pray you, Alleyne, if a man were to take a ship and spread sail across yonder waters, where might he hope to arrive?"

The youth pondered and drew a plan amongst the rushes with the point of his staff. "Holy father," said he, "he would come upon those parts of France which are held by the King's Majesty. But if he trended to the south he might reach Spain and the Barbary States. To his north would be Flanders and the country of the Eastlanders and of the Muscovites."

"True. And how if, after reaching the King's possessions, he still journeyed on to the eastward?"

"He would then come upon that part of France which is still in dispute, and he might hope to reach the famous city of Avignon, where dwells our blessed father, the prop of Christendom." [1]

"And then?"

"Then he would pass through the land of the Almains and the great Roman Empire, and so to the country of the Huns and of the Lithuanian pagans, beyond which lies the great city of Constantine and the kingdom of the unclean followers of Mahmoud."

"And beyond that, fair son?"

"Beyond that is Jerusalem and the Holy Land, and the great river which hath its source in the Garden of Eden."

"And then?"

"Nay, good father, I cannot tell. Methinks the end of the world is not far from there."

"Then we can still find something to teach thee, Alleyne," said the Abbot. "Know that many strange nations lie betwixt

[1] The Pope lived at that time in Avignon, in France, instead of in Rome.

there and the end of the world. There is the country of the Amazons, and the country of the dwarfs, and the country of the fair but evil women who slay with beholding, like the basilisk. These things I know for very sooth, for I had them from that pious Christian and valiant knight, Sir John de Mandeville, who stopped twice at Beaulieu on his way to and from Southampton, and discoursed to us concerning what he had seen, from the reader's desk in the refectory, until there was many a good brother who got neither bit nor sup, so stricken were they by his strange tales."

"I would fain know, father," asked the young man, "what there may be at the end of the world?"

"There are some things," replied the Abbot gravely, "into which it was never intended that we should inquire. But you have a long road before you. Whither will you first turn?"

"To my brother's at Minstead. If he be indeed an ungodly and violent man, there is the more need that I should seek him out and see whether I cannot turn him to better ways."

The Abbot shook his head. "The Socman of Minstead hath earned an evil name over the countryside," he said. "If you must go to him, see at least that he doth not turn you from the narrow path upon which you have learned to tread. But you are in God's keeping, and Godward should you ever look in danger and in trouble. Above all, shun the snares of women, for they are ever set for the foolish feet of the young. Kneel down, my child, and take an old man's blessing."

Alleyne Edricson bent his head while the Abbot poured out his heartfelt supplication that Heaven would watch over this young soul, now going forth into the darkness and danger of the world. It was no mere form for either of them. To them the outside life of mankind did indeed seem to be one of violence and of sin, beset with physical and still more with spiritual danger. Heaven, too, was very near to them in those days. God's direct agency [1] was to be seen in the thunder and the rainbow, the whirlwind and the lightning. To the believer, clouds of angels and confessors and martyrs, armies of the sainted and the saved, were ever stooping over their struggling brethren upon earth, raising, encouraging, and supporting them. It was, then, with a lighter heart and a stouter courage that the young man turned

[1] *agency* (ā′jĕn·sĭ): action.

from the Abbot's room, while the latter, following him to the stairhead, finally commended him to the protection of the holy Julian, patron of travelers.

Underneath, in the porch of the abbey, the monks had gathered to give him a last God-speed. Many had brought some parting token by which he should remember them. There was brother Bartholomew with a crucifix of rare carved ivory, and brother Luke with a white-backed psalter adorned with golden bees, and brother Francis with the "Slaying of the Innocents" most daintily set forth upon vellum. All these were duly packed away deep in the traveler's scrip, and above them old pippin-faced brother Athanasius had placed a parcel of simnel bread and rammel cheese, with a small flask of the famous blue-sealed Abbey wine. So, amid hand-shakings and laughings and blessings, Alleyne Edricson turned his back upon Beaulieu.

At the turn of the road he stopped and gazed back. There was the wide-spread building which he knew so well, the Abbot's house, the long church, the cloisters with their line of arches, all bathed and mellowed in the evening sun. There too was the broad sweep of the river Exe, the old stone well, the canopied niche of the Virgin, and in the center of all the cluster of white-robed figures who waved their hands to him. A sudden mist swam up before the young man's eyes, and he turned away upon his journey with a heavy heart and a choking throat.

Chapter 3

HOW HORDLE JOHN COZENED [1] THE FULLER [2] OF LYMINGTON

It is not, however, in the nature of things that a lad of twenty, with young life glowing in his veins and all the wide world before him, should spend his first hours of freedom in

[1] *cozen* (kŭz'n): to cheat. [2] *fuller* (fo͝ol'ẽr): one who thickens cloth.

mourning for what he had left. Long ere Alleyne was out of sound of the Beaulieu bells he was striding sturdily along, swinging his staff and whistling as merrily as the birds in the thicket. It was an evening to raise a man's heart. The sun shining slantwise through the trees threw delicate traceries across the road, with bars of golden light between. Away in the distance before and behind, the green boughs, now turning in places to a coppery redness, shot their broad arches across the track. The still summer air was heavy with the resinous smell of the great forest. Here and there a tawny brook prattled out from among the underwood and lost itself again in the ferns and brambles upon the further side. Save the dull piping of insects and the sough of the leaves, there was silence everywhere—the sweet restful silence of nature.

And yet there was no want of life—the whole wide wood was full of it. Now it was a lithe, furtive stoat which shot across the path upon some fell errand of its own; then it was a wild cat which squatted upon the outlying branch of an oak and peeped at the traveler with a yellow and dubious eye. Once it was a wild sow which scuttled out of the bracken, with two young sounders at her heels, and once a lordly red staggard walked daintily out from among the tree trunks and looked around him with the fearless gaze of one who lived under the King's own high protection. Alleyne gave his staff a merry flourish, however, and the red deer bethought him that the King was far off, so streaked away from whence he came.

The youth had now journeyed considerably beyond the furthest domains of the abbey. He was the more surprised therefore when, on coming round a turn in the path, he perceived a man clad in the familiar garb of the order, and seated in a clump of heather by the roadside. Alleyne had known every brother well, but this was a face which was new to him—a face which was very red and puffed, working this way and that, as though the man were sore perplexed in his mind. Once he shook both hands furiously in the air, and twice he sprang from his seat and hurried down the road. When he rose, however, Alleyne observed that his robe was much too long and loose for him in every direction, trailing upon the ground and bagging about his ankles, so that even with trussed-up skirts he could make little progress. He ran once, but the long gown clogged him so that he slowed down into a shambling walk and finally plumped into the heather once more.

"Young friend," said he, when Alleyne was abreast of him, "I fear from thy garb that thou canst know little of the abbey of Beaulieu."

"Then you are in error, friend," the clerk answered, "for I have spent all my days within its walls."

"Hast so indeed?" cried he. "Then perhaps canst tell me the name of a great loathly lump of a brother wi' freckled face an' a hand like a spade. His eyes were black an' his hair was red an' his voice like the parish bull. I trow [1] that there cannot be two alike in the same cloisters."

"That surely can be no other than brother John," said Alleyne. "I trust he has done you no wrong, that you should be so hot against him."

"Wrong, quotha!" cried the other, jumping out of the heather. "Wrong! why he hath stolen every plack of clothing off my back, if that be a wrong, and hath left me here in this sorry [2] frock of white falding,[3] so that I have shame to go back to my wife, lest she think that I have donned her old kirtle.[4] Harrow and alas that ever I should have met him!"

"But how came this?" asked the young clerk, who could scarce keep from laughter at the sight of the hot little man so swathed in the great white cloak.

"It came in this way," he said, sitting down once more: "I was passing this way, hoping to reach Lymington ere nightfall, when I came on this red-headed knave seated even where we are sitting now. I uncovered and louted [5] as I passed, thinking that he might be a holy man at his orisons, but he called to me and asked me if I had heard speak of the new indulgence [6] in favor of the Cistercians. 'Not I,' I answered. 'Then the worse for thy soul!' said he; and with that he broke into a long tale how that on account of the virtues of the Abbot Berghersh it had been decreed by the Pope that whoever should wear the habit of a monk of Beaulieu for as long as he might say the seven psalms of David should be assured of the kingdom of Heaven. When I heard this I prayed him on my knees that he would give me the use of

[1] *trow* (trō): to believe. [2] *sorry:* poor and pitiful. [3] *falding* (fôl′-dĭng): rough cloth. [4] *kirtle* (kûr′t'l): a gown. [5] *lout* (lout): to bow. [6] *indulgence* (ĭn·dŭl′jĕns): a special privilege.

his gown, which after many contentions he at last agreed to do, on my paying him three marks towards the regilding of the image of Laurence the martyr. Having stripped his robe, I had no choice but to let him have the wearing of my good leathern jerkin and hose, for, as he said, it was chilling to the blood and unseemly to the eye to stand frockless whilst I made my orisons. He had scarce got them on, and it was a sore labor, seeing that my inches will scarce match my girth—he had scarce got them on, I say, and I not yet at the end of the second psalm, when he bade me do honor to my new dress, and with that set off down the road as fast as feet would carry him. For myself, I could no more run than if I had been sewn in a sack; so here I sit, and here I am like to sit, before I set eyes upon my clothes again."

"Nay, friend, take it not so sadly," said Alleyne, clapping the disconsolate one upon the shoulder. "Canst change thy robe for a jerkin once more at the abbey, unless perchance you have a friend near at hand."

"That have I," he answered, "and close; but I care not to go nigh him in this plight, for his wife hath a gibing tongue, and will spread the tale until I could not show my face in any market from Fordingbridge to Southampton. But if you, fair sir, out of your kind charity would be pleased to go a matter of two bowshots out of your way, you would do me such a service as I could scarce repay."

"With all my heart," said Alleyne readily.

"Then take this pathway on the left, I pray thee, and then the deer track which passes on the right. You will then see under a great beech tree the hut of a charcoal-burner. Give him my name, good sir, the name of Peter the fuller, of Lymington, and ask him for a change of raiment, that I may pursue my journey without delay. There are reasons why he would be loath to refuse me."

Alleyne started off along the path indicated and soon found the log hut where the burner dwelt. He was away faggot-cutting in the forest, but his wife, a ruddy bustling dame, found the needful garments and tied them into a bundle. While she busied herself in finding and folding them, Alleyne Edricson stood by the open door looking in at her with much interest and some distrust, for he had never been so nigh to a woman before. She had round red arms, a dress of some sober woolen stuff, and a brass brooch the size of a cheesecake stuck in the front of it.

"Peter the fuller!" she kept repeating. "Marry come up! if I were Peter the fuller's wife, I would teach him better than to give his clothes to the first knave who asks for them. But he was always a poor, fond, silly creature, was Peter, though we are beholden to him for helping to bury our second son Wat, who was a 'prentice to him at Lymington in the year of the Black Death. But who are you, young sir?"

"I am a clerk on my road from Beaulieu to Minstead."

"Aye, indeed! Hast been brought up at the abbey then. I could read it from thy reddened cheek and downcast eye. Hadst learned from the monks, I trow, to fear a woman as thou wouldst a lazar-house.[1] Out upon them! that they should dishonor their own mothers by such teaching. A pretty world it would be with all the women out of it."

"Heaven forfend [2] that such a thing should come to pass!" said Alleyne.

"Amen and amen! But thou art a pretty lad, and the prettier for thy modest ways. It is easy to see from thy cheek that thou hast not spent thy days in the rain and the heat and the wind, as my poor Wat hath been forced to do."

"I have indeed seen little of life, good dame."

"Wilt find nothing in it to pay for the loss of thy own freshness. Here are the clothes, and Peter can leave them when next he comes this way. Holy Virgin! see the dust upon thy doublet! It were easy to see that there is no woman to tend to thee. So!—that is better. Now buss me, boy."

Alleyne stooped and kissed her, for the kiss was the common salutation of the age, and, as Erasmus long afterwards remarked, more used in England than in any other country. Yet it sent the blood to his temples again, and he wondered, as he turned away, what the Abbot Berghersh would have answered to so frank an invitation. He was still tingling from this new experience when he came out upon the highroad and saw a sight which drove all other thoughts from his mind.

Some way down from where he had left him, the unfortunate Peter was stamping and raving tenfold worse than before.

[1] *lazar-house* (lā'zĕr—): a house for lepers or diseased people. [2] *forfend* (fôr·fĕnd'): to prevent.

Now, however, instead of the great white cloak, he had no clothes on at all, save a short woolen shirt and a pair of leather shoes. Far down the road a long-legged figure was running, with a bundle under one arm and the other hand to his side, like a man who laughs until he is sore.

"See him!" yelled Peter. "Look to him! You shall be my witness. He shall see Winchester jail for this. See where he goes with my cloak under his arm!"

"Who then?" cried Alleyne.

"Who but that cursed brother John. He hath not left me clothes enough to make a gallybagger.[1] The double thief hath cozened me out of my gown."

"Stay though, my friend, it was his gown," objected Alleyne.

"It boots not. He hath them all—gown, jerkin, hosen, and all. Gramercy [2] to him that he left me the shirt and the shoon. I doubt not that he will be back for them anon."

"But how came this?" asked Alleyne, open-eyed with astonishment.

"Are those the clothes? For dear charity's sake give them to me. Not the Pope himself shall have these from me, though he sent the whole college of cardinals to ask it. How came it? Why, you had scarce gone ere this loathly John came running back again, and, when I oped mouth to reproach him, he asked me whether it was indeed likely that a man of prayer would leave his own godly raiment in order to take a layman's jerkin. He had, he said, but gone for a while that I might be the freer for my devotions. On this I plucked off the gown, and he, with much show of haste, did begin to undo his points; but when I threw his frock down, he clipped it up and ran off all untrussed, leaving me in this sorry plight. He laughed so the while, like a great croaking frog, that I might have caught him had my breath not been as short as his legs were long "

The young man listened to this tale of wrong with all the seriousness that he could maintain; but at the sight of the pursy red-faced man and the dignity with which he bore him, the laughter came so thick upon him that he had to lean up against a tree trunk. The fuller looked sadly and gravely at him; but finding that he still laughed, he bowed with much mock politeness

[1] *gallybagger* (găl′ĭ·băg′ẽr): a scarecrow. [2] *gramercy* (grȧ·mûr′sĭ): thanks.

and stalked onwards in his borrowed clothes. Alleyne watched him until he was small in the distance, and then, wiping the tears from his eyes, he set off briskly once more upon his journey.

Chapter 4

HOW THE BAILIFF[1] OF SOUTHAMPTON SLEW THE TWO MASTERLESS MEN

The road along which he traveled was scarce as populous as most other roads in the kingdom, and far less so than those which lie between the larger towns. Yet from time to time Alleyne met other wayfarers, and more than once was overtaken by strings of pack mules and horsemen journeying in the same direction as himself. Once a begging friar came limping along in a brown habit, imploring in a most dolorous voice to give him a single groat to buy bread wherewith to save himself from impending death. Alleyne passed him swiftly by, for he had learned from the monks to have no love for the wandering friars, and, besides, there was a great half-gnawed mutton bone sticking out of his pouch to prove him a liar. Swiftly as he went, however, he could not escape the curse of the four blessed evangelists which the mendicant[2] howled behind him. So dreadful were his execrations that the frightened lad thrust his fingers into his ear-holes and ran until the fellow was but a brown smirch upon the yellow road.

Further on, at the edge of the woodland, he came upon a chapman[3] and his wife, who sat upon a fallen tree. He had put his pack down as a table, and the two of them were devouring a great pasty and washing it down with some drink from a stone jar. The chapman broke a rough jest as he passed, and the woman called shrilly to Alleyne to come and join them, on which the man, turning suddenly from mirth to wrath, began to belabor her

[1] *bailiff* (bāl′ĭf): an officer representing the king and the law. [2] *mendicant* (mĕn′dĭ·kănt): a beggar. [3] *chapman* (chăp′măn): a peddler.

with his cudgel. Alleyne hastened on, lest he make more mischief, and his heart was heavy as lead within him. Look where he would, he seemed to see nothing but injustice and violence and the hardness of man to man.

But even as he brooded sadly over it and pined for the sweet peace of the abbey, he came on an open space dotted with holly bushes, where was the strangest sight that he had yet chanced upon. Near to the pathway lay a long clump of greenery, and from behind this there stuck straight up into the air four human legs clad in parti-colored hosen, yellow and black. Strangest of all was when a brisk tune struck suddenly up and the four legs began to kick and twitter in time to the music. Walking on tiptoe round the bushes, he stood in amazement to see two men bounding about on their heads, while they played, the one a viol and the other a pipe, as merrily and as truly as though they were seated in a choir. Alleyne crossed himself as he gazed at this unnatural sight and could scarce hold his ground with a steady face, when the two dancers, catching sight of him, came bouncing in his direction. A spear's length from him, they each threw a somersault into the air and came down upon their feet with smirking faces and their hands over their hearts.

"A guerdon [1]—a guerdon, my knight of the staring eyes!" cried one.

"A gift, my prince!" shouted the other. "Any trifle will serve—a purse of gold, or even a jeweled goblet."

Alleyne thought of what he had read of demoniac possession [2]—the jumpings, the twitchings, the wild talk. It was in his mind to repeat over the exorcism proper to such attacks; but the two burst out a-laughing at his scared face and turning on to their heads once more, clapped their heels in derision.

"Hast never seen tumblers before?" asked the elder, a black-browed, swarthy man, as brown and supple as a hazel twig. "Why shrink from us, then, as though we were the spawn of the Evil One?" [3]

"Why shrink, my honey-bird? Why so afeard, my sweet cinnamon?" exclaimed the other, a loose-jointed lanky youth with a dancing, roguish eye.

[1] *guerdon* (gûr′dŭn): a reward. [2] *demoniac* (dē·mō′nĭ·ăk) *possession:* being possessed by a devil; containing an evil spirit. [3] *spawn* (spôn) *of the Evil One:* children of the Devil.

"Truly, sirs, it is a new sight to me," the clerk answered. "When I saw your four legs above the bush I could scarce credit my own eyes. Why is it that you do this thing?"

"A dry question to answer," cried the younger, coming back on to his feet. "A most husky question, my fair bird! But how? A flask, a flask!—by all that is wonderful!" He shot out his hand as he spoke, and plucking Alleyne's bottle out of his scrip, he deftly knocked the neck off and poured the half of it down his throat. The rest he handed to his comrade, who drank the wine and then, to the clerk's increasing amazement, made a show of swallowing the bottle, with such skill that Alleyne seemed to see it vanish down his throat. A moment later, however, he flung it over his head and caught it bottom downwards upon the calf of his left leg.

"We thank you for the wine, kind sir," said he, "and for the ready courtesy wherewith you offered it. Touching your question, we may tell you that we are strollers and jugglers, who, having performed with much applause at Winchester fair, are now on our way to the great Michaelmas market at Ringwood. As our art is a very fine and delicate one, however, we cannot let a day go by without exercising ourselves in it, to which end we choose some quiet and sheltered spot where we may break our journey. Here you find us; and we cannot wonder that you, who are new to tumbling, should be astounded, since many great barons, earls, marshals, and knights, who have wandered as far as the Holy Land, are of one mind in saying that they have never seen a more noble or gracious performance. If you will be pleased to sit upon that stump, we will now continue our exercise."

Alleyne sat down willingly as directed with two great bundles on either side of him which contained the strollers' dresses —doublets of flame-colored silk and girdles of leather, spangled with brass and tin. The jugglers were on their heads once more, bounding about with rigid necks, playing the while in perfect time and tune. It chanced that out of one of the bundles there stuck the end of what the clerk saw to be a cittern,[1] so, drawing it forth, he tuned it up and twanged a harmony to the merry lilt which the dancers played. On that they dropped their own instruments, and putting their hands to the ground they hopped

[1] *cittern* (sĭt'ẽrn): a string instrument played by plucking.

about faster and faster, ever shouting to him to play more briskly, until at last for very weariness all three had to stop.

"Well played, sweet poppet!" cried the younger. "Hast a rare touch on the strings."

"How knew you the tune?" asked the other.

"I knew it not. I did but follow the notes I heard."

Both opened their eyes at this and stared at Alleyne with as much amazement as he had shown at them.

"You have a fine trick of ear then," said one. "We have long wished to meet such a man. Wilt join us and jog on to Ringwood? Thy duties shall be light, and thou shalt have twopence a day and meat for supper every night."

"With as much beer as you can put away," said the other, "and a flask of Gascon wine on Sabbaths."

"Nay, it may not be. I have other work to do. I have tarried with you overlong," quoth Alleyne, and resolutely set forth upon his journey once more. They ran behind him some little way, offering him first fourpence and then sixpence a day, but he only smiled and shook his head, until at last they fell away from him. Looking back, he saw that the smaller had mounted on the younger's shoulders, and that they stood so, some ten feet high, waving their adieus to him. He waved back to them and then hastened on, the lighter of heart for having fallen in with these strange men of pleasure.

Alleyne had gone no great distance for all the many small passages that had befallen him. Yet to him, used as he was to a life of such quiet that the failure of a brewing or the altering of an anthem had seemed to be of the deepest import, the quick changing play of the lights and shadows of life was strangely startling and interesting. A gulf seemed to divide this brisk uncertain existence from the old steady round of work and of prayer which he had left behind him. The few hours that had passed since he saw the abbey tower stretched out in his memory until they outgrew whole months of the stagnant life of the cloister. As he walked and munched the soft bread from his scrip, it seemed strange to him to feel that it was still warm from the ovens of Beaulieu.

When he passed Penerley, where were three cottages and a barn, he reached the edge of the tree country and found the great barren heath of Blackdown stretching in front of him, all pink with heather and bronzed with the fading ferns. On the left the woods were still thick, but the road edged away from them and wound over the open. The sun lay low in the west upon a purple cloud, whence it threw a mild, chastening light over the wild moorland and glittered on the fringe of forest, turning the withered leaves into flakes of dead gold, the brighter for the black depths behind them. To the seeing eye decay is as fair as growth, and death as life. The thought stole through Alleyne's heart as he looked upon the autumnal countryside and marveled at its beauty. He had little time to dwell upon it, however, for there were still six good miles between him and the nearest inn. He sat down by the roadside to partake of his bread and cheese, and then with a lighter scrip he hastened upon his way.

There appeared to be more wayfarers on the down than in the forest. First he passed two Dominicans in their long black dresses, who swept by him with downcast looks and pattering lips, without so much as a glance at him. Then there came a gray friar, or minorite, with a good paunch upon him, walking slowly and looking about him with the air of a man who was at peace with himself and with all men. He stopped Alleyne to ask him whether it was not true that there was a hostel somewhere in those parts which was especially famous for the stewing of eels. The clerk having made answer that he had heard the eels of Sowley well spoken of, the friar sucked in his lips and hurried forward. Close at his heels came three laborers walking abreast, with spade and mattock over their shoulders. They sang some rude chorus right tunefully as they walked, but their English was so coarse and rough that to the ears of a cloister-bred man it sounded like a foreign and barbarous tongue. One of them carried a young bittern which they had caught upon the moor, and they offered it to Alleyne for a silver groat. Very glad he was to get safely past them, for, with their bristling red beards and their fierce blue eyes, they were uneasy men to bargain with upon a lonely moor.

Yet it is not always the burliest and the wildest who are the most to be dreaded. The workers looked hungrily at him and then jogged onwards upon their way in slow, lumbering Saxon style. A worse man to deal with was a wooden-legged cripple who came hobbling down the path, so weak and so old to all appearance that a child need not stand in fear of him. Yet when Alleyne had passed him, of a sudden, out of pure devilment, he screamed out a curse at him and sent a jagged flint stone hurtling past his ear. So horrid was the causeless rage of the crooked creature, that the clerk came over a cold thrill and took to his heels until he was out of shot from stone or word. It seemed to him that in this country of England there was no protection for a man save that which lay in the strength of his own arm and the speed of his own foot. In the cloisters he had heard vague talk of the law—the mighty law which was higher than prelate [1] or baron, yet no sign could he see of it. What was the benefit of a law written fair upon parchment, he wondered, if there were no officers to enforce it? As it fell out, however, he had that very evening, ere the sun had set, a chance of seeing how stern was the grip of the English law when it did happen to seize the offender.

A mile or so out upon the moor the road takes a very sudden dip into a hollow, with a peat-colored stream running swiftly down the center of it. To the right of this stood, and stands to this day, an ancient barrow, or burying mound, covered deeply in a bristle of heather and bracken. Alleyne was plodding down the slope upon one side, when he saw an old dame coming towards him upon the other, limping with weariness and leaning heavily upon a stick. When she reached the edge of the stream she stood helpless, looking to right and to left for some ford. Where the path ran down, a great stone had been fixed in the center of the brook, but it was too far from the bank for her aged and uncertain feet. Twice she thrust forward at it, and twice she drew back, until at last, giving up in despair, she sat herself down by the brink and wrung her hands wearily. There she still sat when Alleyne reached the crossing.

"Come, mother," quoth he, "it is not so very perilous a passage."

"Alas! good youth," she answered, "I have a humor in the eyes, and though I can see that there is a stone there, I can by no means be sure as to where it lies."

"That is easily amended," said he cheerily and picking her lightly up, for she was much worn with time, he passed across with her. He could not but observe, however, that as he placed

[1] *prelate* (prĕl′ĭt): a high official of the church.

her down, her knees seemed to fail her, and she could scarcely prop herself up even with her staff.

"You are weak, mother," said he. "Hast journeyed far, I wot?"

"From Wiltshire, friend," said she, in a quavering voice; "three days have I been on the road. I go to my son, who is one of the King's regarders [1] at Brockenhurst. He has ever said that he would care for me in mine old age."

"And rightly too, mother, since you cared for him in his youth. But when have you broken fast?"

"At Lyndenhurst; but alas! my money is at an end, and I could but get a dish of bran porridge from the nunnery. Yet I trust that I may be able to reach Brockenhurst tonight, where I may have all that heart can desire; for oh! sir, but my son is a fine man, with a kindly heart of his own, and it is as good as food to me to think that he should have a doublet of Lincoln green to his back and be the King's own paid man."

"It is a long road yet to Brockenhurst," said Alleyne; "but here is such bread and cheese as I have left, and here, too, is a penny which may help you to supper. May God be with you!"

"May God be with you, young man!" she cried. "May He make your heart as glad as you have made mine!" She turned away, still mumbling blessings, and Alleyne saw her short figure and her long shadow stumbling slowly up the slope.

He was moving away himself, when his eyes lit upon a strange sight, and one which sent a tingling through his skin. Out of the tangled scrub on the old overgrown barrow, two human faces were looking out at him; the sinking sun glimmered full upon them, showing up every line and feature. The one was an oldish man with a thin beard, a crooked nose, and a broad red smudge from a birthmark over his temple; the other was a Negro, a thing rarely met in England at that day, and rarer still in the quiet southland parts. Alleyne had read of such folk, but had never seen one before, and could scarce take his eyes from the fellow's broad pouting lip and shining teeth. Even as he gazed, however, the two came writhing out from among the heather and came down towards him with such a guilty, slinking carriage that the clerk felt that there was no good in them and hastened onwards upon his way.

He had not gained the crown of the slope, when he heard

[1] *regarder* (rē·gär′dẽr): an inspector of the forests.

a sudden scuffle behind him and a feeble voice bleating for help. Looking round, there was the old dame down upon the roadway, with her red wimple flying on the breeze, while the two rogues, black and white, stooped over her, wresting away from her the penny and such other poor trifles as were worth the taking. At the sight of her thin limbs struggling in weak resistance, such a glow of fierce anger passed over Alleyne as set his head in a whirl. Dropping his scrip, he bounded over the stream once more and made for the two villains, with his staff whirled over his shoulder and his gray eyes blazing with fury.

The robbers, however, were not disposed to leave their victim until they had worked their wicked will upon her. The black man, with the woman's crimson scarf tied round his swarthy head, stood forward in the center of the path, with a long dull-colored knife in his hand, while the other, waving a ragged cudgel, cursed at Alleyne and dared him to come on. His blood was fairly aflame, however, and he needed no such challenge. Dashing at the black man, he smote at him with such good will that the other let his knife tinkle into the roadway and hopped howling to a safer distance. The second rogue, however, made of sterner stuff, rushed in upon the clerk and clipped him round the waist with a grip like a bear, shouting the while to his comrade to come round and stab him in the back. At this the Negro took heart of grace, and picking up his dagger again he came stealing with prowling step and murderous eye, while the two swayed backwards and forwards, staggering this way and that. In the very midst of the scuffle, however, whilst Alleyne braced himself to feel the cold blade between his shoulders, there came a sudden scurry of hoofs, and the black man yelled with terror and ran for his life through the heather. The man with the birthmark, too, struggled to break away, and Alleyne heard his teeth chatter and felt his limbs grow limp to his hand. At this sign of coming aid, the clerk held on the tighter, and at last was able to pin his man down, and glanced behind him to see where all the noise was coming from.

Down the slanting road there was riding a big, burly man, clad in a tunic of purple velvet and driving a great black horse as hard as it could gallop. He leaned well over its neck as he rode and made a heaving with his shoulders at every bound as though he were lifting the steed instead of it carrying him. In the rapid glance Alleyne saw that he had white doeskin gloves, a curling white feather in his flat velvet cap, and a broad gold-embroidered baldric [1] across his bosom. Behind him rode six others, two and two, clad in sober brown jerkins, with the long yellow staves of their bows thrusting out from behind their right shoulders. Down the hill they thundered, over the brook, and up to the scene of the contest.

"Here is one!" said the leader, springing down from his reeking horse and seizing the white rogue by the edge of his jerkin. "This is one of them. I know him by that devil's touch upon his brow. Where are your cords, Peterkin? So!—bind him hand and foot. His last hour has come. And you, young man, who may you be?"

"I am a clerk, sir, traveling from Beaulieu."

"A clerk!" cried the other. "Art from Oxenford or from Cambrig? Hast thou a letter from the chancellor of thy college giving thee a permit to beg? Let me see thy letter." He had a stern, square face, with bushy side whiskers and a very questioning eye.

"I am from Beaulieu Abbey, and I have no need to beg," said Alleyne, who was all of a tremble now that the ruffle was over.

"The better for thee," the other answered. "Dost know who I am?"

"No, sir, I do not."

"I am the law!"—nodding his head solemnly. "I am the law of England and the mouthpiece of his most gracious and royal majesty, Edward the Third."

Alleyne louted low to the King's representative. "Truly you came in good time, honored sir," said he. "A moment later and they would have slain me."

"But there should be another one," cried the man in the purple coat. "There should be a black man. A shipman with St. Anthony's fire, and a black man who had served him as cook—those are the pair that we are in chase of."

"The black man fled over to that side," said Alleyne, pointing towards the barrow.

"He could not have gone far, sir bailiff," cried one of the archers, unslinging his bow. "He is in hiding somewhere, for he

[1] *baldric* (bôl′drĭk): a belt.

knew well, black paynim[1] as he is, that our horses' four legs could outstrip his two."

"Then we shall have him," said the other. "It shall never be said, whilst I am bailiff of Southampton, that any waster, riever, draw-latch, or murtherer came scathless away from me and my posse. Leave that rogue lying. Now stretch out in line, my merry ones, with arrow on string, and I shall show you such sport as only the King can give. You on the left, Howett, and Thomas of Redbridge upon the right. So! Beat high and low among the heather, and a pot of wine to the lucky marksman."

As it chanced, however, the searchers had not far to seek. The Negro had burrowed down into his hiding place upon the barrow, where he might have lain snug enough, had it not been for the red gear upon his head. As he raised himself to look over the bracken at his enemies, the staring color caught the eye of the bailiff, who broke into a long screeching whoop and spurred forward, sword in hand. Seeing himself discovered, the man rushed out from his hiding place and bounded at the top of his speed down the line of archers, keeping a good hundred paces to the front of them. The two who were on either side of Alleyne bent their bows as calmly as though they were shooting at the popinjay at the village fair.

"Seven yards windage,[2] Hal," said one, whose hair was streaked with gray.

"Five," replied the other, letting loose his string. Alleyne gave a gulp in his throat, for the yellow streak seemed to pass through the man; but he still ran forward.

"Seven, you jack-fool," growled the first speaker, and his bow twanged like a harp string. The black man sprang high up into the air and shot out both his arms and his legs, coming down all a-sprawl among the heather. "Right under the blade bone!" quoth the archer, sauntering forward for his arrow.

"The old hound is the best when all is said," quoth the bailiff of Southampton, as they made back for the roadway. "That means a quart of the best malmsey[3] in Southampton this very night, Matthew Atwood. Art sure that he is dead?"

"Dead as Pontius Pilate, worshipful sir."

[1] *paynim* (pā′nĭm): a pagan, not a Christian. [2] *windage* (wĭn′dĭj): compensation for the force of the wind. [3] *malmsey* (mäm′zĭ): a sweet wine.

"It is well. Now, as to the other knave. There are trees and to spare over yonder, but we have scarce leisure to make for them. Draw thy sword, Thomas of Redbridge, and hew me his head from his shoulders."

"A boon,[1] gracious sir, a boon!" cried the condemned man.

"What then?" asked the bailiff.

"I will confess to my crime. It was indeed I and the black cook, both from the ship 'La Rose de Gloire,' of Southampton, who did set upon the Flanders merchant and rob him of his spicery and his mercery,[2] for which, as we well know, you hold a warrant against us."

"There is little merit in this confession," quoth the bailiff sternly. "Thou hast done evil within my bailiwick, and must die."

"But, sir," urged Alleyne, who was white to the lips at these bloody doings, "he hath not yet come to trial."

"Young clerk," said the bailiff, "you speak of that of which you know nothing. It is true that he hath not come to trial, but the trial hath come to him. He hath fled the law and is beyond its pale.[3] Touch not that which is no concern of thine. But what is this boon, rogue, which you would crave?"

"I have in my shoe, most worshipful sir, a strip of wood which belonged once to the bark wherein the blessed Paul was dashed up against the island of Melita. I bought it for two rose nobles from a shipman who came from the Levant. The boon I crave is that you will place it in my hands and let me die still grasping it. In this manner, not only shall my own eternal salvation be secured, but thine also, for I shall never cease to intercede for thee."

At the command of the bailiff they plucked off the fellow's shoe, and there, sure enough, at the side of the instep, wrapped in a piece of fine sendal, lay a long, dark splinter of wood. The archers doffed[4] caps at the sight of it, and the bailiff crossed himself devoutly as he handed it to the robber.

"If it should chance," he said, "that through the surpassing merits of the blessed Paul your sin-stained soul should gain a way into paradise, I trust that you will not forget that intercession which you have promised. Bear in mind, too, that it is Herward the bailiff for whom you pray, and not Herward the sheriff, who

[1] *boon* (bo͞on): a favor. [2] *mercery* (mûr′sẽr·ĭ): cloth, textiles. [3] *pale:* protection. [4] *doff* (dŏf): to take off.

is my uncle's son. Now, Thomas, I pray you dispatch, for we have a long ride before us, and sun has already set."

Alleyne gazed upon the scene—the portly velvet-clad official, the knot of hard-faced archers with their hands to the bridles of their horses, the thief with his arms trussed back and his doublet turned down upon his shoulders. By the side of the track the old dame was standing, fastening her red wimple once more round her head. Even as he looked, one of archers drew his sword with a sharp whirr of steel and stepped up to the lost man. The clerk hurried away in horror; but, ere he had gone many paces, he heard a sudden, sullen thump, with a choking, whistling sound at the end of it. A minute later the bailiff and four of his men rode past him on their journey back to Southampton, the other two having been chosen as gravediggers. As they passed, Alleyne saw that one of the men was wiping his sword-blade upon the mane of his horse. A deadly sickness came over him at the sight, and sitting down by the wayside he burst out weeping, with his nerves all in a jangle. It was a terrible world, thought he, and it was hard to know which were the most to be dreaded, the knaves or the men of the law.

Chapter 5

HOW A STRANGE COMPANY GATHERED AT THE "PIED MERLIN"

The night had already fallen, and the moon was shining between the rifts of ragged, drifting clouds before Alleyne Edricson, footsore and weary from the unwonted[1] exercise, found himself in front of the forest inn which stood upon the outskirts of Lyndhurst. The building was long and low, standing back a little from the road, with two flambeaux[2] blazing on either side

[1] *unwonted* (ŭn·wŭn′tĕd): unaccustomed. [2] *flambeaux* (flăm′bō): flaming torches.

of the door as a welcome to the traveler. From one window there thrust forth a long pole with a bunch of greenery tied to the end of it—a sign that liquor was to be sold within. As Alleyne walked up to it, he perceived that it was rudely fashioned out of beams of wood, with twinkling lights all over where the glow from within shone through the chinks. The roof was poor and thatched; but in strange contrast to it there ran all along under the eaves a line of wooden shields, most gorgeously painted with every heraldic [1] device.[2] By the door a horse stood tethered, the ruddy glow beating strongly upon his brown head and patient eyes, while his body stood back in the shadow.

Alleyne stood still in the roadway for a few minutes, reflecting upon what he should do. It was, he knew, only a few miles further to Minstead, where his brother dwelt. On the other hand, he had never seen this brother since childhood, and the reports which had come to his ears concerning him were seldom to his advantage. By all accounts he was a hard and a bitter man.

It might be an evil start to come to his door so late and claim the shelter of his roof. Better to sleep here at this inn and then travel on to Minstead in the morning. If his brother would take him in, well and good.

He would bide with him for a time and do what he might to serve him. If, on the other hand, he should have hardened his heart against him, he could only go on his way and do the best he might by his skill as a craftsman and a scrivener.[3] At the end of a year he would be free to return to the cloisters, for such had been his father's bequest. A monkish upbringing, one year in the world after the age of twenty, and then a free selection one way or the other—it was a strange course which had been marked out for him. Such as it was, however, he had no choice but to follow it, and if he were to begin by making a friend of his brother he had best wait until morning before he knocked at his dwelling.

The rude plank door was ajar, but as Alleyne approached it, there came from within such a gust of rough laughter and clatter of tongues that he stood irresolute upon the threshold. Sum-

[1] *heraldic* (hĕ·răl′dĭk): having to do with **heraldry** (hĕr′ăld·rĭ), the art of recording family histories on shields, banners, and so forth. [2] *device* (dē·vīs′): a design. [3] *scrivener* (skrĭv′nẽr): a person who writes for those who do not know how to write.

moning courage, however, and reflecting that it was a public dwelling, in which he had as much right as any other man, he pushed it open and stepped into the common room.

Though it was an autumn evening and somewhat warm, a huge fire of heaped billets of wood crackled and sparkled in a broad, open grate, some of the smoke escaping up a rude chimney, but the greater part rolling out into the room, so that the air was thick with it, and a man coming from without could scarce catch his breath. On this fire a great cauldron bubbled and simmered, giving forth a rich and promising smell. Seated round it were a dozen or so folk, of all ages and conditions, who set up such a shout as Alleyne entered that he stood peering at them through the smoke, uncertain what this riotous greeting might portend.

"A rouse! [1] A rouse!" cried one rough-looking fellow in a tattered jerkin. "One more round of mead or ale, and the score [2] to the last comer."

" 'Tis the law of the 'Pied Merlin,' " shouted another. "Ho, there, Dame Eliza! Here is fresh custom come to the house, and not a drain for the company."

"I will take your orders, gentles; [3] I will assuredly take your orders," the landlady answered, bustling in with her hands full of leathern drinking-cups. "What is it that you drink, then? Beer for the lads of the forest, mead for the gleeman, strong waters for the tinker, and wine for the rest. It is an old custom of the house, young sir. It has been the use at the 'Pied Merlin' this many a year back that the company should drink to the health of the last comer. Is it your pleasure to humor it?"

"Why, good dame," said Alleyne, "I would not offend the customs of your house, but it is only sooth [4] when I say that my purse is a thin one. As far as twopence will go, however, I shall be right glad to do my part."

"Plainly said and bravely spoken, my sucking friar," roared a deep voice, and a heavy hand fell upon Alleyne's shoulder. Looking up, he saw beside him his former cloister companion, the renegade monk,[5] Hordle John.

[1] *rouse* (rouz): a glass or cup of liquor. [2] *score:* amount due; he means the Alleyne shall pay for the liquor. [3] *gentle:* a gentleman. [4] *sooth* (so͞oth): true. [5] *renegade* (rĕn′ē·gād) *monk:* a monk who has deserted his monastery.

"By the thorn of Glastonbury! ill days are coming upon Beaulieu," said he. "Here they have got rid in one day of the only two men within their walls—for I have had mine eyes upon thee, youngster, and I know that for all thy baby-face there is the making of a man in thee. Then there is the Abbot, too. I am no friend of his, nor he of mine; but he has warm blood in his veins. He is the only man left among them. The others, what are they?"

"They are holy men," Alleyne answered gravely.

"Holy men? Holy cabbages! Holy bean-pods! What do they do but live and suck in sustenance and grow fat? If that be holiness, I could show you hogs in this forest who are fit to head the calendar.[1] Think you it was for such a life that this good arm was fixed upon my shoulder, or that head placed upon your neck? There is work in the world, man, and it is not by hiding behind stone walls that we shall do it."

"Why, then, did you join the brothers?" asked Alleyne.

"A fair enough question; but it is as fairly answered. I joined them because Margery Alspaye, of Bolder, married Crooked Thomas of Ringwood, and left a certain John of Hordle in the cold, for that he was a ranting, roving blade who was not to be trusted in wedlock. That was why, being fond [2] and hotheaded, I left the world; and that is why, having had time to take thought, I am right glad to find myself back in it once more. Ill betide the day that ever I took off my yeoman's jerkin to put on the white gown!"

Whilst he was speaking, the landlady came in again, bearing a broad platter, upon which stood all the beakers and flagons charged to the brim with the brown ale or the ruby wine. Behind her came a maid with a high pile of wooden plates and a great sheaf of spoons, one of which she handed round to each of the travelers.

Two of the company, who were dressed in the weather-stained green doublet of foresters, lifted the big pot off the fire, and a third, with a huge pewter ladle, served out a portion of steaming collops [3] to each guest. Alleyne bore his share and his ale mug away with him to a retired trestle in the corner, where he could sup in peace and watch the strange scene, which was

[1] *calendar:* the calendar (or list) of saints. [2] *fond:* foolish. [3] *collop* (kŏl′ŭp): a piece of meat.

so different to those silent and well-ordered meals to which he was accustomed.

The room was not unlike a stable. The low ceiling, smoke-blackened and dingy, was pierced by several square trap doors with rough-hewn ladders leading up to them. The walls of bare unpainted planks were studded here and there with great wooden pins, placed at irregular intervals and heights, from which hung over-tunics, wallets, whips, bridles, and saddles. Over the fire-place were suspended six or seven shields of wood, with coats of arms rudely daubed upon them, which showed by their varying degrees of smokiness and dirt that they had been placed there at different periods. There was no furniture, save a single long dresser covered with coarse crockery, and a number of wooden benches and trestles, the legs of which sank deeply into the soft clay floor, while the only light, save that of the fire, was furnished by three torches stuck in sockets on the wall, which flickered and crackled, giving forth a strong resinous odor. All this was novel and strange to the cloister-bred youth; but most interesting of all was the motley circle of guests who sat eating their collops round the blaze. They were a humble group of wayfarers, such as might have been found that night in any inn through the length and breadth of England; but to him they represented that vague world against which he had been so frequently and so earnestly warned. It did not seem to him from what hc could see of it to be such a very wicked place after all.

Three or four of the men round the fire were evidently under-keepers and verderers from the forest, sunburned and bearded, with the quick restless eye and lithe movements of the deer among which they lived. Close to the corner of the chimney sat a middle-aged gleeman,[1] clad in a faded garb of Norwich cloth, the tunic of which was so outgrown that it did not fasten at the neck and at the waist. His face was swollen and coarse, and his watery protruding eyes spoke of a life which never wandered very far from the wine-pot. A gilt harp, blotched with many stains and with two of its strings missing, was tucked under one of his arms, while with the other he scooped greedily at his platter. Next to him sat two other men of about the same age, one with a trimming of fur to his coat, which gave him a dignity which was evidently dearer to him than his comfort, for he still

[1] *gleeman* (glē′mă̆n): a minstrel, singer.

drew it round him in spite of the hot glare of the faggots. The other, clad in a dirty russet suit with a long sweeping doublet, had a cunning, foxy face with keen, twinkling eyes and a peaky beard. Next to him sat Hordle John, and beside him three other rough unkempt fellows with tangled beards and matted hair—free laborers from the adjoining farms, where small patches of freehold [1] property had been suffered [2] to remain scattered about in the heart of the royal demesne.[3] The company was completed by a peasant in a rude dress of undyed sheepskin, with the old-fashioned galligaskins [4] about his legs, and a gayly dressed young man with striped cloak, jagged at the edges, and particolored hosen, who looked about him with high disdain upon his face, and held a blue smelling-flask to his nose with one hand, while he brandished a busy spoon with the other. In the corner a very fat man was lying all a-sprawl upon a truss, snoring stertorously, and evidently in the last stage of drunkenness.

"That is Wat the limner," [5] quoth the landlady, sitting down beside Alleyne and pointing with the ladle to the sleeping man. "That is he who paints the signs and the tokens. Alack and alas that ever I should have been fool enough to trust him! Now, young man, what manner of a bird would you suppose a pied merlin to be—that being the proper sign of my hostel?"

"Why," said Alleyne, "a merlin is a bird of the same form as an eagle or a falcon. I can well remember that learned brother Bartholomew, who is deep in all the secrets of nature, pointed one out to me as we walked together near Vinney Ridge."

"A falcon or an eagle, quotha? And pied, that is of two several colors. So any man would say except this barrel of lies. He came to me, look you, saying that if I would furnish him with a gallon of ale, wherewith to strengthen himself as he worked, and also the pigments and a board, he would paint for me a noble pied merlin which I might hang along with the blazonry [6] over my door. I, poor simple fool, gave him the ale and all that he craved, leaving him alone too, because he said that a man's mind must be left untroubled when he had great work to do. When I came back the gallon jar was empty, and he lay as you see him,

[1] *freehold* (frē′hōld′): freely owned, not rented. [2] *suffer:* to allow. [3] *royal demesne* (dē·mān): land owned by the king. [4] *galligaskins* (găl′ĭ-găs′kĭnz): leggings. [5] *limner* (lĭm′nẽr): a painter. [6] *blazonry* (blā′z′n·rĭ): coats of arms (see *heraldry,* p. 310).

with the board in front of him with this sorry device." She raised up a panel which was leaning against the wall, and showed a rude painting of a scraggy and angular fowl, with very long legs and a spotted body.

"Was that," she asked, "like the bird which thou hast seen?"

Alleyne shook his head, smiling.

"No, nor any other bird that ever wagged a feather. It is most like a plucked pullet which has died of the spotted fever. And scarlet too! What would the gentles Sir Nicholas Boarhunte, or Sir Bernard Brocas, of Rochecourt, say if they saw such a thing—or, perhaps, even the King's own Majesty himself, who often has ridden past this way, and who loves his falcons as he loves his sons? It would be the downfall of my house."

"The matter is not past mending," said Alleyne. "I pray you, good dame, to give me those three pigment-pots and the brush, and I shall try whether I cannot better his painting."

Dame Eliza looked doubtfully at him, as though fearing some other stratagem, but, as he made no demand for ale, she finally brought the paints and watched him as he smeared on his background, talking the while about the folk round the fire.

"The four forest lads must be jogging soon," she said. "They bide at Emery Down, a mile or more from here, and tend to the King's hunt. The gleeman is called Floyting Will. He comes from the north country, but for many years he hath gone the round of the forest from Southampton to Christchurch. He drinks much and pays little; but it would make your ribs crackle to hear him sing the 'Jest of Hendy Tobias.' Mayhap he will sing it when the ale has warmed him."

"Who are those next to him?" asked Alleyne, much interested. "He of the fur mantle has a wise and reverent face."

"He is a seller of pills and salves, very learned in humors, and rheums, and fluxes, and all manner of ailments. May good St. Thomas of Kent grant that it may be long before either I or mine need his help! He is here tonight for herbergage,[1] as are the others except the foresters. His neighbor is a tooth-drawer. That bag at his girdle is full of the teeth that he drew at Winchester fair. I warrant that there are more sound ones than sorry, for he is quick at his work and a trifle dim in the eye. The lusty man next him with the red head I have not seen before. The four on

[1] *herbergage* (hĕr′bĕr·gä′jĕ): lodging.

this side are all workers, three of them in the service of the bailiff of Sir Baldwin Redvers, and the other, he with the sheepskin, is, as I hear, a villein [1] from the midlands who hath run from his master. His year and day are well-nigh up, when he will be a free man."

"And the other?" asked Alleyne in a whisper. "He is surely some very great man, for he looks as though he scorned those who were about him."

The landlady looked at him in a motherly way and shook her head. "You have had no great truck with the world," she said, "or you would have learned that it is the small men and not the great who hold their noses in the air. Look at those shields upon my wall and under my eaves. Each of them is the device of some noble lord or gallant knight who hath slept under my roof at one time or another. Yet milder men or easier to please I have never seen: eating my bacon and drinking my wine with a merry face, and paying my score with some courteous word or jest which was dearer to me than my profit. Those are the true gentles. But your chapman or your bearward will swear that there is a lime in the wine, and water in the ale, and fling off at the last with a curse instead of a blessing. This youth is a scholar from Cambrig, where men are wont to be blown out by a little knowledge and lose the use of their hands in learning the laws of the Romans. But I must away to lay down the beds. So may the saints keep you and prosper you in your undertaking!"

Thus left to himself, Alleyne drew his panel of wood where the light of one of the torches would strike full upon it and worked away with all the pleasure of the trained craftsman, listening the while to the talk which went on round the fire. The peasant in the sheepskins, who had sat glum and silent all evening, had been so heated by his flagon of ale that he was talking loudly and angrily, with clenched hands and flashing eyes.

"Sir Humphrey Tennant of Ashby may till his own fields," he cried. "The castle has thrown its shadow upon the cottage overlong. For three hundred years my folk have swinked [2] and sweated, day in and day out, to keep the wine on the lord's table and the harness [3] on the lord's back. Let him take off his plates [4] and delve [5] himself, if delving must be done."

[1] *villein* (vĭl′ĭn): a peasant, serf. [2] *swink:* to labor; slave. [3] *harness:* military equipment. [4] *plates:* armor. [5] *delve* (dĕlv): to dig.

"A proper spirit, my fair son!" said one of the free laborers. "I would that all men were of thy way of thinking."

"He would have sold me with his acres," the other cried, in a voice which was hoarse with passion. " 'The man, the woman, and their litter'—so ran the words of the dotard[1] bailiff. Never a bullock on the farm was sold more lightly. Ha! he may wake some black night to find the flames licking about his ears—for fire is a good friend to the poor man, and I have seen a smoking heap of ashes where overnight there stood just such another castlewick as Ashby."

"This is a lad of mettle!" shouted another of the laborers. "He dares to give tongue to what all men think. Are we not all from Adam's loins, all with flesh and blood, and with the same mouth that must needs have food and drink? Where all this difference then between the ermine cloak and the leathern tunic,[2] if what they cover is the same?"

"Aye, Jenkin," said another, "our foeman is under the stole and the vestment as much as under the helmet and plate of proof.[3] We have as much to fear from the tonsure as from the hauberk. Strike at the noble and the priest shrieks, strike at priest and the noble lays his hands upon glaive.[4] They are twin thieves who live upon our labor."

"It would take a clever man to live upon thy labor, Hugh," remarked one of the foresters, "seeing that the half of thy time is spent in swilling mead at the 'Pied Merlin.' "

"Better that than stealing the deer that thou art placed to guard, like some folk I know."

"If you dare open that swine's mouth against me," shouted the woodman, "I'll crop your ears for you before the hangman has the doing of it, thou long-jawed lack-brain."

"Nay, gentles, gentles!" cried Dame Eliza, in a singsong heedless voice, which showed that such bickerings were nightly things among her guests. "No brawling or brabbling, gentles! Take heed to the good name of the house."

"Besides, if it comes to the cropping of ears, there are other folk who may say their say," quoth the third laborer. "We are

[1] *dotard* (dō′tẽrd): foolish, senile. [2] *ermine cloak and the leathern tunic:* the clothes of the nobles and those of the common people. [3] *our foeman . . . proof:* our enemy is as much the men of the church as the noble men of war. [4] *glaive* (glāv): sword.

all freemen, and I trow that a yeoman's cudgel is as good as a forester's knife. By St. Anselm! it would be an evil day if we had to bend to our master's servants as well as to our masters."

"No man is my master save the King," the woodman answered. "Who is there, save a false traitor, who would refuse to serve the English king?"

"I know not about the English king," said the man Jenkin. "What sort of English king is it who cannot lay his tongue to a word of English? You mind last year when he came down to Malwood, with his inner marshal and his outer marshal, his justiciar, his seneschal, and his four and twenty guardsmen. One noontide I was by Franklin Swinton's gate, when up he rides with an attendant at his heels. 'Ouvre,' [1] he cried, 'ouvre,' or some such word, making signs for me to open the gate; and then 'Merci,' [2] as though he were afraid of me. And you talk of an English king?"

"I do not marvel at it," cried the Cambridge scholar, speaking in the high drawling voice which was common among his class. "It is not a tongue for men of sweet birth and delicate upbringing. It is a foul, snorting, snarling manner of speech. For myself, I swear by the learned Polycarp that I have most ease with Hebrew, and after that perchance with Arabian."

"I will not hear a word said against old King Ned," cried Hordle John in a voice like a bull. "What if he is fond of a bright eye and a saucy face? I know one of his subjects who could match him at that. If he cannot speak like an Englishman I trow that he can fight like an Englishman, and he was hammering at the gates of Paris while alehouse topers [3] were grutching and grumbling at home."

This loud speech, coming from a man of so formidable an appearance, somewhat daunted the disloyal party, and they fell into a sullen silence, in the midst of which the gleeman placed his battered harp upon his knee and began to pick out a melody upon the frayed strings.

"Elbow room for Floyting Will!" cried the woodmen. "Twang us a merry lilt."

"Aye, aye, the 'Lasses of Lancaster,' " one suggested.

"Or 'St. Simeon and the Devil.' "

[1] *ouvre:* French for "open." [2] *merci:* French for "Thank you." [3] *toper* (tōp'ẽr): a drunkard.

"Or the 'Jest of Henry Tobias.' "

To all these suggestions the gleeman made no response, but sat with his eye fixed abstractedly upon the ceiling, as one who calls words to his mind. Then, with a sudden sweep across the strings, he broke out into a song so gross and so foul that ere he had finished a verse the pure-minded lad sprang to his feet with the blood tingling in his face.

"How can you sing such things?" he cried. "You, too, an old man who should be an example to others."

The wayfarers all gazed in the utmost astonishment at the interruption.

"By the holy Dicon of Hampole! our silent clerk has found his tongue," said one of the woodmen. "What is amiss with the song then? How has it offended your babyship?"

"A milder and better-mannered song hath never been heard within these walls," cried another. "What sort of talk is this for a public inn?"

"Shall it be a litany,[1] my good clerk?" shouted a third; "or would a hymn be good enough to serve?"

The gleeman had put down his harp in high dudgeon.[2] "Am I to be preached to by a child?" he cried, staring across at Alleyne with an inflamed and angry countenance. "Is a hairless infant to raise his tongue against me, when I have sung in every fair from Tweed to Trent, and have twice been named aloud by the High Court of the Minstrels at Beverley? I shall sing no more tonight."

"Nay, but you will so," said one of the laborers. "Hi, Dame Eliza, bring a stoup of your best to Will to clear his throat. Go forward with thy song, and if our girl-faced clerk does not love it he can take to the road and go whence he came."

"Nay, but not too fast," broke in Hordle John. "There are two words in this matter. It may be that my little comrade has been overquick in reproof, he having gone early into the cloisters and seen little of the rough ways and words of the world. Yet there is truth in what he says, for, as you know well, the song was not of the cleanest. I shall stand by him, therefore, and he shall neither be put out on the road, nor shall his ears be offended indoors."

"Indeed, your high and mighty grace," sneered one of the yeomen, "have you in sooth so ordained?"

[1] *litany* (lĭt′*ȧ*·nĭ): a prayer. [2] *dudgeon* (dŭj′*ŭ*n): anger.

"By the Virgin!" said a second, "I think that you may both chance to find yourselves upon the road before long."

"And so belabored as to be scarce able to crawl along it," cried a third.

"Nay, I shall go! I shall go!" said Alleyne hurriedly, as Hordle John began to slowly roll up his sleeve and bare an arm like a leg of mutton. "I would not have you brawl about me."

"Hush! lad," he whispered, "I count them not a fly. They may find they have more tow on their distaff than they know how to spin.[1] Stand thou clear and give me space."

Both the foresters and the laborers had risen from their bench, and Dame Eliza and the traveling doctor had flung themselves between the two parties with soft words and soothing gestures, when the door of the "Pied Merlin" was flung violently open, and the attention of the company was drawn from their own quarrel to the newcomer who had burst so unceremoniously upon them.

Chapter 6

HOW SAMKIN AYLWARD WAGERED HIS FEATHERBED

He was a middle-sized man, of most massive and robust build, with an arching chest and extraordinary breadth of shoulder. His shaven face was as brown as a hazelnut, tanned and dried by the weather, with harsh, well-marked features, which were not improved by a long white scar which stretched from the corner of his left nostril to the angle of the jaw. His eyes were bright and searching, with something of menace and of authority in their quick glitter, and his mouth was firm-set and hard, as be-

[1] *they may . . . spin:* they may have bitten off more than they can chew.

fitted one who was wont [1] to set his face against danger. A straight sword by his side and a painted longbow jutting over his shoulder proclaimed his profession, while his scarred brigandine of chain mail and his dinted steel cap showed that he was no holiday soldier, but one who was even now fresh from the wars. A white surcoat with the lion of St. George in red upon the center covered his broad breast, while a sprig of new-plucked broom at the side of his headgear gave a touch of gaiety and grace to his grim, war-worn equipment.

"Ha!" he cried, blinking like an owl in the sudden glare. "Good even to you, comrades! Holà! a woman, by my soul!" and in an instant he had clipped Dame Eliza round the waist and was kissing her violently. His eye happening to wander upon the maid, however, he instantly abandoned the mistress and danced off after the other, who scurried in confusion up one of the ladders and dropped the heavy trap door upon her pursuer. He then turned back and saluted the landlady once more with the utmost relish and satisfaction.

"La petite [2] is frightened," said he. "Ah, c'est l'amour, l'amour! Curse this trick of French, which will stick to my throat. I must wash it out with some good English ale. By my hilt! camarades, there is no drop of French blood in my body, and I am a true English bowman, Samkin Aylward by name; and I tell you, mes amis,[3] that it warms my very heart-roots to set my feet on the dear old land once more. When I came off the galley at Hythe, this very day, I down on my bones, and I kissed the good brown earth, as I kiss thee now, ma belle, for it was eight long years since I had seen it. The very smell of it seemed life to me. But where are my six rascals? Holà, there! En avant!"

At the order, six men, dressed as common drudges, marched solemnly into the room, each bearing a huge bundle upon his head. They formed in military line, while the soldier stood in front of them with stern eyes, checking off their several packages.

"Number one—a French featherbed with the two counterpanes of white sendal," said he.

"Here, worthy sir," answered the first of the bearers, laying a great package down in the corner.

"Number two—seven ells [4] of red Turkey cloth and nine

[1] *wont* (wŭnt): accustomed. [2] *petite:* French for "young girl." [3] *mes amis:* French for "my friends." [4] *ell* (ĕl): twenty-seven inches.

ells of cloth of gold. Put it down by the other. Good dame, I prythee give each of these men a bottrine of wine or a jack of ale. Three—a full piece of white Genoan velvet with twelve ells of purple silk. Thou rascal, there is dirt on the hem! Thou hast brushed it against some wall, coquin!"

"Not I, most worthy sir," cried the carrier, shrinking away from the fierce eyes of the bowman.

"I say yes, dog! By the three kings! I have seen a man gasp out his last breath for less. Had you gone through the pain and unease that I have done to earn these things you would be at more care. I swear by my ten finger bones that there is not one of them that hath not cost its weight in French blood! Four—an incense-boat, a ewer of silver, a gold buckle, and a cope worked in pearls. I found them, camarades, at the Church of St. Denis in the harrying of Narbonne, and I took them away with me lest they fall into the hands of the wicked. Five—a cloak of fur turned up with miniver, a gold goblet with stand and cover, and a box of rose-colored sugar. See that you lay them together. Six—a box of moneys, three pounds of Limousin gold-work, a pair of boots, silver tagged, and, lastly, a store of naping linen. So, the tally is complete! Here is a groat apiece, and you may go."

"Go whither, worthy sir?" asked one of the carriers.

"Whither? To the devil if ye will. What is it to me? Now, ma belle, to supper. A pair of cold capons, a mortress of brawn, or what you will, with a flask or two of the right Gascony. I have crowns in my pouch, my sweet, and I mean to spend them. Bring in wine while the food is dressing. Buvons,[1] my brave lads; you shall each empty a stoup with me."

Here was an offer which the company in an English inn at that or any other date are slow to refuse. The flagons were regathered and came back with the white foam dripping over their edges. Two of the woodmen and three of the laborers drank their portions off hurriedly and trooped off together, for their homes were distant and the hour late. The others, however, drew closer, leaving the place of honor, to the right of the gleeman, to the free-handed newcomer. He had thrown off his steel cap and his brigandine,[2] and had placed them with his sword, his quiver and

[1] *Buvons:* French for "Let us drink." [2] *brigandine* (brĭg′ăn·dīn): coat of body armor.

his painted longbow on the top of his varied heap of plunder in the corner. Now, with his thick and somewhat bowed legs stretched in front of the blaze, his green jerkin thrown open, and a great quart pot held in his corded fist, he looked the picture of comfort and of good-fellowship. His hard-set face had softened, and the thick crop of crisp brown curls which had been hidden by his helmet grew low upon his massive neck. He might have been forty years of age, though hard toil and harder pleasure had left their grim marks upon his features. Alleyne had ceased painting his pied merlin, and sat, brush in hand, staring with open eyes at a type of man so strange and so unlike any whom he had met. Men had been good or had been bad in his catalogue, but here was a man who was fierce one instant and gentle the next, with a curse on his lips and a smile in his eye. What was to be made of such a man as that?

It chanced that the soldier looked up and saw the questioning glance which the young clerk threw upon him. He raised his flagon and drank to him, with a merry flash of his white teeth.

"A toi, mon garçon," [1] he cried. "Hast surely never seen a man-at-arms, that thou shouldst stare so?"

"I never have," said Alleyne frankly, "though I have oft heard talk of their deeds."

"By my hilt!" cried the other, "if you were to cross the narrow sea, you would find them as thick as bees at a tee-hole. Couldst not shoot a bolt down any street of Bordeaux, I warrant, but you would pink archer, squire, or knight. There are more breastplates than gaberdines to be seen, I promise you."

"And where got you all these pretty things?" asked Hordle John, pointing at the heap in the corner.

"Where there is as much more waiting for any brave lad to pick it up. Where a good man can always earn a good wage, and where he need look upon no man as his paymaster, but just reach his hand out and help himself. Aye, it is a goodly and a proper life. And here I drink to mine old comrades, and the saints be with them! Arouse all together, mes enfants, under pain of my displeasure. To Sir Claude Latour and the White Company!"

"Sir Claude Latour and the White Company!" shouted the travelers, draining off their goblets.

[1] *A toi, mon garçon:* French for "To thee, my boy."

"Well quaffed, mes braves! It is for me to fill your cups again, since you have drained them to my dear lads of the white jerkin. Holà! mon ange, bring wine and ale. How runs the old stave?"

We'll drink all together
To the gray goose feather
And the land where the gray goose flew.

He roared out the catch in a harsh, unmusical voice, and ended with a shout of laughter. "I trust that I am a better bowman than a minstrel," said he.

"Methinks I have some remembrance of the lilt," remarked the gleeman, running his fingers over the strings. "Hoping that it will give thee no offense, most holy sir"—with a vicious snap at Alleyne—"and with the kind permit of the company, I will even venture upon it."

Many a time in the after days, Alleyne Edricson seemed to see that scene, for all that so many which were stranger and more stirring were soon to crowd upon him. The fat, red-faced gleeman, the listening group, the archer with upraised finger beating in time to the music, and the huge sprawling figure of Hordle John, all thrown into red light and black shadow by the flickering fire in the center—memory was to come often lovingly back to it. At the time he was lost in admiration at the deft way in which the jongleur disguised the loss of his two missing strings, and the lusty, hearty fashion in which he trolled out his little ballad of the outland bowmen, which ran in some such fashion as this:

What of the bow?
The bow was made in England:
Of true wood, of yew wood,

The wood of English bows;
So men who are free
Love the old yew tree
And the land where the yew tree grows.

What of the cord?
The cord was made in England:
A rough cord, a tough cord,
A cord that bowmen love;
So we'll drain our jacks
To the English flax
And the land where the hemp was wove.

What of the shaft?
The shaft was cut in England:
A long shaft, a strong shaft,
Barbed and trim and true;
So we'll drink together
To the gray goose feather
And the land where the gray goose flew.

What of the men?
The men were bred in England:
The bowman—the yeoman—
The lads of dale and fell.
Here's to you—and to you!
To the hearts that are true
And the land where the true hearts dwell.

"Well sung, by my hilt!" shouted the archer in high delight. "Many a night have I heard that song, both in the old wartime and after in the days of the White Company, when Black Simon of Norwich would lead the stave, and four hundred of the best bowmen that ever drew string would come roaring in upon the chorus. I have seen old John Hawkwood, the same who has led half the Company into Italy, stand laughing in his beard as he heard it, until his plates rattled again. But to get the full smack of it, ye must yourselves be English bowmen and be far off upon an outland soil."

Whilst the song had been singing, Dame Eliza and the maid had placed a board across two trestles and had laid upon it the knife, the spoon, the salt, the tranchoir of bread, and finally the smoking dish which held the savory supper. The archer settled himself to it like one who had known what it was to find good food scarce; but his tongue still went as merrily as his teeth.

"It passes me," he cried, "how all you lusty fellows can bide scratching your backs at home when there are such doings over the seas. Look at me—what have I to do? It is but the eye to the cord, the cord to the shaft, and the shaft to the mark.[1] There is the whole song of it. It is but what you do yourselves for pleasure upon a Sunday evening at the parish village butts."

"And the wage?" asked a laborer.

"You see what the wage brings," he answered. "I eat of the best, and I drink deep. I treat my friend, and I ask no friend to treat me. I clap a silk gown on my girl's back. Never a knight's

[1] *but the eye . . . the mark:* nothing but shooting arrows from the bow.

lady shall be better betrimmed and betrinketed. How of all that mon garçon? And how of the heap of trifles that you can see for yourselves in yonder corner? They are from the South French, every one, upon whom I have been making war. By my hilt! camarades, I think that I may let my plunder speak for itself."

"It seems indeed to be a goodly service," said the tooth-drawer.

"Tête bleu! yes, indeed. Then there is the chance of a ransom. Why, look you, in the affair at Brignais some four years back, when the companies slew James of Bourbon and put his army to the sword, there was scarce a man of ours who had not count, baron, or knight. Peter Karsdale, who was but a common country lout newly brought over, with the English fleas still hopping under his doublet, laid his great hands upon the Sieur Amaury de Chatonville, who owns half Picardy, and had five thousand crowns out of him, with his horse and harness. 'Tis true that a French wench took it all off Peter as quick as the Frenchman paid it; but what then? By the twang of string! it would be a bad thing if money was not made to be spent; and how better than on woman—eh, ma belle?"

"It would indeed be a bad thing if we had not our brave archers to bring wealth and kindly customs into the country," quoth Dame Eliza, on whom the soldier's free and open ways had made a deep impression.

"A toi, ma chérie!" said he, with his hand over his heart. "Holà! there is la petite peeping from behind the door. A toi, aussi, ma petite! Mon Dieu! but the lass has a good color!"

"There is one thing, fair sir," said the Cambridge student in his piping voice, "which I would fain [1] that you would make more clear. As I understand it, there was peace made at the town of Bretigny some six years back between our most gracious monarch and the King of the French. This being so, it seems most passing strange that you should talk so loudly of war and of companies when there is no quarrel between the French and us."

"Meaning that I lie," said the archer, laying down his knife.

"May heaven forfend!" cried the student hastily. "*Magna est veritas set rara,*[2] which means in the Latin tongue that archers

[1] *fain* (fān): to wish. [2] *Magna . . . rara:* This actually means "Truth is great, but rare."

are all honorable men. I come to you seeking knowledge, for it is my trade to learn."

"I fear that you are yet a 'prentice to that trade," quoth the soldier; "for there is no child over the water but could answer what you ask. Know then that though there may be peace between our own provinces and the French, yet within the marches [1] of France there is always war, for the country is much divided against itself, and is furthermore harried by bands of flayers, skinners, Brabaçons, and the rest of them. When every man's grip is on his neighbor's throat, and every five-sous-piece of a baron is marching with tuck of drum to fight whom he will, it would be a strange thing if five hundred brave English boys could not pick up a living. Now that Sir John Hawkwood hath gone with the East Anglian lads and the Nottingham woodmen into the service of the Marquis of Montferrat to fight against the Lord of Milan, there are but ten score of us left, yet I trust that I may be able to bring some back with me to fill the ranks of the White Company. By the tooth of Peter! it would be a bad thing if I could not muster many a Hamptonshire man who would be ready to strike in under the red flag of St. George, and the more so if Sir Nigel Loring, of Christchurch, should don hauberk [2] once more and take the lead of us."

"Ah, you would indeed be in luck then," quoth a woodman; "for it is said that, setting aside the prince, and mayhap good old Sir John Chandos, there was not in the whole army a man of such tried courage."

"It is sooth, every word of it," the archer answered. "I have seen him with these two eyes in a stricken field, and never did man carry himself better. Mon Dieu! yes, ye would not credit it to look at him or to hearken to his soft voice, but from the sailing from Orwell down to the foray to Paris, and that is clear twenty years, there was not a skirmish, onfall, sally, bushment, escalado, or battle, but Sir Nigel was in the heart of it. I go now to Christchurch with a letter to him from Sir Claude Latour to ask him if he will take the place of Sir John Hawkwood; and there is the more chance that he will if I bring one or two likely men at my heels. What say you, woodman: wilt leave the bucks to loose a shaft at a nobler mark?"

[1] *marches:* frontiers or borderlands. [2] *don hauberk* (dŏn hô′bûrk): to put on armor.

The forester shook his head. "I have wife and child at Emery Down," quoth he; "I would not leave them for such a venture."

"You, then, young sir?" asked the archer.

"Nay, I am a man of peace," said Alleyne Edricson. "Besides, I have other work to do."

"Peste!" growled the soldier, striking his flagon on the board until the dishes danced again. "What, in the name of the devil, hath come over the folk? Why sit ye all moping by the fireside, like crows round a dead horse, when there is man's work to be done within a few short leagues of ye? Out upon you all, as a set of laggards and hang-backs! By my hilt, I believe that the men of England are all in France already, and that what is left behind are in sooth the women dressed up in their paltocks and hosen."

"Archer," quoth Hordle John, "you have lied more than once and more than twice; for which, and also because I see much in you to dislike, I am sorely tempted to lay you upon your back."

"By my hilt! then, I have found a man at last!" shouted the bowman. "And, 'fore God, you are a better man than I take you for if you can lay me on my back, mon garçon. I have won the ram more times than there are toes to my feet, and for seven long years I have found no man in the Company who could make my jerkin dusty."

"We have had enough bobance and boasting," said Hordle John, rising and throwing off his doublet. "I will show you that there are better men left in England than ever went thieving to France."

"Pasques Dieu!" cried the archer, loosening his jerkin and eyeing his foeman over with the keen glance of one who is a judge of manhood. "I have only once before seen such a body of a man. By your leave, my red-headed friend, I should be right sorry to exchange buffets with you; and I will allow that there is no man in the Company who would pull against you on a rope; so let that be a salve to your pride. On the other hand I should judge that you have led a life of ease for some months back, and that my muscle is harder than your own. I am ready to wager upon myself against you if you are not afeard."

"Afeard, thou lurdan!" [1] growled big John. "I never saw the

[1] *lurdan* (lûr′dăn): a stupid, lazy fellow.

face yet of the man that I was afeard of. Come out, and we shall see who is the better man."

"But the wager?"

"I have naught to wager. Come out for the love and the lust of the thing."

"Naught to wager!" cried the soldier. "Why, you have that which I covet above all things. It is that big body of thine that I am after. See, now, mon garçon. I have a French featherbed there, which I have been at pains to keep these years back. I had it at the sacking of Issodun, and the King himself hath not such a bed. If you throw me, it is thine; but, if I throw you, then you are under a vow to take bow and bill, and hie with me to France, there to serve in the White Company as long as we be enrolled."

"A fair wager!" cried all the travelers, moving back their benches and trestles, so as to give fair field for the wrestlers.

"Then you may bid farewell to your bed, soldier," said Hordle John.

"Nay; I shall keep the bed, and I shall have you to France in spite of your teeth, and you shall live to thank me for it. How shall it be, then, mon enfant? Collar and elbow, or close-lock, or catch how you can?"

"To the devil with your tricks," said John, opening and shutting his great red hands. "Stand forth, and let me clip thee."

"Shalt clip me as best you can then," quoth the archer, moving out into the open space and keeping a most wary eye upon his opponent. He had thrown off his green jerkin, and his chest was covered only by a pink silk jupon, or undershirt, cut low in the neck and sleeveless. Hordle John was stripped from his waist upwards, and his huge body, with his great muscles swelling out like the gnarled roots of an oak, towered high above the soldier. The other, however, though near a foot shorter, was a man of great strength; and there was a gloss upon his white skin which was wanting in the heavier limbs of the renegade monk. He was quick on his feet, too, and skilled at the game; so that it was clear, from the poise of head and shine of eye, that he counted the chances to be in his favor. It would have been hard that night, through the whole length of England, to set up a finer pair in face of each other.

Big John stood waiting in the center with a sullen, menacing eye, and his red hair in a bristle, while the archer paced lightly and swiftly to the right and the left with crooked knee and hands advanced. Then with a sudden dash, so swift and fierce that the eye could scarce follow it, he flew in upon his man and locked his leg round him. It was a grip that, between men of equal strength, would mean a fall; but Hordle John tore him off from him as he might a rat and hurled him across the room, so that his head cracked up against the wooden wall.

"Ma foi!" cried the bowman, passing his fingers through his curls, "you were not far from the featherbed then, mon gar. A little more and this good hostel would have a new window."

Nothing daunted, he approached his man once more; but this time with more caution than before. With a quick feint he threw the other off his guard and then, bounding upon him, threw his legs round his waist and his arms round his bull-neck, in the hope of bearing him to the ground with the sudden shock. With a bellow of rage, Hordle John squeezed him limp in his huge arms and then, picking him up, cast him down upon the floor with a force which might well have splintered a bone or two, had not the archer with the most perfect coolness clung to the other's forearms to break his fall. As it was, he dropped upon his feet and kept his balance, though it sent a jar through his frame which set every joint a-creaking. He bounded back from his perilous foeman; but the other, heated by the bout, rushed madly after him and so gave the practiced wrestler the very vantage for which he had planned. As big John flung himself upon him, the archer ducked under the great red hands that clutched for him and, catching his man round the thighs, hurled him over his shoulder—helped as much by his own mad rush as by the trained strength of the heave. To Alleyne's eye, it was as if John had taken unto himself wings and flown. As he hurtled through the air, with giant limbs revolving, the lad's heart was in his mouth; for surely no man ever yet had such a fall and came scathless out of it. In truth, hardy as the man was, his neck had been assuredly broken had he not pitched head first on the very midriff of the drunken artist, who was slumbering so peacefully in the corner, all unaware of these stirring doings. The luckless limner, thus suddenly brought out from his dreams, sat up with a piercing yell, while Hordle John bounded back into the circle almost as rapidly as he had left it.

"One more fall, by all the saints!" he cried, throwing out his arms.

"Not I," quoth the archer, pulling on his clothes, "I have come well out of the business. I would sooner wrestle with the great bear of Navarre."

"It was a trick," cried John.

"Aye was it! By my ten finger bones! it is a trick that will add a proper man to the ranks of the Company."

"Oh, for that," said the other, "I count it not a fly; for I had promised myself a good hour ago that I should go with thee, since the life seems to be a goodly and proper one. Yet I would fain have had the featherbed."

"I doubt it not, mon ami," quoth the archer, going back to his tankard. "Here is to thee, lad, and may we be good comrades to each other! But, holà! what is it that ails our friend of the wrathful face?"

The unfortunate limner had been sitting up, rubbing himself ruefully and staring about with a vacant gaze, which showed that he knew neither where he was nor what had occurred to him. Suddenly, however, a flash of intelligence had come over his sodden features, and he rose and staggered for the door. " 'Ware [1] the ale!" he said in a hoarse whisper, shaking a warning finger at the company. "Oh, holy Virgin, 'ware the ale!" and clapping his hands to his injury, he flitted off into the darkness, amid a shout of laughter, in which the vanquished joined as merrily as the victor. The remaining forester and the two laborers were also ready for the road, and the rest of the company turned to the blankets which Dame Eliza and the maid had laid out for them upon the floor. Alleyne, weary with the unwonted excitements of the day, was soon in a deep slumber, broken only by fleeting visions of the many strange folk whom he had met that day.

[1] *'ware* (wār): beware of.

Chapter 7

HOW THE THREE COMRADES JOURNEYED THROUGH THE WOODLANDS

At early dawn the country inn was all alive, for it was rare indeed that an hour of daylight would be wasted at a time when lighting was so scarce and dear. Indeed, early as it was when Dame Eliza began to stir, it seemed that others could be earlier still, for the door was ajar, and the learned student of Cambridge had taken himself off, with a mind which was too intent upon the high things of antiquity to stoop to consider the fourpence which he owed for bed and board. It was the shrill outcry of the landlady when she found her loss, and the clucking of the hens, which had streamed in through the open door, that first broke in upon the slumbers of the tired wayfarers.

Once afoot, it was not long before the company began to disperse. A sleek mule with red trappings was brought round from some neighboring shed for the physician, and he ambled away with much dignity upon his road to Southampton. The tooth-drawer and the gleeman called for a cup of small ale apiece and started off together for Ringwood fair, the old jongleur looking very yellow in the eye and swollen in the face after his overnight potations. The archer, however, who had drunk more than any man in the room, was as merry as a grig, and having kissed the matron and chased the maid up the ladder once more, he went out to the brook and came back with the water dripping from his face and hair.

"Holà! my man of peace," he cried to Alleyne, "whither are you bent this morning?"

"To Minstead," quoth he. "My brother Simon Edricson is socman there, and I go to bide with him for a while. I prythee, let me have my score, good dame."

"Score, indeed!" cried she, standing with upraised hands in front of the panel on which Alleyne had worked the night before. "Say, rather, what it is that I owe to thee, good youth. Aye, this is indeed a pied merlin, and with a leveret [1] under its claws, as I

[1] *leveret* (lĕv′ĕr·ĕt): a young hare.

am a living woman. By the rood of Waltham! but thy touch is deft and dainty."

"And see the red eye of it!" cried the maid.

"Aye, and the open beak."

"And the ruffled wing," added Hordle John.

"By my hilt!" cried the archer, "it is the very bird itself."

The young clerk flushed with pleasure at this chorus of praise, rude and indiscriminate indeed, and yet so much heartier and less grudging than any which he had ever heard from the critical brother Jerome, or the short-spoken Abbot. There was, it would seem, great kindness as well as great wickedness in this world of which he had heard so little that was good. His hostess would hear nothing of his paying either for bed or for board, while the archer and Hordle John placed a hand upon either shoulder and led him off to the board, where some smoking fish, a dish of spinach, and a jug of milk were laid out for their breakfast.

"I should not be surprised to learn, mon camarade," said the soldier, as he heaped a slice of fish upon Alleyne's tranchoir of bread, "that you could read written things, since you are so ready with your brushes and pigments."

"It would be shame to the good brothers of Beaulieu if I could not," he answered, "seeing that I have been their clerk this ten years back."

The bowman looked at him with great respect. "Think of that!" said he. "And you with not a hair to your face, and a skin like a girl. I can shoot three hundred and fifty paces with my little popper there, and four hundred and twenty with the great war bow; yet I can make nothing of this, nor read my own name if you were to set 'Sam Aylward' up against me. In the whole Company there was only one man who could read, and he fell down a well at the taking of Ventadour, which proves that the thing is not suited to a soldier, though most needful to a clerk."

"I can make some show at it," said big John; "though I was scarce long enough among the monks to catch the whole trick of it."

"Here, then, is something to try upon," quoth the archer, pulling a square of parchment from the inside of his tunic. It was tied securely with a broad band of purple silk, and firmly sealed at either end with a large red seal. John pored long and earnestly over the inscription upon the back, with his brows bent as one who bears up against great mental strain.

"Not having read much of late," he said, "I am loath to say too much about what this may be. Some might say one thing and some another, just as one bowman loves the yew, and a second will not shoot save with the ash. To me, by the length and the look of it, I should judge this to be a verse from one of the Psalms."

The bowman shook his head. "It is scarce likely," he said, "that Sir Claude Latour should send me all the way across seas with naught more weighty than a psalm verse. You have clean overshot the butts this time, mon camarade. Give it to the little one. I will wager my featherbed that he makes more sense of it."

"Why, it is written in the French tongue," said Alleyne, "and in a right clerkly hand. This is how it runs: 'A le moult puissant et moult honorable chevalier, Sir Nigel Loring de Christchurch, de son trés fidèle ami Sir Claude Latour, capitaine de la Compagnie blanche, châtelain de Biscar, grand seigneur de Montchâteau, vavaseur de le renommé Gaston, Comte de Foix, tenant les droits de la haute justice, de la milieu, et de la basse.' Which signifies in our speech: 'To the very powerful and very honorable knight, Sir Nigel Loring of Christchurch, from his very faithful friend Sir Claude Latour, captain of the White Company, chatelain of Biscar, grand lord of Montchâteau and vassal to the renowned Gaston, Count of Foix, who holds the rights of the high justice, the middle, and the low.' "

"Look at that now!" cried the bowman in triumph. "That is just what he would have said."

"I can see now that it is even so," said John, examining the parchment again. "Though I scarce understand this high, middle, and low."

"By my hilt! you would understand it if you were Jacques Bonhomme.[1] The low justice means that you may fleece him, and the middle that you may torture him, and the high that you may slay him. That is about the truth of it. But this is the letter which I am to take; and since the platter is clean, it is time that we trussed up and were afoot. You come with me, mon gros Jean; and as to you, little one, where did you say that you journeyed?"

"To Minstead."

[1] *Jacques Bonhomme:* the nickname for French peasants as a class.

"Ah, yes. I know this forest country well, though I was born myself in the hundred of Easebourne, in the borough of Chichester, hard by the village of Midhurst. Yet I have not a word to say against the Hampton men, for there are no better comrades or truer archers in the whole Company than some who learned to loose the string in these very parts. We shall travel round with you to Minstead, lad, seeing that it is little out of our way."

"I am ready," said Alleyne, right pleased at the thought of such company upon the road.

"So am not I. I must store my plunder at this inn, since the hostess is an honest woman. Holà! ma chérie, I wish to leave with you my gold-work, my velvet, my silk, my featherbed, my incense boat, my ewer, my naping linen, and all the rest of it. I take only the money in a linen bag, and the box of rose-colored sugar which is a gift from my captain to the Lady Loring. Wilt guard my treasure for me?"

"It shall be put in the safest loft, good archer. Come when you may, you shall find it ready for you."

"Now, there is a true friend!" cried the bowman, taking her hand. "There is a bonne amie! English land and English women, say I, and French wine and French plunder. I shall be back anon, mon ange. I am a lonely man, my sweeting, and I must settle some day when the wars are over and done. Mayhap you and I— Ah, méchante,[1] méchante! There is la petite peeping from behind the door. Now, John, the sun is over the trees; you must be brisker than this when the bugleman blows 'Bows and Bills.' "

"I have been waiting this time back," said Hordle John gruffly.

"Then we must be off. Adieu, ma vie! The two livres shall settle the score and buy some ribbons against the next kermesse.[2] Do not forget Sam Aylward, for his heart shall ever be thine alone—and thine, ma petite! So, marchons, and may St. Julian grant us as good quarters elsewhere!"

The sun had risen over Ashurst and Denny woods, and was shining brightly, though the eastern wind had a sharp flavor to it, and the leaves were flickering thickly from the trees.

The wayfarers passed through Lyndhurst, struck through the scattered huts of Emery Down, and out on to the broad roll-

[1] *méchante:* French for "naughty." [2] *kermesse* (kûr′mĕs): an outdoor festival or fair.

ing heath covered deep in ferns and in heather, where droves of the half-wild black forest pigs were rooting about amongst the hillocks. The woods about this point fall away to the left and the right, while the road curves upwards and the wind sweeps keenly over the swelling uplands. The broad strips of bracken glowed red and yellow against the black peaty soil, and a queenly doe who grazed among them turned her white front and her great questioning eyes towards the wayfarers. Alleyne gazed in admiration at the supple beauty of the creature; but the archer's fingers played with his quiver, and his eyes glistened with the fell instinct which urges a man to slaughter.

"Tête Dieu!" he growled, "were this France, or even Guienne, we should have a fresh haunch for our none-meat. Law or no law, I have a mind to loose a bolt at her."

"I would break your stave across my knee first," cried John, laying his great hand upon the bow. "What! man, I am forest-born, and I know what comes of it. In our own township of Hordle two have lost their eyes and one his skin for this very thing. On my troth, I felt no great love when I first saw you, but since then I have conceived overmuch regard for you to wish to see the verderer's flayer at work upon you."

"It is my trade to risk my skin," growled the archer; but none the less he thrust his quiver over his hip again and turned his face for the west.

As they advanced, the path still tended upwards, running from heath into copses of holly and yew, and so back into heath again. It was joyful to hear the merry whistle of blackbirds as they darted from one clump of greenery to the other. Now and again a peaty amber-colored stream rippled across their way, with ferny overgrown banks, where the blue kingfisher flitted busily from side to side, or the gray and pensive heron, swollen with trout and dignity, stood ankle-deep among the sedges. Chattering jays and loud wood-pigeons flapped thickly overhead, while ever and anon the measured tapping of Nature's carpenter, the great green woodpecker, sounded from each wayside grove. On either side, as the path mounted, the long sweep of country broadened and expanded, sloping down on the one side through yellow forest and brown moor to the distant smoke of Lymington and the blue misty channel which lay alongside the sky line, while to the north the woods rolled away, grove topping grove, to where in the furthest distance the white spire of Salisbury stood out hard and clear against the cloudless sky. To Alleyne, whose days had been spent in the low-lying coastland, the eager upland air and the wide free countryside gave a sense of life and of the joy of living which made his young blood tingle in his veins. Even the heavy John was not unmoved by the beauty of their road, while the bowman whistled lustily or sang snatches of French love songs in a voice which might have scared the most stouthearted maiden that ever hearkened to serenade.

"I'm a fighting man," he remarked presently. "I warm to one who cares not overmuch for his skin. And he must have good power of hatred and some gall in his liver."

"Ah me!" sighed Alleyne. "Would it not be better if he had some love in his heart?"

"I would not say nay to that. By my hilt! I shall never be said to be traitor to the little King. Let a man love the sex. Pasques Dieu! they are made to be loved, les petites, from wimple down to shoestring! I am right glad, mon garçon, to see that the good monks have trained thee so wisely and so well."

"Nay, I meant not worldly love, but rather that his heart should soften towards those who have wronged him."

The archer shook his head. "A man should love those of his own breed," said he. "But it is not nature that an English-born man should love a Scot or a Frenchman. Ma foi! you have not seen a drove of Nithsdale raiders on their Galloway nags or you would not speak of loving them. I would as soon take Beelzebub himself to my arms. I fear, mon gar, that they have taught thee but badly at Beaulieu, for surely a bishop knows more of what is right and what is ill than an abbot can do, and I myself with these very eyes saw the Bishop of Lincoln hew into a Scottish hobeler with a battle-ax, which was a passing strange way of showing him that he loved him."

Alleyne scarce saw his way to argue in the face of so decided an opinion on the part of a high dignitary of the Church. "You have borne arms against the Scots, then?" he asked.

"Why, man, I first loosed string in battle when I was but a lad, younger by two years than you, at Neville's Cross, under the Lord Mowbray. Later, I served under the Warden of Berwick, who held the King of Scots to ransom. Ma foi! it is rough soldiering, and a good school for one who would learn to be hardy and war-wise."

"I have heard that the Scots are good men of war," said Hordle John.

"For axmen and for spearmen I have not seen their match," the archer answered. "They can travel, too, with bag of meal and grid-iron slung to their sword belt, so that it is ill to follow them. There are scant crops and few beeves in the borderland, where a man must reap his grain with sickle in one fist and brown bill [1] in the other. On the other hand, they are the sorriest archers that I have ever seen and cannot so much as aim with the arbalest, to say nought of the longbow. Again, they are mostly poor folk, even the nobles among them, so that there are few who can buy as good a brigandine of chain mail as that which I am wearing, and it is ill for them to stand up against our own knights, who carry the price of five Scotch farms upon their chest and shoulders. Man for man, with equal weapons, they are as worthy and valiant men as could be found in the whole of Christendom."

"And the French?" asked Alleyne, to whom the archer's light gossip had all the relish that the words of the man of action have for the recluse.

"The French are also very worthy men. We have had great good fortune in France, and it hath led to much bobance and campfire talk, but I have ever noticed that those who know the most have the least to say about it. I have seen Frenchmen fight both in open field, in the intaking and the defending of towns or castlewicks, in escalados,[2] camisades,[3] night forays, bushments, sallies, outfalls,[4] and knightly spear-runnings. Their knights and squires, lad, are every whit as good as ours, and I could pick out a score of those who ride behind Du Guesclin who would hold the lists with sharpened lances against the best men in the army of England. On the other hand, their common folk are so crushed down with gabelle,[5] and poll tax, and every manner of cursed tallage,[6] that the spirit has passed right out of them. It is a fool's plan to teach a man to be a cur in peace and think that he will be a

[1] *brown bill:* a spear having a hooked point. [2] *escalado* (ĕs′kȧ·lä′dō): an attack on a fortified place, in which ladders are used. [3] *camisade* (kăm′ĭ·sād′): a night attack. [4] *outfall* (out′fŏl′): a quick attack. [5] *gabelle* (gȧ·bĕl′): a tax on salt. [6] *tallage* (tăl′ĭj): a tax paid by a tenant to his lord.

lion in war. Fleece them like sheep and sheep they will remain. If the nobles had not conquered the poor folk, it is like enough that we should not have conquered the nobles."

"But they must be sorry folk to bow down to the rich in such a fashion," said big John. "I am but a poor commoner of England myself, and yet I know something of charters, liberties, franchises, usages, privileges, customs, and the like. If these be broken, then all men know that it is time to buy arrowheads."

"Aye, but the men of the law are strong in France as well as the men of war. By my hilt! I hold that a man has more to fear there from the inkpot of the one than from the iron of the other. There is ever some cursed sheepskin in their strong boxes to prove that the rich man should be richer and the poor man poorer. It would scarce pass in England, but they are quiet folk over the water."

"And what other nations have you seen in your travels, good sir?" asked Alleyne Edricson. His young mind hungered for plain facts of life, after the long course of speculation and of mysticism on which he had been trained.

"I have seen the low countryman in arms, and I have nought to say against him. Heavy and slow is he by nature, and is not to be brought into battle for the sake of a lady's eyelash or the twang of a minstrel's string, like the hotter blood of the south. But ma foi! lay hand on his wool-bales, or trifle with his velvet of Bruges, and out buzzes every stout burgher, like bees from the tee-hole, ready to lay on as though it were his one business in life. By Our Lady! they have shown the French at Courtrai and elsewhere that they are as deft in wielding steel as in welding it."

"And the men of Spain?"

"They, too, are very hardy soldiers, the more so as for many hundred years they have had to fight hard against the cursed followers of the black Mahound, who have pressed upon them from the south, and still, as I understand, hold the fairer half of the country. I had a turn with them upon the sea when they came over to Winchelsea, and the good Queen with her ladies sat upon the cliffs looking down at us, as if it had been joust or tourney. By my hilt! it was a sight that was worth the seeing, for all that was best in England was out on the water that day. We went forth in little ships and came back in great galleys—for of fifty tall ships of Spain, over two score flew the Cross of St. George ere the sun had set. But now, youngster, I have answered you freely, and I trow it is time that you answered me. Let things be plat and plain between us. I am a man who shoots straight at his mark. You saw the things I had with me at yonder hostel: name which you will, save only the box of rose-colored sugar which I take to the Lady Loring, and you shall have it if you will but come with me to France."

"Nay," said Alleyne, "I would gladly come with ye to France or where else ye will, just to list to your talk, and because ye are the only two friends that I have in the whole wide world outside of the cloisters; but, indeed, it may not be, for my duty is towards my brother, seeing that father and mother are dead, and he may elder. Besides, when ye talk of taking me to France, ye do not conceive how useless I should be to you, seeing that neither by training nor by nature am I fitted for the wars, and there seems to be nought but strife in those parts."

"That comes from my fool's talk," cried the archer; "for being a man of no learning myself, my tongue turns to blades and targets, even as my hand does. Know then that for every parchment in England there are twenty in France. For every statue, cut gem, shrine, carven screen, or what else might please the eye of a learned clerk, there are a good hundred to our one. At the spoiling of Carcasonne I have seen chambers stored with writing, though not one man in our Company could read them. Again, in Arles, and Nîmes, and other towns that I could name, there are the great arches and fortalices still standing which were built of old by giant men who came from the south. Can I not see by your brightened eye how you would love to look upon these things? Come, then, with me, and, by these ten finger bones! there is not one of them which you shall not see."

"I should indeed love to look upon them," Alleyne answered; "but I have come from Beaulieu for a purpose, and I must be true to my service, even as thou art true to thine."

"Bethink you again, mon ami," quoth Aylward, "that you might do much good yonder, since there are three hundred men in the Company, and none who has ever a word of grace for them, and yet the Virgin knows that there was never a set of men who were in more need of it. Sickerly [1] the one duty may balance the other. Your brother hath done without you this many a year,

[1] *sickerly* (sĭk'ẽr·lĭ): surely.

and, as I gather, he hath never walked as far as Beaulieu to see you during all that time, so he cannot be in any great need of you."

"Besides," said John, "the Socman of Minstead is a byword through the forest, from Bramshaw Hill to Holmesley Walk. He is a drunken, brawling, perilous churl,[1] as you may find to your cost."

"The more reason that I should strive to mend him," quoth Alleyne. "There is no need to urge me, friends, for my own wishes would draw me to France, and it would be a joy to me if I could go with you. But, indeed and indeed, it cannot be, so here I take my leave of you, for yonder square tower amongst the trees upon the right must surely be the church of Minstead, and I may reach it by this path through the woods."

"Well, God be with thee, lad!" cried the archer, pressing Alleyne to his heart. "I am quick to love, and quick to hate, and 'fore God I am loath to part."

"Would it not be well," said John, "that we should wait here and see what manner of greeting you have from your brother? You may prove to be as welcome as the King's purveyor [2] to the village dame."

"Nay, nay," he answered; "ye must not bide for me, for where I go, I stay."

"Yet it may be as well that you should know whither we go," said the archer. "We shall now journey south through the woods until we come out upon the Christchurch Road, and so onwards, hoping tonight to reach the castle of Sir William Montacute, Earl of Salisbury, of which Sir Nigel Loring is constable.[3] There we shall bide, and it is like enough that for a month or more you may find us there, ere we are ready for our viage back to France."

It was hard indeed for Alleyne to break away from these two new but hearty friends, and so strong was the combat between his conscience and his inclinations that he dared not look round, lest his resolution should slip away from him. It was not until he was deep among the tree trunks that he cast a glance backwards, when he found that he could still see them through

[1] *churl* (chûrl): a selfish, unpleasant, low person. [2] *purveyor* (pûr-vā′ēr): an officer who had the right to demand provisions. [3] *constable* (kŭn′stȧ·b'l): the keeper, or highest officer.

the branches on the road above him. The archer was standing with folded arms, his bow jutting from over his shoulder, and the sun gleaming brightly upon his headpiece and the links of his chain mail, and beside him stood his giant recruit. Even as Alleyne watched them they turned upon their heels and plodded off together upon their way.

Chapter 8

HOW STRANGE THINGS BEFELL IN MINSTEAD WOOD

The path which the young clerk had now to follow lay through a magnificent forest of the very heaviest timber, where the giant boles of oak and of beech formed long aisles in every direction, shooting up their huge branches to build the majestic arches of Nature's own cathedral. Beneath lay a broad carpet of the softest and greenest moss, flecked over with fallen leaves, but yielding pleasantly to the foot of the traveler. The track which guided him was one so seldom used that in places it lost itself entirely among the grass, to reappear as a reddish rut between the distant tree trunks. It was very still here in the heart of the woodlands. The gentle rustle of the branches and the distant cooing of pigeons were the only sounds which broke in upon the silence, save that once Alleyne heard afar off a merry call upon a hunting bugle and the shrill yapping of the hounds.

It was not without some emotion that he looked upon the scene around him, for, in spite of his secluded life, he knew enough of the ancient greatness of his own family to be aware that the time had been when they had held undisputed sway over all that tract of country. His father could trace his pure Saxon lineage back to that Godfrey Malf who had held the manors of Bisterne and of Minstead at the time when the Norman first set mailed foot upon English soil. The afforestation [1] of the district,

[1] *afforestation* (ă·fŏr·ĕs·tā·shŭn): conversion into hunting land.

however, and its conversion into a royal demesne had clipped off a large section of his estate. The fate of the ancestor had been typical of that of his descendants. During three hundred years their domains had gradually contracted, sometimes through royal or feudal encroachment, and sometimes through such gifts to the Church as that with which Alleyne's father had opened the doors of Beaulieu Abbey to his younger son. The importance of the family had thus dwindled, but they still retained the old Saxon manor-house, with a couple of farms and a grove large enough to afford pannage [1] to a hundred pigs—"sylva de centum porcis," as the old family parchments describe it. Above all, the owner of the soil could still hold his head high as the veritable Socman of Minstead—that is, as holding the land in free socage, with no feudal superior, and answerable to no man lower than the King. Knowing this, Alleyene felt some little glow of worldly pride as he looked for the first time upon the land with which so many generations of his ancestors had been associated. He pushed on the quicker, twirling his staff merrily, and looking out at every turn of the path for some sign of the old Saxon residence. He was suddenly arrested, however, by the appearance of a wild-looking fellow armed with a club, who sprang out from behind a tree and barred his passage. He was a rough, powerful peasant, with cap and tunic of untanned sheepskin, leather breeches, and galligaskins round legs and feet.

"Stand!" he shouted, raising his heavy cudgel to enforce the order. "Who are you who walk so freely through the wood? Whither would you go, and what is your errand?"

"Why should I answer your questions, my friend?" said Alleyne, standing on his guard.

"Because your tongue may save your pate. But where have I looked upon your face before?"

"No longer ago than last night at the 'Pied Merlin,' " the clerk answered, recognizing the escaped serf who had been so outspoken as to his wrongs.

"By the Virgin! yes. You were the little clerk who sat so mum in the corner, and then cried fy on the gleeman. What hast in the scrip?"

"Naught of any price."

"How can I tell that, clerk? Let me see."

[1] *pannage* (păn′ĭj): grazing ground.

"Not I."

"Fool! I could pull you limb from limb like a pullet. What would you have? Hast forgot that we are alone far from all men? How can your clerkship help you? Wouldst lose scrip and life too?"

"I will part with neither without fight."

"A fight, quotha? A fight betwixt spurred cock and new-hatched chicken! Thy fighting days may soon be over."

"Hadst asked me in the name of charity, I would have given freely," cried Alleyne. "As it stands, not one farthing shall you have with my free will, and when I see my brother, the Socman of Minstead, he will raise hue and cry from vill to vill, from hundred to hundred, until you are taken as a common robber and a scourge to the country."

The outlaw sank his club. "The Socman's brother!" he gasped. "Now, by the keys of Peter! I had rather that hand withered and tongue was palsied ere I had struck or miscalled you. If you are the Socman's brother, you are one of the right side, I warrant, for all your clerkly dress."

"His brother I am," said Alleyne. "But if I were not, is that reason why you should molest me on the King's ground?"

"I give not the pip of an apple for King or for noble," cried the serf passionately. "Ill have I had from them, and ill I shall repay them. I am a good friend to my friends, and, by the Virgin! an evil foeman to my foes."

"And, therefore, the worst of foemen to thyself," said Alleyne. "But I pray you, since you seem to know him, to point out to me the shortest path to my brother's house."

The serf was about to reply, when the clear ringing call of a bugle burst from the wood close behind them, and Alleyne caught sight for an instant of the dun side and white breast of a lordly stag glancing swiftly betwixt the distant tree trunks. A minute later came the shaggy deerhounds, a dozen or fourteen of them, running on a hot scent, with nose to earth and tail in air. As they streamed past, the silent forest around broke suddenly into loud life, with galloping of hoofs, crackling of brushwood, and the short, sharp cries of the hunters. Close behind the pack rode a fourrier [1] and a gentleman attendant, whooping on the laggards and encouraging the leaders in the shrill half-French

[1] *fourrier* (fo͞or′ēr): one who rides ahead of the hunters.

jargon which was the language of venery[1] and woodcraft.[2] Alleyne was still gazing after them, listening to the loud "Hyke-a-Bayard! Hyke-a-Pomers! Hyke-a-Lebryt!" with which they called upon their favorite hounds, when a group of horsemen crashed out through the underwood at the very spot where the serf and he were standing.

The one who led was a man between fifty and sixty years of age, war-worn and weather-beaten, with a broad, thoughtful forehead, and eyes which shone brightly from under his fierce and overhung brows. His beard, streaked thickly with gray, bristled forward from his chin, and spoke of a passionate nature, while the long, finely cut face and firm mouth marked the leader of men. His figure was erect and soldierly, and he rode his horse with the careless grace of a man whose life had been spent in the saddle. In common garb, his masterful face and flashing eye would have marked him as one who was born to rule; but now, with his silken tunic powdered with golden fleurs-de-lis,[3] his velvet mantle lined with the royal miniver, and the lions of England stamped in silver upon his harness, none could fail to recognize the noble Edward, most warlike and powerful of all the long line of fighting monarchs who had ruled the Anglo-Norman race. Alleyne doffed hat and bowed head at the sight of him, but the serf folded his hands and leaned them upon his cudgel, looking with little love at the knot of nobles and knights-in-waiting who rode behind the King.

"Ha!" cried Edward, reining up for an instant his powerful black steed. "Le cerf est passé? Non? Ici, Brocas; tu parles anglais."[4]

"The deer, clowns?" said a hard-visaged, swarthy-faced man, who rode at the king's elbow. "If ye have headed it back, it is as much as your ears are worth."

"It passed by the blighted beech there," said Alleyne, pointing, "and the hounds were hard at its heels."

"It is well," cried Edward, still speaking in French; for, though he could understand English, he had never learned to express himself in so barbarous and unpolished a tongue. "By my

[1] *venery* (vĕn′ĕr·ĭ): hunting. [2] *woodcraft:* skill in anything having to do with the woods. [3] *fleur-de-lis:* the lily of France, an emblem worn by English kings at this time. [4] *"Le cerf . . . . Anglais."* "Did the deer pass this way? No? Here, Brocas; you speak English."

faith, sirs," he continued, half-turning in his saddle to address his escort, "unless my woodcraft is sadly at fault, it is a stag of six tines [1] and the finest that we have roused this journey. A golden St. Hubert to the man who is the first to sound the mort." [2] He shook his bridle as he spoke, and thundered away, his knights lying low upon their horses and galloping as hard as whip and spur would drive them, in the hope of winning the King's prize. Away they drove down the long green glade—bay horses, black and gray, riders clad in every shade of velvet, fur, or silk, with glint of brazen horn and flash of knife and spear. One only lingered, the black-browed Baron Brocas, who, making a gambade which brought him within arm-sweep of the serf, slashed him across the face with his riding-whip. "Doff, dog, doff," he hissed, "when a monarch deigns to lower his eyes to such as you!"—then spurred through the underwood and was gone, with a gleam of steel shoes and flutter of dead leaves.

The villein took the cruel blow without wince or cry, as one to whom stripes are a birthright and an inheritance. His eyes flashed, however, and he shook his bony hand with a fierce wild gesture after the retreating figure.

"Black hound of Gascony," he muttered, "evil the day that you and those like you set foot in free England! I know thy kennel of Rochecourt. The night will come when I may do to thee and thine what you and your class have wrought upon mine and me. May God smite me if I fail to smite thee, thou French robber, with thy wife and thy child and all that is under thy castle roof!"

"Forbear!" cried Alleyne. "Mix not God's name with these unhallowed threats! And yet it was a coward's blow, and one to stir the blood and loose the tongue of the most peaceful. Let me find some soothing simples [3] and lay them on the weal to draw the sting."

"Nay, there is but one thing that can draw the sting, and that the future may bring to me. But, clerk, if you would see your brother you must on, for there is a meeting today, and his merry men will await him ere the shadows turn from west to east. I pray you not to hold him back, for it would be an evil thing if all the stout lads were there and the leader a-missing. I

[1] *tine* (tīn): the prong of an antler. [2] *mort* (môrt): the note blown on the hunting horn at the kill. [3] *simple:* a remedy, medicine.

would come with you, but sooth to say I am stationed here and may not move. The path over yonder, betwixt the oak and the thorn, should bring you out into his nether field."

Alleyne lost no time in following the directions of the wild, masterless man, whom he left among the trees where he had found him. His heart was the heavier for the encounter, not only because all bitterness and wrath were abhorrent to his gentle nature, but also because it disturbed him to hear his brother spoken of as though he were a chief of outlaws or the leader of a party against the state. Indeed, of all the things which he had seen yet in the world to surprise him there was none more strange than the hate which class appeared to bear to class. The talk of laborer, woodman, and villein in the inn had all pointed to the widespread mutiny, and now his brother's name was spoken as though he were the very center of the universal discontent. In good truth, the commons throughout the length and breadth of the land were heart-weary of this fine game of chivalry [1] which had been played so long at their expense. So long as knight and baron were a strength and a guard to the kingdom they might be endured, but now, when all men knew that the great battles in France had been won by English yeomen and Welsh stabbers, warlike fame, the only fame to which his class had ever aspired, appeared to have deserted the plat-clad horsemen. The sports of the lists had done much in days gone by to impress the minds of the people, but the plumed and unwieldy champion was no longer an object either of fear or of reverence to men whose fathers and brothers had shot into the press at Crécy or Poitiers and seen the proudest chivalry in the world unable to make head against the weapons of disciplined peasants. Power had changed hands. The protector had become the protected, and the whole fabric of the feudal system was tottering to a fall. Hence the fierce mutterings of the lower classes and the constant discontent. What Alleyne saw and wondered at in Hampshire would have appealed equally to the traveler in any other English county from the Channel to the marches of Scotland.

He was following the track, his misgivings increasing with every step which took him nearer to that home which he had never seen, when of a sudden the trees began to thin and the sward to spread out into a broad, green lawn, where five cows

[1] *chivalry* (shĭv'ăl·rĭ): the code and system of knighthood.

lay in the sunshine and droves of black swine wandered unchecked. A brown forest stream swirled down the center of this clearing, with a rude bridge flung across it, and on the other side was a second field sloping up to a long, low-lying wooden house, with thatched roof and open squares for windows. Alleyne gazed across at it with flushed cheeks and sparkling eyes—for this, he knew, must be the home of his fathers. A wreath of blue smoke floated up through a hole in the thatch and was the only sign of life in the place, save a great black hound which lay sleeping chained to the doorpost. In the yellow shimmer of the autumn sunshine it lay as peacefully and as still as he had oft pictured it to himself in his dreams.

He was roused, however, from his pleasant reverie by the sound of voices, and two people emerged from the forest some little way to his right and moved across the field in the direction of the bridge. The one was a man with yellow flowing beard and very long hair of the same tint drooping over his shoulders; his dress of good Norwich cloth and his assured bearing marked him as a man of position, while the somber hue of his clothes and the absence of all ornament contrasted with the flash and glitter which had marked the King's retinue. By his side walked a woman, tall and slight and dark, with lithe, graceful figure and clear-cut, composed features. Her jet-black hair was gathered back under a light pink coif, her head poised proudly upon her neck, and her step long and springy, like that of some wild, tireless woodland creature. She held her left hand in front of her, covered with a red velvet glove, and on the wrist a little brown falcon, very fluffy and bedraggled, which she smoothed and fondled as she walked. As she came out into the sunshine, Alleyne noticed that her light gown, slashed with pink, was all stained with the earth and with moss upon one side from shoulder to hem. He stood in the shadow of an oak, staring at her with parted lips, for this woman seemed to him to be the most beautiful and graceful creature that mind could conceive of. Such had he imagined the angels, and such he had tried to paint them in the Beaulieu missals; but here there was something human, were it only in the battered hawk and discolored dress, which sent a tingle and thrill through his nerves such as no dream of radiant and stainless spirit had ever yet been able to conjure up.

The two walked swiftly across the meadow to the narrow

bridge, he in front and she a pace or two behind. There they paused, and stood for a few minutes face to face talking earnestly. Alleyne had read and had heard of love and of lovers. Such were these, doubtless—this golden-bearded man and the fair damsel with the cold, proud face. Why else should they wander together in the woods or be so lost in talk by rustic streams? And yet as he watched, uncertain whether to advance from the cover or to choose some other path to the house, he soon came to doubt the truth of this first conjecture.[1] The man stood, tall and square, blocking the entrance to the bridge, and throwing out his hands as he spoke in a wild, eager fashion, while the deep tones of his stormy voice rose at times into accents of menace and of anger.

She stood fearlessly in front of him, still stroking her bird; but twice she threw a swift questioning glance over her shoulder, as one who is in search of aid. So moved was the young clerk by these mute appeals, that he came forth from the trees and crossed the meadow, uncertain what to do, and yet loath to hold back from one who might need his aid. So intent were they upon each other that neither took note of his approach; until, when he was close upon them, the man threw his arm roughly round the damsel's waist and drew her towards him, she straining her lithe, supple figure away and striking fiercely at him, while the hooded hawk screamed with ruffled wings and pecked blindly in its mistress' defense. Bird and maid, however, had but little chance against their assailant, who, laughing loudly, caught her wrist in one hand while he drew her towards him with the other.

"The best rose has ever the longest thorns," said he. "Quiet, little one, or you may do yourself a hurt. Must pay Saxon toll on Saxon land, my proud Maude, for all your airs and graces."

"You boor!" she hissed. "You base, underbred clod! Is this your care and your hospitality? I would rather wed a branded serf from my father's fields. Leave go, I say— Ah! good youth, Heaven has sent you. Make him loose me! By the honor of your mother, I pray you to stand by me and to make this knave loose me."

"Stand by you I will, and that blithely,"[2] said Alleyne.

[1] *conjecture* (kŏn·jĕk′tûr): an opinion. [2] *blithely* (blīth′lĭ): gladly.

"Surely, sir, you should take shame to hold the damsel against her will."

The man turned a face upon him which was lionlike in its strength and in its wrath. With his tangle of golden hair, his fierce blue eyes, and his large, well-marked features, he was the most comely man whom Alleyne had ever seen; and yet there was something so sinister and so fell [1] in his expression that child or beast might well have shrunk from him. His brows were drawn, his cheek flushed, and there was a mad sparkle in his eyes which spoke of a wild, untamable nature.

"Young fool!" he cried, holding the woman still to his side, though every line of her shrinking figure spoke her abhorrence. "Do you keep your spoon in your own broth. I rede [2] you to go on your way, lest worse befall you. This little wench has come with me and with me she shall bide."

"Liar!" cried the woman; and, stooping her head, she suddenly bit fiercely into the broad brown hand which held her. He whipped it back with an oath, while she tore herself free and slipped behind Alleyne, cowering up against him like the trembling leveret who sees the falcon poising for the swoop above him.

"Stand off my land!" the man said fiercely, heedless of the blood which trickled freely from his fingers. "What have you to do here? By your dress you should be one of those cursed clerks who overrun the land like vile rats, poking and prying into other men's concerns, too caitiff [3] to fight and too lazy to work. By the rood! if I had my will upon ye, I should nail you upon the abbey doors, as they hang vermin before their holes. Art neither man nor woman, young shaveling. Get thee back to thy fellows ere I lay hands upon you: for your foot is on my land, and I may slay you as a common drawlatch." [4]

"Is this your land, then?" gasped Alleyne.

"Would you dispute it, dog? Would you wish by trick or quibble to juggle me out of these last acres? Know, base-born knave, that you have dared this day to stand in the path of one whose race have been the advisers of kings and the leaders of hosts ere ever this vile crew of Norman robbers came into the land or such half-blood hounds as you were let loose to preach

[1] *fell:* cruel. [2] *rede* (rēd): to advise. [3] *caitiff* (kā'tĭf): mean. [4] *drawlatch:* a thief.

that the thief should have his booty and the honest man should sin if he strove to win back his own."

"You are the Socman of Minstead?"

"That am I; and the son of Edric the Socman, of the pure blood of Godfrey the Thane, by the only daughter of the house of Aluric, whose forefathers held the white-horse banner at the fatal fight where our shield was broken and our sword shivered. I tell you, clerk, that my folk held this land from Bramshow Wood to the Ringwood Road; and, by the soul of my father! it will be a strange thing if I am to be bearded upon the little that is left of it. Begone, I say, and meddle not with my affair."

"If you leave me now," whispered the woman, "then shame forever upon your manhood."

"Surely, sir," said Alleyne, speaking in as persuasive and soothing a way as he could, "if your birth is gentle, there is the more reason that your manners should be gentle too. I am well persuaded that you did but jest with this lady, and that you will now permit her to leave your land either alone or with me as a guide, if she should need one, through the wood. As to birth, it does not become me to boast, and there is sooth in what you say as to the unworthiness of clerks, but it is none the less true that I am as well born as you."

"Dog!" cried the furious Socman, "there is no man in the south who can say as much."

"Yet can I," said Alleyne, smiling; "for, indeed, I also am the son of Edric the Socman, of the pure blood of Godfrey the Thane, by the only daughter of Aluric of Brockenhurst. Surely, dear brother," he continued, holding out his hand, "you have a warmer greeting than this for me. There are but two boughs left upon this old, old Saxon trunk."

His elder brother dashed his hand aside with an oath, while an expression of malignant hatred passed over his passion-drawn features. "You are the young cub of Beaulieu, then," said he. "I might have known it by the sleek face and the slavish manner, too monk-ridden and craven in spirit to answer back a rough word. Thy father, shaveling, with all his faults, had a man's heart; and there were few who could look him in the eyes on the day of his anger. But you! Look there, rat, on yonder field where the cows graze, and on that other beyond, and on the orchard hard by the church. Do you know that all these were squeezed out of your dying father by greedy priests, to pay for your upbringing in the cloisters? I, the Socman, am shorn of my lands that you may snivel Latin and eat bread for which you never did hand's turn. You rob me first, and now you would come preaching and whining, in search mayhap of another field or two for your priestly friends. Knave! my dogs shall be set upon you; but, meanwhile, stand out of my path, and stop me at your peril!" As he spoke he rushed forward and, throwing the lad to one side, caught the woman's wrist. Alleyne, however, as active as a young deerhound, sprang to her aid and seized her by the other arm, raising his iron-shod staff as he did so.

"You may say what you will to me," he said between his clenched teeth—"it may be no better than I deserve; but, brother or no, I swear by my hopes of salvation that I will break your arm if you do not leave hold of the maid."

There was a ring in his voice and a flash in his eyes which promised that the blow would follow quick at the heels of the word. For a moment the blood of the long line of hotheaded thanes was too strong for the soft whisperings of the doctrine of meekness and mercy. He was conscious of a fierce, wild thrill through his nerves and a throb of mad gladness at his heart, as his real human self burst for an instant the bonds of custom and of teaching which had held it so long. The Socman sprang back, looking to left and to right for some stick or stone which might serve him for weapon; but finding none, he turned and ran at the top of his speed for the house, blowing the while upon a shrill whistle.

"Come!" gasped the woman. "Fly, friend, ere he come back."

"Nay, let him come!" cried Alleyne. "I shall not budge a foot for him or his dogs."

"Come, come!" she cried, tugging at his arm. "I know the man: he will kill you. Come, for the Virgin's sake, or for my sake, for I cannot go and leave you here."

"Come, then," said he; and they ran together to the cover of the woods. As they gained the edge of the brushwood, Alleyne, looking back, saw his brother come running out of the house again, with the sun gleaming upon his hair and his beard. He held something which flashed in his right hand, and he stooped at the threshold to unloose the black hound.

"This way!" the woman whispered, in a low eager voice. "Through the bushes to that forked ash. Do not heed me; I can run as fast as you, I trow. Now into the stream—right in, over ankles, to throw the dog off, though I think it is but a common cur, like its master." As she spoke, she sprang herself into the shallow stream and ran swiftly up the center of it, with the brown water bubbling over her feet and her hand outstretched toward the clinging branches of bramble or sapling. Alleyne followed close at her heels, with his mind in a whirl at this black welcome and sudden shifting of all his plans and hopes. Yet, grave as were his thoughts, they would still turn to wonder as he looked at the twinkling feet of his guide and saw her lithe figure bend this way and that, dipping under boughs, springing over stones, with a lightness and ease which made it no small task for him to keep up with her. At last, when he was almost out of breath, she suddenly threw herself down upon a mossy bank, between two holly bushes, and looked ruefully at her own dripping feet and bedraggled skirt.

"Holy Mary!" said she, "what shall I do? Mother will keep me to my chamber for a month and make me work at the tapestry of the nine bold knights. She promised as much last week, when I fell into Wilverly bog, and yet she knows that I cannot abide [1] needlework."

Alleyne, still standing in the stream, glanced down at the graceful pink-and-white figure, the curve of raven-black hair, and the proud, sensitive face which looked up frankly and confidingly at his own.

"We had best on," he said. "He may yet overtake us."

"Not so. We are well off his land now, nor can he tell in this great wood which way we have taken. But you—you had him at your mercy. Why did you not kill him?"

"Kill him! My brother?"

"And why not?"—with a quick gleam of her white teeth. "He would have killed you. I know him, and I read it in his eyes. Had I had your staff, I would have tried—aye, and done it, too." She shook her clenched white hand as she spoke, and her lips tightened ominously.

"I am already sad in heart for what I have done," said he, sitting down on the bank and sinking his face into his hands.

[1] *abide* (ȧ·bīd′): to bear, tolerate.

"God help me!—all that is worst in me seemed to come uppermost. Another instant, and I had smitten him: the son of my own mother, the man whom I have longed to take to my heart. Alas! that I should still be so weak."

"Weak!" she exclaimed, raising her black eyebrows. "I do not think that even my father himself, who is a hard judge of manhood, would call you that. But it is, as you may think, sir, a very pleasant thing for me to hear that you are grieved at what you have done, and I can but rede that we should go back together, and you should make your peace with the Socman by handing back your prisoner. It is a sad thing that so small a thing as a woman should come between two who are of one blood."

Simple Alleyne opened his eyes at this little spurt of feminine bitterness. "Nay, lady," said he, "that were worst of all. What man would be so caitiff and thrall [1] as to fail you at your need? I have turned my brother against me, and now, alas! I appear to have given you offense also with my clumsy tongue. But, indeed, lady, I am torn both ways and can scarce grasp in my mind what it is that has befallen."

"Nor can I marvel at that," said she, with a little tinkling laugh. "You came in as the knight does in the jongleur's romances, between dragon and damsel, with small time for the asking of questions. Come," she went on, springing to her feet, and smoothing down her rumpled frock, "let us walk through the shaw [2] together, and we may come upon Bertrand with the horses. If poor Troubadour had not cast a shoe, we should not have had this trouble. Nay, I must have your arm: for, though I speak lightly now that all is happily over, I am as frightened as my brave Roland. See how his chest heaves, and his dear feathers all awry—the little knight who would not have his lady mishandled." So she prattled on to her hawk, while Alleyne walked by her side, stealing a glance from time to time at this queenly and wayward woman. In silence they wandered together over the velvet turf and on through the broad Minstead woods, where the old lichen-draped beeches threw their circles of black shadow upon the sunlit sward.

"You have no wish, then, to hear my story?" said she at last.

"If it pleases you to tell it me," he answered.

[1] *thrall* (thrôl): enslaved. [2] *shaw* (shô): a small woods.

"Oh!" she cried, tossing her head, "if it is of so little interest to you, we had best led it bide."

"Nay," said he eagerly, "I would fain hear it."

"You have a right to know it, if you have lost a brother's favor through it. And yet— Ah, well, you are, as I understand, a clerk, so I must think of you as one step further in orders and make you my father-confessor. Know then that this man has been a suitor for my hand, less, as I think, for my own sweet sake than because he hath ambition and had it on his mind that he might improve his fortunes by dipping into my father's strong box—though the Virgin knows that he would have found little enough therein. My father, however, is a proud man, a gallant knight and tried soldier of the oldest blood, to whom this man's churlish birth and low descent— Oh, lackaday! I had forgot that he was of the same strain as yourself."

"Nay, trouble not for that," said Alleyne, "we are all from good mother Eve."

"Streams may spring from one source, and yet some be clear and some be foul," quoth she quickly. "But, to be brief over the matter, my father would have none of his wooing, nor, in sooth, would I. On that he swore a vow against us, and as he is known to be a perilous man, with many outlaws and others at his back, my father forbade that I should hawk or hunt in any part of the Wood to the north of the Christchurch Road. As it chanced, however, this morning my little Roland here was loosed at a strong-winged heron, and page Bertrand and I rode on, with no thoughts but for the sport, until we found ourselves in Minstead Woods. Small harm, then, but that my horse Troubadour trod with a tender foot upon a sharp stick, rearing and throwing me to the ground. See to my gown, the third that I have befouled within the week. Woe worth me when Agatha the tirewoman [1] sets eyes upon it!"

"And what then, lady?" asked Alleyne.

"Why, then away ran Troubadour, for belike I spurred him in falling, and Bertrand rode after him as hard as hoofs could bear him. When I rose, there was the Socman himself by my side, with the news that I was on his land, but with so many courteous words besides, and such gallant bearing, that he prevailed upon me to come to his house for shelter, there to wait until the page

[1] *tirewoman* (tīr′wo͝om′ăn): the maid in charge of a lady's wardrobe.

return. By the grace of the Virgin and the help of my patron St. Magdalen, I stopped short ere I reached his door, though, as you saw, he strove to hale me up to it. And then—ah-h-h-h!"—she shivered and chattered like one in an ague fit.

"What is it?" cried Alleyne, looking about in alarm.

"Nothing, friend, nothing! I was but thinking how I bit into his hand. Sooner would I bite living toad or poisoned snake. Oh, I shall loathe my lips forever! But you—how brave you were, and how quick! How meek for yourself, and how bold for a stranger! If I were a man, I should wish to do what you have done."

"It was a small thing," he answered, with a tingle of pleasure at these sweet words of praise. "But you—what will you do?"

"There is a great oak near here, and I think that Bertrand will bring the horses there, for it is an old hunting tryst of ours. Then hey for home, and no more hawking today! A twelve-mile gallop will dry feet and skirt."

"But your father?"

"Not one word shall I tell him. You do not know him; but I can tell you he is not a man to disobey as I have disobeyed him. He would avenge me, it is true, but it is not to him that I shall look for vengeance. Some day, perchance, in joust [1] or in tourney,[2] knight may wish to wear my colors, and then I shall tell him that if he does indeed crave my favor, there is wrong unredressed, and the wronger, the Socman of Minstead. So my knight shall find a venture such as bold knights love, and my debt shall be paid, and my father none the wiser, and one rogue the less in the world. Say, is not that a brave plan?"

"Nay, lady, it is a thought which is unworthy of you. How can such as you speak of violence and of vengeance? Are none to be gentle and kind, none to be piteous and forgiving? Alas! it is a hard, cruel world, and I would that I had never left my abbey cell. To hear such words from your lips is as though I heard an angel of grace preaching the devil's own creed."

She started from him as a young colt who first feels the bit. "Gramercy for your rede,[3] young sir!" she said, with a little curt-

[1] *joust* (jŭst): a combat between two knights. [2] *tourney* (to͝or′ni): a contest between armed knights. [3] *Gramercy for your rede:* Thanks for your advice.

sey. "As I understand your words, you are grieved that you ever met me, and look upon me as a preaching devil. Why, my father is a bitter man when he is wroth, but hath never called me such a name as that. It may be his right and duty, but certes it is none of thine. So it would be best, since you think so lowly of me, that you should take this path to the left, while I keep on upon this one; for it is clear that I can be no fit companion for you." So saying, with downcast lids and a dignity which was somewhat marred by her bedraggled skirt, she swept off down the ruddy track, leaving Alleyne standing staring ruefully after her. He waited in vain for some backward glance or sign of relenting, but she walked on with a rigid neck until her dress was only a white flutter among the leaves. Then, with a sunken head and a heavy heart, he plodded wearily down the other path, wroth with himself for the rude and uncouth tongue which had given offense where so little was intended.

He had gone some way, lost in doubt and in self-reproach, his mind all tremulous with a thousand new-found thoughts and fears and wonderments, when of a sudden there was a light rustle of the leaves behind him, and, glancing round, there was this graceful, swift-footed creature, treading in his very shadow, with her proud head bowed, even as his was—the picture of humility and repentance.

"I shall not vex you, nor even speak," she said; "but I would fain keep with you while we are in the wood."

"Nay, you cannot vex me," he answered, all warm again at the very sight of her. "It was my rough words which vexed you; but I have been thrown among men all my life, and, indeed, with all the will, I scarce know how to temper my speech to a lady's ear."

"Then unsay it," cried she quickly; "say that I was right to wish to have vengeance on the Socman."

"Nay, I cannot do that," he answered gravely.

"Then who is ungentle and unkind now?" she cried in triumph. "How stern and cold you are for one so young! Art surely no mere clerk, but bishop or cardinal at the least. Shouldst have crozier [1] for staff and miter [2] for cap. Well, well, for your sake I will forgive the Socman and take vengeance on none but on my

[1] *crozier* (krō′zhẽr): a bishop's staff. [2] *miter* (mī′tẽr): a bishop's headdress.

own willful self who must needs run into danger's path. So will that please you, sir?"

"There spoke your true self," said he; "and you will find more pleasure in such forgiveness than in any vengeance."

She shook her head, as if by no means assured of it, and then with a sudden little cry, which had more of surprise than of joy in it, "Here is Bertrand with the horses!"

Down the glade there came a little green-clad page with laughing eyes, and long curls floating behind him. He sat perched on a high bay horse and held on to the bridle of a spirited black palfrey, the hides of both glistening from a long run.

"I have sought you everywhere, dear Lady Maude," said he in a piping voice, springing down from his horse and holding the stirrup. "Troubadour galloped as far as Holmhill ere I could catch him. I trust that you have had no hurt or scath?" He shot a questioning glance at Alleyne as he spoke.

"No, Bertrand," said she, "thanks to this courteous stranger. And now, sir," she continued, springing into her saddle, "it is not fit that I leave you without a word more. Clerk or no, you have acted this day as becomes a true knight. King Arthur and all his table could not have done more. It may be that, as some small return, my father or his kin may have power to advance your interest. He is not rich, but he is honored and hath great friends. Tell me what is your purpose, and see if he may not aid it."

"Alas! lady, I have now no purpose. I have but two friends in the world, and they have gone to Christchurch, where it is likely I shall join them."

"And where is Christchurch?"

"At the castle which is held by the brave knight Sir Nigel Loring, constable to the Earl of Salisbury."

To his surprise she burst out a-laughing and, spurring her palfrey, dashed off down the glade, with her page riding behind her. Not one word did she say, but as she vanished amid the trees she half-turned in her saddle and waved a last greeting. Long time he stood, half-hoping that she might again come back to him; but the thud of the hoofs had died away, and there was no sound in all the woods but the gentle rustle and dropping of the leaves. At last he turned away and made his way back to the highroad—another person from the lighthearted boy who had left it a short three hours before.

Chapter 9

HOW HORDLE JOHN FOUND A MAN WHOM HE MIGHT FOLLOW

If he might not return to Beaulieu within the year, and if his brother's dogs were to be set upon him if he showed face upon Minstead land, then indeed he was adrift upon earth. North, south, east, and west—he might turn where he would, but all was equally chill and cheerless. The Abbot had rolled ten silver crowns in a lettuce leaf and hid them away in the bottom of his scrip, but that would be a sorry support for twelve long months. In all the darkness there was but the one bright spot of the sturdy comrades whom he had left that morning; if he could find them again, all would be well. The afternoon was not very advanced, for all that had befallen him. When a man is afoot at cockcrow, much may be done in the day. If he walked fast, he might yet overtake his friends ere they reached their destination. He pushed on, therefore, now walking and now running. As he journeyed he bit into a crust which remained from his Beaulieu bread, and he washed it down by a draught from a woodland stream.

It was no easy or light thing to journey through this great forest, which was some twenty miles from east to west and a good sixteen from Bramshaw Woods in the north to Lymington in the south. Alleyne, however, had the good fortune to fall in with a woodman, ax upon shoulder, trudging along in the very direction that he wished to go. With his guidance he passed the fringe of Bolderwood Walk, famous for old ash and yew, through Mark Ash with its giant beech trees, and on through the Knightwood groves, where the giant oak was already a great tree, but only one of many comely brothers. They plodded along together, the woodman and Alleyne, with little talk on either side, for their thoughts were as far asunder as the poles. The peasant's gossip had been of the hunt, of the bracken, of the gray-headed kites that had nested in Wood Fidley, and of the great catch of herring brought back by the boats of Pitt's Deep. The clerk's mind was on his brother, on his future—above all on this strange, fierce, melting, beautiful woman who had broken so suddenly into his life, and as suddenly passed out of it again. So distrait [1] was he and so random his answers, that the woodman took to whistling and soon branched off upon the track to Burley, leaving Alleyne upon the main Christchurch Road.

Down this he pushed as fast as he might, hoping at every turn and rise to catch sight of his companions of the morning.

After passing Holmesley Walk and the Wooton Heath, the forest began to shred out into scattered belts of trees, with gleam of cornfield and stretch of pasture land between. Here and there by the wayside stood little knots of wattle-and-daub huts with shock-haired laborers lounging by the doors and red-cheeked children sprawling in the roadway. Back among the groves he could see the high gable ends and thatched roofs of the franklin's houses, on whose fields these men found employment, or more often a thick dark column of smoke marked their position and hinted at the coarse plenty within. By these signs Alleyne knew that he was on the very fringe of the forest, and therefore no great way from Christchurch. The sun was lying low in the west and shooting its level rays across the long sweep of rich green country, glinting on the white-fleeced sheep, and throwing long shadows from the red kine who waded knee-deep in the juicy clover. Right glad was the traveler to see the high tower of Christchurch Priory gleaming in the mellow evening light, and gladder still when, on rounding a corner, he came upon his comrades of the morning seated astraddle upon a fallen tree. They had a flat space before them, on which they alternately threw little square pieces of bone, and were so intent upon their occupation that they never raised eye as he approached them. He observed with astonishment, as he drew near, that the archer's bow was on John's back, the archer's sword by John's side, and the steel cap laid upon the tree trunk between them.

"Mort de ma vie!" Aylward shouted, looking down at the dice. "Never had I such cursed luck, A murrain [2] on the bones! I have not thrown a good main since I left Navarre. A one and a three! En avant, camarade!"

"Four and three," cried Hordle John, counting on his great fingers, "that makes seven. Ho, archer, I have thy cap! Now have at thee for thy jerkin!"

[1] *distrait* (dĭs·trā′): distracted. [2] *murrain* (mûr′ĭn): plague.

"Mon Dieu!" he growled, "I am like to reach Christchurch in my shirt." Then suddenly glancing up, "Holà, by the splendor of heaven, here is our cher petit! [1] Now, by my ten finger bones! this is a rare sight to mine eyes." He sprang up and threw his arms round Alleyne's neck, while John, no less pleased, but more backward and Saxon in his habits, stood grinning and bobbing by the wayside, with his newly won steel cap stuck wrong side foremost upon his tangle of red hair.

"Hast come to stop?" cried the bowman, patting Alleyne all over in his delight. "Shall not get away from us again!"

"I wish no better," said he, with a pringling in the eyes at this hearty greeting.

"Well said, lad!" cried big John. "We three shall to the wars together, and the devil may fly away with the Abbot of Beaulieu! But your feet and hosen are all besmudged. Hast been in the water, or I am the more mistaken."

"I have, in good sooth," Alleyne answered, and then as they journeyed on their way he told them the many things that had befallen him, his meeting with the villein, his sight of the King, his coming upon his brother, with all the tale of the black welcome and of the fair damsel. They strode on either side, each with an ear slanting towards him, but ere he had come to the end of his story the bowman had spun round upon his heel, and was hastening back the way they had come, breathing loudly through his nose.

"What then?" asked Alleyne, trotting after him and gripping at his jerkin.

"I am back for Minstead, lad."

"And why, in the name of sense?"

"To thrust a handful of steel into the Socman. What! hale a demoiselle against her will, and then loose dogs at his own brother! Let me go!"

"Nenny, nenny!" cried Alleyne, laughing. "There was no scath done. Come back, friend"—and so, by mingled pushing and entreaties, they got his head round for Christchurch once more. Yet he walked with his chin upon his shoulder, until, catching sight of a maiden by a wayside well, the smiles came back to his face and peace to his heart.

"But you," said Alleyne, "there have been changes with

[1] *cher petit: French for "dear little one."*

you also. Why should not the workman carry his tools? Where are bow and sword and cap—and why so warlike, John?"

"It is a game which friend Aylward hath been a-teaching of me."

"And I found an overapt pupil," grumbled the bowman. "He hath stripped me as though I had fallen into the hands of the tardvenus. But, by my hilt! you must render them back to me, camarade, lest you bring discredit upon my mission, and I will pay you for them at armorers' prices."

"Take them back, man, and never heed the pay," said John. "I did but wish to learn the feel of them, since I am like to have such trinkets hung to my own girdle for some years to come."

"Ma foi, he was born for a free companion!" cried Aylward. "He hath the very trick of speech and turn of thought. I take them back, then, and indeed it gives me unease not to feel my yew stave [1] tapping against my leg bone. But see, mes garçons, on this side of the church rises the square and darkling tower of Earl Salisbury's castle, and even from here I seem to see on yonder banner the red roebuck of the Montacutes."

"Red upon white," said Alleyne, shading his eyes; "but whether roebuck or no is more than I could vouch. How black is the great tower, and how bright the gleam of arms upon the wall! See below the flag, how it twinkles like a star!"

"Aye, it is the steel headpiece of the watchman," remarked the archer. "But we must on, if we are to be there before the drawbridge rises at the vespers bugle; for it is likely that Sir Nigel, being so renowned a soldier, may keep hard discipline within the walls and let no man enter after sundown." So saying, he quickened his pace, and the three comrades were soon close to the straggling and broad-spread town which centered round the noble church and the frowning castle.

It chanced on that very evening that Sir Nigel Loring, having supped before sunset, as was his custom, and having himself seen that Pommers and Cadsand, his two war horses, with the thirteen hacks, the five jennets, my lady's three palfreys, and the great dapple-gray roussin, had all their needs supplied, had taken his dogs for an evening breather. Sixty or seventy of them, large and small, smooth and shaggy—deerhound, boarhound, blood-

[1] *yew stave* (yōō′ stāv′): a staff made of yew. He means his bow.

hound, wolfhound, mastiff, alaun, talbot, lurcher, terrier, spaniel—snapping, yelling, and whining, with score of lolling tongues and waving tails, came surging down the narrow lane which leads from the Twynham kennels to the bank of Avon. Two russet-clad varlets,[1] with loud halloo and cracking whips, walked thigh-deep amid the swarm, guiding, controlling, and urging. Behind came Sir Nigel himself, with Lady Loring upon his arm, the pair walking slowly and sedately, as befitted both their age and their condition, while they watched, with a smile in their eyes, the scrambling crowd in front of them. They paused, however, at the bridge, and, leaning their elbows upon the stonework, they stood looking down at their own faces in the glassy stream, and at the swift flash of speckled trout against the tawny gravel.

Sir Nigel was a slight man of poor stature, with soft lisping voice and gentle ways. So short was he that his wife, who was no very tall woman, had the better of him by the breadth of three fingers. His sight having been injured in his early wars by a basketful of lime which had been emptied over him when he led the Earl of Derby's stormers up the breach at Bergerac, he had contracted something of a stoop, with a blinking, peering expression of face. His age was six and forty, but the constant practice of arms, together with a cleanly life, had preserved his activity and endurance unimpaired, so that from a distance he seemed to have the slight limbs and swift grace of a boy. His face, however, was tanned of a dull yellow tint, with a leathery, poreless look, which spoke of rough outdoor doings, and the little pointed beard which he wore, in deference to the prevailing fashion, was streaked and shot with gray. His features were small, delicate, and regular, with clear-cut, curving nose, and eyes which jutted forward from the lids. His dress was simple and yet spruce. A Flandrish hat of beaver, bearing in the band the token of Our Lady of Embrun, was drawn low upon the left side to hide that ear which had been partly shorn from his head by a Flemish man-at-arms in a camp broil before Tournay. His cote-hardie, or tunic, and trunk-hosen were of a purple plum color, with long weepers [2] which hung from either sleeve to below his knees. His shoes were of red leather, daintily pointed at the toes, but not yet prolonged to the extravagant lengths which the succeeding

[1] *varlet* (vär'lĕt): a servant. [2] *weeper* (wēp'ẽr): a cloth cuff ornament.

reign was to bring into fashion. A gold-embroidered belt of knighthood encircled his loins, with his arms, five roses gules [1] on a field [2] argent,[3] cunningly worked upon the clasp. So stood Sir Nigel Loring upon the bridge of Avon and talked lightly with his lady.

And, certes, had the two visages alone been seen, and the stranger been asked which were the more likely to belong to the bold warrior whose name was loved by the roughest soldiery of Europe, he had assuredly selected the lady's. Her face was large and square and red, with fierce, thick brows, and the eyes of one who was accustomed to rule. Taller and broader than her husband, her flowing gown of sendal, and fur-lined tippet [4] could not conceal the gaunt and ungraceful outlines of her figure. It was the age of martial [5] women. The deeds of black Agnes of Dunbar, of Lady Salisbury, and of the Countess of Montfort, were still fresh in the public minds. With such examples before them, the wives of the English captains had become as warlike as their mates, and ordered their castles in their absence with the prudence and discipline of veteran seneschals.[6] Right easy were the Montacutes of their Castle of Twynham, and little had they to dread from roving galley or French squadron, while Lady Mary Loring had the ordering of it. Yet even in that age it was thought that, though a lady might have a soldier's heart, it was scarce as well that she should have a soldier's face. There were men who said that of all the stern passages and daring deeds by which Sir Nigel Loring had proved the true temper of his courage, not the least was his wooing and winning of so forbidding a dame.

"I tell you, my fair lord," she was saying, "that it is no fit training for a demoiselle: hawks and hounds, rotes and citoles, singing a French rondel, or reading the Gestes de Doon de Mayence, as I found her yesternight, pretending sleep, the artful, with the corner of the scroll thrusting forth from under her pillow. Lent her by Father Christopher of the priory, forsooth—that is ever her answer. How shall all this help her when she has

[1] *gules* (gūlz): red. Roses gules: red roses (*see heraldry*, p. 310). [2] *field:* the whole surface or background of a shield, on which the arms are painted. [3] *argent* (är′jĕnt): silver. [4] *tippet* (tĭp′ĕt): a hanging ornamental cloth. [5] *martial* (mär′shăl): warlike. [6] *seneschal* (sĕn′ĕ·shăl): an estate manager.

castle of her own to keep, with a hundred mouths all agape for beef and beer?"

"True, my sweet bird, true," answered the knight, picking a comfit[1] from his gold drageoir.[2] "The maid is like the young filly, which kicks heels and plunges for very lust of life. Give her time, dame, give her time."

"Well, I know that my father would have given me, not time, but a good hazel stick across my shoulders. Ma foi! I know not what the world is coming to, when young maids may flout their elders. I wonder that you do not correct her, my fair lord."

"Nay, my heart's comfort, I never raised hand to woman yet, and it would be a passing strange thing if I began on my own flesh and blood. It was a woman's hand which cast this lime into mine eyes, and though I saw her stoop, and might well have stopped her ere she threw, I deemed it unworthy of my knighthood to hinder or balk one of her sex."

"The hussy!" cried Lady Loring, clenching her broad right hand. "I would I had been at the side of her!"

"And so would I, since you would have been the nearer me, my own. But I doubt not that you are right, and that Maude's wings need clipping, which I may leave in your hands when I am gone, for, in sooth, this peaceful life is not for me, and were it not for your gracious kindness and loving care I could not abide it a week. I hear that there is talk of warlike muster at Bordeaux once more, and by St. Paul! it would be a new thing if the lions of England and the red pile of Chandos were to be seen in the field, and the roses of Loring were not waving by their side."

"Now woe worth me but I feared it!" cried she, with the color all struck from her face. "I have noted your absent mind, your kindling eye, your trying and riveting of old harness. Consider, my sweet lord, that you have already won much honor, that we have seen but little of each other, that you bear upon your body the scar of over twenty wounds received in I know not how many bloody encounters. Have you not done enough for honor and the public cause?"

"My lady, when our liege lord, the King, at three score years, and my Lord Chandos at three score and ten, are blithe and ready to lay lance in rest for England's cause, it would ill be-

[1] *comfit* (kŭm′fĭt): a preserved, dried fruit. [2] *drageoir* (drȧ′zhwȧr′): a box for sweets.

seem me to prate of service done. It is sooth that I have received seven and twenty wounds. There is the more reason that I should be thankful that I am still long of breath and sound in limb. I have also seen some bickering and scuffling. Six great land battles I count, with four upon sea, and seven and fifty on falls, skirmishes, and bushments. I have held two and twenty towns, and I have been at the intaking of thirty-one. Surely, then, it would be bitter shame to me, and also to you, since my fame is yours, that I should now hold back if a man's work is to be done. Besides, bethink you how low is our purse, with bailiff and reeve[1] ever croaking of empty farms and wasting lands. Were it not for this constableship which the Earl of Salisbury hath bestowed upon us, we could scarce uphold the state which is fitting to our degree. Therefore, my sweeting, there is the more need that I should turn to where there is good pay to be earned and brave ransoms to be won."

"Ah, my dear lord," quoth she, with sad, weary eyes. "I thought that at last I had you to mine own self, even though your youth had been spent afar from my side. Yet my voice, as I know well, should speed you on to glory and renown, not hold you back when fame is to be won. Yet what can I say, for all men know that your valor needs the curb and not the spur. It goes to my heart that you should ride forth now, a mere knight bachelor, when there is no noble in the land who hath so good a claim to the square pennon, save only that you have not the money to uphold it."

"And whose fault that, my sweet bird?" said he.

"No fault, my fair lord, but a virtue: for how many rich ransoms have you won, and yet have scattered the crowns among page and archer and varlet, until in a week you had not as much as would buy food and forage. It is a most knightly largesse, and yet withouten money how can man rise?"

"Dirt and dross!" cried he. "What matter rise or fall, so that duty be done and honor gained? Bannaret or bachelor, square pennon or forked, I would not give a denier for the difference, and the less since Sir John Chandos, chosen flower of English chivalry, is himself but a humble knight. But meanwhile fret not thyself, my heart's dove, for it is like that there may be no war

[1] *reeve* (rēv): an official.

waged, and we must await the news. But here are three strangers, and one, as I take it, a soldier fresh from service. It is likely that he may give us word of what is stirring over the water."

Lady Loring, glancing up, saw in the fading light three companions walking abreast down the road, all gray with dust and stained with travel, yet chattering merrily between themselves. He in the midst was young and comely, with boyish open face and bright gray eyes which glanced from right to left as though he found the world around him both new and pleasing. To his right walked a huge red-headed man, with broad smile and merry twinkle, whose clothes seemed to be bursting and splitting at every seam, as though he were some lusty chick who was breaking bravely from his shell. On the other side, with his knotted hand upon the young man's shoulder, came a stout and burly archer, brown and fierce-eyed, with sword at belt and long yellow yew stave peeping over his shoulder. Hard face, battered headpiece, dinted brigandine, with faded red lion of St. George ramping on a discolored ground, all proclaimed as plainly as words that he was indeed from the land of war. He looked keenly at Sir Nigel as he approached, and then, plunging his hand under his breastplate, he stepped up to him with a rough, uncouth bow to the lady.

"Your pardon, fair sir," said he, "but I know you the moment I clap eyes on you, though in sooth I have seen you oftener in steel than in velvet. I have drawn string beside you at La Roche-d'Errien, Romorantin, Maupertuis, Nogent, Auray, and other places."

"Then, good archer, I am right glad to welcome you to Twynham Castle, and in the steward's room you will find provant for yourself and comrades. To me also your face is known, though mine eyes play such tricks with me that I can scarce be sure of my own squire. Rest awhile, and you shall come to the hall anon and tell us what is passing in France, for I have heard that it is likely that our pennons may flutter to the south of the great Spanish mountains ere another year be passed."

"There was talk of it in Bordeaux," answered the archer, "and I saw myself that the armorers and smiths were as busy as rats in a wheat rick. But I bring you this letter from the valiant Gascon knight, Sir Claude Latour. And to you, lady," he added after a pause, "I bring from him this box of red sugar of Narbonne, with every courteous and knightly greeting which a gallant cavalier may make to a fair and noble dame."

This little speech had cost the blunt bowman much pains and planning; but he might have spared his breath, for the lady was quite as much absorbed as her lord in the letter, which they held between them, a hand on either corner, spelling it out very slowly, with drawn brows and muttering lips. As they read it, Alleyne, who stood with Hordle John a few paces back from their comrade, saw the lady catch her breath, while the knight laughed softly to himself.

"You see, dear heart," said he, "that they will not leave the old dog in his kennel when the game is afoot. And what of this White Company, archer?"

"Ah, sir, you speak of dogs," cried Aylward; "but there are a pack of lusty hounds who are ready for any quarry, if they have but a good huntsman to halloo them on. Sir, we have been in the wars together, and I have seen many a brave following, but never such a set of woodland boys as this. They do but want you at their head, and who will bar the way to them!"

"Pardieu!" said Sir Nigel, "if they are all like their messenger, they are indeed men of whom a leader may be proud. Your name, good archer?"

"Sam Aylward, sir, of the hundred of Easebourne and the borough of Chichester."

"And this giant behind you?"

"He is Big John, of Hordle, a forest man, who hath now taken service in the Company."

"A proper figure of a man-at-arms," said the little knight. "Why, man, you are no chicken, yet I warrant him the stronger man. See to that great stone from the coping which hath fallen upon the bridge. Four of my lazy varlets strove this day to carry it hence. I would that you two could put them to shame by budging it, though I fear that I overtask you, for it is of a grievous weight."

He pointed as he spoke to a huge rough-hewn block which lay by the roadside, deep sunken from its own weight in the reddish earth. The archer approached it, rolling back the sleeves of his jerkin, but with no very hopeful countenance, for indeed it was a mighty rock. John, however, put him aside with his left hand, and, stooping over the stone, he plucked it singlehanded from its soft bed and swung it far into the stream. There it fell with mighty splash, one jagged end peaking out above the surface, while the waters bubbled and foamed with far-circling eddy.

"Good lack!" cried Sir Nigel, and "Good lack!" cried his lady, while John stood laughing and wiping the caked dirt from his fingers.

"I have felt his arms round my ribs," said the bowman, "and they crackle yet at the thought of it. This other comrade of mine is a right learned clerk, for all that he is so young, hight [1] Alleyne, the son of Edric, brother to the Socman of Minstead."

"Young man," quoth Sir Nigel sternly, "if you are of the same way of thought as your brother, you may not pass under portcullis [2] of mine."

"Nay, fair sir," cried Aylward hastily, "I will be pledge for it that they have no thought in common; for this very day his brother hath set his dogs upon him, and driven him from his lands."

"And are you, too, of the White Company?" asked Sir Nigel. "Hast had small experience of war, if I may judge by your looks and bearing."

"I would fain [3] to France with my friends here," Alleyne answered; "but I am a man of peace—a reader, exorcist, acolyte, and clerk."

"That need not hinder," quoth Sir Nigel.

"No, fair sir," cried the bowman joyously. "Why, I myself have served two terms with Arnold de Cervolles, he whom they called the archpriest. By my hilt! I have seen him ere now, with monk's gown trussed to his knees, over his sandals in blood in the forefront of the battle. Yet, ere the last string had twanged, he would be down on his four bones among the stricken, and have them all houseled and shriven,[4] as quick as shelling peas. Ma foi! there were those who wished that he would have less care for their souls and a little more for their bodies!"

"It is well to have a learned clerk in every troop," said Sir Nigel. "By St. Paul, there are men so caitiff that they think more of a scrivener's pen than of their lady's smile, and do their

[1] *hight* (hīt): named. [2] *portcullis* (pōrt·kŭl′ĭs): an iron gate which can be raised or lowered. [3] *fain* (fān): gladly. [4] *houseled and shriven* (hou′z'ld; shrĭv′vĕn): offered confessions and received the Eucharist.

devoir [1] in hopes that they may fill a line in a chronicle or make a tag to a jongleur's romance. I remember well that, at the siege of Retters, there was a little, sleek, fat clerk of the name of Chaucer, who was so apt at rondel, sirvente, or tonson, that no man dare give back a foot from the walls, lest he find it all set down in his rimes and sung by every underling and varlet in the camp. But, my soul's bird, you hear me prate as though all were decided, when I have not yet taken counsel either with you or with my lady-mother. Let us to the chamber, while these strangers find such fare as pantry and cellar may furnish."

"The night air strikes chill," said the lady, and turned down the road with her hand upon her lord's arm. The three comrades dropped behind and followed: Aylward much the lighter for having accomplished his mission, Alleyne full of wonderment at the humble bearing of so renowned a captain, and John loud with snorts and sneers, which spoke his disappointment and contempt.

"What ails the man?" asked Aylward in surprise.

"I have been cozened and bejaped," quoth he gruffly.

"By whom, Sir Samson the strong?"

"By thee, Sir Balaam the false prophet."

"By my hilt!" cried the archer, "though I be not Balaam, yet I hold converse with the very creature that spake to him. What is amiss, then, and how have I played you false?"

"Why, marry, did you not say, and Alleyne here will be my witness, that, if I would hie to the wars with you, you would place me under a leader who was second to none in all England for valor? Yet here you bring me to a shred of a man, peaky and ill-nourished, with eyes like a molting owl, who must needs, forsooth, take counsel with his mother ere he buckle sword to girdle."

"Is that where the shoe galls?" cried the bowman, and laughed aloud. "I will ask you what you think of him three months hence, if we be all alive; for sure I am that—"

Aylward's words were interrupted by an extraordinary hubbub which broke out that instant some little way down the street in the direction of the Priory. There was deep-mouthed shouting of men, frightened shrieks of women, howling and barking of curs, and over all a sullen, thunderous rumble, indescribably

[1] *devoir* (dĕ·vwär′): duty.

menacing and terrible. Round the corner of the narrow street there came rushing a brace of whining dogs with tails tucked under their legs, and after them a white-faced burgher, with outstretched hands and widespread fingers, his hair all abristle and his eyes glinting back from one shoulder to the other, as though some great terror were at his very heels. "Fly, my lady, fly!" he screeched and whizzed past them like bolt from bow; while close behind came lumbering a huge black bear, with red tongue lolling from his mouth, and a broken chain jangling behind him. To right and left the folk flew for arch and doorway. Hordle John caught up the Lady Loring as though she had been a feather and sprang with her into an open porch; while Aylward, with a whirl of French oaths, plucked at his quiver and tried to unsling his bow. Alleyne, all unnerved at so strange and unwonted a sight, shrunk up against the wall with his eyes fixed upon the frenzied creature, which came bounding along with ungainly speed, looking the larger in the uncertain light, its huge jaws agape, with blood and slaver trickling to the ground. Sir Nigel alone, unconscious to all appearance of the universal panic, walked with unfaltering step up the center of the road, a silken handkerchief in one hand and his gold comfit-box in the other. It sent the blood cold through Alleyne's veins to see that as they came together—the man and the beast—the creature reared up, with eyes ablaze with fear and hate, and whirled its great paws about the knight to smite him to the earth. He, however, blinking with puckered eyes, reached up his kerchief and flicked the beast twice across the snout with it. "Ah, saucy! saucy," quoth he, with gentle chiding; on which the bear, uncertain and puzzled, dropped its four legs to earth again, and, waddling back, was soon swathed in ropes by the bear ward and a crowd of peasants who had been in close pursuit.

A scared man was the keeper; for, having chained the brute to a stake while he drank a stoup of ale at the inn, it had been baited by stray curs until, in wrath and madness, it had plucked loose the chain and smitten or bitten all who came in its path. Most scared of all was he to find that the creature had come nigh to harm the Lord and Lady of the castle, who had power to place him in the stretch-neck or to have the skin scourged from his shoulders. Yet, when he came with bowed head and humble entreaty for forgiveness, he was met with a handful of small silver from Sir Nigel, whose dame, however, was less charitably disposed, being much ruffled in her dignity by the manner in which she had been hustled from her lord's side.

As they passed through the castle gate, John plucked at Aylward's sleeve, and the two fell behind.

"I must crave your pardon, comrade," said he, bluntly. "I was a fool not to know that a little rooster may be the gamest. I believe that this man is indeed a leader whom we may follow."

Chapter 10

HOW A YOUNG SHEPHERD HAD A PERILOUS FLOCK

Black was the mouth of Twynham Castle, though a pair of torches burning at the further end of the gateway cast a red glare over the outer bailey [1] and sent a dim, ruddy flicker through the rough-hewn arch, rising and falling with fitful brightness. Over the door the travelers could discern the escutcheon of the Montacutes, a roebuck gules on a field argent, flanked on either side by smaller shields which bore the red roses of the veteran constable. As they passed over the drawbridge, Alleyne marked the gleam of arms in the embrasures to right and left, and they had scarce set foot upon the causeway ere a hoarse blare burst from a bugle, and, with screech of hinge and clank of chain, the ponderous bridge swung up into the air, drawn by unseen hands. At the same instant the huge portcullis came rattling down from above and shut off the last fading light of day. Sir Nigel and his lady walked on in deep talk, while a fat understeward took charge of the three comrades and led them to the buttery, where beef, bread, and beer were kept ever in readiness for the wayfarer. After a hearty meal and a dip in the trough to wash the dust from them, they strolled forth into the bailey, where the bowman

[1] *bailey* (bā'lĭ): the courtyard of a feudal castle.

peered about through the darkness at wall and at keep [1] with the carping eyes of one who has seen something of sieges, and is not likely to be satisfied. To Alleyne and to John, however, it appeared to be as great and as stout a fortress as could be built by the hands of man.

Erected by Sir Baldwin de Redvers in the old fighting days of the twelfth century, when men thought much of war and little of comfort, Castle Twynham had been designed as a stronghold pure and simple, unlike those later and more magnificent structures where warlike strength had been combined with the magnificence of a palace. From the time of the Edwards such buildings as Conway or Caernarvon castles, to say nothing of Royal Windsor, had shown that it was possible to secure luxury in peace as well as security in times of trouble. Sir Nigel's trust, however, still frowned above the smooth-flowing waters of the Avon, very much as the stern race of early Anglo-Normans had designed it. There were the broad outer and inner baileys, not paved, but sown with grass to nourish the sheep and cattle which might be driven in on sign of danger. All round were high and turreted walls, with, at the corner, a bare square-faced keep, gaunt and windowless, rearing up from a loftly mound, which made it almost inaccessible to an assailant. Against the bailey walls were rows of frail wooden houses and leaning sheds, which gave shelter to the archers and men-at-arms who formed the garrison. The doors of these humble dwellings were mostly open, and against the yellow glare from within Alleyne could see the bearded fellows cleaning their harness, while their wives would come out for a gossip, with their needlework in their hands, and their long black shadows streaming across the yard. The air was full of the clack of their voices and the merry prattling of children, in strange contrast to the flash of arms and constant warlike challenge from the walls above.

"Methinks a company of school lads could hold this place against an army," quoth John.

"And so say I," said Alleyne.

"Nay, there you are wide of the clout," [2] the bowman said gravely. "By my hilt! I have seen a stronger fortalice carried in a summer evening. I remember such a one in Picardy, with a name as long as Gascon's pedigree. It was when I served under Sir

[1] *keep:* the main tower of a feudal castle. [2] *clout:* in archery, a target.

Robert Knolles, before the days of the Company; and we came by good plunder at the sacking of it. I had myself a great silver bowl, with two goblets, and a plastron of Spanish steel. Pasques Dieu! there are some fine women over yonder! Mort de ma vie! see to that one in the doorway! I will go speak to her. But whom have we here?"

"Is there an archer here hight Sam Aylward?" asked a gaunt man-at-arms, clanking up to them across the courtyard.

"My name, friend," quoth the bowman.

"Then sure I have no need to tell thee mine," said the other.

"By the rood! if it is not Black Simon of Norwich!" cried Aylward. "A mon cœur, camarade, à mon cœur! Ah, but I am blithe to see thee!" The two fell upon each other and hugged like bears.

"And where from, old blood and bones?" asked the bowman.

"I am in service here. Tell me, comrade, is it sooth that we shall have another fling at these Frenchmen? It is so rumored in the guardroom, and that Sir Nigel will take the field once more."

"It is like enough, mon gar, as things go."

"Now may the Lord be praised!" cried the other. "This very night will I set apart a golden ouche to be offered on the shrine of my name saint. I have pined for this, Aylward, as a young maid pines for her lover."

"Art so set on plunder then? Is the purse so light that there is not enough for a rouse? I have a bag at my belt, camarade, and you have but to put your fist into it for what you want. It was ever share and share between us."

"Nay, friend, it is not the Frenchman's gold, but the Frenchman's blood that I would have. I should not rest quiet in the grave, coz, if I had not another turn at them. For with us in France it has ever been fair and honest war—a shut fist for the men, but a bended knee for the woman. But how was it at Winchelsea when their galleys came down upon it some few years back? I had an old mother there, lad, who had come down thither from the Midlands to be the nearer her son. They found her afterwards by her own hearthstone, thrust through by a Frenchman's bill. My second sister, my brother's wife, and her two children, they were but ash heaps in the smoking ruins of their house. I will not say that we have not wrought great scath upon France, but women and children have been safe from us. And so, old friend, my heart is hot within me, and I long to hear the old battle cry again, and, by God's truth! if Sir Nigel unfurls his pennon, here is one who will be right glad to feel the saddle flaps under his knees."

"We have seen good work together, old war dog," quoth Aylward; "and, by my hilt! we may hope to see more ere we die. But we are more like to hawk at the Spanish woodcock than at the French heron, though, certes, it is rumored that Du Guesclin with all the best lances of France have taken service under the lions and towers of Castile. But, comrade, it is in my mind that there is some small matter of dispute still open between us."

" 'Fore God, it is sooth!" cried the other; "I had forgot it. The provost marshal and his men tore us apart when last we met."

"On which, friend, we vowed that we should settle the point when next we came together. Hast thy sword, I see, and the moon throws glimmer enough for such old night bards as we. On guard, mon gar! I have not heard clink of steel this month or more."

"Out from the shadow then," said the other, drawing his sword. "A vow is a vow, and not lightly to be broken."

"A vow to the saints," cried Alleyne, "is indeed not to be set aside; but this is a devil's vow, and, simple clerk as I am, I am yet the mouthpiece of the true church when I say that it were mortal sin to fight on such a quarrel. What! shall two grown men carry malice for years and fly like snarling curs at each other's throats?"

"No malice, my young clerk, no malice," quoth Black Simon. "I have not a bitter drop in my heart for mine old comrade; but the quarrel, as he hath told you, is still open and unsettled. Fall on, Aylward!"

"Not whilst I can stand between you," cried Alleyne, springing before the bowman. "It is shame and sin to see two Christian Englishmen turn swords against each other like a frenzied bloodthirsty paynim."

"And, what is more," said Hordle John, suddenly appearing out of the buttery with the huge board upon which the pastry was rolled, "if either raise sword I shall flatten him like a Shrovetide pancake. By the black rood! I shall drive him into the earth, like a nail into a door, rather than see you do scath to each other."

" 'Fore God, this is a strange way of preaching peace," cried Black Simon. "You may find the scath yourself, my lusty friend, if you raise your great cudgel to me. I had as lief have the castle drawbridge drop upon my pate."

"Tell me, Aylward," said Alleyne earnestly, with his hands outstretched to keep the pair asunder, "what is the cause of quarrel, that we may see whether honorable settlement may not be arrived at?"

The bowman looked down at his feet and then up at the moon. "Parbleu!" he cried, "the cause of quarrel? Why, mon petit, it was years ago in Limousin, and how can I bear in mind what was the cause of it? Simon there hath it at the end of his tongue."

"Not I, in troth," replied the other; "I have had other things to think of. There was some sort of bickering over dice, or wine, or was it a woman, coz?"

"Pasques Dieu! but you have nicked it," cried Aylward. "It was indeed about a woman; and the quarrel must go forward, for I am still of the same mind as before."

"What of the woman, then?" asked Simon. "May the murrain strike me if I can call to mind aught about her."

"It was La Blanche Rose, maid at the sign of the 'Trois Corbeaux' at Limoges. Bless her pretty heart! Why, mon gar, I loved her."

"So did a many," quoth Simon. "I call her to mind now. On the very day that we fought over the little hussy, she went off with Evan ap Rice, a long-legged Welsh dagsman. They have a hostel of their own now, somewhere on the banks of the Garonne, where the landlord drinks so much of the liquor that there is little left for the customers."

"So ends our quarrel, then," said Aylward, sheathing his sword. "A Welsh dagsman, i' faith! C'était mauvais goût,[1] camarade, and the more so when she had a jolly archer and a lusty man-at-arms to choose from."

"True, old lad. And it is as well that we can compose our differences honorably, for Sir Nigel had been out at the first clash of steel; and he hath sworn that if there be quarreling in the garri-

[1] *C'était mauvais goût:* French for "It was bad taste."

son, he would smite the right hand from the broilers. You know him of old, and that he is like to be as good as his word."

"Mort Dieu! yes. But there are ale, mead, and wine in the buttery, and the steward a merry rogue, who will not haggle over a quart or two. Buvons, mon gar, for it is not every day that two old friends come together."

The old soldiers and Hordle John strode off together in all good-fellowship. Alleyne had turned to follow them, when he felt a touch upon his shoulder and found a young page by his side.

"The Lord Loring commands," said the boy, "that you will follow me to the great chamber and await him there."

"But my comrades?"

"His commands were for you alone."

Alleyne followed the messenger to the east end of the courtyard, where a broad flight of steps led up to the doorway of the main hall, the outer wall of which is washed by the waters of the Avon. As designed at first, no dwelling had been allotted to the lord of the castle and his family but the dark and dismal basement story of the keep. A more civilized or more effeminate generation, however, had refused to be pent up in such a cellar, and the hall with its neighboring chambers had been added for their accommodation. Up the broad steps Alleyne went, still following his boyish guide, until at the folding oak doors the latter paused and ushered him into the main hall of the castle.

On entering the room the clerk looked round; but, seeing no one, he continued to stand, his cap in his hand, examining with the greatest interest a chamber which was so different to any to which he was accustomed. The days had gone by when a nobleman's hall was but a barn-like, rush-strewn enclosure, the common lounge and eating-room of every inmate of the castle. The Crusaders had brought back with them experiences of domestic luxuries, of Damascus carpets and rugs of Aleppo, which made them impatient of the hideous bareness and want of privacy which they found in their ancestral strongholds. Still stronger, however, had been the influence of the great French war; for, however well matched the nations might be in martial exercises, there could be no question but that our neighbors were infinitely superior to us in the arts of peace. A stream of returning knights, of wounded soldiers, and of unransomed French noblemen, had been for a quarter of a century continually pouring into England, every one of whom exerted an influence in the direction of greater domestic refinement, while shiploads of French furniture from Calais, Rouen, and other plundered towns had supplied our own artisans with models on which to shape their work. Hence, in most English castles, and in Castle Twynham among the rest, chambers were to be found which would seem to be not wanting either in beauty or in comfort.

In the great stone fireplace a log fire was spurting and crackling, throwing out a ruddy glare which, with the four bracket lamps which stood at each corner of the room, gave a bright and lightsome air to the whole apartment. Above was a wreathwork of blazonry, extending up to the carved and corniced oaken roof; while on either side stood the high canopied chairs placed for the master of the house and for his most honored guest. The walls were hung all round with most elaborate and brightly colored tapestry, representing the achievements of Sir Bevis of Hampton, and behind this convenient screen were stored the tables dormant and benches which would be needed for banquet or high festivity. The floor was of polished tiles, with a square of red and black diapered Flemish carpet in the center; and many settees, cushions, folding chairs, and carved bancals littered all over it. At the further end was a long black buffet, or dresser, thickly covered with gold cups, silver salvers, and other such valuables. All this Alleyne examined with curious eyes; but most interesting of all to him was a small ebony table at his very side, on which, by the side of a chessboard and the scattered chessmen, there lay an open manuscript written in a right clerkly hand and set forth with brave flourishes and devices along the margins. In vain Alleyne bethought him of where he was, and of those laws of good breeding and decorum which should restrain him: those colored capitals and black even lines drew his hand down to them, as the loadstone draws the needle, until, almost before he knew it, he was standing with the romance of Garin de Montglane before his eyes, so absorbed in its contents as to be completely oblivious both of where he was and why he had come there.

He was brought back to himself, however, by a sudden little ripple of quick feminine laughter. Aghast, he dropped the manuscript upon the chessmen and stared in bewilderment round the room. It was as empty and as still as ever. Again he stretched his hand out to the romance, and again came that roguish burst of merriment. He looked up at the ceiling, back at the closed door, and round at the stiff folds of motionless tapestry. Of a sudden, however, he caught a quick shimmer from the corner of a high-backed bancal in front of him and, shifting a pace or two to the side, saw a white slender hand, which held a mirror of polished silver in such a way that the concealed observer could see without being seen. He stood irresolute, uncertain whether to advance or to take no notice; but, even as he hesitated, the mirror was whipped in, and a tall and stately young lady swept out from behind the oaken screen, with a dancing light of mischief in her eyes. Alleyne started with astonishment as he recognized the very maiden who had suffered from his brother's violence in the forest. She no longer wore her gay riding-dress, however, but was attired in a long sweeping robe of black velvet of Bruges, with delicate tracery of white lace at neck and at wrist, scarce to be seen against her ivory skin. Beautiful as she had seemed to him before, the lithe charm of her figure and the proud, free grace of her bearing were enhanced now by the rich simplicity of her attire.

"Ah, you start," said she, with the same sidelong look of mischief, "and I cannot marvel at it. Didst not look to see the distressed damosel again. Oh, that I were a minstrel, that I might put it into rime, with the whole romance—the luckless maid, the wicked Socman, and the virtuous clerk! So might our frame have gone down together for all time, and you be numbered with Sir Percival or Sir Galahad or all the other rescuers of oppressed ladies."

"What I did," said Alleyne, "was too small a thing for thanks; and yet, if I may say it without offense, it was too grave and near a matter for mirth and raillery. I had counted on my brother's love, but God has willed that it should be otherwise. It is a joy to me to see you again, lady, and to know that you have reached home in safety, if this be indeed your home."

"Yes, in sooth, Castle Twynham is my home, and Sir Nigel Loring my father. I should have told you so this morning, but you said that you were coming thither, so I bethought me that I might hold it back as a surprise to you. Oh, dear, but it was brave to see you!" she cried, bursting out a-laughing once more and standing with her hand pressed to her side, and her half-closed eyes twinkling with amusement. "You drew back and came forward with your eyes upon my book there, like the mouse who sniffs the cheese and yet dreads the trap."

"I take shame," said Alleyne, "that I should have touched it."

"Nay, it warmed my very heart to see it. So glad was I, that I laughed for very pleasure. My fine preacher can himself be tempted then, thought I; he is not made of another clay to the rest of us."

"God help me! I am the weakest of the weak," groaned Alleyne. "I pray that I may have more strength."

"And to what end?" she asked sharply. "If you are, as I understand, to shut yourself forever in your cell within the four walls of an abbey, then of what use would it be were your prayer to be answered?"

"The use of my own salvation."

She turned from him with a pretty shrug and wave. "Is that all?" she said. "Then you are no better than Father Christopher and the rest of them. Your own, your own, ever your own! My father is the King's man, and when he rides into the press of fight he is not thinking ever of the saving of his own poor body; he recks little enough if he leave it on the field. Why then should you, who are soldiers of the Spirit, be ever moping or hiding in cell or in cave, with minds full of your own concerns, while the world, which you should be mending, is going on its way and neither sees nor hears you? Were ye all as thoughtless of your own souls as the soldier is of his body, ye would be of more avail to the souls of others."

"There is sooth in what you say, lady," Alleyne answered; "and yet I scarce can see what you would have the clergy and the Church to do."

"I would have them live as others and do men's work in the world, preaching by their lives rather than their words. I would have them come forth from their lonely places, mix with the borel [1] folks, feel the pains and the pleasures, the cares and the rewards, the temptings and the stirrings of the common people. Let them toil, and swinken, and labor, and plow the land, and take wives to themselves—"

"Alas! alas!" cried Alleyne aghast, "you have surely sucked

[1] *borel* (bŏr′ĕl): rough or rude.

this poison from the man Wicliffe, of whom I have heard such evil things."

"Nay, I know him not. I have learned it by looking from my own chamber window and marking these poor monks of the priory, their weary life, their profitless round. I have asked myself if the best which can be done with virtue is to shut it within high walls as though it were some savage creature. If the good will lock themselves up, and if the wicked will still wander free, then alas for the world!"

Alleyne looked at her in astonishment, for her cheek was flushed, her eyes gleaming, and her whole pose full of eloquence and conviction. Yet in an instant she had changed again to her old expression of merriment leavened with mischief.

"Wilt do what I ask?" said she.

"What is it, lady?"

"Oh, most ungallant clerk! A true knight would never have asked, but would have vowed upon the instant. 'Tis but to bear me out in what I say to my father."

"In what?"

"In saying, if he ask, that it was south of the Christchurch Road that I met you. I shall be shut up with the tirewomen else, and have a week of spindle and bodkin, when I would fain be galloping Troubadour up Wilverly Walk, or loosing little Roland at the Vinney Ridge herons."

"I shall not answer him if he ask."

"Not answer! But he will have an answer. Nay, but you must not fail me, or it will go ill with me."

"But, lady," cried poor Alleyne in great distress, "how can I say that it was to the south of the road when I know well that it was four miles to the north?"

"You will not say it?"

"Surely you will not, too, when you know that it is not so?"

"Oh, I weary of your preaching!" she cried, and swept away with a toss of her beautiful head, leaving Alleyne as cast down and ashamed as though he had himself proposed some infamous thing. She was back again in an instant, however, in another of her varying moods.

"Look at that, my friend!" said she. "If you had been shut up in abbey or in cell this day you could not have taught a wayward maiden to abide by the truth. Is it not so? What avail is the shepherd if he leaves his sheep?"

"A sorry shepherd!" said Alleyne humbly. "But here is your noble father."

"And you shall see how worthy a pupil I am. Father, I am much beholden to this young clerk, who was of service to me and helped me this very morning in Minstead Woods, four miles to the north of the Christchurch Road, where I had no call to be, you having ordered it otherwise." All this she reeled off in a loud voice and then glanced with sidelong, questioning eyes at Alleyne for his approval.

Sir Nigel, who had entered the room with a silvery-haired old lady upon his arm, stared aghast at this sudden outburst of candor.

"Maude, Maude!" said he, shaking his head, "it is more hard for me to gain obedience from you than from the ten score drunken archers who followed me to Guienne. Yet, hush! little one, for your fair lady-mother will be here anon, and there is no need that she should know it. We will keep you from the provost marshal this journey. Away to your chamber, sweeting, and keep a blithe face, for she who confesses is shriven. And now, fair mother," he continued, when his daughter had gone, "sit you here by the fire, for your blood runs colder than it did. Alleyne Edricson, I would have a word with you, for I would fain that you should take service under me. And here in good time comes my lady, without whose counsel it is not my wont to decide aught of import; but, indeed, it was her own thought that you should come."

"For I have formed a good opinion of you, and can see that you are one who may be trusted," said the Lady Loring. "And, in good sooth, my dear lord hath need of such a one by his side, for he recks so little of himself that there should be one there to look to his needs and meet his wants. You have seen the cloisters; it were well that you should see the world too, ere you make choice for life between them."

"It was for that very reason that my father willed that I should come forth into the world at my twentieth year," said Alleyne.

"Then your father was a man of good counsel," said she, "and you cannot carry out his will better than by going on this path, where all that is noble and gallant in England will be your companions."

"You can ride?" asked Sir Nigel, looking at the youth with puckered eyes.

"Yes, I have ridden much at the abbey."

"Yet there is a difference betwixt a friar's hack and a warrior's destrier. You can sing and play?"

"On citole, flute, and rebeck."

"Good! You can read blazonry?"

"Indifferent well."

"Then read this," quoth Sir Nigel, pointing upwards to one of the many quarterings which adorned the wall over the fireplace.

"Argent," Alleyne answered, "a fess azure charged with three lozenges dividing three mullets sable. Over all, on an escutcheon of the first, a jambe gules."

"A jambe gules erased," said Sir Nigel, shaking his head solemnly. "Yet it is not amiss for a monk-bred man. I trust that you are lowly and serviceable?"

"I have served all my life, my lord."

"Canst carve too?"

"I have carved two days a week for the brethren."

"A model truly! Wilt make a squire of squires. But tell me, I pray, canst curl hair?"

"No, my lord, but I could learn."

"It is of import," said he, "for I love to keep my hair well-ordered, seeing that the weight of my helmet for thirty years hath in some degree frayed it upon the top." He pulled off his velvet cap of maintenance as he spoke, and displayed a pate which was as bald as an egg and shone bravely in the firelight. "You see," said he, whisking round, and showing one little strip where a line of scattered hairs, like the last survivors in some fatal field, still barely held their own against the fate which had fallen upon their comrades; "these locks need some little oiling and curling, for I doubt not that if you look slantwise at my head, when the light is good, you will yourself perceive that there are places where the hair is sparse."

"It is for you also to bear the purse," said the lady; "for my sweet lord is of so free and gracious a temper that he would give it gayly to the first who asked alms of him. All these things, with some knowledge of venery and of the management of horse, hawk, and hound, with the grace and hardihood and courtesy which are proper to your age, will make you a fit squire for Sir Nigel Loring."

"Alas! lady," Alleyne answered, "I know well the great honor that you have done me in deeming me worthy to wait upon so renowned a knight, yet I am so conscious of my own weakness that I scarce dare incur duties which I might be so ill-fitted to fulfill."

"Modesty and a humble mind," said she, "are the very first and rarest gifts in page or squire. Your words prove that you have these, and all the rest is but the work of use and time. But there is no call for haste. Rest upon it for the night and let your orisons ask for guidance in the matter. We knew your father well, and would fain help his son, though we have small cause to love your brother the Socman, who is forever stirring up strife in the county."

"We can scarce hope," said Nigel, "to have all ready for our start before the feast of St. Luke, for there is much to be done in the time. You will have leisure, therefore, if it please you to take service under me, in which to learn your devoir. Bertrand, my daughter's page, is hot to go; but in sooth he is over-young for such rough work as may be before us."

"And I have one favor to crave from you," added the lady of the castle, as Alleyne turned to leave their presence. "You have, as I understand, much learning which you have acquired at Beaulieu."

"Little enough, lady, compared with those who were my teachers."

"Yet enough for my purpose, I doubt not. For I would have you give an hour or two a day whilst you are with us in discoursing with my daughter, the Lady Maude; for she is somewhat backward, I fear, and hath no love for letters, save for these poor fond romances, which do but fill her empty head with dreams of enchanted maidens and of errant cavaliers. Father Christopher comes over after nones from the priory, but he is stricken with years and slow of speech, so that she gets small profit from his teaching. I would have you do what you can with her, and with Agatha, my young tirewoman, and with Dorothy Pierpoint."

And so Alleyne found himself not only chosen as squire to

a knight but also as squire to three damosels, which was even further from the part which he had thought to play in the world. Yet he could but agree to do what he might, and so went forth from the castle hall with his face flushed and his head in a whirl at the thought of the strange and perilous paths which his feet were destined to tread.

Chapter 11

HOW ALLEYNE LEARNED MORE THAN HE COULD TEACH

And now there came a time of stir and bustle, of furbishing of arms and clang of hammer, from all the southland counties. Fast spread the tidings from thorpe [1] to thorpe and from castle to castle that the old game was afoot once more, and the lions and lilies to be in the field with the early spring. Great news this for that fierce old country, whose trade for a generation had been war, her exports archers and her imports prisoners. For six years her sons had chafed under an unwonted peace. Now they flew to their arms as to their birthright. The old soldiers of Crécy, of Nogent, and of Poitiers were glad to think that they might hear the war trumpet once more, and gladder still were the hot youth who had chafed for years under the martial tales of their sires. To pierce the great mountains of the south, to fight the tamers of the fiery Moors, to follow the greatest captain of the age, to find sunny cornfields and vineyards, when the marches of Picardy and Normandy were as bare and bleak as the Jedburgh forests—here was a golden prospect for a race of warriors. From sea to sea there was stringing of bows in the cottage and clang of steel in the castle.

Nor did it take long for every stronghold to pour forth its

[1] *thorpe* (thôrp): a small group of houses.

cavalry, and every hamlet its footmen. Through the late autumn and the early winter every road and country lane resounded with nakir and trumpet, with the neigh of the war horse and the clatter of marching men. From the Wrekin in the Welsh marches to the Cotswolds in the west or Butser in the south there was no hilltop from which the peasant might not have seen the bright shimmer of arms, the toss and flutter of plume and of pensil. From bypath, from woodland clearing, or from winding moorside track these little rivulets of steel united in the larger roads to form a broader stream, growing ever fuller and larger as it approached the nearest or most commodious seaport. And there all day, and day after day, there was bustle and crowding and labor, while the great ships loaded up, and one after the other spread their white pinions and darted off to the open sea, amid the clash of cymbals and rolling of drums and lusty shouts of those who went and of those who waited. From Orwell to the Dart there was no port which did not send forth its little fleet, gay with streamer and bunting, as for a joyous festival. Thus, in the season of the waning days, the might of England put forth on to the waters.

In the ancient and populous county of Hampshire there was no lack of leaders or of soldiers for a service which promised either honor or profit. Greatest of all the musters, however, was that of Twynham Castle, for the name and the fame of Sir Nigel Loring drew towards him the keenest and boldest spirits, all eager to serve under so valiant a leader. Archers from the New Forest and the Forest of Bere, billmen from the pleasant country which is watered by the Stour, the Avon, and the Itchen, young cavaliers from the ancient Hampshire houses, all were pushing for Christchurch to take service under the banner of the five scarlet roses.

And now, could Sir Nigel have shown the bachelles of land which the laws of rank required, he might well have cut his forked pennon into a square banner,[1] and taken such a following into the field as would have supported the dignity of a banneret. But poverty was heavy upon him, his land was scant, his coffers empty, and the very castle which covered him the holding of another. Sore was his heart when he saw rare bowmen and war-hardened spearmen turned away from his gates for the lack of the money which might equip and pay them. Yet the letter which

[1] *cut . . . banner:* risen in rank.

Aylward had brought him gave him powers which he was not slow to use. In it Sir Claude Latour, the Gascon lieutenant of the White Company, assured him that there remained in his keeping enough to fit out a hundred archers and twenty men-at-arms, which, joined to the three hundred veteran companions already in France, would make a force which any leader might be proud to command. Carefully and sagaciously the veteran knight chose out his men from the swarm of volunteers. Many an anxious consultation he held with Black Simon, Sam Aylward, and other of his more experienced followers, as to who should come and who should stay. By All Saints' Day, however, ere the last leaves had fluttered to earth in the Wilverley and Holmesley glades, he had filled up his full numbers and mustered under his banner as stout a following of Hampshire foresters as ever twanged their war bows. Twenty men-at-arms, too, well mounted and equipped, formed the cavalry of the party, while young Peter Terlake of Fareham, and Walter Ford of Botley, the martial sons of martial sires, came at their own cost to wait upon Sir Nigel and to share with Alleyne Edricson the duties of his squireship.

Yet, even after the enrollment, there was much to be done ere the party could proceed upon its way. For armor, swords, and lances there was no need to take much forethought, for they were to be had both better and cheaper in Bordeaux than in England. With the longbow, however, it was different. Yew staves, indeed, might be got in Spain, but it was well to take enough and to spare with them. Then three spare cords should be carried for each bow, with a great store of arrowheads, besides the brigandines of chain mail, the wadded steel caps, and the brassarts, or arm guards, which were the proper equipment of the archer. Above all, the women for miles round were hard at work cutting the white surcoats which were the badge of the Company and adorning them with the red lion of St. George upon the center of the breast. When all was completed, and the muster called in the castle yard, the oldest soldier of the French wars was fain to confess that he had never looked upon a better-equipped or more warlike body of men, from the old knight with his silk jupon, sitting his great black war horse in the front of them, to Hordle John, the giant recruit, who leaned carelessly upon a huge black bowstave in the rear. Of the six score, fully half had seen service before, while a fair sprinkling were men who had followed the wars all their lives, and had a hand in those battles which had made the whole world ring with the fame and the wonder of the island infantry.

Six long weeks were taken in these preparations, and it was close on Martinmas ere all was ready for a start. Nigh two months had Alleyne Edricson been in Castle Twynham—months which were fated to turn the whole current of his life. Already he had learned to bless his father for that wise provision which had made him seek to know the world ere he had ventured to renounce it.

For it was a different place from that which he had pictured—very different from that which he had heard described when the master of the novices held forth to his charges upon the ravening wolves who lurked for them beyond the peaceful folds of Beaulieu. There was cruelty in it, doubtless, and lust and sin and sorrow; but were there not virtues to atone, robust positive virtues, which did not shrink from temptation, which held their own in all the rough blasts of the workaday world? Monk-bred as he was, Alleyne had native shrewdness and a mind which was young enough to form new conclusions and to outgrow old ones. Abbot Berghersh was a good man, but how was he better than this kindly knight, who lived as simple a life, held as lofty and inflexible an ideal of duty, and did with all his fearless heart whatever came to his hand to do? In turning from the service of the one to that of the other, Alleyne could not feel that he was lowering his aims in life. True that his gentle and thoughtful nature recoiled from the grim work of war, yet in those days of martial orders and militant brotherhoods there was no gulf fixed betwixt the priest and the soldier. The man of God and the man of the sword might without scandal be united in the same individual. Why, then, should he, a mere clerk, have scruples when so fair a chance lay in his way of carrying out the spirit as well as the letter of his father's provision? Much struggle it cost him, anxious spirit-questionings and midnight prayings, with many a doubt and a misgiving; but the issue was that ere he had been three days in Castle Twynham he had taken service under Sir Nigel, and had accepted horse and harness, the same to be paid for out of his share of the profits of the expedition. Henceforth for seven hours a day he strove in the tiltyard [1] to qualify

[1] *tiltyard* (tĭlt'yärd'): a yard for fighting with spears and on horseback.

himself to be a worthy squire to so worthy a knight. Young, supple, and active, with all the pent energies from years of pure and healthy living, it was not long before he could manage his horse and his weapon well enough to earn an approving nod from critical men-at-arms, or to hold his own against Terlake and Ford, his fellow servitors.

But were there no other considerations which swayed him from the cloisters towards the world? To Alleyne had been opened now a side of life of which he had been as innocent as a child, but one which was of such deep import that it could not fail to influence him in choosing his path. A woman, in monkish precepts, had been the embodiment and concentration of what was dangerous and evil—a focus whence spread all that was to be dreaded and avoided. Yet here, day after day, for an hour after nones, and for an hour before vespers, he found himself in close communion with three maidens, all young, all fair, and all therefore doubly dangerous from the monkish standpoint. Yet he found that in their presence he was conscious of a quick sympathy, a pleasant ease, a ready response to all that was most gentle and best in himself, which filled his soul with a vague and new-found joy.

And yet the Lady Maude Loring was no easy pupil to handle. An older and more world-wise man might have been puzzled by her varying moods, her sudden prejudices, her quick resentment at all constraint and authority. Did a subject interest her, was there space in it for either romance or imagination, she would fly through it with her subtle, active mind, leaving her two fellow students and even her teacher toiling behind her. On the other hand, were there dull patience needed, with steady toil and strain of memory, no single fact could by any driving be fixed in her mind. Alleyne might talk to her of the stories of old gods and heroes, of gallant deeds and lofty aims, or he might hold forth upon moon and stars, and let his fancy wander over the hidden secrets of the universe, and he would have a wrapt listener with flushed cheeks and eloquent eyes, who could repeat after him the very words which had fallen from his lips. But when it came to the counting of figures and reckoning of epicycles, away would go her thoughts to horse and hound, and a vacant eye and listless face would warn the teacher that he had lost his hold upon his scholar. Then he had but to bring out the old romance book from the priory, with befingered cover of sheepskin and gold letters upon a purple ground, to entice her wayward mind back to the paths of learning.

At times, too, when the wild fit was upon her, she would break into pertness and rebel openly against Alleyne's gentle firmness. Yet he would jog quietly on with his teachings, taking no heed to her mutiny, until suddenly she would be conquered by his patience, and break into self-revilings, a hundred times stronger than her fault demanded. It chanced, however, that, on one of these mornings when the evil mood was upon her, Agatha, the young tirewoman, thinking to please her mistress, began also to toss her head and make tart rejoinder to the teacher's questions. In an instant the Lady Maude had turned upon her two blazing eyes and a face which was blanched with anger.

"You would dare!" said she. "You would dare!" The frightened tirewoman tried to excuse herself. "But my fair lady," she stammered, "what have I done? I have said no more than I heard."

"You would dare!" repeated the lady in a choking voice. "You, a graceless baggage, a foolish lack-brain, with no thought above the hemming of shifts. And he so kindly and hendy and long-suffering! You would—ha, you may well flee the room!"

She had spoken with a rising voice, and a clasping and opening of her long white fingers, so that it was no marvel that ere the speech was over, the skirts of Agatha were whisking round the door and the click of her sobs to be heard dying swiftly away down the corridor.

Alleyne stared open-eyed at this tigress who had sprung so suddenly to his rescue. "There is no need for such anger," he said mildly. "The maid's words have done me no scath. It is you yourself who have erred."

"I know it," she cried. "I am a most wicked woman. But it is bad enough that one should misuse you. Ma foi! I will see that there is not a second one."

"Nay, nay, no one has misused me," he answered. "But the fault lies in your hot and bitter words. You have called her a baggage and a lack-brain and I know not what."

"And you are he who taught me to speak the truth!" she cried. "Now I have spoken it, and yet I cannot please you. Lack-brain she is, and lack-brain I shall call her."

Such was a sample of the sudden janglings which marred the peace of that little class. As the weeks passed, however, they became fewer and less violent, as Alleyne's firm and constant nature gained sway and influence over the Lady Maude. And yet, sooth to say, there were times when he had to ask himself whether it was not the Lady Maude who was gaining sway and influence over him. If she were changing, so was he. In drawing her up from the world, he was day by day being himself dragged down towards it. In vain he strove and reasoned with himself as to the madness of letting his mind rest upon Sir Nigel's daughter. What was he—a younger son, a penniless clerk, a squire unable to pay for his own harness—that he should dare to raise his eyes to the fairest maid in Hampshire? So spake reason; but, in spite of all, her voice was ever in his ears, and her image in his heart.

And yet it was a surprise and a shock to himself to find how deeply she had entered into his life; how completely those vague ambitions and yearnings which had filled his spiritual nature centered themselves now upon this thing of earth. He had scarce dared to face the change which had come upon him, when a few sudden chance words showed it all up hard and clear, like a lightning flash in the darkness.

He had ridden over to Poole, one November day, with his fellow squire, Peter Terlake, in quest of certain yew staves from Wat Swathling, the Dorsetshire armorer. The day for their departure had almost come, and the two youths spurred it over the lonely downs at the top of their speed on their homeward course, for evening had fallen and there was much to be done. Peter was a hard, wiry, brown-faced, country-bred lad, who looked on the coming war as the schoolboy looks on his holidays. This day, however, he had been somber and mute, with scarce a word a mile to bestow upon his comrade.

"Tell me, Alleyne Edricson," he broke out, suddenly, as they clattered along the winding track which leads over the Bournemouth hills, "has it not seemed to you that of late the Lady Maude is paler and more silent than is her wont?"

"It may be so," the other answered shortly.

"And would rather sit distrait by her oriel [1] than ride gayly to the chase as of old. Methinks, Alleyne, it is this learning which you have taught her that has taken all the life and sap from her.

[1] *oriel* (ō′rĭ·ĕl): a bay window.

It is more than she can master, like a heavy spear to a light rider."

"Her lady-mother has so ordered it," said Alleyne.

"By Our Lady! and withouten disrespect," quoth Terlake, "it is in my mind that her lady-mother is more fitted to lead a company to a storming than to have the upbringing of this tender and milk-white maid. Hark ye, lad Alleyne, to what I never told man or woman yet. I love the fair Lady Maude and would give the last drop of my heart's blood to serve her." He spoke with a gasping voice, and his face flushed crimson in the moonlight.

Alleyne said nothing, but his heart seemed to turn to a lump of ice in his bosom.

"My father has broad acres," the other continued, "from Fareham Creek to the slope of the Portsdown Hill. There is filling of granges, hewing of wood, malting of grain, and herding of sheep as much as heart could wish, and I the only son. Sure am I that Sir Nigel would be blithe at such a match."

"But how of the lady?" asked Alleyne, with dry lips.

"Ah, lad, there lies my trouble. It is a toss of the head and a droop of the eyes if I say one word of what is in my mind. 'Twere as easy to woo the snow dame that we shaped last winter in our castle yard. I did but ask her yesternight for her green veil, that I might bear it as a token, or lambrequin, upon my helm; [1] but she flashed out at me that she kept it for a better man and then all in a breath asked pardon for that she had spoke so rudely. Yet she would not take back the words either, nor would she grant the veil. Has it seemed to thee, Alleyne, that she loves anyone?"

"Nay, I cannot say," said Alleyne, with a wild throb of sudden hope in his heart.

"I have thought so, and yet I cannot name the man. Indeed, save myself, and Walter Ford, and you, who are half a clerk, and Father Christopher of the priory, and Bertrand the page, who is there whom she sees?"

"I cannot tell," quoth Alleyne shortly; and the two squires rode on again, each intent upon his own thoughts.

Next day at morning lesson the teacher observed that his pupil was indeed looking pale and jaded, with listless eyes and a

[1] *helm* (hĕlm): helmet.

weary manner. He was heavyhearted to note the grievous change in her.

"Your mistress, I fear, is ill, Agatha," he said to the tirewoman when the Lady Maude had sought her chamber.

The maid looked aslant at him with laughing eyes. "It is not an illness that kills," quoth she.

"Pray God not!" he cried. "But tell me, Agatha, what it is that ails her."

"Methinks that I could lay my hand upon another who is smitten with the same trouble," said she, with the same sidelong look. "Canst not give a name to it, and thou so skilled in leechcraft?" [1]

"Nay, save that she seems aweary."

"Well, bethink you that it is but three days ere you will all be gone, and Castle Twynham be as dull as the priory. Is there not enough there to cloud a lady's brow?"

"In sooth, yes," he answered; "I had forgot that she is about to lose her father."

"Her father!" cried the tirewoman, with a little trill of laughter. "Oh, simple, simple!" And she was off down the passage like arrow from bow, while Alleyne stood gazing after her, betwixt hope and doubt, scarce daring to put faith in the meaning which seemed to underlie her words.

Chapter 12

HOW THE WHITE COMPANY SET FORTH TO THE WARS

St. Luke's Day had come and had gone, and it was in the season of Martinmas, when the oxen are driven in to the slaughter, that the White Company was ready for its journey.

[1] *leechcraft* (lēch′kráft′): the practice of medicine.

Loud shrieked the brazen bugles from keep and from gateway, and merry was the rattle of the war drum, as the men gathered in the outer bailey, with torches to light them, for the morn had not yet broken. Alleyne, from the window of the armory, looked down upon the strange scene—the circles of yellow flickering light, the lines of stern and bearded faces, the quick shimmer of arms, and the lean heads of the horses. In front stood the bowmen, ten deep, with a fringe of underofficers, who paced hither and thither marshaling the ranks with curt precept or short rebuke. Behind were the little clump of steel-clad horsemen, their lances raised, with long pensils [1] drooping down the oaken shafts. So silent and still were they that they might have been metal-sheathed statues, were it not for the occasional quick, impatient stamp of their chargers, or the rattle of chamfron [2] against neckplates as they tossed and strained. A spear's length in front of them sat the spare and long-limbed figure of Black Simon, the Norwich fighting man, his fierce, deep-lined face framed in steel, and the silk guidon [3] marked with the five scarlet roses slanting over his right shoulder. All round, in the edge of the circle of the light, stood the castle servants, the soldiers who were to form the garrison, and little knots of women, who sobbed in their aprons and called shrilly to their name saints to watch over the Wat or Will or Peterkin who had turned his hand to the work of war.

The young squire was leaning forward, gazing at the stirring and martial scene, when he heard a short, quick gasp at his shoulder, and there was the Lady Maude, with her hand to her heart, leaning up against the wall, slender and fair, like a half-plucked lily. Her face was turned away from him, but he could see, by the sharp intake of her breath, that she was weeping bitterly.

"Alas! alas!" he cried, all unnerved at the sight, "why is it that you are so sad, lady?"

"It is the sight of these brave men," she answered; "and to think how many of them go and how few are like to find their way back. I have seen it before, when I was a little maid, in the year of the Prince's great battle. I remember then how they mustered in the bailey, even as they do now, and my lady-mother holding me in her arms at this very window that I might see the show."

[1] *pensil:* a small, narrow flag. [2] *chamfron:* the headpiece of a horse's armor. [3] *guidon* (gī′dŭn): a small flag or streamer carried by troops.

"Please God, you will see them all back ere another year be out," said he.

She shook her head, looking round at him with flushed cheeks and eyes that sparkled in the lamplight. "Oh, but I hate myself for being a woman!" she cried, with a stamp of her little foot. "What can I do that is good? Here I must bide, and talk and sew and spin, and spin and sew and talk. Ever the same dull round, with nothing at the end of it. And now you are going, too, who could carry my thoughts out of these gray walls and raise my mind above tapestry and distaffs. What can I do? I am of no more use or value than that broken bowstave."

"You are of such value to me," he cried, in a whirl of hot, passionate words, "that all else has become naught. You are my heart, my life, my one and only thought. Oh, Maude, I cannot live without you, I cannot leave you without a word of love. All is changed to me since I have known you. I am poor and lowly and all unworthy of you; but if great love may weigh down such defects, then mine may do it. Give me but one word of hope to take to the wars with me—but one. Ah, you shrink, you shudder! My wild words have frightened you."

Twice she opened her lips, and twice no sound came from them. At last she spoke in a hard and measured voice, as one who dare not trust herself to speak too freely.

"This is oversudden," she said; "it is not so long since the world was nothing to you. You have changed once; perchance you may change again."

"Cruel!" he cried, "who hath changed me?"

"And then your brother," she continued, with a little laugh, disregarding his question. "Methinks this hath become a family custom amongst the Edricsons. Nay, I am sorry; I did not mean a jibe. But, indeed, Alleyne, this hath come suddenly upon me, and I scarce know what to say."

"Say some word of hope, however distant—some kind word that I may cherish in my heart."

"Nay, Alleyne, it were a cruel kindness, and you have been too good and true a friend to me that I should use you despitefully. There cannot be a closer link between us. It is madness to think of it. Were there no other reasons, it is enough that my father and your brother would both cry out against it."

"My brother, what has he to do with it? And your father—"

"Come, Alleyne, was it not you who would have me act fairly to all men, and, certes, to my father amongst them?"

"You say truly," he cried, "you say truly. But you do not reject me, Maude? You give me some ray of hope? I do not ask pledge or promise. Say only that I am not hateful to you—that on some happier day I may hear kinder words from you."

Her eyes softened upon him, and a kind answer was on her lips, when a hoarse shout, with the clatter of arms and stamping of steeds, rose up from the bailey below. At the sound her face set, her eyes sparkled, and she stood with flushed cheek and head thrown back—a woman's body, with a soul of fire.

"My father hath gone down," she cried. "Your place is by his side. Nay, look not at me, Alleyne. It is no time for dallying. Win my father's love, and all may follow. It is when the brave soldier hath done his devoir that he hopes for his reward. Farewell, and may God be with you!" She held out her white, slim hand to him, but as he bent his lips over it she whisked away and was gone, leaving in his outstretched hand the very green veil for which poor Peter Terlake had craved in vain. Again the hoarse cheering burst out from below, and he heard the clang of the rising portcullis. Pressing the veil to his lips, he thrust it into the bosom of his tunic, and rushed as fast as feet could bear him to arm himself and join the muster.

The company had marched to the turn of the road ere Sir Nigel Loring rode out from the gateway, mounted on Pommers, his great black war horse, whose ponderous footfall on the wooden drawbridge echoed loudly from the gloomy arch which spanned it. Sir Nigel was still in his velvet dress of peace, with flat velvet cap of maintenance and curling ostrich feather clasped in a golden brooch. To his three squires riding behind him it looked as though he bore the bird's egg as well as its feather, for the back of his bald pate shone like a globe of ivory. He bore no arms save the long and heavy sword which hung at his saddlebow; but Terlake carried in front of him the high wivern-crested basinet,[1] Ford the heavy ash spear with swallowtail pennon, while Alleyne was entrusted with the emblazoned shield. The Lady Loring rode her palfrey at her lord's bridle arm, for she would see him as far as the edge of the forest; and ever and anon she

[1] *basinet:* a light steel helmet.

turned her hard-lined face up wistfully to him and ran a questioning eye over his apparel and appointments.[1]

"I trust that there is nothing forgot," she said, beckoning to Alleyne to ride on her further side. "I trust him to you, Edricson. Hosen, shirts, cyclas, and under-jupons are in the brown basket on the left side of the mule. His wine he takes hot when the nights are cold, malvoisie or vernage, with as much spice as would cover the thumbnail. See that he hath a change if he come back hot from the tilting. There is goosegrease in a box, if the old scars ache at the turn of the weather. Let his blankets be dry and—"

"Nay, my heart's life," the little knight interrupted, "trouble not now about such matters. Why so pale and wan, Edricson? Is it not enow to make a man's heart dance to see this noble Company, such valiant men-at-arms, such lusty archers? By St. Paul! I should be ill to please if I were not blithe to see the red roses flying at the head of so noble a following!"

"The purse I have already given you, Edricson," continued the lady. "There are in it twenty-three marks, one noble, three shillings, and fourpence, which is a great treasure for one man to carry. And I pray you to bear in mind, Edricson, that he hath two pair of shoes, those of red leather for common use, and the others with golden toechains, which he may wear should he chance to drink wine with the Prince or with Chandos."

"My sweet bird," said Sir Nigel, "I am right loath to part from you, but we are now at the fringe of the forest, and it is not right that I should take the chatelaine too far from her trust."

"But, oh, my dear lord," she cried with a trembling lip, "let me bide with you for one furlong further—or one and a half perhaps. You may spare me this out of the weary miles that you will journey alone."

"Come, then, my heart's comfort," he answered. "But I must crave a gage [2] from thee. It is my custom, dearling, and hath been since I have first known thee, to proclaim by herald in such camps, townships, or fortalices as I may chance to visit that, my ladylove being beyond compare the fairest and sweetest in Christendom, I should deem it great honor and kindly condescension if any cavalier would run three courses against me with sharpened

[1] *appointments:* equipment. [2] *gage* (gāj): the symbol of a pledge of loyalty.

lances, should he chance to have a lady whose claim he was willing to advance. I pray you, then, my fair dove, that you will vouchsafe to me one of those doeskin gloves, that I may wear it as the badge of her whose servant I shall ever be."

"Alack and alas for the fairest and sweetest!" she cried. "Fair and sweet I would fain be for your dear sake, my lord, but old I am, and ugly, and the knights would laugh should you lay lance in rest in such a cause."

"Edricson," quoth Sir Nigel, "you have young eyes, and mine are somewhat bedimmed. Should you chance to see a knight laugh, or smile, or even, look you, arch his brows, or purse his mouth, or in any way show surprise that I should uphold the Lady Mary, you will take particular note of his name, his coat armor, and his lodging. Your glove, my life's desire!"

The Lady Mary Loring slipped her hand from her yellow leather gauntlet, and he, lifting it with dainty reverence, bound it to the front of his velvet cap.

"It is with mine other guardian angels," quoth he, pointing at the saints' medals which hung beside it. "And now, my dearest, you have come far enow. May the Virgin guard and prosper thee! One kiss!" He bent down from his saddle, and then, striking spurs into his horse's sides, he galloped at top speed after his men, with his three squires at his heels. Half a mile further, where the road topped a hill, they looked back, and the Lady Mary on her white palfrey was still where they had left her. A moment later they were on the downward slope, and she had vanished from their view.

For a time Sir Nigel was very moody and downcast, with bent brows, and eyes upon the pommel of his saddle. Edricson and Terlake rode behind him in little better case, while Ford, a careless and lighthearted youth, grinned at the melancholy of his companions and flourished his lord's heavy spear, making a point to right and a point to left, as though he were a paladin [1] contending against a host of assailants. Sir Nigel happening, however, to turn himself in his saddle—Ford instantly became as stiff and as rigid as though he had been struck with a palsy. The four rode alone, for the archers had passed a curve in the road, though Alleyne could still hear the heavy clump, clump of their marching, or catch a glimpse of the sparkle of steel through the tangle of leafless branches.

[1] *paladin* (păl′ȧ·dĭn): champion or hero.

"Ride by my side, friends, I entreat of you," said the knight, reining in his steed that they might come abreast of him. "For, since it hath pleased you to follow me to the wars, it were well that you should know how you may best serve me. I doubt not, Terlake, that you will show yourself a worthy son of a valiant father; and you, Ford, of yours; and you, Edricson, that you are mindful of the old-time house from which all men know that you are sprung. And first I would have you bear very steadfastly in mind that our setting forth is by no means for the purpose of gaining spoil or exacting ransom, though it may well happen that such may come to us also. We go to France, and from thence, I trust, to Spain, in humble search of a field in which we may win advancement and perchance some small share of glory. For this purpose I would have you know that it is not my wont to let any occasion pass where it is in any way possible that honor may be gained. I would have you bear this in mind and give great heed to it, that you may bring me word of all cartels,[1] challenges, wrongs, tyrannies, infamies, and wronging of damsels. Nor is any occasion too small to take note of, for I have known such trifles as the dropping of a gauntlet or the flicking of a breadcrumb, when well and properly followed up, lead to a most noble spear-running. But, Edricson, do I not see a cavalier who rides down yonder road amongst the nether shaw? It would be well, perchance, that you should give him greeting from me. And, should he be of gentle blood, it may be that he would care to exchange thrusts with me."

"Why, my lord," quoth Ford, standing in his stirrups and shading his eyes, "it is old Hob Davidson, the fat miller of Milton!"

"Ah, so it is, indeed," said Sir Nigel, puckering his cheeks; "but wayside ventures are not to be scorned, for I have seen no finer passages than are to be had from such chance meetings, when cavaliers are willing to advance themselves. I can well remember that two leagues from the town of Rheims I met a very valiant and courteous cavalier of France, with whom I had gentle and most honorable contention for upwards of an hour. It hath ever grieved me that I had not his name, for he smote upon me with a mace and went upon his way ere I was in condition to have much speech with him."

[1] *cartel:* a letter of challenge to single combat.

The bleak, hard, wind-swept road dipped down in front of them into a little valley and then, writhing up the heathy slope upon the other side, lost itself among the gaunt pine trees. Far away between the black lines of trunks the quick glitter of steel marked where the Company pursued its way. To the north stretched the tree country, but to the south, between two swelling downs, a glimpse might be caught of the cold gray shimmer of the sea, with the white fleck of a galley sail upon the distant sky line.

Chapter 13

HOW THE YELLOW COG[1] SAILED FORTH FROM LEPE

That night the Company slept at St. Leonard's, in the great monastic barns and spicarium—ground well known both to Alleyne and to John, for they were almost within sight of the abbey of Beaulieu. A strange thrill it gave to the young squire to see the well-remembered white dress once more, and to hear the measured tolling of the deep vespers bell. At early dawn they passed across the broad, sluggish, reed-girt stream—men, horses, and baggage in the flat ferry barges—and so journeyed on through the fresh morning air past Exbury to Lepe. Topping the heathy down, they came of a sudden full in sight of the old sea-port—a cluster of houses, a trail of blue smoke, and a bristle of masts. To right and left the long blue curve of the Solent[2] lapped in a fringe of foam upon the yellow beach. Some way out from the town a line of pessoners, creyers, and other small craft were rolling lazily on the gentle swell. Further out still lay a great merchant ship, high ended, deep waisted, painted of a canary yellow, and towering above the fishing boats like a swan among ducklings.

[1] *cog* (kŏg): a ship with a high prow and stern. [2] *Solent* (sō′lĕnt): the channel between the Isle of Wight and the southern coast of England.

"By St. Paul!" said the knight, "our good merchant of Southampton hath not played us false, for methinks I can see our ship down yonder. He said that she would be of great size and of a yellow shade."

"By my hilt, yes!" muttered Aylward; "she is yellow as a kite's claw, and would carry as many men as there are pips [1] in a pomegranate."

"It is as well," remarked Terlake; "for methinks, my fair lord, that we are not the only ones who are waiting a passage to Gascony. Mine eye catches at times a flash and sparkle among yonder houses which assuredly never came from shipman's jacket or the gaberdine of a burgher."

"I can also see it," said Alleyne, shading his eyes with his hand. "And I can see men-at-arms in yonder boats which ply betwixt the vessel and the shore. But methinks that we are very welcome here, for already they come forth to meet us."

A tumultuous crowd of fishermen, citizens, and women had indeed swarmed out from the northern gate, and approached them up the side of the moor, waving their hands and dancing with joy, as though a great fear had been rolled back from their minds. At their head rode a very large and solemn man with a long chin and a drooping lip. He wore a fur tippet round his neck and a heavy gold chain over it, with a medallion which dangled in front of him.

"Welcome, most puissant [2] and noble lord," he cried, doffing his bonnet to Black Simon. "I have heard of your lordship's valiant deeds, and in sooth they might be expected from your lordship's face and bearing. Is there any small matter in which I may oblige you?"

"Since you ask me," said the man-at-arms, "I would take it kindly if you could spare a link or two of the chain which hangs round your neck."

"What, the corporation chain!" cried the other in horror. "The ancient chain of the township of Lepe! This is but a sorry jest, Sir Nigel."

"What the plague did you ask me for then?" said Simon. "But if it is Sir Nigel Loring with whom you would speak, that is he upon the black horse."

[1] *pip* (pĭp): seed. [2] *puissant* (pū'ĭ·sănt): powerful.

The Mayor of Lepe gazed with amazement on the mild face and slender frame of the famous warrior.

"Your pardon, my gracious lord," he cried. "You see in me the mayor and chief magistrate of the ancient and powerful town of Lepe. I bid you very heartily welcome, and the more so as you are come at a moment when we are sore put to it for means of defense."

"Ha!" cried Sir Nigel, pricking up his ears.

"Yes, my lord, for the town being very ancient and the walls as old as the town, it follows that they are very ancient too. But there is a certain villainous and bloodthirsty Norman pirate hight Tête-noire, who, with a Genoan called Tito Caracci, commonly known as Spade-beard, hath been a mighty scourge upon these coasts. Indeed, my lord, they are very cruel and blackhearted men, graceless and ruthless, and if they should come to the ancient and powerful town of Lepe, then—"

"Then good-by to the ancient and powerful town of Lepe," quoth Ford, whose lightness of tongue could at times rise above his awe of Sir Nigel.

The knight, however, was too much intent upon the matter in hand to give heed to the flippancy of his squire. "Have you then cause," he asked, "to think that these men are about to venture an attempt upon you?"

"They have come in two great galleys," answered the mayor, "with two bank of oars on either side, and great store of engines of war and of men-at-arms. At Weymouth and at Portland they have murdered and ravished. Yesterday morning they were at Cowes, and we saw the smoke from the burning crofts. Today they lie at their ease near Freshwater, and we fear much lest they come upon us and do us a mischief."

"We cannot tarry," said Sir Nigel, riding towards the town, with the mayor upon his left side; "the Prince awaits us at Bordeaux, and we may not be behind the general muster. Yet I will promise you that on our way we shall find time to pass Freshwater and to prevail upon these rovers to leave you in peace."

"We are much beholden to you!" cried the mayor. "But I cannot see, my lord, how, without a warship, you may venture against these men. With your archers, however, you might well hold the town and do them great scath if they attempt to land."

"There is a very proper cog out yonder," said Sir Nigel; "it would be a very strange thing if any ship were not a warship when it had such men as these upon her decks. Certes, we shall do as I say, and that no later than this very day."

"My lord," said a rough-haired, dark-faced man, who walked by the knight's other stirrup, with his head sloped to catch all that he was saying. "By your leave, I have no doubt that you are skilled in land fighting and the marshaling of lances, but, by my soul! you will find it another thing upon the sea. I am the master shipman of this yellow cog, and my name is Goodwin Hawtayne. I have sailed since I was as high as this staff, and I have fought against these Normans and against the Genoese, as well as the Scotch, the Bretons, the Spanish, and the Moors. I tell you, sir, that my ship is overlight and overfrail for such work, and it will but end in our having our throats cut or being sold as slaves to the Barbary heathen."

"I also have experienced one or two gentle and honorable ventures upon the sea," quoth Sir Nigel, "and I am right blithe to have so fair a task before us. I think, good master shipman, that you and I may win great honor in this matter, and I can see very readily that you are a brave and stout man."

"I like it not," said the other sturdily. "In God's name, I like it not. And yet Goodwin Hawtayne is not the man to stand back when his fellows are for pressing forward. By my soul! be it sink or swim, I shall turn her beak into Freshwater Bay, and if good Master Witherton, of Southampton, like not my handling of his ship, then he may find another master shipman."

They were close by the old north gate of the little town, and Alleyne, half-turning in his saddle, looked back at the motley crowd who followed. The bowmen and men-at-arms had broken their ranks and were intermingled with the fishermen and citizens, whose laughing faces and hearty gestures bespoke the weight of care from which this welcome arrival had relieved them. Here and there among the moving throng of dark jerkins and of white surcoats were scattered dashes of scarlet and blue, the wimples or shawls of the women. Aylward, with a fishing lass on either arm, was vowing constancy alternately to her on the right and her on the left, while big John towered in the rear with a little chubby maiden enthroned upon his great shoulder, her soft white arm curled round his shining headpiece. So the throng moved on, until at the very gate it was brought to a stand by a wondrously fat man, who came darting forth from the town with rage in every feature of his rubicund face.

"How now, Sir Mayor?" he roared, in a voice like a bull. "How now, Sir Mayor? How of the clams and the scallops!"

"By Our Lady! my sweet Sir Oliver," cried the mayor. "I have had so much to think of, with these wicked villains so close upon us, that it had quite gone out of my head."

"Words, words!" shouted the other furiously. "Am I to be put off with words? I say to you again, how of the clams and scallops?"

"My fair sir, you flutter me," cried the mayor. "I am a peaceful trader, and I am not wont to be so shouted at upon so small a matter."

"Small!" shrieked the other. "Small! Clams and scallops! Ask me to your table to partake of the dainty of the town, and when I come, a barren welcome and a bare board! Where is my spear-bearer?"

"Nay, Sir Oliver, Sir Oliver!" cried Sir Nigel, laughing. "Let your anger be appeased, since instead of this dish you come upon an old friend and comrade."

"By St. Martin of Tours!" shouted the fat knight, his wrath all changed in an instant to joy, "if it is not my dear little game rooster of the Garonne. Ah, my sweet coz, I am right glad to see you. What days we have seen together!"

"Aye, by my faith," cried Sir Nigel, with sparkling eyes, "we have seen some valiant men, and we have shown our pennons in some noble skirmishes. By St. Paul! we have had great joys in France."

"And sorrows also," quoth the other. "I have some sad memories of the land. Can you recall that which befell us at Libourne?"

"Nay, I cannot call to mind that we ever so much as drew sword at the place."

"Man, man," cried Sir Oliver, "your mind still runs on naught but blades and basinets. Hast no space in thy frame for the softer joys? Ah, even now I can scarce speak of it unmoved. So noble a pie, such tender pigeons, and sugar in the gravy instead of salt! You were by my side that day, as were Sir Claude Latour and the Lord of Pommers."

"I remember it," said Sir Nigel, laughing, "and how you harried the cook down the street, and spoke of setting fire to the inn. By St. Paul! most worthy mayor, my old friend is a perilous man, and I rede you that you compose your difference with him on such terms as you may."

"The clams and scallops shall be ready within the hour," the mayor answered. "I had asked Sir Oliver Buttesthorn to do my humble board the honor to partake at it of the dainty upon which we take some little pride, but in sooth this alarm of pirates hath cast a shadow on my wits. But I trust, Sir Nigel, that you will also partake of none-meat with me?"

"I have overmuch to do," Sir Nigel answered, "for we must be aboard, horse and man, as early as we may. How many do you muster, Sir Oliver?"

"Three and forty. The forty are drunk, and the three are but indifferent sober. I have them all safe upon the ship."

"They had best find their wits again, for I shall have work for every man of them ere the sun set. It is my intention, if it seems good to you, to try a venture against these Norman and Genoese rovers."

"They carry caviar and certain very noble spices from the Levant aboard of ships from Genoa," quoth Sir Oliver. "We may come to great profit through the business. I pray you, master shipman, that when you go on board you pour a helmetful of sea water over any of my rogues whom you may see there."

Leaving the lusty knight and the Mayor of Lepe, Sir Nigel led the Company straight down to the water's edge, where long lines of flat lighters swiftly bore them to their vessel. Horse after horse was slung by main force up from the barges, and after kicking and plunging in empty air was dropped into the deep waist of the yellow cog, where rows of stalls stood ready for their safe keeping. Englishmen in those days were skilled and prompt in such matters, for it was not so long before that Edward had embarked as many as fifty thousand men in the port of Orwell, with their horses and their baggage, all in the space of four-and-twenty hours. So urgent was Sir Nigel on the shore, and so prompt was Goodwin Hawtayne on the cog, that Sir

Oliver Buttesthorn had scarce swallowed his last scallop ere the peal of the trumpet and clang of nakir announced that all was ready and the anchor drawn. In the last boat which left the shore the two commanders sat together in the sheets, a strange contrast to one another, while under the feet of the rowers was a litter of huge stones which Sir Nigel had ordered to be carried to the cog. These once aboard, the ship set her broad mainsail, purple in color, and with a golden St. Christopher bearing Christ upon his shoulder in the center of it. The breeze blew, the sail bellied, over heeled the portly vessel, and away she plunged through the smooth blue rollers, amid the clang of the minstrels on her poop and the shouting of the black crowd who fringed the yellow beach. To the left lay the green Island of Wight, with its long, low, curving hills peeping over each other's shoulders to the sky line; to the right, the wooded Hampshire coast as far as eye could reach; above, a steel-blue heaven, with a wintry sun shimmering down upon them, and enough of frost to set the breath a-smoking.

"By St. Paul!" said Sir Nigel gayly, as he stood upon the poop and looked on either side of him, "it is a land which is very well worth fighting for, and it were pity to go to France for what may be had at home. Did you not spy a crooked man upon the beach?"

"Nay, I spied nothing," grumbled Sir Oliver, "for I was hurried down with a clam stuck in my gizzard and an untasted goblet of Cyprus on the board behind me."

"I saw him, my fair lord," said Terlake, "an old man with one shoulder higher than the other."

" 'Tis a sign of good fortune," quoth Sir Nigel, "so all should be well with us. What say you, Edricson?"

"I cannot tell, my fair lord. The Romans of old were a very wise people, yet, certes, they placed their faith in such matters. So, too, did the Greeks, and divers other ancient peoples who were famed for their learning. Yet of the moderns there are many who scoff at all omens."

"There can be no manner of doubt about it," said Sir Oliver Buttesthorn. "I can well remember that in Navarre one day it thundered on the left out of a cloudless sky. We knew that ill would come of it, nor had we long to wait. Only thirteen days after, a haunch of prime venison was carried from my very tent door by the wolves, and on the same day two flasks of old vernage turned sour."

"You may bring my harness from below," said Sir Nigel to his squires, "and also, I pray you, bring up Sir Oliver's, and we shall don it here. Ye may then see to your own gear; for this day you will, I hope, make a very honorable entrance into the field of chivalry and prove yourselves to be very worthy and valiant squires. And now, Sir Oliver, as to our dispositions: would it please you that I should order them or will you?"

"You, my cockerel, you. By Our Lady! I am no chicken, but I cannot claim to know as much of war as the squire of Sir Walter Manny. Settle the matter to your own liking."

"You shall fly your pennon upon the fore part, then, and I upon the poop.[1] For foreguard I shall give you your own forty men, with two score archers. Two score men, with my own men-at-arms and squires, will serve as a poop guard. Ten archers, with thirty shipmen, under the master, may hold the waist while ten lie aloft with stones and arbalests. How like you that?"

"Good, by my faith, good! But here comes my harness, and I must to work, for I cannot slip into it as I was wont when first I set my face to the wars."

Meanwhile there had been bustle and preparation in all parts of the great vessel. The archers stood in groups about the decks, new-stringing their bows, and testing that they were firm at the nocks.[2] Among them moved Aylward and other of the older soldiers, with a few whispered words of precept here and of warning there.

"Stand to it, my hearts of gold," said the old bowman as he passed from knot to knot. "By my hilt! we are in luck this journey. Bear in mind the old saying of the Company."

"What is that, Aylward?" cried several, leaning on their bows and laughing at him.

" 'Tis the master bowyer's rede: 'Every bow well bent. Every shaft well sent. Every stave well nocked. Every string well locked.' There, with that jingle in his head, a bracer on his left hand, a shooting glove on his right, and a farthing's worth of wax in his girdle, what more doth a bowman need?"

"It would not be amiss," said Hordle John, "if under his girdle he had four farthings' worth of wine."

[1] *poop* (po͞op): the stern section of a ship. [2] *nock* (nŏk): notch.

"Work first, wine afterwards, mon camarade. But it is time that we took our order, for methinks that between the Needle rocks and the Alum cliffs yonder I can catch a glimpse of the topmasts of the galleys. Hewett, Cook, Johnson, Cunningham, your men are of the poop guard. Thornbury, Walters, Hackett, Baddlesmere, you are with Sir Oliver on the forecastle. Simon, you bide with your lord's banner; but ten men must go forward."

Quietly and promptly the men took their places, lying flat upon their faces on the deck, for such was Sir Nigel's order. Near the prow was planted Sir Oliver's spear, with his arms—a boar's head gules upon a field of gold. Close by the stern stood Black Simon with the pennon of the house of Loring. In the waist gathered the Southampton mariners, hairy and burly men, with their jerkins thrown off, their waists braced tight, swords, mallets, and poleaxes in their hands. Their leader, Goodwin Hawtayne, stood upon the poop and talked with Sir Nigel, casting his eye up sometimes at the swelling sail, and then glancing back at the two seamen who held the tiller.

"Pass the word," said Sir Nigel, "that no man shall stand to arms or draw his bowstring until my trumpeter shall sound. It would be well that we should seem to be a merchant ship from Southampton and appear to flee from them."

"We shall see them anon," said the master shipman. "Ha, said I not so? There they lie, the water snakes, in Freshwater Bay; and mark the reek of smoke from yonder point, where they have been at their devil's work. See how their shallops pull from the land! They have seen us and called their men aboard. Now they draw upon the anchor. See them like ants upon the forecastle! They stoop and heave like handy shipmen. But, my fair lord, these are no niefs. I doubt but we have taken in hand more than we can do. Each of these ships is a galeasse, and of the largest and swiftest make."

"I would I had your eyes," said Sir Nigel, blinking at the pirate galleys. "They seem very gallant ships, and I trust that we shall have much pleasance from our meeting with them. It would be well to pass the word that we should neither give nor take quarter this day. Have you perchance a priest or friar aboard this ship, Master Hawtayne?"

"No, my fair lord."

"Well, well, it is no great matter for my Company, for they

were all houseled and shriven ere we left Twynham Castle; and Father Christopher of the priory gave me his word that they were as fit to march to heaven as to Gascony. But my mind misdoubts me as to these Winchester men who have come with Sir Oliver, for they appear to be a very ungodly crew. Pass the word that the men kneel, and that the underofficers repeat to them the pater, the ave, and the credo."

With a clank of arms, the rough archers and seamen took to their knees, with bent heads and crossed hands, listening to the hoarse mutter from the file leaders. It was strange to mark the hush; so that the lapping of the water, the straining of the sail, and the creaking of the timbers grew louder of a sudden upon the ear. Many of the bowmen had drawn amulets and relics from their bosoms, while he who possessed some more than usually sanctified treasure passed it down the line of his comrades, that all might kiss and reap the virtue.

The yellow cog had now shot out from the narrow waters of the Solent, and was plunging and rolling on the long heave of the open channel. The wind blew freshly from the east, with a very keen edge to it; and the great sail bellied roundly out, laying the vessel over until the water hissed beneath her lee bulwarks. Broad and ungainly, she floundered from wave to wave, dipping her round bows deeply into the blue rollers, and sending the white flakes of foam in a spatter over her decks. On her larboard quarter lay the two dark galleys, which had already hoisted sail, and were shooting out from Freshwater Bay in swift pursuit, their double line of oars giving them a vantage which could not fail to bring them up with any vessel which trusted to sails alone. High and bluff the English cog; long, black, and swift the pirate galleys, like two fierce lean wolves which have seen a lordly and unsuspecting stag walk past their forest lair.

"Shall we turn, my fair lord, or shall we carry on?" asked the master shipman, looking behind him with anxious eyes.

"Nay, we must carry on and play the part of the helpless merchant."

"But your pennons? They will see that we have two knights with us."

"Yet it would not be to a knight's honor or good name to lower his pennon. Let them be, and they will think that we are a wine ship for Gascony, or that we bear the wool bales of some mercer of the Staple. Ma foi, but they are very swift! They swoop upon us like two goshawks on a heron. Is there not some symbol or device upon their sails?"

"That on the right," said Edricson, "appears to have the head of an Ethiop upon it."

" 'Tis the badge of Tête-noire, the Norman," cried a seaman-mariner. "I have seen it before, when he harried us at Winchelsea. He is a wondrous large and strong man, with no ruth [1] for man, woman, or beast. They say that he hath the strength of six; and, certes, he hath the crimes of six upon his soul. See, now, to the poor souls who swing at either end of his yardarm!"

At each end of the yard there did indeed hang the dark figure of a man, jolting and lurching with hideous jerkings of its limbs at every plunge and swoop of the galley.

"By St. Paul!" said Sir Nigel, "and by the help of St. George and Our Lady, it will be a very strange thing if our black-headed friend does not himself swing thence ere he be many hours older. But what is that upon the other galley?"

"It is the red cross of Genoa. This Spade-beard is a very noted captain, and it is his boast that there are no seamen and no archers in the world who can compare with those who serve the Doge Boccanegra."

"That we shall prove," said Goodwin Hawtayne; "but it would be well, ere they close with us, to raise up the mantlets [2] and pavises [3] as a screen against their bolts." He shouted a hoarse order, and his seamen worked swiftly and silently, heightening the bulwarks and strengthening them. The three ship's anchors were at Sir Nigel's command carried into the waist and tied to the mast, with twenty feet of cable between, each under the care of four seamen. Eight others were stationed with leather water bags to quench any fire arrows which might come aboard, while others were sent up the mast, to lie along the yard and drop stones or shoot arrows as the occasion served.

"Let them be supplied with all that is heavy and weighty in the ship," said Sir Nigel.

"Then we must send them up Sir Oliver Buttesthorn," quoth Ford.

The knight looked at him with a face which struck the

[1] *ruth* (rōōth): pity. [2] *mantlet* (mănt′lĕt): a sheltering screen. [3] *pavise* (păv′ĭs): a protective shield.

smile from his lips. "No squire of mine," he said, "shall ever make jest of a belted knight. And yet," he added, his eyes softening, "I know that it is but a boy's mirth, with no sting in it. Yet I should ill do my part towards your father if I did not teach you to curb your tongueplay."

"They will lay us aboard on either quarter, my lord," cried the master. "See how they stretch out from each other! The Norman hath a mangonel or a trabuch [1] upon the forecastle. See, they bend to the levers! They are about to loose it."

"Aylward," cried the knight, "pick your three trustiest archers, and see if you cannot do something to hinder their aim. Methinks they are within long arrow flight."

"Seventeen score paces," said the archer, running his eye backwards and forwards. "By my ten finger bones! it would be a strange thing if we could not notch a mark at that distance. Here, Watkins of Sowley, Arneld, Long Williams, let us show the rogues that they have English bowmen to deal with."

The three archers named stood at the further end of the poop, balancing themselves with feet widely spread and bows drawn, until the heads of the cloth-yard arrows were level with the center of the stave. "You are the surer, Watkins," said Aylward, standing by them with shaft upon string. "Do you take the rogue with the red coif. You two bring down the man with the headpiece, and I will hold myself ready if you miss. Ma foi! they are about to loose her. Shoot, mes garçons, or you will be too late."

The throng of pirates had cleared away from the great wooden catapult, leaving two of their number to discharge it. One in a scarlet cap bent over it, steadying the jagged rock which was balanced on the spoon-shaped end of the long wooden lever. The other held the loop of the rope which would release the catch and send the unwieldy missile hurtling through the air. So for an instant they stood, showing hard and clear against the white sail behind them. The next, redcap had fallen across the stone with an arrow between his ribs; and the other, struck in the leg and in the throat, was writhing and spluttering upon the ground. As he toppled backwards he had loosed the spring, and the huge beam of wood, swinging round with tremendous force,

[1] *mangonel* (măng′gō·nĕl), *trabuch* (trȧ·bo͞ok′): stone-throwing machines.

cast the corpse of his comrade so close to the English ship that its mangled and distorted limbs grazed her very stern. As to the stone, it glanced off obliquely and fell midway between the vessels. A roar of cheering and of laughter broke from the rough archers and seamen at the sight, answered by a yell of rage from their pursuers.

"Lie low, mes enfants," cried Aylward, motioning with his left hand. "They will learn wisdom. They are bringing forward shield and mantlet. We shall have some pebbles about our ears ere long."

Chapter 14

HOW THE YELLOW COG FOUGHT THE TWO ROVER GALLEYS

The three vessels had been sweeping swiftly westwards, the cog still well to the front, although the galleys were slowly drawing in upon either quarter. To the left was a hard sky line unbroken by a sail. The island already lay like a cloud behind them, while right in front was St. Alban's Head, with Portland looming mistily in the farthest distance. Alleyne stood by the tiller, looking backwards, the fresh wind full in his teeth, the crisp winter air tingling on his face and blowing his yellow curls from under his basinet. His cheeks were flushed and his eyes shining, for the blood of a hundred fighting Saxon ancestors was beginning to stir in his veins.

"What was that?" he asked, as a hissing, sharp-drawn voice seemed to whisper in his ear. The steersman smiled, and pointed with his foot to where a short heavy crossbow quarrel stuck quivering in the boards. At the same instant the man stumbled forward upon his knees and lay lifeless upon the deck, a blood-stained feather jutting out from his back. As Alleyne stooped to raise him, the air seemed to be alive with the sharp zip-zip of the bolts, and he could hear them pattering on the deck like apples at a tree-shaking.

"Raise two more mantlets by the poop lanthorn," said Sir Nigel quietly.

"And another man to the tiller," cried the master shipman.

"Keep them in play, Aylward, with ten of your men," the knight continued. "And let ten of Sir Oliver's bowmen do as much for the Genoese. I have no mind as yet to show them how much they have to fear from us."

Ten picked shots under Aylward stood in line across the broad deck, and it was a lesson to the young squires who had seen nothing of war to note how orderly and how cool were these old soldiers, how quick the command, and how prompt the carrying out, ten moving like one. Their comrades crouched beneath the bulwarks, with many a rough jest and many a scrap of criticism or advice. "Higher, Wat, higher!" "Put thy body into it, Will!" "Forget not the wind, Hal!" So ran the muttered chorus, while high above it rose the sharp twanging of the strings, the hiss of the shafts, and the short "Draw your arrow! Nick your arrow! Shoot wholly together!" from the master bowman.

And now both mangonels were at work from the galleys, but so covered and protected that, save at the moment of discharge, no glimpse could be caught of them. A huge brown rock from the Genoese sang over their heads and plunged sullenly into the slope of a wave. Another from the Norman whizzed into the waist, broke the back of a horse, and crashed its way through the side of the vessel. Two others, flying together, tore a great gap in the St. Christopher upon the sail and brushed three of Sir Oliver's men-at-arms from the forecastle. The master shipman looked at the knight with a troubled face.

"They keep their distance from us," said he. "Our archery is overgood, and they will not close. What defense can we make against the stones?"

"I think I may trick them," the knight answered cheerfully, and passed his order to the archers. Instantly five of them threw up their hands and fell prostrate upon the deck. One had already been slain by a bolt, so that there were but four upon their feet.

"That should give them heart," said Sir Nigel, eyeing the galleys, which crept along on either side, with a slow, measured swing of their great oars, the water swirling and foaming under their sharp stems.

"They still hold aloof!" cried Hawtayne.

"Then down with two more," shouted their leader. "That will do. Ma foi! but they come to our lure like chicks to the fowler. To your arms, men! The pennon behind me, and the squires round the pennon. Stand fast with the anchors in the waist, and be ready for a cast. Now blow out the trumpets, and may God's benison be with the honest men!"

As he spoke a roar of voices and a roll of drums came from either galley, and the water was lashed into spray by the hurried beat of a hundred oars. Down they swooped, one on the right, one on the left, the sides and shrouds black with men and bristling with weapons. In heavy clusters they hung upon the forecastle, all ready for spring—faces white, faces brown, faces yellow, and faces black, fair Norsemen, swarthy Italians, fierce rovers from the Levant, and fiery Moors from the Barbary States, of all hues and countries, and marked solely by the common stamp of a wild beast ferocity. Rasping up on either side, with oars trailing to save them from snapping, they poured in a living torrent with horrid yell and shrill whoop upon the defenseless merchantman.

But wilder yet was the cry, and shriller still the scream, when there rose up from the shadow of those silent bulwarks the long lines of the English bowmen, and the arrows whizzed in a deadly sleet among the unprepared masses upon the pirate decks. From the higher sides of the cog the bowmen could shoot straight down, at a range which was so short as to enable a cloth-yard shaft to pierce through mail coats or to transfix a shield, though it were an inch thick of toughened wood. One moment Alleyne saw the galley's poop crowded with rushing figures, waving arms, exultant faces; the next it was a blood-smeared shambles, with bodies piled three deep upon each other, the living cowering behind the dead to shelter themselves from that sudden storm blast of death. On either side, the seamen whom Sir Nigel had chosen for the purpose had cast their anchors over the side of the galleys, so that the three vessels, locked in an iron grip, lurched heavily forward upon the swell.

And now set in a fell and fierce fight, one of a thousand of which no chronicler has spoken and no poet sung. Through all the centuries and over all those southern waters nameless men have fought in nameless places, their sole monuments a protected coast and an unravaged countryside.

Fore and aft the archers had cleared the galleys' decks, but from either side the rovers had poured down into the waist, where the seamen and bowmen were pushed back and so mingled with their foes that it was impossible for their comrades above to draw string to help them. It was a wild chaos where ax and sword rose and fell, while Englishman, Norman, and Italian staggered and reeled on a deck which was cumbered with bodies and slippery with blood. The clang of blows, the cries of the stricken, the short, deep shout of the islanders, and the fierce whoops of the rovers rose together in a deafening tumult, while the breath of the panting men went up in the wintry air like the smoke from a furnace. The giant Tête-noire, towering above his fellows and clad from head to foot in plate of proof, led on his boarders, waving a huge mace in the air, with which he struck to the deck every man who approached him. On the other side, Spade-beard, a dwarf in height, but of great breadth of shoulder and length of arm, had cut a road almost to the mast, with three score Genoese men-at-arms close at his heels. Between these two formidable assailants the seamen were being slowly wedged more closely together, until they stood back to back under the mast, with the rovers raging upon every side of them.

But help was close at hand. Sir Oliver Buttesthorn with his men-at-arms had swarmed down from the forecastle, while Sir Nigel, with his three squires, Black Simon, Aylward, Hordle John, and a score more, threw themselves from the poop and hurled themselves into the thickest of the fight. Alleyne, as in duty bound, kept his eyes fixed ever on his lord and pressed forward close at his heels. Often had he heard of Sir Nigel's prowess and skill with all knightly weapons, but all the tales that had reached his ears fell far short of the real quickness and coolness of the man. It was as if the devil was in him, for he sprang here and sprang there, now thrusting and now cutting, catching blows on his shield, turning them with his blade, stooping under the swing of an ax, springing over the sweep of a sword, so swift and so erratic that the man who braced himself for a blow at him might find him six paces off ere he could bring it down. Three pirates had fallen before him, and he had wounded Spade-beard in the neck, when the Norman giant sprang at him from the side with a slashing blow from his deadly mace. Sir Nigel stooped to avoid it, and at the same instant turned a thrust from the Genoese swordsman, but, his foot slipping in a pool of blood, he fell heavily to the ground. Alleyne sprang in front of the Norman, but his sword was shattered and he himself beaten to the ground by a second blow from the ponderous weapon. Ere the pirate chief could repeat it, however, John's iron grip fell upon his wrist, and he found that for once he was in the hands of a stronger man than himself. Fiercely he strove to disengage his weapon, but Hordle John bent his arm slowly back until, with a sharp crack, like a breaking stave, it turned limp in his grasp, and the mace dropped from the nerveless fingers. In vain he tried to pluck it up with the other hand. Back and back still his foeman bent him, until, with a roar of pain and of fury, the giant clanged his full length upon the boards, while the glimmer of a knife before the bars of his helmet warned him that short would be his shrift [1] if he moved.

Cowed and disheartened by the loss of their leader, the Normans had given back and were now streaming over the bulwarks on to their own galley, dropping a dozen at a time on to her deck. But the anchor still held them in its crooked claw, and Sir Oliver with fifty men was hard upon their heels. Now, too, the archers had room to draw their bows once more, and great stones from the yard of the cog came thundering and crashing among the flying rovers. Here and there they rushed with wild screams and curses, diving under the sail, crouching behind booms, huddling into corners like rabbits when the ferrets are upon them, as helpless and as hopeless. They were stern days, and if the honest soldier, too poor for a ransom, had no prospect of mercy upon the battlefield, what ruth was there for sea robbers, the enemies of humankind, taken in the very deed, with proofs of their crimes still swinging upon their yardarm?

But the fight had taken a new and a strange turn upon the other side. Spade-beard and his men had given slowly back, hard pressed by Sir Nigel, Aylward, Black Simon, and the poop guard. Foot by foot the Italian had retreated, his armor running blood at every joint, his shield split, his crest shorn, his voice fallen away to a mere gasping and croaking. Yet he faced his foeman

[1] *shrift* (shrĭft): confession of sins.

with dauntless courage, dashing in, springing back, sure-footed, steady-handed, with a point which seemed to menace three at once. Beaten back on to the deck of his own vessel, and closely followed by a dozen Englishmen, he disengaged himself from them, ran swiftly down the deck, sprang back into the cog once more, cut the rope which held the anchor, and was back in an instant among his crossbowmen. At the same time the Genoese sailors thrust with their oars against the side of the cog, and a rapidly widening rift appeared between the two vessels.

"By St. George!" cried Ford, "we are cut off from Sir Nigel."

"He is lost," gasped Terlake. "Come, let us spring for it." The two youths jumped with all their strength to reach the departing galley. Ford's feet reached the edge of the bulwarks, and, his hand clutching a rope, he swung himself on board. Terlake fell short, crashed in among the oars, and bounded off into the sea. Alleyne, staggering to the side, was about to hurl himself after him, but Hordle John dragged him back by the girdle.

"You can scarce stand, lad, far less jump," said he. "See how the blood rips from your basinet."

"My place is by the flag," cried Alleyne, vainly struggling to break from the other's hold.

"Bide here, man. You would need wings ere you could reach Sir Nigel's side."

The vessels were indeed so far apart now that the Genoese could use the full sweep of their oars and draw away rapidly from the cog.

"My God, but it is a noble fight!" shouted big John, clapping his hands. "They have cleared the poop, and they spring into the waist. Well struck, my lord! Well struck, Aylward! See to Black Simon, how he storms among the shipmen! But this Spadebeard is a gallant warrior. He rallies his men upon the forecastle. He hath slain an archer. Ha! my lord is upon him. Look to it, Alleyne! See to the whirl and glitter of it!"

"By heaven, Sir Nigel is down!" cried the squire.

"Up!" roared John. "It was but a feint. He bears him back. He drives him to the side. Ah, by Our Lady, his sword is through him! They cry for mercy. Down goes the red cross, and up springs Simon with the scarlet roses!"

The death of the Genoese leader did indeed bring the resistance to an end. Amid a thunder of cheering from cog and from galleys the forked pennon fluttered upon the forecastle, and the galley, sweeping round, came slowly back, as the slaves who rowed it learned the wishes of their new masters.

The two knights had come aboard the cog, and the grapplings having been thrown off, the three vessels now moved abreast. Through all the storm and rush of the fight Alleyne had been aware of the voice of Goodwin Hawtayne, the master shipman, with his constant "Hale the bowline! Veer the sheet!" and strange it was to him to see how swiftly the blood-stained sailors turned from the strife to the ropes and back. Now the cog's head was turned Francewards, and the shipman walked the deck, a peaceful master mariner once more.

"There is sad scath done to the cog, Sir Nigel," said he. "Here is a hole in the side two ells across, the sail split through the center, and the wood as bare as a friar's poll. In good sooth, I know not what I shall say to Master Witherton when I see the Itchen once more."

"By St. Paul! it would be a very sorry thing if we suffered you to be the worse of this day's work," said Sir Nigel. "You shall take these galleys back with you, and Master Witherton may sell them. Then from the moneys he shall take as much as may make good the damage, and the rest he shall keep until our homecoming, when every man shall have his share. An image of silver fifteen inches high I have vowed to the Virgin, to be placed in her chapel within the priory, for that she was pleased to allow me to come upon this Spade-beard, who seemed to me from what I have seen of him to be a very sprightly and valiant gentleman. But how fares it with you, Edricson?"

"It is nothing, my fair lord," said Alleyne, who had now loosened his basinet, which was cracked across by the Norman's blow. Even as he spoke, however, his head swirled round, and he fell to the deck with the blood gushing from his nose and mouth.

"He will come to anon," said the knight, stooping over him and passing his fingers through his hair. "I have lost one very valiant and gentle squire this day. I can ill afford to lose another. How many men have fallen?"

"I have checked off the tally," said Aylward, who had come aboard with his lord. "There are seven of the Winchester men, eleven seamen, your squire, young Master Terlake, and nine archers."

"And of the others?"

"They are all dead—save only the Norman knight who stands behind you. What would you that we should do with him?"

"He must hang on his own yard," said Sir Nigel. "It was my vow and must be done."

The pirate leader had stood by the bulwarks, a cord round his arms, and two stout archers on either side. At Sir Nigel's words he started violently, and his swarthy features blanched to a livid gray.

"How, Sir Knight?" he cried in broken English. "Que dites-vous? To hang, le mort du chien! To hang!"

"It is my vow," said Sir Nigel shortly. "From what I hear, you thought little enough of hanging others."

"Peasants, base roturiers," cried the other. "It is their fitting death. Mais Le Seigneur d'Andelys, avec le sang des rois dans ses filons! C'est incroyable!" [1]

Sir Nigel turned upon his heel, while two seamen cast a noose over the pirate's neck. At the touch of the cord he snapped the bonds which bound him, dashed one of the archers to the deck, and seizing the other round the waist sprang with him into the sea.

"By my hilt, he is gone!" cried Aylward, rushing to the side. "They have sunk together like a stone."

"I am right glad of it," answered Sir Nigel; "for though it was against my vow to loose him, I deem that he has carried himself like a very gentle [2] and debonair cavalier."

[1] *Mais Le Seigneur . . . incroyable!:* But the Lord of Andelys, with the blood of kings in his veins! It is incredible! [2] *gentle:* well-born.

Chapter 15

HOW SIR NIGEL LORING PUT A PATCH UPON HIS EYE

[The yellow cog and the two captured galleys sail for France. A violent storm overtakes them, and the damage the cog suffered in the fight causes her to leak dangerously. Just when all seems lost the ship's master sights the mouth of the Gironde river on the coast of France.]

It was on the morning of Friday, the eight-and-twentieth day of November, two days before the feast of St. Andrew, that the cog and her two prisoners, after a weary tacking up the Gironde and the Garonne, dropped anchor at last in front of the noble city of Bordeaux. With wonder and admiration, Alleyne, leaning over the bulwarks, gazed at the forest of masts, the swarm of boats darting hither and thither on the bosom of the broad curving stream, and the gray crescent-shaped city which stretched with many a tower and minaret along the western shore. Never had he in his quiet life seen so great a town, nor was there in the whole of England, save London alone, one which might match it in size or in wealth. Here came the merchandise of all the fair countries which are watered by the Garonne and the Dordogne—the cloths of the south, the skins of Guienne, the wines of the Médoc—to be borne away to Hull, Exeter, Dartmouth, Bristol, or Chester, in exchange for the wools and woolfells of England. Here, too, dwelt those famous smelters and welders who had made the Bordeaux steel the most trusty upon earth, and could give a temper to lance or to sword which might mean dear life to its owner. Alleyne could see the smoke of their forges reeking up in the clear morning air. The storm had died down now to a gentle breeze, which wafted to his ears the long-drawn stirring bugle calls which sounded from the ancient ramparts.

"Holà, mon petit!" said Aylward, coming up to where he stood. "Thou art a squire now, and like enough to win the golden spurs, while I am still the master bowman, and master bowman I shall bide. I dare scarce wag my tongue so freely with you as when we tramped together past Wilverley Chase, else I might be your guide now, for, indeed, I know every house in Bordeaux as a friar knows the beads on his rosary."

"Nay, Aylward," said Alleyne, laying his hand upon the sleeve of his companion's frayed jerkin, "you cannot think me so thrall as to throw aside an old friend because I have had some small share of good fortune. I take it unkind that you should have thought such evil of me."

"Nay, mon gar. 'Twas but a flight shot to see if the wind blew steady, though I were a rogue to doubt it."

"Why, had I not met you, Aylward, at the Lyndhurst inn, who can say where I had now been! Certes, I had not gone to Twynham Castle, nor become squire to Sir Nigel, nor met—" He paused abruptly and flushed to his hair, but the bowman was too busy with his own thoughts to notice his young companion's embarrassment.

"It was a good hostel, that of the 'Pied Merlin,' " he remarked. "By my ten finger bones! when I hang bow on nail and change my brigandine for a tunic, I might do worse than take over the dame and her business."

"I thought," said Alleyne, "that you were betrothed to someone at Christchurch."

"To three," Aylward answered moodily, "to three. I fear I may not go back to Christchurch. I might chance to see hotter service in Hampshire than I have ever done in Gascony. But mark you now yonder lofty turret in the center, which stands back from the river and hath a broad banner upon the summit. See, the rising sun flashes full upon it and sparkles on the golden lions. 'Tis the royal banner of England, crossed by the Prince's label. There he dwells in the abbey of St. Andrew, where he hath kept his court these years back. Beside it is the minster of the same saint, who hath the town under his very special care."

"And how of yon gray turret on the left?"

" 'Tis the fane of St. Michael, as that upon the right is of St. Remi. There, too, above the poop of yonder nief, you see the towers of Saint Croix and of Pey Berland. Mark also the mighty ramparts which are pierced by the three water gates, and sixteen others to the landward side."

"And how is it, good Aylward, that there comes so much music from the town? I seem to hear a hundred trumpets, all calling in chorus."

"It would be strange else, seeing that all the great lords of England and of Gascony are within the walls, and each would have his trumpeter blow as loud as his neighbor, lest it might be thought that his dignity had been abated. Ma foi! they make as much louster as a Scotch army, where every man fills himself with griddlecakes and sits up all night to blow upon the toodle-pipe. See all along the banks how the pages water the horses, and there beyond the town how they gallop them over the plain! For every horse you see a belted knight hath herbergage in the town, for, as I learn, the men-at-arms and archers have already gone forward to Dax."

"I trust, Aylward," said Sir Nigel, coming upon deck, "that the men are ready for the land. Go tell them that the boats will be for them within the hour."

The archer raised his hand in salute and hastened forward. In the meantime Sir Oliver had followed his brother knight, and the two paced the poop together, Sir Nigel in his plum-colored velvet suit with flat cap of the same, adorned in front with the Lady Loring's glove and girt round with a curling ostrich feather. The lusty knight, on the other hand, was clad in the very latest mode. A red chaperon, or cap, with long hanging cornette, sat daintily on the back of his black-curled head, while his gold-hued shoes were twisted up *à la poulaine,* as though the toes were shooting forth a tendril which might hope in time to entwine itself around his massive leg.

"Once more, Sir Oliver," said Sir Nigel, looking shorewards with sparkling eyes, "do we find ourselves at the gate of honor, the door which hath so often led us to all that is knightly and worthy. There flies the prince's banner, and it would be well that we haste ashore and pay our obeisance [1] to him. The boats already swarm from the bank."

"There is a goodly hostel near the west gate, which is famed for the stewing of spiced pullets," remarked Sir Oliver. "We might take the edge of our hunger off ere we seek the prince, for though his tables are gay with damask and silver, he is no trencherman himself and hath no sympathy for those who are his betters."

"His betters!"

"His betters before the tranchoir, lad. Sniff not treason

[1] *obeisance* (ō·bā′săns): homage.

where none is meant. I have seen him smile in his quiet way because I had looked for the fourth time towards the carving squire. And, indeed, to watch him dallying with a little gobbet of bread or sipping his cup of thrice-watered wine is enough to make a man feel shame at his own hunger. Yet war and glory, my good friend, though well enough in their way, will not serve to tighten such a belt as clasps my waist."

"Here is our boat, Sir Oliver," said Sir Nigel, "so it seems best to me that we should go to the abbey with our squires, leaving Master Hawtayne to have his own way in the unloading."

The horses both of knights and squires were speedily lowered into a broad lighter, and reached the shore almost as soon as their masters. Sir Nigel bent his knee devoutly as he put foot on land, and taking a small black patch from his bosom he bound it tightly over his left eye.

"May the blessed George and the memory of my sweet lady-love raise high my heart!" quoth he. "And as a token I vow that I will not take this patch from my eye until I have seen something of this country of Spain and done such a small deed as it lies in me to do. And this I swear upon the cross of my sword and upon the glove of my lady."

"In truth, you take me back twenty years, Nigel," quoth Sir Oliver, as they mounted and rode slowly through the water gate. "After Cadsand, I deem that the French thought that we were an army of the blind, for there was scarce a man who had not closed an eye for the greater love and honor of his lady. Yet it goes hard with you that you should darken one side, when with both open you can scarce tell a horse from a mule. In truth, friend, I think that you step over the line of reason in this matter."

"Sir Oliver Buttesthorn," said the little knight shortly, "I would have you to understand that, blind as I am, I can yet see the path of honor very clearly, and that that is the road upon which I do not crave another man's guidance."

"By my soul," said Sir Oliver, "you are as tart as verjuice [1] this morning! If you are bent upon a quarrel with me, I must leave you to your humor and drop into the 'Tête d'Or' here, for I marked a varlet pass the door who bare a smoking dish, which had, methought, a most excellent smell."

[1] *verjuice* (vûr′jo͞os′): the sour juice of green fruit.

"Nenny, nenny," cried his comrade, laying his hand upon his knee; "we have known each other overlong to fall out, Oliver, like two raw pages at their first *épreuves*.[1] You must come with me first to the prince, and then back to the hostel; though sure I am that it would grieve his heart that any gentle cavalier should turn from his board to a common tavern. But is not that my Lord Delewar who waves to us? Ha! my fair lord, God and Our Lady be with you! And there is Sir Robert Cheney. Good morrow, Robert! I am right glad to see you."

The two knights walked their horses abreast, while Alleyne and Ford, with John Norbury, who was squire to Sir Oliver, kept some paces behind them, a spear's-length in front of Black Simon and of the Winchester guidon bearer. Norbury, a lean, silent man, had been to those parts before, and sat his horse with a rigid neck; but the two young squires gazed eagerly to right or left and plucked each other's sleeves to call attention to the many strange things on every side of them.

"See to the brave stalls!" cried Alleyne. "See to the noble armor set forth, and the costly taffeta—and oh, Ford, see to where the scrivener sits with the pigments and the inkhorns and the rolls of sheepskin as white as the Beaulieu napery! Saw man ever the like before?"

"Nay, man, there are finer stalls in Cheapside," answered Ford, whose father had taken him to London on occasion of one of the Smithfield joustings. "I have seen a silversmith's booth there which would serve to buy either side of this street. But mark these houses, Alleyne, how they thrust forth upon the top. And see to the coats of arms at every window, and banner or pensil on the roof."

"And the churches!" cried Alleyne. "The priory at Christchurch was a noble pile, but it was cold and bare, methinks, by one of these, with their frettings and their carvings and their traceries, as though some great ivy plant of stone had curled and wantoned over the walls."

"And hark to the speech of the folk!" said Ford. "Was ever such a hissing and clacking? I wonder that they have not wit to learn English now that they have come under the English crown. By Richard of Hampole! there are fair faces amongst them. See the wench with the brown wimple! Out on you, Al-

[1] *épreuve:* French for "a test or trial."

leyne, that you would rather gaze upon dead stone than on living flesh!"

It was little wonder that the richness and ornament, not only of church and of stall, but of every private house as well, should have impressed itself upon the young squires. The town was now at the height of its fortunes. Besides its trade and its armorers, other causes had combined to pour wealth into it. War, which had wrought evil upon so many fair cities around, had brought naught but good to this one. As her French sisters decayed she increased, for here, from north and from east and from south, came the plunder to be sold and the ransom money to be spent. Through all her sixteen landward gates there had set for many years a double tide of empty-handed soldiers hurrying Francewards, and of enriched and laden bands who brought their spoils home. The Prince's court, too, with its swarm of noble barons and wealthy knights, many of whom, in imitation of their master, had brought their ladies and their children from England, all helped to swell the coffers of the burghers. Now, with this fresh influx of noblemen and cavaliers, food and lodgings were scarce to be had, and the Prince was hurrying forward his forces to Dax in Gascony to relieve the overcrowding of his capital.

In front of the minster and abbey of St. Andrews was a large square crowded with priests, soldiers, women, friars, and burghers, who made it their common center for sight-seeing and gossip. Amid the knot of noisy and gesticulating townsfolk, many small parties of mounted knights and squires threaded their way towards the Prince's quarters, where the huge iron-clamped doors were thrown back to show that he held audience within. Two score archers stood about the gateway, and beat back from time to time with their bowstaves the inquisitive and chattering crowd who swarmed round the portal. Two knights in full armor, with lances raised and closed visors, sat their horses on either side, while in the center, with two pages to tend upon him, there stood a noble-faced man in flowing purple gown, who checked off upon a sheet of parchment the style and title of each applicant, marshaling them in their due order and giving to each the place which his rank demanded. His long white beard and searching eyes imparted to him an air of masterful dignity, which was increased by his vesture [1] and the heraldic cap with triple plume

[1] *vesture:* dress.

which bespoke his office.

"It is Sir William de Pakington, the prince's own herald and scrivener," whispered Sir Nigel, as they pulled up amid the line of knights who waited admission. "Ill fares it with the man who would venture to deceive him. He hath by rote [1] the name of every knight of France or of England, and all the tree of his family, with his kinships, coat armor, marriages, and I know not what beside. We may leave our horses here with the varlets and push forward with our squires."

Following Sir Nigel's counsel, they pressed on upon foot until they were close to the prince's secretary. Sir William's keen eye singled out the five red roses from amid the overlapping shields and cloud of pennons which faced him.

"Ha!" he cried, "the roses of Loring and the boar's head of Buttesthorn may stand back in peace, but by my faith! they are not to be held back in war. Welcome, Sir Oliver, Sir Nigel! Chandos will be glad to his very heart roots when he sees you. This way, my fair sirs. Your squires are doubtless worthy the fame of their masters. Down this passage, Sir Oliver! Edricson! Ha! one of the old strain of Hampshire Edricsons, I doubt not. And Ford—they are of a south Saxon stock, and of good repute. There are Norburys in Cheshire and in Wiltshire, and also, as I have heard, upon the borders. So, my fair sirs, and I shall see that you are shortly admitted."

He had finished his professional commentary by flinging open a folding door, and ushering the party into a broad hall, which was filled with a great number of people who were waiting, like themselves, for an audience. The room was very spacious, lighted on one side by three arched and mullioned windows, while opposite was a huge fireplace in which a pile of faggots was blazing merrily. Many of the company had crowded round the flames, for the weather was bitterly cold; but the two knights seated themselves upon a bancal, with their squires standing behind them. Looking down the room, Alleyne marked that both floor and ceiling were of the richest oak, the latter spanned by twelve arching beams, which were adorned at either end by the lilies and the lions of the royal arms. On the further side was a small door, on each side of which stood men-at-arms. From time to time an elderly man in black, with rounded shoulders,

[1] *rote* (rōt): memory.

and a long white wand in his hand, came softly forth from this inner room and beckoned to one or other of the company, who doffed cap and followed him.

The two knights were deep in talk, when Alleyne became aware of a remarkable individual who was walking round the room in their direction. As he passed each knot of cavaliers every head turned to look after him, and it was evident, from the bows and respectful salutations on all sides, that the interest which he excited was not due merely to his strange personal appearance. He was tall and straight as a lance, though of a great age, for his hair, which curled from under his velvet cap of maintenance, was as white as the new-fallen snow. Yet, from the swing of his stride and the spring of his step, it was clear that he had not yet lost the fire and activity of his youth. His fierce hawklike face was clean-shaven like that of a priest, save for a long thin wisp of white mustache which drooped down halfway to his shoulder. That he had been handsome might be easily judged from his high aquiline nose and clear-cut chin; but his features had been so distorted by the seams and scars of old wounds, and by the loss of one eye which had been torn from the socket, that there was little left to remind one of the dashing young knight who had been fifty years ago the fairest as well as the boldest of the English chivalry. Yet what knight was there in that hall of St. Andrews who would not have gladly laid down youth, beauty, and all that he possessed to win the fame of this man? For who could be named with Chandos, the stainless knight, the wise councilor, the valiant warrior, the hero of Crécy, of Winchelsea, of Poitiers, of Auray, and of as many other battles as there were years to his life?

"Ha, my little heart of gold!" he cried, darting forward suddenly and throwing his arms round Sir Nigel. "I heard that you were here and have been seeking you."

"My fair and dear lord," said the knight, returning the warrior's embrace, "I have indeed come back to you, for where else shall I go that I may learn to be a gentle and a hardy knight?"

"By my troth!" [1] said Chandos with a smile, "it is very fitting that we should be companions, Nigel, for since you have tied up one of your eyes, and I have had the mischance to lose one of mine, we have but a pair between us. Ah, Sir Oliver! you were on the blind side of me and I saw you not. A wise woman hath

[1] *troth* (trŏth): faith.

made prophecy that this blind side will one day be the death of me. We shall go in to the prince anon; but in truth he hath much upon his hands, for what with Pedro, and the King of Majorca, and the King of Navarre, who is no two days of the same mind, and the Gascon barons who are all chaffering for terms like so many hucksters, he hath an uneasy part to play. But how left you the Lady Loring?"

"She was well, my fair lord, and sent her service and greetings to you."

"I am ever her knight and slave. And your journey, I trust that it was pleasant?"

"As heart could wish. We had sight of two rover galleys, and even came to have some slight bickering with them."

"Ever in luck's way, Nigel!" quoth Sir John. "We must hear the tale anon. But I deem it best that ye should leave your squires and come with me, for, howsoe'er pressed the prince may be, I am very sure that he would be loath to keep two old comrades-in-arms upon the further side of the door. Follow close behind me, and I will forestall old Sir William, though I can scarce promise to roll forth your style and rank as is his wont." So saying, he led the way to the inner chamber, the two companions treading close at his heels and nodding to right and left as they caught sight of familiar faces among the crowd.

Chapter 16

HOW THERE WAS A STIR AT THE ABBEY OF ST. ANDREW'S

The Prince's reception room, although of no great size, was fitted up with all the state and luxury which the fame and power of its owner demanded. A high dais at the further end was roofed in by a broad canopy of scarlet velvet spangled with silver fleurs-de-lis, and supported at either corner by silver rods. This was approached by four steps carpeted with the same material, while all round were scattered rich cushions, oriental mats, and costly rugs of fur. The choicest tapestries which the looms of Arras could furnish draped the walls, with crest and lance and banderole, as the naïve artists of the day were wont to depict them. A few rich settles and bancals, choicely carved and decorated with glazed leather hangings of the sort termed *or basané,* completed the furniture of the apartment, save that at one side of the dais there stood a lofty perch, upon which a cast of three solemn Prussian gerfalcons sat, hooded and jesseled, as silent and motionless as the royal fowler who stood beside them.

In the center of the dais were two very high chairs, covered with light-blue silk thickly powdered with golden stars. On that to the right sat a very tall and well-formed man with red hair, a livid face, and a cold blue eye, which had in it something peculiarly sinister and menacing. He lounged back in a careless position and yawned repeatedly as though heartily weary of the proceedings, stooping from time to time to fondle a shaggy Spanish greyhound which lay stretched at his feet. On the other throne there was perched bolt upright, with prim demeanor, as though he felt himself to be upon his good behavior, a little, round, pippin-faced person, who smiled and bobbed to everyone whose eye he chanced to meet. Between and a little in front of them, on a humble charette, or stool, sat a slim, dark young man, whose quiet attire and modest manner would scarce proclaim him to be the most noted prince in Europe. A jupon of dark blue cloth, tagged with buckles and pendants of gold, seemed but a somber and plain attire amidst the wealth of silk and ermine and gilt tissue of fustian with which he was surrounded. He sat with his two hands clasped round his knee, his head slightly bent, and an expression of impatience and of trouble upon his clear, well-chiseled features. Behind the thrones there stood two men in purple gowns, with ascetic, clean-shaven faces, and half a dozen other high dignitaries and office holders of Aquitaine. Below on either side of the steps were forty or fifty barons, knights, and courtiers, ranged in a triple row to the right and the left, with a clear passage in the center.

"There sits the Prince," whispered Sir John Chandos, as they entered. "He on the right is Pedro, whom we are about to put upon the Spanish throne. The other is Don James, whom we purpose with the aid of God to help to his throne in Majorca. Now follow me, and take it not to heart if he be a little short in his speech, for indeed his mind is full of many very weighty concerns."

The Prince, however, had already observed their entrance, and, springing to his feet, he had advanced with a winning smile and the light of welcome in his eyes.

"We do not need your good offices as herald here, Sir John," said he in a low but clear voice; "these valiant knights are very well known to me. Welcome to Aquitaine, Sir Nigel Loring and Sir Oliver Buttesthorn. Nay, keep your knee for my sweet father at Windsor. I would have your hands, my friends. We are like to give you some work to do ere you see the downs of Hampshire once more. Know you aught of Spain, Sir Oliver?"

"Naught, my sire, save that I have heard men say that there is a dish named an olla which is prepared there, though I have never been clear in my mind as to whether it was but a ragout such as is to be found in the south, or whether there is some seasoning such as fennel or garlic which is peculiar to Spain."

"Your doubts, Sir Oliver, shall soon be resolved," answered the prince, laughing heartily, as did many of the barons who surrounded them. "His majesty here will doubtless order that you have this dish hotly seasoned when we are all safely in Castile."

"I will have a hotly seasoned dish for some folk I know of," answered Don Pedro with a cold smile.

"But my friend Sir Oliver can fight right hardily without either bite or sup," remarked the Prince. "Did I not see him at Poitiers, when for two days we had not more than a crust of bread and a cup of foul water, yet carrying himself most valiantly? With my own eyes I saw him in the route sweep the head from a knight of Picardy with one blow of his sword."

"The rogue got between me and the nearest French victual wain," [1] muttered Sir Oliver, amid a fresh titter from those who were near enough to catch his words.

"How many have you in your train?" asked the Prince, assuming a graver mien.

"I have forty men-at-arms, sire," said Sir Oliver.

"And I have one hundred archers and a score of lances, but

[1] *victual wain* (vĭt″l wān): a food wagon.

there are three hundred men who wait for me on this side of the water upon the borders of Navarre."

"And who are they, Sir Nigel?"

"They are a free company, sire, and they are called the White Company."

To the astonishment of the knight, his words provoked a burst of merriment from the barons round, in which the two Kings and the Prince were fain to join. Sir Nigel blinked mildly from one to the other, until at last perceiving a stout black-bearded knight at his elbow, whose laugh rang somewhat louder than the others, he touched him lightly upon the sleeve.

"Perchance, my fair sir," he whispered, "there is some small vow of which I may relieve you. Might we not have some honorable debate upon the matter? Your gentle courtesy may perhaps grant me an exchange of thrusts?"

"Nay, nay, Sir Nigel," cried the Prince, "fasten not the offense upon Sir Robert Briquet, for we are one and all bogged in the same mire. Truth to say, our ears have just been vexed by the doings of the same Company, and I have even now made vow to hang the man who held the rank of captain over it. I little thought to find him among the bravest of my own chosen chieftains. But the vow is now naught, for, as you have never seen your company, it would be a fool's act to blame you for their doings."

"My liege," said Sir Nigel, "it is a very small matter that I should be hanged, albeit the manner of death is somewhat more ignoble than I had hoped for. On the other hand, it would be a very grievous thing that you, the Prince of England and the flower of knighthood, should make a vow, whether in ignorance or no, and fail to bring it to fulfillment."

"Vex not your mind on that," the Prince answered, smiling. "We have had a citizen from Montauban here this very day, who told us such a tale of sack and murder and pillage that it moved our blood; but our wrath was turned upon the man who was in authority over them, and not on him who had never set eyes upon them."

"My dear and honored master," cried Nigel, in great anxiety, "I fear me much that in your gentleness of heart you are straining this vow which you have taken. If there be so much as a shadow of doubt as to the form of it, it were a thousand times best—"

"Peace! peace!" cried the Prince impatiently. "I am very well able to look to my own vows and their performance. We hope to see you both in the banquet hall anon. Meanwhile you will attend upon us with our train." He bowed, and Chandos, plucking Sir Oliver by the sleeve, led them both away to the back of the press of courtiers.

"Why, little coz," he whispered, "you are very eager to have your neck in a noose. By my soul! had you asked as much from our new ally Don Pedro, he had not balked you. Between friends, there is overmuch of the hangman in him, and too little of the prince. But, indeed, this White Company is a rough band, and may take some handling ere you find yourself safe in your captaincy."

"I doubt not, with the help of St. Paul, that I shall bring them to some order," Sir Nigel answered. "But there are many faces here which are new to me, though others have been before me since first I waited upon my dear master, Sir Walter. I pray you to tell me, Sir John, who are these priests upon the dais?"

"The one is the Archbishop of Bordeaux, Nigel, and the other the Bishop of Agen."

"And the dark knight with gray-streaked beard? By my troth, he seems to be a man of much wisdom and valor."

"He is Sir William Felton, who, with my unworthy self, is the chief councilor of the Prince, he being high steward, and I the Seneschal of Aquitaine."

"And the knights upon the right, beside Don Pedro?"

"They are cavaliers of Spain who have followed him in his exile. The one at his elbow is Fernando de Castro, who is as brave and true a man as heart could wish. In front to the right are the Gascon lords. You may well tell them by their clouded brows, for there hath been some ill will of late betwixt the prince and them. The tall and burly man is the Captal de Buch, whom I doubt not that you know, for a braver knight never laid lance in rest. That heavy-faced cavalier who plucks his skirts and whispers in his ear is Lord Oliver de Clisson, known also as the butcher. He it is who stirs up strife and forever blows the dying embers into flame. The man with the mole upon his cheek is the Lord Pommers, and his two brothers stand behind him, with the Lord Lesparre, Lord de Rosem, Lord de Mucident, Sir Perducas d'Albret, the Souldich de la Trane, and others. Further back are knights from Quercy, Limousin, Saintonge, Poitou, and Aquitaine, with the valiant Sir Guiscard d'Angle. That is he in the rose-colored doublet with the ermine."

"And the knights upon this side?"

"They are all Englishmen, some of the household and others who, like yourself, are captains of companies. There is Lord Neville, Sir Stephen Cossington, and Sir Matthew Gourney, with Sir Walter Huet, Sir Thomas Banaster, and Sir Thomas Felton, who is the brother of the high steward. Mark well the man with the high nose and flaxen beard who hath placed his hand upon the shoulder of the dark hard-faced cavalier in the rust-stained jupon."

"Aye, by St. Paul!" observed Sir Nigel, "they both bear the print of their armor upon their cotes-hardies. Methinks they are men who breathe freer in a camp than a court."

"There are many of us who do that, Nigel," said Chandos, "and the head of the court is, I dare warrant, among them. But of these two men the one is Sir Hugh Calverley, and the other is Sir Robert Knolles."

Sir Nigel and Sir Oliver craned their necks to have the clearer view of these famous warriors, the one a chosen leader of free companies, the other a man who by his fierce valor and energy had raised himself from the lowest ranks until he was second only to Chandos himself in the esteem of the army.

"He hath no light hand in war, hath Sir Robert," said Chandos. "If he passes through a country, you may tell it for some years to come. I have heard that in the north it is still the use to call a house which hath but the two gable ends left, without walls or roof, a Knolles' miter."

"I have often heard of him," said Nigel, "and I have hoped to be so far honored as to run a course with him. But hark, Sir John, what is amiss with the Prince?"

Whilst Chandos had been conversing with the two knights, a continuous stream of suitors had been ushered in, adventurers seeking to sell their swords, and merchants clamoring over some grievance, a ship detained for the carriage of troops, or a tun of sweet wine which had the bottom knocked out by a troop of thirsty archers. A few words from the Prince disposed of each case, and, if the applicant liked not the judgment, a quick glance from the Prince's dark eyes sent him to the door with the grievance all gone out of him. The younger ruler had sat listlessly upon his stool with the two puppet monarchs enthroned behind him, but of a sudden a dark shadow passed over his face, and he sprang to his feet in one of those gusts of passion which were the single blot upon his noble and generous character.

"How now, Don Martin de la Carra?" he cried. "How now, sirrah? What message do you bring to us from our brother of Navarre?"

The newcomer to whom this abrupt query had been addressed was a tall and exceedingly handsome cavalier who had just been ushered into the apartment. His swarthy cheek and raven-black hair spoke of the fiery south, and he wore his long black cloak swathed across his chest and over his shoulders in a graceful sweeping fashion, which was neither English nor French. With stately steps and many profound bows, he advanced to the foot of the dais before replying to the prince's question.

"My powerful and illustrious master," he began, "Charles, King of Navarre, Earl of Evreux, Count of Champagne, who also writeth himself Overlord of Bearn, hereby sends his love and greetings to his dear cousin Edward, the Prince of Wales, Governor of Aquitaine, Grand Commander of—"

"Tush! tush! Don Martin!" interrupted the Prince, who had been beating the ground with his foot impatiently during this stately preamble. "We already know our cousin's titles and style, and, certes, we know our own. To the point, man, and at once. Are the passes open to us, or does your master go back from his word pledged to me at Libourne no later than last Michaelmas?"

"It would ill become my gracious master, sire, to go back from promise given. He does but ask some delay, and certain conditions and hostages—"

"Conditions! Hostages! Is he speaking to the Prince of England, or is it to the bourgeois [1] provost [2] of some half-captured town! Conditions, quotha? He may find much to mend in his own condition ere long. The passes are, then, closed to us?"

"Nay, sire—"

"They are open, then?"

"Nay, sire, if you would but—"

"Enough, enough, Don Martin," cried the prince. "It is a

[1] *bourgeois* (bo͞or·zhwä′): middle-class. [2] *provost* (prŏv′ŭst): an official in charge.

sorry sight to see so true a knight pleading in so false a cause. We know the doings of our cousin Charles. We know that while with the right hand he takes our fifty thousand crowns for the holding of the passes open, he hath his left outstretched to Henry of Trastamare, or to the King of France, all ready to take as many more for the keeping them closed. I know our good Charles, and, by my blessed name-saint the Confessor, he shall learn that I know him. He sets his kingdom up to the best bidder, like some scullion farrier selling a glandered horse. He is—"

"My lord," cried Don Martin, "I cannot stand here to hear such words of my master. Did they come from other lips, I should know better how to answer them."

Don Pedro frowned and curled his lip, but the prince smiled and nodded his approbation.

"Your bearing and your words, Don Martin, are such as I should have looked for in you," he remarked. "You will tell the King, your master, that he hath been paid his price, and that if he holds to his promise, he hath my word for it that no scath shall come to his people, nor to their houses or gear. If, however, we have not his leave, I shall come close at the heels of this message without his leave, and bearing a key with me which shall open all that he may close." He stooped and whispered to Sir Robert Knolles and Sir Hugh Calverley, who smiled as men well-pleased, and hastened from the room.

"Our cousin Charles has had experience of our friendship," the Prince continued, "and now, by the Saints! he shall feel a touch of our displeasure. I send now a message to our cousin Charles which his whole kingdom may read. Let him take heed lest worse befall him. Where is my Lord Chandos? Ha, Sir John, I commend this worthy knight to your care. You will see that he hath refection,[1] and such a purse of gold as may defray his charges, for, indeed, it is great honor to any court to have within it so noble and gentle a cavalier. How say you, sire?" he asked, turning to the Spanish refugee, while the herald of Navarre was conducted from the chamber by the old warrior.

"It is not our custom in Spain to reward pertness in a messenger," Don Pedro answered, patting the head of his greyhound. "Yet we have all heard the lengths to which your royal generosity runs."

[1] *refection* (rḗ·fĕk′shŭn): food and drink.

"In sooth, yes," cried the King of Majorca.

"Who should know it better than we?" said Don Pedro bitterly, "since we have had to fly to you in our trouble as to the natural protector of all who are weak."

"Nay, nay, as brothers to a brother," cried the Prince, with sparkling eyes. "We doubt not, with the help of God, to see you very soon restored to those thrones from which you have been so traitorously thrust."

"When that happy day comes," said Pedro, "then Spain shall be to you as Aquitaine,[1] and, be your project what it may, you may ever count on every troop and every ship over which flies the banner of Castile."

"And," added the other, "upon every aid which the wealth and power of Majorca can bestow."

"Touching the hundred thousand crowns in which I stand your debtor," continued Pedro carelessly, "it can no doubt—"

"Not a word, sire, not a word!" cried the Prince. "It is not now when you are in grief that I would vex your mind with such base and sordid matters. I have said once and forever that I am yours with every bowstring of my army and every florin in my coffers."

"Ah! here is indeed a mirror of chivalry," said Don Pedro. "I think, Sir Fernando, since the Prince's bounty is stretched so far, that we may make further use of his gracious goodness to the extent of fifty thousand crowns. Good Sir William Felton, here, will doubtless settle the matter with you."

The stout old English councilor looked somewhat blank at this prompt acceptance of his master's bounty.

"If it please you, sire," he said, "the public funds are at their lowest, seeing that I have paid twelve thousand men of the companies, and the new taxes—the hearth tax and the wine tax —not yet come in. If you could wait until the promised help from England comes—"

"Nay, nay, my sweet cousin," cried Don Pedro. "Had we known that your own coffers were so low, or that this sorry sum could have weighed one way or the other, we had been loath indeed—"

"Enough, sire, enough!" said the Prince, flushing with vexa-

[1] He means that Spain shall be under English rule as Aquitaine (part of France) now is.

tion. "If the public funds be, indeed, so backward, Sir William, there is still, I trust, my own private credit, which hath never been drawn upon for my own uses, but is now ready in the cause of a friend in adversity. Go, raise this money upon our own jewels, if naught else may serve, and see that it be paid over to Don Fernando."

"In security I offer—" cried Don Pedro.

"Tush! tush!" said the Prince. "Your kingly pledge is my security, without bond or seal. But I have tidings for you, my lords and lieges, that our brother of Lancaster is on his way for our capital with four hundred lances and as many archers to aid us in our venture. When he hath come, and when our fair consort is recovered in her health, which I trust by the grace of God may be ere many weeks be past, we shall then join the army at Dax and set our banners to the breeze once more."

A buzz of joy at the prospect of immediate action rose up from the group of warriors. The Prince smiled at the martial ardor which shone upon every face around him.

"It will hearten you to know," he continued, "that I have sure advices that this Henry is a very valiant leader, and that he has it in his power to make such a stand against us as promises to give us much honor and pleasure. Of his own people he hath brought together, as I learn, some fifty thousand, with twelve thousand of the French free companies, who are, as you know, very valiant and expert men-at-arms. It is certain, also, that the brave and worthy Bertrand de Guesclin hath ridden into France to the Duke of Anjou, and purposes to take back with him great levies from Picardy and Brittany. We hold Bertrand in high esteem, for he has oft before been at great pains to furnish us with an honorable encounter. What think you of it, my worthy Captal? He took you at Cocherel, and, by my soul! you will have the chance now to pay that score."

The Gascon warrior winced a little at the allusion, nor were his countrymen around him better pleased, for on the only occasion when they had encountered the arms of France without English aid they had met with a heavy defeat.

"There are some who say, sire," said the burly De Clisson, "that the score is already overpaid, for that without Gascon help, Bertrand had not been taken at Auray, nor had King John been overborne at Poitiers."

"By heaven! but this is too much," cried an English nobleman. "Methinks that Gascony is too small a cock to crow so lustily."

"The smaller cock, my Lord Audley, may have the longer spur," remarked the Captal de Buch.

"May have its comb clipped if it make overmuch noise," broke in an Englishman.

"By Our Lady of Rocamadour!" cried the Lord of Mucident, "this is more than I can abide. Sir John Charnell, you shall answer to me for those words!"

"Freely, my lord, and when you will," returned the Englishman carelessly.

"My Lord de Clisson," cried Lord Audley, "you look somewhat fixedly in my direction. By God's soul! I should be right glad to go further into the matter with you."

"And you, my Lord of Pommers," said Sir Nigel, pushing his way to the front, "it is in my mind that we might break a lance in gentle and honorable debate over the question."

For a moment a dozen challenges flashed backwards and forwards at this sudden bursting of the cloud which had lowered so long between the knights of the two nations. Furious and gesticulating the Gascons, white and cold and sneering the English, while the Prince, with a half-smile, glanced from one party to the other, like a man who loved to dwell upon a fiery scene, and yet dreaded lest the mischief go so far that he might find it beyond his control.

"Friends, friends!" he cried at last, "this quarrel must go no further. The man shall answer to me, be he Gascon or English, who carries it beyond this room. I have overmuch need for your swords that you should turn them upon each other. Sir John Charnell, Lord Audley, you do not doubt the courage of our friends of Gascony?"

"Not I, sire," Lord Audley answered. "I have seen them fight too often not to know that they are very hardy and valiant gentlemen."

"And so say I," quoth the other Englishman; "but, certes, there is no fear of our forgetting it while they have a tongue in their heads."

"Nay, Sir John," said the Prince reprovingly, "all peoples have their own use and customs. There are some who might call us cold and dull and silent. But you hear, my lords of Gascony, that these gentlemen had no thought to throw a slur upon your honor or your valor, so let all anger fade from your mind. Clisson, Captal, De Pommers, I have your word?"

"We are your subjects, sire," said the Gascon barons, though with no very good grace. "Your words are our law."

"Then shall we bury all cause of unkindness in a flagon of malvoise," said the Prince cheerily. "Ho, there! the doors of the banquet hall! I have been overlong from my sweet spouse, but I shall be back with you anon. Let the sewers serve and the minstrels play, while we drain a cup to the brave days that are before us in the south!" He turned away, accompanied by the two monarchs, while the rest of the company, with many a compressed lip and menacing eye, filed slowly through the side door to the great chamber in which the royal tables were set forth.

Chapter 17

HOW ALLEYNE WON HIS PLACE IN AN HONORABLE GUILD

Whilst the prince's council was sitting, Alleyne and Ford had remained in the outer hall, where they were soon surrounded by a noisy group of young Englishmen of their own rank, all eager to hear the latest news from England.

"How is it with the old man at Windsor?" asked one.

"But how of England, my lads of Loring?" asked another.

"I take it," said Ford, "that it is much as it was when you were there last, save that perchance there is a little less noise there."

"And why less noise, young Solomon?"

"Ah, that is for your wit to discover."

"Pardieu! here is a paladin [1] come over, with the Hampshire

[1] *paladin* (păl′ȧ·dĭn): a hero.

mud still sticking to his shoes. He means that the noise is less for our being out of the country."

"They are very quick in these parts," said Ford, turning to Alleyne.

"How are we to take this, sir?" asked the ruffling squire.

"You may take it as it comes," said Ford carelessly.

"Here is pertness!" cried the other.

"Sir, I honor your truthfulness," said Ford.

"Stint it, Humphrey," said the tall squire, with a burst of laughter. "You will have little credit from this gentlemen, I perceive. Tongues are sharp in Hampshire, sir."

"And swords?"

"Hum! we may prove that. In two days' time is the tournament, when we may see if your lance is as quick as your wit."

"All very well, Roger Harcomb," cried a burly, bullnecked young man, whose square shoulders and massive limbs told of exceptional personal strength. "You pass too lightly over the matter. We are not to be so easily overcrowded. The Lord Loring hath given his proofs; but we know nothing of his squires, save that one of them hath a railing tongue. And how of you, young sir?" bringing his heavy hand down on Alleyne's shoulder.

"And what of me, young sir?"

"Ma foi! this is my lady's page come over. Your cheek will be browner and your hand harder ere you see your mother again."

"If my hand is not hard, it is ready."

"Ready? Ready for what? For the hem of my lady's train?"

"Ready to chastise insolence, sir," cried Alleyne with flashing eyes.

"Sweet little coz!" answered the burly squire. "Such a dainty color! Such a mellow voice! Eyes of a bashful maid, and hair like a three years' babe! Voila!" He passed his thick fingers roughly through the youth's crisp golden curls.

"You seek to force a quarrel, sir," said the young man, white with anger.

"And what then?"

"Why, you do it like a country boor, and not like a gentle squire. Hast been ill bred and as ill taught? I serve a master who could show you how such things should be done."

"And how would he do it, oh, pink of squires?"

"He would neither be loud nor would he be unmannerly, but

rather more gentle than is his wont. He would say, 'Sir, I should take it as an honor to do some small deed of arms against you, not for mine own glory or advancement, but rather for the fame of my lady and for the upholding of chivalry.' Then he would draw his glove, thus, and throw it on the ground; or, if he had cause to think that he had to deal with a churl, he might throw it in his face—as I do now!"

A buzz of excitement went up from the knot of squires as Alleyne, his gentle nature turned by this causeless attack into fiery resolution, dashed his glove with all his strength into the sneering face of his antagonist. From all parts of the hall squires and pages came running, until a dense, swaying crowd surrounded the disputants.

"Your life for this!" said the bully, with a face which was distorted with rage.

"If you can take it," returned Alleyne.

"Good lad!" whispered Ford. "Stick to it close as wax."

"I shall see justice," cried Norbury, Sir Oliver's silent attendant.

"You brought it upon yourself, John Tranter," said the tall squire, who had been addressed as Roger Harcomb. "You must ever plague the newcomers. But it were shame if this went further. The lad hath shown a proper spirit."

"But a blow! a blow!" cried several of the older squires. "There must be a finish to this."

"Nay; Tranter first laid hand upon his head," said Harcomb. "How say you, Tranter? The matter may rest where it stands?"

"My name is known in these parts," said Tranter, proudly. "I can let pass what might leave a stain upon another. Let him pick up his glove and say that he has done amiss."

"I should see him in the claws of the devil first," whispered Ford.

"You hear, young sir?" said the peacemaker. "Our friend will overlook the matter if you do but say that you have acted in heat and haste."

"I cannot say that," answered Alleyne.

"It is our custom, young sir, when new squires come amongst us from England, to test them in some such way. Bethink you that if a man have a new lance, he will ever try it in time of peace, lest in days of need it may fail him. How much more, then, is it proper to test those who are our comrades in arms?"

"I should draw out if it may honorably be done," murmured Norbury in Alleyne's ear. "The man is a noted swordsman and far above your strength."

Edricson came, however, of that sturdy Saxon blood which is very slowly heated, but once up not easily to be cooled. The hint of danger which Norbury threw out was the one thing needed to harden his resolution.

"I came here at the beck of my master," he said, "and I looked on every man here as an Englishman and a friend. This gentleman hath shown me a rough welcome, and if I have answered him in the same spirit he has but himself to thank. I will pick the glove up; but, certes, I shall abide what I have done unless he first crave my pardon for what he hath said and done."

Tranter shrugged his shoulders. "You have done what you could to save him, Harcomb," said he. "We had best settle at once."

"So say I," cried Alleyne.

"The council will not break up until the banquet," remarked a gray-haired squire. "You have a clear two hours."

"And the place?"

"The tilting yard is empty at this hour."

"Nay; it must not be within the grounds of the court, or it may go hard with all concerned if it come to the ears of the Prince."

"But there is a quiet spot near the river," said one youth. "We have but to pass through the abbey grounds, along the armory wall, past the church of St. Remy, and so down the Rue des Apôtres."

"En avant, then!" cried Tranter shortly, and the whole assembly flocked out into the open air, save only those whom the special orders of their masters held to their posts. These unfortunates crowded to the small casements and craned their necks after the throng as far as they could catch a glimpse of them.

Close to the banks of the Garonne there lay a little tract of green sward, with the high wall of a prior's garden upon one side and an orchard with a thick bristle of leafless apple trees upon the other. The river ran deep and swift up to the steep bank; but there were few boats upon it, and the ships were moored far out in the center of the stream. Here the two combatants drew their swords and threw off their doublets, for neither had any defensive armor. In such combats, as well as in the more formal sports of the tilting yard, Tranter had won a name for strength and dexterity which had caused Norbury to utter his well-meant warning. On the other hand, Alleyne had used his weapons in constant exercise and practice for every day for many months, and being by nature quick of eye and prompt of hand, he might pass now as no mean swordsman. A strangely opposed pair they appeared as they approached each other: Tranter dark and stout and stiff, with hairy chest and corded arms, Alleyne a model of comeliness and grace, with his golden hair and his skin as fair as a woman's. An unequal fight it seemed to most; but there were a few, and they the most experienced, who saw something in the youth's steady gray eye and wary step which left the issue open to doubt.

"Hold, sirs, hold!" cried Norbury, ere a blow had been struck. "This gentleman hath a two-handed sword, a good foot longer than that of our friend."

"Take mine, Alleyne," said Ford.

"Nay, friends," he answered, "I understand the weight and balance of mine own. To work, sir, for our lord may need us at the abbey!"

Tranter's great sword was indeed a mighty vantage in his favor. He stood with his feet close together, his knees bent outwards, ready for a dash inward or a spring out. The weapon he held straight up in front of him with blade erect, so that he might either bring it down with a swinging blow, or by a turn of the heavy blade he might guard his own head and body. A further protection lay in the broad and powerful guard which crossed the hilt, and which was furnished with a deep and narrow notch, in which an expert swordsman might catch his foeman's blade, and by a quick turn of his wrist might snap it across. Alleyne, on the other hand, must trust for his defense to his quick eye and active foot—for his sword, though keen as a whetstone could make it, was of a light and graceful build, with a narrow, sloping pommel and a tapering steel.

Tranter well knew his advantage and lost no time in putting it to use. As his opponent walked towards him he suddenly bounded forward and sent in a whistling cut which would have severed the other in twain had he not sprung lightly back from it.

Quick as a panther, Alleyne sprang in with a thrust, but Tranter, who was as active as he was strong, had already recovered himself and turned it aside with a movement of his heavy blade. Again he whizzed in a blow which made the spectators hold their breath, and again Alleyne very quickly and swiftly slipped from under it and sent back two lightning thrusts which the other could scarce parry. So close were they to each other that Alleyne had no time to spring back from the next cut, which beat down his sword and grazed his forehead, sending the blood streaming into his eyes and down his cheeks. He sprang out beyond sword sweep, and the pair stood breathing heavily, while the crowd of young squires buzzed their applause.

"Bravely struck on both sides!" cried Roger Harcomb. "You have both won honor from this meeting, and it would be sin and shame to let it go further."

"You have done enough, Edricson," said Norbury.

"You have carried yourself well," cried several of the older squires.

"For my part, I have no wish to slay this young man," said Tranter, wiping his heated brow.

"Does this gentleman crave my pardon for having used me despitefully?" asked Alleyne.

"Nay, not I."

"Then stand on your guard, sir!" With a clatter and dash the two blades met once more, Alleyne pressing in so as to keep within the full sweep of the heavy blade, while Tranter as continually sprang back to have space for one of his fatal cuts. A three-parts-parried blow drew blood from Alleyne's left shoulder, but at the same moment he wounded Tranter slightly upon the thigh. Next instant, however, his blade had slipped into the fatal notch, there was a sharp cracking sound, with a tinkling upon the ground, and he found a splintered piece of steel fifteen inches long was all that remained to him of his weapon.

"Your life is in my hands!" cried Tranter, with a bitter smile.

"Nay, nay, he makes submission!" broke in several squires.

"Another sword!" cried Ford.

"Nay, sir," said Harcomb, "that is not the custom."

"Throw down your hilt, Edricson," cried Norbury.

"Never!" said Alleyne. "Do you crave my pardon, sir?"

"You are mad to ask it."

"Then on guard again!" cried the young squire, and sprang in with a fire and a fury which more than made up for the shortness of his weapon. It had not escaped him that his opponent was breathing in short, hoarse gasps, like a man who is dizzy with fatigue. Now was the time for the purer living and the more agile limb to show their value. Back and back gave Tranter, ever seeking time for a last cut. On and on came Alleyne, his jagged point now at his foeman's face, now at his throat, now at his chest, still stabbing and thrusting to pass the line of steel which covered him. Yet his experienced foeman knew well that such efforts could not be long sustained. Let him relax for one instant, and his deathblow had come. Relax he must! Flesh and blood could not stand the strain. Already the thrusts were less fierce, the foot less ready, although there was no abatement of the spirit in the steady gray eyes. Tranter, cunning and wary from years of fighting, knew that his chance had come. He brushed aside the frail weapon which was opposed to him, whirled up his great blade, sprang back to get the fairer sweep—and vanished into the waters of the Garonne.

So intent had the squires, both combatants and spectators, been on the matter in hand, that all thought of the steep bank and swift, still stream had gone from their minds. It was not until Tranter, giving back before the other's fiery rush, was upon the very brink, that a general cry warned him of his danger. That last spring, which he hoped would have brought the fight to a bloody end, carried him clear of the edge, and he found himself in an instant eight feet deep in the ice-cold stream. Once and twice his gasping face and clutching fingers broke up through the still green water, sweeping outwards in the swirl of the current. In vain were sword sheaths, apple branches, and belts linked together thrown out to him by his companions. Alleyne had dropped his shattered sword and was standing, trembling in every limb, with his rage all changed in an instant to pity. For the third time the drowning man came to the surface, his hands full of green slimy water plants, his eyes turned in despair to the shore. Their glance fell upon Alleyne, and he could not withstand the mute appeal which he read in them. In an instant he, too, was in the Garonne, striking out with powerful strokes for his late foeman.

Yet the current was swift and strong, and, good swimmer as he was, it was no easy task which Alleyne had set himself. To clutch at Tranter and to seize him by the hair was the work of a few seconds, but to hold his head above water and to make their way out of the current was another matter. For a hundred strokes he did not seem to gain an inch. Then at last, amid a shout of joy and praise from the bank, they slowly drew clear into more stagnant water, at the instant that a rope, made of a dozen sword belts linked together by the buckles, was thrown by Ford into their very hands. Three pulls from eager arms, and the two combatants, dripping and pale, were dragged up the bank, and lay panting upon the grass.

John Tranter was the first to come to himself, for although he had been longer in the water, he had done nothing during that fierce battle with the current. He staggered to his feet and looked down upon his rescuer, who had raised himself upon his elbow, and was smiling faintly at the buzz of congratulation and of praise which broke from the squires around him.

"I am much beholden to you, sir," said Tranter, though in no very friendly voice. "Certes, I should have been in the river now but for you, for I was born in Warwickshire, which is but a dry county, and there are few who swim in those parts."

"I ask no thanks," Alleyne answered shortly. "Give me your hand to rise, Ford."

"The river has been my enemy," said Tranter, "but it hath been a good friend to you, for it has saved your life this day."

"That is as it may be," returned Alleyne.

"But all is now well over," quoth Harcomb, "and no scath come of it, which is more than I had at one time hoped for. Our young friend here hath very fairly and honestly earned his right to be craftsman of the Honorable Guild of the Squires of Bordeaux. Here is your doublet, Tranter."

"Alas for my poor sword, which lies at the bottom of the Garonne!" said the squire.

"Here is your pourpoint, Edricson," cried Norbury. "Throw it over your shoulders, that you may have at least one dry garment."

"And now away back to the abbey!" said several.

"One moment, sirs," cried Alleyne, who was leaning on Ford's shoulder, with the broken sword, which he had picked up, still clutched in his right hand. "My ears may be somewhat dulled by the water, and perchance what has been said has escaped me, but I have not yet heard this gentleman crave pardon for the insults which he put upon me in the hall."

"What! do you still pursue the quarrel?" asked Tranter.

"And why not, sir? I am slow to take up such things, but once afoot I shall follow it while I have life or breath."

"Ma foi! you have not too much of either, for you are as white as marble," said Harcomb bluntly. "Take my rede, sir, and let it drop, for you have come very well out from it."

"Nay," said Alleyne, "this quarrel is none of my making; but, now that I am here, I swear to you that I shall never leave this spot until I have that which I have come for: so ask my pardon, sir, or choose another glaive, and to it again."

The young squire was deadly white from his exertions, both on the land and in the water. Soaking and stained, with a smear of blood on his white shoulder and another on his brow, there was still in his whole pose and set of face the trace of an inflexible resolution. His opponent's duller and more material mind quailed before the fire and intensity of a higher spiritual nature.

"I had not thought that you had taken it so amiss," said he awkwardly. "It was but such a jest as we play upon each other, and, if you must have it so, I am sorry for it."

"Then I am sorry too," quoth Alleyne warmly, "and here is my hand upon it."

"And the none-meat horn has blown three times," quoth Harcomb, as they all streamed in chattering groups from the ground. "I know not what the Prince's maître-de-cuisine will say or think. By my troth! master Ford, your friend here is in need of a cup of wine, for he hath drunk deeply of Garonne water. I had not thought from his fair face that he had stood to this matter so shrewdly."

"Faith," said Ford, "this air of Bordeaux hath turned our turtledove into a gamecock. A milder or more courteous youth never came out of Hampshire."

"His master also, as I understand, is a very mild and courteous gentleman," remarked Harcomb; "yet I do not think that they are either of them men with whom it is very safe to trifle."

Chapter 18

HOW AGOSTINO PISANO RISKED HIS HEAD

Even the squires' table at the Abbey of St. Andrew's at Bordeaux was on a very sumptuous scale while the Prince held his court there. Here first, after the meager fare of Beaulieu and the stinted board of the Lady Loring, Alleyne learned the lengths to which luxury and refinement might be pushed. Roasted peacocks, with the feathers all carefully replaced, so that the bird lay upon the dish even as it had strutted in life, boars' heads with the tusks gilded and the mouth lined with silver foil, jellies in the shape of the Twelve Apostles, and a great pasty which formed an exact model of the King's new castle at Windsor—these were a few of the strange dishes which faced him. An archer had brought him a change of clothes from the cog, and he had already, with the elasticity of youth, shaken off the troubles and fatigues of the morning. A page from the inner banqueting hall had come with word that their master intended to drink wine at the lodgings of the Lord Chandos that night, and that he desired his squires to sleep at the hotel of the "Half Moon" on the Rue des Apôtres. Thither then they both set out in the twilight after the long course of juggling tricks and glee-singing with which the principal meal was concluded.

A thin rain was falling as the two youths, with their cloaks over their heads, made their way on foot through the streets of the old town, leaving their horses in the royal stables. An occasional oil lamp at the corner of a street, or in the portico of some wealthy burgher, threw a faint glimmer over the shining cobblestones and the varied motley crowd who, in spite of the weather, ebbed and flowed along every highway. In those scattered circles of dim radiance might be seen the whole busy panorama of life in a wealthy and martial city. Here passed the round-faced burgher, swollen with prosperity, his sweeping dark-clothed gaberdine, flat velvet cap, broad leather belt, and dangling pouch all speaking of comfort and of wealth. Behind him his serving wench, her blue wimple over her head, and one hand thrust forth to bear the lanthorn which threw a golden bar of light along her master's path. Behind them a group of swaggering, half-drunken Yorkshire dalesmen, speaking a dialect which their own southland countrymen could scarce comprehend, their jerkins marked with the pelican, which showed that they had come over in the train of the north-country Stapletons. The burgher glanced back at their fierce faces and quickened his step, while the girl pulled her wimple closer round her, for there was a meaning in their wild eyes, as they stared at the purse and the maiden, which men of all tongues could understand. Then came archers of the guard, shrill-voiced women of the camp, English pages with their fair skins and blue wondering eyes, dark-robed friars, lounging men-at-arms, swarthy loud-tongued Gascon serving-men, seamen from the river, rude peasants of the Médoc, and becloaked and be-feathered squires of the court, all jostling and pushing in an ever-changing, many-colored stream, while English, French, Welsh, Basque, and the varied dialects of Gascony and Guienne filled the air with their babel. From time to time the throng would be burst asunder and a lady's horse litter would trot past towards the abbey, or there would come a knot of torch-bearing archers, walking in front of Gascon baron or English knight as he sought his lodgings after the palace revels. Clatter of hoofs, clinking of weapons, shouts from the drunken brawlers, and high laughter of women, they all rose up, like the mist from a marsh, out of the crowded streets of the dim-lit city.

One couple out of the moving throng especially engaged the attention of the two young squires, the more so as they were going in their own direction and immediately in front of them. They consisted of a man and a girl, the former very tall, with rounded shoulders, a limp of one foot, and a large flat object covered with dark cloth under his arm. His companion was young and straight, with a quick, elastic step and graceful bearing, though so swathed in a black mantle that little could be seen of her face save a flash of dark eyes and a curve of raven hair. The tall man leaned heavily upon her to take the weight off his tender foot, while he held his burden betwixt himself and the wall, cuddling it jealously to his side, and thrusting forward his young companion to act as a buttress whenever the pressure of the crowd threatened to bear him away. The evident anxiety of the man, the appearance of his attendant, and the joint care with which they defended their concealed possession excited the interest of the two young Englishmen who walked within hand-touch of them.

"Courage, child!" they heard the tall man exclaim in strange hybrid French. "If we can win another sixty paces we are safe."

"Hold it safe, father," the other answered in the same soft, mincing dialect. "We have no cause for fear."

"Verily, they are heathens and barbarians," cried the man; "mad, howling, drunken barbarians! Forty more paces, Tita mia, and I swear to the holy Eloi, patron of all learned craftsmen, that I will never set foot over my door again until the whole swarm are safely hived in their camp of Dax, or wherever else they curse with their presence. Twenty more paces, my treasure! Ah, my God! how they push and braw! Get in their way, Tita mia! Put your little elbow bravely out! Set your shoulders squarely against them, girl! Why should you give way to these mad islanders? Ah, cospetto! we are ruined and destroyed!"

The crowd had thickened in front, so that the lame man and the girl had come to a stand. Several half-drunken English archers, attracted, as the squires had been, by their singular appearace, were facing towards them and peering at them through the dim light.

"By the three kings!" cried one, "here is an old dotard shrew to have so goodly a crutch! Use the leg that God hath given you, man, and do not bear so heavily upon the wench."

"Twenty devils fly away with him!" shouted another. "What, how, man! are brave archers to go maidless while an old man uses one as a walking staff?"

"Come with me, my honey bird!" cried a third, plucking at the girl's mantle.

"Nay, with me, my heart's desire!" said the first. "By St. George! our life is short, and we should be merry while we may. May I never see Chester Bridge again if she is not a right winsome lass!"

"What hath the old toad under his arm?" cried one of the others.

"Let us see, old bag of bones; let us see what it is that you have under your arm!" They crowded in upon him, while he, ignorant of their language, could but clutch the girl with one hand

and the parcel with the other, looking wildly about in search of help.

"Nay, lads, nay!" cried Ford, pushing back the nearest archer. "This is but scurvy conduct. Keep your hands off, or it will be the worse for you."

"Keep your tongue still, or it will be the worse for you," shouted the most drunken of the archers. "Who are you to spoil sport?"

"A raw squire, new landed," said another. "By St. Thomas of Kent! we are at the beck of our master, but we are not to be ordered by every babe whose mother hath sent him as far as Aquitaine."

"Oh, gentlemen," cried the girl in broken French, "for dear Christ's sake stand by us, and do not let these terrible men do us an injury."

"Have no fears, lady," Alleyne answered. "We shall see that all is well with you. Take your hand from the girl's wrist, you north-country rogue!"

"Hold to her, Wat!" said a great black-bearded man-at-arms, whose steel breastplate glimmered in the dusk. "Keep your hands from your bodkins, you two, for that was my trade before you were born, and, by my soul! I will drive a handful of steel through you if you move a finger."

"Thank God!" said Alleyne suddenly, as he spied in the lamplight a shock of blazing red hair which fringed a steel cap high above the heads of the crowd. "Here is John, and Aylward, too! Help us, comrades, for there is wrong being done to this maid and to the old man."

"Holà, mon petit," said the old bowman, pushing his way through the crowd, with the huge forester at his heels. "What is all this, then? By the twang of string! I think that you will have some work upon your hands if you are to right all the wrongs that you may see upon this side of the water. It is not to be thought that a troop of bowmen, with the wine buzzing in their ears, will be as soft-spoken as so many young clerks in an orchard. When you have been a year with the Company you will think less of such matters. But what is amiss here? The provost marshal with his archers is coming this way, and some of you may find yourselves in the stretch-neck if you take not heed."

"Why, it is old Sam Aylward of the White Company!"

shouted the man-at-arms. "Why, Samkin, what hath come upon thee? I can call to mind the day when you were as roaring a blade as ever called himself a free companion. By my soul! from Limoges to Navarre, who was there who would kiss a wench or cut a throat as readily as bowman Aylward of Hawkwood's company?"

"Like enough, Peter," said Aylward, "and, by my hilt! I may not have changed so much. But it was ever a fair loose and a clear mark with me. The wench must be willing, or the man must be standing up against me, else, by these ten finger bones! either were safe enough for me."

A glance at Aylward's resolute face, and at the huge shoulders of Hordle John, had convinced the archers that there was little to be got by violence. The girl and the old man began to shuffle on in the crowd without their tormentors venturing to stop them. Ford and Alleyne followed slowly behind them, but Aylward caught the latter by the shoulder.

"By my hilt! camarade," said he, "I hear that you have done great things at the abbey today, but I pray you to have a care, for it was I who brought you into the Company, and it would be a black day for me if aught were to befall you."

"Nay, Aylward, I will have a care."

"Thrust not forward into danger too much, mon petit. In a little time your wrist will be stronger and your cut more shrewd."

Alleyne, slipping through the crowd, rejoined Ford, who was standing in talk with the two strangers who had now reached their own doorstep.

"Brave young signor," cried the tall man, throwing his arms round Alleyne, "how can we thank you enough for taking our parts against those horrible drunken barbarians? What should we have done without you? My Tita would have been dragged away, and my head would have been shivered into a thousand fragments."

"Nay, I scarce think that they would have mishandled you so," said Alleyne in surprise.

"Ho, ho!" cried he with a high crowing laugh, "it is not the head upon my shoulders that I think of. Cospetto! no. It is the head under my arm which you have preserved."

"Perhaps the signori would deign to come under our roof,

father," said the maiden. "If we bide here, who knows that some fresh tumult may not break out?"

"Well said, Tita! Well said, my girl! I pray you, sirs, to honor my unworthy roof so far. A light, Giacomo! There are five steps up. Now two more. So! Here we are at last in safety. Corpo di Baccho! I would not have given ten maravedi for my head when those children of the devil were pushing us against the wall. Tita mia, you have been a brave girl, and it was better that you should be pulled and pushed than that my head should be broken."

"Yes indeed, father," said she earnestly.

"But those English! Ach! Take a Goth, a Hun, and a Vandal; mix them together and add a Barbary rover; then take this creature and make him drunk—and you have an Englishman. My God! were ever such people upon earth! What place is free from them? I hear that they swarm in Italy even as they swarm here. Everywhere you will find them, except in heaven."

"Dear father," cried Tita, still supporting the angry old man, as he limped up the curved oaken stair. "You must not forget that these good signori who have preserved us are also English."

"Ah, yes. My pardon, sirs! Come into my room here. There are some who might find some pleasure in these paintings, but I learn the art of war is the only art which is held in honor in your island."

The low-roofed, oak-paneled room into which he conducted them was brilliantly lit by four scented oil lamps. Against the walls, upon the table, on the floor, and in every part of the chamber were great sheets of glass painted in the most brilliant colors. Ford and Edricson gazed around them in amazement, for never had they seen such magnificent works of art.

"You like them then," the lame artist cried, in answer to the look of pleasure and of surprise in their faces. "There are, then, some of you who have a taste for such trifling."

"I could not have believed it," exclaimed Alleyne. "What color! What outlines! See to this martyrdom of the holy Stephen, Ford. Could you not yourself pick up one of these stones which lie to the hand of the wicked murtherers?"

"And see this stag, Alleyne, with the cross betwixt its horns. By my faith! I have never seen a better one at the Forest of Bere."

"And the green of this grass—how bright and clear! Why, all the painting that I have seen is but child's play beside this. This worthy gentleman must be one of those great painters of whom I have oft heard brother Bartholomew speak at Beaulieu."

The dark mobile face of the artist shone with pleasure at the unaffected delight of the two young Englishmen. His daughter had thrown off her mantle and disclosed a face of the finest and most delicate Italian beauty, which soon drew Ford's eyes from the pictures in front of him. Alleyne, however, continued with little cries of admiration and of wonderment to turn from the walls to the table and yet again to the walls.

"What think you of this, young sir?" asked the painter, tearing off the cloth which concealed the flat object which he had borne beneath his arm. It was a leaf-shaped sheet of glass bearing upon it a face with a halo round it, so delicately outlined, and of so perfect a tint, that it might have been indeed a human face which gazed with sad and thoughtful eyes upon the young squire. He clapped his hands, with that thrill of joy which true art will ever give to a true artist.

"It is great!" he cried. "It is wonderful! But I marvel, sir, that you should have risked a work of such beauty and value by bearing it at night through so unruly a crowd."

"I have indeed been rash," said the artist. "Some wine, Tita, from the Florence flask! Had it not been for you, I tremble to think of what might have come of it. See to the skin tint: it is not to be replaced; for paint as you will, it is not once in a hundred times that it is not either burned too brown in the furnace or else the color will not hold, and you get but a sickly white. There you can see the very veins and the throb of the blood. Yes, diavolo! if it had broken, my heart would have broken too. It is for the choir window of the church of St. Remy, and we had gone, my little helper and I, to see if it was indeed of the size for the stonework. Night had fallen ere we finished, and what could we do save carry it home as best we might? But you, young sir, you speak as if you too knew something of the art."

"So little that I scarce dare speak of it in your presence," Alleyne answered. "I have been cloister-bred, and it was no very great matter to handle the brush better than my brother novices."

"There are pigments, brush, and paper," said the old artist. "I do not give you glass, for that is another matter and takes much skill in the mixing of colors. Now, I pray you to show me a touch of your art. I thank you, Tita! The Venetian glasses, cara mia, and fill them to the brim. A seat, signor!"

While Ford, in his English French, was conversing with Tita in her Italian French, the old man was carefully examining his precious head to see that no scratch had been left upon its surface. When he glanced up again, Alleyne had, with a few bold strokes of the brush, tinted in a woman's face and neck upon the white sheet in front of him.

"Diavolo!" exclaimed the old artist, standing with his head on one side, "you have power; yes, cospetto! you have power. It is the face of an angel!"

"It is the face of the Lady Maude Loring!" cried Ford, even more astonished.

"Why, on my faith, it is not unlike her!" said Alleyne, in some confusion.

"Ah! a portrait! So much the better. Young man, I am Agostino Pisano, the son of Andrea Pisano, and I say again that you have power. Further, I say that, if you will stay with me, I will teach you all the secrets of the glass-stainers' mystery: the pigments and their thickening, which will fuse into the glass and which will not, the furnace and the glazing—every trick and method you shall know."

"I would be right glad to study under such a master," said Alleyne; "but I am sworn to follow my lord whilst this war lasts."

"War! war!" cried the old Italian. "Ever this talk of war. And the men that you hold to be great—what are they? Have I not heard their names? Soldiers, butchers, destroyers! Ah, per Baccho! we have men in Italy who are, in very truth, great. You pull down, you despoil; but they build up, they restore. Ah, if you could but see my own dear Pisa, the Duomo, the cloisters of Campo Santo, the high Campanile, with the mellow throb of her bells upon the warm Italian air! Those are the works of great men. And I have seen them with my own eyes, these very eyes which look upon you. I have seen Andrea Orcagna, Taddeo Gaddi, Giottino, Stefano, Simone Memmi—men whose very colors I am not worthy to mix. Ah, signori, there are the real great men, whose names will be held in honor when your soldiers are shown to have been the enemies of humankind."

"Faith, sir," said Ford, "there is something to say for the

soldiers also, for, unless they be defended, how are all these gentlemen whom you have mentioned to preserve the pictures which they have painted?"

"And all these!" said Alleyne. "Have you indeed done them all?—and where are they to go?"

"Yes, signor, they are all from my hand. Some are, as you see, upon one sheet, and some are in many pieces which may fasten together. There are some who do but paint upon the glass, and then, by placing another sheet of glass upon the top and fastening it, they keep the air from their painting. Yet I hold that the true art of my craft lies as much in the furnace as in the brush. See this rose window, which is from the model of the Church of the Holy Trinity at Vendôme, and this other of the 'Finding of the Grail,' which is for the apse of the abbey church. Time was when none but my countrymen could do these things; but there is Clement of Chartres and others in France who are very worthy workmen. But, ah! there is that ever-shrieking brazen tongue which will not let us forget for one short hour that it is the arm of the savage, and not the hand of the master, which rules over the world."

A stern, clear bugle call had sounded close at hand to summon some following together for the night.

"It is a sign to us as well," said Ford. "I would fain stay here forever amid all these beautiful things"—staring hard at the blushing Tita as he spoke—"but we must be back at our lord's hostel ere he reach it." Amid renewed thanks and with promises to come again, the two squires bade their leave of the old Italian glass-stainer and his daughter.

"Mon Dieu! Alleyne, saw you ever so lovely a face?" cried Ford as they hurried along together. "So pure, so peaceful, and so beautiful!"

"In sooth, yes. And the hue of the skin the most perfect that ever I saw. Marked you also how the hair curled round the brow? It was wonder fine."

"Those eyes, too!" cried Ford. "How clear and how tender—simple, and yet so full of thought!"

"If there was a weakness it was in the chin," said Alleyne.

"Nay, I saw none."

"It was well curved, it is true."

"Most daintily so."

"And yet—"

"What then, Alleyne? Wouldst find flaw in the sun?"

"Well, bethink you, Ford, would not more power and expression have been put into the face by a long and noble beard?"

"Holy Virgin!" cried Ford, "the man is mad. A beard on the face of little Tita!"

"Tita! Who spoke of Tita?"

"Who spoke of aught else?"

"It was the picture of St. Remy, man, of which I have been discoursing."

"You are indeed," cried Ford, laughing, "a Goth, Hun, and Vandal, with all the other hard names which the old man called us. How could you think so much of a smear of pigments, when there was such a picture painted by the good God himself in the very room with you?"

Chapter 19

HOW ENGLAND HELD THE LISTS AT BORDEAUX

So used were the good burghers of Bordeaux to martial display and knightly sport, that an ordinary joust or tournament was an everyday matter with them. The fame and brilliancy of the Prince's court had drawn the knights-errant and pursuivants-of-arms from every part of Europe. In the long lists by the Garonne on the landward side of the northern gate there had been many a strange combat, when the Teutonic knight, fresh from the conquest of the Prussian heathen, ran a course against the knight of Calatrava, hardened by continual struggle against the Moors, or cavaliers from Portugal broke a lance with Scandinavian warriors from the further shore of the great Northern Ocean. Here fluttered many an outland pennon, bearing symbol and blazonry from the banks of the Danube, the wilds of Lithuania, and the mountain strongholds of Hungary; for chivalry was of no clime and of no race, nor was any land so wild that the fame and name of the prince had not sounded through it from border to border.

Great, however, was the excitement through town and district when it was learned that on the third Wednesday in Advent there would be held a passage-at-arms in which five knights of England would hold the lists against all comers. The great concourse of noblemen and famous soldiers, the national character of the contest, and the fact that this was a last trial of arms before what promised to be an arduous and bloody war, all united to make the event one of the most notable and brilliant that Bordeaux had ever seen. On the eve of the contest the peasants flocked in from the whole district of Médoc, and the fields beyond the walls were whitened with the tents of those who could find no warmer lodging. From the distant camp of Dax, too, and all the cluster of flourishing towns which look upon Bordeaux as their mother, there thronged an unceasing stream of horsemen and of footmen, all converging upon the great city. By the morning of the day on which the courses were to be run, not less than eighty thousand people had assembled round the lists and along the low grassy ridge which looks down upon the scene of the encounter.

It was, as may well be imagined, no easy matter among so many noted cavaliers to choose out five on either side who should have precedence over their fellows. A score of secondary combats had nearly arisen from the rivalries and bad blood created by the selection, and it was only the influence of the Prince and the efforts of the older barons which kept the peace among so many eager and fiery soldiers. Not till the day before the courses were the shields finally hung out for the inspection of the ladies and the heralds, so that all men might know the names of the champions and have the opportunity to prefer any charge against them, should there be stain upon them which should disqualify them from taking part in so noble and honorable a ceremony.

Sir Hugh Calverley and Sir Robert Knolles had not yet returned from their raid into the marches of the Navarre, so that the English party were deprived of two of their most famous lances. Yet there remained so many good names that Chandos and Felton, to whom the selection had been referred, had many an earnest consultation, in which every feat of arms and failure or success of each candidate was weighed and balanced against the rival claims of his companions. Lord Audley of Cheshire, the hero of Poitiers, and Loring of Hampshire, who was held to be the second lance in the army, were easily fixed upon. Then, of the younger men, Sir Thomas Percy of Northumberland, Sir Thomas Wake of Yorkshire, and Sir William Beauchamp of Gloucestershire were finally selected to uphold the honor of England. On the other side were the veteran Captal de Buch and the brawny Olivier de Clisson, with the free companion Sir Perducas d'Albret, the valiant Lord of Mucident, and Sigismond von Altenstadt, of the Teutonic Order. The older soldiers among the English shook their heads as they looked upon the escutcheons of these famous warriors, for they were all men who had spent their lives upon the saddle, and bravery and strength can avail little against experience and wisdom of war.

It was indeed an enormous crowd which covered the whole vast plain from the line of vineyards to the river bank. From the northern gate the Prince, arriving with his train of companions, looked down at a dark sea of heads, brightened here and there by the colored hoods of the women, or by the sparkling headpieces of archers and men-at-arms. In the center of this vast assemblage the lists seemed but a narrow strip of green marked out with banners and streamers, while a gleam of white with a flutter of pennons at either end showed where the marquees were pitched which served as the dressing-rooms of the combatants. A path had been staked off from the city gate to the stands which had been erected for the court and the nobility. Down this, amid the shouts of the enormous multitude, the Prince cantered with his two attendant kings, his high officers of state, and his long train of lords and ladies, courtiers, counselors, and soldiers, with toss of plume and flash of jewel, sheen of silk and glint of gold—as rich and gallant a show as heart could wish. The head of the cavalcade had reached the lists ere the rear had come clear of the city gate, for the fairest and the bravest had assembled from all the broad lands which are watered by the Dordogne and the Garonne. Here rode dark-browed cavaliers from the sunny south, fiery soldiers from Gascony, graceful courtiers of Limousin or Saintonge, and gallant young Englishmen from beyond the seas. Here, too, were the beautiful brunettes of the Gironde, with eyes which outflashed their jewels, while beside them rode their blond sisters of England, clear cut and aquiline, swathed in swansdown and in ermine, for the air was biting though the sun was bright. Slowly the long and glittering train wound into the lists, until every horse had been tethered by the varlets in waiting, and every lord and lady seated in the long stands which stretched, rich in tapestry and velvet and blazoned arms, on either side of the center of the arena.

The holders of the lists occupied the end which was nearest to the city gate. There, in front of their respective pavilions, flew the martlets of Audley, the roses of Loring, the scarlet bars of Wake, the lion of the Percies, and the silver wings of the Beauchamps, each supported by a squire clad in hanging green stuff to represent so many Tritons, and bearing a huge conch shell in his left hand. Behind the tents the great war horses, armed at all points, champed and reared, while their masters sat at the doors of their pavilions, with their helmets upon their knees, chatting as to the order of the day's doings. The English archers and men-at-arms had mustered at that end of the lists, but the vast majority of the spectators were in favor of the attacking party. Hence the applause was by no means general when the herald-at-arms proclaimed, after a flourish of trumpets, the names and styles of the knights who were prepared, for the honor of their country and for the love of their ladies, to hold the field against all who might do them the favor to run a course with them. On the other hand, a deafening burst of cheering greeted the rival herald, who, advancing from the other end of the lists, rolled forth the well-known titles of the five famous warriors who had accepted the defiance.

"Ha! my grace D'Armagnac," said the Prince, "it seems that our friends on this side will not grieve if our English champions lose the day."

"It may be so, sire," the Gascon nobleman answered. "I have little doubt that in Smithfield or at Windsor an English crowd would favor their own countrymen."

"By my faith! that's easily seen," said the Prince, laughing, "for a few score English archers at yonder end are bellowing as though they would outshout the mighty multitude. I fear that they will have little to shout over this journey, for my gold vase has small prospect of crossing the water. What are the conditions, John?"

"They are to tilt singly not less than three courses, sire, and the victory to rest with that party which shall have won the greater number of courses, each pair continuing till one or other have the vantage. He who carries himself best of the victors hath the prize, and he who is judged best of the other party hath a jeweled clasp. Shall I order that the nakirs sound, sire?"

The prince nodded, and the trumpets rang out, while the champions rode forth one after the other, each meeting his opponent in the center of the lists. Sir William Beauchamp went down before the practiced lance of the Captal de Buch. Sir Thomas Percy won the vantage over the Lord of Mucident, and the Lord Audley struck Sir Perducas d'Albret from the saddle. The burly De Clisson, however, restored the hopes of the attackers by beating to the ground Sir Thomas Wake of Yorkshire. So far, there was little to choose betwixt challengers and challenged.

"By St. James of Santiago!" cried Don Pedro, with a tinge of color upon his pale cheeks, "win who will, this has been a most noble contest."

"Who comes next for England, John?" the Prince asked Chandos in a voice which quivered with excitement.

"Sir Nigel Loring of Hampshire, sire."

"Ha! he is a man of good courage, and skilled in the use of all weapons."

"He is indeed, sire. But his eyes, like my own, are the worse for wars. Yet he can tilt or play his part at handstrokes as merrily as ever. I have heard that at Twynham Castle there is a buffet which groans beneath the weight of his prizes."

"I pray that my vase may join them," said the prince. "But here is the cavalier of Germany, and by my soul! he looks like a man of great valor and hardiness. Let them run their full three courses, for the issue is overgreat to hang upon one."

As the Prince spoke, amid a loud flourish of trumpets and the shouting of the Gascon party, the last of the assailants rode gallantly into the lists. He was a man of great size, clad in black armor without blazonry or ornament of any kind, for all worldly display was forbidden by the rules of the military brotherhood to which he belonged. No plume or nobloy fluttered from his plain tilting salade, and even his lance was devoid of the customary banderole. A white mantle fluttered behind him, upon the left side of which was marked the broad black cross picked out with silver which was the well-known badge of the Teutonic Order. Mounted upon a horse as large, as black, and as forbidding as himself, he cantered slowly forward, with none of those prancings and gambades with which a cavalier was accustomed to show his command over his charger. Gravely and sternly he inclined his head to the Prince and took his place at the further end of the arena.

He had scarce done so before Sir Nigel rode out from the holders' enclosure and, galloping at full speed down the lists, drew his charger up before the Prince's stand with a jerk which threw it back upon its haunches. With white armor, blazoned shield, and plume of ostrich feathers from his helmet, he carried himself in so jaunty and joyous a fashion, with tossing pennon and curveting charger, that a shout of applause ran the full circle of the arena. With the air of a man who hastes to a joyous festival, he waved his lance in salute and, reining the pawing horse round without permitting its forefeet to touch the ground, he hastened back to his station.

A great hush fell over the huge multitude as the two last champions faced each other. A double issue seemed to rest upon their contest, for their personal fame was at stake as well as their party's honor. Both were famous warriors, but as their exploits had been performed in widely sundered countries, they had never before been able to cross lances. A course between such men would have been enough in itself to cause the keenest interest, apart from its being the crisis which would decide who should be the victors of the day. For a moment they waited—the German somber and collected, Sir Nigel quivering in every fiber with eagerness and fiery resolution. Then, amid a long-drawn breath from the spectators, the glove fell from the marshal's hand, and the two steel-clad horsemen met like a thunderclap in front of the royal stand. The German, though he reeled for an instant before the thrust of the Englishman, struck his opponent so fairly upon the visor that the laces burst, the plumed helmet flew to pieces, and Sir Nigel galloped on down the lists with his bald head shimmering in the sunshine. A thousand waving scarves and tossing caps announced that the first bout had fallen to the popular party.

The Hampshire knight was not a man to be disheartened by a reverse. He spurred back to his pavilion and was out in a few instants with another helmet. The second course was so equal that the keenest judges could not discern any vantage. Each struck fire from the other's shield, and each endured the jarring shock as though welded to the horse beneath him. In the final bout, however, Sir Nigel struck his opponent with so true an aim that the point of the lance caught between the bars of his visor and tore the front of his helmet out, while the German, aiming somewhat low, and half-stunned by the shock, had the misfortune to strike his adversary upon the thigh, a breach of the rules of the tilting yard, by which he not only sacrificed his chances of success, but would also have forfeited his horse and his armor, had the English knight chosen to claim them. A roar of applause from the English soldiers, with an ominous silence from the vast crowd who pressed round the barriers, announced that the balance of victory lay with the holders. Already the ten champions had assembled in front of the prince to receive his award, when a harsh bugle call from the further end of the lists drew all eyes to a new and unexpected arrival.

Chapter 20

HOW A CHAMPION CAME FORTH FROM THE EAST

The Bordeaux lists were, as has already been explained, situated upon the plain near the river upon those great occasions when the tilting ground in front of the Abbey of St. Andrew's was deemed to be too small to contain the crowd. On the eastern side of this plain the countryside sloped upwards, thick with vines in summer, but now ridged with the brown bare enclosures. Over the gently rising plain curved the white road which leads inland, usually flecked with travelers, but now with scarce a living form upon it, so completely had the lists drained all the district of its inhabitants. Strange it was to see such a vast concourse of people, and then to look upon that broad, white, empty highway which wound away, bleak and deserted, until it narrowed itself to a bare streak against the distant uplands.

Shortly after the contest had begun, anyone looking from the lists along this road might have remarked, far away in the extreme distance, two brilliant and sparkling points which glittered and twinkled in the bright shimmer of the winter sun. Within an hour these had become clearer and nearer, until they might be seen to come from the reflection from the headpieces of two horsemen who were riding at the top of their speed in the direction of Bordeaux. Another half-hour had brought them so close that every point of their bearing and equipment could be discerned. The first was a knight in full armor, mounted upon a brown horse with a white blaze upon breast and forehead. He was a short man of great breadth of shoulder, with visor closed, and no blazonry upon his simple white surcoat or plain black shield. The other, who was evidently his squire and attendant, was unarmed save for the helmet upon his head, but bore in his right hand a very long and heavy oaken spear which belonged to his master. In his left hand the squire held not only the reins of his own horse but those of a great black war horse, fully harnessed, which trotted along at his side. Thus the three horses and their two riders rode swiftly to the lists, and it was the blare of the trumpet sounded by the squire as his lord rode into the arena which had broken in upon the prize-giving and drawn away the attention and interest of the spectators.

"Ha, John!" cried the prince, craning his neck, "who is this cavalier, and what is it that he desires?"

"On my word, sire," replied Chandos, with the utmost surprise upon his face, "it is my opinion that he is a Frenchman."

"A Frenchman!" repeated Don Pedro. "And how can you tell that, my Lord Chandos, when he has neither coat armor, crest, or blazonry?"

"By his armor, sire, which is rounder at elbow and at shoulder than any of Bordeaux or of England. Italian he might be were his basinet more sloped, but I will swear that those plates were welded betwixt this and Rhine. Here comes his squire, however, and we shall hear what strange fortune hath brought him over the marches."

As he spoke the attendant cantered up the grassy enclosure and, pulling up his steed in front of the royal stand, blew a second fanfare upon his bugle. He was a raw-boned, swarthy-cheeked man, with black bristling beard and a swaggering bearing. Having sounded his call, he thrust the bugle into his belt, and, pushing his way betwixt the groups of English and of Gascon knights, he reined up within a spear's length of the royal party.

"I come," he shouted in a hoarse, thick voice, with a strong Breton accent, "as squire and herald from my master, who is a very valiant pursuivant-of-arms, and a liegeman [1] to the great and powerful monarch, Charles, King of the French. My master has heard that there is jousting here, and prospect of honorable advancement, so he has come to ask that some English cavalier will vouchsafe [2] for the love of his lady to run a course with sharpened lances with him, or to meet him with sword, mace, battle-ax, or dagger. He bade me say, however, that he would fight only with a true Englishman, and not with any mongrel who is neither English nor French, but speaks with the tongue of the one, and fights under the banner of the other."

"Sir!" cried De Clisson, with a voice of thunder, while his countrymen clapped their hands to their swords. The squire, however, took no notice of their angry faces, but continued with his master's message.

"He is now ready, sire," he said, "albeit his destrier [3] has traveled many miles this day, and fast, for we were in fear lest we come too late for the jousting."

"Ye have indeed come too late," said the Prince, "seeing that the prize is about to be awarded; yet I doubt not that one of these gentlemen will run a course for the sake of honor with this cavalier of France."

"And as to the prize, sire," quoth Sir Nigel, "I am sure that I speak for all when I say this French knight hath our leave to bear it away with him if he can fairly win it."

"Bear word of this to your master," said the Prince, "and ask him which of these five Englishmen he would desire to meet. But stay; your master bears no coat armor, and we have not yet heard his name."

"My master, sire, is under vow to the Virgin neither to reveal

[1] *liegeman* (lēj′măn): a loyal follower. [2] *vouchsafe* (vouch·sāf′): to condescend, be willing. [3] *destrier* (dĕs′trĭ·ẽr): a war horse.

his name nor to open his visor until he is back upon French ground once more."

"Yet what assurance have we," said the Prince, "that this is not some varlet masquerading in his master's harness, or some caitiff knight, the very touch of whose lance might bring infamy upon an honorable gentleman?"

"It is not so, sire," cried the squire earnestly. "There is no man upon earth who would demean himself by breaking a lance with my master."

"You speak out boldly, squire," the Prince answered; "but unless I have some further assurance of your master's noble birth and gentle name I cannot match the choicest lances of my court against him."

"You refuse, sire?"

"I do refuse."

"Then, sire, I was bidden to ask you from my master whether you would consent if Sir John Chandos, upon hearing my master's name, should assure you that he was indeed a man with whom you might yourself cross swords without indignity."

"I ask no better," said the Prince.

"Then I must ask, Lord Chandos, that you will step forth. I have your pledge that the name shall remain ever a secret, and that you will neither say nor write one word which might betray it. The name is—" He stooped down from his horse and whispered something into the old knight's ear which made him start with surprise, and stare with much curiosity at the distant knight, who was sitting his charger at the further end of the arena.

"Is this indeed sooth?" he exclaimed.

"It is, my lord, and I swear it by St. Ives of Brittany."

"I might have known it," said Chandos, twisting his mustache, and still looking thoughtfully at the cavalier.

"What then, Sir John?" asked the Prince.

"Sire, this is a knight whom it is indeed great honor to meet, and I would that your grace would grant me leave to send my squire for my harness, for I would dearly love to run a course with him."

"Nay, nay, Sir John, you have gained as much honor as one man can bear, and it were hard if you could not rest now. But I pray you, squire, to tell your master that he is very welcome to our court, and that wines and spices will be served him, if he would refresh himself before jousting."

"My master will not drink," said the squire.

"Let him then name the gentleman with whom he would break a spear."

"He would contend with these five knights, each to choose such weapons as suit him best."

"I perceive," said the Prince, "that your master is a man of great heart and high of enterprise. But the sun already is low in the west, and there will scarce be light for these courses. I pray you, gentlemen, to take your places, that we may see whether this stranger's deeds are as bold as his words."

The unknown knight had sat like a statue of steel, looking neither to the right nor to the left during these preliminaries. He had changed from the horse upon which he had ridden, and bestrode the black charger which his squire had led beside him. His immense breadth, his stern composed appearance, and the mode in which he handled his shield and his lance were enough in themselves to convince the thousands of critical spectators that he was a dangerous opponent. Aylward, who stood in the front row of the archers with Simon, big John, and others of the Company, had been criticizing the proceedings from the commencement with the ease and freedom of a man who had spent his life under arms and had learned in a hard school to know at a glance the points of a horse and his rider. He stared now at the stranger with a wrinkled brow and the air of a man who is striving to stir his memory.

"By my hilt! I have seen the thick body of him before today. Yet I cannot call to mind where it could have been. At Nogent belike, or was it at Auray? Mark me, lads, this man will prove to be one of the best lances of France, and there are no better in the world."

"It is but child's play, this poking game," said John. "I would fain try my hand at it, for, by the black rood! I think that it might be amended."

"What then would you do, John?" asked several.

"There are many things which might be done," said the forester thoughtfully. "Methinks that I would begin by breaking my spear."

"So they all strive to do."

"Nay, but not upon another man's shield. I would break it over my own knee."

"And what the better for that, old beef and bones?" asked Black Simon.

"So I would turn what is but a lady's bodkin of a weapon into a very handsome club."

"And then, John?"

"Then I would take the other's spear into my arm or my leg or where it pleased him best to put it, and I would dash out his brains with my club."

"By my ten finger bones! old John," said Aylward, "I would give my featherbed to see you at a spear-running. This is a most courtly and gentle sport which you have devised."

"So it seems to me," said John seriously. "Or, again, one might seize the other round the middle, pluck him off his horse, and bear him to the pavilion, there to hold him to ransom."

"Good!" cried Simon, amid a roar of laughter from all the archers round. "By Thomas of Kent! we shall make a camp marshal of thee, and thou shalt draw up rules for our jousting. But, John, who is it that you would uphold in this knightly and pleasing fashion?"

"What mean you?"

"Why, John, so strong and strange a tilter must fight for the brightness of his lady's eyes or the curve of her eyelash, even as Sir Nigel does for the Lady Loring."

"I know not about that," said the big archer, scratching his head in perplexity. "Since Mary hath played me false, I can scarce fight for her."

"Yet any woman will serve."

"There is my mother then," said John. "She was at much pains at my upbringing, and, by my soul! I will uphold the curve of her eyelashes, for it tickleth my very heart root to think of her. But who is here?"

"It is Sir William Beauchamp. He is a valiant man, but I fear that he is scarce firm enough upon the saddle to bear the thrust of such a tilter as this stranger promises to be."

Aylward's words were speedily justified, for even as he spoke, the two knights met in the center of the lists. Beauchamp struck his opponent a shrewd blow upon the helmet, but was met with so frightful a thrust that he whirled out of his saddle and rolled over and over upon the ground. Sir Thomas Percy met with little better success, for his shield was split, his vambrace torn, and he himself wounded slightly in the side. Lord Audley and the unknown knight struck each other fairly upon the helmet; but, while the stranger sat as firm and rigid as ever upon his charger, the Englishman was bent back to his horse's crupper by the weight of the blow, and had galloped halfway down the lists ere he could recover himself. Sir Thomas Wake was beaten to the ground with a battle-ax—that being the weapon which he had selected—and had to be carried to his pavilion. These rapid successes, gained one after the other over four celebrated warriors, worked the crowd up to a pitch of wonder and admiration. Thunders of applause from the English soldiers, as well as from the citizens and peasants, showed how far the love of brave and knightly deeds could rise above the rivalries of race.

"By my soul! John," cried the Prince, with his cheek flushed and his eyes shining, "this is a man of good courage and great hardiness. I could not have thought that there was any single arm upon earth which could have overthrown these four champions."

"He is indeed, as I have said, sire, a knight from whom much honor is to be gained. But the lower edge of the sun is wet, and it will be beneath the sea ere long."

"Here is Sir Nigel Loring, on foot and with his sword," said the prince. "I have heard that he is a fine swordsman."

"The finest in your army, sire," Chandos answered. "Yet I doubt not that he will need all his skill this day."

As he spoke, the two combatants advanced from either end in full armor with their two-handed swords sloping over their shoulders. The stranger walked heavily and with a measured stride, while the English knight advanced as briskly as though there was no iron shell to weigh down the freedom of his limbs. At four paces distance they stopped, eyed each other for a moment, and then in an instant fell to work with a clatter and clang as though two sturdy smiths were busy upon their anvils. Up and down went the long, shining blades, round and round they circled in curves of glimmering light, crossing, meeting, disengaging, with flash of sparks at every parry. Here and there bounded Sir Nigel, his head erect, his jaunty plume fluttering in the air, while his dark opponent sent in crashing blow upon blow, following fiercely up with cut and with thrust, but never once getting past the practiced blade of the skilled swordsman. The crowd roared with delight as Sir Nigel would stoop his head to avoid a blow, or by some slight movement of his body allow some terrible thrust to glance harmlessly past him. Suddenly, however, his time came. The Frenchman, whirling up his sword, showed for an instant a chink betwixt his shoulder piece and the rerebrace which guarded his upper arm. In dashed Sir Nigel, and out again so swiftly that the eye could not follow the quick play of his blade, but a trickle of blood from the stranger's shoulder, and a rapidly widening red smudge upon his white surcoat, showed where the thrust had taken effect. The wound was, however, but a slight one, and the Frenchman was about to renew his onset, when, at a sign from the prince, Chandos threw down his baton, and the marshals of the lists struck up the weapons and brought the contest to an end.

"It were time to check it," said the Prince, smiling, "for Sir Nigel is too good a man for me to lose, and, by the five holy wounds! if one of those cuts came home, I should have fears for our champion. What think you, Pedro?"

"I think, Edward, that the little man was very well able to take care of himself. For my part, I should wish to see so well matched a pair fight on while a drop of blood remained in their veins."

"We must have speech with him. Such a man must not go from my court without rest or sup. Bring him hither, Chandos, and, certes, if the Lord Loring hath resigned his claim upon this goblet, it is right and proper that this cavalier should carry it to France with him as a sign of the prowess that he has shown this day."

As he spoke, the knight-errant, who had remounted his war horse, galloped forward to the royal stand, with a silken kerchief bound round his wounded arm. The setting sun cast a ruddy glare upon his burnished arms and sent his long black shadow streaming behind him up the level clearing. Pulling up his steed, he slightly inclined his head, and sat in the stern and composed fashion with which he had borne himself throughout, heedless of the applauding shouts and the flutter of kerchiefs from the long lines of brave men and of fair women who were looking down upon him.

"Sir knight," said the Prince, "we have all marveled this day at this great skill and valor with which God has been pleased to endow you. I would fain that you should tarry at our court, for a time at least, until your hurt is healed and your horses rested."

"My hurt is nothing, sire, nor are my horses weary," returned the stranger in a deep, stern voice.

"Will you not at least hie back to Bordeaux with us, that you may drain a cup of muscadine and sup at our table?"

"I will neither drink your wine nor sit at your table," returned the other. "I bear no love for you or for your race, and there is naught that I wish at your hands until the day when I see the last sail which bears you back to your island vanishing away against the western sky."

"These are bitter words, sir knight," said Prince Edward, with an angry frown.

"And they come from a bitter heart," answered the unknown knight. "How long is it since there has been peace in my hapless country? Where are the steadings and orchards and vineyards which made France fair? Where are the cities which made her great? From Provence to Burgundy we are beset by every prowling hireling in Christendom, who rend and tear the country which you have left too weak to guard her own marches. Is it not a byword that a man may ride all day in that unhappy land without seeing thatch upon roof or hearing the crow of cock? Does not one fair kingdom content you, that you should strive so for this other one which has no love for you? Pardieu! a true Frenchman's words may well be bitter, for bitter is his lot and bitter his thoughts as he rides through his thrice unhappy country."

"Sir knight," said the Prince, "you speak like a brave man, and our cousin of France is happy in having a cavalier who is so fit to uphold his cause either with tongue or with sword. But if you think such evil of us, how comes it that you have trusted yourselves to us without warranty or safe-conduct?"

"Because I knew that you would be here, sire. Had the man who sits upon your right been ruler of this land, I had indeed thought twice before I looked to him for aught that was knightly or generous." With a soldierly salute, he wheeled round his horse and, galloping down the lists, disappeared amid the dense crowd of footmen and of horsemen who were streaming away from the scene of the tournament.

"The insolent villain!" cried Pedro, glaring furiously after him. "I have seen a man's tongue torn from his jaws for less. Would it not be well even now, Edward, to send horsemen to hale him back? Bethink you that it may be one of the royal house of France, or at least some knight whose loss would be a heavy blow to his master. Sir William Felton, you are well mounted, gallop after the caitiff, I pray you."

"Do so, Sir William," said the Prince, "and give him this purse of a hundred nobles as a sign of the respect which I bear for him; for, by St. George! he has served his master this day even as I would wish liegemen of mine to serve me." So saying, the Prince turned his back upon the King of Spain and, springing upon hs horse, rode slowly homewards to the Abbey of St. Andrew's.

Chapter 21

HOW SIR NIGEL WROTE TO TWYNHAM CASTLE

On the morning after the jousting, when Alleyne Edricson went, as was his custom, into his master's chamber to wait upon him in his dressing and to curl his hair, he found him already up and very busily at work. He sat at a table by the window, a deerhound on one side of him and a lurcher on the other, his feet tucked away under the trestle on which he sat, and his tongue in his cheek, with the air of a man who is much perplexed. A sheet of vellum lay upon the board in front of him, and he held a pen in his hand, with which he had been scribbling in a rude schoolboy hand. So many were the blots, however, and so numerous the scratches and erasures, that he had at last given it up in despair, and sat with his single uncovered eye cocked upwards at the ceiling, as one who waits upon inspiration.

"By St. Paul!" he cried, as Alleyne entered, "you are the man who will stand by me in this matter. I have been in sore need of you, Alleyne."

"God be with you, my fair lord!" the squire answered. "I trust that you have taken no hurt from all that you have gone through yesterday."

"Nay; I feel the fresher for it, Alleyne. It has eased my joints, which were somewhat stiff from these years of peace. I trust, Alleyne, that thou didst very carefully note and mark the bearing and carriage of this knight of France; for it is time, now when you are young, that you should see all that is best, and mold your own actions in accordance. This was a man from whom much honor might be gained, and I have seldom met anyone for whom I have conceived so much love and esteem. Could I but learn his name, I should send you to him with my cartel, that we might have further occasion to watch his goodly feats of arms."

"It is said, my fair lord, that none know his name save only the Lord Chandos, and that he is under vow not to speak it. So ran the gossip at the squires' table."

"Be he who he might, he was a very hardy gentleman. But I have a task here, Alleyne, which is harder to me than aught that was set before me yesterday."

"Can I help you, my lord?"

"That indeed you can. I have been writing my greetings to my sweet wife; for I hear that a messenger goes from the Prince to Southampton within the week, and he would gladly take a packet for me. I pray you, Alleyne, to cast your eyes upon what I have written, and see if they are such words as my lady will understand. My fingers, as you can see, are more used to iron and leather than to the drawing of strokes and turning of letters. What then? Is there aught amiss that you should stare so?"

"It is this first word, my lord. In what tongue were you pleased to write?"

"In English; for my lady talks it more than she doth French."

"Yet this is no English word, my sweet lord. Here are four t's, and never a letter betwixt them."

"By St. Paul! it seemed strange to my eye when I wrote it," said Sir Nigel. "They bristle up together like a clump of lances. We must break their ranks and set them farther apart. The word is 'that.' Now I will read it to you, Alleyne, and you shall write it out fair; for we leave Bordeaux this day, and it would be great joy to me to think that the Lady Loring had word from me."

Alleyne sat down as ordered, with a pen in his hand and a fresh sheet of parchment before him, while Sir Nigel slowly spelled out his letter, running his forefinger on from word to word.

> That my heart is with thee, my dear sweeting, is what thine own heart will assure thee of. All is well with us here, save that Pepin hath the mange on his back, and Pommers hath scarce yet got clear of his stiffness from being four days on shipboard; and the more so because the sea was very high, and we were like to founder on account of a hole in her side, which was made by a stone cast at us by certain sea rovers, who may the saints have in their keeping, for they have gone from amongst us, as has young Terlake, and two score mariners and archers, who would be the more welcome here, as there is like to be a very fine war, with much honor and all hopes of advancement, for which I go to gather my Company together, who are now at Montaubon, where they pillage and destroy; yet I hope that, by God's help, I may be able to show that I am their master, even as, my sweet lady, I am thy servant.

"How of that, Alleyne?" continued Sir Nigel, blinking at his squire, with an expression of some pride upon his face. "Have I not told her all that hath befallen us?"

"You have said much, my fair lord; and yet, if I may say so, it is somewhat crowded together, so that my Lady Loring can, mayhap, scarce follow it. Were it in shorter periods—"

"Nay, it boots not [1] how you marshal them, as long as they are all there at the muster. Let my lady have the words, and she will place them in such order as pleases her best. But I would have you add what it would please her to know."

"That will I," said Alleyne blithely, and bent to the task.

"My fair lady and mistress," he wrote:

> God hath had us in His keeping, and my lord is well and in good cheer. He hath won much honor at the jousting before the Prince, when he alone was able to make it good against a very valiant man from France. Touching the moneys, there is enough and to spare until we reach Montaubon. Herewith, my fair lady, I send my humble regards, entreating you that you will give the same to your daughter, the Lady Maude. May the holy saints have you both in their keeping is ever the prayer of thy servant,
>
> ALLEYNE EDRICSON.

[1] *boots not:* makes no difference.

"That is very fairly set forth," said Sir Nigel, nodding his bald head as each sentence was read to him. "And for thyself, Alleyne, if there be any dear friend to whom you would fain give greeting, I can send it for thee within this packet."

"There is none," said Alleyne, sadly.

"Have you no kinsfolk, then?"

"None, save my brother."

"Ha! I had forgotten that there was ill blood betwixt you. But are there none in all England who love thee?"

"None that I dare say so."

"And none whom you love?"

"Nay, I will not say that," said Alleyne.

Sir Nigel shook his head and laughed softly to himself. "I see how it is with you," he said. "Have I not noted your frequent sighs and vacant eye? Is she fair?"

"She is indeed," cried Alleyne from his heart, all tingling at this sudden turn of the talk.

"And good?"

"As an angel."

"And yet she loves you not?"

"Nay, I cannot say that she loves another."

"Then you have hopes?"

"I could not live else."

"Then must you strive to be worthy of her love. Be brave and pure, fearless to the strong and humble to the weak; and so, whether this love prosper or no, you will have fitted yourself to be honored by a maiden's love, which is, in sooth, the highest guerdon which a true knight can hope for."

"Indeed, my lord, I do so strive," said Alleyne; "but she is so sweet, so dainty, and of so noble a spirit, that I fear me that I shall never be worthy of her."

"By thinking so you become worthy. Is she then of noble birth?"

"She is, my lord," faltered Alleyne.

"Of a knightly house?"

"Yes."

"Have a care, Alleyne, have a care!" said Sir Nigel, kindly. "The higher the steed the greater the fall. Hawk not at that which may be beyond thy flight."

"My lord, I know little of the ways and usages of the world," cried Alleyne, "but I would fain ask your rede upon the matter. You have known my father and my kin: is not my family one of good standing and repute?"

"Beyond all question."

"And yet you warn me that I must not place my love too high."

"Were Minstead yours, Alleyne, then, by St. Paul! I cannot think that any family in the land would not be proud to take you among them, seeing that you come of so old a strain. But while the Socman lives—Ha, by my soul! if this is not Sir Oliver's step I am the more mistaken."

As he spoke, a heavy footfall was heard without, and the portly knight flung open the door and strode into the room.

"Why, my little coz," said he, "I have come across to tell you that I live above the barber's in the Rue de la Tour, and that there is a venison pasty in the oven and two flasks of the right vintage on the table. By St. James! a blind man might find the place, for one has but to get in the wind from it, and follow the savory smell. Put on your cloak, then, and come, for Sir Walter Hewett and Sir Robert Briquet, with one or two others, are awaiting us."

"Nay, Oliver, I cannot be with you, for I must to Montaubon this day."

"To Montaubon? But I have heard that your Company is to come with my forty Winchester rascals to Dax."

"If you will take charge of them, Oliver. For I will go to Montaubon with none save my two squires and two archers. Then, when I have found the rest of my Company I shall lead them to Dax. We set forth this morning."

"Then I must back to my pasty," said Sir Oliver. "You will find us at Dax, I doubt not, unless the Prince throw me into prison, for he is very wroth against me."

"And why, Oliver?"

"Pardieu! because I have sent my cartel, gauntlet, and defiance to Sir John Chandos and to Sir William Felton."

"To Chandos? In God's name, Oliver, why have you done this?"

"Because he and the other have used me despitefully."

"And how?"

"Because they have passed me over in choosing those who

should joust for England. Yourself and Audley I could pass, coz, for you are mature men; but who are Wake and Percy and Beauchamp? By my soul! I was prodding for my food into a camp kettle when they were howling for their pap. Is a man of my weight and substance to be thrown aside for the first three half-grown lads who have learned the trick of the tiltyard? But hark ye, coz, I think of sending my cartel also to the Prince."

"Oliver! Oliver! You are mad!"

"Not I, i' faith! I care not a denier whether he be prince or no. By St. James! I see that your squire's eyes are starting from his head like a trussed crab. Well, friend, we are all three men of Hampshire, and not lightly to be jeered at."

"Has he jeered at you then?"

"Pardieu! yes. 'Old Sir Oliver's heart is still stout,' said one of his court. 'Else had it been out of keeping with the rest of him,' quoth the Prince. 'And his arm is strong,' said another. 'So is the backbone of his horse,' quoth the Prince. This very day I will send him my cartel and defiance."

"Nay, nay, my dear Oliver," said Sir Nigel, laying his hand upon his angry friend's arm. "There is naught in this, for it was but saying that you were a strong and robust man, who had need of a good destrier. And as to Chandos and Felton, bethink you that if when you yourself were young the older lances had ever been preferred, how would you then have had the chance to earn the good name and fame which you now bear? You do not ride as light as you did, Oliver, and I ride lighter by the weight of my hair, but it would be an ill thing if in the evening of our lives we showed that our hearts were less true and loyal than of old. If such a knight as Sir Oliver Buttesthorn may turn against his own prince for the sake of a light word, then where are we to look for steadfast faith and constancy?"

"Ah! my dear little coz, it is easy to sit in the sunshine and preach to the man in the shadow. Yet you could ever win me over to your side with that soft voice of yours. Let us think no more of it then. But, holy Mother! I had forgot the pasty, and it will be as scorched as Judas Iscariot! Come, Nigel, lest the foul fiend get the better of me again."

"For one hour, then; for we march at midday. Tell Aylward, Alleyne, that he is to come with me to Montaubon, and to choose one archer for his comrade. The rest will to Dax when the Prince starts, which will be before the feast of the Epiphany. Have Pommers ready at midday with my sycamore lance, and place my harness on the sumpter mule."

With these brief directions, the two old soldiers strode off together, while Alleyne hastened to get all in order for their journey.

Chapter 22

HOW THE COMRADES CAME OVER THE MARCHES OF FRANCE

It was a bright, crisp winter's day when the little party set off from Bordeaux on their journey to Montaubon, where the missing half of their Company had last been heard of. Sir Nigel and Ford had ridden on in advance, the knight upon his hackney, while his great war horse trotted beside his squire. Two hours later Alleyne Edricson followed; for he had the tavern reckoning to settle, and many other duties which fell to him as squire of the body. With him came Aylward and Hordle John, armed as of old, but mounted for their journey upon a pair of clumsy Landes horses, heavy-headed and shambling, but of great endurance, and capable of jogging along all day, even when between the knees of the huge archer, who turned the scale at two hundred and seventy pounds. They took with them the sumpter mules, which carried in panniers the wardrobe and table furniture of Sir Nigel; for the knight, though neither fop nor epicure, was very dainty in small matters and loved, however bare the board or hard the life, that his napery should still be white and his spoon of silver.

There had been frost during the night, and the white hard road rang loud under their horses' irons as they spurred through the east gate of the town, along the same broad highway which the unknown French champion had traversed on the day of the jousts. The three rode abreast, Alleyne Edricson with his eyes cast down and his mind distrait, for his thoughts were busy with the conversation which he had had with Sir Nigel in the morning. Had he done well to say so much, or had he not done better to have said more? What would the knight have said had he confessed to his love for the Lady Maude? Would he cast him off in disgrace, or might he chide him as having abused the shelter of his roof? It had been ready upon his tongue to tell him all, when Sir Oliver had broken in upon them. Perchance Sir Nigel, with his love of all the dying usages of chivalry, might have contrived some strange ordeal or feat of arms by which his love should be put to the test. Alleyne smiled as he wondered what fantastic and wondrous deed would be exacted from him. Whatever it was, he was ready for it, whether it were to hold the lists in the court of the King of Tartary, to carry a cartel to the Sultan of Bagdad, or to serve a term against the wild heathen of Prussia. Sir Nigel had said that his birth was high enough for any lady, if his fortune could but be amended. Often had Alleyne curled his lip at the beggarly craving for land or for gold which blinded man to the higher and more lasting issues of life. Now it seemed as though it were only by this same land and gold that he might hope to reach his heart's desire. But then, again, the Socman of Minstead was no friend to the Constable of Twynham Castle. It might happen that, should he amass riches by some happy fortune of war, this feud might hold the two families aloof. Even if Maude loved him, he knew her too well to think that she would wed him without the blessing of her father. Dark and murky was it all, but hope mounts high in youth, and it ever fluttered over all the turmoil of his thoughts like a white plume amid the shock of horsemen.

It was evening before the three comrades came into Aiguillon. There they found Sir Nigel Loring and Ford safely lodged at the sign of the "Bâton Rouge," where they supped on good fare and slept between lavender-scented sheets. It chanced, however, that a knight of Poitou, Sir Gaston d'Estelle, was staying there on his way back from Lithuania, where he had served a term with the Teutonic knights under the land master of the presbytery of Marienberg. He and Sir Nigel sat late in high converse as to bushments, outfalls, and the intaking of cities, with many tales of warlike men and valiant deeds. Then their talk turned to minstrelsy, and the stranger knight drew forth a cittern, upon which he played the Minnelieder of the north, singing the while in a high cracked voice of Hildebrand and Brunhild and Siegfried, and all the strength and beauty of the land of Almain. To this, Sir Nigel answered with the romances of Sir Eglamour, and of Sir Isumbras, and so through the long winter night they sat by the crackling wood-fire, answering each other's songs until the crowing cocks joined in their concert. Yet, with scarce an hour of rest, Sir Nigel was as blithe and bright as ever as they set forth after breakfast upon their way.

"This Sir Gaston is a very worthy man," said he to his squires as they rode from the "Bâton Rouge." "He hath a very strong desire to advance himself, and would have entered upon some small knightly debate with me, had he not chanced to have his arm bone broken by the kick of a horse. I have conceived a great love for him, and I have promised him that when his bone is mended I will exchange thrusts with him. But we must keep to this road upon the left."

"Nay, my fair lord," quoth Aylward. "The road to Montaubon is over the river, and so through Quercy and the Agenois."

"True, my good Aylward; but I have learned from this worthy knight, who hath come over the French marches, that there is a company of Englishmen who are burning and plundering in the country round Villefranche. I have little doubt, from what he says, that they are those whom we seek."

"By my hilt! it is like enough," said Aylward. "By all accounts they had been so long at Montaubon that there would be little there worth the taking. Then, as they have already been in the south, they would come north to the country of the Aveyron."

"We shall follow the Lot until we come to Cahors, and then cross the marches into Villefranche," said Sir Nigel. "By St. Paul! as we are but a small band, it is very likely that we may have some very honorable and pleasing adventure, for I hear that there is little peace upon the French border."

All morning they rode down a broad and winding road, barred with the shadows of poplars. Sir Nigel rode in front with his squires, while the two archers followed behind with the sumpter mule between them. They had left Aiguillon and the Garonne far to the south, and rode now by the tranquil Lot, which curves blue and placid through a gently rolling country. Alleyne could not but mark that, whereas in Guienne there had been many townlets and few castles, there were now many castles and few houses. On either hand gray walls and square, grim keeps peeped out at every few miles from amid the forests, while the few villages which they passed were all ringed round with rude walls, which spoke of the constant fear and sudden foray of a wild frontier land. Twice during the morning there came bands of horsemen swooping down upon them from the black gateways of wayside strongholds, with short, stern questions as to whence they came and what their errand. Bands of armed men clanked along the highway, and the few lines of laden mules which carried the merchandise of the trader were guarded by armed varlets, or by archers hired for the service.

"The peace of Bretigny hath not made much change in these parts," quoth Sir Nigel, "for the country is overrun with free companions and masterless men. Yonder towers, between the wood and the hill, mark the town of Cahors, and beyond it is the land of France."

After passing Cahors, the party branched away from the main road and, leaving the river to the north of them, followed a smaller track which wound over a vast and desolate plain. This path led them amid marshes and woods, until it brought them out into a glade with a broad stream swirling swiftly down the center of it. Through this the horses splashed their way, and on the farther shore Sir Nigel announced to them that they were now within the borders of the land of France. For some miles they still followed the same lonely track, which led them through a dense wood, and then widening out, curved down to an open rolling country.

If it were grim and desolate upon the English border, however, what can describe the hideous barrenness of this ten times harried tract of France? The whole face of the country was scarred and disfigured, mottled over with the black blotches of burned farmsteadings, and the gray, gaunt gable ends of what had been châteaux. Broken fences, crumbling walls, vineyards littered with stones, the shattered arches of bridges—look where you might, the signs of ruin and rapine met the eye. Here and there only, on the farthest sky line, the gnarled turrets of a castle, or the graceful pinnacles of church or of monastery showed where the forces of the sword or of the spirit had preserved some small islet of security in this universal flood of misery. Moodily and in silence the little party rode along the narrow and irregular track, their hearts weighed down by this far-stretching land of despair. It was indeed a stricken and a blighted country, and a man might have ridden from Auvergne in the north to the marches of Foix, nor ever seen a smiling village or a thriving homestead.

From time to time as they advanced they saw strange lean figures scraping and scratching amid the weeds and thistles, who, on sight of the band of horsemen, threw up their arms and dived in among the brushwood, as shy and as swift as wild animals. More than once, however, they came on families by the wayside, who were too weak from hunger and disease to fly, so that they could but sit like hares on a tussock, with panting chests and terror in their eyes. So gaunt were these poor folk, so worn and spent—with bent and knotted frames, and sullen, hopeless, mutinous faces—that it made the young Englishman heartsick to look upon them. Indeed, it seemed as though all hope and light had gone so far from them that it was not to be brought back; for when Sir Nigel threw down a handful of silver among them, there came no softening of their lined faces, but they clutched greedily at the coins, peering questioningly at him, and champing with their animal jaws. Here and there amid the brushwood the travelers saw the rude bundle of sticks which served them as a home—more like a fowl's nest than the dwelling place of man. Yet why should they build and strive, when the first adventurer who passed would set torch to their thatch, and when their own feudal lord would wring from them with blows and curses the last fruits of their toil? They sat at the lowest depth of human misery and hugged a bitter comfort to their souls as they realized that they could go no lower. Yet they had still the human gift of speech, and would take council among themselves in their brushwood hovels, glaring with bleared eyes and pointing with thin fingers at the great widespread châteaux which ate like a cancer into the life of the countryside. When such men, who are beyond hope and fear, begin in their dim minds to see the source of their woes, it may be an evil time for those who have wronged them. The weak man becomes strong when he has nothing, for then only can he feel the wild, mad thrill of despair. High and strong the château, lowly and weak the brushwood hut; but God help the seigneur and his lady when the men of the brushwood set their hands to the work of revenge!

Through such country did the party ride for eight, or it might be for nine, miles, until the sun began to slope down in the west and their shadows to stream down the road in front of them. Wary and careful they must be, with watchful eyes to the right and the left, for this was no man's land, and their only passports were those which hung from their belts. Frenchman and Englishman, Gascon and Provençal, Brabanter, tardvenu, scorcher, flayer, and free companion wandered and struggled over the whole of this accursed district. So bare and cheerless was the outlook, and so few and poor the dwellings, that Sir Nigel began to have fears as to whether he might find food and quarters for his little troop. It was a relief to him, therefore, when their narrow track opened out upon a larger road, and they saw some little way down it a square white house with a great bunch of holly hung out at the end of a stick from one of the upper windows.

"By St. Paul!" said he, "I am right glad; for I had feared that we might have neither provant nor herbergage. Ride on, Alleyne, and tell this innkeeper that an English knight with his party will lodge with him this night."

Alleyne set spurs to his horse and reached the inn door a long bowshot before his companions. Neither varlet nor ostler could be seen, so he pushed open the door and called loudly for the landlord. Three times he shouted, but, receiving no reply, he opened an inner door and advanced into the chief guestroom of the hostel.

A very cheerful wood fire was sputtering and cracking in an open grate at the further end of the apartment. At one side of this fire, in a high-backed oak chair, sat a lady, her face turned towards the door. The firelight played over her features, and Alleyne thought that he had never seen such queenly power, such dignity and strength, upon a woman's face. She might have been five-and-thirty years of age, with aquiline nose, firm yet sensitive mouth, dark curving brows, and deep-set eyes which shone and sparkled with a shifting brilliancy. Beautiful as she was, it was not her beauty which impressed itself upon the beholder; it was her strength, her power, the sense of wisdom which hung over the broad white brow, the decision which lay in the square jaw and delicately molded chin. A chaplet of pearls sparkled amid her black hair, with a gauze of silver network flowing back from it over her shoulders; a black mantle was swathed round her, and she leaned back in her chair as one who is fresh from a journey.

In the opposite corner there sat a very burly and broad-shouldered man, clad in a black jerkin trimmed with sable, with a black velvet cap with curling white feather cocked upon the side of his head. A flask of red wine stood at his elbow, and he seemed to be very much at his ease, for his feet were stuck up on a stool, and between his thighs he held a dish full of nuts. These he cracked between his strong white teeth and chewed in a leisurely way, casting the shells into the blaze. As Alleyne gazed in at him he turned his face half-round and cocked an eye at him over his shoulder. It seemed to the young Englishman that he had never seen so hideous a face, for the eyes were of the lightest green, the nose was broken and driven inwards, while the whole countenance was seared and puckered with wounds. The voice, too, when he spoke, was as deep and as fierce as the growl of a beast of prey.

"Young man," said he, "I know not who you may be, and I am not much inclined to bestir myself, but if it were not that I am bent upon taking my ease, I swear, by the sword of Joshua! that I would lay my dog whip across your shoulders for daring to fill the air with these discordant bellowings."

Taken aback at this ungentle speech, and scarce knowing how to answer it fitly in the presence of the lady, Alleyne stood with his hand upon the handle of the door, while Sir Nigel and his companions dismounted. At the sound of these fresh voices, and of the tongue in which they spoke, the stranger crashed his dish of nuts down upon the floor and began himself to call for the landlord until the whole house re-echoed with his roarings. With an ashen face the white-aproned host came running at his call, his hands shaking and his very hair bristling with apprehension. "For the sake of God, sirs," he whispered as he passed, "speak him fair and do not rouse him! For the love of the Virgin, be mild with him!"

"Who is this, then?" asked Sir Nigel.

Alleyne was about to explain, when a fresh roar from the stranger interrupted him.

"Thou villain innkeeper," he shouted, "did I not ask you when I brought my lady here whether your inn was clean?"

"You did, sire."

"Did I not very particularly ask you whether there were any vermin in it?"

"You did, sire."

"And you answered me?"

"That there were not, sire."

"And yet ere I have been here an hour I find Englishmen crawling about within it. Where are we to be free from this pestilent race? Can a Frenchman upon French land not sit down in a French auberge [1] without having his ears pained by the clack of their hideous talk? Send them packing, innkeeper, or it may be the worse for them and for you."

"I will, sire, I will!" cried the frightened host, and bustled from the room, while the soft, soothing voice of the woman was heard remonstrating with her furious companion.

"Indeed, gentlemen, you had best go," said mine host. "It is but six miles to Villefranche, where there are very good quarters at the sign of the 'Lion Rouge.' "

"Nay," answered Sir Nigel, "I cannot go until I have seen more of this person, for he appears to be a man from whom much is to be hoped. What is his name and title?"

"It is not for my lips to name it unless by his desire. But I beg and pray you, gentlemen, that you will go from my house, for I know not what may come of it if his rage should gain the mastery of him."

"By St. Paul!" lisped Sir Nigel, "this is certainly a man whom it is worth journeying far to know. Go tell him that a humble knight of England would make his further honorable acquaintance, not from any presumption, pride, or ill-will, but for the advancement of chivalry and the glory of our ladies. Give him greeting from Sir Nigel Loring, and say that the glove which I bear in my cap belongs to the most peerless and lovely of her sex, whom I am now ready to uphold against any lady whose claim he might be desirous of advancing."

The landlord was hesitating whether to carry this message or no, when the door of the inner room was flung open, and the

[1] *auberge* (ōb′bĕrzh′): French for "inn."

stranger bounded out like a panther from its den, his hair bristling and his deformed face convulsed with anger.

"Still here!" he snarled. "Dogs of England, must ye be lashed hence? Tiphaine, my sword!" He turned to seize his weapon, but as he did so, his gaze fell upon the blazonry of Sir Nigel's shield, and he stood staring, while the fire in his strange green eyes softened into a sly and humorous twinkle.

"Mort Dieu!" cried he, "it is my little swordsman of Bordeaux. I should remember that coat armor, seeing that it is but three days since I looked upon it in the lists by Garonne. Ah! Sir Nigel, Sir Nigel! you owe me a return for this," and he touched his right arm, which was girt round just under the shoulder with a silken kerchief.

But the surprise of the stranger at the sight of Sir Nigel was as nothing compared with the astonishment and the delight which shone upon the face of the knight of Hampshire as he looked upon the strange face of the Frenchman. Twice he opened his mouth, and twice he peered again, as though to assure himself that his eyes had not played him a trick.

"Bertrand!" he gasped at last. "Bertrand du Guesclin!"

"By St. Ives!" shouted the French soldier, with a hoarse roar of laughter, "it is well that I should ride with my visor down, for he that has once seen my face does not need to be told my name. It is indeed I, Sir Nigel, and here is my hand! I give you my word that there are but three Englishmen in this world whom I would touch, save with the sharp edge of the sword: the prince is one, Chandos the second, and you the third; for I have heard much that is good of you."

"I am growing aged, and am somewhat spent in the wars," quoth Sir Nigel; "but I can lay by my sword now with an easy mind, for I can say that I have crossed swords with him who hath the bravest heart and the strongest arm of all this great kingdom of France. I have longed for it, I have dreamed of it, and now I can scarce bring my mind to understand that this great honor hath indeed been mine."

"By the Virgin of Rennes! you have given me cause to be very certain of it," said Du Guesclin, with a gleam of his broad white teeth.

"And perhaps, most honored sir, it would please you to continue the debate. Perhaps you would condescend to go farther into the matter. God He knows that I am unworthy of such honor, yet I can show my four-and-sixty quarterings, and I have been present at some bickerings and scufflings during these twenty years."

"Your fame is very well known to me, and I shall ask my lady to enter your name upon my tablets," said Sir Bertrand. "There are many who wish to advance themselves, and who bide their turn, for I refuse no man who comes on such an errand. At present it may not be, for mine arm is stiff from this small touch, and I would fain do you full honor when we cross swords again. Come in with me, and let your squires come also, that my sweet spouse, the Lady Tiphaine, may say that she hath seen so famed and gentle a knight."

Into the chamber they went in all peace and concord, where the Lady Tiphaine sat like queen on throne for each in turn to be presented to her. Sooth to say, the stout heart of Sir Nigel, which cared little for the wrath of her lionlike spouse, was somewhat shaken by the calm, cold face of this stately dame, for twenty years of camp life had left him more at ease in the lists than in a lady's boudoir. He bethought him, too, as he looked at her set lips and deep-set questioning eyes, that he had heard strange tales of this same Lady Tiphaine du Guesclin. Was it not she who was said to lay hands upon the sick and raise them from their couches when the leeches had spent their last nostrums? Had she not forecast the future, and were there not times when in the loneliness of her chamber she was heard to hold converse with some being upon whom mortal eye never rested—some dark familiar who passed where doors were barred and windows high? Sir Nigel sunk his eye and marked a cross on the side of his leg as he greeted this dangerous dame, and yet ere five minutes had passed he was hers, and not he only but his two young squires as well. The mind had gone out of them, and they could but look at this woman and listen to the words which fell from her lips—words which thrilled through their nerves and stirred their souls like the battle call of a bugle.

Often in peaceful afterdays was Alleyne to think of that scene of the wayside inn of Auvergne. The shadows of evening had fallen, and the corners of the long, low, wood-paneled room were draped in darkness. The sputtering wood fire threw out a circle of red flickering light which played over the little group of wayfarers and showed up every line and shadow upon their faces. Sir Nigel sat with elbows upon knees, and chin upon hands, his patch still covering one eye, but his other shining like a star, while the ruddy light gleamed upon his smooth white head. Ford was seated at his left, his lips parted, his eyes staring, and a fleck of deep color on either cheek, his limbs all rigid, as one who fears to move. On the other side the famous French captain leaned back in his chair, a litter of nutshells upon his lap, his huge head half-buried in a cushion, while his eyes wandered with an amused gleam from his dame to the staring, enraptured Englishmen. Then, last of all, that pale clear-cut face, that sweet clear voice, with its high thrilling talk of the deathlessness of glory, of the worthlessness of life, of the pain of ignoble joys, and of the joy which lies in all pains which lead to a noble end. Still, as the shadows deepened, she spoke of valor and virtue, of loyalty, honor, and fame, and still they sat drinking in her words while the fire burned down and the red ash turned to gray.

"By the sainted Ives!" cried Du Guesclin at last, "it is time that we spoke of what we are to do this night, for I cannot think that in this wayside auberge there are fit quarters for an honorable company."

Sir Nigel gave a long sigh as he came back from the dreams of chivalry and hardihood into which this strange woman's words had wafted him. "I care not where I sleep," said he; "but these are, indeed, somewhat rude lodgings for this fair lady."

"What contents my lord contents me," quoth she. "I perceive, Sir Nigel, that you are under vow," she added, glancing at his covered eye.

"It is my purpose to attempt some small deed," he answered.

"And the glove—is it your lady's?"

"It is indeed my sweet wife's."

"Who is doubtless proud of you."

"Say rather I of her," quoth he quickly. "God He knows that I am not worthy to be her humble servant. It is easy, lady, for a man to ride forth in the light of day, and do his devoir when all men have eyes for him. But in a woman's heart there is a strength and truth which asks no praise, and can but be known to him whose treasure it is."

The Lady Tiphaine smiled across at her husband. "You have

often told me, Bertrand, that there were very gentle knights amongst the English," quoth she.

"Aye, aye," said he moodily. "But to horse, Sir Nigel, you and yours and we shall seek the château of Sir Tristram de Roche-fort, which is two miles on this side of Villefranche. He is Seneschal of Auvergne, and mine old war companion."

"Certes, he would have a welcome for you," quoth Sir Nigel; "but, indeed, he might look askance at one who comes without permit over the marches."

"By the Virgin! when he learns that you have come to draw away these rascals, he will be very blithe to look upon your face. Innkeeper, here are ten gold pieces. What is over and above your reckoning you may take off from your charges to the next needy knight who comes this way. Come then, for it grows late, and the horses are stamping in the roadway."

The Lady Tiphaine and her spouse sprang upon their steeds without setting feet to stirrup, and away they jingled down the white moonlit highway, with Sir Nigel at the lady's bridle arm and Ford a spear's length behind them. Alleyne had lingered for an instant in the passage, and as he did, there came a wild outcry from a chamber upon the left, and out there ran Aylward and John, laughing together like two schoolboys who are bent upon a prank. At sight of Alleyne they slunk past him with somewhat of a shamefaced air and, springing upon their horses, galloped after their party. The hubbub within the chamber did not cease, however, but rather increased, with yells of: "A moi, mes amis! A moi, camarades! A moi, l'honorable champion de l'Evêque de Montaubon! A la recouse de l'église sainte!" [1] So shrill was the outcry that both the innkeeper and Alleyne, with every varlet within hearing, rushed wildly to the scene of the uproar.

It was indeed a singular scene which met their eyes. The room was a long and lofty one, stone floored and bare, with a fire at the further end upon which a great pot was boiling. A deal table ran down the center, with a wooden wine pitcher upon it, and two horn cups. Some way from it was a smaller table, with a single beaker and a broken wine bottle. From the heavy wooden

[1] *"A moi . . . sainte!":* "To me, my friends! To me, comrades! To me, the honorable champion of the Bishop of Montaubon! To the aid of the holy Church!"

rafters which formed the roof there hung rows of hooks which held up sides of bacon, joints of smoked beef, and strings of onions for winter use. In the very center of all these, upon the largest hook of all, there hung a fat little red-faced man with enormous whiskers, kicking madly in the air and clawing at rafters, hams, and all else that was within hand-grasp. The huge steel hook had been passed through the collar of his leather jerkin, and there he hung, like a fish on a line, writhing, twisting, and screaming, but utterly unable to free himself from his extraordinary position. It was not until Alleyne and the landlord had mounted on the table that they were able to lift him down, when he sank, gasping with rage, into a seat and rolled his eyes round in every direction.

"Has he gone?" quoth he.

"Gone? Who?"

"He, the man with the red head, the giant man."

"Yes," said Alleyne, "he hath gone."

"And comes not back?"

"No."

"The better for him!" cried the little man, with a long sigh of relief. "Mon Dieu! What! am I not the champion of the Bishop of Montaubon? Ah, could I have descended, could I have come down, ere he fled! Then you would have seen. You would have beheld a spectacle then. There would have been one rascal the less upon earth. Ma foi, yes!"

"Good master Pelligny," said the landlord, "these gentlemen have not gone very fast, and I have a horse in the stable at your disposal, for I would rather have such bloody doings as you threaten outside the four walls of mine auberge."

"I hurt my leg and cannot ride," quoth the bishop's champion. "I strained a sinew on the day that I slew the three men at Castelnau."

"God save you, master Pelligny!" cried the landlord. "It must be an awesome thing to have so much blood upon one's soul. And yet I do not wish to see so valiant a man mishandled, and so I will, for friendship's sake, ride after this Englishman and bring him back to you."

"You shall not stir," cried the champion, seizing the innkeeper in a convulsive grasp. "I have a love for you, Gaston, and I would not bring your house into ill repute, nor do such scath to these walls and chattels as must befall if two such men as this Englishman and I fall to work here."

"Nay, think not of me!" cried the innkeeper. "What are my walls when set against the honor of François Poursuivant d'Amour Pelligny, champion of the Bishop of Montaubon? My horse, André!"

"By the saints, no! Gaston, I will not have it! You have said truly that it is an awesome thing to have such rough work upon one's soul. I am but a rude soldier, yet I have a mind. Mon Dieu! I reflect, I weigh, I balance. Shall I not meet this man again? Shall I not bear him in mind? Shall I not know him by his great paws and his red head? Ma foi, yes!"

"And may I ask, sir," said Alleyne, "why it is that you call yourself champion of the Bishop of Montaubon?"

"You may ask aught which it is becoming to me to answer. The bishop hath need of a champion, because, if any cause be set to test of combat, it would scarce become his office to go down into the lists with leather and shield and cudgel to exchange blows with any varlet. He looks around him, then, for some tried fighting man, some honest smiter who can give a blow or take one. It is not for me to say how far he hath succeeded, but it is sooth that he who thinks that he hath but to do with the Bishop of Montaubon, finds himself face to face with François Poursuivant d'Amour Pelligny."

At this moment there was a clatter of hoofs upon the road, and a varlet by the door cried out that one of the Englishmen was coming back. The champion looked wildly about for some corner of safety, and was clambering up towards the window, when Ford's voice sounded from without, calling upon Alleyne to hasten, or he might scarce find his way. Bidding adieu to landlord and to champion, therefore, he set off at a gallop, and soon overtook the two archers.

"A pretty thing this, John," said he. "Thou wilt have holy Church upon you if you hang her champions upon iron hooks in an inn kitchen."

"It was done without thinking," he answered apologetically, while Aylward burst into a shout of laughter.

"By my hilt! mon petit," said he, "you would have laughed also could you have seen it. For this man was so swollen with pride that he would neither drink with us, nor sit at the same table with us, nor as much as answer a question, but must needs talk to the varlet all the time that it was well there was peace, and that he had slain more Englishmen than there were tags to his doublet. Our good old John could scarce lay his tongue to French enough to answer him, so he must needs reach out his great hand to him and place him very gently where you saw him. But we must on, for I can scarce hear their hoofs upon the road."

"I think that I can see them yet," said Ford, peering down the moonlit road.

"Pardieu! yes. Now they ride forth from the shadow. And yonder dark clump is the Castle of Villefranche. En avant, camarades! or Sir Nigel may reach the gates before us. But hark, mes amis, what sound is that?"

As he spoke, the hoarse blast of a horn was heard from some woods upon the right. An answering call rung forth upon their left, and hard upon it two others from behind them.

"They are the horns of swineherds," quoth Aylward. "Though why they blow them so late I cannot tell."

"Let us on, then," said Ford, and the whole party, setting their spurs to their horses, soon found themselves at the Castle of Villefranche, where the drawbridge had already been lowered and the portcullis raised in response to the summons of Du Guesclin.

Chapter 23

HOW THE BLESSED HOUR OF SIGHT CAME TO THE LADY TIPHAINE

Sir Tristram de Rochefort, Seneschal of Auvergne and Lord of Villefranche, was a fierce and renowned soldier who had grown gray in the English wars. As lord of the marches and guardian of an exposed countryside, there was little rest for him even in times of so-called peace, and his whole life was spent in raids and outfalls upon the Brabanters, latecomers, flayers, free companions, and roving archers who wandered over his province. At times he would come back in triumph, and a dozen corpses swinging from the summit of his keep would warn evil-doers that there was still a law in the land. At others his ventures were not so happy, and he and his troop would spur it over the drawbridge with clatter of hoofs hard at their heels and whistle of arrows about their ears. Hard he was of hand and harder of heart, hated by his foes, and yet not loved by those whom he protected, for twice he had been taken prisoner, and twice his ransom had been wrung by dint of blows and tortures out of the starving peasants and ruined farmers. Wolves or watchdogs, it was hard to say from which the sheep had most to fear.

The Castle of Villefranche was harsh and stern as its master. A broad moat, a high outer wall turreted at the corners, with a great black keep towering above all—so it lay before them in the moonlight. By the light of two flambeaux protruded through the narrow slit-shaped openings at either side of the ponderous gate, they caught a glimpse of the glitter of fierce eyes and of the gleam of the weapons of the guard. The sight of the two-headed eagle of Du Guesclin, however, was a passport into any fortalice in France, and ere they had passed the gate the old border knight came running forwards with hands out-thrown to greet his famous countryman. Nor was he less glad to see Sir Nigel, when the Englishman's errand was explained to him, for these archers had been a sore thorn in his side and had routed two expeditions which he had sent against them. A happy day it would be for the Seneschal of Auvergne when he should learn that the last yew bow was over the marches.

The material for a feast was ever at hand in days when, if there was grim want in the cottage, there was at least rude plenty in the castle. Within an hour the guests were seated around a board which creaked under the great pasties and joints of meat, varied by those more dainty dishes in which the French excelled, the spiced ortolan and the truffled beccaficoes. The Lady Rochefort, a bright and laughter-loving dame, sat upon the left of her warlike spouse, with Lady Tiphaine upon the right. Beneath sat Du Guesclin and Sir Nigel, with Sir Amory Monticourt, of the order of the Hospitalers, and Sir Otto Harnit, a wandering knight from the kingdom of Bohemia. These, with Alleyne and Ford, four French squires, and the castle chaplain, made the company who sat together that night and made good cheer in the Castle of Villefranche. The great fire crackled in the grate, the hooded hawks slept upon their perches, the rough deerhounds with expectant eyes crouched upon the tiled floor; close at the elbows of the guests stood the dapper little lilac-coated pages; the laugh and jest circled round, and all was harmony and comfort. Little they recked of the brushwood men who crouched in their rags along the fringe of the forest and looked with wild and haggard eyes at the rich, warm glow which shot a golden bar of light from the high arched windows of the castle.

Supper over, the tables dormant were cleared away as by magic, and trestles and bancals arranged around the blazing fire, for there was a bitter nip in the air. The Lady Tiphaine had sunk back in her cushioned chair, and her long dark lashes drooped low over her sparkling eyes. Alleyne, glancing at her, noted that her breath came quick and short, and that her cheeks had blanched to a lily white. Du Guesclin eyed her keenly from time to time, and passed his broad brown fingers through his crisp, curly black hair with the air of a man who is perplexed in his mind.

"These folk here," said the knight of Bohemia, "they do not seem too well fed."

"Ah, canaille!" [1] cried the Lord of Villefranche. "You would scarce credit it, and yet it is sooth that when I was taken at Poitiers, it was all that my wife and foster brother could do to raise the money from them for my ransom. The sulky dogs would rather have three twists of a rack [2] or the thumbkins [3] for an hour, than pay out a denier for their own feudal father and liege lord. Yet there is not one of them but hath an old stocking full of gold pieces hid away in a snug corner."

"Why do they not buy food then?" asked Sir Nigel. "By St. Paul! it seemed to me their bones were breaking through their skin."

"It is their grutching and grumbling which makes them thin. We have a saying here, Sir Nigel, that if you pummel Jacques

[1] *canaille* (kȧ·nāl′): French for "riffraff, low-class people." [2] *rack:* a stretching machine used for torture. [3] *thumbkin* (thŭm′kin): thumbscrew, used for torture.

Bonhomme he will pat you, but if you pat him he will pummel you. Doubtless you find it so in England."

"Ma foi, no!" said Sir Nigel. "I have two Englishmen of this class in my train, who are at this instant, I make little doubt, as full of your wine as any cask in your cellar. He who pummeled them might come by such a pat as he would be likely to remember."

"I cannot understand it," quoth the Seneschal, "for the English knights and nobles whom I have met were not men to brook the insolence of the base born."

"Perchance, my fair lord, the poor folk are sweeter and of a better countenance in England," laughed the Lady Rochefort. "Mon Dieu! you cannot conceive to yourself how ugly they are! Without hair, without teeth, all twisted and bent; for me, I cannot think how the good God ever came to make such people. I cannot bear it, I, and so my trusty Raoul goes ever before me with a cudgel to drive them from my path."

"Yet they have souls, fair lady, they have souls!" murmured the chaplain, a white-haired man with a weary, patient face.

"So I have heard you tell them," said the lord of the castle; "and for myself, father, though I am a true son of holy Church, yet I think that you were better employed in saying your mass and in teaching the children of my men-at-arms than in going over the countryside to put ideas in these folks' heads which would never have been there but for you. I have heard that you have said to them that their souls are as good as ours, and that it is likely that in another life they may stand as high as the oldest blood of Auvergne. For my part, I believe that there are so many worthy knights and gallant gentlemen in heaven who know how such things should be arranged that there is little fear that we shall find ourselves mixed up with base roturiers and swineherds. Tell your beads, father, and con your psalter,[1] but do not come between me and those whom the King has given to me!"

"God help them!" cried the old priest. "A higher king than yours has given them to me, and I tell you here in your own castle hall, Sir Tristram de Rochefort, that you have sinned deeply in your dealings with these poor folk, and that the hour will come, and may even now be at hand, when God's hand will be heavy

[1] *Tell . . . psalter:* he means "stick to your religion."

upon you for what you have done." He rose as he spoke, and walked slowly from the room.

"Peste take him!" cried the French knight. "Now, what is a man to do with a priest, Sir Bertrand?—for one can neither fight him like a man nor coax him like a woman."

"Ah, Sir Bertrand knows, the naughty one!" cried the Lady Rochefort. "Have we not all heard how he went to Avignon and squeezed fifty thousand crowns out of the Pope?"

"Ma foi!" said Sir Nigel, looking with a mixture of horror and admiration at Du Guesclin. "Did not your heart sink within you? Were you not smitten with fears? Have you not felt a curse hang over you?"

"I have not observed it," said the Frenchman carelessly. "But, by St. Ives! Tristram, this chaplain of yours seems to me to be a worthy man, and you should give heed to his words, for though I care nothing for the curse of a bad pope, it would be a grief to me to have aught but a blessing from a good priest."

"Hark to that, my fair lord," cried the Lady Rochefort. "Take heed, I pray thee, for I do not wish to have a blight cast over me, nor a palsy of the limbs. I remember that once before you angered Father Stephen, and my tirewoman said that I lost more hair in seven days than ever before in a month."

"If that be sign of sin, then, by St. Paul! I have much upon my soul," said Sir Nigel, amid a general laugh. "But in very truth, Sir Tristram, if I may venture a word of counsel, I should advise that you make your peace with this good man."

"He shall have four silver candlesticks," said the Seneschal moodily. "And yet I would that he would leave the folk alone. You cannot conceive in your mind how stubborn and brainless they are. Mules and pigs are full of reason beside them. God He knows that I have had great patience with them. It was but last week that, having to raise some money, I called up to the castle Jean Goubert, who, as all men know, has a casketful of gold pieces hidden away in some hollow tree. I give you my word that I did not so much as lay a stripe upon his fool's back, but after speaking with him, and telling him how needful the money was to me, I left him for the night to think over the matter in my dungeon. What think you that the dog did? Why, in the morning we found that he had made a rope from strips of his leathern jerkin and had hung himself to the bar of the window."

"For me, I cannot conceive such wickedness!" cried the lady.

"And there was Gertrude Le Bœuf, as fair a maiden as eye could see, but as bad and bitter as the rest of them. When young Amory de Valance was here last Lammastide he looked kindly upon the girl, and even spoke of taking her into his service. What does she do, with her dog of a father? Why, they tie themselves together and leap into the Linden Pool, where the water is five spears'-lengths deep. I give you my word that it was a great grief to young Amory, and it was days ere he could cast it from his mind. But how can one serve people who are so foolish and so ungrateful?"

Whilst the Seneschal of Villefranche had been detailing the evil doings of his tenants, Alleyne had been unable to take his eyes from the face of Lady Tiphaine. She had lain back in her chair, with drooping eyelids and bloodless face, so that he had feared at first her journey had weighed heavily upon her, and that the strength was ebbing out of her. Of a sudden, however, there came a change, for a dash of bright color flickered up on to either cheek, and her lids were slowly raised again upon eyes which sparkled with such luster as Alleyne had never seen in human eyes before, while their gaze was fixed intently, not on the company, but on the dark tapestry which draped the wall. So transformed and so ethereal was her expression that Alleyne, in his loftiest dream of archangel or of seraph, had never pictured so sweet, so womanly, and yet so wise a face. Glancing at Du Guesclin, Alleyne saw that he also was watching his wife closely, and from the twitching of his features, and the beads upon his brick-colored brow, it was easy to see that he was deeply agitated by the change which he marked in her.

"How is it with you, lady?" he asked at last, in a tremulous voice.

Her eyes remained fixed intently upon the wall, and there was a long pause ere she answered him. Her voice, too, which had been so clear and ringing, was now low and muffled, as that of one who speaks from a distance.

"All is very well with me, Bertrand," said she. "The blessed hour of sight has come round to me again."

"I could see it come! I could see it come!" he exclaimed, passing his fingers through his hair with the same perplexed expression as before.

"This is untoward, Sir Tristram," he said at last. "And I scarce know in what words to make it clear to you, and to your fair wife, and to Sir Nigel Loring, and to these other stranger knights. My tongue is a blunt one, and fitter to shout word of command than to clear up such a matter as this, of which I can myself understand little. This, however, I know, that my wife is come of a very sainted race, whom God hath in His wisdom endowed with wondrous powers, so that Tiphaine Raquenel was known throughout Brittany ere ever I first saw her at Dinan. Yet these powers are ever used for good, and they are the gift of God and not of the devil, which is the difference betwixt white magic and black."

"Perchance it would be as well that we should send for Father Stephen," said Sir Tristram.

"It would be best that he should come," cried the Hospitaler.

"And bring with him a flask of holy water," added the knight of Bohemia.

"Not so, gentlemen," answered Sir Bertrand. "It is not needful that this priest should be called, and it is in my mind that in asking for this ye cast some slight shadow or slur upon the good name of my wife, as though it were still doubtful whether her power came to her from above or below. If ye have indeed such a doubt, I pray that you will say so, that we may discuss the matter in a fitting way."

"For myself," said Sir Nigel, "I have heard such words fall from the lips of this lady that I am of the opinion that there is no woman, save only one, who can be in any way compared to her in beauty and in goodness. Should any gentleman think otherwise, I should deem it great honor to run a small course with him, or debate the matter in whatever way might be most pleasing to him."

"Nay, it would ill become me to cast a slur upon a lady who is both my guest and the wife of my comrade-in-arms," said the Seneschal of Villefranche. "I have perceived also that on her mantle there is marked a silver cross, which is surely sign enough that there is naught of evil in these strange powers which you say that she possesses."

This argument of the Seneschal's appealed so powerfully to the Bohemian and to the Hospitaler that they at once intimated that their objections had been entirely overcome, while even the

Lady Rochefort, who had sat shivering and crossing herself, ceased to cast glances at the door, and allowed her fears to turn to curiosity.

"Among the gifts which have been vouchsafed to my wife," said Du Guesclin, "there is the wondrous one of seeing into the future; but it comes very seldom upon her, and goes as quickly, for none can command it. The blessed hour of sight, as she hath named it, has come but twice since I have known her, and I can vouch for it that all that she hath told me was true, for on the evening of the Battle of Auray she said that the morrow would be an ill day for me and for Charles of Blois. Ere the sun had sunk again he was dead, and I the prisoner of Sir John Chandos. Yet it is not every question that she can answer, but only those—"

"Bertrand, Bertrand!" cried the lady in the same muttering far-away voice, "the blessed hour passes. Use it, Bertrand, while you may."

"I will, my sweet. Tell me, then, what fortune comes upon me?"

"Danger, Bertrand—deadly, pressing danger—which creeps upon you and you know it not."

The French soldier burst into a thunderous laugh, and his green eyes twinkled with amusement. "At what time during these twenty years would not that have been a true word?" he cried. "Danger is in the air that I breathe. But is this so very close, Tiphaine?"

"Here—now—close upon you!" The words came out in broken, strenuous speech, while the lady's fair face was writhed and drawn, like that of one who looks upon a horror which strikes the words from her lips. Du Guesclin gazed round the tapestried room, at the screens, the tables, the abace, the credence, the buffet with its silver salver, and the half-circle of friendly, wondering faces. There was an utter stillness, save for the sharp breathing of the Lady Tiphaine and for the gentle soughing of the wind outside, which wafted to their ears the distant call upon a swineherd's horn.

"The danger may abide," said he, shrugging his broad shoulders. "And now, Tiphaine, tell us what will come of this war in Spain."

"I can see little," she answered, straining her eyes and puckering her brow, as one who would fain clear her sight. "There are mountains, and dry plains, and flash of arms, and shouting of battle cries. Yet it is whispered to me that by failure you will succeed."

"Ha! Sir Nigel, how like you that?" quoth Bertrand, shaking his head. "It is like mead and vinegar, half-sweet, half-sour. And is there no question which you would ask my lady?"

"Certes there is. I would fain know, fair lady, how all things are at Twynham Castle, and above all how my sweet lady employs herself."

"To answer this I would fain lay hand upon one whose thoughts turn strongly to this castle which you have named. Nay, my Lord Loring, it is whispered to me that there is another here who hath thought more deeply of it than you."

"Thought more of mine own home?" cried Sir Nigel. "Lady, I fear that in this matter at least you are mistaken."

"Not so, Sir Nigel. Come hither, young man, young English squire with the gray eyes! Now give me your hand, and place it here across my brow, that I may see that which you have seen. What is this that rises before me? Mist, mist, rolling mist with a square black tower above it. See, it shreds out, it thins, it rises, and there lies a castle in green plain, with the sea beneath it, and a great church within a bowshot. There are two rivers which run through the meadows, and between them lie the tents of the besiegers."

"The besiegers!" cried Alleyne, Ford, and Sir Nigel, all three in a breath.

"Yes, truly, and they press hard upon the castle, for they are an exceeding multitude, and full of courage. See how they storm and rage against the gate, while some rear ladders, and others, line after line, sweep the walls with their arrows. They are many leaders who shout and beckon, and one, a tall man with a golden beard, who stands before the gate stamping his foot and hallooing them on, as a hunter doth the hounds. But those in the castle fight bravely. There is a woman, two women, who stand upon the walls and give heart to the men-at-arms. They shower down arrows, darts, and great stones. Ah! they have struck down the tall leader, and the others give back. The mist thickens, and I can see no more."

"By St. Paul!" said Sir Nigel, "I do not think that there can be any such doings at Christchurch, and I am very easy of the fortalice so long as my sweet wife hangs the key of the outer bailey at the head of her bed. Yet I will not deny that you have pictured the castle as well as I could have done myself, and I am full of wonderment at all that I have heard and seen."

"I would, Lady Tiphaine," cried the Lady Rochefort, "that you would use your power to tell me what hath befallen my golden bracelet, which I wore when hawking upon the second Sunday of Advent, and have never set eyes upon since."

"Nay, lady," said Du Guesclin, "it does not befit so great and wondrous a power to pry and search and play the varlet, even to the beautiful châtelaine of Villefranche. Ask a worthy question, and, with the blessing of God, you shall have a worthy answer."

"Then I would fain ask," cried one of the French squires, "as to which may hope to conquer in these wars betwixt the English and ourselves."

"Both will conquer and each will hold its own," answered the Lady Tiphaine.

"Then we shall still hold Gascony and Guienne?" cried Sir Nigel.

The lady shook her head. "French land, French blood, French speech," she answered. "They are French, and France shall have them."

"But not Bordeaux?" cried Sir Nigel excitedly.

"Bordeaux also is for France."

"But Calais?"

"Calais too."

"Woe worth me then, and ill hail to these evil words! If Bordeaux and Calais be gone, then what is left for England?"

"It seems indeed that there are evil times coming upon your country," said Du Guesclin. "In our fondest hopes we never thought to hold Bordeaux. By St. Ives! this news hath warmed the heart within me. Our dear country will then be very great in the future, Tiphaine?"

"Great and rich and beautiful," she cried. "Far down the course of time I can see her still leading the nations, a wayward queen among the peoples, great in war, but greater in peace, quick in thought, deft in action, with her people's will for her sole monarch, from the sands of Calais to the blue seas of the south."

"Ha!" cried Du Guesclin, with his eyes flashing in triumph, "you hear her, Sir Nigel?—and she never yet said word which was not sooth."

The English knight shook his head moodily. "What of my own poor country?" said he. "I fear, lady, that what you have said bodes but small good for her."

The lady sat with parted lips, and her breath came quick and fast. "My God!" she cried, "what is this that is shown me? Whence come they, these peoples, these lordly nations, these mighty countries which rise up before me? I look beyond, and others rise, and yet others, far and farther to the shores of the uttermost waters. They crowd! They swarm! The world is given to them, and it resounds with the clang of their hammers and the ringing of their church bells. They call them many names, and they rule them this way or that, but they are all English, for I can hear the voices of the people. On I go, and onwards over seas where man hath never yet sailed, and I see a great land under new stars and a stranger sky, and still the land is England. Where have her children not gone? What have they not done? Her banner is planted on ice. Her banner is scorched in the sun. She lies athwart the lands, and her shadow is over the seas. Bertrand, Bertrand! we are undone, for the buds of her bud are even as our choicest flower!" Her voice rose to a wild cry, and throwing up her arms she sank back, white and nerveless, into the deep oaken chair.

"It is over," said Du Guesclin moodily, as he raised her drooping head with his strong brown hand. "Wine for the lady, squire! The blessed hour of sight hath passed."

Chapter 24

HOW THE BRUSHWOOD MEN CAME TO THE CHATEAU OF VILLEFRANCHE

It was late ere Alleyne Edricson, having carried Sir Nigel the goblet of spiced wine which it was his custom to drink after the curling of his hair, was able at last to seek his chamber. It was a stone-flagged room upon the second floor, with a bed in a recess for him, and two smaller pallets on the other side, on which Aylward and Hordle John were already snoring. Alleyne had knelt down to his evening orisons, when there came a tap at his door, and Ford entered with a small lamp in his hand. His face was deadly pale, and his hand shook until the shadows flickered up and down the wall.

"What is it, Ford?" cried Alleyne, springing to his feet.

"I can scarce tell you," said he, sitting down on the side of the couch, and resting his chin upon his hand. "I know not what to say or what to think."

"Has aught befallen you, then?"

"Yes, or I have been slave to my own fancy. I tell you, lad, that I am all undone, like a fretted bowstring. Hark hither, Alleyne! it cannot be that you have forgotten little Tita, the daughter of the old glass-stainer at Bordeaux?"

"I remember her well."

"She and I, Alleyne, broke the lucky groat together ere we parted, and she wears my ring upon her finger. 'Caro mio,' quoth she when last we parted, 'I shall be near thee in the wars, and thy danger will be my danger.' Alleyne, as God is my help, as I came up the stairs this night I saw her stand before me, her face in tears, her hands out as though in warning—I saw it, Alleyne, even as I see those two archers upon their couches. Our very finger tips seemed to meet ere she thinned away like a mist in the sunshine."

"I would not give overmuch thought to it," answered Alleyne. "Our minds will play us strange pranks, and bethink you that these words of the Lady Tiphaine du Guesclin have wrought upon us and shaken us."

Ford shook his head. "I saw little Tita as clearly as though I were back at the Rue des Apôtres at Bordeaux," said he. "But the hour is late, and I must go."

"Where do you sleep, then?"

"In the chamber above you. May the saints be with us all!" He rose from the couch and left the chamber, while Alleyne could hear his feet sounding upon the winding stair. The young squire walked across to the window and gazed out at the moonlit landscape, his mind absorbed by the thought of the Lady Tiphaine, and of the strange words that she had spoken as to what was going forward at Castle Twynham. Leaning his elbows upon the stonework, he was deeply plunged in reverie, when in a moment his thoughts were brought back to Villefranche and to the scene before him.

The window at which he stood was in the second floor of that portion of the castle which was nearest to the keep. In front lay the broad moat, with the moon lying upon its surface, now clear and round, now drawn lengthwise as the breeze stirred the waters. Beyond, the plain sloped down to a thick wood, while further to the left a second wood shut out the view. Between the two an open glade stretched, silvered in the moonshine, with the river curving across the lower end of it.

As he gazed, he saw, of a sudden, a man steal forth from the wood into the open clearing. He walked with his head sunk, his shoulders curved, and his knees bent, as one who strives hard to remain unseen. Ten paces from the fringe of trees he glanced around and, waving his hand, he crouched down, and was lost to sight among a belt of furze bushes. After him there came a second man, and after him a third, a fourth, and a fifth, stealing across the narrow open space and darting into the shelter of the brushwood. Nine-and-seventy Alleyne counted of these dark figures flitting across the line of the moonlight. Many bore huge burdens upon their backs, though what it was that they carried he could not tell at the distance. Out of the one wood and into the other they passed, all with the same crouching, furtive gait, until the black bristle of trees had swallowed up the last of them.

For a moment Alleyne stood in the window, still staring down at the silent forest, uncertain as to what he should think of these midnight walkers. Then he bethought him that there was one beside him who was fitter to judge on such a matter. His fingers had scarce rested upon Aylward's shoulder ere the bowman was on his feet, with his hand outstretched to his sword.

"Qui va?" he cried. "Holà! mon petit. By my hilt! I thought there had been a camisade. What then, mon gar?"

"Come hither by the window, Aylward," said Alleyne. "I have seen four score men pass from yonder shaw across the glade, and nigh every man of them had a great burden on his back. What think you of it?"

"I think nothing of it, mon camarade! There are as many masterless folk in this country as there are rabbits on Cowdray Down, and there are many who show their faces by night but would dance in a hempen collar if they stirred forth in the day. On all the French marches are droves of outcasts, spoilers, and drawlatches, of whom I judge that these are some, though I marvel that they should dare to come so nigh to the castle of the Seneschal. All seems very quiet now," he added, peering out of the window.

"They are in the further wood," said Alleyne.

"And there they may bide. Back to rest, mon petit; for, by my hilt! each day now will bring its own work. Yet it would be well to shoot the bolt in yonder door when one is in strange quarters. So!" He threw himself down upon his pallet and in an instant was fast asleep.

It might have been about three o'clock in the morning when Alleyne was aroused from a troubled sleep by a low cry or exclamation. He listened, but, as he heard no more, he set it down as the challenge of the guard upon the walls and dropped off to sleep once more. A few minutes later he was disturbed by a gentle creaking of his own door, as though someone were pushing cautiously against it, and immediately afterwards he heard the soft thud of cautious footsteps upon the stair which led to the room above, followed by a confused noise and a muffled groan. Alleyne sat up on his couch with all his nerves in a tingle, uncertain whether these sounds might come from a simple cause—some sick archer and visiting leech perhaps—or whether they might have a more sinister meaning. But what danger could threaten them here in this strong castle, under the care of famous warriors, with high walls and a broad moat around them? Who was there that could injure them? He had well-nigh persuaded himself that his fears were a foolish fancy, when his eyes fell upon that which sent the blood cold to his heart and left him gasping, with hands clutching at the counterpane.

Right in front of him was the broad window of the chamber, with the moon shining brightly through it. For an instant something had obscured the light, and now a head was bobbing up and down outside, the face looking in at him, and swinging slowly from one side of the window to the other. Even in that dim light there could be no mistaking those features. Drawn, distorted, and blood-stained, they were still those of the young fellow squire who had sat so recently upon his own couch. With a cry of horror Alleyne sprang from his bed and rushed to the casement, while the two archers, aroused by the sound, seized their weapons and stared about them in bewilderment. One glance was enough to show Edricson that his fears were but too true. Foully murdered, with a score of wounds upon him and a rope round his neck, his poor friend had been cast from the upper window, and swung slowly in the night wind, his body rasping against the wall, and his disfigured face upon a level with the casement.

"My God!" cried Alleyne, shaking in every limb. "What has come upon us? What devil's deed is this?"

"Here is flint and steel," said John stolidly. "The lamp, Aylward! This moonshine softens a man's heart. Now we may use the eyes which God hath given us."

"By my hilt!" cried Aylward, as the yellow flame flickered up, "it is indeed young master Ford, and I think that this Seneschal is a black villain, who dare not face us in the day but would murther us in our sleep. By the twang of string! if I do not soak a goose's feather with his heart's blood, it will be no fault of Samkin Aylward of the White Company."

"But, Aylward, think of the men whom I saw yesternight," said Alleyne. "It may not be the Seneschal. It may be that others have come into the castle. I must to Sir Nigel ere it be too late. Let me go, Aylward, for my place is by his side."

"One moment, mon gar. Put that steel headpiece on the end of my yew stave. So! I will put it first through the door; for it is ill to come out when you can neither see nor guard yourself. Now, camarades, out swords and stand ready! Holà, by my hilt! it is time that we were stirring!"

As he spoke, a sudden shouting broke forth in the castle, with the scream of a woman and the rush of many feet. Then came the sharp clink of clashing steel, and a roar like that of an angry lion—"Notre Dame du Guesclin! St. Ives! St. Ives!" The bowman pulled back the bolt of the door and thrust out the headpiece at the end of the bow. A clash, the clatter of the steel cap upon the ground, and, ere the man who struck could heave up for another blow, the archer had passed his sword through his body. "On, camarades, on!" he cried; and, breaking fiercely past two men who threw themselves in his way, he sped down the broad corridor in the direction of the shouting.

A sharp turning, and then a second one, brought them to the head of a short stair, from which they looked straight down upon the scene of the uproar. A square oak-floored hall lay beneath them, from which opened the doors of the principal guest chambers. This hall was as light as day, for torches burned in numerous sconces upon the walls, throwing strange shadows from the tusked or antlered heads which ornamented them. At the very foot of the stair, close to the open door of their chamber, lay the Seneschal and his wife: she with her head shorn from her shoulders, he thrust through with a sharpened stake, which still protruded from either side of his body. Three servants of the castle lay dead beside them, all torn and draggled, as though a pack of wolves had been upon them. In front of the central guest chamber stood Du Guesclin and Sir Nigel, half-clad and unarmored, with the mad joy of battle gleaming in their eyes. Their heads were thrown back, their lips compressed, their blood-stained swords poised over their right shoulders, and their left feet thrown out. Three dead men lay huddled together in front of them; while a fourth, with the blood squirting from a severed vessel, lay back with updrawn knees, breathing in wheezy gasps. Further back—all panting together, like the wind in a tree—there stood a group of fierce, wild creatures, bare-armed and bare-legged, gaunt, unshaven, with deep-set murderous eyes and wild beast faces. With their flashing teeth, their bristling hair, their mad leapings and screamings, they seemed to Alleyne more like fiends from the pit than men of flesh and blood. Even as he looked, they broke into a hoarse yell and dashed once more upon the two knights, hurling themselves madly upon their sword points; clutching, scrambling, biting, tearing, careless of wounds if they could but drag the two soldiers to earth. Sir Nigel was thrown down by the sheer weight of them, and Sir Bertrand, with his thunderous war cry, was swinging round his heavy sword to clear a space for him to rise, when the whistle of two long English arrows, and the rush of the squire and the two English archers down the stairs, turned the tide of the combat. The assailants gave back, the knights rushed forward, and in a very few moments the hall was cleared, and Hordle John had hurled the last of the wild men down the steep steps which led from the end of it.

"Do not follow them," cried Du Guesclin. "We are lost if we scatter. For myself I care not a denier, though it is a poor thing to meet one's end at the hands of such scum; but I have my dear lady here, who must by no means be risked. We have breathing space now, and I would ask you, Sir Nigel, what it is that you would counsel?"

"By St. Paul!" answered Sir Nigel, "I can by no means understand what hath befallen us, save that I have been woken up by your battle cry, and, rushing forth, found myself in the midst of this small bickering. Harrow and alas for the lady and the Seneschal! What dogs are they who have done this bloody deed?"

"They are the Jacks, the men of the brushwood. They have the castle, though I know not how it hath come to pass. Look from this window into the bailey."

"By heaven!" cried Sir Nigel, "it is as bright as day with the torches. The gates stand open, and there are three thousand of them within the walls. See how they rush and scream and wave! What is it that they thrust out through the postern door? My God! it is a man-at-arms, and they pluck him limb from limb, like hounds on a wolf. Now another, and yet another. They hold the whole castle, for I see their faces at the windows. See, there are some with great bundles on their backs."

"It is dried wood from the forest. They pile them against the walls and set them in a blaze. Who is this who tries to check them? By St. Ives! it is the good priest who spake for them in the hall. He kneels, he prays, he implores! What! villains, would ye raise hands against those who have befriended you? Ah, the butcher has struck him! He is down! They stamp him under their feet! They tear off his gown and wave it in the air! See now, how the flames lick up the walls! Are there none left to rally round us? With a hundred men we might hold our own."

"Oh, for my Company!" cried Sir Nigel. "But where is Ford, Alleyne?"

"He is foully murdered, my fair lord."

"The saints receive him! May he rest in peace! But here come some at last who may give us counsel, for amid these passages it is ill to stir without a guide."

As he spoke, a French squire and the Bohemian knight came rushing down the steps, the latter bleeding from a slash across his forehead.

"All is lost!" he cried. "The castle is taken and on fire, the Seneschal is slain, and there is naught left for us."

"On the contrary," quoth Sir Nigel, "there is much left to us, for there is a very honorable contention before us, and a fair lady for whom to give our lives. There are many ways in which a man might die, but none better than this."

"You can tell us, Godfrey," said Du Guesclin to the French squire: "how came these men into the castle, and what succors can we count upon? By St. Ives! if we come not quickly to some counsel we shall be burned like young rooks in a nest."

The squire, a dark, slender stripling, spoke firmly and quickly, as one who was trained to swift action. "There is a passage under the earth into the castle," said he, "and through it some of the Jacks made their way, casting open the gates for the others. They have had help from within the walls, and the men-at-arms were heavy with wine: they must have been slain in their beds, for these devils crept from room to room with soft step and ready knife. Sir Amory the Hospitaler was struck down with an ax as he rushed before us from his sleeping chamber. Save only ourselves, I do not think that there are any left alive."

"What, then, would you counsel?"

"That we make for the keep. It is unused, save in time of war, and the key hangs from my poor lord and master's belt."

"There are two keys there."

"It is the larger. Once there, we might hold the narrow stair; and at least, as the walls are of a greater thickness, it would be longer ere they could burn them. Could we but carry the lady across the bailey, all might be well with us."

"Nay; the lady hath seen something of the work of war," said Tiphaine, coming forth, as white, as grave, and as unmoved as ever. "I would not be a hamper to you, my dear spouse and gallant friends. Rest assured of this, that if all else fail I have always a safeguard here"—drawing a small silver-hilted poniard [1] from her bosom—"which sets me beyond the fear of these vile and blood-stained wretches."

"Tiphaine," cried Du Guesclin, "I have always loved you; and now, by Our Lady of Rennes! I love you more than ever. Did I not know that your hand will be as ready as your words, I would myself turn my last blow upon you, ere you should fall into their hands. Lead on, Godfrey! A new golden pyx [2] will shine in the minster of Dinan if we come safely through with it."

The attention of the insurgents had been drawn away from murder to plunder, and all over the castle might be heard their cries and whoops of delight as they dragged forth the rich tapestries, the silver flagons, and the carved furniture. Down in the courtyard half-clad wretches, their bare limbs all mottled with bloodstains, strutted about with plumed helmets upon their heads, or with the Lady Rochefort's silken gowns girt round their loins and trailing on the ground behind them. Casks of choice wine had been rolled out from the cellars, and starving peasants squatted, goblet in hand, draining off vintages which De Rochefort had set aside for noble and royal guests. Others, with slabs of bacon and joints of dried meat upon the ends of their pikes, held them up to the blaze or tore at them ravenously with their teeth. Yet all order had not been lost amongst them, for some hundreds of the better-armed stood together in a silent group, leaning upon their rude weapons and looking up at the fire, which had spread so rapidly as to involve one whole side of the castle. Already Alleyne could hear the crackling and roaring of the flames, while the air was heavy with heat and full of the pungent whiff of burning wood.

[1] *poniard* (pŏn′yẽrd): a dagger. [2] *pyx* (pĭks): a vessel used in religious services.

Chapter 25

HOW FIVE MEN HELD THE KEEP OF VILLEFRANCHE

Under the guidance of the French squire the party passed down two narrow corridors. The first was empty, but at the head of the second stood a peasant sentry, who started off at the sight of them, yelling loudly to his comrades. "Stop him, or we are undone!" cried Du Guesclin, and had started to run, when Aylward's great war bow twanged like a harp string, and the man fell forward upon his face, with twitching limbs and clutching fingers. Within five paces of where he lay a narrow and little-used door led out into the bailey. From beyond it came such a babel of hooting and screaming, horrible oaths and yet more horrible laughter, that the stoutest heart might have shrunk from casting down the frail barrier which faced them.

"Make straight for the keep!" said Du Guesclin, in a sharp, stern whisper. "The two archers in front, the lady in the center, a squire on either side, while we three knights shall bide behind and beat back those who press upon us. So! Now open the door, and God have us in his holy keeping!"

For a few moments it seemed that their object would be attained without danger, so swift and so silent had been their movements. They were halfway across the bailey ere the frantic, howling peasants made a movement to stop them. The few who threw themselves in their way were overpowered or brushed aside, while the pursuers were beaten back by the ready weapons of the three cavaliers. Unscathed, they fought their way to the door of the keep and faced round upon the swarming mob, while the squire thrust the great key into the lock.

"My God!" he cried, "it is the wrong key."

"The wrong key!"

"Dolt, fool that I am! This is the key of the castle gate; the other opens the keep. I must back for it!" He turned, with some wild intention of retracing his steps, but at the instant a great jagged rock, hurled by a brawny peasant, struck him full upon the ear, and he dropped senseless to the ground.

"This is key enough for me!" quoth Hordle John, picking up the huge stone, and hurling it against the door with all the strength of his enormous body. The lock shivered, the wood smashed, the stone flew into five pieces, but the iron clamps still held the door in its position. Bending down, he thrust his great fingers under it and, with a heave, raised the whole mass of wood and iron from its hinges. For a moment it tottered and swayed, and then, falling outward, buried him in its ruin, while his comrades rushed into the dark archway which led to safety.

"Up the steps, Tiphaine!" cried Du Guesclin. "Now round, friends, and beat them back!" The mob of peasants had surged in upon their heels, but the two trustiest blades in Europe gleamed upon that narrow stair, and four of their number dropped upon the threshold. The others gave back and gathered in a half-circle round the open door, gnashing their teeth and shaking their clenched hands at the defenders. The body of the French squire had been dragged out by them and hacked to pieces. Three or four others had pulled John from under the door, when he suddenly bounded to his feet and, clutching one in either hand, dashed them together with such force that they fell senseless across each other upon the ground. With a kick and a blow he freed himself from two others who clung to him, and in a moment he was within the portal with his comrades.

Yet their position was a desperate one. The peasants from far and near had been assembled for this deed of vengeance, and not less than six thousand were within or around the walls of the Château of Villefranche. Ill-armed and half-starved, they were still desperate men, to whom danger had lost all fears: for what was death that they should shun it to cling to such a life as theirs? The castle was theirs, and the roaring flames were spurting through the windows and flickering high above the turrets on two sides of the quadrangle. From either side they were sweeping down from room to room and from bastion to bastion in the direction of the keep. Faced by an army, and girt in by fire, were six men and one woman; but some of them were men so trained to danger and so wise in war that even now the combat was less unequal than it seemed. Courage and resource were penned in by desperation and numbers, while the great yellow sheets of flame threw their lurid glare over the scene of death.

"There is but space for two upon a step to give free play to our sword arms," said Du Guesclin. "Do you stand with me, Nigel, upon the lowest. France and England will fight together this night. Sir Otto, I pray you to stand behind us with this young squire. The archers may go higher yet and shoot over our heads. I would that we had our harness, Nigel."

"Often have I heard my dear Sir John Chandos say that a knight should never, even when a guest, be parted from it. Yet it will be more honor to us if we come well out of it. We have a vantage, since we see them against the light, and they can scarce see us. It seems to me that they muster for an onslaught."

"If we can but keep them in play," said the Bohemian, "it is likely that these flames may bring us succor [1] if there be any true men in the country."

"Bethink you, my fair lord," said Alleyne to Sir Nigel, "that we have never injured these men, nor have we cause of quarrel against them. Would it not be well, if but for the lady's sake, to speak them fair and see if we may not come to honorable terms with them?"

"Not so, by St. Paul!" cried Sir Nigel. "It does not accord with mine honor, nor shall it ever be said that I, a knight of England, was ready to hold parley with men who have slain a fair lady and a holy priest."

"As well hold parley with a pack of ravening wolves," said the French captain. "Ha! Notre Dame du Guesclin! St. Ives! St. Ives!"

As he thundered forth his war cry, the Jacks who had been gathering before the black arch of the gateway rushed in madly in a desperate effort to carry the staircase. Their leaders were a small man, dark in the face, with his beard done up in two plaits, and another larger man, very bowed in the shoulders, with a huge club studded with sharp nails in his hand. The first had not taken three steps ere an arrow from Aylward's bow struck him full in the chest, and he fell coughing and spluttering across the threshold. The other rushed onwards, and breaking between Du Guesclin and Sir Nigel he dashed out the brains of the Bohemian with a single blow of his clumsy weapon. With three swords through him he still struggled on, and had almost won his way through them ere he fell dead upon the stair. Close at his heels came a hundred furious peasants, who flung themselves

[1] *succor* (sŭk′ẽr): assistance.

again and again against the five swords which confronted them. It was cut and parry and stab as quick as eye could see or hand act. The door was piled with bodies, and the stone floor was slippery with blood. The deep shout of Du Guesclin, the hard, hissing breath of the pressing multitude, the clatter of steel, the thud of falling bodies, and the screams of the stricken made up such a medley as came often in afteryears to break upon Alleyne's sleep. Slowly and sullenly at last the throng drew off, with many a fierce backward glance, while eleven of their number lay huddled in front of the stair which they had failed to win.

"The dogs have had enough," said Du Guesclin.

"By St. Paul! there appear to be some very worthy and valiant persons among them," observed Sir Nigel. "They are men from whom, had they been of better birth, much honor and advancement might be gained. Even as it is, it is a great pleasure to have seen them. But what is this that they are bringing forward?"

"It is as I feared," growled Du Guesclin. "They will burn us out, since they cannot win their way past us. Shoot straight and hard, archers; for, by St. Ives! our good swords are of little use to us."

As he spoke, a dozen men rushed forward, each screening himself behind a huge fardel of brushwood. Hurling their burdens in one vast heap within the portal, they threw burning torches upon the top of it. The wood had been soaked in oil, for in an instant it was ablaze, and a long, hissing, yellow flame licked over the heads of the defenders and drove them further up to the first floor of the keep. They had scarce reached it, however, ere they found that the wooden joists and planks of the flooring were already on fire. Dry and worm-eaten, a spark upon them became a smolder, and a smolder a blaze. A choking smoke filled the air, and the five could scarce grope their way to the staircase which led up to the very summit of the square tower.

Strange was the scene which met their eyes from this eminence. Beneath them on every side stretched the long sweep of peaceful country, rolling plain, and tangled wood, all softened and mellowed in the silver moonshine. No light, nor movement, nor any sign of human aid could be seen, but far away the hoarse clangor of a heavy bell rose and fell upon the wintry air. Beneath and around them blazed the huge fire, roaring and crackling on every side of the bailey, and even as they looked the two corner turrets fell in with a deafening crash, and the whole castle was but a shapeless mass, spouting flames and smoke from every window and embrasure. The great black tower upon which they stood rose like a last island of refuge amid this sea of fire; but the ominous crackling and roaring below showed that it would not be long ere it was engulfed also in the common ruin. At their very feet was the square courtyard, crowded with the howling and dancing peasants, their fierce faces upturned, their clenched hands waving, all drunk with bloodshed and with vengeance. A yell of execration [1] and a scream of hideous laughter burst from the vast throng as they saw the faces of the last survivors of their enemies peering down at them from the height of the keep. They still piled the brushwood round the base of the tower and gamboled hand in hand around the blaze, screaming out the doggerel lines which had long been the watchword of the Jacquerie:

Cessez, cessez, gens d'armes et piétons,
De piller et manger le bonhomme,
Qui de longtemps Jacques Bonhomme
Se nomme.[2]

Their thin, shrill voices rose high above the roar of the flames and the crash of the masonry, like the yelping of a pack of wolves who see their quarry before them and know that they have well-nigh run him down.

"By my hilt!" said Aylward to John, "it is in my mind that we shall not see Spain this journey. It is a great joy to me that I have placed my featherbed and other things of price with that worthy woman at Lyndhurst, who will now have the use of them. I have thirteen arrows yet, and if one of them fly unfleshed, then, by the twang of string! I shall deserve my doom. First at him who flaunts with my lady's silken frock. Clap in the clout, by God! though a hand's breadth lower than I had meant. Now for the rogue with the head upon his pike. Ha! to the inch, John. When my eye is true, I am better at rovers than at long butts or hoyles. A good shoot for you also, John! The villain hath fallen forward into the fire. But I pray you, John, to loose gently, and not to pluck with the drawing hand, for it is a trick that hath marred many a fine bowman."

[1] *execration* (ĕk·sê·krā′shŭn): hatred. [2] This verse calls upon the gentry to cease tormenting the peasants. It was the rallying cry of the Jacquerie, or rising of the peasants.

Whilst the two archers were keeping up a brisk fire upon the mob beneath them, Du Guesclin and his lady were consulting with Sir Nigel upon their desperate situation.

" 'Tis a strange end for one who has seen so many stricken fields," said the French chieftain. "For me one death is as another, but it is the thought of my sweet lady which goes to my heart."

"Nay, Bertrand, I fear it as little as you," said she. "Had I my dearest wish, it would be that we should go together."

"Well answered, fair lady!" cried Sir Nigel. "And very sure I am that my own sweet wife would have said the same. If the end be now come, I have had great good fortune in having lived in times when so much glory was to be won, and in knowing so many valiant gentlemen and knights. But why do you pluck my sleeve, Alleyne?"

"If it please you, my fair lord, there are in this corner two great tubes of iron, with many heavy balls, which may perchance be those bombards [1] and shot of which I have heard."

"By St. Ives! it is true," cried Sir Bertrand, striding across to the recess where the ungainly, funnel-shaped, thick-ribbed engines were standing. "Bombards they are, and of good size. We may shoot down upon them."

"Shoot with them, quotha?" cried Aylward in high disdain, for pressing danger is the great leveler of classes. "How is a man to take aim with these fool's toys, and how can he hope to do scath with them?"

"I will show you," answered Sir Nigel; "for here is the great box of powder, and if you will raise it for me, John, I will show you how it may be used. Come hither, where the folk are thickest round the fire. Now, Aylward, crane thy neck and see what would have been deemed an old wife's tale when we first turned our faces to the wars. Throw back the lid, John, and drop the box into the fire!"

A deafening roar, a fluff of bluish light, and the great square tower rocked and trembled from its very foundations, swaying this way and that like a reed in the wind. Amazed and dizzy, the defenders, clutching at the cracking parapets for support, saw great stones, burning beams of wood, and mangled bodies hurtling past them through the air. When they staggered to their feet once more, the whole keep had settled down upon one side, so

[1] *bombard* (bŏm′bärd): a cannon.

that they could scarce keep their footing upon the sloping platform. Gazing over the edge, they looked down upon the horrible destruction which had been caused by the explosion. For forty yards round the portal the ground was black with writhing, screaming figures, who struggled up and hurled themselves down again, tossing this way and that, sightless, scorched, with fire bursting from their tattered clothing. Beyond this circle of death their comrades, bewildered and amazed, cowered away from this black tower and from these invincible men, who were most to be dreaded when hope was furthest from their hearts.

"A sally, Du Guesclin, a sally!" cried Sir Nigel. "By St. Paul! they are in two minds, and a bold rush may turn them." He drew his sword as he spoke and darted down the winding stairs, closely followed by his four comrades. Ere he was at the first floor, however, he threw up his arms and stopped. "Mon Dieu!" he said, "we are lost men!"

"What then?" cried those behind him.

"The wall hath fallen in, the stair is blocked, and the fire still rages below. By St. Paul! friends, we have fought a very honorable fight, and may say in all humbleness that we have done our devoir, but I think that we may now go back to the Lady Tiphaine and say our orisons, for we have played our parts in this world, and it is time that we made ready for another."

The narrow pass was blocked by huge stones littered in wild confusion over each other, with the blue choking smoke reeking up through the crevices. The explosion had blown in the wall and cut off the only path by which they could descend. Pent in, a hundred feet from earth, with a furnace raging under them and a ravening multitude all round who thirsted for their blood, it seemed indeed as though no men had ever come through such peril with their lives. Slowly they made their way back to the summit, but as they came out upon it the Lady Tiphaine darted forward and caught her husband by the wrist.

"Bertrand," said she, "hush and listen! I have heard the voices of men all singing together in a strange tongue."

Breathless they stood, and silent, but no sound came up to them, save the roar of the flames and the clamor of their enemies.

"It cannot be, lady," said Du Guesclin. "This night hath overwrought you, and your senses play you false. What men are there in this country who would sing in a strange tongue?"

"Holà!" yelled Aylward, leaping suddenly into the air with waving hands and joyous face. "I thought I heard it ere we went down, and now I hear it again. We are saved, comrades! By these ten finger bones, we are saved! It is the marching song of the White Company. Hush!"

With upraised forefinger and slanting head, he stood listening. Suddenly there came swelling up a deep-voiced, rollicking chorus from somewhere out of the darkness. Never did choice or dainty ditty of Provence or Languedoc sound more sweetly in the ears than did the rough-tongued Saxon to the six who strained their ears from the blazing keep:

We'll drink all together
To the gray goose feather
And the land where the gray goose flew.

"Ha, by my hilt!" shouted Aylward, "it is the dear old bow song of the Company. Here come two hundred as tight lads as ever twirled a shaft over their thumbnails. Hark to the dogs, how lustily they sing!"

Nearer and clearer, swelling up out of the night, came the gay marching lilt:

What of the bow?
  The bow was made in England,
Of true wood, of yew wood,
  The wood of English bows;
For men who are free
Love the old yew tree
  And the land where the yew tree grows.

What of the men?
  The men were bred in England,
The bowmen, the yeomen,
  The lads of the dale and fell,
Here's to you and to you,
To the hearts that are true,
  And the land where the true hearts dwell.

"They sing very joyfully," said Du Guesclin, "as though they were going to a festival."

"It is their wont when there is work to be done."

"By St. Paul!" quoth Sir Nigel, "it is in my mind that they come too late, for I cannot see how we are to come down from this tower."

"There they come, the hearts of gold!" cried Aylward. "See, they move out from the shadow. Now they cross the meadow. They are on the further side of the moat. Holà, camarades, holà! Johnston, Eccles, Cooke, Harward, Bligh! Would ye see a fair lady and two gallant knights done foully to death?"

"Who is there?" shouted a deep voice from below. "Who is this who speaks with an English tongue?"

"It is I, old lad. It is Sam Aylward of the Company; and here is your captain, Sir Nigel Loring, and four others, all laid out to be grilled like an Easterling's herrings."

"Curse me if I did not think that it was the style of speech of old Samkin Aylward," said the voice, amid a buzz from the ranks. "Wherever there are knocks going, there is Sammy in the heart of it. But who are these ill-faced rogues who block the path? To your kennels, canaille! What! you dare look us in the eyes? Out swords, lads, and give them the flat of them! Waste not your shafts upon such runagate knaves."

There was little fight left in the peasants, however, still dazed by the explosion, amazed at their own losses, and disheartened by the arrival of the disciplined archers. In a very few minutes they were in full flight for their brushwood homes, leaving the morning sun to rise upon a blackened and bloodstained ruin, where it had left the night before the magnificent castle of the Seneschal of Auvergne. Already the white lines in the east were deepening into pink as the archers gathered round the keep and took counsel how to rescue the survivors.

"Had we a rope," said Alleyne, "there is one side which is not yet on fire, down which we might slip."

"But how to get a rope?"

"It is an old trick," quoth Aylward. "Holà! Johnston, cast me up a rope, even as you did at Maupertius in the war time."

The grizzled archer thus addressed took several lengths of rope from his comrades and, knotting them firmly together, he stretched them out in the long shadow which the rising sun threw from the frowning keep. Then he fixed the yew stave of his bow upon end and measured the long, thin, black line which it threw upon the turf.

"A six-foot stave throws a twelve-foot shadow," he muttered. "The keep throws a shadow of sixty paces. Thirty paces of rope will be enow and to spare. Another strand, Watkin! Now pull at the end, that all may be safe. So! It is ready for them."

"But how are they to reach it?" asked the young archer beside him.

"Watch and see, young fool's-head," growled the old bowman. He took a long string from his pouch and fastened one end to an arrow.

"All ready, Samkin?"

"Ready, camarade."

"Close to your hand then." With an easy pull he sent the shaft flickering gently up, falling upon the stonework within a foot of where Aylward was standing. The other end was secured to the rope, so that in a minute a good strong cord was dangling from the only sound side of the blazing and shattered tower. The Lady Tiphaine was lowered with a noose drawn fast under the arms, and the other five slid swiftly down, amid the cheers and joyous outcry of their rescuers.

Chapter 26

HOW THE COMPANY TOOK COUNSEL ROUND THE FALLEN TREE

Where is Sir Claude Latour?" asked Sir Nigel, as his feet touched ground.

"He is in camp, near Montpezat, two hours' march from here, my fair lord," said Johnston, the grizzled bowman who commanded the archers.

"Then we shall march thither, for I would fain have you all back at Dax in time to be in the Prince's vanguard." [1]

"My lord," cried Alleyne, joyfully, "here are our chargers in the field, and I see your harness amid the plunder which these rogues have left behind them."

[1] *vanguard* (văn′gärd): the troops in front.

"By St. Ives! you speak sooth, young squire," said Du Guesclin. "There is my horse and my lady's jennet. The knaves led them from the stables, but fled without them. Now, Nigel, it is great joy to me to have seen one of whom I have often heard. Yet we must leave you now, for I must be with the King of Spain ere your army crosses the mountains."

"I had thought that you were in Spain with the valiant Henry of Trastamare."

"I have been there, but I came to France to raise succor for him. I shall ride back, Nigel, with four thousand of the best lances of France at my back, so that your prince may find he hath a task which is worthy of him. God be with you, friend, and may we meet again in better times!"

"I do not think," said Sir Nigel, as he stood by Alleyne's side, looking after the French knight and his lady, "that in all Christendom you will meet with a more stout-hearted man or a fairer and sweeter dame. But your face is pale and sad, Alleyne! Have you perchance met with some hurt during the ruffle?"

"Nay, my fair lord, I was but thinking of my friend Ford, and how he sat upon my couch no later than yesternight."

Sir Nigel shook his head sadly. "Two brave squires have I lost," said he. "I know not why the young shoots should be plucked, and an old weed left standing, yet, certes, there must be some good reason, since God hath so planned it. Did you not note, Alleyne, that the Lady Tiphaine did give us warning last night that danger was coming upon us?"

"She did, my lord."

"By St. Paul! my mind misgives me as to what she saw at Twynham Castle. And yet I cannot think that any Scottish or French rovers could land in such force as to beleaguer the fortalice. Call the Company together, Aylward; and let us on, for it will be shame to us if we are not at Dax upon the trysting day."

The archers had spread themselves over the ruins, but a blast upon a bugle brought them all back to muster, with such booty as they could bear with them stuffed into their pouches or slung over their shoulders.

As they formed into ranks, each man dropping silently into his place, Sir Nigel ran a questioning eye over them, and a smile of pleasure played over his face. Tall and sinewy and brown, clear-eyed, hard-featured, with the stern and prompt bearing of experienced soldiers, it would be hard indeed for a leader to seek for a choicer following. Here and there in the ranks were old soldiers of the French wars, grizzled and lean, with fierce, puckered features and shaggy, bristling brows. The most, however, were young and dandy archers, with fresh English faces, their beards combed out, their hair curling from under their close steel hufkens, with gold or jeweled earrings gleaming in their ears, while their gold-spangled baldrics, their silken belts, and the chains which many of them wore round their thick brown necks, all spoke of the brave times which they had had as free companions. Each had a yew or hazel stave slung over his shoulder, plain and serviceable with the older men, but gaudily painted and carved at either end with the others. Steel caps, mail brigandines, white surcoats with the red lion of St. George, and sword or battle-ax swinging from their belts completed this equipment, while in some cases the murderous maul, or five-foot mallet, was hung across the bowstave, being fastened to their leathern shoulder belt by a hook in the center of the handle. Sir Nigel's heart beat high as he looked upon their free bearing and fearless faces.

For two hours they marched through forest and marshland, along the left bank of the river Aveyron; Sir Nigel riding behind his Company, with Alleyne at his right hand, and Johnston, the old master bowman, walking by his left stirrup. Ere they had reached their journey's end the knight had learned all that he would know of his men, their doings, and their intentions. Once, as they marched, they saw upon the further bank of the river a body of French men-at-arms, riding very swiftly in the direction of Villefranche.

"It is the Seneschal of Toulouse, with his following," said Johnston, shading his eyes with his hand. "Had he been on this side of the water, he might have attempted something upon us."

"I think that it would be well that we should cross," said Sir Nigel. "It were pity to balk this worthy seneschal, should he desire to try some small feat of arms."

"Nay, there is no ford nearer than Tourville," answered the old archer. "He is on his way to Villefranche, and short will be the shrift of any Jacks who come into his hands, for he is a man of short speech. It was he and the Seneschal of Beaucaire who hung Peter Wilkins, of the Company, last Lammastide; for which, by the black rood of Waltham! they shall hang themselves if ever they come into our power. But here are our comrades, Sir Nigel, and here is our camp."

As he spoke, the forest pathway along which they marched opened out into a green glade, which sloped down towards the river. High, leafless trees girt it on three sides, with a thick undergrowth of holly between their trunks. At the farther end of this forest clearing there stood forty or fifty huts, built very neatly from wood and clay, with the blue smoke curling out from the roofs. A dozen tethered horses and mules grazed around the encampment, while a number of archers lounged about: some shooting at marks, while others built up great wooden fires in the open and hung their cooking kettles above them. At the sight of their returning comrades there was a shout of welcome, and a horseman who had been exercising his charger behind the camp came cantering down to them. He was a dapper, brisk man, very richly clad, with a round, clean-shaven face, and very bright black eyes, which danced and sparkled with excitement.

"Sir Nigel!" he cried. "Sir Nigel Loring, at last! By my soul! we have awaited you this month past. Right welcome, Sir Nigel! You have had my letter?"

"It was that which brought me here," said Sir Nigel. "But indeed, Sir Claude Latour, it is a great wonder to me that you did not yourself lead these bowmen, for surely they could have found no better leader?"

"None, none, by the Virgin of L'Esparre!" he cried, speaking in the strange, thick Gascon speech which turns every *v* into a *b*. "But you know what these islanders of yours are, Sir Nigel. They will not be led by any save their own blood and race. There is no persuading them. Not even I, Claude Latour, Seigneur of Montchâteau, master of the high justice, the middle, and the low, could gain their favor. They must needs hold a council and put their two hundred thick heads together, and then there comes this fellow Aylward and another, as their spokesmen, to say that they will disband unless an Englishman of good name be set over them. There are many of them, as I understand, who come from some great forest which lies in Hampi, or Hampti—I cannot lay my tongue to the name. Your dwelling is in those parts, and so their thoughts turned to you as their leader. But we had hoped that you would bring a hundred men with you."

"They are already at Dax, where we shall join them," said

Sir Nigel. "But let the men break their fast, and we shall then take counsel what to do."

"Come into my hut," said Sir Claude. "It is but poor fare that I can lay before you—milk, cheese, wine, and bacon—yet your squire and yourself will doubtless excuse it. This is my house, where the pennon flies before the door—a small residence to contain the Lord of Montchâteau."

Sir Nigel sat silent and distrait at his meal, while Alleyne hearkened to the clattering tongue of the Gascon, and to his talk of the glories of his own estate, his successes in love, and his triumphs in war.

"And now that you are here, Sir Nigel," he said at last, "I have many fine ventures all ready for us. I have heard that Montpezat is of no great strength, and that there are two hundred thousand crowns in the castle. At Castelnau also there is a cobbler who is in my pay, and who will throw us a rope any dark night from his house by the town wall. I promise you that you shall thrust your arms elbow-deep among good silver pieces ere the nights are moonless again; for on every hand of us are fair women, rich wine, and good plunder, as much as heart could wish."

"I have other plans," answered Sir Nigel curtly; "for I have come hither to lead these bowmen to the help of the Prince, our master, who may have sore need of them ere he set Pedro upon the throne of Spain. It is my purpose to start this very day for Dax upon the Adour, where he hath now pitched his camp."

The face of the Gascon darkened, and his eyes flashed with resentment. "For me," he said, "I care little for this war, and I find the life which I lead a very joyous and pleasant one. I will not go to Dax."

"Nay, think again, Sir Claude," said Sir Nigel gently; "for you have ever had the name of a true and loyal knight. Surely you will not hold back now when your master hath need of you."

"I will not go to Dax!" the other shouted.

"But your devoir—your oath of fealty?"

"I say that I will not go."

"Then, Sir Claude, I must lead the Company without you."

"If they will follow," cried the Gascon with a sneer. "These are not hired slaves, but free companions, who will do nothing save by their own good wills. In very sooth, my Lord Loring, they are ill men to trifle with, and it were easier to pluck a bone from a hungry bear than to lead a bowman out of a land of plenty and of pleasure."

"Then I pray you to gather them together," said Sir Nigel, "and I will tell them what is in my mind; for if I am their leader, they must to Dax, and if I am not, then I know not what I am doing in Auvergne. Have my horse ready, Alleyne; for, by St. Paul! come what may, I must be upon the homeward road ere midday."

A blast upon the bugle summoned the bowmen to counsel, and they gathered in little knots and groups around a great fallen tree which lay athwart the glade. Sir Nigel sprang lightly upon the trunk and stood with blinking eye and firm lips, looking down at the ring of upturned warlike faces.

"They tell me, bowmen," said he, "that ye have grown so fond of ease and plunder and high living that ye are not to be moved from this pleasant country. But, by St. Paul! I will believe no such thing of you, for I can readily see that you are all very valiant men, who would scorn to live here in peace when your prince hath so great a venture before him. Ye have chosen me as a leader, and a leader I will be if ye come with me to Spain; and I vow to you that my pennon of the five roses shall, if God give me strength and life, be ever where there is most honor to be gained. But if it be your wish to loll and loiter in these glades, bartering glory and renown for vile gold and ill-gotten riches, then ye must find another leader; for I have lived in honor, and in honor I trust that I shall die. If there be forest men or Hampshire men amongst ye, I call upon them to say whether they will follow the banner of Loring."

"Here's a Romsey man for you!" cried a young bowman with a sprig of evergreen set in his helmet.

"And a lad from Alresford!" shouted another.

"And from Milton!"

"And from Burley!"

"And from Lymington!"

"And a little one from Brockenhurst!" shouted a huge-limbed fellow who sprawled beneath a tree.

"By my hilt! lads," cried Aylward, jumping upon the fallen trunk, "I think that we could not look the girls in the eyes if we let the Prince cross the mountains and did not pull string to clear a path for him. It is very well in time of peace to lead such a life as we have had together, but now the war banner is in the wind once more, and, by these ten finger bones! If it go alone, old Samkin Aylward will walk beside it."

These words from a man so popular as Aylward decided many of the waverers, and a shout of approval burst from his audience.

"Far be it from me," said Sir Claude Latour suavely, "to persuade you against this worthy archer, or against Sir Nigel Loring; yet we have been together in many ventures, and, perchance, it may not be amiss if I say to you what I think upon the matter."

"Peace for the little Gascon!" cried the archers. "Let every man have his word. Shoot straight for the mark, lad, and fair play for all."

"Bethink you, then," said Sir Claude, "that you go under a hard rule, with neither freedom nor pleasure—and for what? For sixpence a day, at the most; while now you may walk across the country and stretch out either hand to gather in whatever you have a mind for. What do we not hear of our comrades who have gone with Sir John Hawkwood to Italy? In one night they have held to ransom six hundred of the richest noblemen of Mantua. They camp before a great city, and the base burghers come forth with the keys, and then they make great spoil; or, if it please them better, they take so many horse-loads of silver as a composition;[1] and so they journey on from state to state, rich and free and feared by all. Now, is not that the proper life for a soldier?"

"The proper life for a robber!" roared Hordle John, in his thundering voice.

"And yet there is much in what the Gascon says," said a swarthy fellow in a weather-stained doublet; "and I for one would rather prosper in Italy than starve in Spain."

"You were always a cur and a traitor, Mark Shaw," cried Aylward. "By my hilt! if you will stand forth and draw your sword, I will warrant you that you will see neither one nor the other."

"Nay, Aylward," said Sir Nigel, "we cannot mend the matter by broiling. Sir Claude, I think that what you have said

[1] *composition:* an agreement or settlement.

does you little honor, and if my words aggrieve you, I am ever ready to go deeper into the matter with you. But you shall have such men as will follow you, and you may go where you will, so that you come not with us. Let all who love their prince and country stand fast, while those who think more of a well-lined purse step forth upon the farther side."

Thirteen bowmen, with hung heads and sheepish faces, stepped forward with Mark Shaw and ranged themselves behind Sir Claude. Amid the hootings and hissings of their comrades, they marched off together to the Gascon's hut, while the main body broke up their meeting and set cheerily to work packing their possessions, furbishing their weapons, and preparing for the march which lay before them. Over the Tarn and the Garonne, through the vast quagmires of Armagnac, past the swift-flowing Losse, and so down the long valley of the Adour, there was many a long league to be crossed ere they could join themselves to that dark war cloud which was drifting slowly southwards to the line of the snowy peaks, beyond which the banner of England had never yet been seen.

Chapter 27

HOW THE ARMY MADE THE PASSAGE OF RONCESVALLES

The whole vast plain of Gascony and of Languedoc is an arid and profitless expanse in winter, save where the swift-flowing Adour and her snow-fed tributaries, the Louts, the Oloron, and the Pau, run down to the sea of Biscay. South of the Adour the jagged line of mountains which fringe the sky line send out long granite claws, running down into the lowlands and dividing them into "gaves," or stretches of valley. Hillocks grow into hills, and hills into mountains, each range overlying its neighbor, until they soar up in the giant chain which raises its spotless and untrodden peaks, white and dazzling, against the pale blue wintry sky.

A quiet land is this—a land where the slow-moving Basque, with his flat biretta-cap, his red sash, and his hempen sandals, tills his scanty farm or drives his lean flock to their hillside pastures. It is the country of the wolf and the izard,[1] of the brown bear and the mountain goat, a land of bare rock and of rushing water. Yet here it was that the will of a great prince had now assembled a gallant army; so that from the Adour to the passes of Navarre the barren valleys and wind-swept wastes were populous with soldiers and loud with the shouting of orders and the neighing of horses. For the banners of war had been flung to the wind once more, and over those glistening peaks was the highway along which Honor pointed in an age when men had chosen her as their guide.

And now all was ready for the enterprise. From Dax to St. Jean Pied-du-Port the country was mottled with the white tents of Gascons, Aquitanians, and English, all eager for the advance. From all sides the free companions had trooped in, until not less than twelve thousand of these veteran troops were cantoned along the frontiers of Navarre. From England had arrived the Prince's brother, the Duke of Lancaster, with four hundred knights in his train and a strong company of archers. Above all, an heir to the throne had been born in Bordeaux, and the Prince might leave his spouse with an easy mind, for all was well with mother and with child.

The keys of the mountain passes still lay in the hands of the shifty and ignoble Charles of Navarre, who had chaffered[2] and bargained both with the English and with the Spanish, taking money from the one side to hold them open and from the other to keep them sealed. The mallet hand of Edward, however, had shattered all the schemes and wiles of the plotter. Neither entreaty nor courtly remonstrance came from the English prince; but Sir Hugh Calverley passed silently over the border with his company, and the blazing walls of the two cities of Miranda and Puenta della Reyna warned the unfaithful monarch that there were other metals besides gold, and that he was dealing with a

[1] *izard* (ĭz′ẽrd): a mountain antelope. [2] *chaffer* (chăf′fẽr): to discuss terms.

man to whom it was unsafe to lie. His price was paid, his objections silenced, and the mountain gorges lay open to the invaders. From the Feast of the Epiphany there was mustering and massing until, in the first week of February—three days after the White Company joined the army—the word was given for a general advance through the defile of Roncesvalles. At five in the cold winter's morning the bugles were blowing in the hamlet of St. Jean Pied-du-Port, and by six Sir Nigel's Company, three hundred strong, were on their way for the defile,[1] pushing swiftly in the dim light up the steep curving road; for it was the Prince's order that they should be the first to pass through, and that they should remain on guard at the further end until the whole army had emerged from the mountains. Day was already breaking in the east, and the summits of the great peaks had turned rosy red, while the valleys still lay in the shadow, when they found themselves with the cliffs on either hand and the long, rugged pass stretching away before them.

Sir Nigel rode his great black war horse at the head of his archers, dressed in full armor, with Black Simon bearing his banner behind him, while Alleyne, at his bridle arm, carried his blazoned shield and his well-steeled ashen spear. A proud and happy man was the knight, and many a time he turned in his saddle to look at the long column of bowmen who swung swiftly along behind him.

"By St. Paul! Alleyne," said he, "this pass is a very perilous place, and I would that the King of Navarre had held it against us, for it would have been a very honorable venture had it fallen to us to win a passage. I have heard the minstrels sing of one Sir Roland who was slain by the infidels in these very parts."

"If it please you, my fair lord," said Black Simon, " I know something of these parts, for I have twice served a term with the King of Navarre. There is a hospice of monks yonder, where you may see the roof among the trees, and there it was that Sir Roland was slain. The village upon the left is Orbaiceta, and I know a house therein where the right wine of Jurançon is to be bought, if it would please you to quaff a morning cup."

"There is smoke yonder upon the right."

"That is a village named Les Aldudes, and I know a hostel there also where the wine is of the best. It is said that the inn-

[1] *defile* (dê·fīl′): a narrow gorge.

keeper hath a buried treasure, and I doubt not, my fair lord, that if you grant me leave I could prevail upon him to tell us where he hath hid it."

"Nay, nay, Simon," said Sir Nigel curtly, "I pray you to forget these free-companion tricks. Ha! Edricson, I see that you stare about you, and, in good sooth, these mountains must seem wondrous indeed to one who hath but seen Butser or the Portsdown hill."

The broken and rugged road had wound along the crests of low hills, with wooded ridges on either side of it over which peeped the loftier mountains, the distant Peak of the South and the vast Altabisca, which towered high above them and cast its black shadow from left to right across the valley. From where they now stood they could look forward down a long vista of beech woods and jagged rock-strewn wilderness, all white with snow, to where the pass opened out upon the uplands beyond. Behind them they could still catch a glimpse of the gray plains of Gascony, and could see her rivers gleaming like coils of silver in the sunshine. As far as eye could see, from among the rocky gorges and the bristles of the pine woods there came the quick twinkle and glitter of steel, while the wind brought with it sudden distant bursts of martial music from the great host which rolled by every road and bypath towards the narrow pass of Roncesvalles. On the cliffs on either side might also be seen the flash of arms and the waving of pennons where the force of Navarre looked down upon the army of strangers who passed through their territories.

"By St. Paul!" said Sir Nigel, blinking up at them, "I think that we have much to hope for from these cavaliers, for they cluster very thickly upon our flanks. Pass word to the men, Aylward, that they unsling their bows, for I have no doubt that there are some very worthy gentlemen yonder who may give us some opportunity for honorable advancement."

"I hear that the Prince hath the King of Navarre as hostage," said Alleyne, "and it is said that he hath sworn to put him to death if there be any attack upon us."

"It was not so that war was made when good King Edward first turned his hand to it," said Sir Nigel sadly. "Ah! Alleyne, I fear that you will never live to see such things, for the minds of men are more set upon money and gain than of old. By St.

Paul! it was a noble sight when two great armies would draw together upon a certain day, and all who had a vow would ride forth to discharge themselves of it. What noble spear-runnings have I not seen, and even in an humble way had a part in, when cavaliers would run a course for the easing of their souls and for the love of their ladies! Never a bad word have I for the French, for, though I have ridden twenty times up to their array, I have never yet failed to find some very gentle and worthy knight or squire who was willing to do what he might to enable me to attempt some small feat of arms. Then, when all cavaliers had been satisfied, the two armies would come to handstrokes, and fight right merrily until one or other had the vantage. By St. Paul! it was not our wont in those days to pay gold for the opening of passes, nor would we hold a king as hostage lest his people come to thrusts with us. In good sooth, if the war is to be carried out in such a fashion, then it is grief to me that I ever came away from Castle Twynham, for I would not have left my sweet lady had I not thought that there were deeds of arms to be done."

"But surely, my fair lord," said Alleyne, "you have done some great feats of arms since we left the Lady Loring."

"I cannot call any to mind," answered Sir Nigel.

"There was the taking of the sea rovers, and the holding of the keep against the Jacks."

"Nay, nay," said the knight, "these were not feats of arms, but mere wayside ventures and the chances of travel. By St. Paul! if it were not that these hills are oversteep for Pommers, I would ride to these cavaliers of Navarre and see if there were not some among them who would help me to take this patch from mine eye. It is a sad sight to see this very fine pass, which my own Company here could hold against an army, and yet to ride through it with as little profit as though it were the lane from my kennels to the Avon."

All morning Sir Nigel rode in a very ill humor, with his Company tramping behind him. It was a toilsome march over broken ground and through snow which came often as high as the knee, yet, ere the sun had begun to sink, they had reached the spot where the gorge opens out on to the uplands of Navarre, and could see the towers of Pampeluna jutting up against the southern sky line. Here the Company were quartered in a scattered mountain hamlet, and Alleyne spent the day looking down upon the swarming army which poured with gleam of spears and flaunt of standards through the narrow pass.

"Holà, mon gar," said Aylward, seating himself upon a boulder by his side. "This is indeed a fine sight upon which it is good to look, and a man might go far ere he would see so many brave men and fine horses. By my hilt! our little lord is wroth because we have come peacefully through the passes, but I will warrant him that we have fighting enow ere we turn our faces northward again. It is said that there are fourscore thousand men behind the King of Spain, with Du Guesclin and all the best lances of France, who have sworn to shed their heart's blood ere this Pedro come again to the throne."

"Yet our own army is a great one," said Alleyne.

"Nay, there are but seven-and-twenty thousand men. Chandos hath persuaded the Prince to leave many behind, and, indeed, I think that he is right, for there is little food and less water in these parts for which we are bound. A man without his meat or a horse without his fodder is like a wet bowstring, fit for little. But voilà, mon petit, here comes Chandos and his company, and there is many a pensil and banderole among yonder squadrons which show that the best blood of England is riding under his banners."

Whilst Aylward had been speaking, a strong column of archers had defiled through the pass beneath them. They were followed by a banner-bearer who held high the scarlet wedge upon a silver field which proclaimed the presence of the famous warrior. He rode himself within a spear's-length of his standard, clad from neck to foot in steel, but draped in the long linen gown, or parement, which was destined to be the cause of his death. His plumed helmet was carried behind him by his body squire, and his head was covered by a small purple cap, from under which his snow-white hair curled downwards to his shoulders. With his long beaklike nose and his single gleaming eye, which shone brightly from under a thick tuft of grizzled brow, he seemed to Alleyne to have something of the look of some fierce old bird of prey. For a moment he smiled, as his eye lit upon the banner of the five roses waving from the hamlet; but his course lay for Pampeluna, and he rode on after the archers.

Close at his heels came sixteen squires, all chosen from the highest families, and behind them rode twelve hundred English knights, with gleam of steel and tossing of plumes, their harness jingling, their long straight swords clanking against their stirrup irons, and the beat of their chargers' hoofs like the low deep roar of the sea upon the shore. Behind them marched six hundred Cheshire and Lancashire archers, bearing the badge of the Audleys, followed by the famous Lord Audley himself. Two hundred heavily armed cavalry rode behind the Audley standard, while close at their heels came the Duke of Lancaster with a glittering train, heralds tabarded with the royal arms riding three deep upon cream-colored chargers in front of him. Away behind him, as far as eye could reach, rolled the far-stretching, unbroken river of steel—rank after rank and column after column, with waving of plumes, glitter of arms, tossing of guidons, and flash and flutter of countless armorial devices. All day Alleyne looked down upon the changing scene, and all day the old bowman stood by his elbow, pointing out the crests of famous warriors and the arms of noble houses. So through the sunny winter day the chivalry of England poured down through the dark pass of Roncesvalles to the plains of Spain.

It was on Monday that the Duke of Lancaster's division passed safely through the Pyrenees. On the Tuesday there was a bitter frost, and the ground rung like iron beneath the feet of the horses; yet, ere evening, the Prince himself, with the main battle of his army, had passed the gorge and united with his vanguard at Pampeluna. With him rode the King of Majorca, the hostage King of Navarre, and the fierce Don Pedro of Spain, whose pale blue eyes gleamed with a sinister light as they rested once more upon the distant peaks of the land which had disowned him. Under the royal banners rode many a bold Gascon baron and many a hot-blooded islander. From dawn to sundown the long train wound through the pass, their breath reeking up upon the frosty air like the steam from a cauldron.

The weather was less keen upon the Wednesday, and the rear guard made good their passage, with the bombards and the wagon train. Free companions and Gascons made up this portion of the army to the number of ten thousand men—war-hardened and veteran companies of English bowmen and others whose very names seem to smack of hard hands and ruthless deeds. With them also were the pick of the Gascon chivalry and a long train of needy and grasping border nobles, with long pedigrees and short purses, who had come down from their hillside strongholds, all hungering for the spoils and the ransoms of Spain. By the Thursday morning the whole army was encamped in the Vale of Pampeluna, and the Prince had called his council to meet in the old palace of the ancient city of Navarre.

Chapter 28

HOW THE COMPANY MADE SPORT IN THE VALE OF PAMPELUNA

Whilst the council was sitting in Pampeluna, the White Company, having encamped in a neighboring valley, close to the companies of La Nuit and of Black Ortingo, were amusing themselves with swordsplay, wrestling, and shooting at the shields which they had placed upon the hillside to serve them as butts. The young archers, with their coats of mail thrown aside, their brown or flaxen hair tossing in the wind, and their jerkins turned back to give free play to their brawny chests and arms, stood in lines, each loosing his shaft in turn, while Johnston, Aylward, Black Simon, and half-a-score of the elders lounged up and down with critical eyes, and a word of rough praise or of curt censure for the marksmen. Behind stood knots of Gascon and Brabant crossbowmen from the companies of Ortingo and of La Nuit, leaning upon their unsightly weapons and watching the practice of the Englishmen.

"A good shot, Hewett, a good shot!" said old Johnston to a young bowman, who stood with his bow in his left hand, gazing with parted lips after his flying shaft. "You see, she finds the ring, as I knew she would from the moment that your string twanged."

"Loose it easy, steady, and yet sharp," said Aylward. "By my hilt! mon gar, it is very well when you do but shoot at a shield, but when there is a man behind the shield, and he rides at you with wave of sword and glint of eyes from behind his visor, you may find him a less easy mark."

"It is a mark that I have found before now," answered the young bowman.

"And shall again, camarade, I doubt not. But holà! Johnston, who is this who holds his bow like a crowkeeper?"

"It is Silas Peterson, of Horsham. Do not wink with one eye and look with the other, Silas, and do not hop and dance after you shoot, with your tongue out, for that will not speed it upon its way. Stand straight and firm, as God made you. Move not the bow arm, and steady with the drawing hand!"

"I' faith," said Black Simon, "I am a spearman myself, and am more fitted for handstrokes than for such work as this. Yet I have spent my days among bowmen, and I have seen many a brave shaft sped. I will not say but that we have some good marksmen here, and that this Company would be accounted a fine body of archers at any time or place. Yet I do not see any men who bend so strong a bow or shoot as true a shaft as those whom I have known."

"You say sooth," said Johnston, turning his seamed and grizzled face upon the man-at-arms. "See yonder," he added, pointing to a bombard which lay within the camp: "there is what hath done scath to good bowmanship, with its filthy soot and foolish roaring mouth. I wonder that a true knight like our prince should carry such a scurvy thing in his train. Robin, thou red-headed lurdan, how oft must I tell thee not to shoot straight with a quarter-wind blowing across the mark?"

"By these ten finger bones! there were some fine bowmen at the intaking of Calais," said Aylward. "I well remember that, on occasion of an outfall, a Genoan raised his arm over his mantlet and shook it at us, a hundred paces from our line. There were twenty who loosed shafts at him, and when the man was afterwards slain it was found that he had taken eighteen through his forearm."

"And I can call to mind," remarked Johnston, "that when the great cog *Christopher*, which the French had taken from us, was moored two hundred paces from the shore, two archers, little Robin Withstaff and Elias Baddlesmere, in four shots each cut every strand of her hempen anchor cord, so that she well-nigh came upon the rocks."

"Good shooting, i' faith rare shooting!" said Black Simon. "But I have seen you, Johnston, and you, Samkin Aylward, and one or two others who are still with us, shoot as well as the best. Was it not you, Johnston, who took the fat ox at Finsbury butts against the pick of London town?"

A sunburnt and black-eyed Brabanter had stood near the old archers, leaning upon a large crossbow and listening to their talk, which had been carried on in that hybrid camp dialect which both nations could understand. He was a squat, bull-necked man, clad in the iron helmet, mail tunic, and woolen gambeson of his class. A jacket with hanging sleeves, slashed with velvet at the neck and wrists, showed that he was a man of some consideration, and underofficer, or file leader, of his company.

"I cannot think," said he, "why you English should be so fond of your six-foot stick. If it amuse you to bend it, well and good; but why should I strain and pull, when my little moulinet [1] will do all for me, and better than I can do it for myself?"

"I have seen good shooting with the prod and with the latch," said Aylward, "but, by my hilt! camarade, with all respect to you and to your bow, I think that is but a woman's weapon, which a woman can point and loose as easily as a man."

"I know not about that," answered the Brabanter, "but this I know, that though I have served for fourteen years, I have never yet seen an Englishman do aught with the longbow which I could not do better with my arbalest. By the three kings! I would even go further and say that I have done things with my arbalest which no Englishman could do with his longbow."

"Well said, mon gar," cried Aylward. "A good cock has ever a brave call. Now, I have shot little of late, but there is Johnston here who will try a round with you for the honor of the Company."

"And I will lay a gallon of Jurançon wine upon the longbow," said Black Simon, "though I had rather, for my own drinking, that it were a quart of Twynham ale."

"I take both your challenge and your wager," said the man of Brabant, throwing off his jacket and glancing keenly about him with his black, twinkling eyes. "I cannot see any fitting mark, for I care not to waste a bolt upon these shields, which a drunken boor could not miss at a village kermesse."

[1] *moulinet* (mōō'lĭ·nĕt'): a winding device for bending a crossbow.

"This is a perilous man," whispered an English man-at-arms, plucking at Aylward's sleeve. "He is the best marksman of all the crossbow companies and it was he who brought down the Constable de Bourbon at Brignais. I fear that your man will come by little honor with him."

"Yet I have seen Johnston shoot this twenty years, and I will not flinch from it. How say you, old war hound, will you not have a flight shot or two with this springald?"

"Tut, tut, Aylward," said the old bowman. "My day is past, and it is for the younger ones to hold what we have gained. I take it unkindly of thee, Samkin, that thou shouldst call all eyes thus upon a broken bowman who could once shoot a fair shaft. Let me feel that bow, Wilkins! It is a Scotch bow, I see, for the upper nock is without and the lower within. By the black rood! it is a good piece of yew, well nocked, well strung, well waxed, and very joyful to the feel. I think even now that I might hit any large and goodly mark with a bow like this. Turn thy quiver to me, Aylward. I love an ash arrow pierced with cornelwood for a roving shaft."

"By my hilt! and so do I," cried Aylward. "These three gander-winged shafts are such."

"So I see, comrade. It has been my wont to choose a saddle-backed feather for a dead shaft, and a swine-backed for a smooth flier. I will take the two of them. Ah! Samkin, lad, the eye grows dim and the hand less firm as the years pass."

"Come, then, are you not ready?" said the Brabanter, who had watched with ill-concealed impatience the slow and methodic movements of his antagonist.

"I will venture a rover with you, or try long butts or hoyles," said old Johnston. "To my mind the longbow is a better weapon than the arbalest, but it may be ill for me to prove it."

"So I think," quoth the other with a sneer. He drew his moulinet from his girdle, and fixing it to the windlass, he drew back the powerful double cord until it had clicked into the catch. Then from his quiver he drew a short, thick quarrel, which he placed with the utmost care upon the groove. Word had spread of what was going forward, and the rivals were already surrounded, not only by the English archers of the Company, but by hundreds of arbalestiers and men-at-arms from the bands of Ortingo and La Nuit, to the latter of which the Brabanter belonged.

"There is a mark yonder on the hill," said he; "mayhap you can discern it."

"I see something," answered Johnston, shading his eyes with his hand; "but it is a very long shoot."

"A fair shoot—a fair shoot! Stand aside, Arnaud, lest you find a bolt through your gizzard. Now, comrade, I take no flight shot, and I give you the vantage of watching my shaft."

As he spoke he raised his arbalest to his shoulder and was about to pull the trigger, when a large gray stork flapped heavily into view, skimming over the brow of the hill, and then soaring up into the air to pass the valley. Its shrill and piercing cries drew all eyes upon it, and, as it came nearer, a dark spot which circled above it resolved itself into a peregrine falcon, which hovered over its head, poising itself from time to time, and watching its chance of closing with its clumsy quarry. Nearer and nearer came the two birds, all absorbed in their own contest, the stork wheeling upwards, the hawk still fluttering above it, until they were not a hundred paces from the camp. The Brabanter raised his weapon to the sky, and there came the short, deep twang of his powerful string. His bolt struck the stork just where its wing meets the body, and the bird whirled aloft in a last convulsive flutter before falling, wounded and flapping, to the earth. A roar of applause burst from the crossbowmen; but at the instant that the bolt struck its mark, old Johnston, who had stood listlessly with arrow on string, bent his bow and sped a shaft through the body of the falcon. Whipping the other from his belt, he sent it skimming some few feet from the earth with so true an aim that it struck and transfixed the stork for the second time ere it could reach the ground. A deep-chested shout of delight burst from the archers at the sight of this double feat, and Aylward, dancing with joy, threw his arms round the old marksman and embraced him with such vigor that their mail tunics clanged again.

"Ah! camarade," he cried, "you shall have a stoup with me for this! What then, old dog, would not the hawk please thee, but thou must have the stork as well. Oh, to my heart again!"

"It is a pretty piece of yew, and well strung," said Johnston, with a twinkle in his deep-set gray eyes. "Even an old broken bowman might find the clout with a bow like this."

"You have done very well," remarked the Brabanter in a surly voice. "But it seems to me that you have not yet shown yourself to be a better marksman than I, for I have struck that at which I aimed, and, by the three kings! no man can do more."

"It would ill beseem me to claim to be a better marksman," answered Johnston, "for I have heard great things of your skill. I did but wish to show that the longbow could do that which an arbalest could not do, for you could not with your moulinet have your string ready to speed another shaft ere the bird drop to the earth."

"In that you have vantage," said the crossbowman. "By St. James! it is now my turn to show you where my weapon has the better of you. I pray you to draw a flight shaft with all your strength down the valley, that we may see the length of your shoot."

"That is a very strong prod of yours," said Johnston, shaking his grizzled head as he glanced at the thick arch and powerful strings of his rival's arbalest. "I have little doubt that you can overshoot me, and yet I have seen bowmen who could send a cloth-yard arrow further than you could speed a quarrel."

"So I have heard," remarked the Brabanter; " and yet it is a strange thing that these wondrous bowmen are never where I chance to be. Pace out the distances with a wand at every five score, and do you, Arnaud, stand at the fifth wand to carry back my bolts to me."

A line was measured down the valley, and Johnston, drawing an arrow to the very head, sent it whistling over the row of wands.

"Bravely drawn! A rare shoot!" shouted the bystanders. "It is well up to the fourth mark."

"By my hilt! it is over it," cried Aylward. "I can see where they have stooped to gather up the shaft."

"We shall hear anon," said Johnston quietly, and presently a young archer came running to say that the arrow had fallen twenty paces beyond the fourth wand.

"Four hundred paces and a score," cried Black Simon. "I' faith, it is a very long flight. Yet wood and steel may do more than flesh and blood."

The Brabanter stepped forward with a smile of conscious triumph and loosed the cord of his weapon. A shout burst from his comrades as they watched the swift and lofty flight of the heavy bolt.

"Over the fourth!" groaned Aylward. "By my hilt! I think that it is well up to the fifth."

"It is over the fifth!" cried a Gascon loudly, and a comrade came running with waving arms to say that the bolt had pitched eight paces beyond the mark of the five hundred.

"Which weapon hath the vantage now?" cried the Brabanter, strutting proudly about with shouldered arbalest, amid the applause of his companions.

"You can overshoot me," said Johnston gently.

"Or any other man who ever bent a longbow," cried his victorious adversary.

"Nay, not so fast," said a huge archer, whose mighty shoulders and red head towered high above the throng of his comrades. "I must have a word with you ere you crow so loudly. Where is my little popper? By sainted Dick of Hampole! it will be a strange thing if I cannot outshoot that thing of thine, which to my eyes is more like a rattrap than a bow. Will you try another flight, or do you stand by your last?"

"Five hundred and eight paces will serve my turn," answered the Brabanter, looking askance at this new opponent.

"Tut, John," whispered Aylward, "you never were a marksman. Why must you thrust your spoon into this dish?"

"Easy and slow, Aylward. There are very many things which I cannot do, but there are also one or two which I have the trick of. It is in my mind that I can beat this shoot, if my bow will but hold together."

"Go on, old babe of the woods!" "Have at it, Hampshire!" cried the archers, laughing.

"By my soul! you may grin," cried John. "But I learned how to make the long shoot from old Hob Miller of Milford." He took up a great black bow, as he spoke, and sitting down upon the ground he placed his two feet on either end of the stave. With an arrow fitted, he then pulled the string towards him with both hands until the head of the shaft was level with the wood. The great bow creaked and groaned and the cord vibrated with the tension.

"Who is this fool's-head who stands in the way of my shoot?" said he, craning up his neck from the ground.

"He stands on the further side of my mark," answered the Brabanter, "so he has little to fear from you."

"Well, the saints assoil him!" cried John. "Though I think he is overnear to be scathed." As he spoke he raised his two feet, with the bowstave upon their soles, and his cord twanged with a deep rich hum which might be heard across the valley. The measurer in the distance fell flat upon his face, and then jumping up again, he began to run in the opposite direction.

"Well shot, old lad! It is indeed over his head," cried the bowmen.

"Mon Dieu!" exclaimed the Brabanter, "who ever saw such a shoot?"

"It is but a trick," quoth John. "Many a time have I won a gallon of ale by covering a mile in three flights down Wilverley Chase."

"It fell a hundred and thirty paces beyond the fifth mark," shouted an archer in the distance.

"Six hundred and thirty paces! Mon Dieu! but that is a shoot! And yet it says nothing for your weapon, mon gros camarade, for it was by turning yourself into a crossbow that you did it."

"By my hilt! there is truth in that," cried Aylward. "And now, friend, I will myself show you a vantage of the longbow. I pray you to speed a bolt against yonder shield with all your force. It is an inch of elm with bull's hide over it."

"I scarce shot as many shafts at Brignais," growled the man of Brabant; "though I found a better mark there than a cantle of bull's hide. But what is this, Englishman? The shield hangs not one hundred paces from me, and a blind man could strike it." He screwed up his string to the furthest pitch, and shot his quarrel at the dangling shield. Aylward, who had drawn an arrow from his quiver, carefully greased the head of it, and sped it at the same mark.

"Run, Wilkins," quoth he, "and fetch me the shield."

Long were the faces of the Englishmen and broad the laugh of the crossbowmen as the heavy mantlet was carried towards them, for there in the center was the thick Brabant bolt driven deeply into the wood, while there was neither sign nor trace of the cloth-yard shaft.

"By the three kings!" cried the Brabanter, "this time at least there is no gainsaying which is the better weapon, or which the truer hand that held it. You have missed the shield, Englishman."

"Tarry a bit! tarry a bit, mon gar!" quoth Aylward, and turning round the shield he showed a round clear hole in the wood at the back of it. "My shaft has passed through it, camarade, and I trow the one which goes through is more to be feared than that which bides on the way."

The Brabanter stamped his foot with mortification, and was about to make some angry reply, when Alleyne Edricson came riding up to the crowds of archers.

"Sir Nigel will be here anon," said he, "and it is his wish to speak with the Company."

In an instant order and method took the place of general confusion. Bows, steel caps, and jacks were caught up from the grass. A long cordon cleared the camp of all strangers, while the main body fell into four lines with underofficers and file leaders in front and on either flank. So they stood, silent and motionless, when their leader came riding towards them, his face shining and his whole small figure swelling with the news which he bore.

"Great honor has been done to us, men," cried he: "for, of all the army, the prince has chosen us out that we should ride onwards into the lands of Spain to spy upon our enemies. Yet, as there are many of us, and as the service may not be to the liking of all, I pray that those will step forward from the ranks who have the will to follow me."

There was a rustle among the bowmen, but when Sir Nigel looked up at them no man stood forward from his fellows, but the four lines of men stretched unbroken as before. Sir Nigel blinked at them in amazement, and a look of the deepest sorrow shadowed his face.

"That I should live to see the day!" he cried. "What! not one—"

"My fair lord," whispered Alleyne, "they have all stepped forward."

"Ah, by St. Paul! I see how it is with them. I could not think that they would desert me. We start at dawn tomorrow, and ye are to have the horses of Sir Robert Cheney's company. Be ready, I pray ye, at early cockcrow."

A buzz of delight burst from the archers as they broke their ranks and ran hither and thither, whooping and cheering like boys who have news of a holiday. Sir Nigel gazed after them with a smiling face, when a heavy hand fell upon his shoulder.

"What ho! my knight-errant of Twynham!" said a voice. "You are off to Ebro, I hear; and, by the holy fish of Tobias! you must take me under your banner."

"What! Sir Oliver Buttesthorn!" cried Sir Nigel. "I had heard that you were come into camp, and had hoped to see you. Glad and proud shall I be to have you with me."

"I have a most particular and weighty reason for wishing to go," said the sturdy knight.

"I can well believe it," returned Sir Nigel; "I have met no man who is quicker to follow where honor leads."

"Nay, it is not for honor that I go, Nigel."

"For what then?"

"For pullets."

"Pullets?"

"Yes, for the rascal vanguard have cleared every hen from the countryside. It was this very morning that Norbury, my squire, lamed his horse in riding round in quest of one, for we have a bag of truffles, and naught to eat with them. Never have I seen such locusts as this vanguard of ours. Not a pullet shall we see until we are in front of them; so I shall leave my Winchester runagates to the care of the provost marshal, and I shall hie south with you, Nigel, with my truffles at my saddlebow."

"Oliver, Oliver, I know you overwell," said Sir Nigel, shaking his head, and the two old soldiers rode off together to their pavilion.

Chapter 29

HOW SIR NIGEL HAWKED[1] AT AN EAGLE

To the south of Pampeluna in the kingdom of Navarre there stretched a high tableland, rising into bare, sterile hills, brown or gray in color, and strewn with huge boulders of granite. On the

[1] *hawk* (hôk): to attempt to capture by means of specially trained hawks.

Gascon side of the great mountains there had been running streams, meadows, forests, and little nestling villages. Here, on the contrary, were nothing but naked rocks, poor pasture, and savage, stone-strewn wastes. Gloomy defiles or barrancas intersected this wild country, with mountain torrents dashing and foaming between their rugged sides. The clatter of waters, the scream of the eagle, and the howling of wolves were the only sounds which broke upon the silence in that dreary and inhospitable region.

Through this wild country it was that Sir Nigel and his Company pushed their way, riding at times through vast defiles where the brown, gnarled cliffs shot up on either side of them, and the sky was but a long winding blue slit between the clustering lines of box which fringed the lips of the precipices; or again leading their horses along the narrow and rocky paths worn by the muleteers upon the edges of the chasm, where under their very elbows they could see the white streak which marked the *gave* which foamed a thousand feet below them. So for two days they pushed their way through the wild places of Navarre, past Fuente, over the rapid Ega, through Estella, until upon a winter's evening the mountains fell away from in front of them, and they saw the broad blue Ebro curving betwixt its double line of homesteads and of villages. The fishers of Viana were aroused that night by rough voices speaking in a strange tongue, and ere morning Sir Nigel and his men had ferried the river and were safe upon the land of Spain.

All the next day they lay in a pine wood near to the town of Logrono, resting their horses and taking counsel as to what they should do. Sir Nigel had with him Sir William Felton, Sir Oliver Buttesthorn, stout old Sir Simon Burley, the Scotch knight-errant, the Earl of Angus, and Sir Richard Causton, all accounted among the bravest knights in the army, together with sixty veteran men-at-arms, and three hundred and twenty archers. Spies had been sent out in the morning, and returned after nightfall to say that the King of Spain was encamped some fourteen miles off in the direction of Burgos, having with him twenty thousand horse and forty-five thousand foot. A dry-wood fire had been lit, and round this the leaders crouched, the glare beating upon their rugged faces, while the hardy archers lounged and chatted amid the tethered horses, while they munched their scanty provisions.

"For my part," said Sir Simon Burley, "I am of opinion that

we have already done that which we have come for. For do we not now know where the King is, and how great a following he hath, which was the end of our journey?"

"True," answered Sir William Felton, "but I have come on this venture because it is a long time since I have broken a spear in war, and, certes, I shall not go back until I have run a course with some cavalier of Spain. Let those go back who will, but I must see more of these Spaniards ere I turn."

"I will not leave you, Sir William," returned Sir Simon Burley; "and yet, as an old soldier and one who hath seen much of war, I cannot but think that it is an ill thing for four hundred men to find themselves between an army of sixty thousand on the one side and a broad river on the other."

"Yet," said Sir Richard Causton, "we cannot for the honor of England go back without a blow struck."

"Nor for the honor of Scotland either," cried the Earl of Angus. "By St. Andrew! I wish that I may never set eyes upon the water of Leith again if I pluck my horse's bridle ere I have seen this camp of theirs."

"By St. Paul! you have spoken very well," said Sir Nigel, "and I have always heard that there were very worthy gentlemen among the Scots, and fine skirmishing to be had upon their border. Bethink you, Sir Simon, that we have this news from the lips of common spies, who can scarce tell us as much of the enemy and of his forces as the Prince would wish to hear."

"You are the leader in this venture, Sir Nigel," the other answered, "and I do but ride under your banner."

"Yet I would fain have your rede and counsel, Sir Simon. But, touching what you say of the river, we can take heed that we shall not have it at the back of us, for the Prince hath now advanced to Salvatierra, and thence to Vittoria, so that if we come upon their camp from the further side we can make good our retreat."

"What then would you propose?" asked Sir Simon, shaking his grizzled head as one who is but half convinced.

"That we ride forward ere the news reach them that we have crossed the river. In this way we may have sight of their army, and, perchance, even find occasion for some small deed against them."

"So be it, then," said Sir Simon Burley; and the rest of the council having approved, a scanty meal was hurriedly snatched, and the advance resumed under the cover of the darkness. All night they led their horses, stumbling and groping through wild defiles and rugged valleys, following the guidance of a frightened peasant who was strapped by the wrist to Black Simon's stirrup leather. With the early dawn they found themselves in a black ravine, with others sloping away from it on either side, and the bare brown crags rising in long bleak terraces all round them.

"If it please you, fair lord," said Black Simon, "this man hath misled us, and since there is no tree upon which we may hang him, it might be well to hurl him over yonder cliff."

The peasant, reading the soldier's meaning in his fierce eyes and harsh accents, dropped upon his knees, screaming loudly for mercy.

"How comes it, dog?" asked Sir William Felton in Spanish. "Where is this camp to which you swore that you would lead us?"

"By the sweet Virgin! By the blessed Mother of God!" cried the trembling peasant, "I swear to you that in the darkness I have myself lost the path."

"Over the cliff with him!" shouted half a dozen voices; but ere the archers could drag him from the rocks to which he clung, Sir Nigel had ridden up and called upon them to stop.

"How is this, sirs?" said he. "As long as the Prince doth me the honor to entrust this venture to me, it is for me only to give orders; and, by St. Paul! I shall be right blithe to go very deeply into the matter with anyone to whom my words may give offense. How say you, Sir William? Or you, my Lord of Angus? Or you, Sir Richard?"

"Nay, nay, Nigel!" cried Sir William. "This base peasant is too small a matter for old comrades to quarrel over. But he hath betrayed us, and, certes, he hath merited a dog's death."

"Hark ye, fellow," said Sir Nigel. "We give you one more chance to find the path. We are about to gain much honor, Sir William, in this enterprise, and it would be a sorry thing if the first blood shed were that of an unworthy boor. Let us say our morning orisons, and it may chance that ere we finish he may strike upon the track."

With bowed heads, and steel caps in hand, the archers stood at their horses' heads, while Sir Simon Burley repeated the pater, the ave, and the credo. Long did Alleyne bear the scene in mind

—the knot of knights in their dull leaden-hued armor, the ruddy visage of Sir Oliver, the craggy features of the Scottish earl, the shining scalp of Sir Nigel, with the dense ring of hard, bearded faces and the long brown heads of the horses, all topped and circled by the beetling cliffs. Scarce had the last deep "amen" broken from the Company, when, in an instant, there rose the scream of a hundred bugles, with the deep rolling of drums and the clashing of cymbals, all sounding together in one deafening uproar. Knights and archers sprang to arms, convinced that some great host was upon them; but the guide dropped upon his knees and thanked Heaven for its mercies.

"We have found them, *caballeros!*" [1] he cried. "This is their morning call. If ye will but deign to follow me, I will set them before you ere a man might tell his beads."

As he spoke he scrambled down one of the narrow ravines, and, climbing over a low ridge at the further end, he led them into a short valley with a stream purling down the center of it and a very thick growth of elder and of box upon either side. Pushing their way through the dense brushwood, they looked out upon a scene which made their hearts beat harder and their breath come faster.

In front of them there lay a broad plain, watered by two winding streams and covered with grass, stretching away to where, in the furthest distance, the towers of Burgos bristled up against the light blue morning sky. Over all this vast meadow there lay a great city of tents—thousands upon thousands of them, laid out in streets and in squares like a well-ordered town. High silken pavilions or colored marquees,[2] shooting up from among the crowd of meaner dwellings, marked where the great lords and barons of Leon and Castile displayed their standards, while over the white roofs, as far as eye could reach, the waving of ancients, pavons, pensils, and banderoles, with flash of gold and glow of colors, proclaimed that all the chivalry of Iberia [3] were mustered in the plain beneath them. Far off, in the center of the camp, a huge palace of red and white silk, with the royal arms of Castile waving from the summit, announced that the gallant Henry lay there in the midst of his warriors.

As the English adventurers, peeping out from behind their

[1] *caballero* (kä'vä·lyā'rō): Spanish for "a knight or horseman." [2] *marquee* (mär·kē'): a field tent. [3] *Iberia* (ī·bēr'ĭ·ȧ): Spain.

brushwood screen, looked down upon this wondrous sight, they could see that the vast army in front of them was already afoot. The first pink light of the rising sun glittered upon the steel caps and breastplates of dense masses of slingers and of crossbowmen, who drilled and marched in the spaces which had been left for their exercise. A thousand columns of smoke reeked up into the pure morning air where the faggots were piled and the camp kettles already simmering. In the open plain, clouds of light horse galloped and swooped with swaying bodies and waving javelins, after the fashion which the Spanish had adopted from their Moorish enemies. All along by the sedgy banks of the rivers long lines of pages led their masters' chargers down to water, while the knights themselves lounged in gayly dressed groups about the doors of their pavilions, or rode out, with their falcons upon their wrists and their greyhounds behind them, in quest of quail or of leveret.

"By my hilt! mon gar," whispered Aylward to Alleyne, as the young squire stood with parted lips and wondering eyes, gazing down at the novel scene before him, "we have been seeking them all night, but now that we have found them I know not what we are to do with them."

"You say sooth, Samkin," quoth old Johnston. "I would that we were upon the far side of Ebro again, for there is neither honor nor profit to be gained here. What say you, Simon?"

"By the rood!" cried the fierce man-at-arms, "I will see the color of their blood ere I turn my mare's head for the mountains. Am I a child, that I should ride for three days and naught but words at the end of it?"

"Well said, my sweet honeysuckle!" cried Hordle John. "I am with you, like hilt to blade. Could I but lay hands upon one of those gay prancers yonder, I doubt not that I should have ransom enough from him to buy my mother a new cow."

"A cow!" said Aylward. "Say rather ten acres and a homestead on the banks of Avon.

"Say you so? Then, by Our Lady! here is for yonder one in the red jerkin!"

He was about to push recklessly forward into the open, when Sir Nigel himself darted in front of him, with his hand upon his breast.

"Back!" said he. "Our time is not yet come, and we must lie

here until evening. Throw off your jacks and headpieces, lest their eyes catch the shine, and tether the horses among the rocks."

The order was swiftly obeyed, and in ten minutes the archers were stretched along by the side of the brook, munching the bread and the bacon which they had brought in their bags, and craning their necks to watch the ever-changing scene beneath them. Very quiet and still they lay, save for a muttered jest or whispered order, for twice during the long morning they heard bugle calls from amid the hills on either side of them, which showed that they had thrust themselves in between the outposts of the enemy. The leaders sat amongst the boxwood and took counsel together as to what they should do; while from below there surged up the buzz of voices, the shouting, the neighing of horses, and all the uproar of a great camp.

"What boots it [1] to wait?" said Sir William Felton. "Let us ride down upon their camp ere they discover us."

"And so say I," cried the Scottish earl; "for they do not know that there is any enemy within thirty long leagues of them."

"For my part," said Sir Simon Burley, "I think that it is madness, for you cannot hope to rout this great army; and where are you to go and what are you to do when they have turned upon you? How say you, Sir Oliver Buttesthorn?"

"By the apple of Eve!" cried the fat knight, "it appears to me that this wind brings a very savory smell of garlic and of onions from their cooking kettles. I am in favor of riding down upon them at once, if my old friend and comrade here is of the same mind."

"Nay," said Sir Nigel, "I have a plan by which we may attempt some small deed upon them, and yet, by the help of God, may be able to draw off again; which, as Sir Simon Burley hath said, would be scarce possible in any other way."

"How then, Sir Nigel?" asked several voices.

"We shall lie here all day; for amid this brushwood it is ill [2] for them to see us. Then when evening comes we shall sally out upon them and see if we may not gain some honorable advancement from them."

"But why then rather than now?"

"Because we shall have nightfall to cover us when we draw off, so that we may make our way back through the mountains.

[1] *What boots it?:* What use is it? [2] *ill:* difficult.

I would station a score of archers here in the pass, with all our pennons jutting forth from the rocks, and as many nakirs and drums and bugles as we have with us, so that those who follow us in the fading light may think that the whole army of the Prince is upon them, and fear to go further. What think you of my plan, Sir Simon?"

"By my troth! I think very well of it," cried the prudent old commander. "If four hundred men must needs run a tilt against sixty thousand, I cannot see how they can do it better or more safely."

"And so say I," cried Felton heartily. "But I wish the day were over, for it will be an ill thing for us if they chance to light upon us."

The words were scarce out of his mouth when there came a clatter of loose stones, the sharp cling of trotting hoofs, and a dark-faced cavalier, mounted upon a white horse, burst through the bushes and rode swiftly down the valley from the end which was farthest from the Spanish camp. Lightly armed, with his visor open and a hawk perched upon his left wrist, he looked about him with the careless air of a man who is bent wholly upon pleasure, and unconscious of the possibility of danger. Suddenly, however, his eyes lit upon the fierce faces which glared out at him from the brushwood. With a cry of terror, he thrust his spurs into his horse's sides and dashed for the narrow opening of the gorge. For a moment it seemed as though he would have reached it, for he had trampled over or dashed aside the archers who threw themselves in his way; but Hordle John seized him by the foot in his grasp of iron and dragged him from the saddle, while two others caught the frightened horse.

"Ho, ho!" roared the great archer. "How many cows wilt buy my mother, if I set thee free?"

"Hush that bull's bellowing!" cried Sir Nigel impatiently. "Bring the man here. By St. Paul! it is not the first time that we have met; for, if I mistake not, it is Don Diego Alvarez, who was once at the Prince's court."

"It is indeed I," said the Spanish knight, speaking in the French tongue, "and I pray you to pass your sword through my heart; for how can I live—I, a caballero of Castile—after being dragged from my horse by the base hands of a common archer?"

"Fret not for that," answered Sir Nigel. "For, in sooth, had he not pulled you down, a dozen cloth-yard shafts had crossed each other in your body."

"By St. James! it were better so than to be polluted by his touch," answered the Spaniard, with his black eyes sparkling with rage and hatred. "I trust that I am now the prisoner of some honorable knight or gentleman."

"You are the prisoner of the man who took you, Sir Diego," answered Sir Nigel. "And I may tell you that better men than either you or I have found themselves before now prisoners in the hands of archers of England."

"What ransom, then, does he demand?" asked the Spaniard.

Big John scratched his red head and grinned in high delight when the question was propounded to him. "Tell him," said he, "that I shall have ten cows and a bull too, if it be but a little one. Also a dress of blue sendal for mother and a red one for Joan; with five acres of pasture land, two scythes, and a fine new grindstone. Likewise a small house, with stalls for the cows, and thirty-six gallons of beer for the thirsty weather."

"Tut, tut!" cried Sir Nigel, laughing. "All these things may be had for money; and I think, Don Diego, that five thousand crowns is not too much for so renowned a knight."

"It shall be duly paid him."

"For some days we must keep you with us; and I must crave leave also to use your shield, your armor, and your horse."

"My harness is yours by the law of arms," said the Spaniard gloomily.

"I do but ask the loan of it. I have need of it this day, but it shall be duly returned to you. Set guards, Aylward, with arrow on string, at either end of the pass; for it may happen that some other cavaliers may visit us ere the time be come." All day the little band of Englishmen lay in the sheltered gorge, looking down upon the vast host of their unconscious enemies. Shortly after midday, a great uproar of shouting and cheering broke out in the camp, with mustering of men and calling of bugles. Clambering up among the rocks, the companions saw a long rolling cloud of dust along the whole eastern sky line, with the glint of spears and the flutter of pennons, which announced the approach of a large body of cavalry. For a moment a wild hope came upon them that perhaps the Prince had moved more swiftly than had been planned, that he had crossed the Ebro, and that this was his vanguard sweeping to the attack.

"Surely I see the red pile of Chandos at the head of yonder squadron!" cried Sir Richard Causton, shading his eyes with his hand.

"Not so," answered Sir Simon Burley, who had watched the approaching host with a darkening face. "It is even as I feared. That is the double eagle of Du Guesclin."

"You say very truly," cried the Earl of Angus. "These are the levies of France, for I can see the ensigns of the Marshal d'Andreghen, with that of the Lord of Antoing and of Briseuil, and of many another from Brittany and Anjou."

"By St. Paul! I am very glad of it," said Sir Nigel. "Of these Spaniards I know nothing; but the French are very worthy gentlemen, and will do what they can for our advancement."

"There are at the least four thousand of them, and all men-at-arms," cried Sir William Felton. "See, there is Bertrand himself, beside his banner, and there is King Henry, who rides to welcome him. Now they all turn and come into the camp together."

As he spoke, the vast throng of Spaniards and of Frenchmen trooped across the plain, with brandished arms and tossing banners. All day long the sound of revelry and of rejoicing from the crowded camp swelled up to the ears of the Englishmen, and they could see the soldiers of the two nations throwing themselves into each other's arms and dancing hand-in-hand round the blazing fires. The sun had sunk behind a cloud bank in the west before Sir Nigel at last gave word that the men should resume their arms and have their horses ready. He had himself thrown off his armor and had dressed himself from head to foot in the harness of the captured Spaniard.

"Sir William," said he, "it is my intention to attempt a small deed, and I ask you, therefore, that you will lead this outfall upon the camp. For me, I will ride into their camp with my squire and two archers. I pray you to watch me, and to ride forth when I am come among the tents. You will leave twenty men behind here, as we planned this morning, and you will ride back here after you have ventured as far as seems good to you."

"I will do as you order, Nigel; but what is it that you propose to do?"

"You will see anon, and, indeed, it is but a trifling matter. Alleyne, you will come with me and lead a spare horse by the bridle. I will have the two archers who rode with us through France, for they are trusty men and of stout heart. Let them ride behind us, and let them leave their bows here among the bushes, for it is not my wish that they should know that we are Englishmen. Say no word to any whom we may meet, and, if any speak to you, pass on as though you heard them not. Are you ready?"

"I am ready, my fair lord," said Alleyne.

"And I," "And I," cried Aylward and John.

"Then the rest I leave to your wisdom, Sir William; and if God sends us fortune we shall meet you again in this gorge ere it be dark."

So saying, Sir Nigel mounted the white horse of the Spanish cavalier and rode quietly forth from his concealment with his three companions behind him, Alleyne leading his master's own steed by the bridle. So many small parties of French and Spanish horse were sweeping hither and thither that the small band attracted little notice, and making its way at a gentle trot across the plain, they came as far as the camp without challenge or hindrance. On and on they pushed, past the endless lines of tents amid the dense swarms of horsemen and of footmen, until the huge royal pavilion stretched in front of them. They were close upon it when, of a sudden, there broke out a wild hubbub from a distant portion of the camp, with screams and war cries and all the wild tumult of battle. At the sound, soldiers came rushing from their tents, knights shouted loudly for their squires, and there was mad turmoil on every hand of bewildered men and plunging horses. At the royal tent a crowd of gorgeously dressed servants ran hither and thither in helpless panic, for the guard of soldiers who were stationed there had already ridden off in the direction of the alarm. A man-at-arms on either side of the doorway were the sole protectors of the royal dwelling.

"I have come for the King," whispered Sir Nigel; "and, by St. Paul! he must back with us or I must bide here."

Alleyne and Aylward sprang from their horses and flew at the two sentries, who were disarmed and beaten down in an instant by so furious and unexpected an attack. Sir Nigel dashed into the royal tent, and was followed by Hordle John as soon as the horses had been secured. From within came wild screamings and the clash of steel, and then the two emerged once more, their swords and forearms reddened with blood, while John bore over his shoulder the senseless body of a man whose gay surcoat, adorned with the lions and towers of Castile, proclaimed him to belong to the royal house. A crowd of white-faced sewers and pages swarmed at their heels, those behind pushing forwards, while the foremost shrank back from the fierce faces and reeking weapons of the adventurers. The senseless body was thrown across the spare horse, the four sprang to their saddles, and away they thundered, with loose reins and busy spurs, through the swarming camp.

But confusion and disorder still reigned among the Spaniards, for Sir William Felton and his men had swept through half their camp, leaving a long litter of the dead and the dying to mark their course. Uncertain who were their attackers, and unable to tell their English enemies from their newly arrived Breton allies, the Spanish knights rode wildly hither and thither in aimless fury. The mad turmoil, the mixture of races, and the fading light were all in favor of the four who alone knew their own purpose among the vast uncertain multitude. Twice ere they reached open ground they had to break their way through small bodies of horses, and once there came a whistle of arrows and singing of stones about their ears; but, still dashing onwards, they shot out from among the tents and found their own comrades retreating for the mountains at no very great distance from them. Another five minutes of wild galloping over the plain, and they were all back in their gorge, while their pursuers fell back before the rolling of drums and blare of trumpets which seemed to proclaim that the whole army of the Prince was about to emerge from the mountain passes.

"By my soul! Nigel," cried Sir Oliver, waving a great boiled ham over his head, "I have come by something which I may eat with my truffles! I had a hard fight for it, for there were three of them with their mouths open and the knives in their hands, all sitting agape round the table, when I rushed in upon them. How say you, Sir William, will you not try the smack of the famed Spanish swine, though we have but the brook water to wash it down?"

"Later, Sir Oliver," answered the old soldier, wiping his

grimed face. "We must further into the mountains ere we be in safety. But what have we here, Nigel?"

"It is a prisoner whom I have taken, and, in sooth, as he came from the royal tent and wears the royal arms upon his jupon, I trust that he is the King of Spain."

"The King of Spain!" cried the companions, crowding round in amazement.

"Nay, Sir Nigel," said Felton, peering at the prisoner through the uncertain light, "I have twice seen Henry of Trastamare, and, certes, this man in no way resembles him."

"Then, by the light of heaven! I will ride back for him," cried Sir Nigel.

"Nay, nay, the camp is in arms, and it would be rank madness. Who are you, fellow?" he added in Spanish, "and how is it that you dare to wear the arms of Castile?"

The prisoner was but recovering the consciousness which had been squeezed from him by the grip of Hordle John. "If it please you," he answered, "I and nine others are the body squires of the King and must ever wear his arms, so as to shield him from even such perils as have threatened him this night. The King is at the tent of the brave Du Guesclin, where he will sup tonight. But I am a caballero of Aragon, Don Sancho Penelosa, and, though I be no king, I am yet ready to pay a fitting price for my ransom."

"By St. Paul! I will not touch your gold," cried Sir Nigel. "Go back to your master and give him greeting from Sir Nigel Loring of Twynham Castle, telling him that I had hoped to make his better acquaintance this night, and that, if I have disordered his tent, it was but in my eagerness to know so famed and courteous a knight. Spur on, comrades! for we must cover many a league ere we can venture to light fire or to loosen girth. I had hoped to ride without this patch tonight, but it seems that I must carry it yet a little longer."

Chapter 30

HOW SIR NIGEL TOOK THE PATCH FROM HIS EYE

It was a cold, bleak morning in the beginning of March, and the mist was drifting in dense rolling clouds through the passes of the Cantabrian mountains. The Company, who had passed the night in a sheltered gully, were already astir, some crowding round the blazing fires and others romping or leaping over each other's backs, for their limbs were chilled, and the air biting. Here and there, through the dense haze which surrounded them, there loomed out huge pinnacles and jutting boulders of rock: while high above the sea of vapor there towered up one gigantic peak, with the pink glow of the early sunshine upon its snow-capped head. The ground was wet, the rocks dripping, the grass and evergreens sparkling with beads of moisture; yet the camp was loud with laughter and merriment, for a messenger had ridden in from the Prince with words of heart-stirring praise for what they had done, and with orders that they should still abide in the forefront of the army.

Round one of the fires were clustered four or five of the leading men of the archers, cleaning the rust from their weapons, and glancing impatiently from time to time at a great pot which smoked over the blaze. There was Aylward squatting cross-legged in his shirt, while he scrubbed away at his chain-mail brigandine, whistling loudly the while. On one side of him sat old Johnston, who was busy in trimming the feathers of some arrows to his liking; and on the other Hordle John, who lay with his great limbs all asprawl, and his headpiece balanced upon his uplifted foot. Black Simon of Norwich crouched amid the rocks, crooning an Eastland ballad to himself, while he whetted his sword upon a flat stone which lay across his knees; while beside him sat Alleyne Edricson and Norbury, the silent squire of Sir Oliver, holding out their chilled hands towards the crackling faggots.

"Cast on another culpon, and stir the broth with thy sword sheath," growled John, looking anxiously for the twentieth time at the reeking pot.

"By my hilt!" cried Aylward, "now that John hath come by this great ransom, he will scarce abide the fare of poor archer lads. How say you, camarade? When you see Hordle once more, there will be no penny ale and fat bacon, but Gascon wines and baked meats every day of the seven."

"I know not about that," said John, kicking his helmet up into the air and catching it in his hand. "I do but know that whether the broth be ready or no, I am about to dip this into it."

"It simmers and it boils," cried Johnston, pushing his hard-lined face through the smoke. In an instant the pot had been plucked from the blaze, and its contents had been scooped up in half a dozen steel headpieces, which were balanced betwixt their owners' knees, while, with spoon and gobbet of bread, they devoured their morning meal.

"It is ill weather for bows," remarked John at last, when, with a long sigh, he drained the last drop from his helmet. "My strings are as limp as a cow's tail this morning."

"You should rub them with water glue," quoth Johnston. "You remember, Samkin, that it was wetter than this on the morning of Crécy, and yet I cannot call to mind that there was aught amiss with our strings."

"It is in my thoughts," said Black Simon, still pensively grinding his sword, "that we may have need of your strings ere sundown. I dreamed of the red cow last night."

"And what is this red cow, Simon?" asked Alleyne.

"I know not, young sir; but I can only say that on the eve of Cadsand, and on the eve of Crécy, and on the eve of Nogent, I dreamed of a red cow; and now the dream has come upon me again, so I am now setting a very keen edge to my blade."

"Well said, old war dog!" cried Aylward. "By my hilt! I pray that your dream may come true, for the Prince hath not set us out here to drink broth or to gather whortleberries. One more fight, and I am ready to hang up my bow, marry a wife, and take to the fire. But how now, Robin? Who is it that you seek?"

"The Lord Loring craves your attendance in his tent," said a young archer to Alleyne.

The squire rose and proceeded to the pavilion, where he found the knight seated upon a cushion, with his legs crossed in front of him and a broad ribbon of parchment laid across his knees, over which he was poring with frowning brows and pursed lips.

"It came this morning by the Prince's messenger," said he, "and was brought from England by Sir John Fallislee, who is new come from Sussex. What make you of this upon the outer side?"

"It is fairly and clearly written," Alleyne answered, "and it signifies 'To Sir Nigel Loring, Knight Constable of Twynham Castle, by the hand of Christopher, the servant of God at the Priory of Christchurch.' "

"So I read it," said Sir Nigel. "Now I pray you to read what is set forth within."

Alleyne turned to the letter, and, as his eyes rested upon it, his face turned pale, and a cry of surprise and grief burst from his lips.

"What then?" asked the knight, peering up at him anxiously. "There is naught amiss with the Lady Mary or with the Lady Maude?"

"It is my brother—my poor unhappy brother!" cried Alleyne, with his hand to his brow. "He is dead."

"By St. Paul! I have never heard that he had shown so much love for you that you should mourn him so."

"Yet he was my brother—the only kith or kin that I had upon earth. Mayhap he had cause to be bitter against me, for his land was given to the abbey for my upbringing. Alas! alas! and I raised my staff against him when last we met! He has been slain—and slain, I fear, amidst crime and violence."

"Ha!" said Sir Nigel. "Read on, I pray you."

" 'God be with thee, my honored lord, and have thee in his holy keeping. The Lady Loring hath asked me to set down in writing what hath befallen at Twynham, and all that concerns the death of thy ill neighbor, the Socman of Minstead. For when ye had left us, this evil man gathered around him all outlaws, villeins, and masterless men, until they were come to such a force that they slew and scattered the King's men who went against them. Then, coming forth from the woods, they laid siege to thy castle, and for two days they girt us in and shot hard against us, with such numbers as were a marvel to see. Yet the Lady Loring held the place stoutly, and on the second day the Socman was slain—by his own men, as some think—so that we were delivered from their hands; for which praise be to all the saints, and more especially to the holy Anselm, upon whose feast it came to pass. The Lady Loring and the Lady Maude, thy fair daughter, are in good health; and so also am I, save for an imposthume of the toe joint, which hath been sent me for my sins. May all the saints preserve thee!' "

"It was the vision of the Lady Tiphaine," said Sir Nigel, after a pause. "Marked you not how she said that the leader was one with a yellow beard, and how he fell before the gate? But how came it, Alleyne, that this woman, to whom all things are as crystal, and who hath not said one word which has not come to pass, was yet so led astray as to say that your thoughts turned to Twynham Castle even more than my own?"

"My fair lord," said Alleyne, with a flush on his weather-stained cheeks, "the Lady Tiphaine may have spoken sooth when she said it; for Twynham Castle is in my heart by day and in my dreams by night."

"Ha!" cried Sir Nigel, with a sidelong glance.

"Yes, my fair lord; for, indeed, I love your daughter, the Lady Maude; and, unworthy as I am, I would give my heart's blood to serve her."

"By St. Paul! Edricson," said the knight coldly, arching his eyebrows, "you aim high in this matter. Our blood is very old."

"And mine also is very old," answered the squire.

"And the Lady Maude is our single child. All our name and lands center upon her."

"Alas! that I should say it, but I also am now the only Edricson."

"And why have I not heard this from you before, Alleyne? In sooth, I think that you have used me ill."

"Nay, my fair lord, say not so; for I know not whether your daughter loves me, and there is no pledge between us."

Sir Nigel pondered for a few moments, and then burst out a-laughing. "By St. Paul!" said he, "I know not why I should mix in the matter; for I have ever found that the Lady Maude was very well able to look to her own affairs. Since first she could stamp her little foot, she hath ever been able to get that for which she craved; and if she set her heart on thee, Alleyne, and thou on her, I do not think that this Spanish king, with his three-score thousand men, could hold you apart. Yet this I will say, that I would see you a full knight ere you go to my daughter with words of love. I have ever said that a brave lance should wed her; and, by my soul! Edricson, if God spare you, I think that you will acquit yourself well. But enough of such trifles, for we have our work before us, and it will be time to speak of this matter when we see the white cliffs of England once more. Go to Sir William Felton, I pray you, and ask him to come hither, for it is time that we were marching. There is no pass at the further end of the valley, and it is a perilous place, should an enemy come upon us."

Alleyne delivered his message and then wandered forth from the camp, for his mind was all in a whirl with this unexpected news, and with his talk with Sir Nigel. Sitting upon a rock, with his burning brow resting upon his hands, he thought of his brother, of their quarrel, of the Lady Maude in her bedraggled riding dress, of the gray old castle, of the proud pale face in the armory, and of the last fiery words with which she had sped him on his way. Then he was but a penniless, monk-bred lad, unknown and unfriended. Now he was himself Socman of Minstead, the head of an old stock, and the lord of an estate which, if reduced from its former size, was still ample to preserve the dignity of his family. Further, he had become a man of experience, was counted brave among brave men, had won the esteem and confidence of her father, and, above all, had been listened to by him when he told him the secret of his love. As to the gaining of knighthood, in such stirring times it was no great matter for a brave squire of gentle birth to aspire to that honor. He would leave his bones among these Spanish ravines, or he would do some deed which would call the eyes of men upon him.

Alleyne was still seated on the rock, his griefs and his joys drifting swiftly over his mind like the shadow of clouds upon a sunlit meadow, when of a sudden he became conscious of a low, deep sound which came booming up to him through the fog. Close behind him he could hear the murmur of the bowmen, the occasional bursts of hoarse laughter, and the champing and stamping of their horses. Behind it all, however, came that low-pitched, deep-toned hum which seemed to come from every quarter and to fill the whole air. In the old monastic days he remembered to have heard such a sound when he had walked out one windy night at Bucklershard and had listened to the long waves breaking upon the shingly shore. Here, however, was neither wind nor sea, and yet the dull murmur rose ever louder and stronger out of the heart of the rolling sea of vapor. He turned and ran to the camp, shouting an alarm at the top of his voice.

It was but a hundred paces, and yet, ere he had crossed it, every bowman was ready at his horse's head, and the group of knights were out and listening intently to the ominous sound.

"It is a great body of horse," said Sir William Felton, "and they are riding very swiftly hitherwards."

"Yet they must be from the Prince's army," remarked Sir Richard Causton, "for they come from the north."

"Nay," said the Earl of Angus, "it is not so certain; for the peasant with whom we spoke last night said that it was rumored that Don Tello, the Spanish king's brother, had ridden with six thousand chosen men to beat up the Prince's camp. It may be that on their backward road they have come this way."

"By St. Paul!" cried Sir Nigel, "I think that it is even as you say, for that same peasant had a sour face and a shifting eye, as one who bore us little good will. I doubt not that he has brought these cavaliers upon us."

"But the mist covers us," said Sir Simon Burley. "We have yet time to ride through the further end of the pass."

"Were we a troop of mountain goats, we might do so," answered Sir William Felton, "but it is not to be passed by a company of horsemen. If these be indeed Don Tello and his men, then we must bide where we are and do what we can to make them rue the day that they found us in their path."

"Well spoken, William!" cried Sir Nigel, in high delight. "If there be so many as has been said, then there will be much honor to be gained from them, and every hope of advancement. But the sound has ceased, and I fear that they have gone some other way."

"Or mayhap they have come to the mouth of the gorge, and are marshaling their ranks. Hush and hearken! for they are no great way from us."

The Company stood peering into the dense fog wreath, amidst a silence so profound that the dripping of the water from the rocks and the breathing of the horses grew loud upon the ear. Suddenly from out the sea or mist came the shrill sound of a neigh, followed by a long blast upon a bugle.

"It is a Spanish call, my fair lord," said Black Simon. "It is used by their riders and huntsmen when the beast hath not fled, but is still in its lair."

"By my faith!" said Sir Nigel, smiling, "if they are in a humor for venerie, we may promise them some sport ere they sound the mort over us. But there is a hill in the center of the gorge on which we might take our stand."

"I marked it yesternight," said Felton, "and no better spot could be found for our purpose, for it is very steep at the back. It is but a bowshot to the left, and, indeed, I can see the shadow of it."

The whole Company, leading their horses, passed across to the small hill which loomed in front of them out of the mist. It was indeed admirably designed for defense, for it sloped down in front, all jagged and boulder-strewn, while it fell away behind in a sheer cliff of a hundred feet or more. On the summit was a small uneven plateau, with a stretch across of a hundred paces, and a depth of half as much again.

"Unloose the horses!" said Sir Nigel. "We have no space for them, and if we hold our own, we shall have horses and to spare when this day's work is done. Nay, keep yours, my fair sirs, for we may have work for them. Aylward, Johnston, let your men form a harrow [1] on either side of the ridge. Sir Oliver and you, my Lord Angus, I give you the right wing, and the left to you, Sir Simon, and to you, Sir Richard Causton. I and Sir William Felton will hold the center with our men-at-arms. Now order the ranks, and fling wide the banners, for our souls are God's and our bodies the King's, and our swords for St. George and for England!"

Sir Nigel had scarcely spoken, when the mist seemed to thin in the valley and to shred away into long ragged clouds which trailed from the edges of the cliffs. The gorge in which they had camped was a mere wedge-shaped cleft among the hills, three-quarters of a mile deep, with the small rugged rising upon which they stood at the further end, and the brown crags walling it in on three sides. As the mist parted, and the sun broke through, it gleamed and shimmered with dazzling brightness upon the armor and headpieces of a vast body of horsemen, who stretched across the barranca from one cliff to the other and extended backwards

[1] *harrow* (hăr′ō): a diagonal formation.

until their rear guard were far out upon the plain beyond. Line after line, and rank after rank, they choked the neck of the valley with a long vista of tossing pennons, twinkling lances, waving plumes, and streaming banderoles, while the curvets and gambades of the chargers lent a constant motion and shimmer to the glittering, many-colored mass. A yell of exultation and a forest of waving steel through the length and breadth of their column announced that they could at last see their entrapped enemies, while the swelling notes of a hundred bugles and drums, mixed with the clash of Moorish cymbals, broke forth into a proud peal of martial triumph. Strange it was to these gallant and sparkling cavaliers of Spain to look upon this handful of men upon the hill, the thin lines of bowmen, the knots of knights and men-at-arms, with armor rusted and discolored from long service, and to learn that these were indeed the soldiers whose fame and prowess had been the campfire talk of every army in Christendom. Very still and silent they stood, leaning upon their bows, while their leaders took counsel together in front of them. No clang of bugle rose from their stern ranks, but in the center waved the leopards of England, on the right the ensign of their Company with the roses of Loring, and on the left, over three score of Welsh bowmen, there floated the red banner of Merlin with the boars' heads of the Buttesthorns. Gravely and sedately they stood beneath the morning sun, waiting for the onslaught of their foemen.

"By St. Paul!" said Sir Nigel, gazing with puckered eye down the valley, "there appear to be some very worthy people among them. What is this golden banner which waves upon the left?"

"It is the ensign of the Knights of Calatrava," answered Felton.

"And the other upon the right?"

"It marks the Knights of Santiago, and I see by his flag that their grand master rides at their head. There, too, is the banner of Castile amid yonder sparkling squadron which heads the main battle. There are six thousand men-at-arms, with ten squadrons of slingers, as far as I may judge their numbers."

"There are Frenchmen among them, my fair lord," remarked Black Simon. "I can see the pennons of De Couvette, De Brieux, Saint Pol, and many others who struck in against us for Charles of Blois."

"You are right," said Sir William, "for I can also see them. There is much Spanish blazonry also, if I could but read it. Don Diego, you know the arms of your own land. Who are they who have done us this honor?"

The Spanish prisoner looked with exultant eyes upon the deep and serried ranks of his countrymen.

"By St. James!" said he, "if ye fall this day, ye fall by no mean hands, for the flower of the knighthood of Castile ride under the banner of Don Tello, with the chivalry of Asturias, Toledo, Leon, Cordova, Galicia, and Seville. I see the guidons of Albornez, Caçorla, Rodriguez, Tavora, with the two great orders, and the knights of France and of Aragon. If you will take my rede you will come to a composition with them, for they will give you such terms as you have given me."

"Nay, by St. Paul! it were pity if so many brave men were drawn together, and no little deed of arms to come of it. Ha! William, they advance upon us; and, by my soul! it is a sight that is worth coming over the seas to see."

As he spoke, the two wings of the Spanish host, consisting of the Knights of Calatrava on the one side and of Santiago upon the other, came swooping swiftly down the valley, while the main body followed more slowly behind. Five hundred paces from the English the two great bodies of horse crossed each other and, sweeping round in a curve, retired in feigned confusion towards their center. Often in bygone wars had the Moors tempted the hot-blooded Spaniards from their places of strength by such pretended flights, but there were men upon the hill to whom every ruse and trick of war were as their daily trade and practice. Again and even nearer came the rallying Spaniards, and again with cry of fear and stooping bodies they swerved off to right and left, but the English still stood stolid and observant among their rocks. The vanguard halted a long bowshot from the hill and with waving spears and vaunting shouts challenged their enemies to come forth, while two cavaliers, spurring forward from the glittering ranks, walked their horses slowly between the two arrays, with targets braced and lances in rest, like the challengers in a tourney.

"By St. Paul!" cried Sir Nigel, with his one eye glowing like an ember, "these appear to be two very worthy and debonair gentlemen. I do not call to mind when I have seen any people who seemed of so great a heart and so high of enterprise. We have our horses, Sir William: shall we not relieve them of any vow which they may have upon their souls?"

Felton's reply was to bound upon his charger, and to urge it down the slope, while Sir Nigel followed not three spears'-lengths behind him. It was a rugged course, rocky and uneven, yet the two knights, choosing their men, dashed onwards at the top of their speed, while the gallant Spaniards flew as swiftly to meet them. The one to whom Felton found himself opposed was a tall stripling with a stag's head upon his shield, while Sir Nigel's man was broad and squat, with plain steel harness, and a pink and white torse bound round his helmet. The first struck Felton on the target with such force as to split it from side to side, but Sir William's lance crashed through the camail which shielded the Spaniard's throat, and he fell, screaming hoarsely, to the ground. Carried away by the heat and madness of fight, the English knight never drew rein, but charged straight on into the array of the knights of Calatrava. Long time the silent ranks upon the hill could see a swirl and eddy deep down in the heart of the Spanish column, with a circle of rearing chargers and flashing blades. Here and there tossed the white plume of the English helmet, rising and falling like the foam upon a wave, with the fierce gleam and sparkle ever circling round it, until at last it had sunk from view, and another brave man had turned from war to peace.

Sir Nigel, meanwhile, had found a foeman worthy of his steel, for his opponent was none other than Sebastian Gomez, the picked lance of the monkish Knights of Santiago, who had won fame in a hundred bloody combats with the Moors of Andalusia. So fierce was their meeting that their spears shivered up to the very grasp, and the horses reared backwards until it seemed that they must crash down upon their riders. Yet with consummate horsemanship they both swung round in a long curve, and then plucking out their swords they lashed at each other like two lusty smiths hammering upon an anvil. The chargers spun round each other, biting and striking, while the two blades wheeled and whizzed and circled in gleams of dazzling light. Cut, parry, and thrust followed so swiftly upon each other that the eye could not follow them, until at last, coming thigh to thigh, they cast their arms around each other and rolled off their saddles to the ground. The heavier Spaniard threw himself upon his enemy and, pinning him down beneath him, raised his sword to slay him, while a shout of triumph rose from the ranks of his countrymen. But the fatal blow never fell, for even as his arm quivered before descending, the Spaniard gave a shudder and, stiffening himself, rolled heavily over upon his side, with the blood gushing from his armpit and from the slit of his visor. Sir Nigel sprang to his feet with his bloody dagger in his left hand and gazed down upon his adversary, but that fatal and sudden stab in the vital spot, which the Spaniard had exposed by raising his arm, had proved instantly mortal. The Englishman leaped upon his horse and made for the hill, at the very instant that a yell of rage from a thousand voices and the clang of a score of bugles announced the Spanish onset.

But the islanders were ready and eager for the encounter. With feet firmly planted, their sleeves rolled back to give free play to their muscles, their long yellow bowstaves in their left hands, and their quivers slung to the front, they had waited in the four-deep harrow formation which gave strength to their array and yet permitted every man to draw his arrow freely, without harm to those in front. Aylward and Johnston had been engaged in throwing light tufts of grass into the air to gauge the wind force, and a hoarse whisper passed down the ranks from the file leaders to the men, with scraps of advice and admonition.

"Do not shoot outside the fifteen score paces," cried Johnston. "We may need all our shafts ere we have done with them."

"Better to overshoot than to undershoot," added Aylward. "Better to strike the rear guard than to feather a shaft in the earth."

"Loose quick and sharp when they come," added another. "Let it be the eye to the string, the string to the shaft, and the shaft to the mark. By Our Lady! their banners advance, and we must hold our ground now if ever we are to see Southampton Water again."

Alleyne, standing with his sword drawn amidst the archers, saw a long toss and heave of the glittering squadrons. Then the front ranks began to surge slowly forward, to trot, to canter, to gallop, and in an instant the whole vast array was hurtling onward, line after line, the air full of the thunder of their cries, the ground shaking with the beat of their hoofs, the valley choked with the rushing torrent of steel, topped by the waving plumes, the slanting spears, and the fluttering banderoles. On they swept, over the level and up to the slope, ere they met the blinding storm of the English arrows. Down went the whole ranks in a whirl of mad confusion, horses plunging and kicking, bewildered men falling, rising, staggering on or back, while ever new lines of horsemen came spurring through the gaps and urged their chargers up the fatal slope. All around him Alleyne could hear the stern, short orders of the master bowmen, while the air was filled with the keen twanging of the strings and the swish and patter of the shafts. Right across the foot of the hill there had sprung up a long wall of struggling horses and stricken men, which ever grew and heightened as fresh squadrons poured on the attack. One young knight on a gray jennet leaped over his fallen comrades and galloped swiftly up the hill, shrieking loudly upon St. James, ere he fell within a spear-length of the English line, with the feathers of arrows thrusting out from every crevice and joint of his armor. So for five long minutes the gallant horsemen of Spain and of France strove ever and again to force a passage, until the wailing note of a bugle called them back, and they rode slowly out of bowshot, leaving their best and their bravest in the ghastly, blood-mottled heap behind them.

But there was little rest for the victors. Whilst the knights had charged them in front, the slingers had crept round upon either flank and had gained a footing upon the cliffs and behind the outlying rocks. A storm of stones broke suddenly upon the defenders, who, drawn up in lines upon the exposed summit, offered a fair mark to their hidden foes. Johnston, the old archer, was struck upon the temple and fell dead without a groan, while fifteen of his bowmen and six of the men-at-arms were struck down at the same moment. The others lay on their faces tc avoid the deadly hail, while at each side of the plateau a fringe of bowmen exchanged shots with the slingers and crossbowmen among the rocks, aiming mainly at those who had swarmed up the cliffs, and bursting into laughter and cheers when a well-aimed shaft brought one of their opponents toppling down from his lofty perch.

"I think, Nigel," said Sir Oliver, striding across to the little knight, "that we should all acquit ourselves better had we our none-meat, for the sun is high in the heaven."

"By St. Paul!" quoth Sir Nigel, plucking the patch from his

eye, "I think that I am now clear of my vow, for this Spanish knight was a person from whom much honor might be won. Indeed, he was a very worthy gentleman, of good courage and great hardiness, and it grieves me that he should have come by such a hurt. As to what you say of food, Oliver, it is not to be thought of, for we have nothing with us upon the hill."

"Nigel!" cried Sir Simon Burley, hurrying up with consternation upon his face, "Aylward tells me that there are not ten score arrows left in all their sheaves. See! they are springing from their horses and cutting their sollerets [1] that they may rush upon us. Might we not even now make a retreat?"

"My soul will retreat from my body first!" cried the little knight. "Here I am, and here I bide, while God gives me strength to lift a sword."

"And so say I!" shouted Sir Oliver, throwing his mace high into the air and catching it again by the handle.

"To your arms, men!" roared Sir Nigel. "Shoot while you may, and then out sword, and let us live or die together!"

[1] *solleret* (sŏl′ẽr·ĕt): an armored shoe.

Chapter 31

HOW THE WHITE COMPANY CAME TO BE DISBANDED

Then uprose from the hill in the rugged Cantabrian valley a sound such as had not been heard in those parts before, nor was again, until the streams which rippled amid the rocks had been frozen by over four hundred winters and thawed by as many returning springs. Deep and full and strong it thundered down the ravine, the fierce battle call of a warrior race, the last stern welcome to whoso should join with them in that world-old game where the stake is death. Thrice it swelled forth and thrice it sank away, echoing and reverberating amidst the crags. Then, with set faces, the Company rose up among the storm of stones and looked down upon the thousands who sped swiftly up the slope against them. Horse and spear had been set aside, but on foot, with sword and battle-ax, their broad shields slung in front of them, the chivalry of Spain rushed to the attack.

And now arose a struggle so fell, so long, so evenly sustained, that even now the memory of it is handed down amongst the Cantabrian mountaineers, and the ill-omened knoll is still pointed out by fathers to their children as the "Altura de los Ingleses," where the men from across the sea fought the great fight with the knights of the south.

The last arrow was quickly shot, nor could the slingers hurl their stones, so close were friend and foe. From side to side stretched the thin line of the English, lightly armed and quick-footed, while against it stormed and raged the pressing throng of fiery Spaniards and of gallant Bretons. The clink of crossing sword blades, the dull thudding of heavy blows, the panting and gasping of weary and wounded men, all rose together in a wild, long-drawn note, which swelled upwards to the ears of the wondering peasants who looked down from the edges of the cliffs upon the swaying turmoil of the battle beneath them.

Back and forward reeled the leopard banner, now borne up the slope by the rush and weight of the onslaught, now pushing downwards again as Sir Nigel, Burley, and Black Simon, with their veteran men-at-arms, flung themselves madly into the fray. Alleyne, at his lord's right hand, found himself swept hither and thither in the desperate struggle, exchanging savage thrusts one instant with a Spanish cavalier, and the next torn away by the whirl of men and dashed up against some new antagonist. To the right, Sir Oliver, Aylward, Hordle John, and the bowmen of the Company fought furiously against the monkish Knights of Santiago, who were led up the hill by their prior—a great, deep-chested man, who wore a brown monastic habit over his suit of mail. Three archers he slew in three giant strokes, but Sir Oliver flung his arms round him, and the two, staggering and straining, reeled backwards and fell, locked in each other's grasp, over the edge of the steep cliff which flanked the hill. In vain his knights stormed and raved against the thin line which barred their path; the sword of Aylward and the great ax of John gleamed in the forefront of the battle, and huge jagged pieces of rock, hurled by the strong arms of the bowmen, crashed and hurtled amid their ranks. Slowly they gave back down the hill, the archers still hanging upon their skirts, with a long litter of writhing and twisted figures to mark the course which they had taken. At the same instant the Welshmen upon the left, led on by the Scotch earl, had charged out from among the rocks which sheltered them and, by the fury of their outfall, had driven the Spaniards in front of them in headlong flight down the hill.

In the center only, things seemed to be going ill with the defenders. Black Simon was down—dying as he would wish to have died, like a grim old wolf in its lair—with a ring of his slain around him. Twice Sir Nigel had been overborne, and twice Alleyne had fought over him until he had staggered to his feet once more. Burley lay senseless, stunned by a blow from a mace, and half of the men-at-arms lay littered upon the ground around him. Sir Nigel's shield was broken, his crest shorn, his armor cut and smashed, and the visor torn from his helmet; yet he sprang hither and thither, with light foot and ready hand, engaging two Bretons and a Spaniard at the same instant—thrusting, stooping, dashing in, springing out—while Alleyne still fought by his side, stemming with a handful of men the fierce tide which surged up against them. Yet it would have fared ill with them had not the archers from either side closed in upon the flanks of the attackers and pressed them very slowly and foot by foot down the long slope, until they were on the plain once more, where their fellows were already rallying for a fresh assault.

But terrible indeed was the cost at which the last had been repelled. Of the three hundred and seventy men who had held the crest, one hundred and seventy-two were left standing, many of whom were sorely wounded and weak from loss of blood. Sir Oliver Buttesthorn, Sir Richard Causton, Sir Simon Burley, Black Simon, Johnston, a hundred and fifty archers, and forty-seven men-at-arms had fallen, while the pitiless hail of stones was already whizzing and piping once more about their ears, threatening every instant to further reduce their numbers.

Sir Nigel looked about him at his shattered ranks, and his face flushed with a soldier's pride.

"By St. Paul!" he cried, "I have fought in many a little bickering, but never one that I would be more loath to have missed than this. But you are wounded, Alleyne?"

"It is naught," answered his squire, stanching the blood which dripped from a sword cut across his forehead.

"These gentlemen of Spain seem to be most courteous and worthy people. I see that they are already forming to continue this debate with us. Form up the bowmen two deep instead of four. By my faith! some very brave men have gone from among us. Aylward, you are a trusty soldier, for all that your shoulder has never felt accolade,[1] nor your heels worn the gold spurs. Do you take charge of the right; I will hold the center, and you, my Lord of Angus, the left."

"Ho! for Sir Samkin Aylward!" cried a rough voice among the archers, and a roar of laughter greeted their new leader.

"By my hilt!" said the old bowman, "I never thought to lead a wing in a stricken field. Stand close, camarades, for, by these finger bones! we must play the man this day."

"Come hither, Alleyne," said Sir Nigel, walking back to the edge of the cliff which formed the rear of their position. "And you, Norbury," he continued, beckoning to the squire of Sir Oliver, "do you also come here."

The two squires hurried across to him, and the three stood looking down into the rocky ravine which lay a hundred and fifty feet beneath them.

"The Prince must hear of how things are with us," said the knight. "Another onfall we may withstand, but they are many and we are few, so that the time must come when we can no longer form line across the hill. Yet if help were brought us we might hold the crest until it comes. See yonder horses which stray among the rocks beneath us?"

"I see them, my fair lord."

"And see yonder path which winds along the hill upon the further end of the valley?"

"I see it."

"Were you on those horses, and riding up yonder track, steep and rough as it is, I think that ye might gain the valley beyond. Then on to the Prince, and tell him how we fare."

"But, my fair lord, how can we hope to reach the horses?" asked Norbury.

[1] *accolade* (ăk′ô·lād′): the tap of a sword used in conferring knighthood.

"Ye cannot go round to them, for they would be upon ye ere ye could come to them. Think ye that ye have heart enough to clamber down this cliff?"

"Had we but a rope."

"There is one here. It is but one hundred feet long, and for the rest ye must trust to God and to your fingers. Can you try it, Alleyne?"

"With all my heart, my dear lord, but how can I leave you in such a strait?"

"Nay, it is to serve me that ye go. And you, Norbury?"

The silent squire said nothing, but he took up the rope, and, having examined it, he tied one end firmly round a projecting rock. Then he cast off his breastplate, thigh pieces, and greaves, while Alleyne followed his example.

"Tell Chandos or Calverley or Knolles, should the Prince have gone forward," cried Sir Nigel. "Now, may God speed ye, for ye are brave and worthy men."

It was, indeed, a task which might make the heart of the bravest sink within him. The thin cord dangling down the face of the brown cliff seemed from above to reach little more than half-way down it. Beyond stretched the rugged rock, wet and shining, with a green tuft here and there thrusting out from it, but little sign of ridge or foothold. Far below, the jagged points of the boulders bristled up, dark and menacing. Norbury tugged thrice with all his strength upon the cord and then lowered himself over the edge, while a hundred anxious faces peered over at him as he slowly clambered downwards to the end of the rope. Twice he stretched out his foot, and twice he failed to reach the point at which he aimed, but even as he swung himself for a third effort a stone from a sling buzzed like a wasp from amid the rocks and struck him full upon the side of his head. His grasp relaxed, his feet slipped, and in an instant he was a crushed and mangled corpse upon the sharp ridges beneath him.

"If I have no better fortune," said Alleyne, leading Sir Nigel aside, "I pray you, my dear lord, that you will give my humble service to the Lady Maude, and say to her that I was ever her true servant and most unworthy cavalier."

The old knight said no word, but he put a hand on either shoulder and kissed his squire, with the tears shining in his eyes. Alleyne sprang to the rope and, sliding swiftly down, soon found himself at its extremity. From above, it seemed as though rope and cliff were well-nigh touching, but now, when swinging a hundred feet down, the squire found that he could scarce reach the face of the rock with his foot, and that it was as smooth as glass, with no resting place where a mouse could stand. Some three feet lower, however, his eye lit upon a long jagged crack which slanted downwards, and this he must reach if he would save not only his own poor life but that of the eight score men above him. Yet it were madness to spring for that narrow slit with naught but the wet, smooth rock to cling to. He swung for a moment, full of thought, and even as he hung there another of the hellish stones sang through his curls, and struck a chip from the face of the cliff. Up he clambered a few feet, drew up the loose end after him, unslung his belt, held on with knee and with elbow while he spliced the long, tough leathern belt to the end of the cord; then lowering himself as far as he could go, he swung backwards and forwards until his hand reached the crack, when he left the rope and clung to the face of the cliff. Another stone struck him on the side, and he heard a sound like a breaking stick, with a keen stabbing pain which shot through his chest. Yet it was no time now to think of pain or ache. There were his lord and his eight score comrades, and they must be plucked from the jaws of death. On he clambered, with his hand shuffling down the long sloping crack, sometimes bearing all his weight upon his arms, at others finding some small shelf or tuft on which to rest his foot. Would he never pass over that fifty feet? He dared not look down, and could but grope slowly onwards, his face to the cliff, his fingers clutching, his feet scraping and feeling for a support. Every vein and crack and mottling of that face of rock remained forever stamped upon his memory. At last, however, his foot came upon a broad resting place and he ventured to cast a glance downwards. Thank God! he had reached the highest of those fatal pinnacles upon which his comrade had fallen. Quickly now he sprang from rock to rock until his feet were on the ground, and he had his hand stretched out for the horse's rein, when a sling stone struck him on the head, and he dropped senseless upon the ground.

An evil blow it was for Alleyne, but a worse one still for him who struck it. The Spanish slinger, seeing the youth lie slain, and judging from his dress that he was no common man, rushed forward to plunder him, knowing well that the bowmen above him had expended their last shaft. He was still three paces, however, from his victim's side when John, upon the cliff, plucked up a huge boulder and, poising it for an instant, dropped it with fatal aim upon the slinger beneath him. It struck upon his shoulder and hurled him, crushed and screaming, to the ground, while Alleyne, recalled to his senses by these shrill cries in his very ear, staggered onto his feet and gazed wildly about him. His eyes fell upon the horses grazing upon the scanty pasture, and in an instant all had come back to him—his mission, his comrades, the need for haste. He was dizzy, sick, faint, but he must not die, and he must not tarry, for his life meant many lives that day. In an instant he was in his saddle and spurring down the valley. Loud rang the swift charger's hoofs over rock and reef, while the fire flew from the stroke of iron, and the loose stones showered up behind him. But his head was whirling round, the blood was gushing from his brow, his temple, his mouth. Ever keener and sharper was the deadly pain which shot like a red-hot arrow through his side. He felt that his eye was glazing, his senses slipping from him, his grasp upon the reins relaxing. Then, with one mighty effort, he called up all his strength for a single minute. Stooping down, he loosened the stirrup straps, bound his knees tightly to his saddle flaps, twisted his hands in the bridle, and then, putting the gallant horse's head for the mountain path, he dashed the spurs in and fell forward fainting with his face buried in the coarse, black mane.

Little could he ever remember of that wild ride. Half conscious, but ever with the one thought beating in his mind, he goaded the horse onwards, rushing swiftly down steep ravines, over huge boulders, along the edges of black abysses. Dim memories he had of beetling cliffs, of a group of huts with wondering faces at the doors, of foaming, clattering water, and of a bristle of mountain beeches. Once, ere he had ridden far, he heard behind him three deep, sullen shouts, which told him that his comrades had set their faces to the foe once more. Then all was blank until he woke to find kindly blue English eyes peering down upon him and to hear the blessed sound of his country's speech. They were but a foraging party—a hundred archers and as many men-at-arms—but their leader was Sir Hugh Calverley, and he was not a man to bide idle when good blows were to be had not three leagues from him. A scout was sent flying with a message to the camp, and Sir Hugh, with his two hundred men, thundered off to the rescue. With them went Alleyne, still bound to his saddle, still dripping with blood, and swooning and recovering, and swooning once again. On they rode, and on, until, at last, topping a ridge, they looked down upon the fateful valley. Alas! and alas! for the sight that met their eyes.

There, beneath them, was the blood-bathed hill, and from the highest pinnacle there flaunted the yellow and white banner with the lions and the towers of the royal house of Castile. Up the long slope rushed ranks and ranks of men—exultant, shouting, with waving pennons and brandished arms. Over the whole summit were dense throngs of knights, with no enemy that could be seen to face them, save only that at one corner of the plateau an eddy and swirl amid the crowded mass seemed to show that all resistance was not yet at an end. At the sight, a deep groan of rage and of despair went up from the baffled rescuers, and, spurring on their horses, they clattered down the long and winding path which led to the valley beneath.

But they were too late to avenge, as they had been too late to save. Long ere they could gain the level ground, the Spaniards, seeing them riding swiftly amid the rocks, and being ignorant of their numbers, drew off from the captured hill and, having secured their few prisoners, rode slowly in a long column, with drum-beating and cymbal-clashing, out of the valley. Their rear ranks were already passing out of sight ere the newcomers were urging their panting, foaming horses up the slope which had been the scene of that long-drawn and bloody fight.

And a fearsome sight it was that met their eyes! Across the lower end lay the dense heap of men and horses where the first arrow storm had burst. Above, the bodies of the dead and the dying—French, Spanish, and Aragonese—lay thick and thicker, until they covered the whole ground two and three deep in one dreadful tangle of slaughter. Above them lay the Englishmen in their lines, even as they had stood, and higher yet upon the plateau a wild medley of the dead of all nations, where the last deadly grapple had left them. In the further corner, under the shadow of a great rock, there crouched seven bowmen, with great John in the center of them— all wounded, weary, and in sorry case, but still unconquered, with their blood-stained weapons waving and their voices ringing a welcome to their countrymen. Alleyne rode across to John, while Sir Hugh Calverley followed close behind him.

"By St. George!" cried Sir Hugh, "I have never seen signs of so stern a fight, and I am right glad that we have been in time to save you."

"You have saved more than us," said John, pointing to the banner which leaned against the rock behind him.

"You have done nobly," cried the old free companion, gazing with a soldier's admiration at the huge frame and bold face of the archer. "But why is it, my good fellow, that you sit upon this man?"

"By the rood! I had forgot him," John answered, rising and dragging from under him no less a person than the Spanish caballero, Don Diego Alvarez. "This man, my fair lord, means to me a new house, ten cows, one bull—if it be but a little one—a grindstone, and I know not what besides; so that I thought it well to sit upon him, lest he should take a fancy to leave me."

"Tell me, John," cried Alleyne faintly, "where is my dear lord, Sir Nigel Loring?"

"He is dead, I fear. I saw them throw his body across a horse and ride away with it, but I fear the life had gone from him."

"Now woe worth me! And where is Aylward?"

"He sprang upon a riderless horse and rode after Sir Nigel to save him. I saw them throng around him, and he is either taken or slain."

"Blow the bugles!" cried Sir Hugh, with a scowling brow. "We must back to camp, and, ere three days, I trust that we may see these Spaniards again. I would fain have ye all in my company."

"We are of the White Company, my fair lord," said John.

"Nay, the White Company is here disbanded," answered Sir Hugh solemnly, looking round him at the lines of silent figures. "Look to the brave squire, for I fear that he will never see the sun rise again."

Chapter 32

OF THE HOME–COMING TO HAMPSHIRE

It was a bright July morning four months after that fatal fight in the Spanish barranca. A blue heaven stretched above, a green rolling plain undulated below, intersected with hedgerows and flecked with grazing sheep. The sun was yet low in the heaven, and the red cows stood in the long shadow of the elms, chewing the cud and gazing with great vacant eyes at two horsemen who were spurring it down the long white road which dipped and curved away back to where the towers and pinnacles beneath the flat-topped hill marked the old town of Winchester.

Of the riders one was young, graceful, and fair, clad in plain doublet and hosen of blue Brussels cloth, which served to show his active and well-knit figure. A flat velvet cap was drawn forward to keep the glare from his eyes, and he rode with lips compressed and anxious face, as one who has much care upon his mind. Young as he was, and peaceful as was his dress, the dainty golden spurs which twinkled upon his heels proclaimed his knighthood, while a long seam upon his brow and a scar upon his temple gave a manly grace to his refined and delicate countenance. His comrade was a large, red-headed man upon a great black horse, with a huge canvas bag slung from his saddlebow, which jingled and clinked with every movement of his steed. His broad, brown face was lighted up by a continual smile, and he looked slowly from side to side with eyes which twinkled and shone with delight. Well might John rejoice, for was he not back in his native Hampshire, had he not Don Diego's five thousand crowns rasping against his knee, and, above all, was he not himself squire now to Sir Alleyne Edricson, the young Socman of Minstead, lately knighted by the sword of the Black Prince himself, and esteemed by the whole army as one of the most rising of the soldiers of England?

For the last stand of the Company had been told throughout Christendom wherever a brave deed of arms was loved, and honors had flowed in upon the few who had survived it. For two months Alleyne had wavered betwixt death and life, with a broken rib and a shattered head; yet youth and strength and a cleanly life were all upon his side, and he awoke from his long delirium to find that the war was over, that the Spaniards and their allies had been crushed at Navaretta, and that the Prince had himself heard the tale of his ride for succor and had come in person to his bedside to touch his shoulder with his sword and to insure that so brave and true a man should die, if he could not live, within the order of chivalry. The instant that he could set foot to ground Alleyne had started in search of his lord, but no word could he hear of him, dead or alive, and he had come home now, sad-hearted, in the hope of raising money upon his estates and so starting upon his quest once more. Landing at London, he had hurried on with a mind full of care, for he had heard no word from Hampshire since the short note which had announced his brother's death.

"By the rood!" cried John, looking around him exultantly, "where have we seen, since we left, such noble cows, such fleecy sheep, grass so green, or a man so drunk as yonder rogue who lies in the gap of the hedge?"

"Ah, John," Alleyne answered wearily, "it is well for you, but I never thought that my home-coming would be so sad a one. My heart is heavy for my dear lord and for Aylward, and I know not how I may break the news to the Lady Mary and to the Lady Maude, if they have not yet had tidings of it."

John gave a groan which made the horses shy. "It is indeed a black business," said he. "But be not sad, for I shall give half these crowns to my old mother, and half will I add to the money which you may have, and so we shall buy that yellow cog wherein we sailed to Bordeaux, and in it we shall go forth and seek Sir Nigel."

Alleyne smiled, but shook his head. "Were he alive we should have had word of him ere now," said he. "But what is this town before us?"

"Why, it is Romsey!" cried John. "See the tower of the old gray church, and the long stretch of the nunnery. But here sits a very holy man, and I shall give him a crown for his prayers."

Three large stones formed a rough cot by the roadside, and beside it, basking in the sun, sat the hermit, with clay-colored face, dull eyes, and long withered hands. With crossed ankles and sunken head, he sat as though all his life had passed out of him, with the beads slipping slowly through his thin, yellow fingers. Behind him lay the narrow cell, clay-floored and damp, comfortless, and sordid. Beyond it there lay, amid the trees, the wattle-and-daub hut of a laborer, the door open, and the single room exposed to the view. The man, ruddy and yellow-haired, stood leaning upon the spade wherewith he had been at work upon the garden patch. From behind him came the ripple of a happy woman's laughter, and two young urchins darted forth from the hut, bare-legged and towsy, while the mother, stepping out, laid her hand upon her husband's arm and watched the gambols of the children. The hermit frowned at the untoward noise which broke upon his prayers, but his brow relaxed as he looked upon the broad silver piece which John held out to him.

"There lies the image of our past and of our future," cried Alleyne, as they rode on upon their way. "Now, which is better, to till God's earth, to have happy faces round one's knee, and to love and be loved, or to sit forever moaning over one's own soul, like a mother over a sick babe?"

"I know not about that," said John, "for it casts a great cloud over me when I think of such matters. But I know that my crown was well spent, for the man had the look of a very holy person. As to the other, there was naught holy about him that I could see, and it would be cheaper for me to pray for myself than to give a crown to one who spent his days in digging for lettuces."

Ere Alleyne could answer, there swung round the curve of the road a lady's carriage drawn by three horses abreast with a postilion upon the outer one. Very fine and rich it was, with beams painted and gilt, wheels and spokes carved in strange figures, and over all an arched cover of red and white tapestry. Beneath its shade there sat a stout and elderly lady in a pink cote-hardie, leaning back among a pile of cushions, and plucking out her eyebrows with a small pair of silver tweezers. None could seem more safe and secure and at her ease than this lady, yet here also was a symbol of human life, for in an instant, even as Alleyne reined aside to let the carriage pass, a wheel flew out from among its fellows, and over it all toppled—carving, tapestry, and gilt—in one wild heap, with the horses plunging, the postilion shouting, and the lady screaming from within. In an instant Alleyne and

John were on foot, and had lifted her forth, all in a shake with fear but little the worse for her mischance.

"Now woe worth me!" she cried, "and ill fall on Michael Easover of Romsey! for I told him that the pin was loose, and yet he must needs gainsay me, like the daffe that he is."

"I trust that you have taken no hurt, my fair lady," said Alleyne, conducting her to the bank, upon which John had already placed a cushion.

"Nay, I have had no scath, though I have lost my silver tweezers. Now, lackaday! did God ever put breath into such a fool as Michael Easover of Romsey? But I am much beholden to you, gentle sirs. Soldiers ye are, as one may readily see. I am myself a soldier's daughter," she added, casting a somewhat languishing glance at John, "and my heart ever goes out to a brave man."

"We are indeed fresh from Spain," quoth Alleyne.

"From Spain, say you? Ah! it was an ill and sorry thing that so many should throw away the lives that Heaven gave them. In sooth, it is bad for those who fall, but worse for those who bide behind. I have but now bid farewell to one who hath lost all in this cruel war."

"And how that, lady?"

"She is a young damsel of these parts, and she goes now into a nunnery. Alack! it is not a year since she was the fairest maid from Avon to Itchen, and now it was more than I could abide to wait at Romsey Nunnery to see her put the white veil upon her face, for she was made for a wife and not for the cloister. Did you ever, gentle sir, hear of a body of men called 'The White Company' over yonder?"

"Surely so," cried both the comrades.

"Her father was the leader of it, and her lover served under him as squire. News hath come that not one of the Company was left alive, and so, poor lamb, she hath—"

"Lady!" cried Alleyne, with catching breath, "is it the Lady Maude Loring of whom you speak?"

"It is, in sooth."

"Maude! And in a nunnery! Did, then, the thought of her father's death so move her?"

"Her father!" cried the lady, smiling. "Nay; Maude is a good daughter, but I think it was this young golden-haired squire of whom I have heard who has made her turn her back upon the world."

"And I stand talking here!" cried Alleyne wildly. "Come, John, come!"

Rushing to his horse, he swung himself into the saddle and was off down the road in a rolling cloud of dust as fast as his good steed could bear him.

Great had been the rejoicing amid the Romsey nuns when the Lady Maude Loring had craved admission into their order—for was she not sole child and heiress of the old knight, with farms and fiefs which she could bring to the great nunnery? Long and earnest had been the talks of the gaunt lady abbess in which she had conjured the young novice to turn forever from the world, and to rest her bruised heart under the broad and peaceful shelter of the church. And now, when all was settled, and when abbess and lady superior had had their will, it was but fitting that some pomp and show should mark the glad occasion. Hence was it that the good burghers of Romsey were all in the streets, that gay flags and flowers brightened the path from the nunnery to the church, and that a long procession wound up to the old arched door, leading up the bride to these spiritual nuptials. There was lay sister Agatha, with the high gold crucifix, and the three incense-bearers, and the two-and-twenty garbed in white who cast flowers upon either side of them and sang sweetly the while. Then, with four attendants, came the novice, her drooping head wreathed with white blossoms, and, behind, the abbess and her council of older nuns, who were already counting in their minds whether their own bailiff could manage the farms of Twynham or whether a reeve would be needed beneath him to draw the utmost from these new possessions which this young novice was about to bring them.

But alas for plots and plans when love and youth and nature, and above all, fortune are arrayed against them. Who is this travel-stained youth who dares to ride so madly through the lines of staring burghers? Why does he fling himself from his horse and stare so strangely about him? See how he has rushed through the incense-bearers, thrust aside lay sister Agatha, scattered the two-and-twenty damosels who sang so sweetly—and he stands before the novice with his hands outstretched and his face shining and the light of love in his gray eyes. Her foot is on the very lintel of the church, and yet he bars the way—and she, she thinks no more of the wise words and holy rede of the lady abbess, but she hath given a sobbing cry and hath fallen forward with his arms around her drooping body and her wet cheek upon his breast. A dank, cold air comes out from the black arch before them. Without, the sun shines bright and the birds are singing amid the ivy on the drooping beeches. Their choice is made, and they turn away, hand-in-hand, with their backs to the darkness and their faces to the light.

Very quiet was the wedding in the old priory church at Christchurch, where Father Christopher read the service and there were few to see, save the Lady Loring and John and a dozen bowmen from the castle. The Lady of Twynham had drooped and pined for weary months, so that her face was harsher and less comely than before, yet she still hoped on, for her lord had come through so many dangers that she could scarce believe that he might be stricken down at last. It had been her wish to start for Spain and to search for him, but Alleyne had persuaded her to let him go in her place. There was much to look after, now that the lands of Minstead were joined to those of Twynham, and Alleyne had promised her that if she would but bide with his wife he would never come back to Hampshire again until he had gained some news, good or ill, of her lord and lover.

The yellow cog had been engaged, with Goodwin Hawtayne in command, and a month after the wedding Alleyne rode down to Bucklershard to see if she had come round yet from Southampton. On the way he passed the fishing village of Pitt's Deep and marked that a little creyer or brig was tacking off the land, as though about to anchor there. On the way back, as he rode towards the village, he saw that she had indeed anchored, and that many boats were round her, bearing cargo to the shore.

A bowshot from Pitt's Deep there was an inn a little back from the road, very large and wide-spread, with a great green bush hung upon a pole from one of the upper windows. At this window he marked, as he rode up, that a man was seated who appeared to be craning his neck in his direction. Alleyne was still looking up at him, when a woman came rushing from the open door of the inn and made as though she would climb a tree, looking back the while with a laughing face. Wondering what these doings might mean, Alleyne tied his horse to a tree, and was walking amid the trunks towards the inn, when there shot from the entrance a second woman who made also for the trees. Close at her heels came a burly, brown-faced man, who leaned against the doorpost and laughed loudly with his hand to his side. "Ah, mes belles!" he cried, "and is it thus you treat me? Ah, mes petites! I swear by these finger bones that I would not hurt a hair of your pretty heads; but I have been among the black paynim, and, by my hilt! it does me good to look at your English cheeks. Come, drink a stoup of muscadine with me, mes anges, for my heart is warm to be among ye again."

At the sight of the man Alleyne had stood staring, but at the sound of his voice such a thrill of joy bubbled up in his heart that he had to bite his lip to keep himself from shouting outright. But a deeper pleasure yet was in store. Even as he looked, the window above was pushed outwards, and the voice of the man whom he had seen there came out from it. "Aylward," cried the voice, "I have seen just now a very worthy person come down the road, though my eyes could scarce discern whether he carried coat armor. I pray you to wait upon him and tell him that a very humble knight of England abides here, so that if he be in need of advancement, or have any small vow upon his soul, or desire to exalt his lady, I may help him to accomplish it."

Aylward at this order came shuffling forward amid the trees, and in an instant the two men were clinging in each other's arms, laughing and shouting and patting each other in their delight; while old Sir Nigel came running with his sword, under the impression that some small bickering had broken out, only to embrace and be embraced himself, until all three were hoarse with their questions and outcries and congratulations.

On their journey home through the woods Alleyne learned their wondrous story: how, when Sir Nigel came to his senses, he with his fellow captive had been hurried to the coast and conveyed by sea to their captor's castle; how, upon the way, they had been taken by a Barbary rover, and how they exchanged their light captivity for a seat on a galley bench and hard labor at the pirate's oars; how, in the port at Barbary, Sir Nigel had slain the Moorish captain and had swum with Aylward to a small coaster which they had taken, and so made their way to England with a rich cargo to reward them for their toils. All this Alleyne listened to, until the dark keep of Twynham towered above them in the gloaming, and they saw the red sun lying athwart the rippling Avon. No need to speak of the glad hearts at Twynham Castle that night, nor of the rich offerings from out that Moorish cargo which found their way to the chapel of Father Christopher.

Sir Nigel Loring lived for many years, full of honor and laden with every blessing. He rode no more to the wars, but he found his way to every jousting within thirty miles; and the Hampshire youth treasured it as the highest honor when a word of praise fell from him as to their management of their horses or their breaking of their lances. So he lived and so he died, the most revered and the happiest man in all his native shire.

For Sir Alleyne Edricson and for his beautiful bride the future had also naught but what was good. Twice he fought in France, and came back each time laden with honors. A high place at court was given to him, and he spent many years at Windsor under the second Richard and the fourth Henry—where he received the honor of the Garter [1] and won the name of being a brave soldier, a true-hearted gentleman, and a great lover and patron of every art and science which refines or ennobles life.

As to John, he took unto himself a village maid and settled in Lyndhurst, where his five thousand crowns made him the richest franklin for many miles around. For many years he drank his ale every night at the "Pied Merlin," which was now kept by his friend Aylward, who had wedded the good widow to whom he had committed his plunder. The strong men and the bowmen of the country round used to drop in there of an evening to wrestle a fall with John or to shoot a round with Aylward; but, though a silver shilling was to be the prize of the victory, it has never been reported that any man earned much money in that fashion. So they lived, these men, in their own lusty, cheery fashion—rude and rough, but honest, kindly, and true.

A NOTE ON HERALDRY

In all parts of the world and in all ages, men have adopted symbols to stand for their families, their tribes, their occupation, or for some particular belief or endeavor. The cross used on the shields and banners of the Crusaders, for instance, is, in turn, the emblem of

[1] *Garter:* the Order of the Garter, the highest order of knighthood in England.

Christianity. And today, national flags, military insignia and decorations, and even barber poles are forms of this ancient practice.

At the time this story takes place all kinds of designs and symbols, in various colors and combinations, were used by different families in their "blazonry," or coat of arms. Some were simple enough, a "bend" being a band drawn slantwise. But the variety is almost unlimited. We find trees, flowers and leaves, towers, weapons, forts, and so on. Animals were a particular favorite. Sometimes a symbol was chosen as a pun on a family's name. A family called Lambton, for instance, chose lambs; a goat's head was chosen by the Gateshead family. Sometimes the designs of two or more branches of a family were combined to show the family's descent.

One of Alleyne Edricson's duties as Sir Nigel's squire was to have a wide knowledge of these "devices." They made up a kind of sign language by which the knights could recognize each other. You see how the emblazoned shields and banners added to color and splendor of tournaments. But it was not all glitter and pageantry. Their most practical purpose was as a kind of ancestor to military uniforms. For without some identification, knights in the crush of battle (and particularly in their closed helmets) would not even be able to tell friend from foe.

Blazonry was also used for more peaceful purposes. For example, it could be found as decoration on household objects, in seals on documents, and on tombs.

GLOSSARY

angelus: a bell sounding a call to prayer
arbalest: a steel crossbow
argent: silver
ave: the Hail Mary prayer

bailey: the courtyard of a feudal castle
bailiff: an officer representing the king and the law
basinet: a light steel helmet
blazonry: coats of arms (see **heraldry**)
blithely: gladly
bombard: a cannon
boon: a favor
boots not: makes no difference
brigandine: coat of body armor

caitiff: mean
camisade: a night attack
canaille: riffraff, low-class people
chapman: a peddler
chérie: dear, darling
chivalry: the code and system of knighthood
churl: a selfish, unpleasant, low person
cittern: a stringed instrument played by plucking
cog: a ship with a high prow and stern

collop: a piece of meat
constable: the keeper, or highest officer
cozen: to cheat

defile: a narrow gorge
deign: to think it worthy
demesne: an estate, land owned
destrier: a war horse
device: a design
devoir: duty
doff: to take off, as a hat
don: to put on
drawlatch: a thief

ell: twenty-seven inches
ere: before
escalado: an attack on a fortified place, in which ladders are used

fain: gladly, *or* to wish
falding: rough cloth
fell: cruel
filch: to steal
flambeaux: flaming torches
fleur-de-lis: the lily of France, an emblem worn by English kings at this time
forfend: to prevent
franklin: a landowner
fuller: one who thickens cloth

gabelle: a tax on salt
garçon: a boy
gentle: well-born *or* a gentleman
glaive: sword
gleeman: a minstrel, singer
gramercy: thanks
gules: red

habit: clothes
harrow: a diagonal formation
hauberk: armor
heraldry: the art of recording family histories on shields, banners, and so forth
herbergage: lodging
hide: about 100 acres
hight: named
houseled: having received the Eucharist
hundred: a division of a county

ill: difficult

jerkin: a jacket
joust: a combat between two knights

keep: the main tower of a feudal castle

laud: a morning prayer
leechcraft: the practice of medicine
leveret: a young hare
liegeman: a loyal follower
limner: a painter
list: a field of combat
lout: to bow
lurdan: a stupid, lazy fellow

malmsey: a sweet wine
mangonel: a stone-throwing machine
march: a frontier or borderland
martial: warlike
matin: a morning prayer
mercery: cloth, textiles
mort: the note blown on the hunting horn at the kill

napery: table linen
nock: a notch, *or* to notch
none-meat: afternoon meal
novice: one who is training to be a monk

orison: prayer
outfall: a quick attack

palmer: a pilgrim who has visited the holy land
pate: the head
pater: the Lord's prayer
paynim: pagan, not a Christian
petite: a young girl
poll: the head

prie-dieu: a prayer desk
provost: an official in charge
provost marshal: the officer in charge of prisoners on trial

recreant: not faithful to duty
rede: advice, *or* to advise
rood: a crucifix or cross
rote: memory
ruth: pity

scath: harm
score: a bill, amount due
scourge: to whip
scrivener: a person who writes for those who do not know how to write
seneschal: an estate manager
shrift: confession of sins before death
shriven: having confessed and been forgiven
socman: a feudal landholder
sooth: true
sorry: poor and pitiful
suffer: to allow
swink: to labor; slave

tallage: a tax paid by a tenant to his lord
thrall: enslaved
tiltyard: a yard for fighting with spears and on horseback
tirewoman: the maid in charge of a lady's wardrobe
tonsured: shaved on the top
tourney: a contest between armed knights
troth: faith
trow: to believe

unwonted: unaccustomed

varlet: a servant
venery: hunting
villein: a peasant, serf

windage: compensation for the force of the wind
wont: accustomed

AFTERWORD

One of the oldest and best kind of stories is one in which a boy becomes a man. There are many such stories among the Greek myths. *Treasure Island* is that kind of story. *The White Company* is such a story. When we first meet Alleyne Edricson he is about to set off on a journey into the great outer world. His life in the abbey has been like life in school. He has learned many useful things. He has found joy and pleasure and comfort in his studies. But, by the terms of his father's will, he has to test himself against the world. He is to have a year in which to discover whether he should spend his life as a monk and a scholar, or leave it all behind in favor of whatever new life he should prefer.

In many ways the outer world that Alleyne first sees is as strange to him as it is to us. It is violent and colorful. It is dangerous and beautiful. It is noisy and coarse. It is puzzling but it is exciting. Life in the abbey, in the monastery, was orderly. The abbot was harsh but fair. Everyone knew what to do and when to do it. The world beyond its walls seems at first to be without any order at all. But, then, isn't this the way anything strange and new appears to be?

Conan Doyle is able to make this world seem very real. He does this by his descriptions of the road along which Alleyne walks. When he introduces a new character he immediately tells you something by which that person can be easily remembered. Hordle John has red hair, bulging muscles, and a huge body. Samkin Aylward always says "by these ten finger bones" when he gets excited. And the way the old archer mixes French words in his speech reminds us how much time he has spent fighting in France.

But it is in his descriptions of places that Conan Doyle is at his best. We can actually walk into the "Pied Merlin," peer through the smoke, see the foresters and other folk sitting about the tables, see the colorful wooden shields on the wall, and even hear Dame Eliza shouting at her maid. We can see the deep forests with the slanting sunlight cutting through the mists, and hear the birds singing deep among the underbrush. We watch the jugglers doing their practice tricks in the glade, and with our own imagination we can add the details that the author leaves out. This is good writing.

The author is the storyteller of *The White Company*. He uses the third person narrative. That is, he introduces a scene by saying that so-and-so looked a certain way and then said this or that. In between the talk, or dialogue, he uses simple storytelling. We call this narrative. Now, there is an advantage to the third person narrative, as you can see. It allows the author to tell you what the same thing looks like to several different people. He can tell you how anyone feels. In the first person narrative, the author must tell the whole story through the eyes of one person or another. There are advantages for each method.

We began by saying that *The White Company* is the story of a boy who becomes a man. It is more than this. It is the story of the choice between two different ways of living. Monastery life is one way; life in the open world is another. The first is called religious, or more specifically, monastic; we call the second way the secular life. Each has its advantages. The monastery offers security, quiet, safety, and a chance to study and worship undisturbed. The secular life offers adventure, opportunity for many careers—such as the life of the soldier, the lord of the manor, knighthood—and the opportunity to raise a family. But in that world of the late Middle Ages, it was a very dangerous life.

You must have noticed that there were two other ways of life to be considered. They were both secular. One was the life of chivalry in which knights followed their hearts, as we say. It was courtly, formal, and filled with strange rules and practices. It was an old way of life and it was passing away. The other way of life does not have a specific name. The best we can say is that it had the beginnings of what has become democracy. You noticed that the common people of France were not only very poor, but they seemed to have no real sense of their own worth and no real ability to do things on their own. The ordinary English soldier was a free man. The brushwood men who attacked the castle of Villefranche were worse than slaves. This was partly because the English felt that they belonged to a country while the ordinary Frenchman felt that he was owned by the lord of the manor.

So we might say that *The White Company* is a story of the last days of chivalry. Sir Nigel Loring is probably one of the best examples of the men who led a chivalrous life. He takes his vows of knighthood with great seriousness. He defends the weak, rights wrongs, punishes evil-doers—but he does all this for the love of his lady or for some special vow that he has taken at the time. He does odd things, such as wearing a patch over one eye even when his sight with both eyes is not very good. He wears his lady's glove in his cap as a sign that he is ever ready to defend her honor, and he is always looking for a fight. But notice that he never calls it a fight; he uses words like "bickering" or "debate," or he says of the other knight, "perhaps I may be able to relieve him of some vow." In plain language, however, he means he wants to start a fight.

Remember how Sir Nigel seeks out the pirate ships? Although the odds are against him, he welcomes the engagement. This seems to be a wild and even improbable battle (although such sea fights took place quite often), but even here, the code of knighthood is respected by Sir Nigel; when he slays the pirate he speaks of him with fondness: "He was a valiant foeman." It is almost as if he considered the fight more important than the victory.

We often speak of the way the English understate the importance of an event. During World War II, after a heavy bombing of London, a British announcer would say: "We had a bit of a *do* tonight"—when half the city was in flames. Remember how Sir Nigel refers to the sea fight? "We had sight of two rover galleys, and even came to have some slight bickering with them."

Now we must not laugh at Sir Nigel. Such men as he have done great and noble deeds throughout history. The Greek hero Achilles was as much a knight as Sir Nigel. The pilots of our fighter planes in the last war were probably the last of the knights. Many of them wore their lady's handkerchief or glove on their helmet as they flew into combat. Some tank commanders did the same thing. So, although the age of chivalry and the kind of civilization in which it flourished was beginning to die out during the Middle Ages, some of the habits and manners of knighthood are with us even today, and some of them are worth keeping.

This book seems to have been put together almost like a medieval tapestry. One colorful scene follows another, from the very beginning. And, as was said before, the author always allows room for the reader's imagination to add the details: the scene in the Prince's chamber with the two exiled Spaniards; the old lame Italian artist showing his stained glass window pieces (and here the artist is shown as a man of peace); the great tournament with its huge crowd of eighty thousand people, the chargers, the banners, the trumpet calls; the fight in the tower of the burning castle—an artist would have a wonderful time illustrating these scenes, but he could never capture all that the reader's mind can imagine.

But this book is also filled with wonderful sounds, not only those that must be described at secondhand, such as battle cries, the din of the market place, or the roistering of the soldiers at the inn, but the sound of the English language itself as it is being freed from the mixture of French and Anglo-Saxon. Someday you will learn more about this, but for now notice how in the speech of knights, soldiers, and common people these words occur: rede, sooth, quotha, bobance and boasting, fain. In addition there are quite a few French words and phrases, some of which you can easily understand, such as Samkin Aylward's statement: "La petite is frightened." Remember when we first meet him he says this and then adds, "Curse this trick of French, which will stick to my throat." At that time French was still the language of the upper classes and nobility in England. There are many ordinary English words today which came directly from the French language: table, garage, trouble. But it is important to understand that in the fourteenth century, especially through the writings of Geoffrey Chaucer, and even of clerks like Alleyne, the English language was becoming very much what it is today. And although you will have some trouble understanding Chaucer's poetry, you will be surprised how much of this old language will be familiar to you.

This is a historical novel; we can even call it a historical romance, using that word the way we shall for *Treasure Island*. It is teeming with adventure. It is colorful and exciting. There are heroes and villains. But in addition to all these there is a background of fact. During the year 1366 there were such companies of Englishmen fighting in France. There was such a man as Sir John Chandos, and he was actually the adviser to Prince Edward and as great a man as he appears in our story. The French knight Bertrand Du Guesclin was a great hero to his people. The people in our story speak of Chaucer, "a fat clerk." He was one of the greatest poets of the English language and probably did more than any man except Shakespeare to make the English language what it is today. There are many other examples which you can find for yourselves—but the important point here is that, in addition to entertaining you, a historical romance, if it is as well written as *The White Company,* can teach you quite a bit about the way people lived and thought long ago.

But the story itself is always the most important thing. It moves swiftly from episode to episode. The way of the hero is always blocked by something. He wishes to go to his home, but he meets Lady Maude and is driven away by his brother. He then chooses the life of his comrades with the White Company. He is accepted as a squire by Sir Nigel, partly because he is well born and partly because he is educated and can read and write. He is then swept up into the life of the fighting man even though he is still a man of peace. In fact it is not until he is challenged by another squire at the river's edge in France that he finally proves himself to be a soldier.

His love for Lady Maude makes Alleyne choose the life of chivalry. Notice that Alleyne begins to use the language of Sir Nigel; he talks of vows and honor. He dreams of "sallies and intakings and ambuscades." He seeks to do some service by which he can bring fame to his family name. All the while Samkin Aylward and Hordle John remain common soldiers. He has close ties of friendship with them, but it is like the friendship between an officer and an enlisted man. He does not speak their rough language. He does not think as they do.

Notice the manner in which Sir Arthur Conan Doyle introduces each character. It is almost as if he had sound motion-picture equipment with him, and a time machine to take him back to the fourteenth century. Take, for example,

Hordle John:

> He was a man of huge stature, dark-eyed and red-headed, with a peculiar half-humorous, half-defiant expression upon his bold, well-marked features. His cowl was thrown back upon his shoulders, and his gown, unfastened at the top, disclosed a round, sinewy neck, ruddy and corded like the bark of a fir.

Or Alleyne Edricson:

> He was a thin-faced, yellow-haired youth, rather above middle size, comely and well shapen, with straight, lithe figure and eager, boyish features. His clear, pensive gray eyes and quick, delicate expression spoke of a nature which had unfolded far from the boisterous joys and sorrows of the world.

And again Samkin Aylward:

> He was a middle-sized man, of most massive and robust build, with an arching chest and extraordinary breadth of shoulder. His shaven

> face was as brown as a hazelnut, tanned and dried by the weather, with harsh, well-marked features, which were not improved by a long white scar which stretched from the corner of his left nostril to the angle of the jaw.

In addition to these descriptions we are told how these men walk and talk. Alleyne is educated and careful in his speech. Samkin is a rough soldier and sounds like soldiers always sound. Hordle John is a big, good-natured country boy who is open and honest with both word and action.

When we first meet Sir Nigel and Lady Loring, we see

> . . . the pair walking slowly and sedately, as befitted both their age and their condition. . . .

Then we are told that:

> Sir Nigel was a slight man of poor stature, with soft lisping voice and gentle ways. So short was he that his wife, who was no very tall woman, had the better of him by the breadth of three fingers.

We find out that his eyes were injured with lime during a campaign and because of this he walks with a slight stoop. But he has the grace of a boy in his movements.

> His age was six and forty, but the constant practice of arms, together with a cleanly life, had preserved his activity and endurance . . . his face, however, was tanned to a dull yellow tint, with a leathery, poreless look, which spoke of rough outdoor doings, and a little pointed beard he wore, in deference to the prevailing fashion, which was streaked and shot through with gray.

But in describing both Sir Nigel and Lady Loring, the author really sums them up when he says:

> And certes, had the two visages alone been seen, and the stranger been asked which were the more likely to belong to the bold warrior . . . he had assuredly selected the lady's.

One of the marks of the good storyteller is that you can see his people and places clearly even though they have strange looks and stranger manners. He is able to do this because underneath any strangeness of time and place human beings are much the same. They have hopes and fears. They try to get ahead in the world. They struggle with their consciences about what is right and wrong. They are honorable or they are mean. They are lazy or they are hard-working. They get hungry, tired, angry. In other words, they are like us—underneath their strangeness. A good storyteller makes this plain.

This point must be repeated: *The White Company* is the story of the last days of chivalry and the coming of public law and order. The knight-errant was the protector of the poor and the oppressed. He was the defender of faith and honor. The vows he made could be broken only by death. And he did all this for the greater glory of his lady, whether she was his wife or his sweetheart. His language was an extravagant mixture of love words and battle words. But whenever he spoke of himself or his achievements, he spoke in understatement. He spoke of himself as "humble" or "worthless." No matter how great the wound he suffered from, he would call it a "trifle" or a "naughty scratch." A great battle he would call a "bickering." When he issues a challenge to a joust, he does so with great courtesy. Courtesy is in fact the key word to all knightly behavior. "I shall be very blithe to go into the matter further with you," or "I would debate with you in a very honorable way."

These things *The White Company* tells us: There were great changes going on all over Western Europe during the fourteenth century. Some of these were in the relationships between people—between knight and squire; between lord and vassal; between king and country. This was the time when "knighthood was in flower." And like a flower it was a beautiful blossom while it lasted. It was a colorful way of life. It made good manners important even though it went to strange extremes. It taught loyalty and truth to the people. In fact it made possible the feeling we have today toward our country, which we call patriotism.

It made the ordinary languages of the people popular. In earlier times only Latin was the proper language for important matters.

It developed another kind of language, the language of heraldry. By looking at a knight's shield, on which was painted his coat of arms, you could tell not only his name and rank, but even his whole family history. The language of heraldry used strange words, and stranger meanings for ordinary words. It would be interesting to look up the subject in a reliable encyclopedia. One could say that this is a bonus for the reading and the enjoyment of a fine story.

Alleyne becomes a knight as the story closes. We can be sure that in many ways he will be a very different kind of knight from Sir Nigel. He will be as brave; he has already proven that. But, because of the education he has received from the Abbot Berghersh, he will become a better lord and leader. He belongs to one of the great younger generations that have done so much to make what is good and great in the modern world, for it was Alleyne's generation that helped to lead England out of the Dark Ages toward a rebirth, or renaissance.

STUDY QUESTIONS

CHAPTERS 1 TO 7

1. The first chapter of *The White Company* tells how Hordle John leaves Beaulieu Abbey. Who do you think is in the right in the dispute: Abbot Berghersh, Hordle John, or both? What makes it certain that John will leave?

2. Alleyne Edricson's departure from Beaulieu is quite different from that of Hordle John. Why is Alleyne leaving? What is his attitude toward the monastery? What is the Abbot's attitude toward Alleyne?

3. What are Alleyne's impressions of the "strange company" at the "Pied Merlin"? On the whole, are they favorable or unfavorable?

4. Why do Hordle John and Samkin Aylward wrestle? What is at stake in the wrestling match? Why do you think they become friends?

5. What do you know by this time about the White Company?

CHAPTERS 8 TO 11

1. When Alleyne first enters his brother's land, he meets several people. Who are they?

2. Who is the Socman of Minstead? What is a socman? What sort of person is this socman?

3. When in these first chapters do you realize that Alleyne Edricson is not merely a sweet-natured boy, but rather has within himself the courage and strength of manhood? Do you think this change in him is for the better, or not?

4. In their talk, after Alleyne has rescued the lady from the socman, what do they quarrel about? How does this show a difference in their characters?

5. Why is Hordle John at first very unhappy about having decided to follow Sir Nigel Loring? What event changes his mind?

6. What is Alleyne first asked to do as Sir Nigel's squire? How does this change some of his ideas about the world outside the monastery?

CHAPTERS 12 TO 21

1. What is your first impression of Sir Oliver Buttesthorn?

2. Describe how Sir Nigel first shows his skill as a fighter.

3. Why does Aylward say to Alleyne that their friendship has changed, and what is Alleyne's answer?

4. What do you learn about the two rulers Prince Edward hopes to restore to their thrones?

5. What are Alleyne's first two tastes of armed conflict? How does he conduct himself?

6. What is the difference between Alleyne's and Ford's reaction to their visit to the artist's house?

7. How does Alleyne tell Sir Nigel about the secret in his heart?

CHAPTERS 22 TO 27

1. What do you learn about the condition of the peasants as the companions cross the marches of France?

2. From what you have read so far describe Sir Nigel Loring's principal object in life.

3. At the Chateau of Villefranche, what is the attitude of Sir Tristram de Rocheforte and his wife toward the neighboring peasants? What do you think of it?

4. Describe the attack on the

castle and the reasons that lay behind it.

5. In what condition does Sir Nigel find the White Company when he first makes their acquaintance? How does Sir Nigel appeal to them and how do they respond?

CHAPTERS 28 TO 32

1. What happens during Hordle John's sojourn in Spain that enables him eventually to settle down in ease and comfort?

2. What is Sir Nigel's reaction when Alleyne confesses his love for Lady Maude? Does his attitude seem fair or unfair to you? Explain.

3. How does Sir Nigel keep the vow he made before the expedition?

4. What does Sir Hugh mean when he says, "The White Company is here disbanded"?

5. Does Alleyne's decision at the end of a year to choose the life of the outside world instead of that of the monastery surprise you? What are the reasons for his choice? Does he have any reason to regret not returning to a sheltered religious life?

General Questions

1. What were the attractions of being a member of a free company of soldiers like the White Company? Why do you think men were willing to leave their homes and risk their lives to join?

2. Many, perhaps most, of the characters in *The White Company* are types; that is, they are overdrawn so that they are not quite real but rather typical of a class or group of people. These overdrawn characters are one of the delights of the book, even though we know that no real person would ever have behaved exactly as they do. Discuss Sir Nigel Loring, Sir Oliver Buttesthorn, Abbot Berghersh, Samkin Aylward, and Lady Maude. What group does each typify? What are the principal characteristics of each? What is unreal about each?

3. There are some passages in the book which strike us as delightful nonsense, and where it seems that Sir Arthur is laughing affectionately at his characters. Can you mention some such passages?

4. There are a number of minor characters in *The White Company* who are vividly described and hard to forget. Mention two or three of these whom you especially enjoyed.

5. *The White Company* tells, among other things, about the breaking down of the world of knights and ladies, the world of chivalry, and about the beginning of a different sort of life, in which the common people were to have much more to say about how the affairs of nations should be run. Can you recall events in the book that seem to foretell such a new way of life?

6. Do you notice any difference in the attitude of the French nobles toward their common people and of the English nobles toward theirs? How does the attitude of the common people of the two countries toward themselves differ?

7. Nowadays, we do not particularly admire a person who is always looking for a fight. Yet this is exactly what Sir Nigel Loring was doing. Do you admire him or not? Explain.

8. Would you describe the plot of *The White Company* as simple or complicated? Explain your answer.

9. Sir Arthur Conan Doyle is by no means blind to the evils and

hardships caused by the class system he describes both in England and in France. What injustices does he describe? What examples are there of violent discontent of certain groups of people? Which does Doyle think had the crueler social system, England or France? Explain your answer.

10. There are many interesting words in *The White Company,* words which you probably did not know when you came upon them and yet which are necessary if the author is to write fluently about fourteenth-century Europe. Can you tell the meaning of the following: blazonry, boon, chivalry, demesne, gentle, gramercy, heraldry, jerkin, joust, orison, rood, shriven, sooth, troth, varlet? See if you can use each in a sentence that will illustrate its meaning. If you need help, use the glossary on pages 311–13.

Gods, Heroes, and Men of Ancient Greece

by W. H. D. Rouse

DEDICATED

TO THE INTELLIGENT BOYS
OF THE PERSE SCHOOL, CAMBRIDGE,
WHO LISTENED TO THESE STORIES
AND WHEN THEY HEARD A GOOD THING
KNEW THAT IT WAS GOOD

WHEN you hear these stories of the Greek gods, you must be careful not to confuse them with your own God; for although the same name is used, it means different things. The Greeks thought the world was managed by a multitude of beings, like another human world in general, but consisting of beings who had different powers from men. The chief of these were very powerful, and the little ones had greater power than men. They loved and hated and quarreled with each other like men; they even fought battles like men; and one dynasty of kings supplanted another; but they could not kill each other, for they were immortal. They could only kill the monsters and giants who were also commonly to be found. And all these were themselves subject to something higher than themselves, which they called Necessity. It is this highest power of all that we call God, and the Greeks were feeling their way toward it, but they thought less about it than they did about the lower powers. These stories concern these lower powers, and how they were mixed up with mankind.

Many of the Greek stories are beautiful, but not all; and they seem to say that the gods rose out of savages, just as men did, and learned by degrees what was good and noble. All these stories fit into a picture where each has its place. The Greeks knew them well, and they were always taken for granted at the back of their minds; so that without them we cannot understand the Greeks at all. The ordinary people believed them; they thought of the gods as friendly creatures, rather like themselves, who enjoyed a bit of fun as much as they did; but they also feared them as terrible and strong and ready to punish wrongdoing. By degrees the wisest of the Greeks looked for a meaning in these stories, and did not believe them exactly; they thought of them as poetry, or fairy tales. But their ideas of right and wrong were much the same as ours, and they revered all that was good in their gods as much as we revere our own God.

—W. H. D. ROUSE

Contents

Myth is a strange word. Look it up in a small dictionary and you will learn that it has to do with fables, folklore, and fairy tales. Look in a larger dictionary and you will learn that myths are very ancient stories, so old that no one can tell when or just where they were first told. Look into an encyclopedia and you will find many pages giving examples of myths from many different times and countries, and many more pages explaining the meanings of certain myths. Go to a big library and you will find shelves with hundreds of books listed under myth. Some of these will be collections of myths. Others will be reports of scholars, archaeologists, and other scientists who have studied and thought about what myths are and how they might have developed. Finally, look back in this book to the table of contents on the preceding page. See how many names you recognize. Myth is indeed a strange word, but something you have known about for a long time. How is this possible?

"He is as strong as Hercules." "I am interested in Project Mercury." "The kite is caught in a maze of branches." "That was a titanic explosion." "She is a regular Venus." In each one of those sentences, one of the words refers to some one of the myths you will be reading about. The meaning of those words tells you something about the myth itself. So, you can understand that one of the ways in which myth works is to serve as explanations for things and happenings that are not easy to talk about in ordinary words.

Myths have another use. You will find, as you read them here, that many of the stories are very familiar. This is not because you have read them before, although you might have read some of them. It is because most of the great stories of all time are based upon myths in some way. They deal with the same kinds of subjects. They tell about wonderful adventures. They explain puzzling things. They describe acts of great courage and of terrible fears. They tell of love and hate, of friendship and faithfulness. They tell about the meaning of truth and beauty and justice. And the Greek myths, because they have been used for so long in our civilization, have given us the words we ordinarily use when we talk about things of this sort. You might almost say that the Greek myths have given us our vocabulary of great ideas. They also seem to have given us the plots for most of the great stories we have read or ever will read. In fact, while you are reading the myths in this section, you might keep a watch for stories on television that seem to have plots like the stories the Greeks told about their gods and heroes.

These great stories have been popular for so many centuries that artists and writers have used them again and again. Most of the great painters have used them as their subjects. Go to a library and look at any book of fine paintings, or better still, visit a museum if you can and see for yourself how the artists have used these myths. Poets and playwrights, both ancient and modern, have used the same subjects. Sometimes they use only the names of these mythical people to give special meaning to what they write. This is why it is useful as well as interesting to learn about myths.

In order to help you at the beginning, turn to the pronunciation guide on page 500 and become familiar with the names. Turn also, to the genealogical table (really, a family tree) to learn how the gods, heroes, and monsters were thought to be related to one another.

You will be reading about these myths in one form or another many times during your life. The more you learn about them, the more you will understand what they have meant to people in the past. They will help you to appreciate how the ancient people looked at the world they lived in. They are still very good stories. They are often wonderful ways of looking at and understanding what is odd, puzzling, and strange about the world and the people who live in it.

PART ONE

Chapter 1 THE BEGINNING OF THINGS

In the beginning there was Chaos, a great hollow Void, in which the seeds or beginnings of all things were mixed up together in a shapeless mass, all moving about in all directions. By degrees these beginnings slowly sorted themselves out; the heavier parts gathered together and became Earth; the lighter parts flew up and became the sky, with air between; and under the earth was a dark place called Tartarus. In the heavens, the sun, moon, and stars appeared one by one; on earth, the land separated from the sea; rain fell, and the rivers ran down from the hills; trees grew up, and the world became something like what we know, and it had the shape of a great round ball, or a disk, like a large plate.

From Chaos, the great Void, came forth many and strange children; but first and most wonderful of all was Eros, or Love, who came no one knows how, and was quite different from all the others; he outlived them all, and still lives, the most mighty of all divine powers. From Chaos came forth also Erebus and black Night; and their child was the Day.

From Chaos, lastly, came into being Father Uranus, or Heaven; and Pontus, the Sea; and Mother Earth. Heaven and Earth were parents of a great brood of children. These were called, in general, the Titans. The brood began with monsters, but they improved as they went on. Among the monsters were three, with fifty heads apiece and a hundred hands; their names were Cottus, Gyges, and Briareus. Three others were named the Cyclopes; Cyclops means "goggle-eyed," and each Cyclops had one huge eye in the middle of his forehead, with one huge and bushy eyebrow above it. There were others, some of whom we shall meet later; and then came a superior brood of children. I will not tell you the names of all these now, but one was Oceanus, the ocean stream, which runs like a great river all round the earth; and one was Hyperion, who took charge of the light by night and day. He was the father of Eos, the Dawn, and Helios, the Sun, and Selene, the Moon. And the youngest of the children of Heaven and Earth was named Cronus: the youngest but the most terrible of them all.

Now Uranus hated his children and feared them; and as each was born, he hid them in secret places of the earth and kept them prisoners in darkness. But Mother Earth was angry to see her children so badly treated; so she persuaded them to rebel, and they did so, and cast down Uranus from the sky. They cast him down into Tartarus, the dark region below the earth. In the fight he was wounded by Cronus; drops of his blood fell on the sea, and from these drops sprang up Aphrodite, who became the goddess of beauty and love. Her name means "daughter of the foam," because she came up out of the foam of the sea. Other drops of his blood fell on the earth; and from these sprang up the Giants and the Furies. We shall hear of these later, for the Giants made war on the gods long afterwards; and the Furies used to range about the world, when men were created, chasing and punishing those men who shed blood.

Cronus was leader of this rebellion, and he became King of Heaven in his father's place. When he became king, he cast down his brothers and sisters into Tartarus, except one, Rhea, whom he married. But he was not so careful about their children. Some of them were useful, like Dawn, and Sun, and Moon, so he left them alone. Another of the Titans had five sons. Atlas was one of those sons, and he was made to stand by the gate of Tartarus and to hold up the sky on his shoulders. Two others of this family were very famous afterwards. Their names were Prometheus and Epimetheus, that is to say, Forethought and Afterthought. Prometheus was the cleverest of all the Titans, and he went to live on the earth. There he used to wander about making models out of mud to amuse himself.

Now at that time things were not quite sorted out from Chaos, and there were bits of life still in the mud or clay of the earth. So when Prometheus made this clay into all sorts of odd shapes, the shapes came alive as he made them, and became worms, and snakes, and crocodiles, and all kinds of strange creatures, which you can see in museums. As he grew more skillful, he made also birds and animals, and at last he thought he could make something in the shape of the immortals. His first attempt went on four legs, like the other animals, and had a tail like them; it was a monkey in fact. He tried all sorts of monkeys, big and small, until he found out how to make his model stand upright. Then he cut off the tail and lengthened the thumbs of the hands and twisted them inwards. That may seem a very little thing, but it makes all the difference between a monkey's hands and a man's; just try and see how many things you cannot do if you tie your thumb fast to your first finger. And if you look at the skeleton of a man in the museum, you will see that you have a tiny tail in the right place, or at least the bones of it, all that is left after Prometheus cut it off.

Thousands of years afterwards, the Greeks used to show in one of their temples lumps of clay, which they said were left over after Prometheus had made the first man. This clay was the color of mud and smelled a little like human flesh.

Prometheus was very much pleased with his new pet. He used to watch men hunting for food and living in caves and holes, like ants or badgers. He determined to educate men as well as he could, and he was always their friend. Cronus did not take notice of what he was doing; and now we must turn to Cronus and see what he was doing himself.

Chapter 2 THE GODS

Cronus had married one of the Titans, named Rhea; and he was determined that his children should not rebel against him, as he had rebelled against his father, so as soon as one was born, he swallowed it whole. Five he swallowed up in this way; but then Rhea grew tired of this, as she wanted babies to play with, so when the sixth was born, she determined to save him. She took a big stone of the same size as a baby and wrapped it in swaddling clothes and presented it to Cronus as the last baby. Cronus promptly swallowed the stone, and was quite contented. This was really a thing easy to manage, because no doubt the gods used to do with their babies just as the Greek mothers used to do: they wrapped them round and round with a long narrow cloth, until they looked like a chrysalis,[1] or a long plum, with the baby's head sticking out of the end. Then Rhea took the real baby, whose name was Zeus, and hid him in the island of Crete, in a cave which you can still see at this day. He was put in the charge of two nymphs, who fed him on goat's milk, and the cave was watched by armed guards; whenever the baby cried, the guards made such a din by clashing their spears on their shields that Cronus heard nothing of its cries.

Rhea bided her time; and when Zeus grew up, she told him how Cronus had swallowed his brothers and sisters, and how she had saved Zeus himself; and they made a plot against Cronus, as Cronus had done against his father. Together they managed to give Cronus a strong dose of medicine. This made Cronus very sick, and he disgorged all the children, one after another. First came the stone which Rhea had made him swallow; and Cronus was very much surprised to see that. You may see the stone, if you wish, for it was placed in the sacred place of Delphi, and it is still there, in the Museum. Then came the five others in order. I must tell you their names now, because they all come into the story; they were Hestia, Demeter, Hera, Hades, and Poseidon. Strange to say, they had all grown up quite well inside their father, and now they were as big as Zeus, and ready to join in the plot. Then they all made war upon Cronus, and the war went on for ten years, but neither party could win.

Cronus got friends to help him, as far as he could, and one of them was the wise Prometheus. As the war went on, Prometheus said, "Sir, I advise you to bring up your brothers from Tartarus." But Cronus was afraid of his brothers; he said, "No, thank you, no brothers for me." When Prometheus found that Cronus was too stupid to take good advice, he went over to the side of Zeus. To Zeus he gave the same advice; and although Zeus was not very wise, he was wise enough to take this advice.

[1] *chrysalis* (krĭs′ȧ·lĭs): a cocoon.

So he set free the three Cyclopes named Thunderer, Lightener, and Shiner; and they were so grateful that they gave Zeus a gift each—the thunder and the lightning and the thunderbolt. They also gave Hades a cap which made him invisible when he put it on; and they gave Poseidon a trident, or three-pronged spear. Next Zeus set free the three monsters with fifty heads and a hundred hands. You see what an advantage that gave to Zeus. Each of them was like a quick-firing gun, and could throw a hundred stones for Cronus' one.

Now Zeus made a feast for his friends. He gave them nectar, the drink of the gods, and ambrosia, the food of the gods, which was the food of immortality; and he said, "Now let us fight, and make an end of this long war."

Then there was a terrible battle. The three monsters caught up a rock in each of their three hundred hands, and cast them in volleys at Cronus. Zeus thundered and lightened and launched his thunderbolts. The earth shook, the sea boiled, the forests caught fire and burned, blustering winds made confusion all round. In the end, they conquered Cronus and bound him in chains and shut him up in dark Tartarus.

As far as heaven is high above the earth, so deep is Tartarus below the earth. Nine days and nine nights a stone would fall from heaven to earth; nine days and nine nights it would fall from earth to deep Tartarus. A brazen [1] wall runs round it, and brazen gates close it in; there Cronus was in prison, guarded by the Cyclopes and the three hundred-handed monsters. In front of the gate stands Atlas, immovable, bearing the heavens upon his shoulders. A fearful watchdog guards the gates, Cerberus, with three heads and three gaping mouths. When anyone goes in, Cerberus fawns upon him and licks his hands with his three tongues; but if anyone tries to go out, Cerberus devours him up. There Night and Day meet together and greet one another, as one passes in and the other passes out. Within dwell Sleep and Death, brothers, the children of Night. Sleep can wander over the earth at will, seizing men and letting them go; but Death, once he gets hold of a man, never lets him go again, for there is no pity in his heart.

And there dwells Styx, the lady of the black river of Hate, eldest daughter of Oceanus. When quarrels arise among the im-

[1] *brazen* (brā′z'n): made of brass.

mortal gods, then Zeus sends his messenger Iris with a golden jug to bring some of the waters of Styx, which falls from a high and beetling rock. The gods must swear an oath by this water. If any of them breaks the oath, for one year he lies breathless, and cannot partake of sweet nectar and ambrosia; after that year he is cut off from the meeting of the gods for nine years more, and then only may he come back and join their company.

In that dark place the banished Titans dwell, guarded by the monsters. And the Cyclopes are always busy, forging the thunderbolts of Zeus.

After the victory, Zeus and his two brothers were ready to fight each other to decide which should be king; but the wise Prometheus persuaded them to cast lots and to share the sovereignty among them. So lots were cast. Zeus became King of Heaven, and Poseidon King of the Sea, and Hades King of dark Tartarus; but the earth belonged to them all.

Chapter 3 PROMETHEUS

Prometheus, you may remember, was an inventor, and he had filled the earth with animals of his molding, among them Man. He had made Man's body to be like the gods; and into him he put a speck of all the creatures on earth which he had already made, to see what would come of the mixture. There was a speck of the lion and of the deer, a speck of the cow and of the serpent, a speck of the dog and of the fox, of the monkey and of the owl, the dove and the vulture. It was, indeed, a strange mixture, and so are we still, are not we? Sometimes brave and sometimes timid, now calm and now spiteful, truthful or cunning, mischievous or solemn, gentle or greedy! I have often seen boys very much like monkeys, all but the tail. We need a lot of training before we can get all this chaos into order. Prometheus knew that, and he did his best to train up mankind in the way they should go.

He soon found he could not do much without fire. You remember that fire was a great novelty even to the gods; Zeus got it as a gift from the Cyclopes; and he soon began to use it for cooking and for making things. He set up one of his sons, named Hephaestus, as the blacksmith and goldsmith by appointment to the heavenly court. Hephaestus also became a builder and architect, and a fine workman he was. So Prometheus, when he saw all these things, understood that he must get fire by hook or by crook. But Zeus did not like the idea at all. When he turned his attention to the earth and saw all the creatures that Prometheus had been making, he thought them a poor lot. "I will not give fire to such creatures as those," he said. "The earth is a fine place, and it is wasted on them. Let us destroy them and make a better sort of creatures."

But Prometheus, of course, would not agree to that. Zeus could not do everything, as you must have noticed, and he could not wipe out mankind offhand. There is a gap in the story here, and we do not know what happened. But it is clear that there was some sort of war, and that Prometheus did his best to protect his friends, for the next thing we hear of is that Prometheus is making peace between gods and men. They had come to an agreement of some sort, and as usual when a quarrel was made up, there was to be a solemn sacrifice. Some animal was killed, and the gods were to have part of the animal, and men were to have part. In later days, the gods' part used to be burnt, because in that way it could go up to heaven in smoke; but at this time there was no fire on earth, so Zeus came to the place himself to receive his part.

Now Prometheus thought of a way to let his beloved men get the best part. He cut up the victim and put the tidbits into a bladder and wrapped round it a rough piece of hide. Then he put all the bones together in a bundle and wrapped round it a layer of fat. He knew Zeus was rather greedy and had a tooth for fat; so he waited to see what would happen.

When Zeus saw the two parcels, he said, laughing, "Why, my good Titan, this is not a fair division at all. What is that dry old bag?" But Prometheus said, "It is quite fair, sir, we are well satisfied; take your choice, I pray you." As he expected, Zeus chose the enticing parcel of fat. But when he opened it, and saw nothing but bones inside, he was very angry. However, he hid his anger, and pretended he knew about it all the time. "I see this is another of your tricks!" he said. "You are a clever fellow, indeed! Well, never mind." But he had really been taken in, and he did not forget it. He just waited for a chance to pay men out; and when Prometheus begged again for a spark of fire, Zeus flatly refused.

But Prometheus was not to be beaten so easily; and he thought of another trick. He took a long fennel stalk, and dried it, and cut it in half; and as he passed by the hearth where the fire was always kept burning, he poked the stalk in, and let the pith catch fire inside it. He carried out the stalk, and fastened the other half to it, and left the pith smoldering in the middle. Then he calmly walked out of Olympus, with the fennel stalk for a walking stick, and walked down to earth, and nobody noticed anything about it.

Now he had the fire, he began to teach men in earnest. He showed them how to cook and how to keep themselves warm, how to bake bricks and burn pottery, how to melt metals and make tools. Men lived no longer in caves and holes in the earth, but made houses to live in. Prometheus taught them how to write and how to do arithmetic; he taught them about the stars and gave them medicine to cure their diseases; and they learned how to tame the horse and the ass and the camel, that these might carry their burdens, and sheep and cows, to give them milk and meat and to clothe them with skins and fleecy wool.

In fact, he taught them the beginnings of all the arts, and he gave them one blessing above all others. Hitherto they had known the future; they saw trouble and death coming upon them, and they could do nothing to help it, so they were always miserable. But Prometheus took away from men all knowledge of the future; and in its place he put in their hearts blind hopes, which saw nothing, but made them to be always happy. And he gathered together all the evil things that were in the earth, war and quarrel, hatred and greed, pains and diseases, and put them into a large jar; he put a lid on the pot and sealed it and gave it to his brother Epimetheus. "Take care of this, my brother," he said, "and never leave it out of your charge. And when I am away, be very careful not to receive any gift from Zeus. He is man's enemy, and I fear he may try to do him a mischief."

Meanwhile, Zeus had other things to concern him. But when by chance his eye fell upon the earth, what should he see but gleams of fire! How came fire to be on earth? Prometheus must be at the bottom of that! But Prometheus was nowhere to be found; he was busy on earth, as you know. Zeus determined to have his revenge.

So he sent for Hephaestus, the clever craftsman, and told him to make a woman. For there had been only men upon earth so far, and they managed without women as best they could. Hephaestus took a lump of clay and molded it into the shape of one of the immortal goddesses. He molded a beautiful creature, like a modest maid; and all the gods and goddesses gave her gifts. The goddess Athena dressed her in fine clothes and taught her spinning and weaving and needlework. Aphrodite, goddess of beauty, filled her with grace and made her such that every man would wish her to be his own. Gold necklaces and bracelets were put upon her, and garlands of flowers crowned her head. Hermes, the Crier of the gods, put lovely speech into her mouth, and all sorts of trickery into her mind. They named her Pandora, or All-gifts, because all the gods and goddesses had brought her a gift. Then Zeus sent Hermes to take Pandora down to the earth, and to give her to Epimetheus.

Now Epimetheus was not like his brother Prometheus, who always thought of things beforehand, and looked before he leaped. Epimetheus was a fool, who used to do foolish things first, and afterwards thought, "What a fool I have been!" He was like the man who shut the stable door after the horse was stolen. While Prometheus was busy teaching men, Epimetheus sat at home, taking care of his jar. But when he saw Hermes bringing in this beautiful creature, Pandora, and when Hermes said, "Good day to you! Here is a gift from Zeus, Pandora, to be your wife!" Epimetheus was delighted. He forgot all about his brother's warning and thanked Hermes and took the gods' gift, Pandora, with her beautiful voice. She became his wife, and she was the mother of all women upon the earth, who were both a bane [1] and a blessing to men: for they were lovely and charming, and yet they were full of deceit. Of course this was in those early days. They have become better since then, as men have.

It was not long before Pandora began her mischief. She was full of curiosity, and wanted to know about the big jar. "What is in that jar, my husband?" she asked. "You never open it to take out corn or oil or anything we use." Epimetheus said, "My dear,

[1] *bane* (bān): cause of harm.

that is no business of yours. It belongs to my brother, and he will not have it meddled with." Pandora pretended to be satisfied, but she only waited till Epimetheus was out of the way, and then she went straight to the jar and took off the lid.

In a moment, out flew a swarm of horrid things, looking like bluebottle flies, and beetles, and wasps, fat and black and ugly, buzzing and darting about everywhere. She clapped on the lid again, but it was too late. They all went flying over the world: plague, pestilence, and all uncharitableness—the evils of the whole world, which the wise Prometheus had shut up safely in the great jar. And that is how mankind has been so unhappy ever since. And when Prometheus came home and saw what had been done, all that his brother could say was, "What a fool I have been!"

Prometheus himself was cruelly punished for stealing the fire, for Zeus ordered Hephaestus to carry him far away to Mount Caucasus, and there to nail him to a rock, while an eagle came and gnawed at his liver. (Whatever the eagle ate in the day grew again at night.) And there Prometheus was left, until long afterwards he was set free, as you shall hear in due time.

After that Zeus seemed to be content with his revenge. For he made friends with mankind, and men honored him and sacrificed to him; and by degrees gods and men came to depend on one another. The gods would have missed men's sacrifices and men's worship; and men looked to the gods for help and the punishment of wrongdoing. Henceforward the histories of gods and men go together.

Chapter 4 DEMETER

You remember that Demeter was one of the family of Cronus; and while Prometheus was amusing himself with making clay models, and Zeus was concerned with getting his kingdom in order, you must not suppose that Demeter was doing nothing at all. She was also interested in the earth, as Prometheus was; indeed, her name means "Mother Earth," although she was not the same as the old Mother Earth who was her own mother, and the mother of so many strange monsters. The new Mother Earth, if I may call her so, had now a daughter of her own, called Persephone, who was very beautiful; and Hades, the King of Tartarus, fell in love with her, but Demeter would not hear of the match. Persephone used to live in our world, which had become a beautiful place, full of flowers and fruit and the songs of birds; she had a number of friends, the daughters of Oceanus, the Ocean, who was himself one of the sons of the old Mother Earth. They used to play about in the fields and groves, and plucked the flowers, singing and dancing together.

Now Zeus was in favor of his brother's wish; and he asked the old Mother Earth to produce a wonderful flower, in order to attract Persephone to the proper spot, where Hades was to carry her off. There was a meadow in the island of Sicily, where all sorts of flowers grew: rose and crocus and violet, iris and hyacinth; and there Mother Earth put forth the best of all, a splendid tuft of narcissus, one hundred blooms upon one stalk, which smelled so sweetly that heaven and earth and sea laughed for joy. The maiden Persephone put out her hand to take the beautiful flower; but the earth gaped open, and a golden chariot issued forth, drawn by immortal black horses and driven by King Hades himself. Out leaped the King and caught her up and carried her in his chariot down to his dark kingdom. As he bore her along, she cried loudly for help, but no one heard her cry, except Hecate, the goddess of the Moon, who heard her voice from her cave; and Helios, the Sun, who saw her from his chariot in the sky; and except her own mother, Demeter, who heard her voice, but saw nothing.

Then Demeter in sorrow sped over land and sea, searching for her daughter; but no man and no bird of course could tell her anything. For nine days she sought her, and found her not; and for nine nights, carrying flaming torches in her hands; but on the tenth dawn she was met by Hecate, who also bore a torch, and Hecate said, "I heard her voice, although I saw not where she was, but be sure that Helios, the Sun, who sees all things, must have seen her." So Demeter sped on, until she found Helios; and standing in front of his horse, she said, "Helios, you see everything, tell me truly of my daughter; for I heard her voice, but saw not where she was."

Helios said, "I pity you, Demeter, and I will tell you. Zeus has done this; he gave her to Hades, his brother, and Hades seized her and carried her down to his kingdom in the dark. He is no unfitting husband for your daughter, for he is lord of one-third part of the great universe."

But Demeter was very angry with Zeus, and she would not come to Olympus, but disguised herself and went down among the cities and fields of men. No one knew her, and, in course of time, she came to the town of Eleusis, not far from the city of Athens. There she sat down by the Maidens' Well, where the women of the place used to come for water.

Four maidens, daughters of Celeus, who was chief lord of that place, saw her sitting by the well, like an old woman, tired and travel-stained. One of them said, "Why do you sit here, mother? Come to our house, and you will be welcome."

Demeter said, "I thank you, maidens, and I will tell you my story. My name is Doso, the Giver, and I have now come from Crete; not by my will, for pirates carried me off from my home. They have brought the ship to shore not far off, and while they were all making ready their meal, I slipped away from them, and then I wandered until I came here. Now may you all have what your hearts wish; but tell me of some house where I may go and do such work as an old woman can do. I am a good nurse and I can attend a young child or teach the younger women their work."

One of the maidens answered her, "Mother, what the gods send we must bear; for they are stronger than we. There are many good houses in our town where you could find refuge; but we invite you to our house, where our mother is now nursing her youngest son, but lately born, a child of many prayers. If you can bring him up to be a goodly youth, our mother would give you many gifts, so that other people would envy you. We will go now and tell her." They did so, and returned quickly, running along, to bid the stranger follow. And Demeter followed, with her head veiled, and wearing a dark cloak; and her heart was full of sorrow.

They entered the portico of the house, and there by a pillar they saw the great lady sitting, Metaneira, holding her youngest son to her breast. The girls ran up to her, and Demeter followed; but as she crossed the threshold, she seemed taller to look at, and full of majesty, and Metaneira rose from her couch and bade her be seated. But Demeter would not sit upon the couch to which she was invited; for her heart was too full of sorrow, and she waited until one of the maidens brought her a stool. There she sat, holding her veil before her face. She spoke no word, she would neither eat nor drink, until an old crone[1] made a merry jest; and Demeter laughed for the first time, and felt cheered in heart. Then she accepted a drink, not wine, which she said was not lawful for her, but meal and water mixed with mint in a posset.[2]

Then Metaneira said, "Welcome, lady, for I can see you are no common woman, so full as you are of dignity and grace. But we must all bear what the gods choose to send us. And what I can give you shall be yours in my house. Take this, my son, and nurse him for me; and when he grows up to be a big lad, I will reward you, so that you shall be the envy of others."

Demeter said, "I accept the charge gladly; there shall be no heedlessness in me. No witchcraft shall touch him, and no gnawing worm, for I know charms that are stronger than worms and witchcraft."

She took the baby, and tended him; and he grew up without food or milk, like something divine. For Demeter would anoint him with the ambrosia of immortality, and she would breathe softly upon him as she held him to her breast; but at night, unknown to his parents, she would plunge him like a brand into the fire. And they all wondered to see him grow so big and strong; he seemed to be more than a mortal babe. Indeed, Demeter would have made him immortal; but it so happened that Metaneira watched, and saw what she did, and cried out, "Demophon, my son, this strange woman is burying you deep in the fire! What will become of me!"

Demeter was angry when she heard this. She caught up the boy out of the fire, and threw him down on the ground, and cried out:

"What fools you mortals are! You cannot foresee either good or evil. And now you have done a mischief past all healing. I would have made your boy immortal, free from death and old

[1] *crone* (krōn): a wrinkled old woman. [2] *posset* (pŏs′ĕt): hot spiced curdled milk.

age; but now he must abide his fate and die when his time comes. Yet he shall have everlasting honor, since he has lain upon my knees and slept in my arms. For I am that Demeter, whom both gods and men delight in. Now let all the people build me a temple here in Eleusis, and I will teach you my holy rites, to celebrate here forever."

As she said this, the goddess threw off her aspect of an old woman, beauty spread round about her, and a lovely fragrance was wafted from her robes, and a light shone from her body, and golden hair streamed down over her shoulders, so that the whole house was filled with brightness. And so she went out.

Metaneira remained speechless and amazed, and forgot all about her son, lying on the ground; but he cried pitifully, and his sisters heard him, and ran quickly from their beds. One picked up the baby, and laid him in her bosom; one revived the fire, one looked to their mother: then they gathered about the babe, and washed him; but he was not comforted, for they were less skillful nurses than the goddess.

In the morning they told Celeus what had happened; and he gave orders for a temple to be built, as the goddess had commanded. The temple was built, and there Demeter sat; but she would not be comforted, for she still mourned her lost daughter. She caused a dreadful year for mankind; the seed would not sprout, no fruit would grow, no flowers were to be seen. And famine would have destroyed the whole race of men, out and out; but Zeus observed it and sent down Iris, the messenger of the gods.

Iris came down to Eleusis, and saw Demeter sitting there in her temple; and she said, "Demeter, I have a message from Zeus, who bids you come to the meeting place of the gods." But Demeter said, "I will not come"; nor would she move, although Zeus sent each of the gods in turn to call her, and they made her great promises and offered choice gifts. Still, she declared that she would never set foot on Olympus or let the earth bring forth her fruits, until she should see her daughter once again.

Then Zeus sent his herald and crier, Hermes, down to the realms of Hades in the dark underworld. And he found Hades reclining upon his couch with Persephone beside him, his unwilling bride, sad and sorrowful as her mother. And Hermes said, "King Hades, I am sent by Zeus to bring up Persephone to the gods, that her mother may see her again; for she threatens to destroy the whole race of men with famine, and then there will be no one to honor the gods and to do them sacrifice."

Hades smiled grimly when he heard the behest of Zeus; and he said, "Go now, Persephone, and be kind to me; I am no unfitting husband for you, for I am brother to Father Zeus. And while you are here, you shall rule all that lives and moves, and all shall worship you and pay you due offerings, or he shall be punished." But before she went, he managed to make her eat some pomegranate seed, for he wanted to bring her back again; if she had not eaten, she could have remained with her mother forever, but she did not know that. Then Hades brought out the golden chariot and the black horses, and Hermes took the reins and drove them over land and sea, until they came to Eleusis, where Demeter sat in her temple.

When Demeter saw Persephone, she ran out, and Persephone leaped down from the chariot, and they fell into each other's arms. But as she held her daughter, Demeter's heart misgave her, and she said, "Tell me, my daughter, did you taste any food while you were away? If you have not, you may live with me and your father among the immortal gods; but if you have eaten anything in the dark underworld, you must go back there. And how were you carried away?"

Persephone said, "Mother, when Hermes came to bring me back to you, I sprang up at once for joy; but Hades put a pomegranate seed into my mouth and forced me to swallow it against my will. And I was carried off as I plucked a lovely narcissus bloom, while I was playing with my friends."

So they comforted one another: partly in joy and partly in sorrow, for since Persephone had eaten the pomegranate seed, she was bound to return to the dark world.

Then Hecate came up, and embraced Persephone, and from that time Hecate became her servant and companion.

Then Rhea, the mother of Zeus, came and led Demeter and her daughter into the presence of Zeus. And Zeus promised all honor to Demeter among the immortal gods, and she might have whatever rights she would choose; and Demeter was pacified and allowed the seed to sprout and the fruits of the earth to grow, and all the flowers of spring blossomed forth again. And she went again to Eleusis, and taught the princes of Eleusis all her secrets.

She gave to Triptolemus, the son of Celeus, the seeds of wheat and sent him in a chariot drawn by winged dragons all over the earth to teach men ploughing and sowing. She also established a feast in her temple, where the people every four years celebrated great Mysteries, in which they were taught holy doctrines and the laws of good life.

Her daughter Persephone had eaten in the world below, and she must return there; but Zeus ordained that she should remain there only one-third part of the year, and that for the other two parts of the year she should live with her mother. So for one-third of the year, Persephone lives underground, and then it is winter, and the leaves fall, and all seems dead upon the earth; but in the springtime, when Persephone comes up again, the trees put forth leaves, and the flowers bloom, and the kindly fruits of the earth grow up, and men are able to live and be happy.

Chapter 5 ATHENA

Some of the Greek stories are beautiful, like that which you have just heard about Persephone. But some stories are wild and savage, because they belong to the early beginnings of Greek religion, which rose out of chaos very much as our world rose out of chaos. Yet these stories, both ugly and beautiful, were all in the minds of the Greeks; and I tell both kinds to you, or else you would know only part of the Greeks. You may see how their religion and their poetry is like the history of mankind itself, which begins in savagery and rises to something noble and fine. So you must be prepared to hear other childish stories before you come to learn the thoughts and beliefs of the wisest Greeks.

One such tale is the birth of the goddess Athena, a maiden goddess who never married a husband, but was like a strong man, clothed in armor and always ready to fight. This is how the birth came about.

Zeus had for his wife Hera, daughter of old Cronus the Titan, as you remember; but he was not content with one wife.

Like King Solomon, he had many wives; and one of them, Metis, caused him great anxiety; for Mother Earth told him that if Metis bore a son, that son should be lord of heaven. Zeus accordingly remembered his father Cronus, and what does he do but swallows up his wife whole. Before long he had a bad headache, which got worse and worse until he could bear it no longer. So he sent for Hephaestus, his son, the clever smith, and told him to chop open his head with an ax. "Why, sir," said Hephaestus, "that will kill you!" "Nonsense!" said Zeus, "gods cannot die: chop away!" And Hephaestus raised his ax and brought it down with a great crash on the head of Zeus and split it open: and out of the split jumped a little figure, a young goddess it seemed, clad in armor, which rapidly grew bigger until she was full size. As she leaped out, she uttered a loud battle cry; the heaven shivered, and Mother Earth did quake. The split in the head of Zeus closed up again, and now the headache was quite well. This was the goddess Athena, whom Zeus always loved very much after that. She was daughter of Metis, which name means "Cleverness," and she came out of the head of Zeus; she was the cleverest of the goddesses, and afterwards taught people how to spin and weave and sew, and how to paint and carve and do all kinds of clever things, better than Prometheus had done.

Chapter 6 THE OLYMPIAN HOUSEHOLD

And now we have some kind of order in the universe. The three brothers have each his own department, and each his own home. Zeus and his gods live in heaven, that is in the sky, or as the Greeks sometimes said, on Mount Olympus, because that was the highest mountain in Greece and nearest the sky. The Greeks were rather muddled about this, but it does not really matter. In any case, the gods were called Olympians, and they had a regular court up there, wherever it was: a palace, with apartments or separate houses for the inhabitants, horses and chariots, food and drink, regular hours for meals, and everything very much as it was to be later in a royal palace on earth. Hephaestus was the general craftsman; he had a smithy, where he made wonderful works in gold and silver and bronze, even little chairs that could roll about of themselves. Athena, whose birth you have heard of, soon settled down as court dressmaker, spinning yarn and weaving and sewing and embroidering, like any good housewife. She invented all sorts of arts besides, such as pottery and painting, for she was a clever creature.

The household included the old persons we know, although we do not hear much of most of them. Zeus was there, of course, with his mother Rhea the Titan, and Hera his wife; Demeter, now she was reconciled again, and Persephone in the summer; Aphrodite, goddess of love and beauty. Aphrodite was married to Hephaestus, which is surprising, for she was the loveliest creature alive, and he was ugly and hairy and swarthy; they must have been like Beauty and the Beast. Hephaestus was not quite equal to the others in rank, for Hera, his mother, disliked him because he was ugly, and he used to serve the nectar at table. I do not know who did the cooking, but if Olympus was like a good Greek house, the goddesses of the household did it. There were many others connected with this household, who must have been there or at least nearby; for it was increasing by the various sons and daughters of Zeus. Hera was the mother of Ares, the god of War, and the goddesses of Youth and Birth, Hebe and Eileithyia. Another wife of Zeus bore to him the three Horae, or Seasons, named Law, Justice, and Peace, and the three Fates: Spinner, Portioner, and Never-turn-back. Another was mother of the three Graces, Brightness, Bloom, and Merryheart. Another wife brought him the nine Muses, who loved singing and dancing. There were also a great number of divine beings, not so important as these, who lived in different parts of the universe; they were all related, and all knew each other, wherever they were, but they lived in the country and did not come regularly to Olympus.

Zeus was the head of the family; and on the whole, he managed his big household with tact. He was an easygoing creature who loved peace and quiet, and he let them alone as long as he could; but sometimes they made such a to-do, he could stand it no longer, and then he would lose his temper, and knock the gods all over the place, for he was very strong. He said to them once:

"Just listen to me: you may try it if you like. Fasten a golden chain to me, and pull on it, all of you, gods and goddesses together, and you will never pull great Zeus down to earth, however hard you may try. But if I choose, I can pull you all up, with earth and sea too, and fasten you to a peak of Olympus, and there in the air you shall all hang."

Hera in particular was a great trial to him. She had a bad temper and a sharp tongue; and once when she had tried him too far, he hung her over the edge of heaven by her hands, with a big stone fastened to each foot. On this occasion, her son Hephaestus tried to help her, whereupon Zeus picked him up by the leg, and threw him out of heaven. All day long he fell, and in the evening, down he came plump into the island of Lemnos. The fall hurt his legs badly, and the people of Lemnos nursed him back to health. After that he had to keep hidden for a long time; in the end he came back to Olympus, but he was always lame, and when he carried the nectar round it was a great joke to laugh at his hobbling gait. But he was a good-humored creature, and bore no grudge.

Chapter 7 APOLLO AND ARTEMIS

One of the quarrels of Hera concerned a maiden of the Titans, named Leto, who was always mild and gentle, kind to both men and gods, gentlest creature in all Olympus. Zeus loved her, because she was so gentle, and made her one of his wives; but Hera was not gentle at all, she was jealous, and vowed that Leto should have no children. She drove Leto out of Olympus, and laid her commands on earth and sea, that no place should give harborage to Leto. So Leto wandered all over the world distracted, praying every land and every island to help her; but they all refused, for fear of Hera's commands. At last Leto espied an island, floating on the top of the sea, so that it was no part either of sea or land; this was the little island of Delos. Then by the power of Zeus, four pillars of adamant [1] grew up from below sea, and rooted Delos to the bottom of the sea; and there the children of Leto were born, by the side of a beautiful palm tree.

These children were twins, Apollo and Artemis. A nurse gave them nectar, the drink of the gods, then ambrosia, the food of immortality; and as gods do, the children quickly grew strong and wise, and Apollo cried out:

"I shall ever love music and the bow, and I will declare to men the will of Zeus in truthfulness." And to the amazement of all who saw it, he began to walk upon the earth; and the island of Delos burst into bloom with golden flowers. Artemis also, his twin sister, loved the bow, as Apollo did; she became afterwards great at hunting, and ranged the woods and forests with bow and arrows, attended by a train of nymphs, who were something like the gods, but inferior. Both of them had many temples and many worshipers.

But Apollo out of all his sacred places, all over the world, on mountainsides and by the flowing rivers, always loved best of all the little island of Delos and its little hill, because there he was born; and from the little hill, Cynthus, he took one of his favorite titles, and was called the Cynthian. On this hill is still to be seen his sacred cave, where he was worshiped ever after, until the Greek gods all passed away, and the Christian God took their place. There he had an oracle,[2] giving answers with divine voice to all who sought his aid, the first of many such oracles of Apollo; and there he had great feasts, with splendid processions and ceremonies, with dancing and singing of hymns, and games and sports to amuse the people. Trains of young men and young women sang in honor of Apollo and Artemis, whose arrows bring death and pestilence upon men if they are offended, and punishment upon evildoers; and these worshipers could imitate the strange languages and chatterings of all the races of men, so that a foreigner would think that his own people were singing.

But I am going on too fast in the story, for as yet Apollo is only a beginner. He has to make his way in the world, and to earn a place in the divine court. And so he became a great traveler and

[1] *adamant* (ăd′ȧ·mănt): an imaginary hard stone. [2] *oracle* (ŏr′ȧ·k'l): the place where truth and wisdom are revealed, usually by a priest or priestess.

colonizer, seeking everywhere for places where he might settle; and he did not scruple to take possession of a convenient shrine, even if someone was there before him. This is what he did at Delphi, as I shall now explain to you.

He passed over the sea, then, this way and that, sitting upon a tripod, which served him instead of a ship. A tripod is a three-legged stool; and this tripod was a fine one, made all of gold, as was proper for a god, and having two wings where the handles of the tripod usually are: thus it could skim along the surface of the sea, like a flying fish, and round about it the dolphins leaped out to see what was coming, and dived back again. I cannot tell you all his travels, but I will tell you now how he came to Delphi.

Apollo had already been to report himself in Olympus. We do not know how the gods received him, but I should think they may have been doubtful at first of the stranger, and snubbed him. In any case, he thought he had better look out for a more notable place to settle than the little island of Delos, which Hera sneered at, we may be sure. So he came down from Mount Olympus, and passed over to the great island of Euboea, but found nothing there. Then he crossed the narrow strait which divides Euboea from the mainland, about fifty yards wide, and passed over the place where the city of Thebes was afterwards to be. A few miles from Thebes, he came to a likely place, where there was a spring of water, named after the nymph who lived in it, Telephus. Apollo was pleased with the place, and said, "Telephus, I think this place will do nicely for me, so I will just build a temple here."

This did not suit Telephus at all; she wanted to keep her own place for herself, and who was this upstart that he should calmly take possession of it? So she answered, "If I may say so frankly, I do not think you will like this place. Horses and mules are passing by all day long, and they all drink of my water; I am sure the noise of their trampling will disturb you. Besides, the people will be eager to gaze at a well-built chariot, or a well-matched team, and they will not pay proper attention to your temple, where, by the way, they will be expected to make some offering themselves. But I can tell you the very place—you know best, of course. You see that great mountain, Parnassus, with its peaks covered with snow? In the dell just below it is a place called Crissa, and there is room to build you a fine temple. The path is too narrow for chariots, and you will have none to disturb you, but all those who dwell around will bring you offerings, and seek your help."

Apollo was persuaded, and went on his way, along the lakeside and into the mountain glens, by a path which was to be famous in years to come. As he crossed the summit of the pass, he saw before him a deep valley, with steep rocks on either side, but at the bottom, a watercourse, and trees growing thick. At the end of the valley was a wide and fertile plain, full of trees. It was like a river of trees flowing into a sea of trees, and beyond sparkled the real sea in the distance.

When he had come about halfway down toward the plain, he saw the little town of Crissa, and above it a dark cleft in the rock, from which a stream came bubbling out. There was room for a temple here; but here, also, someone was settled before him. For here was a sacred place of Mother Earth, a hole or cave where gusts of strange vapor came out of the rock, and the place was guarded by a dragon, a great bloated monster, which used to destroy the crops with her breath and to devour the farmers' cattle and sheep—a terrible and bloodthirsty pest was this dragon. Apollo shot the monster with arrows from his bow. She writhed about and tried to bite him, but could not, nor could her deadly breath hurt an immortal; so there the dragon died.

And Apollo said, "Rot there, you monster; you shall do no more harm to man." And the dragon rotted; and the place was called Pytho, which means "the rotting place," and Apollo took a title himself from this place and was called Pythian Apollo, for he took possession of the sacred cave, where Mother Earth had her oracle, and of the sacred spring, Castalia. Close by he built his own temple, not very large at first, but it was to grow great by and by; and underneath the temple, in a small chamber cut out of the rock, he made the vapor come up, which had such strange effects on those who breathed it.

Apollo now had a temple, but he had no servants and priests. What was he to do? As he was wondering, he saw from afar—for the gods can see farther than we can—a ship leaving the coasts of Crete, full of Cretans. Apollo knew that the Cretans were great men for sacrifices and for laws, and that it was the Cretans who guarded Zeus, the father of Apollo, when Zeus was a baby in the Cretan cave.

Apollo therefore took the form of a dolphin, swiftest of fishes, and he sped through the sea until he reached the Cretan ship. Then with a great leap, he shot out of the water and leaped against the side of the ship, making its timbers quiver and shake. The sailors did not know who he was, but they sat still in fear, and kept on their course as it was set, toward the northwest; and by the will of Zeus, a southeast wind blew them quickly forward. Past the Laconian coast they sped, and on toward the coast of Elis, and when they would have put in to land, the ship would not obey the helm, but Apollo guided it whither he would. And when they came over against the mouth of the Gulf of Corinth, the wind veered to the west and blew them straight into the little bay which lay by the plain of Crissa.

Then Apollo leaped out from the sea, like a shining star, and sped to his temple, from which he returned in the shape of a handsome young man, with long hair flowing over his shoulders, and he said, "Strangers, who are you?"

They said, "Sir—though you look more like a god than a man—hail to you! Now tell us, what is this place? We are Cretans, and we were bound elsewhere, but some god has brought us here against our will."

Apollo replied, "Strangers from woody Crete, I am Apollo, the son of Zeus; and you have been brought here to keep my rich temple, which shall be honored among men. Take in your sails, and draw up the ship on the sand, and upon the shore build an altar and sacrifice to Apollo the Dolphin. Then take your meal, and follow me to my temple at Delphi."

They did so, and followed him up the slope, singing the Healer's Hymn which they had been used to sing in Crete. Then Apollo showed them his temple, and said, "Here you shall abide, and care for my temple; and you will not need to plow the land or to keep herds; for my worshipers will come from far and near, and they will bring many sheep for sacrifice."

He procured priestesses, also, to help in the oracle. In turns they sat on a tripod in the secret cell under the temple; and the priestess, as she drank in the wonderful vapor, became inspired, and uttered strange words in an unknown tongue.

The priests could not interpret the words, nor indeed could Apollo himself; but he knew one who could, and that was the ancient god Pan, who lived in Arcadia. And Apollo went to Pan, and learned from him the art of divining, and taught his priests; so that after that the priests were able to tell the meaning of the words which the priestess uttered, and to answer the questions which the worshipers put to the god.

Chapter 8 PAN

Pan was one of the old ancient gods, a strange creature unlike the rest. Some say he was the son of Zeus, but some again say he was the son of Cronus, and I am inclined to think that this is true, for the children of Zeus were all like the gods, even Hephaestus. For although Hephaestus was ugly (so that Hera his mother hated him), he had two arms and two legs, and was clearly one of the divine race; but Pan was half a goat, and that looks like the old generation. It looks like a son of Cronus too; for such another son of Cronus was Chiron, half man and half horse. Pan was shaggy with hair all over, and he had two short horns on his head; from his waist downward he was like a goat, with a tail, and his knees turned the wrong way, and he had goat's hooves. Whoever his father was, and whoever was his mother (for that is uncertain too), he was born in Arcadia, among the mountains, and there he dwelt, the friend of the herdsmen and the hunters and the fishermen. He was attended by a troop of servants, like himself, at least insofar that each had a long tail, and some had also goat's feet. These were called Satyrs.

He was fond of all the nymphs of the trees and the springs and the hills, and one of them always attended him, the nymph Echo; so that when he uttered his piercing cry in the forests, high up on the mountainside Echo would answer him. Pan quite fell in love with Echo, and often chased her about the hills; but he never caught her, for she was always just before him, or just behind him, giving back his cry. The hunters and herdsmen all loved him, but they feared him also, because his loud cry sometimes put a sudden terror into men's hearts, so that they ran away helter-skelter, without knowing why; this they called Pan's terror, or a panic, as we call it still. He would do this even in war, if he chose to help any army of fighting men; and long ages afterward, he is said to have raised his cry among the Persians at the battle of Marathon, and made the Athenians drive them in rout. Then the Athenians took him into their city of Athens as one of their gods, and gave him a cavern which you can still see on the side of the Acropolis hill.

But that was long after; the time we now speak of was when Apollo was just making his way in the world, and there were no great cities of men as yet. The hunters and the herdsmen, who go up into the mountains in the springtime, when the Pleiades rise in the sky, and stay there until they set in October, asked his help in tending their herds and hunting their game; and they made him thank-offerings, head and horns or a skin, which they would hang on the branches of some large tree. Pan was fond of music and dancing, and he invented the panspipes, seven hollow reeds of different lengths, giving different notes, which he fixed in a row, with the hollow ends upward, and played by blowing into them under his lip. You can hear the panspipes if ever you find a Punch-and-Judy show. As Pan played on the pipes, the Satyrs would all dance around; and the hunters and herdsmen imitated him, and danced, and tootled on their pipes. At midday he would sleep, in some shady spot by a spring of water; and the people were very much afraid of disturbing Pan at midday. A Greek poetess, named Anyte, has written this verse about Pan:

> Why in this dark lone forest do you play,
> O rustic Pan, on a melodious reed?
> That on the dreary hills my heifers may
> Have pasture, and on bearded grain may feed.

Pan knew all the secrets of the forest and of the earth, for he lived close to Mother Earth; and he had this gift of divining, which he taught to Apollo, as you have heard.

Chapter 9 HERMES

But the art of divining was not all that Apollo had to learn. He loved music and singing, but he had no instrument to play on, and before you hear how he got one, you must listen to the story of Hermes.

He has already come into this history, but I cannot keep all the things exactly in order as they happened, or the stories would be a collection of bits all mixed up. So now I must tell you how Hermes came to join the company of the gods. Hermes was himself a son of Zeus, and his mother, Maia, lived in a cave on Mount Cyllene in Arcadia; and there he was born—a marvelous baby! For he was born in the morning, at midday he played on the harp, and in the evening he stole Apollo's cattle. He was to be the prince of tricksters, the cleverest creature in the world, a friend of cattle, a bringer of dreams, a giver of good luck, who could outwit both gods and men. He even made the tortoise sing; and this is the story.

As soon as he was born, and laid in the cradle, he leaped out, and went off in search of Apollo's cattle. Just outside the cave, what should he see but a big tortoise, waddling along. Hermes laughed, and said:

"Here is a sign of good luck, the first thing! Good day to you! I am glad to see you, tortoise. Where did you get that dappled shell to cover you with, a fine treasure here in the hills? I will take you inside, and you shall profit me greatly. I will show you the greatest respect. But it is a pity for you that you came out this morning. There is no place like home; it is dangerous out of doors. Alive, you are useful to keep off the witches, but if you die I will teach you to sing."

No sooner said than done. He took the tortoise into the cave. Then he cut off its head and legs, and scooped out all the flesh, and cut away the lower part of the shell. He bored holes in the upper round of the shell, and fixed reeds across the inside, and stretched a piece of skin tight across the hollow part of the shell over the reeds. Then he fixed two horns in the upper part of the shell, and joined their tops by a bridge. Lastly, he tied seven strings of sheep's gut to the bridge, each one a little tighter than the last, and fastened the ends at the bottom of the shell. He touched each string in turn, and each gave a different note, because they were each of different thickness and tightness; then he played tunes, while he sang little ditties, full of mirth and fun.

But his mind was now bent on other things; so he laid his newly made harp in the cradle and ran out to find something to eat.

He climbed a hill which overlooked a plain where the cattle of the gods were feeding. Thither he descended, and cut out fifty of the best cows, and drove them to a lonely spot, driving them backward, that he might spoil the tracks. He tied under his feet bundles of myrtle twigs, so that they would not make a mark like feet.

On his way, he passed an old man, digging about his vines; and he said, "Old man, I think these vines will bear you a good vintage, and you will make plenty of wine with the fruit, if you can keep a quiet tongue in your head, and remember to forget what you have seen." And on he went, until as night drew to an end, he reached the byres and drinking troughs by the river Alpheus. There he fed the kine, and gave them drink. And then he gathered a pile of brushwood, and prepared to make fire, for it was Hermes who found out the way to make fire with two sticks. He took a block of dry wood, and a dry stick which he sharpened; then he twisted the point of the stick round and round on the block, until a little sawdust wore out of it, and by and by this grew hot, and at last kindled into flame. And he piled the brushwood into a trench, and set fire to it. If only he had been in the world before, he might have saved some trouble for Prometheus.

Then he threw down two cows, and bent their heads to their flanks, and cut the vital spot. He flayed them, and laid their skins on the rocks; then he cut out the choicest parts, and pierced them with spits, and roasted chine [1] and paunch [2] over the fire. He laid out the meat on flat stones and divided it into twelve parts as offerings to the twelve great gods; and although he would have liked very much to eat some, being a god he contented himself with the smell. And after that, he burned up the heads, and hooves, and left no trace of his theft. He threw his footgear into the river, and passed quietly back to his cave, where he snuggled down into the cradle, with his beloved harp by his side.

[1] *chine* (chīn): backbone and attached parts. [2] *paunch* (pänch): belly.

But his mother saw him; and she said, "Naughty rogue! What have you been doing out in the night, clothed in shamelessness as a garment? I think Apollo will soon have you out of this place, tied up in ropes like a thief that you are. You are born to be a nuisance to gods and men!"

Hermes said, "Mother, why do you scold me as if I were a feeble babe? No, no, I will make your fortune. Why should we live here in a cave, with no followers and no offerings? We are gods, and we may as well be rich and enjoy life as they do. I will be Apollo's equal, or else I will be prince of robbers. I will break into his great house at Pytho, and take his tripod and his other treasures, see if I don't!"

By this time, as the sun rose, Apollo had gone to the place where his cattle were kept, and he soon missed the stolen cows; so he set out in search of them. Before long he came across the old man, who was then grazing his beast; and he said, "Old man, I am seeking my cattle, fifty fine cows, which have strayed away. Have you seen anyone driving cows?"

The old man said, "Good sir, it's hard to tell all that one's eyes do see. Many travelers pass this way, some honest, and some not, and it is difficult to know one from another. However, I was digging about my vines all day, and I think I saw, but I do not know for certain, I think I saw a child, whoever he was, with some cattle; he had a long stick, and he kept walking from side to side, and driving the cattle backward, with their heads toward him."

So Apollo went on, and by and by he came on the tracks of the cattle. "Here they are," he said, "turned toward the meadow, it is true; but the other tracks—what can they be? No man or woman can have made them, no wolf or bear or lion. Wonderful tracks they are indeed, each more wonderful than the last!"

And so he followed on, until he came to Cyllene and the cave; and he went in. But Hermes snuggled down in his cradle, and cuddled himself up in the swaddlings, squeezing head and hands and feet into a ball, and he made as though he were asleep; but he was really wide awake, and held his harp under his arm-pit. Apollo looked at the mother and child, and opened the chests that lay there, but found nothing. But Apollo knew by his power that the child was the thief; so he said to him:

"Child, confess about the cows, or I will cast you into the

darkness of Tartarus, where you will have to be a baby forever, and you shall be the babies' prince, if you like!"

And Hermes said, "Apollo, what unkind words you have spoken! Are you looking for cows? I have seen none; I have heard none, no one has told me anything about them; I can give you no news, nor earn your reward, if you offer a reward. Do I look like a cow-lifter? All I care for is sleep, and milk, and a warm bath. Do not let anyone hear of this dispute; how surprised the gods will be that a newborn baby should drive a herd of cows! I was born yesterday, my feet are soft and the ground is rough; but if you wish, I will swear a great oath by my father's head that I did not steal your cows, and I do not know who did, whatever cows may be; for I never saw one, and have only heard the word cow."

As he said this, Hermes darted his glances this way and that, wrinkling his brows, and then he began to whistle aloud, as if Apollo's talk was just an idle tale. But Apollo laughed softly, and said to him, "Oh, you little rogue! You talk so innocently that I think you must have had good practice in thieving. I daresay you have stripped many a house last night, and left the poor owners not a stool to sit on. Many a herdsman will you plague in days to come, when you have a hankering for meat. But come now, if you don't want to sleep your last sleep in that cradle; get out, you comrade of dark night. You shall have the title Prince of Thieves among the immortal gods."

Then Apollo caught him up in his arms, but the child gave a loud sneeze, and Apollo dropped him down on the ground, and said, "Fear not, swaddling baby, son of Zeus and Maia. By that omen, I shall find my cattle, sure enough." Hermes jumped up, and pushed his covering up to his ears, and said, "Where are you taking me in all this haste? Is it the loss of your cows that makes you so angry? I wish all the cows in the world might perish. I don't know who stole them, and I don't know even what a cow is. Let us put the case before Zeus, and he shall decide between us."

For now, Hermes saw it was of no use to resist. He began to walk over the sand, and Apollo came after, and they climbed up to the top of Mount Olympus, where Zeus their father holds the scales of judgment. There was an assembly on that day of the Olympian gods, and the two stood before the knees of Zeus.

Then Zeus said, "Where do you come from now, Apollo, driving this rich booty before you? A newborn babe—but he marches in front like a herald! This must be some weighty matter for us to decide."

And Apollo said, "Sir, it is a weighty matter, although you are pleased to make fun of me, as if I were the only god on the lookout for spoils. Here is a child, a thief and a robber, whom I found on the hill of Cyllene. Never in all my days have I seen one so pert as he is. He stole my cows, and drove them away last evening to Pylos, and wonderful tracks they made. The cows seemed to be going to the place they came from, but he himself strayed all over the place, walking neither on his feet nor on his hands, but somehow, as it seemed, on a lot of twigs. I tracked him over the sand, and when he got upon the hard ground, I found an old man who had noticed him. So when he had shut up the cattle somewhere, he went home and lay down in his cradle in the dark cave. When I found him, he rubbed his eyes, and said, 'I have not seen them, or heard of them, so it is of no use to offer me a reward for the finding.' "

Then Hermes said, pointing his finger at Apollo, "Father, I am a truthful child; I cannot tell a lie. He came to our cave at sunrise, looking for his cows. He brought no witnesses, but violently ordered me to confess, or he would throw me down into Tartarus. For he is strong, and I was only born yesterday, not at all like a cow-lifter. Believe me, I did not drive his cows to the house, I never crossed the threshold. Helios the Sun sees everything, but he never saw that. You know I am not guilty. I swear it by your house! Someday I will punish him for this cruel accusation; but now, help the younger!"

And as he spoke, his eyes kept shooting sidelong glances, to see how they all took it, and he held his clothes tight over his shoulders. But Zeus laughed aloud at the cunning little knave, and said:

"Go now, both of you, and you, Hermes, show where you have hidden the cattle." With these words he bowed his head, and at that sign all must obey. So Hermes led Apollo to the place by the river Alpheus, where he had shut up the cows; and as he drove them out, Apollo saw the two hides lying upon the rocks, and said:

"You crafty rogue, how were you able to flay two cows, and

you a newborn babe? I fear the strength you shall have one day; you will not need long to grow!"

He caught up strong withies,[1] and tried to bind Hermes; but the bonds fell off, and as they struggled, Apollo caught sight of the harp, which Hermes had kept all this time hidden under his armpit. Then he coaxed the child, and at last made him friendly; and Hermes took the harp with his left hand, and with his right he touched each of the strings, which gave out their notes; and Apollo laughed aloud, for the music went to his soul. And Hermes played sweetly upon the harp, and sang to its music in a lovely voice: he sang all the story of the gods, how they came to be out of chaos, each in his turn, and how each received his portion. Then he sang praises of Memory, mother of the nine Muses. And Apollo said:

"That song of yours is worth fifty cows, and I believe we shall soon settle our quarrel in peace. But tell me, who gave you this wonderful thing and who taught you to sing? For I vow no one on Olympus has ever heard such singing, or seen such a treasure as this thing. We have our songs, and we have our flutes, but I never cared much for them. Here is a choice of three things at once—mirth or love or sleep; they are all in your music. Now sit down, dear boy, and respect the words of your elder. I promise you great fame, both you and your mother; I will make you a leader renowned among the gods; I will give you great gifts."

Hermes understood quite well what Apollo meant; and he said:

"You put your questions well; but I am not jealous, I am quite willing that you should learn my art. You shall learn it this day. I mean to be your friend. Now you know everything, since you are one of the gods' company, and Zeus has given you his oracles, and taught you his laws. So you can easily learn what you please, but since you are determined to play on the harp, then take this as a gift from me. Play and sing and be merry. Bring it in boldly to the feast and the dance, to be a joy by night and by day. He who inquires of this with skill and wisdom is taught by its sound all things that delight the mind, as he caresses it with gentle friendliness; but he who is ignorant and inquires of it with violence, to him it chatters vanity and folly. So I give you this harp, noble son of Zeus, and I will be keeper of the roving cattle.

[1] *withy* (wĭth'ĭ): a willow twig.

Then there is no need for you to be angry, although you are a hard bargainer."

Then Hermes held out the harp, and Apollo took it and gave to Hermes his whip and made him keeper of the herds: and ever since, Hermes Eriunius, or "All-wool," has been the helper and guardian of herdsmen and shepherds; and he became also the god and patron of all traders, who make bargains together.

So these two, Apollo and Hermes, returned to Olympus in friendship. But Apollo said, "Cunning rogue, I fear you may steal my harp from me, and my bow too. Swear me then a great oath, to do nothing but what will be pleasing to me."

And Hermes nodded his head, like Zeus, and promised never to steal anything that belonged to Apollo, and never to enter his treasury; but Apollo swore always to love Hermes, and none better than Hermes. Then Apollo said, "I will give you a staff of riches, a golden wand, which will keep you safe as long as you do good deeds. But I cannot teach you the art of divining, which I know you wish to possess, though you have only hinted at it. I alone may know the wise counsel of Zeus, and I have sworn him an oath that no other god shall know it, save insofar as he bids me reveal it. As for men, if they come to me guided by birds of true omen,[1] I will tell them the truth, and I will not deceive them; but if any trust to idly chattering birds, and invoke me against my will, wishing to know more than the gods do, it shall be a vain errand, yet their gifts I will take. But there are three ancient sisters, having wings, who fly about feeding on honey, like bees; and when the honey inspires them, they are willing to speak truth, but if they are deprived of it, they speak falsely, and go buzzing round each other. These sisters I give to you; inquire of them, and delight your heart, and teach men to do the same, if you will."

So Zeus, remembering how Hermes came before Apollo like a herald, made Hermes the herald and crier of the gods, with a place in Olympus, and he made him his own particular messenger. With his magical wand he was ordered to lead the ghosts of men down to Hades, for a touch of it makes the sleeping eyes wake, and the waking eyes close in sleep. He was to preside over all games and contests of men, and to stand in the wrestling school and the gymnasium, with the title of Hermes-in-the-Ring.

[1] *omen* (ō′mĕn): telling of the future.

He was to be giver of luck, that whenever anyone should find a good thing, he would thank Hermes, and call his find Hermaion, or "Hermes' gift." And Hermes was to be lord of birds of omen, and lord of the beasts of the forest and the beasts of the field. He plays no more on the harp, but tootles his tunes on the panspipes, which some even say that he invented.

And Apollo now is ever welcome to the immortals. He plays lovely music upon the harp, and all the Muses together sing as he plays, while the Graces and the Seasons dance, with Harmony and Youth and Aphrodite, holding each other by the wrist. His sister Artemis also joins in the dance, and the other gods listen and look on.

Chapter 10 ARTEMIS

Thus Apollo won a place of welcome in heaven, nor was his sister Artemis slow to make good her footing there.

There are three goddesses in Olympus whose hearts were never touched by Aphrodite, the goddess of love.

One is Hestia, which means "the Hearth," eldest born of the children of Cronus, and youngest too; for she was born first by her mother, and swallowed first by her father, so that when he came to disgorge his children, Hestia came forth last. Both Poseidon and Apollo sought to wed her, but she refused outright; and touching the head of Zeus, she swore to remain a maiden all her days. So Zeus gave her a high place in the house, and a rich portion. There she guards the hearth, and tends the fire, like a good housewife. In all the temples of the gods she has a share of honor, and a chief place in all the cities and homes of men, for in every house and in every town hall is a sacred hearth, and the sacred fire was kept burning.

The second is Athena, who cares nothing for love, but delights in war, and in practicing all clever arts and crafts, which she taught to men. And the third is Artemis, who loves hunting and archery, and the harp with its dances and songs.

You see Hestia lived the natural life of a woman, such as the eldest daughter has lived in many a household on earth; but the other two were quite out of the way. Athena was like a man, as born of a man's head, all brain, with a man's courage too; but Artemis, I think, wanted to show that she could do as well as her brother. She was not originally like Apollo, she was not charming like him, and she never dreamed of oracles; but as he used the bow, she used the bow, and they were often linked together in worship. Thus she gained a good share of honor and profit along with her brother.

But they were a pushing pair of young gods, and not easily satisfied. Apollo was not content with taking the oracle of Delphi from old Mother Earth; he actually took over the sun, and Artemis, not to be beaten, took over the moon.

Both sun and moon were already well looked after by those of the old Titan stock, Helios and Selene. When the universe was being brought into order, you may remember that the sun was taken in charge by Hyperion, the fourth son of Uranus and Mother Earth, who used to drive the sun's chariot from morning to evening, and looked after the horses. Hyperion married Thea, the Divine, a most venerable and radiant goddess, and his children were Eos, Helios, and Selene. He then divided the duties among them: Eos took over the dawn, Helios the sun, and Selene the moon. Helios used to drive over the sky all day the team of four horses, which were named Fiery, Shiny, Scorcher, and Blazer; and in the evening, when they dipped down into the ocean, a golden boat used to carry them round over the ocean stream behind the earth, so as to be ready for next morning. Helios had temples in every part of Greece, on the tops of the hills; the most famous were on the acropolis of Corinth, and in the island of Rhodes. How he got that last is a pretty story.

When Zeus and the Immortals were dividing the earth among them, so that each should have his own particular part, they forgot all about the Sun-god, for he was busy about his duties, out of sight, out of mind, and no place was allotted to him. But when he next came to visit Zeus, he said, "Sir, what place have you allotted to me?" Zeus was very much put out. "Why," he said, "we forgot all about you. But never mind, we will cast lots again." "Oh, no," said Helios, "pray do not do that. I saw just the place for me, as I was driving high over the sea; down in the depths of the sea was a beautiful island, rising gradually up towards the top. Let the Portioner lift up her hands, and swear an oath that it shall be mine." She did so, and the famous island of Rhodes came up from the depths. Helios took it for his own, and wedded Rhodos, the nymph of the island, and she bore him three sons, who built them a city each, and divided the island among them. But Apollo, I suppose, did not like another god to dispute his omniscience; and it was Apollo's right alone, he thought, to see everything and to know everything, so he turned out Helios, although no one had ever made any complaint as to the way he did his duty.

Selene, sister of Helios, and like him a Titan, drove a silver chariot with two white horses over the nightly sky, but not every night: she had no light of her own, but borrowed some from her brother. She was a loving creature, and one of the wives of Zeus, but she herself was deeply in love with a man, named Endymion, a beautiful youth whom she saw sleeping upon a mountain. She crept down to him and kissed him, and there she kept him in perpetual sleep, that she might visit him whenever she wished. Artemis then, not to be outdone by her brother, turned out Selene, and took over the moon.

But this happened long ages after the time I am now speaking of, near the end of the career of the enterprising twins, Apollo and Artemis. At present Artemis is only beginning her course, and she sought to win her footing in Olympus.

Artemis used to hunt the wild boar, surrounded by a company of maidens who attended her. She was a hard-hearted goddess, and deeply resented any slight or rudeness. Once, for example, a young man named Actaeon happened to see her quite by accident, as she was bathing in a pool, and he went away at once; but she turned him into a deer, and his own dogs killed him. Another time, when her sacrifices were forgotten, she sent a large boar into the countryside, which dealt ruin all around; but that belongs to another story, which you shall hear in its place. On the occasion which I am to describe, she turned her hunting to good account.

You remember that Zeus at the beginning of his reign had terrible battles with monsters, which he destroyed; but these were not the only rebellions he had to deal with. Poseidon, lord of the sea, had two sons, named Otus and Ephialtes, who were a remarkable pair of beings. Each year they grew one cubit [1] in breadth, and one fathom [2] in height; so at nine years old, they were fifty-four feet high, and thirteen feet six inches broad; and they thought they were a match for a common sort of god like Zeus. So they determined to conquer Zeus, and to rule the universe themselves. They piled Mount Ossa upon Mount Olympus, and Mount Pelion upon Ossa, and they meant thus to climb up into heaven and turn Zeus out. They caught Ares, the War-god, and shut him up in a brazen pot, with the lid on, where they kept him for thirteen months; but he was rescued by Hermes and came out quite exhausted. Zeus was pleased with Hermes, because this proved that he had been wise to welcome Hermes into Olympus. But Zeus did not seem to take much notice of the big boys; however, Artemis did, because they were great huntsmen, and she knew all about them and how they grew. She changed herself therefore into the shape of a deer; and one day, when they were hunting, she ran between them. Each threw a spear at her, but she skipped nimbly out of the way; so the spear of Otus pierced Ephialtes, and the spear of Ephialtes pierced Otus, and that was the end of them. I do not know what they might have done if they had lived to grow up.

So Artemis had now shown that she was a person of importance; and she began to spread her worship about the world. Whenever she saw a center of worship with some animal in it, she took possession herself. There were two of them in Crete. One goddess named Britomartis protected the hunters, and one named Dictynna, our Lady of Nets, protected the fishers. Artemis turned them both out, and took possession of their worship and their revenues. In Thrace was another, Bendis, who was a protector of hunters, and she also had something to do with the moon. She used to have a relay race of men on horseback, carrying torches, which must not go out. In Athens, again, there was a ceremony connected with bears. Once a year all the little girls, at ten years of age, had to dress up in brown clothes, and go into the goddess' temple; and if they did not do that, they would not be allowed to marry when they grew up. They were called the Little She-bears. Artemis took over this temple and the Little Bears, and she did

[1] *cubit* (kū′bĭt): the distance from the elbow to the end of the middle finger. [2] *fathom* (făth′ŭm): six feet.

the same for Bendis and her torch race. She even went over to Asia, and she did not despise the ugliest goddess in the whole world, who had a great temple at Ephesus. This was the goddess about whom St. Luke wrote, when he described how the people all cried out by the space of two hours, "Great is Diana of the Ephesians!" For Diana was the Roman name for Artemis.

She also took to herself the worship of Hecate. You remember Hecate, who used to attend upon Persephone, she who met Demeter on her search and carried two torches. Hecate was a Night-goddess, who had something to do with the moon, and knew all about witches. She helped to bring children into the world, and presided over funerals when men died. Artemis took over all Hecate's work, and the result was she was thought to be three goddesses in one, Persephone, Artemis, and the Moon. So her statue often had three heads on one body. It was set up at the crossroads, and people used to drop cakes and nuts and such things by her statue, for anyone to eat. They called it Hecate's dinner.

PART TWO

Chapter 11 THE FLOOD

You have heard how Zeus by degrees put his kingdom in order, and made the beginning of law in Olympus. There he held a court of justice and heard pleadings and gave his decision according to his laws. These laws were so far the decision of his will, from which there was no appeal. When Zeus bowed his head all must obey. He demanded an oath by the river Styx, and there were penalties for falsehood. And he was beginning to make his will felt among men; they also had their oaths and their beginnings of justice, their compacts, and their sacrifices; and they worshiped the gods, who could not do without the gifts and the burnt offerings of men, for although they were nourished upon nectar and ambrosia, still the odor of burnt sacrifice, rising in the smoke, was pleasant to them, and they seemed to have got more than pleasure from it somehow. The gods, however, used to travel among men; they shared the feasts and the life of men, if they were pleased with them, and often in the shape of beggars and strangers. They watched to see who did good and who did evil. And when men did evil they were punished; sometimes in this world, especially in matters of bloodshed, when the Furies chased the guilty until he was purified; and after death there was also a judgment, of which you will hear by and by. So you will see that gods and men were all mixed up together.

But we cannot sort out all these things into their proper time; gods and men were both growing up side by side, and my stories of the two societies overlap now and then. Prometheus, as you know, was the great friend of man, and he gave him fire, and he taught him everything; but Zeus came to take interest in man more and more, as he became educated himself and wiser with experience. Once, you remember, he desired to destroy man altogether and make a new creature to put in his place; and once, but at what time exactly we do not know, he nearly did destroy mankind. For he sent a great flood upon the world, which drowned everyone that it came near. This is how it came about.

We are told that there were Four Ages of Man, of which the first was the best. I suppose that was when all the miseries of mankind were shut up in a jar, and kept safe by Epimetheus, before women came into the world with Pandora, who let out all our troubles by taking off the lid from the jar. The first was the Golden Age, called also the Age of Cronus, before the reign of Zeus began. If Cronus was a savage himself, at least he had sense enough to leave Prometheus alone; and the Golden Age ought rather to be called the Age of Prometheus, I think. In the Golden Age it was very much like the Garden of Eden. Men lived like the gods, free from sorrow and free from disease. They feasted and made merry so long as they lived. They had no hard work to do, for the earth brought forth her kindly fruits without tillage, so that cabbages and lettuces grew like weeds, and men were content with acorns from the oak or fruit from the trees or such things as came out of the ground. They had no disease and never grew old; but when they came to the limit of their days, death came upon them in their sleep and they passed away in peace.

Nor did death end them; for their spirits dwelt on the earth, and still do so, watching and helping mortal man. They are clothed in mist, and seen of none, but they see all the doings of man, whether they be good or evil.

After this generation of men had passed away, came the Silver Age, less noble than the first in body and spirit. For a hundred years they lived like children; then for a short time they lived in foolishness and wickedness, and neglected to worship the gods, and then they perished.

When these came to an end, a third generation came up called the Age of Brass, terrible and strong. They built houses of brass, and made armor and weapons of brass, and tilled the earth with brazen tools, for there was no iron as yet. The men of this race fought together, and perished by their own hands. But in among them there grew up another race, half gods and half men, called the heroes, of whom there are many stories yet to tell. The best of the human race are descended from them.

And when the men of brass had perished by their own hands, there came a fourth race upon the earth in the Iron Age, which still goes on. Iron is their metal, and they make tools and armor of iron. They never cease to toil and labor day or night, and they never cease fighting with one another. The father does not agree with his children, nor the children with their father, nor guest with host, nor comrade with comrade. Sons do not repay their parents for their love and care; promises are broken, and evildoers are honored. This race also will come to an end, and all that is evil in it will perish utterly; but the good will have their reward.

Now in this Iron Age, Zeus visited the earth, to see whether men were as bad as they were said to be; and he came to the realm of one Lycaon, who was King in Arcadia. Lycaon laughed, on hearing that Zeus had come, and said, "Now then, let us see if he is really a god!" So he killed an innocent man, a hostage in fact, whom he was bound to protect, and cooked his flesh, and set it before Zeus his guest, to see if he would eat it. But Zeus struck the King's house with a thunderbolt, and Lycaon fled terrified to the hills. His rough coat changed into bristling hairs all over his body. He tried to shout, and out came a snarl, for he had turned into a wolf, destined to delight in blood all the rest of his days.

Zeus called a council of the gods, and told them what had been done; and then he declared that he thought it best to destroy mankind. The others said, "But what shall we do? There will be no one to offer sacrifices to the gods." "Never mind for that," said Zeus. "I will provide." The question then came, whether he should launch his thunderbolts on the world, and set it afire; but Zeus was afraid that so great a conflagration might rise to the upper air, and set that also on fire, so that the Olympians themselves would be burned up.

It seemed best therefore to use water. The winds were bidden to gather the clouds; the rains descended, and the floods came and overwhelmed the whole country of Greece, so that all who dwelt there were drowned. Men and beasts, wolves and sheep, lions and tigers were carried down to the sea, and seals and dolphins swam about in the forests.

But one solitary pair remained: Deucalion, a son of Prometheus, and his wife, Pyrrha, the daughter of Epimetheus. They were good people both, no one more just and no one more strict in worshiping the gods. They had got into a little chest or ark, which was in the house, and the waters carried them to the slopes of Mount Parnassus, close to the cleft where Mother Earth had an oracle. The shrine at that time was in charge of Themis, goddess of Justice, for Apollo had not yet come that way. They gave thanks to Themis, and prayed to the nymphs of that place. When Zeus saw that this innocent pair had been saved, he told Poseidon to recall his floods, and Poseidon bade his trumpeter Triton sound the recall. Triton blew a blast into his hollow shell, and the waves were stayed. Then Zeus made a great hole in the earth, and the waters all ran down, and the land began to appear. For thousands of years, this hole used to be shown in the sacred place of Olympia.

Deucalion looked around on the world, all shining with mud, and said to Pyrrha, "My wife, see, we are the whole population of the world! And the clouds are still dark above us. What should I do, if I were alone? or you, without me? Let us ask what is the will of God."

So they entered the shrine of Themis, and said, "Themis, if the anger of Zeus is satisfied, tell us how to recover the human race." And Themis said, "Go down to the plain, and cover your heads with a veil, and throw behind you your mother's bones."

They went out, and Pyrrha said to her husband, "I am afraid, my dear husband. How can we find our mother's bones? And if we could find them, would it not be wicked to disturb them?"

But Deucalion was not his father's son for nothing; he had some of this father's wisdom, and he replied, "Wife, the gods often speak in riddles. I think Themis means the bones of Mother Earth, that is, stones. Let us try them, it can do no harm to try."

Then they veiled their heads, and each of them picked up stones, and threw them behind their backs. Perhaps you will hardly believe it, but the stones as they fell took on human shapes. Deucalion's became men, and Pyrrha's became women. Even now we show traces of this origin; for we have veins in our bodies, like the veins in a piece of marble, both called by the same name; and men are called peoples, because they grew out of pebbles.

Chapter 12 ATHENA AND POSEIDON

As men multiplied upon the earth, and built cities, they built also temples to the gods. Generally each place had a chief god, which it honored more than the rest, and we do not always know why they were chosen. Not all the gods pushed their way in like Apollo and Artemis; but there was some rivalry between them, naturally enough. Poseidon was god of the sea, so he did not find it as easy as the others to get places on the land. He got Corinth without much difficulty, because Corinth lay between two seas, and depended for her wealth on the sea. He also wanted Athens; and you might have thought that very proper, because in later years Athens was the great sea power of Greece, but in the early days Athens did not think much about the sea. Athens lay three miles from the shore, and had no harbor then.

Athena also wanted Athens, and they were told to decide it by giving a gift to mankind: whichever gave the best gift should win. You see how far we have come from the time when Zeus would not give men fire, and only Prometheus gave them anything good! The gods thought of men more kindly now.

So they came to the contest, on the acropolis hill. Poseidon struck his trident upon the rock—you may still see the cleft it made, under the porch of an old temple—and out sprang a horse. Poseidon was a great god for horses, and in later times, he held famous horse races. The sea is full of horses, you know, and you can observe their white manes all over it, as they leap about in stormy weather. That was indeed a noble gift to man. It is true, they had horses already, as you heard in the story of Prometheus; but this was a noble breed, like the Arab, better than their heavy horses with big heads.

Athena came with a little olive tree, which she planted in a garden close by the place where Poseidon struck. I do not think this tree had been know before; it was a new gift, all her own. It is said to have come from the paradise beyond the North Wind. The tree was adjudged to be the best gift, and the King chose Athena for the chief goddess of Athens, and named the city after her. And it was a wise choice, for the olive became the great wealth of Athens. It fed the people with its fruit, as it does to this day, and it provided a soft and precious oil for their use, to put in their food, and to rub their bodies with when they were tired. They planted the tree everywhere, and made oil for other people to buy, and so they became rich.

Athena's temple at Athens became the most lovely of all Greek temples, and you may still see it, lovely even in ruins. I want you to remember this temple, because it will come into the very last part of our history.

Just before this, the island of Rhodes had come up out of the sea, as you may remember, and the sons of Helios were building new cities there. The men of one of these cities, Lindos, thought they would like their great goddess to be Athena, who had lately sprung out of the head of Zeus, to the amazement of all the world. The new goddess would suit the new island. They hoped to be first in the field, before anyone else could come in. Helios agreed. "But be careful," he said. "Do not waste time; build up an altar at once, and make a sacrifice, and you will have the first claim.

The Athenians were also trying hard, and it was a near thing. In fact, the Lindians got ready their altar first, and the sacrifice, but they were in such a hurry that they forgot to bring fire up the hill. So they had to make a fireless sacrifice. The Athenians were second in time, but they had fire and everything necessary, so that the smoke might rise to Olympus. Therefore Athena made Athens her chief seat. But she was pleased also with Lindos, and sorry for the hard luck of that place. Zeus sent a shower of gold to fall upon Lindos; and Athena taught them to be the cleverest workers in metal of all the world.

Chapter 13 THE HEROES: HERCULES

Gods and men had another fight before them, this time as allies; but before we come to that, I must tell you about the Heroes, who came up in the world, as you remember, at some time in man's history. They were half god and half man. The gods were always mixing with men; they had to visit their temples, and receive worship and sacrifice, and they had also to travel about and see how men were behaving; and it often happened that one of the gods would fall in love with a beautiful maiden among mankind, and they would wed with these maidens. Their children were the Heroes. These Heroes lived in the world among mankind, and did many wonderful deeds, but they were not immortal; their bodies died, and after death they were worshiped on earth, but their souls lived still, and some went to the Islands of the Blessed, while some were even caught up into heaven.

The greatest of all the Heroes was Hercules. He was the son of Zeus and Alcmena, Princess of Thebes, and there was great excitement over his birth. Hera was jealous and angry; and as soon as he was born, with his twin brother Iphicles, she sent two large serpents into the chamber, to kill the babies. But Hercules lifted up his head, and clutched the throats of the two serpents, and held them writhing until their lives were throttled[1] out of them. Up jumped his mother, and ran to help, and all the women shrieked out, "He's dead!" In came the men, clad in full armor; in came Prince Amphitryon, holding a drawn sword in his hand. When he saw the baby Hercules, with a serpent hanging limp from each hand, he cried out, "Who told me the baby was dead? It is the serpents that are dead!" But glad as he was, there was something about it which he could not understand; so he went to find old Teiresias, the Theban seer, who lived next door. "Come out, neighbor!" he said. "What does this mean?" And Teiresias told him by prophecy the mighty deeds which the baby was destined to do when he grew up. "And now," he went on, "gather up twigs of briar and wild pear, and with these burn the bodies of these two serpents; and let some one take up the ashes, and throw them into the river, and return without looking behind him; then the river shall carry them out of your country into the sea."

So Hercules grew up; and the best masters taught him to shoot arrows from the bow, and to box, and wrestle, and fight in every manner, and to read and write, to sing and to play upon the harp. Prince Amphitryon taught him to drive the chariot, and Castor himself, the Horseman-god, taught him how to manage a horse, and to use the sword and the javelin, and to fight in armor, and how to lead men in time of war.

[1] throttle (thrŏt′'l): to choke.

So he grew up till his eighteenth year, and then a surprising thing happened. He was thinking what his future life was likely to be; probably he had heard something of the prophecies of Teiresias, and perhaps he shrank from the danger a little. But he saw, or he thought he saw, two women approaching him. And one of them ran in front, to get the first word; and he saw that she was tall and handsome, and decked out in gay finery, with her cheeks rather too red to be natural; and she said to him, "Young man, I see you are in doubt what to do, and what path of life to follow. I invite you to follow me; you shall have the easiest and pleasantest life in the world, no hard work and no dangers; you shall eat, drink, and be merry, others shall work and you shall have the enjoyment, and you shall be as happy as the day is long." And Hercules said, "What is your name?" The woman answered, "My real name is Pleasure, but my enemies call me Vice."

By this time, the second woman had come up. Hercules saw this one also to be tall and handsome, but after a different fashion; for she was stately and dignified, and of a noble look; her dress was all white, truth was in her eyes, and modesty in her manners. She said, "Young sir, I know your parents and your breeding, and how you have been educated and brought up; which makes me hope that you will be a good workman of noble deeds. I will not deceive you with promises of pleasant things, but I will tell you the truth. Nothing that is really good can be got without labor and hardship, for so the gods have ordained. If you wish to enjoy the fruits of the earth, you must plow and sow, and reap and mow. So if you wish your body to be strong, you must make your body the servant to your mind, and fear not labor and sweat. And just in the same way, if you wish for the gods' favor, you must serve the gods; if you wish for the love of friends, you must do good to your friends; if you wish for honor from your city or your native land, you must work for their benefit, and you must defend them from enemies without and tyrants within. Follow me, and I can make you great, and truly happy." Hercules said, "And what is your name?" She answered, "My name is Virtue."

Then Pleasure said, "See, Hercules, what a hard road she puts before you! Not a scrap of pleasure in it!" But Virtue said, "Such pleasure as hers leads only to surfeit and weariness. He that tries to be happy, never succeeds, but he that does noble deeds gains happiness without trying."

And Hercules resolved to follow the hard road, and to put away from his mind the craving for pleasure.

So Hercules made his choice. But his first task was to master himself, before he could do great deeds with his own strength, for he had a violent temper. And so once he quarreled with his music master, who found fault with him and struck him; then Hercules lifted up his harp and struck the man down, and killed him. He was not found guilty of murder, since the other had struck first, but Prince Amphitryon sent him to work on the cattle farm, that he might school himself and master his temper. While he was there a lion came down from the hills and attacked the cattle, but Hercules killed the lion, called the Lion of Cithaeron, which was the name of the hill country whence he came.

After this he gathered together the young men of the city of Thebes, and they fought against a neighboring king who held Thebes under tribute, and set Thebes free from the tribute, for which the King of Thebes, whose name was Creon, gave Hercules his daughter Megara for a wife.

But soon after this a terrible misfortune happened to Hercules, for madness came upon him, sent by the goddess Hera, who was always his enemy, and Hercules in his madness killed his own children. When he recovered, he sought how he might atone for his deed, and asked the oracle at Delphi what he should do. The oracle told him that he must live at Tiryns, an ancient city in south Greece, and for years he must serve Eurystheus, King of Mycenae, and do what he commanded. Each year therefore Eurystheus set him a hard task to do, and these are called the Twelve Labors of Hercules.

(1) The First Labor was the Nemean Lion. There was a terrible lion that ranged on the mountains not far from Tiryns. You should look up this country on the map, for it comes often into the stories of Greece. There is a fertile plain on the east side of Greece, looking towards Asia, which contained three ancient cities, built in the beginning of time by great warriors who came from Asia. Near the coast is the first, Tiryns, and you may see the ruins there to this day, for it was built of huge stones, and everyone who sees it is amazed. In the middle of the plain is a large rock, and upon this the second city was built, named Argos; and at the end of the plain is the third city, Mycenae, which is also to be seen still, in ruins, with a wonderful gate built of huge

stones, called the Lion Gate, because above it are the figures of two lions rampant. The whole plain is called the Plain of Argos.

Now at Mycenae the hills and mountains begin, and a few miles from it is the valley of Nemea, where this lion of Nemea used to range about. This lion was of huge size. He was a son of the monster Typhon, whom we shall hear of soon; and he could not be wounded with iron or bronze or stone. He had a den in one of the rocks, a long tunnel with two openings, where he used to live; and if he were chased he ran into one end, and ran out of the other. Eurystheus commanded Hercules to bring him the skin of this lion.

So Hercules took with him his bow and a quiver full of arrows and a heavy club which he used to carry. When he came to the place, he could find no tracks, nor could he ask news from anyone, for all the people were afraid to come out and there was no one in the fields. Toward evening, the lion came to his den full-fed, with his mouth and chest all spotted with blood, and licking his chops. Hercules hid by the way, and let fly a shaft at him; but the arrow slid off his skin, for he could not be wounded by iron or bronze or stone. Hercules shot him again, full in the chest, but the arrow fell useless to the ground. The lion rolled his eyes, and saw Hercules; then lashing his flanks with his tail, he gathered himself up for a spring. As he leaped, Hercules held up his left arm wrapped in his cloak, and brought down his club with a bang on the lion's head; the club splintered in fragments, but it checked the spring, and the lion stood wagging his head and dizzy with the blow. Then Hercules threw down his bow and arrows and leaped on the lion's back, treading down the lion's hind legs with his own feet, while he put his hands round the lion's neck and pulled up one foreleg; then he got this leg under his arm, and gripped the lion's throat with his two hands, and bending him backwards, throttled him.

There lay the lion dead on the ground; but how could Hercules skin him? No iron could cut the skin, no bronze, and no stone; but a thought came into his mind, that he should cut off the skin of the lion with the lion's own claws. And so he did. He brought back the skin to Eurystheus, but he would not give it up; and ever after that he wore that skin as a garment, with the forepaws over his shoulder, and the head like a helmet over his own head, which looked out of the lion's jaws. This is what you always see in the pictures of Hercules.

(2) The Second Labor was the Lernaean Hydra. There was a marsh in the Plain of Argos called Lerna, and in it there was a huge serpent with nine heads, called Hydra the Watersnake, because she lived in the marsh; and her middle head was immortal. Some say she had a hundred heads, and it is difficult to say how many there were, you will soon hear why. Hercules was commanded to kill this Hydra; so off he went in a chariot, driven by his charioteer, Iolaus, his nephew. When they came to the place, Hercules jumped out and shot the serpent with his arrows, but she did not seem to mind that; then he attacked her with his club, but she did not mind that; then he took a sickle, and cut off head after head, but whenever he cut off one head, two grew in its place.

As he was cutting away, he felt a nip on his leg, and what should he see but an enormous crab come to help his friend the serpent. "That is not fair, two to one!" said Hercules. "Iolaus, come and help me!" So Iolaus came with another sickle, but that only made matters worse. Suddenly Hercules had a happy thought. "Get me some sticks," he said, "and burn the place!" Iolaus made a fire, and brought up the brands; and as Hercules cut off a head, Iolaus burned the place so that new ones could not grow. Then Hercules cut off the immortal head, and buried it under a rock; and if it has not been moved, I suppose it is there still. In any case, the marsh is there still, and it still breeds a lot of ugly snakes. The crab was killed too, and actually became a constellation in the sky, but I really cannot see why. From this a proverb grew up in Greece,

> Even Hercules is done,
> In a fight of two to one.

Hercules kept the bile of the serpent to dip his arrows in, and thus a wound from his arrows brought death with it.

(3) The Third Labor was the Arcadian Deer. This was a doe, but nevertheless she had antlers, golden antlers and brazen feet, and she wandered all over Arcadia free, for she was sacred to Artemis. Why that was so is another story which I cannot tell you now, for there are so many stories in Greece that there is no end to them. Hercules chased the doe for a whole year; and we

do not know quite how he caught her, for some say it was in a net, and some say he found her asleep. But in the end, catch her he did, and brought her home on his back. On the way, Artemis met him, and wanted to know what he was doing with her doe. She was very angry, but Hercules said, "I can't help it: Zeus commands me to obey Eurystheus, and Eurystheus commands me to bring him this doe. So what can I do?" Thus he managed to make peace with Artemis, and brought the doe to his tyrannical master.

(4) The Fourth Labor was the Erymanthian Boar. Like the lion and the Hydra, this boar was a nuisance to the countryside, where it destroyed cattle and crops, and attacked the people who lived there. Eurystheus told him this time that he must bring in the boar alive, which seems to be just spiteful, since Hercules had done the other tasks so well. He had to be careful, you see, not to use too much strength, or too little; for if he used too much, he would kill the boar, and if he used too little, the boar might kill him, or at least damage him.

He set out then, and on his way he passed through the country of the Centaurs. These were monsters, you remember, half horse and half man; they had a man's head and shoulders, and a horse's body; some were a whole man, legs and all, with half a horse growing out behind. They were as swift as a horse and as strong as a wild beast and as wise as men. One of them, named Pholus, had a cask of wine, and he said, when he saw Hercules, "Come into my cave, sir, and let me entertain you; I have a fine drink here which I have been keeping specially for your visit." Hercules thanked him, and came in. Pholus set cooked meat before him, but he ate his own meat raw.

Then the cask was opened. The wine was a hundred years old. It was indeed a delicious drink, which Hercules had never tasted before, and it spread abroad such a delicious scent that the neighborhood became full of it and the other Centaurs smelled it and galloped up to Pholus' cave, to see what it was. When they saw what it was, they crowded into the cave and began to drink it, which made them wilder than ever.

Now Pholus was frightened, and ran to hide himself, leaving Hercules to face the furious monsters. They tore up trees by the roots to attack him, and threw great stones at him, and some even picked up axes to cut him down, or drove at him with firebrands. Their mother, the Cloud, helped them by pouring about them a thick mist, which did little hindrance to the beasts with four legs, but made it difficult not to slip for Hercules with only two. Yet he was a match for them; he did not even need help this time, and so perhaps he had learned something from his fight with the Hydra. He killed a large number, and the rest he drove away. Among the killed Centaurs were Horsey and Hilley and Black-mane, Hit-for-hit, Thumper, and Bristler. Pholus came back when the fight was over, and looking at the dead bodies, he pulled out one of the arrows. "How strange," he said, "that a little thing like that could kill such great creatures!" and he dropped it down on the ground; but in dropping, the point scratched his foot, and as the arrow was poisoned, Pholus died too.

After this, Hercules went on in search of the boar; and he chased him about in the snow, until the boar fell exhausted in a thicket. Then Hercules heaved the boar up on his shoulders and carried it back to Eurystheus. He marched into the hall, where Eurystheus was sitting, and made as though to throw down the boar at his feet; but Eurystheus, who was a coward himself, became terrified at the sight, and ran away, until he saw a large wine jar buried in the ground with the neck open. Into this jar he jumped to hide himself. The boar did no mischief to Eurystheus, but Eurystheus went on to find more labors for Hercules.

(5) The Fifth Labor was to clean the Stables of Augeas. This Augeas was King of Elis. He had thirty thousand cattle, and their stables had not been cleaned for thirty years; but Hercules was commanded to clean them in one day. He offered to clean them out if Augeas would give him one-tenth of the cattle, and Augeas agreed. Then Hercules made gaps in the walls of the stables, one at each end, and turned the course of two rivers toward the upper end; the water ran in at the upper end and ran out at the lower end, carrying all the dirt with it. Augeas, however, made an excuse to avoid paying what he had promised. Hercules punished King Augeas afterwards, for he killed him, and carried off the spoil of the country; and with this spoil he founded the great games at Olympia.

(6) The Sixth Labor was to destroy the Stymphalian Birds. These birds had brazen claws and brazen wings and brazen beaks. They used to shoot out their brazen feathers like arrows, and kill people with them, and then they ate their bodies. The birds were gathered about Lake Stymphalis in Arcadia; thence they flew

out in swarms, and settled on the fields, and devoured all the crops. Hercules saw that he could not kill all these birds; but Athena came to his help, and gave him a huge rattle of brass. Hercules rattled and made a great noise, and the birds rose up; he shot his arrows, and killed some, and the rest flew away. What became of most of them I do not know, but we shall hear of some of them later. At least the Stymphalian lake and the land of Arcadia were quite cleared.

(7) The Seventh Labor was the Cretan Bull. This was a wonderful and beautiful bull, belonging to King Minos of Crete, which had gone mad. Hercules caught this bull and carried him on his shoulders to King Eurystheus; then he let the bull loose again, and the bull wandered all over Greece, and did damage everywhere, until he came to Marathon; and at Marathon he remained, but we shall hear of him also again.

(8) The Eighth Labor was to capture the Mares of Diomedes. This man was a savage king of Thrace. He kept his mares fastened with iron chains to mangers of brass, and he used to feed them with the flesh of men. Hercules called for volunteers to help him; and they went to Thrace and attacked Diomedes, and gave him to his own mares to eat. The mares then became quiet and tame, and Hercules easily brought them to Eurystheus.

(9) The Ninth Labor was the Girdle of the Queen of the Amazons. The Amazons were a tribe of women who fought on horseback like men; and their Queen Hippolyte had a splendid girdle. Hercules led another body of volunteers against these. When he came to their country, which was in Asia Minor, he demanded the girdle, and Hippolyte came to him quite ready to give it; but the other Amazons thought their queen was being made prisoner, so they attacked Hercules and his companions. There was a battle, and the Amazons were defeated, and Hercules brought the girdle back.

(10) The Tenth Labor was the Oxen of Geryon. This was a horrid monster with three bodies joined at the waist, who lived in an island off the coast of Spain. His oxen were guarded by another monster, and by a dog with two heads. This was a tremendous journey for Hercules; you see he had been to the far east, and to the north, and now he went to the west, traversing the north part of Africa. Wherever he went, he cleared the country of wild beasts and serpents, and punished lawless men; for as you

remember from the story of his youth, all his life was given to the service of mankind, and he did all his great works without payment.

When he came to the Straits of Gibraltar, he set up two pillars, one on each side, to mark the extreme limit of travel; for the sea and the countries outside the straits were unknown in these early days. These were called ever afterwards, the Pillars of Hercules.

He then attacked the two-headed dog and killed it with his club; after which he killed the guardian monster, and shot the three-bodied monster Geryon with his arrows, and drove the cattle back by land, clearing out the wild beasts on his way, and settling the people in orderly government.

(11) The Eleventh Labor was to fetch the Golden Apples of the Hesperides. This task was more difficult than usual, because he did not know where they were. So he hunted for them all over the world, and in the course of his journey he had many adventures; among them he came to the place where Prometheus was nailed to the rock. Hercules was angry at the fate of Prometheus; so he set him free, and persuaded Zeus to be kind to him again, and to receive him into the company of Olympus. Prometheus advised Hercules to find Atlas, his brother, and to ask him where the apples were. For Atlas was the father of the maidens called the Hesperides, and they had a garden in the far west, in Spain, where they guarded the golden apples with the help of a dragon.

You remember old Atlas, the Titan, who bore up the heavens upon his shoulders. Hercules accordingly sought him out, and asked him kindly to show the way to the Garden of Hesperides, that he might get the golden apples. Atlas said, "I must not do that, but I will tell you what I will do: I will fetch the apples for you, if you will just hold up the heavens a bit. But I do not think you are strong enough for that." "Not strong enough!" said Hercules, "I will soon show you." So he stood by Atlas, and Atlas carefully shifted the weight of the heavens upon his head, and Hercules held it up with his hands.

It was terribly heavy, much worse than he expected. Some of the stars fell out as he held it, because he was new to the job, and very glad he was when he saw Atlas coming back. "Here you are," said Atlas, showing him the apples. "What do you want them for?" Hercules said, "To give to Eurystheus." Then Atlas said, "I can do that, it is no trouble at all," and began to go off. You see, he thought it a great piece of luck that some one had come to relieve him of his job. And Hercules saw that he was in for it, if he was not careful. No doubt his talk with Prometheus had sharpened his wits, for he did not show anger or apprehension, whatever he felt; but all he said was, "I thank you; I am much obliged, but just give me a little help first. I am not used to this weight, and it is rather uncomfortable. Hold it a minute while I make a pad for my head." Atlas was not clever like his brother Prometheus, who had all the brains of the family; he was a stupid thing like his uncle Cronus: so he agreed at once, and laid the apples down on the ground. Then Hercules thanked him and shifted the heavens upon Atlas' shoulders again, and picked up the apples, and went off to Eurystheus. I do not know what Atlas said. The heaven has not fallen down yet, so we may suppose the old Titan still does his duty; but we shall see.

(12) The Last Labor was to fetch up the dog Cerberus from Tartarus. There is a dark cave in Mount Taínaron, which is the entrance to Tartarus, and a dark tunnel downward; and by this way Hercules went down. He had some adventures in the lower world which you will hear of later; and Hades allowed him to take Cerberus, if he could do so without using his weapons. Hercules therefore seized the dog with his hands, and crushed him tight until his spirit was tamed; then he carried him up into the world, and showed him to Eurystheus, after which he brought him back to remain as the watchdog of Hades.

And so you see Hercules led the life he had chosen when he was a young man; and these years of penance under Eurystheus he spent in exploring the world, and clearing it of dangerous monsters, and making it better for men to live in. I have not told you half his great deeds yet; many of them come in among his Labors, but it is convenient to keep the Twelve Labors together.

One of these deeds was the battle with the Giants. Zeus had already got rid of most of the ancient monsters, but a troop of giants remained, and to conquer these the oracle declared it necessary to seek the help of a mortal. Hercules therefore was summoned to help; and the battle was joined on the plain of Phlegra.

The Giants, like other such, used huge rocks and trees to throw at their enemies, and burning firebrands. One of them split off a chunk of the island Cos, and threw it at his enemy; you may see today how large it was, for it fell in the sea, and is now called the island of Nisyros. Another of them, Alcyoneus, whenever he was knocked down, jumped up again stronger than ever. For it was fated that he could not be killed upon the land where he was born. So the goddess Athena, who had plenty of sense, told Hercules to drag him over the boundary of his land, into the next; and there they killed him easily enough. Zeus struck some with his thunderbolt; Athena and Poseidon, Apollo and Artemis, all took part, and Hercules was not wanting. The Giants were destroyed, and their bodies were buried under volcanoes, and islands in the sea. So now we see gods and men on the same side. Men were becoming better, and Zeus was more friendly toward them, for there was no more talk of destroying mankind. And in fact, gods and men are now so mixed up that it is impossible to tell of them separately.

Madness came upon Hercules once more, which led to a strange adventure. In his madness he killed a friend without knowing what he did. When he recovered his senses, he went to the oracle of Apollo, at Delphi, to ask what he should do, in order to be made pure from this deed of bloodshed; but the priestess would give him no answer. This made him angry, and he said, "Very well, I will make an oracle of my own!" Then he seized Apollo's tripod, where the priestess used to sit, and began to carry it off. As he went off, who should meet him at the door of the temple but Apollo himself! Apollo took hold of one leg of the tripod, Hercules held to the other two, and there was a great fight, Hercules pulling one way and Apollo the other. I do not know which would have won; but while they were pulling away, Zeus came between them. He said, "What is the meaning of this? No fighting in the family, please; you will only break the thing, if you pull it like that." Then he dropped a little speck of a thunderbolt between them which fizzled up and startled them both. "Now," he said, "put it back; and give Hercules his answer."

So Hercules got his answer, and the answer was this: he was to be sold as a slave, and to work for three years, and then he was to pay the price paid for him to the soul of the man he had killed.

So Hermes sold him, and he was bought by Omphale, Queen of Lydia, and she set him many tasks to do. Some of them were worthy of Hercules, for she made him clear out the robbers and brigands from her country. One of these was named the Stripper. He used to catch wayfarers, and rob them, and make them dig about his vines with a spade; Hercules knocked him on the head with his own spade.

There were also two brothers, full of mischief, who used to creep into the houses and steal. Their mother knew about their doings, but all she did was to give them a warning, "Beware Hercules!"

Then one day Hercules caught them. He trussed them up like a pair of fowl, and hung them head downward on the two ends of a pole, and then he set off, carrying the pole across his shoulders, like a milkman. The boys were quite cheerful, and did nothing but crack jokes. "Who are you, pray?" they asked. He said, "I am Hercules." As they were hanging head downward, they had a good view of his legs, which were all covered with black hair; and one said, "You call yourself Hercules, do you? I call you Hairy-knees!" This pleased Hercules, who liked a joke himself; so he let them off easily. Omphale also liked a joke; so she used to make Hercules put on her dress, and she put on his lionskin, and then she gave him a distaff and spindle, and made him spin wool into thread. When the three years were up, he paid the fine, and he was now held to be free from guilt.

Hercules also joined the quest of the Golden Fleece, a great adventure, but I leave that until I come to the story of the Argonauts. He also once met Theseus, a great hero like himself, and he had many other adventures which I must pass over; but there is one that I must tell, because that is the beginning of the story of Troy.

It begins in the early days of the reign of Zeus, when he had troubles without and troubles within. Only a hint has come down in memory; we only know that there was a conspiracy of the gods against Zeus. A party of them wanted to dethrone him, and put him in prison; and in this party were his wife Hera, and his daughter Athena, with his brother Poseidon, and his son Apollo. That might have been the end of Zeus, but for the sea nymph Thetis, who was afterward mother of Achilles. Thetis had a happy idea: why not call in the help of the hundred-handed monster, Briareus? And so he did: Briareus came to help his old friend, who had set him free once upon a time. You may imagine how it amazed the gods, plotting together in the corner, when they saw the monster march in, full of pride and power, waving his hundred hands about, and saw him sit down by the side of Zeus! Zeus punished Apollo and Poseidon by sending them down to earth, and commanding them to serve the King of Troy for wages, one year long. They had to build the walls of Troy, and hard work it was, as Poseidon said afterward; but when the year was up, and they asked for their wages, the King gave them none; he only said, "Get out, or I will cut off both your ears, and sell you to be slaves in the islands!"

I suppose he did not know who they were, but he soon found out, when they became gods again. For Apollo sent a pestilence, and Poseidon sent a sea monster, who caught the people and swallowed them up. This went on until the King inquired of an oracle, which told him that he would be free if he gave his daughter to the monster. Accordingly he left his daughter on the seashore, securely tied, for the monster to eat. But he asked Hercules to deliver her, and promised that if he did, he would give as a reward his precious mares to Hercules; for he had some wonderful mares of a divine breed. Then Hercules attacked the monster. It was a terrible monster; Hercules leaped into its mouth, and went down into its belly; there he was three days and nights, cutting and hacking, until he cut his way out, and made an end of it at last.

So Hercules killed the monster and delivered the maiden. He told her that she was free to go home, unless she would rather come away with him; she said she would rather come with him, for fear another monster might come along later. But the King refused to give either his daughter or the mares. He was as bad as ever, you see. Then Hercules went away, and soon came back with a fleet; they besieged Troy, and broke through the wall, and stormed the city. The King was killed, and Hercules made one of his sons king in his place. This man was called King Priam, who comes in Homer's story of the great Trojan War.

We are now coming to the last scene in the life of Hercules. His home now was in Calydon, a district in north Greece, not far from the place where the English poet, Lord Byron, died, in 1824, helping to make the Greeks free. The King of Calydon had a beautiful daughter, named Deianira, and she was wooed by the god of the great river Achelous, which runs through the country. The wooer was rather alarming, for he appeared first in the form of a bull, then in the form of a serpent with shining coils, then like a man with a bull's head. You may imagine that Deianira was pleased when a proper man appeared, that is Hercules himself. There was a great fight between Hercules and the bull, but Hercules won; and the maiden became his wife. But she lived in great anxiety, because Hercules had to go away upon so many adventures; and she was a little jealous too, for fear he should fall in love with someone else on his travels.

It happened that they had to travel away from Calydon together; and on the way, there was a river to cross. At the crossing, there was a Centaur, half man and half horse, named Nessus, who used to ferry travelers over the river. Hercules told Nessus to carry over his wife; but when Nessus was across on the bank, he laid hold of her, and began to carry her off. Hercules saw this from the other side, and at once shot an arrow, which struck the deathblow of Nessus.

But Nessus was an evil creature, and guessing that Deianira might be jealous, he said to her, "Now I am about to die, I wish to make up to you for my evil attempt. Catch some of my blood as it drops from the wound, and it shall be a charm for you. If your husband ever ceases to love you, this charm will win back his love. Keep it carefully away from the sun, and far from the fire, and when you want to use it, put it like ointment upon him." She caught the blood in a jar, and the Centaur died; and she kept his blood secretly, with great care, sealed up in the jar, away from fire and sunlight.

Now when Hercules was coming back from one of his adventures, victorious as usual, and with a long train of captives, she found out that one of the captives was a very beautiful maiden, and they said that Hercules was in love with her. So Deianira took out her jar, and poured the blood upon the inside of a long robe which she had woven herself, and sent it to her husband by a messenger. The robe was folded up, and laid in a box to carry. She told the messenger to give it to her husband, that he might wear it when he did sacrifice in thanksgiving for a safe return.

But when the messenger was gone, she was terribly frightened. As she was spreading the stuff upon the robe, a drop had fallen upon a piece of wool that lay near, and when the robe was gone, she happened to look at the wool, and saw that it was smoldering—then it broke into a flame, and all shriveled up into ashes. She waited in great anxiety until the messenger should return; and there was good reason for it, for by and by the messenger did return, and she heard an awful story.

Hercules took the robe and put it on and began his sacrifice. But the sunlight worked on the stuff through the robe, and he felt first a tickling, then a burning. The robe clung close to his limbs, and by degrees burned into his flesh. They laid him down on a couch, and in a short time he perished. But his soul went to heaven, and there dwelt among the gods. They gave him a house to live in, and a heavenly bride, Hebe, the goddess of Youth; as if to say that Hercules, after all his troubles, was to live forever young and strong as he was in his youth. So the prophecy was fulfilled that he heard in his young days. He lived a noble life; he had many troubles; and in the end he gained fame and immortality.

Chapter 14 TYPHON

Zeus had his faults, but he was not a bad king; indeed, he was just the king who was wanted in those early days, when the chief need was to put things in order. Without order and discipline, you cannot have peace; and without power to punish, you cannot have order. Zeus had no courts of law, and no police, no army and navy; he had nothing but his own will and his own strength to back him. Anyone with supreme power is sure to make mistakes, however good he may be; and he is very likely to use his power sometimes to indulge his pleasures. Zeus did so and so did the other gods.

Besides this, those who are kept in order do not always like it. The gods were an unruly company, and they were apt to rebel if they could, since each thought he could do the job better than Zeus, and wanted to be on the top. You have heard of one rebellion, and how it was put down by the help of Briareus, who came in like a constable to keep order. I daresay there were other rebellions, but if so, they came to nothing.

Zeus had dangers from outside also to fight against. He had just conquered the Giants, as you have heard, but the last and worst of the monsters remained. Old Mother Earth, who had never forgiven Zeus for casting her sons into prison, made a last attempt to get the better of him. She produced her last offspring, last and most terrible, named Typhon, which we call in English the typhoon—that terrible waterspout which seems to join sea to clouds with a black tower, and rolls the waters round in a whirlpool, and bursts upon fleets of ships, so that they are never more seen.

The monster Typhon was more terrible still. From his shoulders grew a hundred dragons' heads, with black flickering tongues, and fierce fire blazed from their eyes. All manner of voices came out of the dragons' mouths. Sometimes they would utter words that the gods understood, for the gods had their own language; sometimes they would speak in the language of men; again it might be the noise of a bull bellowing in fury or the roar of a ravening lion or the hissing of serpents.

This monster was biding his time; and he found it through a fault of Zeus himself. For Zeus had fallen in love, and he left his post of duty; but as he did not wish to frighten the maiden, he hid thunderbolt and lightning in a rocky cave. But such things could not be hidden, for volumes of black smoke rolled from the cave, and sparks of fire shot out of the smoke, and the mountain rumbled. So Mother Earth saw it, and called to her son Typhon, "Up, Typhon, now is your time! I can show you where Zeus has hidden his lightning. Take it, and fight him with his own weapons!"

Typhon came forth in his might. The dragons' heads, which were shaped like those of lions, tigers, bulls, or horrid things without a name, stood out of his shoulders on monstrous necks, and every head roared or bellowed or hissed. Typhon seized the lightnings and the thunderbolts in his innumerable hands, and cast them over the skies.

Then indeed there was consternation in earth and heaven. The rocks melted and the seas dried up; and all the constellations of the sky were shaken. You know perhaps that the stars of heaven, like everything else, had been coming into order. Here and there a number of them joined into groups, like families, and called themselves by various names. We call some of them the Signs of the Zodiac. These signs, twelve in number, are named in the following lines:

> The Ram, the Bull, the Heavenly Twins,
> And next the Crab, the Lion shines,
> The Virgin and the Scales,
> The Scorpion, Archer, and the Goat,
> The Man who bears the Watering Pot,
> The Fish with shining tails.

There were many other groups; as the Great Bear, or Plow, or Charles' Wain,[1] with its guardian, the Oxdriver; the Little Bear, the Swan, the Kids, the Snake, the Eagle, the Whale, the Great Dog, and the Little Dog, and Orion the Hunter. Look up into the sky, and see how many of these you can make out. I am sure you know the Great Bear, but what about the others? Imagine now what a fuss there was among these! The Bull bellowed, the Lion roared, the Bear tried to climb up the North Pole, but Typhon pulled him down; he caught the Morning Star in one hand, and with another whipped up the horses of the Sun till they ran away; he threw the Bull across the sky, shining like a second Moon. The others did what they could: Orion shot at him, and his dogs barked, but the fixed stars alone stood immovable, far away from the fight.

Meanwhile, Zeus had returned from his excursion, and found his thunder and lightnings gone, and confusion all over the high heaven. What was he to do? He went down to earth, and there he met a man called Cadmus; you have not heard of Cadmus before, but I will tell you his story soon. So Zeus came to Cadmus, taking with him his friend Pan, and they gave him a flock of sheep and goats and a herd of cattle, and built him a hut of reeds. Pan gave him the panspipes, and Zeus said to him, "Pipe away, Cadmus, and we shall have peace in heaven. How old Cronus would laugh, if he could see me brought low by my own thunderbolts! But I know these monsters. You can charm them with tootling, as you charm a serpent! And he is a hundred serpents!"

So Cadmus dressed up like a shepherd and sat down leaning against a tree and tootled away on his pipes where Typhon could

[1] *wain* (wān): a wagon.

hear him. Typhon heard him, and pricked up his ears, and crept toward the beautiful sound of the pipes; but he left his lightnings behind him in the cave, deep in the bosom of Mother Earth. He came up to Cadmus, and held out one of his fifty right hands. He smiled as well as he could with his middle face, a big one in the middle of the hundred, which was in shape like a man's face, but bright red in color; and he opened his mouth, and said:

"Why do you fear me, herdsman? Why do you cover your eyes with your hand? I will do you no harm; you may keep your pipes and welcome, for I have another instrument which has a voice of its own. Let us have a friendly match. You make your reedy tune, and I will make a thundery tune. Puff your cheeks and blow with your lips—the blasts of the North Wind shall blow out my booming thunderbolts! When I am King of Heaven, I will set you there, cattle and all, if you like; I will not part you from them. You shall be close to the heavenly Goat, or if you prefer it, beside the Bull. Pipe away, happy shepherd, today on earth, tomorrow in heaven. You shall have Athena to wife, or any other you like, except Hera; for I mean to keep Hera for myself. If you have a brother who can drive a team, he shall have the horses of the Sun. Pipe away, for my victory! Your pipes shall be sounded in heaven, and made equal to the heavenly harp!"

Cadmus made answer, "My pipes have pleased you a little. What would you say if you could hear me play on the harp? I had a harp once, but Zeus destroyed it because he was jealous for the sake of his son Apollo. But one of these days we will have a match in heaven, Apollo and I. When you strike down the others, be sure to spare him; and then we will see which of us can sing best the praises of victorious Typhon; and you must spare the Muses, that they may dance for us."

Typhon nodded his heads in delight, and shook all his locks of hair; and a shower of poison drops was scattered around. He thrust out all his heads, and pricked up all his ears, and stood enchanted with the melody of the pipes.

While Typhon was listening to the tune, Zeus crept into the cave, unseen and unheard, and once more took possession of his lightnings and thunders.

What need is there to tell of the last battle? Typhon piled up rocks and crags for his two hundred hands to throw; and he shouted loud boasts to the winds. But when he has to face Zeus armed with his lightnings, Victory marching in front, with Fear on his right hand, and Terror on his left, no monster can stand. Typhon was struck down, his eyes blinded, his hands all shriveled up. The last revolt was ended. There were no more.

Chapter 15 CADMUS

Zeus, you remember, had come away from his post when the last monster appeared. He had seen a beautiful maiden in Phoenicia, where the Philistines were in the time of King David, but this was long before David's time. The maiden was Europa, and Zeus determined to carry her off. So he changed himself into a bull, and wandered along the shore. Europa was playing there with her friends. When she saw the bull, she was delighted with his looks, and ran up to pat his neck. She threw a wreath of flowers over his horns, and as he seemed to be friendly, she even climbed on to his back. Then the bull began to walk slowly about, and by degrees he came near to the sea. All at once, he set off running into the sea. Europa was very much frightened, but she did not dare to slip off. She held fast to his neck and back, clutching hold of the hairy coat; and very soon he was quietly swimming out to sea.

She cried loudly for help, and her friends all came running down to the beach. They stood in a row by the edge of the water, crying also, but that did no good; the bull swam on and on; Europa cried till she was tired, then sank down on the bull's back, and made the best of it.

I have no doubt that Zeus could swim faster than most bulls; but even so, it was a long journey, until at last she espied land ahead. Zeus brought her to land in the island of Crete; and there he placed her in the sacred cave on Mount Dicte, where he had been kept as a baby. She lived long enough to bear two sons, named Minos and Rhadamanthus. We do not know much more about Europa, but she had the honor of giving her name to the continent of Europe. Her son Minos became King of Crete, and Rhadamanthus became a famous judge. There is more to tell of them, but we must leave them now, and see what happened when she was carried off.

Her father was distressed at her loss, and sent off his sons to search for her, all over the world; but none of them ever found her. One of these sons was Cadmus, who met us in the last story. After many wanderings he came to Delphi and asked the oracle where he should find his sister.

Apollo gave him an oracle in these words:

> Cadmus, you waste your time in wandering round
> To seek a bull that never can be found.
> Outside my sanctuary as you pass
> You'll see a dun cow feeding on the grass,
> Marked with a moon of white on either side;
> Follow her footsteps, let her be your guide;
> Follow her, till at length she lays her down;
> There in that place abide, and build a town.

Cadmus did as he was told. He followed the cow over hill and dale, until in the middle of a plain he came to a small hill with a spring flowing from it. There the cow lay down. But the spring was guarded by a terrible dragon, which darted forth and bit one man and strangled another, until Cadmus' company ran off in dismay. But Cadmus caught up a huge stone, and heaved it at the monster. The stone crushed his head, and Cadmus ran in and cut the head off with his sword.

It was a huge head, and the mouth was full of teeth. Cadmus pulled out all the teeth, and gathered them in a helmet; then he took out a handful of the teeth, and scattered them over the ground, like seed corn. But as each tooth fell, up sprang from the place a warrior in full armor. Then this crop of warriors all began fighting with each other, until all were dead except five. Cadmus founded the city of Thebes; and the five survivors became the ancestors of the Thebans.

Cadmus did a great service to his new country, for he taught them the alphabet. Perhaps you will think there is not much in the alphabet; but suppose there were none, how would you write, and what would you read? Somebody must have invented the alphabet, and it was a very clever thing to do. I could tell you a long story about that which would surprise you; but there is no time now. You remember that Prometheus first taught men to write; but he made them draw pictures to begin with. If they wanted to write *tree,* they drew a picture of a tree, and so on, and then he left them to learn more by themselves. They soon found it a long job to put everything into pictures. How would you write home in pictures: "Dear Father, please send me five dollars; your affectionate son, John"? Then someone hit on the idea of using the picture of a thing for the first letter of its name, as *tree* for T, and so he could spell words which have no picture, like *time.* Cadmus knew this plan, and he taught the alphabet to the Greeks; and thousands of years later, the Greeks taught it to the Romans; and the Romans passed it on to us. So when you write home for five dollars, remember Cadmus, who showed you how to do it. We still use one of his pictures at the beginning of the alphabet. For if you draw a cow's head and horns like this

 you have only to turn it upside down, and then you have

a big  which was the first letter of his word for a cow.

You have already heard how Cadmus helped Zeus, when the monster Typhon attacked him. For this help Zeus rewarded him by giving him a wife. This wife was Harmonia, herself of divine birth; for her father was Ares, god of War, and her mother was Aphrodite, goddess of Love. Her name means friendship and agreement and anything that fits nicely together like a tune of music or a fine piece of carpentry; and we have borrowed her name in English for this kind of thing, when we use the word *harmony.*

Cadmus and Harmonia had a grand wedding feast; the gods were their guests, and sat upon golden thrones. This was the first time the gods ever attended the marriage feast of a mortal man. Many gifts were given, but the most famous was a necklace which one of the gods gave to Harmonia. It was a beautiful necklace, but afterward it brought ruin on all who possessed it. Harmonia did not know that; but she found it out, and her four daughters found it out, when each of them perished in turn. Three of them I will leave, for the present, but the fourth, Semele, was the most famous of all.

For Zeus himself fell in love with Semele, and made her his

wife. But Semele was not contented to be the wife of Zeus. She became jealous of Hera, the divine wife in Olympus, and forgot that she was only a mortal. Zeus did not forget; he never showed her his lightnings and his thunderbolts, as he did to Hera, and Semele fretted and fumed and gave him no peace. Zeus warned her that it was dangerous, and told her she could not see him in all his glory and live; but you know he was rather too easygoing, and did not like to refuse what he was asked, so in the end he consented. He came to Semele, with lightning and thunder playing about his head; and the lightning burned her up. She perished therefore; but Zeus caught hold of her little baby, his own son, and took care of it as if he were the mother. The baby was the god Dionysus, or Bacchus, and I will tell you next what happened to him, and how he was admitted into the family of the Olympians. Zeus actually made a little pocket in his own leg, by cutting the skin, and there he kept the baby, like a kangaroo, until he could find a good nurse.

Chapter 16 DIONYSUS

Hermes laughed when he saw Zeus limping about with a pocket in his leg; and when Zeus opened the pocket and pulled out the baby and gave it to Hermes and told him to find a nurse, Hermes said, "Let us name him Dionysus," or "Zeus's limp," for that is what the word meant, or so he said. Then he took the baby and dandled him on his arm and flew off to find a nurse. First he tried some nymphs; but Hera pursued the baby and frightened the nymphs, and Hermes carried him off to his aunt, Ino, who nursed him with her own baby. Then she handed him over to a nursemaid who took care of him all day and kept on the watch for some trick of Hera's. She used to amuse him with a rattle and drums. She put a wreath of vine leaves about his head and wrapped up a pine branch in ivy for him to play with. She dressed him in the dappled skins of fawns, and even wreathed a festoon of long snakes about his neck and arms.

But Hera pursued him still, wherever he went. Hermes, however, took care of him; and at last, after many adventures, he carried the baby to old Rhea, the Titan, mother of Zeus, who used to visit Asia Minor, and had her worshipers there. She used to ride in a car drawn by lions, and all round her were her attendants and guardians, the Corybantes, who used to dance and clash their swords on their shields. Rhea taught the child to ride bareback on her lions, and to fear none of the wild beasts. When he was nine years old, he could catch hares by running on his own feet. He hunted the deer, and carried the tigers on his shoulders. He used to bring in lion cubs as a gift for his grandmother, and even brought full-grown lions for her car. Zeus would laugh with joy to see it. When he grew older the boy used to dress in the skins of the wild beasts, and he had a car of his own, drawn by a team of leopards. He would put his hand into a bear's mouth, and the shaggy beast would lick the fingers, quite tame.

But now Dionysus was fully grown, and Zeus sent him a message by Hermes, in these words: "My boy, it is time you should earn a place in Olympus. You will not get it without hard work, for the gods have placed hard work in front of all good things. I did not win my own place without hard work, nor did my servant Hermes, who brings this message. He set Ares free from the brazen jar, and he killed the shepherd Argus, at my bidding. Perhaps you have not heard that story, so I will tell it to you.

"There was a beautiful maiden, Io, whom I loved dearly; but Hera was jealous, and turned her into a white cow. The cow was distracted, and ran after her father and sisters. She tried to say, 'I am Io,' but all she could do was to give a gentle moo. They patted the pretty creature, and her father offered her a bunch of hay to eat; she only licked his hands, and dropped tears out of her eyes, but her tongue would not obey her wishes. Then she scratched in the sand with her hoof, first *I* and then *O*, over and over again. At last her father took notice, and understood that lament, and he could not even keep his daughter, for Hera soon sent her a guardian. This guardian was a wonderful creature, named Argus, very strong, who had a circle of eyes all round his head, and eyes spotted all over his body. These eyes used to sleep in turn, a few at a time while the rest kept watch. Argus drove away her father, and led Io into the mountains. He tethered her to a tree and sat down himself where he could watch the whole countryside.

"But I called my servant Hermes, and told him to rescue Io. Hermes put on his cap, and the wings on his feet, and took his magic wand in his hand, and away he went over hill and dale, until he came to the place where Argus watched. When he came near the place, he laid aside his cap and his wings, and gathered a flock of wild goats, which was easy for a god to do; but he kept his magic wand in his hand, and walked along like a goatherd, tootling upon the pipes. Argus heard the tune, and called out, 'Come this way, my friend, whoever you are. You might sit down with me on this rocky seat; you will find here the best of food for your goats, and it is a nice shady place for fellows like us.' So Hermes sat down, and they passed the time in talking.

"Argus asked him, 'What is that pretty pipe of yours?' 'Oh,' he said, 'that is a long story. There was once a beautiful nymph, and Pan fell in love with her.' Then he tootled a tune, and went on, 'But the nymph did not like the looks of Pan, with his horns and tail and goat's hooves, so she ran away. She ran and ran till she could run no more; then she came to a river, with reeds growing along the bank. She plunged into the reed bed, and cried to the reeds, "Save me, my sisters!" And the reeds gathered all round her, and she changed into the shape of the reeds herself. Then Pan came running up, and saw her disappear into the reeds. He clasped her in his arms, or what he thought was his nymph, but found he was holding a bunch of reeds; and as he tried to kiss her and to whisper gentle words in her ear, the breath of his lips made music among the reeds. "Ah well," he said, "I will keep you always with me"; and he arranged a row of reeds on a frame, and carried them with him wherever he went. Whenever he wanted to kiss the nymph, or to whisper to her, he blew upon the reeds, and made this lovely tune which you hear. And the pipes bear the name of Syrinx, which was the name of the nymph, and the reeds are called Syrinx too.'

"But before he finished his tale, what with the tale and what with the talking, Argus became sleepy, and his eyes began to close. Now Hermes took his magic wand, which with a touch can send waking eyes to sleep, and stroked round the head of Argus, and stroked down his body, until all his eyes were fast closed in sleep, and his head nodded down on his breast. Then Hermes took up his sickle, and with one blow cut off Argus' head.

"I will not tell you now what happened to Io because that is another long story; for Hera sent a gadfly to sting her, and drove her wandering all over the world, where she had many adventures, until at last she was happy. But Hera took all the eyes of her servant Argus, and set them in the peacock's tail, where they are to this day; and that is why the peacock is her favorite bird. But I leave all this, for it is Hermes I wish to tell of now, and how he won a place among the Olympians. Just as he won his place by good service, so must you. Like Io, you must travel all over the world, and you must do what you can for mankind."

You remember that Dionysus had been taught by Rhea how to tame the wild beasts; and in the stories about him, he is often represented as a bull, a bear, or lion, or panther. He had also learned from her the secrets of her worship, and how to play on the flute and the timbrel and the drum. And he made a wonderful discovery, the fruit of the vine.

For he had a beloved friend and playmate who died, and Dionysus would not be comforted. But his friend was buried, and from the place where he lay buried grew up a plant, with leaves curling like the boy's hair, and clusters of grapes blushing like the boy's cheeks. Dionysus caught a cluster of grapes and squeezed it in his hand and the juice trickled into a hollow horn which he had in the other hand. He touched the horn with his lips and tasted the juice, and as he drank, his sorrow went from him. He cried out:

"There is life in you still, my friend! Figs and olives are good, and so is wheaten bread, but they give pleasure only as far as the tooth. You run through all my veins like my blood, and my friend becomes a part of me! Here is my nectar, and Olympus can have no better. You shall give joy to the feast; when men shall drink of you, those who are poor will become rich, those who mourn will forget their sorrow."

After this, wherever he went he was attended by troops of followers: old Silenus, a lover of wine, but sage and prudent; frisky Satyrs, bold as lions before a fight, timid as hares in the fight; women maddened with wine, for they never knew when to stop; nymphs, and graces, and dancing maids. They dressed in the skins of fawn or panther, and put on their heads wreaths of vine or ivy, and twined serpents about their arms and necks. Each held a long fennel stalk, or a light rod, with ivy twined round it and a fir cone on the top. All night long they used to dance, waving torches of pine wood, to the music of drums and flutes. Dionysus led his troops all over the world, even as far as India, and sometimes he had to fight battles; but in the end, he gave to all mankind his precious gift of wine. But he was careful to warn them not to drink too much. If they were moderate, they had nothing but joy; but if they took more and more, they became angry and quarrelsome and violent, and did evil deeds. He showed them how to mix water with their wine, that they might not be maddened by it.

Dionysus had many adventures. Once he was standing upon a rocky headland, looking like a young man, with long hair flowing over his shoulders, and clad in a purple robe. A ship passed by; and the mariners saw him there, and made a plot to carry him off and make some profit by him. So they ran ashore and surrounded him and carried him on board ship. They tied him fast with ropes; but the ropes slipped off his limbs and left him free. The steersman called out, "You fools, do not you see this is a god? Zeus perhaps or Apollo or Poseidon? You cannot hold him. Let us put him back on shore." But the captain said, "You lend a hand with the sail, and then look to the wind. You may be an old woman, but there are men here to look after that fellow. He will soon send word to his family, and there will be a good ransom, now that we have got him by a piece of good luck."

So they hoisted the sail, and got under way—and then miracles began to happen. Wine ran down the mast, and a beautiful scent was spread abroad. Vine leaves and tendrils budded out of the sails on each side, and bunches of grapes hung down, while ivy crawled up the mast. Suddenly a lion appeared on the forecastle, and roamed about, and amidships a shaggy bear, growling and glaring. All the crew huddled together upon the poop.[1] The lion leaped on the captain and tore him to pieces; the other seamen dived into the sea, and as they dived they were turned into dolphins. But Dionysus spared the worthy steersman, and made him a happy man.

[1] *poop* (po͞op): the high part of a ship's hull, in the stern.

Old Silenus himself had an adventure which is worth telling. He was fond of wine, as you have heard, and once he took too much wine and went to sleep. While he was asleep the country people found him, and tied his hands together, and led him to their King, Midas, King of Phrygia in Asia Minor. "See here," they said, "my lord King, what a queer creature we have found! He seems to be only half a man—look at his tail!"

But Midas knew the old man; so he said, "Let him go, I know him; he is a friend of Dionysus." The countrymen untied his hands, and Midas took him back to Dionysus himself.

"Oh, here is my friend!" said Dionysus, "I thought you were lost for good! And you, my worthy Midas, you deserve a reward. Ask what you will, you shall have it."

Midas was a rich man, but like many rich men, he wanted to be richer; so he said at once, "I ask that everything I touch may turn into gold!"

Dionysus could not help thinking this was a greedy wish, but he had promised, and he said, "Be it so: everything you touch shall turn into gold."

Midas went off delighted. He plucked a twig from a tree—twig, leaves, and all turned into gold. He touched a stone—the stone turned into gold. He patted his favorite dog—the dog at once froze into gold, and stood there, a golden image; Midas did not know whether to be glad or sorry at that, but he kept his fingers from his attendants, for fear they might turn into gold too.

When he came home, he had recovered his spirits a little, and he said, "Let us have a grand feast tonight, to celebrate this occasion." He was careful to eat nothing meanwhile, so that he might have more room for the feast when it came.

The feast was ready; the courtiers were in their places, and Midas began by taking up a goblet of wine, to drink their health. "Your good health, gentlemen!" he cried, and raised it to his lips. The goblet was gold already, but as soon as the wine touched his lips, it turned into liquid gold. He did not like this at all, and spat out the drop he had taken. "What's this!" he cried, but nobody else knew what it was; they only looked at him in surprise. He sat down, and took up a piece of bread—it turned into gold. He passed a bit of game to his lips—it turned into gold. The guests were eating and drinking away comfortably, and did not notice the King, until he suddenly said, "Look here, all my food is turning into gold, and I shall starve!"

How they all stared at him, and tried not to laugh. They gave him tidbits with their own hands, but no sooner did the food touch his lips, than it was gold. The King left the table, and went to his room, and spent a very unhappy night.

Next day things were no better, and he went off posthaste to Dionysus. When he found the god, Midas looked so pale and unhappy, that Dionysus asked, "Why, what is the matter?"

Midas said, "Your gift!"

Dionysus said, "What is the matter with my gift? Didn't it come off?"

"Only too well!" said Midas. "All my food turns to gold, and I shall just starve to death!"

"Well," said Dionysus, "I gave you what you asked, so don't blame me. However, if you are tired of it, go down to the river Tmolus, and bathe in the water." It is rather like Naaman and his leprosy,[1] isn't it?

Off went Midas, as fast as he could, and bathed in the river Tmolus, and all the gold was washed out of him into the river. And ever afterwards, you had only to sift the sands of the river, and specks of gold were found there, as they still are, I believe.

Midas was a stupid old man, as you see, and now he was so sick of gold, that he spent his time in wandering about the woods. One day he found a contest going on between Apollo and Pan. Old Pan was proud of his pipes, and challenged Apollo to a musical match; so they met in a glade of the woods and chose a judge, and Pan piped away, and Apollo played on the harp. Meanwhile Midas had crept up, and hid in a bush, all ears. He was delighted with the music, but on the whole he preferred Pan.

When the judge was asked, "Which is the better?" he said at once, "Apollo"; but Midas could not contain himself, and he sang out from his bush, "I think Pan is the best myself!"

"Who is that?" cried Apollo, and pulled him out from the bush. "Why, it is King Midas, the man of gold!" and he laughed aloud. "So you think Pan is better than I am, do you?"

"Yes, I do," said Midas.

[1] *Naaman and his leprosy* (nā′ă·măn): a Syrian captain cured of leprosy by the prophet Elisha who instructed him to bathe in the river Jordan.

"Well," said Apollo, "you have not much of an ear. I will give you a better pair." Then he waved his hands, and Midas' ears grew up about a foot high, and covered themselves with fur and fluff, and lo and behold, Midas had a fine pair of ass's ears. "There you are," said Apollo; and as Midas listened to him, he did not turn his head toward him, as a man does, but waggled his two ears in that direction, like an ass, and all the company roared with laughter.

Midas went off in a great state, and slunk indoors after dark. He went up to his chamber, and told his slave to wrap a grand turban about his head, to cover the ears. "Now then, young man," he said, "not a word to anyone, or off comes your head." Then he went into his court, and nobody was the wiser.

But the wretched slave did not know what to do. He was amazed and dumfounded, and bursting with a fine piece of gossip which he dared not tell to a soul. Imagine how you would feel with such a piece of news, if your master had a long pair of ass's ears, and you could not tell anyone! He kept it to himself as long as he could; and when he could hold it no longer, he rushed down to the riverside, and dug a deep hole, and whispered into the hole, "Midas has a pair of ears like a jackass!" Then he filled up the hole with earth, and came home again, feeling much better.

But that was not the end of it. Reeds grew up out of the hole, and there was a great rustling among the reeds, and some boys who were surprised at the noise happened to listen, and this is what they heard, a loud whisper carried through the air—"Midas has the ears of a jackass! Midas has the ears of a jackass!" They told their friends, and before long everybody about the court was whispering, and choking with laughter, "Midas has the ears of a jackass under that fine turban!"

At last Midas himself caught the whisper, and the courtiers could see his whole turban waggle as his ears turned to the sound. He was furious, and I am afraid the slave's head was cut off, but now the King had to make the best of it.

Dionysus carried his wine all over Greece, and found worshipers everywhere, who built him temples; and everywhere those who used his gift well were made happy by it, and those who used it badly were made furious or mad. So it is with all the gifts of God. They are given to us for use, not for misuse, and we learn by experience.

Lastly, having done his work in the world, Dionysus wished to take his place in Olympus; but he would not go without his mother, Semele. She was a mortal, and she had died, and now she was in the dark house of Hades; so Dionysus resolved to go and fetch her. But he did not know the way, until a man who knew told him. There was a pool in the marsh of Lerna, where Hercules had his fight with the water snake, if you have not forgotten. This pool was bottomless, and that was one way to the lower world.

Dionysus dived in, and in due time came to the dark house of Hades. He begged for his mother's life; and King Hades, who was never willing to let anyone go when once he had him, refused at first; but at last he agreed, if Dionysus would send him down in exchange one of those whom he loved best, a life for a life. Dionysus promised, and led his mother up once more to the earth, where she had been so happy and so unhappy, and thence to Olympus, where they both joined the company of the immortal gods. He did not forget his promise to Hades. What he loved most on earth were three things, the vine, the ivy, and the myrtle; so he sent Hades a myrtle plant, a life for a life. Perhaps that was not quite a fair exchange. What do you think?

You may still see the place where Dionysus dived, on his way to the house of Hades. It is a pool of dark waters, smooth and glassy, with great reeds growing round it, and a circle of tall white poplars with silvery stems. The people still say that it is bottomless. You may still see the place where he came up with his mother, a beautiful plain on the bay of Troezen, with groves of oranges and lemons, and rows of tall cypress trees. But the deep cleft in the rock by which they came is closed now forever.

Chapter 17 ASCLEPIUS

One more god has to be added, and then the number of the Olympians will be complete. After that we have to do with their dealings among mankind. This god was named Asclepius, and he was the god of healing, one who did only kind things, and never pushed out anyone else; but all men loved him and worshipped him for his deeds of kindness.

He was the son of Apollo; but when he was born, he was left out among the mountains, to live or die. There a nanny goat found him, and gave him milk, and a dog watched over him, until a shepherd came and found him. He was put in the charge of a wonderful creature named Chiron, a Centaur; that is to say, he was half man and half horse.

Chiron was himself the son of old Cronus the Titan; and he lived in a cave on Mount Pelion. He was the wisest and most just of all creatures on earth. He knew all the healing herbs that grow, to cure the diseases which men have. He could heal wounds, and sing magical ditties which soothed the sick and made them well. He could chase and catch the wild animals. In his cave among the hills he lived a happy life at home with his wife and mother; and all the young heroes used to be brought to him, and left to be taught, like schoolboys in a boarding school. He taught them how to ride on his own back and how to hunt and how to fight and how to use healing herbs; and he taught them the rules of good conduct. His most famous rule was: Honor Zeus first among gods, and among men honor first thy father.

Asclepius learned all this from him, but he paid most attention to the healing herbs and the salves for curing wounds and the magical ditties, for he cared nothing about hunting or war. When he grew up, he became famous for his cures; but he went too far in this. He happened one day to kill a snake; and as the dead snake lay on the ground, by and by another snake crept up, and laid an herb on the dead snake's mouth. Then the dead snake came to life again, and they both went away together. Asclepius noticed what the herb was—for he had not learned about this one from Chiron; and he used it to bring a dead man back to life.

This made Hades angry, and he complained to Zeus. "Look

here, sir," he said, "if this man goes on, my kingdom will be empty. It is not fair to me." Then Zeus struck Asclepius with a thunderbolt, and killed him. But Apollo his father begged Zeus to relent, and Zeus revived Asclepius, and placed him among the stars. I do not think he used to visit Olympus and to join the company of the gods there. He seems to have been much more interested in mankind, and did not care for grandeur. He soon had temples all over Greece, and men were glad to worship him.

These places were much more than temples. Besides the temple, there was always a place where sick people could stay while they were being cured. They used to lie in rows along a sort of portico, like what you see outside a house, only much longer and much finer, built of stone, with pillars and open on the warm side. There in the night they had dreams, and the dreams told them what to do to be cured. Or else the god himself, with his sons and daughters, used to make the rounds, and give the sick people medicines or ointments.

He had several sons and daughters, who helped him. Three of the daughters were named Health and Healing and Allcure, and we have actually borrowed two of their names in English. One of them is Panacea, which we used to mean a drug that cures everything; and one is Hygeia, which people who like long words use instead of health, when they talk about "hygiene," just to show off. Besides the sons and daughters, the god used to be helped by his famous snakes. These snakes lived in a hole under the temple, and they used to crawl about among the sick people and lick their eyes or their wounds. In the morning, the proper thing was to drop a cake into the snakes' hole, besides making a sacrifice to the god.

You may still see the ruins of some of these places, and the thank-offerings of those who were healed. Sometimes they used to give a little model of what was cured: an eye, if they had sore eyes, or a tooth or an arm or leg. Sometimes they put up the story of what happened, carved on the stones of the wall. One of them says he had had a lance head in his jaw for six years. He slept in the corridor; and dreamed the god came, and drew it out, and put it into his hands. Next morning, he woke, and found the lance head in his hand. Another man had a long beard and a bald head, and the boys used to laugh at him, which he did not like; but the god put some ointment upon his head, and in the morning he found a fine crop of hair.

When the Greek gods came to an end, and the Christian religion took their place, the Christian churches took over some of their ancient customs. So even now, sick people come and sleep in the courtyard of a church; and if they are healed, they offer to the saint of the church little silver models of hands or feet or teeth or the whole body, whatever part may have been ailing. Thus we may think that the kind, good Asclepius is not quite dead and finished, even now.

PART THREE

Chapter 18 JASON

We now come to one of the most wonderful stories, the Quest of the Golden Fleece; and I must tell you how it began.

Jason was the son of a man who was rightful king of a place in Thessaly; but the king's cousin, Pelias, took the kingdom for himself. The banished king could do nothing. A son was born to him, and he was afraid that Pelias might kill the child; so he pretended that the child was dead. The women set up a loud lamentation in the house, they beat their breasts, they tore their hair, as the fashion was; finally, they made a funeral and draped the bier [1] with purple and pretended to bury the child. But what they really did was this: they put the child in the charge of faithful persons, and sent him away secretly, by night, into the mountains, to the cave of the Centaur Chiron. You remember Chiron the Centaur, half man and half horse, who was the son of Cronus the old Titan; he had been trained in hunting and gymnastics—as far as a horse could manage—in music and medicine, and in the art of prophecy. He knew all about all the animals on the hills and all the trees of the forest and all the herbs of healing which grow in the ground. Indeed, he became the wisest of creatures, kind and good. He lived in a cave on Mount Pelion, with his wife and his old mother, and it was the custom to send young boys to him, like a sort of training school for the heroes. He taught all his boys to honor Zeus, and to honor their fathers, besides the arts I have mentioned. So to him Jason came; and there he remained for twenty years, learning to be a brave man, and a wise man.

[1] *bier* (bēr): a coffin.

Now Pelias was always uneasy in his mind. He knew he had no right to be king, and he feared the gods might punish him; so he became more anxious than ever, when a strange oracle was given him by Apollo, "Beware of the man with one understanding!" He could not quite make out what this meant, and he brooded over it, as he was meant to do.

Then one day he heard everybody in the palace talking about a piece of news. "Have you heard?" they said. "A young fellow has just appeared in the market place, a stranger. He is dressed in a close-fitting tunic, with a leopard skin thrown over it; he carries a pair of spears, and he has thick chestnut hair falling to his shoulders. Come and see!"

They came to see, but no one knew him. "A fine fellow, this!" they said. "He can hardly be Apollo, or the god of war, and those big boys, Otus and Ephialtes, are dead, as we know. But who can he be?"

Pelias came to see also. He got into his mule car, and came galloping along the street. When he saw the man, he was struck with fear; for he had one foot bare, and a boot on his right foot only, since he had lost the other in crossing a river. When Pelias saw this, he thought, "Here is the man with one understanding!" That is quite a good name for a boot, isn't it? No doubt Apollo meant to puzzle Pelias. And Pelias was very much afraid; but he hid his fear, and to hide it, he spoke very rudely to the young man. "Where do you come from, young stranger?" he said. "What old drab was your mother? What ditch were you born in? Tell the truth, and do not try to deceive me."

But Jason returned a soft answer. "Sir, I will show you what Chiron's training is, for I come from his cave, and from the gentle breeding of his mother and his wife. Twenty years I have spent there, and I have never done a deed or said a word to make them ashamed of me. Now I come to my own home and claim the honor which is mine by inheritance. For I am informed that Pelias has robbed my father of his rights. And now can any of you kind people tell me where my father lives? I am Jason, the son of Aeson."

They led him to the place, and his father knew him, and wept for joy to see his beautiful son. Soon his two brothers came from their homes, and his cousins, and there was a family feast. Jason did the honors; and after they had feasted and talked, he said, "Now for a serious word. Come with me to Pelias and let us hear what he will say."

Straight from the feast they made their way to the palace; and there Jason said, still speaking gently:

"My lord, I do not complain or threaten. We ought to rule our passions, and so to act that happiness may follow. You and I are of the same race, and it is a shame for kinsmen to quarrel and fight. Keep your flocks and herds, keep your house and your wealth; but give me the scepter and the throne which belonged to my father, that no violence may arise between us."

Pelias answered, "I will do as you wish. I am old, and you are young, and you may be able to quell the anger of the gods below. For Phrixus bids me bring him home, and the golden fleece of the ram which saved him. That is what he tells me in a dream; I have inquired of Apollo's oracle, and he tells me the same. Go to the far east, and bring them back, and I swear an oath to you that I will hand over my throne to you." So they agreed; but before I tell you how Jason accomplished the quest, I must tell the story of the ram with a golden fleece.

Chapter 19 THE RAM WITH A GOLDEN FLEECE

Phrixus was the son of the King of Boeotia, and he had a sister named Helle; their mother was Nephele, the Cloud. It must be awkward to have a Cloud for your wife; you never know when she will be at home and when she will be flying about in the sky. And so the King seems to have found it, for he married a second wife, named Ino, who was one of the daughters of Cadmus. You remember Cadmus, no doubt, and his wedding, and the necklace given to his wife, which brought misfortune wherever it went. It brought misfortunes to Ino, one of them a very great misfortune, that is, jealousy, which makes the person who has it miserable, and everyone who comes near miserable too. Ino had children of her own, and she was jealous of Phrixus and Helle, and wanted to get rid of them.

So she made the following plan. First, she got hold of the seed corn which was to be sown in the land for next year; and she had it all parched, over the fire, so that it was dead and could not grow. Then she put it back where it came from. In due time, the corn was sown; but no shoots came up—there was not a leaf, or an ear of corn, in the whole country. The people were in despair and did not know what to do.

Next, Ino persuaded her husband to inquire of the oracle at Delphi; and when he sent to inquire, she bribed the messengers who went there. She told them then to come back and pretend that they had asked the oracle, and that the oracle said, "Kill Phrixus and Helle at the altar for a sacrifice, or your corn will grow no more." This was a dreadful blow to the King; but he had to obey what he believed to be God's wish, like Abraham and Isaac in the Bible. And in this case too there was a ram, but a different sort of ram from the ram which was sacrificed instead of Isaac.

This was a wonderful ram, with a golden fleece, which Nephele from the clouds provided at the altar. There stood the two children, ready to be killed; there stood the sacrificer with his knife; there stood the King, full of sorrow, and jealous Ino, full of joy; and lo and behold, down came the golden ram, and up got the boy and girl upon his back, and away he flew into the sky.

For a long time, all was well; they passed over land and sea, making for the far east. But after a while, Helle grew tired, and could not hold on any longer. She just dropped down into the sea, and was drowned; and the place where she fell is still called Hellespont, or the "Sea of Helle."

Phrixus could do nothing, and the ram went on, until he came to the far end of the Black Sea, to the east, to the land of the Colchians; and there he came down. The King of this land was named Aeëtes, the brother of the witch Circe, whom you will hear of in the story of Odysseus, if you can find someone to tell it to you. The ram was sacrificed, and his golden fleece was nailed to a tree in a sacred grove of oaks, and guarded by a terrible dragon which never slept.

This Phrixus, who was a cousin of Pelias and of Jason, was

the man who appeared in a dream to Pelias and told him to bring him back home and lay his ghost. At least, that was what Pelias said; but perhaps he made it up, because he thought that Jason would probably be killed in trying to get the Golden Fleece.

King Aeëtes gave his daughter to Phrixus, when he was old enough to marry, and there he lived and died. But his sons returned to their father's old home, to claim his inheritance. And ever after they had to obey a strange rule. The eldest son, the head of the family, was never allowed to enter the town hall. He might go anywhere else he liked, but if he entered the town hall, he could not go out again unless he were taken to the altar, and sacrificed on the spot. You will not be surprised to hear that the eldest sons, from generation to generation, preferred to go away and settle in some foreign land.

Chapter 20 THE ARGONAUTS

You know now what a task Jason had to do. People knew very little about the world, then; and they had only very small sailing ships or galleys that used oars, in which they were at the mercy of winds and waters. This voyage was aimed at the far end of the Black Sea, a dangerous sea which no one knew well: indeed, its proper name was the Unfriendly Sea; only men called it the Friendly Sea for fear of offending it. A noble ship was built for the voyage. The goddess Athena helped in the building and set up as the stem a great beam of oak, which was brought from the sacred grove at Dodona. This great oaken stem had a voice, and spoke sometimes to the crew. The ship was named Argo, and the sailors were called the Argonauts, or Sailors of Argo.

All the great heroes of Greece came to take part in the voyage: their names you will hear often in Greek story. Hercules came, with Castor and Polydeuces, all sons of Zeus; Orpheus came, the great singer; Holdfast and Pullhard, sons of Hermes;

Zetes and Calais, sons of the North Wind, and each had a pair of wings on his shoulders, shivering with purple feathers; Tiphys the steersman, and Mopsus the seer. And there on the shore was the old Centaur Chiron, with his wife, who held young Achilles on her arm, to wish good-by to his father Peleus, and a happy voyage.

Across the Aegean Sea they sailed, and through the Hellespont, where Helle had fallen and died; and over the Propontis, a little sea between Hellespont and Bosporus, where they had many adventures. They had to fight with a tribe of huge men who had six arms: two grew from their shoulders, and four from their sides. In one place, where they went to get water, they lost the boy, Hylas. As he let down his urn into a pool, the nymph of the pool saw this beautiful boy and stretched up her arm to embrace him. She loved him so much that she drew him down to the water, and he was seen no more. But Hercules sought for him high and low, and he wandered so far that the others put off without missing him, and left him behind. When they found he was missing, they were about to turn back for him; but a Sea-god put up his head and shoulders out of the water, and said, "Why do you wish to take Hercules in search of the Golden Fleece? It is his duty to serve King Eurystheus, and to perform the labors which the King ordains." So they went on, and Hercules went about his proper work.

Again they had to put in, to the place where poor old Phineus lived by the sea. He had the gift of foretelling the future, and he told too much; so blindness was sent upon him by Zeus, and he was persecuted by the Harpies. These were huge great birds with sharp wings and claws. Whenever Phineus took a meal, the Harpies would swoop down upon him from the clouds, and snatched the food from his hands, and even from his mouth; worse than that, they covered the rest of it with filth, so that he could not eat any of it, and he had to live by what kind neighbors brought him secretly. This was to cease, as he knew by his power, when Jason should come and deliver him.

He heard the tramp of the heroes, and came down to meet them, like a lifeless dream, bowed over his staff, and crept to the door on his withered feet, feeling the walls; his limbs trembled for weakness, and his parched skin was caked with dirt, and only the skin held his bones together. He sat on the threshold of the courtyard, and the earth seemed to reel under his feet. At last he said:

"Listen, brave men, if you are they whom Jason leads in the ship Argo. Save me, and leave me not in my misery. I am blind, as you see, and I can eat no meat; for the Harpies snatch the food from my mouth, and bespatter all the place with filth. The oracle declares that I shall be saved by the sons of the North Wind, and let me tell you, I am no stranger to them, for their sister was my wife."

So they got ready a feast, the last prey for the Harpies. And no sooner had he touched the food, than out of the clouds swooped the horrible birds, like flashes of lightning, and clutched the food from the old man's hand, and sped away over the sea. But the two sons of the North Wind unfolded their purple wings, and sped away in pursuit, holding their swords in hand. They came up with the Harpies, until they just grazed their feathers with their finger tips; and they would have destroyed them, but Iris, the messenger of the gods, met them, and said, "It is not lawful to kill the hounds of Zeus, but I swear to you that they shall visit old Phineus no more." So they turned back, and the Harpies flew on to their den in distant Crete.

The heroes washed the old man's skin, and made sacrifices, and set out a new feast, which he enjoyed for the first time in many long years. And the old man said, "Listen now, and I will tell you what it is lawful for you to know. For I have learned that Zeus desires to reveal his oracles to men incomplete, that they may not know too much. But this I may tell you. You will soon see, at the mouth of the Bosporus, two rocks, called the Clashers, which constantly clash together, and then move apart. You must take with you a dove, and when you come to the rocks, let her go; then watch if she passes through. If she escapes, you may follow; and row hard, for in that passage, rowing will be better than praying. But if she is caught, then turn back; for it is better to yield to the will of the gods." Then he told them of other perils, and said that they should reach their goal, and that a god would guide them on their way home. Lastly he said, "Take thought of Aphrodite, goddess of love, for your success will depend upon her help. I may tell you no more."

Then the two sons of the North Wind returned, panting from

their long chase, and said, "Sir, you are free from the Harpies forever."

When the time came for departure, the heroes embarked, not forgetting to take the dove with them.

At the mouth of the Bosporus, they saw two huge rocks rushing violently together. The rocks met with a crash and sent up the sea in clouds of spray; then they leaped apart, and the sea rushed in to fill the gap and met in the middle, rising like a great mountain of water. There was a swift current against them, and a wind blowing them on, which nearly matched, so they were obliged to put out the oars.

As the rocks drew together again, they let the dove go, and all craned their necks to see. Clash, went the rocks! As they went back, the heroes could see the dove had got through, only the rocks had caught one of her tail feathers. They were able to see this, because one of them, named Lynceus, had eyes so sharp, that he could see everything under the sky, as clearly as if it were close.

The waves whirled the ship round; but the helmsman shouted out—"Row, you men! she's through!" And they rowed with all their might. As the rocks moved apart, a huge wave rose up in front of them and carried them back; but another wave rose behind them and carried them onward. The rocks were now rushing together again, nearer and nearer, but the men rowed as they never had rowed before, and the wave carried them out clear into the sea. The two rocks crashed together, and there they remained, joined into one. They stood still, and they have never moved since.

Then the heroes gave thanks to Athena, who had built the ship Argo so strongly that she was proof against all the perils of the sea.

They passed on, and came in due time to the island of Ares, where old Phineus had told them to land. This island was haunted by flocks of terrible birds, with brazen beaks and brazen feathers. You remember these—how Hercules had scared them away from the Stymphalian lake. These birds used to shoot out their feathers like arrows, and the first notice of them which the heroes had was that one of them shot out a bronze feather, and it struck one of the heroes on his shoulder.

"What's that?" he cried in dismay. Some one drew out the feather, and bound up the wound; and another said, "These are the birds of Ares! It is of no use to shoot arrows against them, they are too many and too strong; but I remember what Hercules did, for I was there and saw it. He shook a rattle of brass and frightened them away. Let us divide ourselves: one half shall row, and one half shall put on their helmets, with nodding plumes, and hold up their spears and make a roof over the rowers with their shields. When we come near the island, these will shout and rattle the spears on the shields."

So they did. They shouted and rattled, and the birds shot their feathers in clouds, but they crashed on the shields and only made a louder din. So the birds were frightened, and all flew away to the mountains opposite.

The heroes landed, and now they found out why Phineus had told them to land there; for on the shore they found the four sons of Phrixus himself, who had set out for home in order to claim their inheritance, and here they had been shipwrecked. They were glad to get on board, and Jason hoped they might be useful when the ship came to Colchis.

The heroes sailed away, and coasted along by the Caucasus Mountains, where Prometheus was nailed to a rock. There they saw the great eagle, sailing high, near the clouds, and they heard the whir of his wings, and the fanning of the wings shook their sails, high as he was. He sailed along with his wings pushed far out on both sides, like a ship with long shining oars. And soon they heard the bitter cry of Prometheus, as the eagle swooped down and tore at his liver. At last they came to the Colchian land. They entered the mouth of the river and let the ship ride at anchor off the shore.

Chapter 21 CUPID AND HIS MOTHER

While the heroes were hidden among the reeds, their friends in Olympus were not forgetful of them. Hera in particular sought out Athena, and said, "What shall we do about the Golden Fleece? Do you think Jason will be able to persuade King Aeëtes to part with it? He has a wonderful tongue to persuade, and he always loves gentle words. Or will they have to fight for it? And how can so few fight against so many? Give me your advice."

Athena said, "Really I do not know what to say. I have been considering many plans, but I cannot think of a good one."

They were silent awhile, with their eyes fixed on the ground. Then Hera said:

"I will tell you what. The King's daughter, Medea, is skilled in all sorts of charms and spells. Would she help? What if she were to fall in love with Jason? Suppose we ask the help of Aphrodite."

"Well," said Athena, "I do not understand those things, I never cared much myself for gods or men, but by all means let us try."

So they went to the house which Hephaestus, the Smith-god, had built for Aphrodite when he married her. He was away at the forge; but they found the goddess on a seat facing the door. Her golden hair was loose, and covered her shoulders; she was parting it with a golden comb, and just about to bind it up into braids. When she saw them, she rose, and greeted them, and gave them seats, gathering up her long hair in one hand, and said:

"Good friends, what brings you here? I have not seen you this long time; you do not often visit my humble home."

She said this because her husband was not quite of the first rank, and Hera disliked him, although he was her own son. Aphrodite thus felt her vanity hurt a little. But Hera said:

"Ah, you are making fun of us! But this is a serious matter which we come about. Jason and his company are now on the river Phasis in quest of the Golden Fleece, and I do not see how they can get it. Jason at least I am determined to save. I cannot abide that Pelias, who neglects my sacrifices; but I do love the young man. Once I was on earth, trying men, to see how they behaved. I took on me the likeness of an ugly old crone, and sat down by the side of a rushing river, when he came along. Then I begged him to help an old woman, and he took me up on his shoulders, ugly though I was, and carried me across the river. So I will certainly save him, and punish Pelias for his neglect."

"Well," said Aphrodite, "what can I do? I will help you if I can."

Hera said, "You can help us, indeed. Just tell your boy Cupid to shoot one of his arrows at Medea, and make her fall in love with Jason."

"Ah, if he will!" said Aphrodite. "He is a naughty boy, and will not do what I tell him. He is more likely to listen to you than to me. I mean to break his bow and arrows before his eyes, the little wretch! And he says that if I touch him, he will make me repent it!"

The goddesses smiled, and looked at each other. This vexed Aphrodite, and she went on, "Yes, you only laugh at my troubles; I get no sympathy from anyone, and I ought not to have said anything about it. However, I will try and see if I can coax him."

Hera smiled gently, and took her hand, and said, "Do try, my dear, and don't be angry with the boy. I am sure he will be a good boy, and do what his mother asks him."

So they went out into the orchard, and there they found Cupid playing with young Ganymede, a boy whom Zeus had taken a fancy to, and so had sent his eagle which caught him up into the skies and brought him to Olympus to be his cupbearer at table. They were playing for golden dice. Cupid was holding his hand full of the dice close to his breast, and laughing at Ganymede, who was then casting the last two, with gloomy looks; for he did not like losing. He lost them too, and went off in the sulks, without noticing the goddesses. Then Aphrodite said:

"You rogue, have you cheated the innocent child? Shame upon you! Come now, do something for me, like a good boy, and I will give you a beautiful ball, the one which Zeus played with in his cave when he was a baby. A golden ball, with blue circles round it! If you throw it up, it leaves a flaming track in the sky, like a comet! That is what I will give you, if you will shoot one of your arrows at Medea, and make her love Jason."

"Give it me now!" he cried, and dropped his golden dice on

the ground. "Now, now!" and he clutched hold of her dress on both sides, and clung to her. She smiled at him, and kissed him, and said:

"No, not now, but I promise to give it as soon as you have shot one arrow at Medea."

Without another word the boy slung his quiver across his shoulder, and caught up his bow, and away he ran; through the orchard, out of the gates of Olympus, down through the air, until he saw the earth stretched beneath him, the sea spread wide and the mountains rising into the sky.

Chapter 22 JASON AND MEDEA

Meanwhile, the heroes were taking counsel together, what was best to do. And Jason said to them, "My friends, it is always best to try persuasion first. Gentle words have great power. Let me go with one or two others, and let us take the sons of Phrixus to be our guides, and open the matter with King Aeëtes. If he will not listen, we can discuss whether it will be well to use force."

So Jason left the ship, with his comrades, and he held in his hand the wand that Hermes had given him to show that his errand was peaceful. They passed over a plain with lines of willows on which was a strange sight. The Colchians are a wild race of men; and when a man dies, they do not bury him or burn him, but they wrap up the body in an oxhide and hang it up in a tree. So in these trees were hanging long rows of bundles in which were the bodies of their dead.

Then the heroes came to the King's palace, and a wonderful place it was. The god Hephaestus built it with walls and towers and roomy chambers; and in the courtyard he built four fountains, one running with milk, one with wine, one with fragrant oil, one with water which grew warm at the setting of the Pleiades, and at their rising it became cold as ice. He also made for him bulls with feet of brass and mouths of brass, who breathed fire out of their jaws; and a great plow of adamant, all in one piece.

Medea saw them coming. She was there in the company of her sister, the wife of Phrixus, and she cried aloud when she saw Jason with his friends. And the mother lifted up her hands and cried out and ran up to embrace her sons, and sobbing, she said:

"So you did not go far, my boys, and here you are back again! Why did you leave your mother?"

Meanwhile Cupid passed unseen, and glided close by Jason. He put arrow to bowstring and drew it and shot straight at Medea, who stood gazing at Jason. The arrow went deep into her heart, like a burning flame, and filled her with amazement until her soul melted; and from that moment there was only one thought in her, the love for Jason.

That night there was a banquet, and King Aeëtes questioned his guests as to their coming. The eldest son of Phrixus answered: "My lord, our ship was wrecked, and we were saved by this stranger, who has come on a useless quest. His ship was built by the goddess Athena, and no storms can hurt it; and he is sent by one Pelias, who wishes to lay the ghost of Phrixus by asking the gift of the Golden Fleece. Be it as you will, for they do not offer force, although the ship is full of the chief heroes of Hellas." [1]

This filled the King with fury, and he cried out, "Begone, you traitors! It is my throne you want, and that is why you have brought all these armed men into my house! If you had not tasted my food, and so become my guests, I would have cut out your tongues and cut off your hands and left you only your feet to run away!"

The young man would have answered angrily, but Jason checked him and said, "My lord, bear with us. We have no such desires; for who would cross the wide seas for another man's goods? Fate has sent us, and the bidding of a presumptuous King. Great is your power, and your name shall be published abroad in all Hellas."

These gentle words calmed the King, but he brooded hate and suspicion all the same. However, he thought he might try what these heroes could do, so he said:

"I bear no grudge against brave men, least of all if they have the blood of the gods in their veins. I will give you the

[1] *Hellas:* Greece.

Golden Fleece when I have tried you. I will ask you to do only what I can do myself. I have two bulls with brazen feet and brazen mouths who breathe fire out of their mouths. These bulls I yoke, and plow the fields of Ares; and into the furrows I cast not seed, but teeth from the Theban dragon, which Athena gave me when the dragon was killed by Cadmus. Then a crop of armed men grows up, and as they rise against me, I kill them all. If you can yoke the bulls and plow the field and kill the crop of armed men, I will give you the Golden Fleece. If not, I will keep it, for it is not right that a brave man should yield to a coward."

Jason was abashed by this. He did not know what to say; and the King sat, smiling grimly at him. At last he made answer, "My lord, you set me a hard task. But I accept the contest even though it be my doom to die. Necessity brought me here and I must do my part."

So he went away with his friends; and Medea watched him as he went, and her soul crept after him like a dream, for she was possessed now of this terrible passion and could think of nothing but Jason. But when the heroes were by themselves, the son of Phrixus said, "There is one thing that can help us. There is a maiden here who knows all manner of drugs and spells; if she would help us, we might succeed. I will ask my mother to entreat her." Jason said, "Very well then, go and try; but it is a pitiful thing that we must depend on the help of women." So far he had not noticed Medea, and did not know who she was. Meanwhile the King laid his plans, so that when the bulls should have killed Jason, he would attack the heroes and kill them, and burn the ship Argo to ashes.

But Medea had no rest for love of Jason. And after restless sleep and bad dreams, she got up to seek her sister for comfort. As she opened the door, there on the threshold her sister stood, also in distress, and she cried, "Medea, what is the matter? Why do you weep so?"

Medea shrank from telling her secret; she said, "Sister, I have had terrible dreams. I fear the King may be plotting against your sons, along with the strangers!"

The sister said, "Ah me, I am afraid too! But first swear to help me, and to tell no one what I shall say."

Medea said, "I swear to keep all secret, and to help as far as I can."

Then her sister said, "Can you think of any way to win the contest, for the sake of my sons? I have left them in my chamber. Come to pray for help."

Medea's heart leaped for joy. "I love you, my sister," she said, "and your sons. I will find out a charm to conquer the bulls."

And so Medea prepared to keep her promise. She could see that disgrace would fall upon her, and perhaps death, for taking the stranger's part against her own father; but she could not help it, for she was filled with an overpowering passion, sent from the gods, like that terrible passion which seized Helen in later days and brought the ruin of Troy and the death of thousands of brave men. She could think only of one thing, how to help Jason, although she spoke of her sister and the sons of her sister. She opened her casket of drugs, and took out a wonderful root, called the root of Prometheus because it grew up from the ground where the eagle had let fall a drop of blood from his liver, or rather a drop of that fluid which runs in the veins of the gods, for they have not blood like men. If a man should anoint his body with this, for one day he would be safe against any blow from anything made of brass, and safe from fire.

Chapter 23

THE BRAZEN BULLS AND THE DRAGON'S TEETH

When day dawned, Medea put on a beautiful robe and a veil over it, shining like silver; and calling her twelve maids, she said, "Make ready the mule car and come with me to the shrine of Hecate." They put the mules to, and Medea mounted the car and took up the reins and whip and trotted down the street. The maidens trussed up their skirts and laid hold of the car, six on each side, and ran along with it. So they came to the shrine of Hecate, goddess of night, lady of spells and charms and potions.

Then Medea said to the maidens, "Listen to me. You saw the stranger, and you know what he has come for. My sister and her sons beg me to accept his gifts, and protect him against the brazen bulls. I have summoned him to meet me here, and you shall have a good share of what he gives." The maidens were pleased to agree to this, and were ready to take part with their mistress.

Meanwhile the sons of Phrixus had returned to Jason and told him to meet Medea at the shrine of Hecate. Led by them, Jason came to the tryst, and Medea saw him come. She sent her maidens apart, and Jason advanced alone.

Never was there so noble a young man as Jason. As Medea gazed at him, her knees trembled, and she could not address him. They stood face to face speechless.

At last, Jason said, "Maiden, why do you fear me so much? I am not a man of violence. I come in friendship to this holy place, as your suppliant, to crave your help. For surely one so lovely as you are must be full of gentle courtesy."

Her heart grew warm within her and melted like dew upon a rose. She said, "Take heed what I say. When the day for your trial is fixed, and my father has given you the dragon's teeth to sow, on the midnight before, bathe in the river, alone; and then put on a black robe, and dig a pit, and there sacrifice a ewe to Hecate, pouring out before her a pot of honey. Then go away without looking back, no matter what noises you hear. At dawn, soak this root which I give you in water, strip, and anoint your whole body with the water, as if with oil, and sprinkle it over your shield and sword. Then for one day no fire can hurt you, and no strokes from the spears of earthborn men. One thing more: when you have plowed the soil and sown the seed and the earthborn men spring up, cast among them a large stone. They will fight for it together and kill each other. Then you may take away the Golden Fleece, and may happiness go with you, wherever you go." Then she took courage and caught hold of his right hand and said, "Remember me when you come to your own land, and I will remember you, in despite of my father. If you forget me, may a messenger bird come over the sea and tell me; and may I be wafted through the air, as an unexpected guest to remind you how I helped you to escape!" So she said, with tears running down her cheeks. And Jason replied, "Speak not of birds and unexpected guests! If you will come with me, you shall be honored in all Hellas, and if you will be my wife, only death shall part us."

Then Medea was glad, but she was unhappy too, for she foresaw that troubles were to come.

And so they parted. Jason returned to his friends, and Medea passed through her maidens and saw none of them. She mounted her car and drove home and walked through the company and past her sister without seeing anyone. She sat down by her bed, with her heart full of thoughts.

The time came. Jason did as he had been told and anointed himself and his weapons and in the morning he was ready. King Aeëtes was in full armor, and handed to Jason the helmet with the dragon's teeth; and they repaired to the spot. There the King plumped down the plow in front of Jason, and said with a laugh, "There is your task, my good man! Get on with it!"

Then Jason set up his spear in the ground by a tree and leaned his helmet against it and slung his sword over his shoulder; but he bore no armor upon his body, only took the shield with him, as he examined the tracks of the bulls in the soil and went to meet them. Both bulls rushed out of their lair together, breathing fire and smoke. Jason held his shield before him to meet their attack. They struck it with their mighty horns but could not move him. Then he caught one bull by the horn and dragged it to the yoke and struck its brazen leg with his foot and forced it down on the knee. He forced down the other bull beside it, then threw down his shield and held them both on their fore-knees, while two of his comrades passed him the yoke. He fastened both bulls to the yoke, and lifting the brazen pole between them, made it fast. Then Jason slung his shield behind his back and took up the helmet with the teeth and his own spear, which he used to prick the sides of the bulls and to drive them along.

The bulls bellowed and spouted flame, but it was of no use—go they must, and they drew the great plow and cut a deep furrow behind them. As they went, Jason dropped the dragon's teeth in the furrow, turning round ever and anon to see whether the earthborn men should rise too soon. But the time was not yet. The field was plowed. He loosed the oxen and let them go, while he filled the helmet with water from the river and quenched his thirst.

By this time, the crop began to appear: helmets and shining spears thrust up from the ground, and soon the men were ready to fight. Then Jason took up a great stone and hurled it among them. The earthborn men yelled, and rushed together, fighting over the stone; and Jason rushed on them, hewing them down, some with head and shoulders above the ground, some half risen to the air, some just standing upright, or making their first rush to battle. He cut them down as you cut corn with a sickle; and there they lay, biting the earth with their teeth.

Chapter 24 THE GOLDEN FLEECE

But King Aeëtes did not keep his word. He would not give up the Golden Fleece, and he pondered in his mind how he could destroy the heroes and their ship. Medea was plunged in trouble to think what must come next; and in the night, she went secretly to the shore and called out to her kinsmen, "Save me and save yourselves while there is yet time, before the king can get his men together. I will charm the serpent, and I will help you to get the Golden Fleece."

So she guided the ship to the place where the fleece hung, in the sacred grove of Ares. She led Jason to the huge oak tree upon which it was hung. As they came near, the serpent, which never slept, saw them with his keen eyes and hissed loudly at them, wreathing his coils all about. And Medea sang a soft song, and while she sang, the serpent's head drooped and nodded, and his coils relaxed; while she sang she sprinkled his eyes with her magical brew, and he let his jaw sink down and slept. Then she smeared ointment upon his head, while Jason took down the Golden Fleece, heavy and thick, and draped it over his left shoulder.

What joy there was in the ship, when they saw Jason return, bearing the Golden Fleece! He led Medea to a seat in the stern, and said:

"Now, men, for the homeward voyage! Let a part of you row, and the rest hold their shields along the sides to protect us from the shafts of our enemies."

By this time, Medea's flight was known, and the people saw that the ship Argo was gone from her moorings. The King came into the market place, holding a torch, and called upon all to give chase. So they manned their ships and launched into the river; but the ship Argo was now well on her way.

It would be too long to tell of their journey home. It would be very puzzling too, for the earth must have had an odd shape in those days, as you will see. They came in due time to the mouth of the Danube; and while they were there one of the Colchian ships caught them up. The other ships had gone in different directions, and lost them altogether, but this ship was commanded by Absyrtus, Medea's own brother, and it was full of fighting men. This was the cause of a dreadful crime, for which Jason and Medea paid heavily. They arranged a meeting with Absyrtus, in order to make peace together; and when Absyrtus came to the meeting, Jason killed him with his sword. The Argonauts then set upon the Colchians, unexpectedly, and destroyed them.

After this, storms fell upon the heroes, and they would never have got home, but for the speaking stem which Athena had put in the bow of the ship. This stem uttered a voice and spoke and told them that Jason and Medea must be purified from the murder by the witch Circe, who lived in the far west in an island.

Then they passed into the Danube and rowed up the stream until, after a long time, they passed from the Danube into the Rhone, and from the Rhone into the Rhine, and from the Rhine into the Ocean Stream which encompasses the earth all around. Then they came into the quicksands and marshes of the African coast and into a lake from which they could not get out. Still they endured and carried the ship Argo on their shoulders over the sand, twelve days and twelve nights. When they came to the sea again, they still had dangers to meet, Scylla and Charybdis, and the Sirens, whom I cannot tell you about now, but at last they found Circe's island, and Circe purified them from the murder.

While Jason was away, Pelias had killed his old father, for he never expected Jason to return and never meant to keep his promise and make Jason king. Jason was very angry at this, as you may imagine, and asked Medea to punish the treachery of Pelias.

So Medea spoke to the daughters of Pelias in a friendly way. "What a pity it is," she said, "that your father is such an old man, and cannot enjoy his kingdom!" "Well," said they, "it cannot be helped, can it?" "Can it not!" said Medea. "I will show you." She got an old ram and cut it up and boiled it in a caldron with some of her magical drugs and sang charms about it, and lo and behold, out of the caldron skipped a young lamb!

So she persuaded them to kill old Pelias and boil him too. But no young Pelias came out of the caldron; he was dead and done for.

Then the son of Pelias banished Jason and Medea to Corinth.

But still trouble did not leave them. Medea had been maddened by Cupid's arrow, as you have heard, and Jason seems to have been infected by her madness. He was at first, as you know, a man of peace and gentle and just and not willing to shed blood if he could help it. He also had fine manners, as he showed by helping what seemed to be an ugly old crone. But he was now cruel and heartless too. He became tired of Medea and married another wife. Medea then destroyed the new wife by her magic and killed her own two sons and fled in an air chariot drawn by dragons to Athens. In Athens she married the old king, and we shall hear of her fate later, when we come to the story of Theseus.

PART FOUR

Chapter 25 THESEUS AND THE ROBBERS

There is another hero of many great deeds who was as famous as Hercules, and that is Theseus. He was the great hero of the Athenians, and he became their king; but first I must tell you of his young days.

Athens lies on the north side of a gulf of the sea which separates the two parts of Greece on the eastern side, as the Gulf of Corinth does on the western side; between these two gulfs is a neck of land joining the two parts of Greece, called the Isthmus of Corinth.

On the south side of this gulf, opposite Athens, is a strip of land close to the sea on which was a small city called Troezen; behind it rise the mountains, and behind the mountains is the plain of Argos, with its three mighty fortresses, which I have told of before. In the gulf of the sea between Athens and Troezen are many islands; the chief of these islands were famous in Greek history, namely, Aegina and Salamis.

Now the King of Athens, named Aegeus, happened to visit this little city of Troezen on his travels. He was anxious to have a son, and he had been to consult the oracle of the gods on that matter, when he came to Troezen, and the King of Troezen entertained him. But the King of Troezen had a beautiful daughter, named Aethra, and King Aegeus fell in love with her and married her secretly., for he was not quite safe on his throne. His brother had fifty sons, and he had none; so he feared their enmity. By and by he went back to Athens, but he left Aethra behind. When he left her, he said:

"My wife, if you bear a son, bring him up well and when he is old enough, send him to me at Athens."

She said, "How shall I know when he will be old enough?"

Then King Aegeus said, "See here," and he lifted up a great piece of rock, for he was a strong man, "see here: I lay under this rock my sword and my shoes which I wear on my feet. When the boy shall be strong enough to lift this rock, let him take my sword and my shoes and bring them to me, and I shall be able to know him by that sign."

Then he bade her farewell and went away. And then he forgot all about her.

In due time a boy was born, and they called his name Theseus. Aethra and her father brought him up and taught him to be strong and brave and wise; for her father was a wise man, so wise that some of his sayings used to be repeated by the Greeks in later ages. One was a very simple saying, but very sensible, and it showed that he was a just man when he might have been unjust. It was this:

> Give your servants all their pay;
> Keep your word, without delay.

Theseus became strong and healthy in body, and in particular he learned all the art of wrestling, which proved useful to him by and by. Both in wrestling and in all he did, he depended not on brute force, but on skill and intelligence. His mother did not tell him who his father was, but brought him up quietly in their little town.

Hercules himself once passed that way and paid them a visit. He walked up, clad in his lionskin, and at this sight everybody else ran away except Theseus. He thought it was a lion, walking on its hindlegs, but he was not afraid. Boy as he was, he picked up a thick stick and ran at the lion.

Then Hercules laughed and said, "Don't kill me, my good boy! I won't hurt you."

Theseus stopped in surprise and asked, "Then who are you?"

Hercules said, "Did you never hear my name? I am Hercules, and this is the skin of a lion which I once killed when I was not much older than you."

Theseus was delighted, and they made great friends. Hercules told him his own story, and Theseus made up his mind that he would do things like that when he should grow up, but he said nothing about it to the other.

Thus time went on until he became sixteen years of age. At that age it was proper to cut off his long hair and make it sacred to some god, as the boys used to do when they became men. Theseus cut off only the front part of his hair and dedicated it to Apollo, leaving the rest as it was. He must have let his hair grow again, for thus it is in all his pictures; but some warriors of that day used to keep the front of their heads shaven, so that their enemies might not be able to catch hold of it in battle. They shaved off their beards too, for the same reason: it would not be pleasant in the midst of battle, if someone caught you by the beard and pulled you down. They left the hair growing behind—why, do you think? Because they did not expect to run away.

And now Aethra thought she would tell Theseus who his father was, although she felt anxious because he seemed to have forgotten all about her, and never sent to inquire how she was doing, and whether he had a son or no. She took Theseus to the rock and said, "You are quite a man now, my son. Try if you can lift up that rock." Then she pointed out the rock, all overgrown in the moss and weeds.

Theseus tried, and he found it a very heavy rock. At first he could not move it, but at last he gave a great heave, and up it came.

"Why, what's this!" he cried. "A sword and a pair of shoes!"

"Your father's sword and shoes," said Aethra; and as he gazed at her in astonishment, she went on, "Your father is King of Athens, over on the other side of the sea. He left us here for good reasons of his own and told me that when you were strong enough to lift that rock, you were to put on the shoes and sling the sword over your shoulder and go to him at Athens."

"And what then?" said Theseus.

"I don't know what he means to do with you," she replied. "Perhaps you will be king too, but in any case, you must do what he tells you. I will get a ship and send you across."

"No, no," said Theseus, "no ship! What do the shoes mean? They mean I must walk; and the sword means I must fight my way."

"Oh," said Aethra, "don't do that, my boy! Thy road is full

of robbers and bloodthirsty men who are much too strong for you, my boy!"

But he cried out, "Robbers! Then I will kill them, like Hercules!"

This made Aethra very sad, and she did her best to persuade him not to go by land; but all in vain, and go he would.

So he thanked his mother and his good grandfather for their kindness and prepared for the journey. He put on a tunic of deep crimson and a leather bonnet and slung his father's sword over his left shoulder. With the shoes on his feet and a thick woolen mantle and a couple of lances in his left hand, he set out on the path which was to lead him through a long life of noble deeds, until he came to be honored like Hercules.

He took the road into the hills, and he had not gone far, before a huge giant rushed out at him, brandishing a thick club. Theseus, who knew all the tricks of boxing and wrestling, laid down his lances and let him come up; then he lightly stepped aside and caught the giant's right arm and twisted it, so that he let fall the club. In a trice Theseus picked up the club and brought it down on the giant's head, and that was the end of him. You see he had made a good beginning to his journey. He took the club along with him, in case it might be useful.

That night he slept in the woods, breathing the sweet smell of pine trees; and next morning he walked on to the Isthmus. But there on his road he saw another giant robber, named Sinis. They called him the Pine-bender, for he was so strong, that he could catch a pine tree by the top and bend it down to the ground. When strangers came that way, he used to say, "Please help me with this pine tree"; and as soon as the stranger had got his arms round the top of the tree, Sinis used to laugh, and let go, and the pine tree used to spring up and shoot off the man like a stone from a catapult. Or he would pull down two trees and would fasten the man one arm and one leg to each, and then let the trees go. This used to tear the man in half, so people said. Theseus no doubt had heard about Sinis; so when Sinis came up smiling and asked his help to bend down a tree, Theseus gave him a tap on the head with the club, which stunned him. Then he pulled down two pine trees and tied their tops down. He fastened Sinis between them and let the tops go, and so Sinis was treated as he used to treat strangers.

As Theseus went on, he met a savage wild sow which gave him some trouble, but he ran his lance through her and then finished her off with his sword.

All this happened on the level ground, but now the ground began to rise until the way became only a narrow path leading round a high cliff, halfway up the side. As he came round a bend, he saw in front of him a small piece of flat ground with grass growing upon it, and a spring of fresh water bubbling out; and in the middle was a huge man, looking wild and fierce, sitting upon a seat with a large basin full of water at his feet.

"Who are you, stranger?" said he.

"And who are you?" said Theseus.

"I am Sciron," said the other. "And now, who are you?"

Theseus said, "I am a traveler, on the way to Athens."

"Ha!" said the man, "I hope you may get there! But that depends upon me. No traveler may pass me, without paying toll."

"What is the toll?" said Theseus.

"To wash my feet," said the robber.

"What!" said Theseus, "I, a free man, to do the work of a slave!"

"If you do not," said Sciron, "look down the cliff, and see what will become of you."

Theseus looked down the cliff, and at the bottom what should he see but a huge tortoise, looking up at the cliff with gaping mouth; and well he might, for that was where his food came from. Sciron, you see, used to make travelers wash his feet, and if they would not, then he kicked them over the cliff. But if they did wash his feet, he kicked them down all the same, only he did not tell Theseus that. Theseus saw the huge tortoise, and he noticed a great quantity of bones lying about, so he could easily guess what happened. However, he pretended to be frightened, and turned back to the bowl.

"Very well," he said, "I suppose I must. But, sir, this water will never do to wash your noble feet. It is full of dirt, let me get you some more," and without waiting for an answer, he tilted up the bowl and let the water run out, and then he picked up the bowl and brought it down with a crash on Sciron's head. Sciron fell down half dazed, and Theseus kicked him over the cliff. As he looked down he could see the huge tortoise joyfully waddling up and gnawing the flesh off the robber's bones. But the tortoise did not know that he would never get another meal of that sort.

Theseus had earned a rest now, and that night he slept in the robber's own cave which he saw in the side of the rock. There was plenty of food there, and all he wanted.

Next day, he passed out of the dangerous path and walked over hill and dale until he came to another fertile spot. Here he found a fourth robber, who was not such a savage as the others. At least he gave the travelers a chance, for he used to challenge them to a wrestling match. You may imagine that this suited Theseus quite well. He hung up his sword on a tree, and he leaned his club and his lances against it; then he stripped for the bout. The robber had no art or skill in his wrestling, but Theseus knew all the tricks of the ring, as I have told you. The robber stepped up cautiously, spreading his arms wide to get a grip as far outside his enemy as he could; but Theseus quickly stepped in, with his hands close together. He got his left arm over the robber's neck, so that he held the robber's head tight under his left armpit, and with his right hand he got hold of the robber's body from underneath; then he gave a great heave, and threw him backward over his own head, the throw that wrestlers call the Flying Mare. The robber fell on his head and broke his neck.

Theseus was now near Athens, and only one more robber was left to deal with, who lived on the last hill before you come to Athens by the shore path. This robber was named Procrustes, the Hammerer. It was evening as Theseus drew near, and he saw Procrustes sitting at the door of his home. Procrustes called out:

"Welcome, stranger, may I offer you a bed for the night?"

"I thank you," said Theseus, "I should be very glad of a bed; it is evening, and I have had a long day."

"Well," said Procrustes, "come in, and take your choice."

That sounded an odd way of speaking, but Theseus came in, and there he saw two beds, one very long and one very short.

"I do not know, really," said Theseus. "The small one seems too short for me, but I should not like to deprive you of yours."

"Ha-ha!" said Procrustes, "you need not worry—I can make you fit either of them!" and roaring with laughter, he took up a saw in one hand, and a hammer in the other. "All I do is to put long men on the short bed and saw off the ends that stick out; and I put short men on the long bed and hammer out their legs till they fit!" He roared with laughter again.

But you understand that Theseus was not so simple as he seemed. He had been watching all this time, and now with a quick leap, he had hold of the robber's right hand and arm, which he twisted in his clever way, and made him drop the hammer. Then Theseus picked up the hammer and hammered out Procrustes on his own bed, until his life departed from him.

Chapter 26 THESEUS AND MEDEA

But rumor runs fast, and it came to Athens. The people were all summoned by sound of trumpet, and when they met in the market place, there was Aegeus, the King. The spokesman of the people lifted up his voice, and said:

"My lord, why did the trumpet call us together? Is there danger of war. Are bands of robbers lifting the cattle and sheep? Or what trouble is there?"

The King said, "A messenger has come from the Isthmus, who tells of prodigious deeds done by a mighty man. Sinis the Pine-bender is dead; the wild sow is dead, which killed men and laid waste the countryside; Sciron lies at the foot of his cliff; the wrestling school of Cercyon is shut up for good; Procrustes has been hammered on his own bed."

The spokesman said, "Who is the man, sir, who does these mighty deeds? For such things are not done without the help of the gods. Is he alone, or at the head of an army?"

The King said, "He has a couple of servants with him, so I am told; he wears a crimson tunic and a leather headpiece upon his nut-brown hair; he carries two lances and a club; a sword with ivory hilt is slung over his shoulder, and a woolen mantle covers all."

The people dispersed, and welcomed Theseus in crowds along the way; and the King made a banquet to do him honor. He had forgotten all about Aethra, and never knew who Theseus was; but his wife the queen was Medea, whom you have heard of already, a beautiful and terrible witch, and she knew him at once by her magical power.

But she bided her time; and by and by she said to the King, "Who is this young man?" He said, "I don't know, but he is a fine fellow." Medea said, "Yes indeed he is. He has destroyed all those robbers and the wild sow. Why not send him after the Bull of Marathon?" For at Marathon, not far from Athens, was the Cretan bull which, as you remember, Hercules had brought there from Crete; and this bull was doing a great deal of damage. Medea hoped that the bull would kill Theseus, and then her own son might be king when Aegeus died.

Aegeus agreed, and Theseus set off for Marathon, with a strong rope to bring back the bull. He made a noose in this rope, and laid a plan to tackle the bull; for, as you remember, he did his great deeds by cleverness, not by brute force. I do not know exactly how he managed it; but the picture which the Greeks made shows him lying under the bull, so I suppose he did something like what the Spanish bullfighters do. He took off his crimson tunic and carried it bundled up in one hand, holding the noose in the other. Then he walked quietly up to the bull, and as the bull stood pawing the ground and preparing to charge, he spread out the red cloth suddenly toward the left, fluttering in the air. This caught the bull's eye, for they hate red cloth, and as he moved his head toward the red cloth, Theseus threw it down, and dived under him on the near side, and got the noose over his hind legs; then he pulled the noose tight, and there was the bull, caught fast. Theseus brought the bull back to Athens, and it was killed at a solemn sacrifice.

Thus Medea's first plan was foiled; but she made a second plot, to poison Theseus. She kept on dropping hints and talking to Aegeus and pretending she feared that the young man might plot against the King. He was so popular in the city, she said, that he might lead the people to rebel against him. It would be impossible now to send him away, and the only thing was to poison him. Aegeus did not like this plan, but he was persuaded by his wicked wife, and at last he agreed.

So the next time they were dining together, Medea put poison in the wine cup and handed it to Theseus. But just as Theseus lifted the cup to his lips, Aegeus happened to notice the sword which was slung over his shoulder. He had never seen it so close before, and when he saw it, he knew it as his own. At once he dashed the cup from the lips of Theseus and cried out, "You are my son!" Then Theseus showed him the sword and the shoes, which Aegeus had never looked at before, and told him the whole story. Aegeus was very much ashamed that he had neglected his son so long, but he was much more glad that he had been saved from murdering him. He was very angry with Medea and banished her from the country, and Theseus was acknowledged as his true son and heir. Although Aegeus was still afraid of his brother and his brother's fifty sons, Theseus was safe enough, because all the people loved him and admired him.

Chapter 27 THESEUS AND THE MINOTAUR

But Theseus had not done with bulls; and his last fight was the most terrible of all. The bull of Marathon, you remember, had been brought from Crete by Hercules; and he left a son behind him in Crete, who was half bull and half man, named the Minotaur, which means the Bull of Minos, King of Crete. Minos made a pet of this bull, as he had done with the sire, and he had a wonderful house built for it. There was a very clever man living in Crete, named Daedalus, an architect and an inventor, who could make houses and statues and all sorts of machines such as people had then. In fact, they say his statues could even walk. Daedalus built a house for the Minotaur, which was called the Labyrinth. It was a maze full of winding passages, like the maze of Hampton Court, only more mazy still, and all of stone. The paths led to a cave in the middle, where the Minotaur slept. But most horrible of all, this monster was fed with the flesh of men who were turned into the Labyrinth. Once in, they soon lost their way and kept wandering about; but the Minotaur knew all the ways, and it gave him sport to hunt them until he caught them and killed them and ate them up.

Now Minos had had a quarrel with the city of Athens because his son had been killed there, perhaps by accident, perhaps not. This son had been victorious in the Athenian games and had gone afterward to tackle the bull of Marathon, which came from Crete as you remember, and the bull had killed him—at least, that was one story. But Minos made war on King Aegeus in consequence and forced him to pay a tribute every year, but not a tribute of money: he was forced to send to Minos every year seven young men and seven young maidens whom Minos turned into the Labyrinth for the Minotaur to eat. This was more bitter for Aegeus than all his other fears and anxieties.

The time was now come for the tribute to be paid; and lots were to be cast for the young men and maidens. Then Theseus spoke out boldly:

"Father, it is a shameful thing to send these boys and girls to be cruelly killed by a monster. Let me go with them, and I will kill the beast!"

All were astonished, Aegeus was dismayed, but Theseus stuck to it. Go he would! Never would he put up with this cruel tribute. And like a true leader of men, he would never command one of his subjects to do anything which he was not ready to do himself. So the lots were cast for the others, and they went down in a sad procession to the place where the ship lay that was to take them to Crete. Minos was on board the ship himself.

Now this ship bore a black sail, in token of mourning; and King Aegeus on parting gave Theseus a white sail, with the words, "My son, if the gods make you able to destroy the monster, put up this white sail on your return, that I may see it far away on the water and know that my son is safe." This Theseus promised to do.

The ship set sail. A fair breeze from the north blew it over the waters. On board were Theseus and the other victims, unarmed and helpless, for such was the will of Minos; and Minos himself looked at them, gloating with joy. He even put out his hand, and rudely stroked the cheeks of one of the maidens, who cried out, "Help me, Theseus!"

Then Theseus rolled his dark eyes in anger, and said, "Son of Zeus, that is not lawful. You have dropped the rudder of your mind. Hold back your violent hand! God's destiny rules all, and what he has decreed, the scales of justice shall weigh out for us.

That fate we shall fulfill, when it comes. Until then, hold your harsh purpose. If Zeus was your father, I am akin to Poseidon, and indeed I may call him father, and the nymphs of the sea gave my mother a golden veil at her wedding. Therefore control yourself, for I would not care to see the light of day if you should do violence to one of this company. Before that, we two will come to a trial of strength, and destiny shall decide between us."

The sailors were amazed to hear these bold words. Minos had no will to try his strength with the invincible wrestler; but he thought of a new plan, and cried out, "Zeus, my father, give me a sign with thy lightning! And you, if you are akin to Poseidon, the Earth-shaker, dive down to his abode and bring me back this ring that glistens on my hand! Now you shall see if the lord of thunder hears my prayer!"

At these words the lightning flashed; and Minos threw the ring into the sea and said, "Look now at the clear sign of Zeus! Into the sea with you, and Poseidon will give you fame over all the earth."

Theseus was not afraid; he stood up on the stern and dived down into the sea out of sight. The steersman would have brought up the ship to await him, but Minos would not allow it. He called out, "Keep her before the wind," in hope that if Theseus did come up again, he might be left behind to drown. Little did he know the counsels of the gods! So the ship sped on before the wind, and the young Athenians shuddered and wept at their coming fate and the loss of their champion.

But the champion was quite safe. As soon as he dived beneath the surface, a pair of dolphins caught him up, one under each arm, and carried him down and down through the water, clear as crystal, with a delicate tinge of green; among the shoals of fishes, which stared at them with great round eyes, through the seaweeds, to a coral cave, where the daughters of the sea used to dwell. Their radiant forms shone with splendor like fire through soft transparent robes, like silvery muslin, and golden bands were round their heads. They were all dancing gracefully in the coral cave.

There he saw the Queen of the Sea, Amphitrite, who threw about him a purple robe, and set a wreath of dark red roses upon his head. She said:

"Why have you come, my boy?"

Theseus answered, "To fetch the ring of King Minos, who has just thrown it into the sea."

The nymphs had ceased dancing when he came in; and now one of them glided up—they do not need to walk, they can glide up, or down, or all along, whenever they will, as swift as a tunny fish; and she held out the ring to Theseus, saying, "Here it is; I caught it as he threw."

They delayed him no longer. The dolphins took him back between them, far swifter than a ship, and brought him up on the ship's quarter [1] where he appeared to the amazement of the whole company and the secret wrath of Minos. And, most wonderful of all, when he emerged from the sea and stood once more on the deck to return his ring to Minos, Theseus was quite dry. See what wonders the gods can do!

Now they came to the Cretan haven; and now the great procession marched up from the haven to the city, with the fourteen young men and maidens in their midst, sad and mournful; but the city was full of rejoicing, for there was a feast to celebrate this tribute and this sacrifice to the terrible Minotaur. The whole road, three miles long, was thronged with people in gay clothes, shouting and waving their hands, as you can see today in the pictures they made themselves; and the women looked out of the upper windows of the houses, with bare necks and shoulders, after their country fashion, and with tight bodices and flounces on their skirts.

Among them was Ariadne, daughter of King Minos, who with her friends sat on an upper balcony of the King's palace. "Look," she said, "there are the victims. Poor things, how sad they look! But who is that marching at the head of them? He is not sad like the rest; he is proud and brave and holds up his head."

One of the ladies in waiting said, "Why, that's the young son of the King of Athens. And what do you think they say? He was not taken by lot; he came of his own free will and says he will fight with the monster."

"Brave boy!" said Ariadne. "It is a shame he should die." And she fell silent and let the others talk, for the instant she saw Theseus, love struck her heart, and she determined to help him.

But what could she do? If he killed the monster, he would

[1] *quarter:* one side or another off a ship's stern.

never get out of the Labyrinth; and would he kill him? How could he, without a weapon? You see, she did not know the story of Theseus, as you do, or how good he was at wrestling. At last she went to Daedalus, the architect of the Labyrinth, and asked him how she could help the young prince to find his way out of the Labyrinth. Daedalus was very much afraid to meddle, but he was an Athenian himself, and wished well to Theseus. At last he thought of something that could not easily be found out, and he said:

"Madam, all that I can do is this. Take this ball of thread and convey it to him. Tell him to tie one end to the post of the door and to unroll it as he goes. Then if he succeeds in killing the monster, he can roll it up as he comes out, and nobody will ever know how he managed."

Ariadne thanked Daedalus; and that night she sent her old nurse, with the ball of thread tied in a corner of her dress. Some say she sent also a sword, but I do not think she did that, although we often see it in the pictures of Theseus. It would be difficult for an old woman to hide a sword, and if she were searched she would be suspected of some mischief, but who would suspect a ball of thread?

The old woman managed somehow to see Theseus. She gave him the ball of thread and the message and added, "The Princess says that she loves you and prays you to take her away with you, if you win the fight." "That I will indeed," said Theseus, and they parted.

The procession of youths and maidens came to the Labyrinth. The gates were opened, and they were led in. Then the gates were shut. There they stood, helpless and hopeless, for they knew nothing of the ball of thread, and they did not really believe that Theseus would win. But Theseus said:

"Be of good cheer, my friends. God is with us! Did you not see me come out of the water? And now—this place is full of winding ways, and no one who gets in can ever find his way out; so you must stay here, and not stir one step from the gates. Leave the rest to me."

So saying, he drew out the ball of thread from his breast and tied one end of it to the doorpost; then he moved away into the dark paths, unrolling the thread as he went. The others were all attention, for here was something new which they did not understand, but it made them hope once more, for hope is always with us—Prometheus did well to put blind hope in our hearts, a more precious thing than knowledge.

So Theseus moved cautiously on, coming now to a blank wall, now to a place with many turnings; and although he tried to keep his direction toward the middle, as true as he could, yet before long he really did not know which way he was going. Well was the place called the maze; it was enough to maze anyone. But at last he came to an open space where he saw a black cave; and on the floor of the cave lay the monster like a strong giant with the head of a bull and bull's horns.

Up leaped the monster and let out a great roar and rushed at Theseus. What happened then I do not know, for I was not there, and no one was there to see; nor did Theseus tell tales about it afterward, for he was no boaster, as some of the heroes were. Some of his pictures show him holding a sword; but, as I said before, I do not think he had one, for all the captives were unarmed, and the old nurse brought him none. I am sure that he used all the art of wrestling and boxing which he knew so well, and that the gods put strength into his limbs, as they so often do when the weaker man defends the right. It was of no use for Theseus to strike at the bull's head or neck, as he would have done with a man; so he must have struck at the heart, or the mark, or used the wrestler's trippings and grapplings. In the end, the monster was killed.

But there was no time to rest. Theseus offered a prayer of thankfulness and once more picked up his ball of thread; then he went back by the way he had come, a long roundabout, winding up the thread as he went, for he wished to leave no trace to make Minos think that someone had helped him. And you may imagine the joy of his friends when they saw him return, bruised and covered with blood, but victorious over the horrible monster.

How they got out, I do not know. Perhaps the guards had left the door unlocked, because they never expected anyone to come out alive; perhaps (as I think) the old nurse was there, waiting, for you may be sure Ariadne was waiting somewhere. But get out they did. It was night. The city was asleep, and the prisoners crept down the long road to the harbor. Somewhere they met Ariadne, wrapped up so that no one could tell who she was. Quietly they climbed into their ship; quietly they hoisted the sail; and before anyone was awake in the morning, the ship was sailing away far over the seas.

I need not tell you of Ariadne's joy, or the love of Theseus for her kind heart. They were happy together, and when they came to a pleasant island next day, they landed there, and stayed there quite a long time. And they might have lived happily ever after; but it so happened that the goddess Artemis killed her, I do not know why, but Artemis was a hard and cruel goddess, and easily offended. They do say that the god Dionysus then raised her to heaven as his wife, and placed among the stars the crown he gave her at his marriage. Others say that Theseus deserted her, but there are always those who will say unkind things. I think myself he was a noble and true gentleman, and it does not seem like him to desert the girl who saved him. At least what happened next shows that he was very much hurt by her loss. His mind was so troubled that he forgot his promise to his old father—he forgot to put up the white sail to show that he was safe, and the ship came sailing home with the old black sail hoisted.

Every day King Aegeus would climb the Acropolis hill, which stands in the middle of Athens, and sit there watching the distant sea for his son's ship. He sat on that projecting rock which you can see in front of the great gate. There is a beautiful little temple built on it now, the temple of Wingless Victory, as if the people meant that Victory sat on their hill and could never fly away. There sat Aegeus; and there one morning he spied a sail. The sun shone upon it, and he could not tell for a long time what color the sail was; but as the ship drew nearer, he saw it was black. The old man's heart broke, and he fell down from the rock, and died. The sea is still called the Aegean Sea, after King Aegeus, and some believed that he threw himself into the sea; but the sea is some distance from this rocky hill, and I think I have told you the true story. So the people did not go down to the sea to meet the ship, for they thought all was lost: but when Theseus and the young men and maidens came out, and the news ran to their parents, then there was rejoicing and feasting. Only Theseus was sad, for his old father was dead.

Chapter 28

DAEDALUS AND ICARUS, AND THE END OF THESEUS

You wonder perhaps what was happening in Crete. Minos was in a great fury when he heard how his Minotaur was dead and the prisoners escaped. He inquired of everybody and found out about the ball of thread and how Daedalus had provided it; so he took Daedalus and his son Icarus and shut them up in the Labyrinth which Daedalus had made.

But Daedalus was too clever to be kept in the Labyrinth. And yet how was he to get out? The walls were high, the gates were locked and barred—nothing but a bird could get out. Very well: he determined to be a bird. He was always inventing things. He had invented the saw, among other things. He had noticed someone rubbing a snake's jaw, which is all jagged, against a piece of stick which he soon rubbed through; and the idea came to him that he might make a metal tool like the snake's jaw, with teeth, which cuts easily through wood, when it might take a long time to chop it with an ax. So there was nothing strange when he asked for his tools and his materials. Minos thought he might as well make something useful instead of wasting his time. It seemed likely to be something quite new, as he kept asking for wax and reeds and eagles' feathers.

What do you think Daedalus was making? Wings! He fitted the feathers in proper order along a frame, and fixed them with wax, just as you make the panspipes. Before long he had a fine large pair of wings ready to fit on his arms and shoulders, and a smaller pair for Icarus. He tried them and flapped about, and after a little practice, he found he could fly almost as well as a bird. Then he taught Icarus; but he warned him to be careful. "As we fly over the sea," he said, "do not fly too low, or you will be drenched by the spray, and the wings will be clogged; and do not fly too high, for if you go near the sun, he will melt you." Icarus promised everything; and then, boylike, he forgot all about it.

So one fine day, the people of Crete were astonished to see

two birds rise from the Labyrinth, huge creatures, bigger than any bird they had seen in their lives before. Then they looked harder and saw it was Daedalus and his son, flapping away for dear life. They told Minos the news, and great was his rage; but he could do nothing. Away they flew, farther and farther, until they were only dots in the sky; and at last they were seen no more.

Icarus was delighted. He flew steadily at first, but when they had got clear out of sight of the haven, he became excited and dived about like a real eagle. Down he went almost into the sea, up again higher into the air. "Take care, my boy," cried his father, again and again, but the boy took no notice. Higher and higher he went, until he came too close to the sun, and the sun melted the wax, and the feathers fell out of his wings, and he dropped into the sea like a stone. The part where he fell is still called the Icarian Sea.

Daedalus himself escaped to Sicily and thought he was safe. Minos sailed everywhere with ships of war to bring him back, if he could find him; but he did not say what he wanted. All he did was, wherever he came, to put a puzzle to those he met. He knew that Daedalus would try his wits on any puzzle he came across, and he did not think anyone else would solve his puzzle. This was the puzzle: he offered a shell, twisted round and round like a turret staircase, and said, "If anyone can pass a thread through this shell, I will give him a large reward."

He came at last to the city where Daedalus was, and the king of the place entertained him. In the course of talk, Minos said, "Here is a puzzle, my friend; can you thread this shell?" The king took it and turned it over and over, and looked wise. At last he said, "Well, if you leave it with me, I think I can manage it"—not that he really thought anything of the kind, but Daedalus was then hiding in his house, and he thought that if Daedalus could solve the puzzle, he might get the credit himself.

So Minos left the shell, and the king went straight off to Daedalus with it. Daedalus looked at it a minute, then he said, "Find me an ant." The ant was found, and Daedalus tied a fine thread round the ant, then he bored a hole in the top of the shell, and put the ant in at the bottom. The ant tried to escape, and ran straight up the shell, and round and round the curls of the spiral, and out at the top, pulling the thread behind him. Daedalus cut the thread, saying, "Good-by, ant, and many thanks," and let the ant go. Then he gave the shell back to the King, with a thread running right through it, and the King took it to Minos.

Then Minos said, "I know who did that! No one but Daedalus could have done it, and you have got him here! Hand over the man to me, or it shall be the worse for you." The king was afraid of Minos, and he promised to hand over Daedalus that night after dinner. But when Minos went to the bath before dinner, he was drowned in the bath. So Daedalus was safe, and I do not think you will feel very sorry for cruel King Minos.

There is still something left to tell of Theseus when he found himself King of Athens, after his old father's death. He had a hard fight to establish himself. His fifty cousins fought against him, and he was obliged to defend himself; but in the end he killed all the fifty and brought his enemies low. He joined Hercules in the war against the Amazons, and defeated the Amazons again in Athens itself, for they had invaded Athens and made their camp on the lower part of the Acropolis hill, a flat rock overlooking the market place, which is called Areopagus. In the New Testament it is called Mars' Hill, and it is the place where St. Paul preached a sermon once in Athens. There Theseus defeated this strange tribe of fighting women.

Theseus made a great friend of a man named Pirithoüs, and when Pirithoüs wanted to carry off Persephone from the lower world, Theseus helped him. You remember Persephone, daughter of Demeter, who was carried off by King Hades and made queen of the dark world below. Pirithoüs thought he would do her a good turn if he carried her off himself and made her his wife. But it was a great mistake for a mortal man to dare such a thing, and Pirithoüs paid dearly for it, as you will hear.

Theseus and Pirithoüs got down safely to Tartarus, but Hades outwitted them. He received them kindly and bade them be seated, but he made them seat themselves in the Chair of Forgetfulness, cut out of the rock. As they sat down, they forgot all the past; and the arms and sides of the chair grew round them, so that they became part of the rock. There sat Pirithoüs, and there he must sit forever; there also would Theseus have sat forever, but after a long time Hercules came down and brought him away. But Theseus left a bit of his legs sticking to the rock; and they say all the Athenians who were born afterward had the same bit of their legs wanting, but I have not noticed that in the Athenians I have seen.

When Theseus returned to Athens, he did great things for his city. It was only a small place, and the people lived all over the country in villages; but Theseus collected them together into the city of Athens, and fortified it and made it strong. Thus they could till their farms while there was peace, but when war came, they gathered together into the city to defend themselves. And he appears now and then in the Greek stories: a great king and lawgiver, a friend of those who were in trouble, and one who did good to mankind, like his friend and comrade Hercules. And there we will leave him.

Chapter 29 MELEAGER AND THE BRAND

You remember how Chiron bade farewell to Jason, and his wife stood by, holding the infant Achilles in her arms. I am now to tell you the story of the child's father, whose name was Peleus. He had many adventures before the boy was born, and one of them was in hunting the Calydonian Boar.

He was one of the Argonauts, who brought back the Golden Fleece, and with him was young Meleager, the son of a prince of Calydon in northwestern Greece. When Meleager came home, he found his father's kingdom in confusion. The king had forgotten to make due sacrifice to Artemis, who as you have heard, was a cruel and hard goddess. To punish the mistake, she sent upon Calydon a monstrous boar which breathed fire and destroyed all the crops and stock of the countryside. Meleager therefore collected a band of friends to encounter this boar; among them was Atalanta, a very manlike young woman. She was a great huntress and fighter. She actually took part in the quest of the Golden Fleece, and now she was eager to join in the new quest. Atalanta was the first to hit the boar with an arrow, then another shot him in the eye, but Meleager killed him with a blow in the side. Then he gave the skin to Atalanta, because he was in love with her. This enraged the others, who said the skin ought not to be given to a woman. A fight followed, and in the fight Meleager killed the brothers of Althaea, his mother.

Althaea saw the victorious band returning from the hunt with Atalanta and the spoils of the terrible boar. They went up to the temple to give thanks for their victory, but behind them came the dead bodies of those who had been slain. "Who are these?" cried Althaea; and when she heard who they were, "Who killed them?" Imagine her horror, when she was told that her own son had killed her brothers. Her love for her son turned to hatred, and she remembered a strange event which happened when the boy was a baby.

Seven days after his birth the Three Fates appeared and looked at the baby. Then one of the Fates said, in a solemn voice, "This child will live as long as that brand on the hearth shall burn. When it is burned up, the child will die." Althaea had instantly caught up the brand from the fire and put it out and laid it aside carefully in a chest where she had kept it ever since.

And now she made haste to the chest and unlocked it and took up the brand and cast it upon the fire. As it burned, Meleager in the temple felt as if fire were burning within him and fell down on the ground. Before long the brand was burned and Meleager was dead.

When this deed was done, Althaea came to her senses and bitterly repented, but that was of no use; she could not bring her son back to life, and in despair she made away with herself. The young man's sisters wept so much that even Artemis took pity on them; she touched them with a rod and turned them into guinea hens which cackle all day and all night in a melancholy way. It was no great kindness, you may think, but Artemis meant well, for those who worshiped Artemis took care never to eat guinea fowl. The sisters went on weeping, and some say their tears turned into drops of amber.

Chapter 30 ATALANTA

You may like to hear the rest of Atalanta's history before we go on. Her father had wanted a son, and when Atalanta was born, he said, "What's the use of a girl to me? Put her out on the mountains and let her die." So the servants put her out on the mountains. There a she-bear came along and took a fancy to the strange little thing and fed her with her own milk. By and by some hunters passed that way and found her and saved her and brought her up.

She became a hard woman, like her hard father, and like the hard life she was forced to lead. She cared for no hardship; she shrank from no toil; she feared no wild beast of the forest. Even when two terrible Centaurs attacked her, she cared nothing, but killed them both. When she grew up, she found out her father and came to live in his house. She made a great name for herself in running and wrestling and other manly sports; she even wrestled with Peleus and beat him. She must have been a handful to manage; so her father soon became tired of her, and did his best to find a husband who would relieve him of his troublesome daughter. At first she would not hear of a husband; but at last she agreed, on certain conditions.

The conditions were that if anyone wanted to marry her, he must run a race with her; if he lost the race, he was to lose his life. But she was so beautiful that many young men were willing to try, even on those terms; many did try and failed, and they were put to death.

One young man, named Milanion, a fine young fellow, laughed at this. "What fools you are," said he, "to run such a risk for a girl! Are there not plenty of girls in the country? You will not catch me risking my neck for one, no matter how beautiful she may be."

"That is all very well," said the young men, "but you have not seen her. Come with us to the next race, and then you may talk." "All right," he said, "I will come," and he went with them to see the race.

There they stood at the starting post: Atalanta, like Artemis herself, as beautiful and as hard; and the young man, full of strength and grace, and confident that he would win. Off they went: he was quick on his feet, but nothing to Atalanta who sped off like the wind and easily came in first. Then the young man was led off to his death.

But would you believe it, no sooner had Milanion set eyes on Atalanta, then he fell in love as deeply as the rest. He thought he had never seen anything so beautiful as Atalanta, and on the spot he declared that he would try his luck. Atalanta herself was sorry, as she saw this fine young man. "You are only a boy," she said, "and why should you throw your life away? Think how many lives have been wasted already!" For she had grown tired of this; indeed, she thought the condition would have kept men away, and all she wanted was to be left alone. But in fact, she fell a little in love with Milanion too, and she did her best to dissuade him. Why she did not accept him at once, if she liked him, I do not know; but perhaps she felt that it would make her look small before the world, and she did not really love him enough, as yet. So a day was fixed for the new race.

Milanion was not quite so cheerful when he got away. He did not feel so sure he would win; and now that he could not see her, he did not feel so sure she was worth it. But he felt he could not back out of the challenge. Then he prayed to the goddess Aphrodite to help him, and she heard his prayer, for she did not like this hard maiden who made light of the goddess of love. She had a wonderful tree in her grove which bore golden apples. Three of these apples she picked and gave them to Milanion and told him what to do.

The day came. There were crowds of people to see the race: the king was there, with his court; Atalanta was there, girt in a short tunic, like Artemis, and ready to run. Milanion came, with the golden apples tucked into a corner of his tunic. They made rather a bulge, but no one noticed it in all that excitement.

The two runners stood at the starting point: the signal was given—they were off. Atalanta did not run as swiftly as usual, for her own heart weakened a little to see this beautiful young man running for his life. For a little time, they ran neck and neck, but the ardor of the race took hold of Atalanta, and she shot ahead.

Then Milanion pulled out one of his apples and rolled it ahead of Atalanta. She caught sight of the bright thing and hesitated and stopped in her course to pick it up. Milanion passed her, and sped away at full speed. But Atalanta tucked her apple into her bosom, and off she went again; she soon passed Milanion and left him behind her. Now Milanion pulled out another apple and sent it rolling a little to one side. Once more Atalanta saw the apple and darted away from the course to pick it up; once more Milanion ran ahead, and this time he gained a good deal of ground.

But the pace was telling on Milanion. He began to pant, and his breath came dry from his throat; run as he would, he could not keep ahead, and now he took out his last apple. This time, he threw it as hard as he could, right away to one side, but so that Atalanta could see it. And as before, Atalanta darted in pursuit, and ran right out of the course until she was able to catch it, and tucked it way with the rest.

They were not yet at the end of the race, and Atalanta began to gain on Milanion; but Aphrodite was watching, unseen, and she made the apples grow heavier and heavier, until Atalanta felt as if she were carrying a weight of lead in her bosom. She went slower and slower, and Milanion kept ahead and won the race.

Then there were great rejoicings, and Atalanta was no less pleased than the rest, althouh she did not say much about it. So they were married, and they deserved to live happily ever after, but unluckily they did not. For they gave offense to Zeus, and he turned them into a pair of lions. Perhaps after all, Atalanta was more happy as a lioness than she would have been as a woman, but we do not know her side of the story, because she could no longer tell it.

Chapter 31 PELEUS AND THETIS

We return to Peleus, the father of the little boy whom Chiron's wife held in her arms.

Peleus was the son of Aeacus, Prince of Aegina, who was himself a son of Zeus. Aegina is a very important island in Greek history, and the heroes who were of the family of Aeacus played a great part. Aeacus himself was a just man, so that he was even asked to settle disputes among his kinsmen, the Immortals, and after death he became one of the Judges of the dead, in the dark house of Hades.

Once upon a time, when Peleus was hunting on Mount Pelion, a certain prince hid the sword of Peleus as he slept, and left him alone among the wild beasts. There he would have perished, for the Centaurs caught him; but old Chiron the Centaur saved his life, and afterward found his sword. For some time after that, he lived with Chiron and hunted the wild beasts.

There was a sea nymph, named Thetis, who was so beautiful that two of the great gods fell in love with her. One was Poseidon, lord of the sea, who knew all the Nereids that lived in the coral caves under the waters; but he had never seen the equal of Thetis, and he wanted to make her his wife. The other god was Zeus himself. No doubt he had heard Poseidon talking about this young beauty and went to have a look at her himself.

At all events, the brothers fell out about it; and as they could not agree, they asked the advice of the wise Themis, the goddess of justice and law. She said at once, "Before I give my opinion, I ought to tell you one thing: her son will be stronger than his father. I should advise you to let her marry a mortal man, and that will be better for both of you."

The gods were persuaded at once. "No stronger sons for me," said Zeus, "that is my view, whatever you may think of it, brother Poseidon." "I agree with that," said Poseidon. "Well, who shall be her husband?" Zeus answered, "She shall have a good one, and I know a man who has lately distinguished himself by honorable conduct, one Peleus, who is living at present with old Chiron in his cave."

Then a message was sent to Peleus, telling him that Zeus was ready to give him a beautiful nymph of the sea, on condition that he must catch her first. Chiron told him about it. He said, "Like the other creatures of the sea, she can change her shape. If you want her for a wife, you must catch her and hold her fast."

Peleus felt sure he would win. Perhaps he had learned something from his wrestling match with Atalanta; but at least he knew now that the gods were on his side. So he went down to the seashore with Chiron; and there was Thetis, waiting for him;

there were the nymphs of the sea, all looking on; and there were the gods, as pleased as possible to see a new kind of wrestling match.

Peleus caught hold of the two wrists of Thetis, and held fast. Thetis changed first into a tree, and he held fast to the two branches he found in his hands; that was easy enough. Next, she became an eagle, and he held her two wings. And then suddenly he found himself holding the strong paws of a tiger. Still he would not let go; and now he was holding a great lion. I suppose Thetis was losing her patience, for the next thing she did was to change into wind. I do not know how he held the wind, but he did; and so he did when she changed into fire which scorched him, and then water which put out the fire. His hands were still clenched when he saw that he held two of the long arms of a giant squid. But that was a mistake on the part of Thetis, for he held these arms so tight that she could not change any more, and so she became at last Thetis.

Now Thetis knew that she was beaten, so she put a good face on the matter and agreed to be married to Peleus. And it was indeed a magnificent wedding which was remembered all through Greek history. There was a grand feast; there were visitors from far and near; and to cap all, there was a half circle of noble thrones, and the gods themselves seated upon them to share in the feasts, while the Muses sang and played on the flute and harp, and the Seasons danced in the midst. The Fates also sang, the Spinner, the Portioner, and Never-turn-back. They sang:

Fortunate pair! Your child shall be a boy
Who shall lay low the enemy hosts at Troy.
No other man shall be so brave and strong.
Run on, my spindles, pull the thread along!

Chiron gave Peleus a great ashen spear, which we often hear of in the stories about him; Poseidon gave him two immortal horses, named Chestnut and Bay, and the other gods gave him weapons and armor.

Peleus had now got his wish and a divine wife, but he found out, as many men have done, that it is better to marry one of your own rank in life. Thetis bore a son, Achilles, and she loved him very much, but she wanted to make him immortal, like herself. She dipped him in the awful river of Styx to make his body safe against wounds; but she had to hold him by the heel and ankle, and so his heel was left unprotected, and it was a wound in the heel that killed him in the end. Not content with a water bath, she used fire too. Every night she used to lay him in the fire, as Demeter did to another baby, if you remember. This was done to burn away all of him that was mortal, and in the day she used to anoint him with the gods' own ambrosia which made them immortal. But one night Peleus caught her at it, and when he saw the child writhing amid the flames, he cried out. Then Thetis caught up the child and threw him down on the ground and fled away shrieking to the sea. Into the sea she plunged and returned to her father Nereus and the sea nymphs her sisters, and came back no more. Peleus lived sad and deserted in his palace halls.

But he took the child Achilles, and gave him over to Chiron to train him up. Chiron fed him on the marrow of lions to make him brave and strong, and on the marrow of stags to make him swift of foot. He became so swift that he could catch any animal by running after it, and he was always called by everyone Swift-foot Achilles. When he grew older, Chiron made him a little sword and a little spear and a little shield and little bow and arrows, and sent him out to catch what he could. So he practiced the arts of war on mice and moles, which he was to practice later in real battle. There we will leave him to grow up, while we turn to other things that were happening in the world.

Chapter 32 APOLLO AND ADMETUS

You remember how Zeus once had to prevent a rebellion among the gods, and how Apollo and Poseidon were punished by doing a year's hard labor on earth. Zeus had to punish Apollo again for another offense; and this time he had to be a man's servant again for a year. So he came down into Thessaly.

Admetus was King of Pherae in Thessaly, and when he was engaging his servants for the year, he saw a noble young man waiting to offer himself. "Who are you?" he asked. "You are a stranger to me." "Yes, sir," said Apollo, for he it was. "I am a good hand with sheep and cattle, and I will serve you well." So he was engaged; and so well he did his work that in the spring all the cows had twin calves and all the ewes had twin lambs and all the nanny goats had twin kids, safe and sound. Admetus was very much pleased with his man and made much of him.

Sometimes the young herdsman used to bring out a strange instrument, made of a tortoise shell with strings fixed across it; he used to touch the strings with his fingers, and bring out beautiful music that made them all want to dance. But sometimes the King met him early in the morning and saw wreaths of flowers about his head; he would stand still to gaze at the rising sun, and seemed not to see Admetus at all. But strangest of all, when sacrifice was made to the gods, the stranger was never there.

Admetus was a great horseman, for the Thessalians loved horses; and once he went to the games at the court of King Pelias, whom you remember in the story of Jason. He won all his contests, but he lost his heart; for his eyes fell on Alcestis, the daughter of Pelias, and he fell in love with her at once. When he asked Pelias for his daughter, everyone thought it would be a fine match for her with the rich Thessalian king; but Pelias, who was a proud man, smiled grimly and said, "It is no light honor to wed a maiden who has divine blood in her veins. One who woos her must drive up to my door in a chariot drawn by a lion and a boar. If not, it is fated that she must die on her wedding day."

Admetus, also a proud man, said at once, "Fear nothing for that; you shall see the sight you ask for, without fail." But in his mind he did not think he could do it; so with all his prizes, he returned home downcast and gloomy.

As he walked in the evening and thought what a fool he had been to make such a promise, he saw his young herdsman, and greeted him. Apollo said, "You seem to be unhappy, sir; what is it?" "I have been a fool," said Admetus. "I asked Pelias for his daughter, and he told me that I must come to fetch her, driving a lion and a wild boar." Apollo said, "I think I can help you, if you will let me go away for a few days." Admetus was glad to consent, for what else could he do? So he returned to his palace, and Apollo took his bow and arrows and set off for the mountains.

The days were long while Admetus waited; but at last came

a morning, when he opened his eyes to see the young herdsman standing by his bed, and he heard him call out, "Awake, King Admetus! Your team is ready." Then he arose and came down to the door, and there stood an ivory chariot with a lion and a boar under the yoke. "Farewell," said Apollo, "but be sure to return this evening, for at sunset the beasts will be wild again." Admetus leaped lightly into the chariot and caught up the reins and away.

How the people stared to see this new team go by! And when he came to the city of Pelias, what commotion there was in the streets, what amazement to hear the padding of the lion's paws and the clatter of the boar's hoofs, and their growls as they ran through the streets! To the palace of Pelias they came and drew up at the door. "Welcome!" said Pelias—"here is your bride! And you, my daughter, thank the man who has taken away your curse, and made you able to be a happy wife and mother. But you, sir, pray deign to stay this night with us, and let us hold a feast to do you honor."

"No," said Admetus, remembering what Apollo had told him; "I cannot delay. I must be gone at once." So he led Alcestis to the chariot, and they both mounted, and away drove Admetus with his bride. When they came to the sacred grove close by his own city, there stood the young herdsman. The beasts at once came to a stop, and would not move; so the pair dismounted and left the team with him and made the rest of their way on foot.

There was great joy when they arrived, although everyone was surprised to see them walking. Sacrifices were made to the gods, and all made ready for the wedding. But in the excitement, Artemis was forgotten; there was no sacrifice for her, and the hard goddess never failed to punish that slight. So when Admetus opened the door of his bridal chamber, he saw a heap of snakes writhing on the floor. He understood this to be a sign of the anger of some deity.

Admetus again asked the help of Apollo; and Apollo succeeded in making Artemis friendly again. I do not know how he did it, but Artemis was his sister, and no doubt she knew that Apollo could do her many a good turn if he liked. She forgave Admetus, at all events; and Apollo persuaded the Fates to grant him a special favor: that when his time came to die, his life might be saved if someone else would die for him.

Soon after that Apollo's year was up, and he returned to Olympus.

Time went on. Alcestis bore two children; Admetus was happy; his kingdom was prosperous—but a day came when he fell ill, and he knew that he was to die. He turned his face to the wall and said nothing, for he did not wish to ask another to die for him.

Everyone knew what the Fates had promised, but no one came forward to offer his life for the King. Of course they all talked about it, and everyone thought that everyone else ought to die, but no one was anxious to be the man. "Why does not his old father die?" they said. "He has had his life; there is not much left for him anyhow." But the old man did not see it like that. "I am sorry for my son," he said. "Poor fellow! To die so young, and so happy. But I am quite happy too; life is sweet. Why should one give it up before the gods call him? Let every man bear his own fate." Even the old queen thought much the same. They were sorry for their son, but sorrier for themselves: and Admetus prepared to die.

But Alcestis said nothing at all. She came in the evening and lay down by her husband's side; and in her heart she said, "I will die for my husband." So she went quietly to sleep, and in the morning she lay there dead.

Admetus awoke to find himself as strong and well as ever he was. He could not understand why, until he looked on his wife's face and saw that she was dead. Then he understood that she had given her life for him. But life was too dear at such a price. He knew that his happiness was over, but there was no help for it; and Alcestis was prepared for burial and carried out to the tomb.

Just at this moment, who should come up but Hercules. Admetus was bound by the laws of hospitality to entertain a guest; so Hercules was led apart from the signs of mourning, and the servants provided him with all he needed. After his dinner, he asked where Admetus was. Some excuse was made, but at last he began to suspect something. "Why do you look so gloomy, man?" he said. And by degrees the story came out.

Then Hercules was angry. "He should not have let me feast," said he, "with mourning in the house, and especially with his own wife dead. But it was a noble hospitality, after all! Perhaps I can do something to repay it." Then a thought came into his mind. "Where is the tomb?" he asked. "Let me go and pay my respects to the Queen." They showed him, and he entered the tomb.

He was there a long time, and there were sounds of a struggle, which disturbed the servants, but they did not like to go in. For King Hades himself was within that place, and Hercules wrestled with King Hades until he consented to let Alcestis come back to life. So Hercules raised up Alcestis from her bier and led her, veiled, to the palace; and there, to the amazement of the world, he gave back Alcestis to her husband, safe and sound.

Chapter 33 HELIOS AND PHAËTHON

When Apollo used to gaze at the sun, at the time he was herdsman to Admetus, I think he was making a plan already to take it over himself; for you know he was an ambitious young god. But so far the sun was in the charge of Helios, one of the old Titans, and a nephew of Cronus. Zeus left him alone, because he did his job all right and never wanted to rebel.

But Helios had a boy of his own, a young fellow named Phaëthon, or "the Shiner"; and Phaëthon was as ambitious as Apollo.

He often watched his father driving the horses of the sun. So easily he did it, that Phaëthon thought he could do the same. But he did not dare to say so plainly; he made a roundabout plan to get what he wanted.

So one evening, when Helios sat down to rest, Phaëthon said to him, "Father, am I really your son? You are so magnificent that I feel very small beside you."

Helios answered, "Indeed you are my son; and to prove it, I will grant you anything you may choose to ask."

Phaëthon said, "I thank you, my father! and I will prove that I am your son indeed! Let me drive your horses for one day!"

Then Helios struck his forehead with his hand; he saw what a fool he had been to make such a promise. But the promise was made, and even the gods cannot recall their gifts. He said, at last:

"Ah, that was a rash promise. That is the only thing I would deny you, my boy. You are mortal, and no mortal can do that task. Indeed, even Zeus himself could not do it; he can manage a thunderbolt, but he cannot drive the horses of the sun. Let me persuade you to choose something else. Think now, while I tell you how difficult is the task. The first part of the way is a steep ascent, and the horses find it all they can do to climb up. Then you are in high heaven, and to look down on the sea and the earth makes even me dizzy. And last there is a steep way downward which needs all my strength and skill to hold the horses back. Every evening the goddess of the sea trembles with fear that I may fall headlong and make the waters boil. And think of the dangers of the way! All the while, the heavens are whirling around at a great rate, and you may easily dash the chariot against the North or South Pole. And there are strange monsters on all sides: a wild Bull, thrusting his horns at you; an Archer, shooting his arrows; a Scorpion, with a sharp sting; and a Crab, sweeping his great claws all around. And the horses are breathing out flame from their mouths and nostrils the whole time."

But Phaëthon would not listen; indeed, all this made him more eager to try.

So next morning, when Eos opened the gates of the dawn, and all the stars were driven away, and the moon faded, Helios led Phaëthon to his car and commanded the Seasons to put his horses to the yoke. Phaëthon gazed in wonder at the car: its wheels were of gold, with silver spokes, and jewels flashed from the fittings. Still more did he wonder at the horses, as they pranced out breathing fire. Helios with a sad heart anointed his son's face with sacred ointment, to protect him from the fire, and placed on his head his own crown with its golden spikes. Then he said:

"Be careful, my son, and spare the lash. Look for the tracks of my wheels; for the course is not straight through the heavens, but it goes slantwise, in a wide curve which keeps clear of both North Pole and South Pole alike. Now take the reins, unless you will be well advised at the last moment, and choose another gift."

"No, my father," said Phaëthon, "I fear nothing; I will show that I am your son!" And he mounted the car, and took the reins.

The four horses, Fiery, Shiny, Scorcher, and Blazer, snorted and champed; and at once they felt the light weight of the boy, and his unskillful hands. They took the bit between their teeth and leaped up, tossing the chariot about, and dashed straight up the sky. They did not keep to the proper path, but went straight for the Bear, who had never been so hot before in his life. Phaëthon looked down and his head swam; he looked back, but that way he could not go; he looked forward to the west, and how far off that seemed! He saw the Crab, waving his claws, and he saw the Scorpion with the great sting in his tail—a panic seized him, and he dropped the reins. When the horses felt the reins on their backs, they just ran away.

Then the earth began to feel it: the forests caught fire, Athos was in a blaze; Caucasus and Ida melted their snows; and all the people of Africa were burned black, as they have been ever since. Phaëthon choked with the flames about him. But Zeus had pity on the world. He sent a thunderbolt and struck Phaëthon; down fell the chariot into the sea; and down fell Phaëthon into the river Eridanus. The horses went at top speed to the west, and there they were rubbed down, and put in the golden boat to carry them back to the east.

Phaëthon's sisters wept and lamented his death; they wept and would not be comforted, as they stood by their brother's tomb. Indeed, they stood there weeping so long that gradually they felt themselves growing into the soil. Bark grew up around them, from the feet upward, and they became poplar trees. But their tears continued to flow, and as they flowed, the tears became drops of amber.

Helios was full of sorrow, and said, "I have had enough of this task; anyone may drive the horses of the sun for me. Let me rest." But Zeus would not allow it. He provided a new chariot, and commanded Helios to drive as before, and so he did, until at a later time, Apollo turned him out and took over the sun himself.

PART FIVE

Chapter 34 ORPHEUS AND EURYDICE

Orpheus was one of the heroes who went in quest of the Golden Fleece. I did not tell you then all the things he did, because there were so many other things to tell; but I will tell you some now. To the sound of his harp, the ship Argo glided down into the sea. The sound of his harp made the Clashing Rocks stand still just one minute, when the Argo was passing through. The sound of his harp helped to send the sleepless dragon to sleep.

You see he was a rare hand with the harp; and no wonder, for his father was Apollo, and Apollo taught him to play upon his own harp. He played so beautifully that all the wild beasts on Mount Olympus used to come and lie down all around him, to listen. More than that, even the trees would pluck up their roots, if they were not too old and too deep, and hop along to listen. Even the rocks rolled out of their places and came to listen. All the country people were enchanted; the wild Satyrs used to dance around him, wagging their tails.

He married a wife named Eurydice, whom he loved very much. One day Eurydice trod on a snake, which bit her foot, and she died.

Orpheus would not be comforted. He played on his harp no more; he wandered over the mountains, and through the forests, and mourned his lost wife. At last he determined that he would go down to the dark house of Hades, and bring her back.

So he entered the dark cave, and traversed the dark tunnel which led through the earth, to the dark house of Hades. When he came to the gate, the three-headed dog Cerberus growled and would have bitten him; but Orpheus played a soft tune on his harp, and the dog dropped his three heads on his paws and gently wagged his tail and let Orpheus go by.

When he came to the great hall of Hades, what a sight met his eyes! There sat King Hades and Queen Persephone, on their thrones. There sat the three Judges of the Dead: Minos, Rhadamanthus and Aeacus—for there is justice in the house of Hades. Every soul, when it comes into that place, must give account for deeds done in the body: those who are good are dismissed to the Elysian Fields, to be at peace; those who are bad receive punishment proper to their deeds.

There Orpheus saw some of the great sinners enduring their punishment. He saw a family of nine-and-forty sisters, the Danaïdes, who had all been married on one day, and had murdered their husbands in the night. They were condemned to draw water and carry it in jars to a huge vessel with holes in the bottom, so as fast as they poured the water in, it ran out.

He saw the punishment of the cruel King Tantalus. In his life on earth, Tantalus once entertained the gods at a feast. Like the wicked King of Arcadia, he wanted to see if they really had more wisdom than men. So he killed his own son Pelops and cooked the body and offered it to the gods to eat. They all knew it at once and refused, except Demeter, who ate a bit of the shoulder, because she had just lost her daughter and did not know what she was doing. Pelops was brought back to life and made well again, all but the bit of his shoulder, which was missing; but Demeter put an ivory shoulder in its place. This Tantalus was punished by being hungry and thirsty forever. He stood in the middle of a lake of water: when he bent down his head to drink, the water all slid away; if he scooped up a handful, the water ran through his fingers. All round the water grew trees laden with fruit: apples and pears, figs and grapes, and oranges; when he stretched out his hand to pluck one, the tree whisked it away into the air above him. Did your father ever call you a tantalizing brat? If so, he was reminding you of Tantalus, who was always disappointed when he hoped for something good.

He saw Sisyphus, the most cunning and deceitful of men, who had betrayed the secrets of the gods. His punishment was to roll a huge stone up to the top of a hill. He pushed with head and shoulders, panting and sweating and covered with dust; but whenever he got to the top, the stone would gently slide off on one side or the other, and roll down to the bottom. Then he had to begin all over again.

He saw Ixion, who also had committed an act of treachery to the gods. His punishment was the strangest of all. He was fastened to a wheel with four spokes, one for each leg and arm, and the wheel went round and round forever.

That was the scene which met the eye of Orpheus, as he entered the dark house of Hades. The soul of Eurydice was there waiting, for her case had not yet been heard; there were so many waiting for judgment. But Orpheus pleaded with Hades, that he might take her back to life.

Hades said, "Why should I treat her otherwise than I treat the other souls?"

Orpheus was silent; then his eyes flashed, and he said, in a loud voice, "This is why!" and struck up a tune on his harp. The melody began soft, then rose and rang loudly through the dark hall: and as the melody sounded, Hades leaned forward on his throne and listened; Persephone turned her head and sat still and listened; the three judges ceased their questions and listened; the Danaïdes stood still and listened and let the water do what it would—the water ceased to run out of the holes; Tantalus' lake stood still and Tantalus had a good drink, then he listened too; the stone of Sisyphus rolled up to Orpheus and lay still; Ixion's wheel stood still and Ixion with it, to listen to the wonderful sounds. At last Hades said: "Your music is worth a life. Take her and go, but be very careful never to look back at her till you come to your own door."

Orpheus was glad enough to have her on any conditions; so he turned round, and went towards the gate, still playing upon his harp, and Eurydice followed him. Out of the gate he went, still playing, past the three-headed Cerberus, along the dark tunnel, out of the dark cave, and then he thought to himself, "I wonder if Eurydice is following," for he could not hear her footsteps. Without thinking, he turned to look: there she was, close behind—but even as he looked, she uttered a cry; she began to fade; and in a few moments, like a wisp of smoke, she had vanished.

Now there was no hope for Orpheus. But he seems to have learned the wisdom of the gods by his journey to the house of Hades; for he no longer played on his harp, but he made wonderful poems, telling mankind what to do if they wished to please the gods and to be happy after death. Some say he also taught them to eat only vegetables and not to kill animals for food. Perhaps he remembered how sensible the animals were in listening to his music; but that can hardly be the reason, for the trees listened too, and no doubt the vegetables would have listened if they had been handy.

But Orpheus would not marry another wife. There were a number of wild women in Thrace, where he lived, and they used to hold feasts in honor of Dionysus every year and madden themselves with wine. Some say they were angry because Orpheus would not take one of them to wife. Whatever the reason may be, these women set on him and killed him and cut off his head and threw it into the river Hebrus. The river carried it into the sea, and it floated across to the island of Lesbos, by the town of Methymna, where it was washed ashore. And ever since that time, right down to our own day, the nightingales in the olive trees round Methymna sing more sweetly than any other nightingales in the world.

Chapter 35

DANAË AND THE SHOWER OF GOLD

You remember the Danaïdes in the dark house of Hades who had to fill up a huge vessel with holes in the bottom. Their father was Danaüs, who had fifty daughters, but his brother Aegyptus (or Egypt) had fifty sons. Danaüs was afraid that the fifty sons were going to kill him. He agreed that they should be married to his fifty daughters, and then he gave each of the daughters a dagger and told them to kill their husbands as soon as they fell asleep. Forty-nine of them did so, but the fiftieth did not, and I think I may tell you her name, as I have spared you the names of the other nine-and-forty. It was Hypermnestra. She did not kill her husband, and after many years we come now to the story of her grandsons, Acrisius and his brother Proetus.

That is a long rigmarole, to be sure, but we have come to the point at last.

Acrisius and his twin brother Proetus were always fighting together, as brothers often do; and when they grew up, Acrisius drove his brother out, and remained King of Argos by himself. But an oracle foretold that he was to be killed by his grandson, if there should be one. He had a daughter Danaë, and he determined to make sure that she should never have a son: so he built a strong tower of brass, and shut her up in the tower, along with her waiting women, and allowed no one else to go in.

This was a cruel fate, and Danaë was very unhappy; but what could she do? She could see from her tower all the people going about their business, and enjoying their life: feasts and processions, weddings and dances, and there she was, left all alone and bored to death. No one dared to come in, and the attendants and guards were too much afraid of the King to allow anyone to visit her.

But Zeus, who sees all things, saw Danaë in her tower; and as she was beautiful, Zeus fell in love with her and resolved to make her his wife. It was easy enough for him, but he did not march up to the door and demand admittance; he made another plan, quite a new one.

So it happened that one day, as Danaë sat melancholy in her chamber at the top of the tower, she saw the air become thick with a kind of mist. Soon the mist grew into soft flakes of gold, like a golden snow, and fell all over the room. Then the flakes gathered up into a solid shape; and she saw standing before her what she thought was a noble young man, and his body was covered with bright clothing that shone like gold.

"Who are you?" said Danaë, astonished.

"Do not fear me," said he, "for I have heard of your sad fate, and I have come to comfort you, if you will be my lover."

Danaë was delighted to have so noble a lover, when she expected none at all, not even an ugly one. So after that, Zeus would often come and visit her in a shower of golden snowflakes, unknown to all, and after his visit, he would melt into golden snowflakes again, and pass away on the wind.

Acrisius knew nothing of all this; and what was his amazement, one day, when a messenger came panting before him, and said:

"Sir, your daughter has borne a son!"

"What!" said he, "did I not forbid you to let anyone go in?"

"Sir," he answered, "we have let no one go in; we know nothing about it! Do not blame us; we have done our duty, I swear it."

Then Acrisius was angry and frightened at once. Whatever the cause, there was his grandson, and the oracle said he was to kill Acrisius one day. Acrisius did not like to murder his daughter and the baby outright; but he quieted his conscience by saying they should have a chance. So he put both of them into a large chest, or hutch, and fastened the cover on it, with holes to let in the air; and then he set them adrift on the sea.

The winds blew, and the waves rose, and the foam drenched the mother and her son, as they lay in the chest. The tears ran down her cheeks, and she threw her arms about the boy and said, "Ah, my baby, what sorrow is yours! And yet you weep not. You sleep quiet like a suckling babe in this dark chest; you care not for the salt foam on your hair, nor for the whistling wind, as you lie in your purple wrappings, with your soft cheek against mine. If you knew your danger, you would open your little ear to my words. Sleep on, my babe, and may the sea sleep, and may Zeus your father send us help!"

Chapter 36

PERSEUS AND THE GORGON MEDUSA

Zeus heard the mother's prayer; the chest was washed up on the shore of a little island named Seriphos. A man of the island came along and saw the chest, which was richly carved, and he thought it a great find. But when he prized off the lid, what was his surprise to see Danaë and the baby inside! He was a kind man, and took them in, and they lived in his house while the boy grew up.

The boy's name was Perseus; and he grew up to be strong and brave and handsome, and won prizes in the athletic games of the island. So he was noticed by the King, Polydectes; and before long the King caught sight of his mother, Danaë, and determined to make her his wife.

But Danaë would not hear of it: she, the wife of the immortal Zeus, to give herself to the petty chief of a small island! The King persecuted her, but he was afraid of Perseus; and he soon saw that Perseus must be got out of the way.

Accordingly, he pretended to flatter him on his success in the games. "You are a fine boy," he said, "you can beat every one in this island at running and boxing and wrestling. In fact, you are wasted in a small place like this. You ought to try some great task, and make a name in the world, like the real heroes." You see, he did not know that Perseus was a real hero, as being a son of Zeus; Danaë kept that secret to herself.

"What do you mean, sir?" asked Perseus. "Just tell me something worth trying for!"

"I will," said the King. "Go and bring me Medusa's head."

Perseus asked, "Who is Medusa?"

The King said, "There are three awful sisters, the three Gorgons, named the Strong, the Leaper, and the Queen, that is Medusa. Strong and Leaper are ugly things, but the Gorgon Medusa is the most beautiful creature in the world. I want her head; never mind why."

"Where can they be found?" asked Perseus.

The King said, "Far away in the west, in the land of darkness. You must find you own way, for I do not know any more about it."

This fired the ambition of Perseus, and he determined to fetch Medusa's head.

The gods knew all this, of course; and as Perseus was thinking what to do, suddenly Athena appeared to him, and said:

"Perseus, do you know me?"

"Indeed I do!" said Perseus. "You are the great goddess Athena."

"Well," said Athena, "we gods are going to help you. First

of all look at this," and she showed him the image of a head: the face was very beautiful, but cruel and cold and unhappy, and instead of hair, it had curling ringlets of snakes all round. "That is the Gorgon Medusa," she said, "but if you look at the real face, you will be turned into stone."

"Then how can I get the head?" said Perseus.

"Take this shield," and she gave him a shield, smooth and shining, like a mirror, "and when you come to Medusa, keep your back to her, and see her image in the shield, so as to strike back over your shoulder. Then cut off her head, and put it in this bag," and she gave him a large bag of leather. "Be careful to leave her sisters alone, for they are immortal; Medusa alone is mortal, and she can be killed."

"But how shall I find the way?" he asked.

"Wait a minute," said Athena, and then all of a sudden, there were Hermes and Hades, who appeared out of nothing, as the gods can do. But Hermes said, "See here, I lend you my winged shoes; put them on your feet, and you will fly through the air like a bird. And here is a sharp sickle to cut off Medusa's head." Then Hades said, "And I lend you my cap of darkness; when you have it on, you will be invisible, and no one will see you."

"And now," said Athena, "you must fly away to the west, until you come to the Three Old Hags, who alone know the way to the Gorgons. They have only one eye between them and one tooth, which they lend about as they want them. Their names are the Buzzer, the Terror, and the Fury, and they keep watch over their sisters, the Gorgons. They live in the west, beyond the sun and moon, and you will have to persuade them to tell you the way."

This did not sound hopeful, but there was no more to be done as the three gods had all disappeared.

So Perseus slung the shield and the sickle about his shoulders and hung the bag over his back and put on the cap of darkness and fastened the winged shoes to his feet; then he rose in the air.

On and on he flew, over land and sea, over mountain and forest, beyond the sun and the moon into the dark regions of the west. No doubt the winged shoes guided him, for he came straight to the place where the Three Old Hags had their dwelling.

Terror said, "I hear a noise in the air. What is it?"

Fury said, "Give me the tooth, and let me bite it!" So the tooth was passed to Fury, but she could see nothing because the eye was in the socket of Buzzer.

Terror said, "Sister, what can you see?"

Buzzer said, "I can see nothing at all, but I hear a shivering in the air"; for the cap of darkness made Perseus invisible.

"Pass me the eye!" said Fury, "you are as blind as a bat!" She put the eye into her own socket, but saw nothing. Then Terror said, "Pass it here, will you!"

But as Fury took out the eye and held it toward her sister, Perseus neatly swooped in between them and caught it. "Now then," said Fury, "can *you* see anything?" for she thought Terror had taken it, and of course the eye could see nothing as it passed between them, with no socket to sit in.

"Give me the eye!" said Terror.

"I have given it!" said Fury, "and I felt you take it!"

"I did not!" said Terror.

"Here," said Fury, "take the tooth, and give her a nip," but as she held out the tooth, Perseus swooped down quickly and caught it. Then there was a frightful quarrel, as each Old Hag thought the others were playing a trick on her. In the midst of it, Perseus called out:

"Fear nothing, mighty beings, the eye and the tooth are safe: I hold them in my hand."

There was a sudden silence. Then they all cried out at once, "Who is that?"

He replied, "I am Perseus, and I come to ask you the way to the place where the Gorgons are."

"We will not tell you!" they all cried out.

"Then I will not give you back the eye and the tooth. Good-by," and he made as if to go.

"Wait, wait, wait!" they cried. They did their best to persuade Perseus to give back the eye and the tooth, but he was firm, and in the end, they had to tell him the way to go. Then he flew off, saying, "When I come back, you shall have your eye and your tooth safe and sound."

Thus the Three Old Hags could not defend their sisters, the Gorgons, and Perseus came to the place where they were.

He found the Gorgons asleep. Two of them had golden

wings and bronze claws and enormous teeth, and they would have made short work of Perseus if they had caught him. But he was careful to be quiet; and approaching Medusa backward, he looked at her image in the bright shield and struck a blow behind him and killed her. Then he cut off the head and put it into his bag. Drops of blood fell from the neck: and from them sprang up Pegasus, the winged horse, who flew away to the stables of Zeus. The two sisters awoke and tried to catch Perseus in their claws; but he was too quick for them. He flew back to the Three Old Hags, and gave them the eye in turn and let them have a look at him when he took off his cap. He gave back the tooth too, but he took care to give it just as he was about to fly away, and he gave it to one who had not the eye at that moment.

Chapter 37 PERSEUS AND ANDROMEDA

The journey back was more of a roundabout. No doubt Perseus thought he would never have a better chance of seeing the world. He seems to have flown over Africa and Asia, and he even visited the people who live behind the North Wind. These were a very happy people who had a kind of earthly paradise, almost as good as the Islands of the Blessed, where all the great heroes went, and lived forever at peace.

As he passed over Africa, he saw a huge figure with its head in the clouds, and when he looked close, it was old Atlas the Titan, holding up the heavens upon his shoulder.

Old Atlas hailed him and said, "Stranger, you must be the hero Perseus, who according to the oracle will set me free. Show me the Gorgon's head!" He was weary of holding up the heavens, and he thought with pleasure of the short holiday he had when Hercules paid him a visit.

Perseus took the head out of his bag and held it out toward Atlas, but he was careful to turn his own head away. Then he put it back in the bag; and when he looked at Atlas, he saw that his body had changed into a great rock, his hair and beard into forests. So Atlas rested at last from his long labor. If you look on the map, there you will see the Atlas Mountains still, and they hold up the heavens quite as well as the old Titan did.

As Perseus came nearer home, on a bright sunny day, he looked down: and there on the coast of Palestine, near the port of Joppa, which you have read of in the Bible, he saw a long procession of people moving toward the sea. They were leading a beautiful maiden, and soon they bound her fast with chains to a rock and went away weeping and wailing loud.

This maiden was named Andromeda, and she was daughter to the King of that place. Her mother was a vain and foolish woman, and she had boasted that her daughter was more beautiful than all the nymphs of the sea. Accordingly the god of the sea, Poseidon, the father of these nymphs, was very angry, and he flooded the coast and sent a sea monster to devour anyone he could catch. At last, after many prayers, he consented to spare the people, if the King would give his daughter for the sea monster to devour; and that was why they left her chained to a rock, and went away.

Perseus did not know this. He only saw the maiden chained to a rock, and an ugly monster swimming in from the sea. The maiden gazed at the monster with staring eyes, full of horror; the monster lashed the sea with his tail, and his green sides shone in the sunlight with scales of hard horn; his mouth opened and showed a red throat and sharp rows of teeth. Neither of them looked up, to see a new kind of bird swoop down from the sky. Down came Perseus like an eagle, holding the sickle of Hermes which had cut off the Gorgon's head. He attacked the monster from behind, and gave him a deep cut on the neck. Then there was a terrible fight, but the monster could not reach Perseus, and Perseus flew in and out like an eagle, cutting under the monster's scales, until at last he cut its throat, and the body fell back lifeless upon the sea.

You may imagine how glad Andromeda was, and how Perseus loosed her chains and led her back to her father, and how glad her father was, and how willingly he consented when Perseus asked him that Andromeda might be his wife. Had he not well earned the prize?

There was only one difficulty: that the King had promised her to someone else. This was a man named Phineus, who came up in a rage and said, "Where is my bride?"

Perseus said, "Where were you when the sea monster was going to devour your bride?"

Phineus said, "I could not help her; why should I be swallowed too?"

Perseus said, "If you did not care enough for your bride to strike a blow for her life, you have no claim now."

Phineus said, "We will see about that. Here, you men!" and he called to his bodyguard, who stood under arms, with threatening looks. But Perseus did not wait for more. He took out the Gorgon's head from his bag, and showed it to them: and there they stood, turned into stone.

Then there was a grand wedding and high rejoicings. But Perseus had to leave his bride there for the time being because he must go back to Seriphos, and hand over the Gorgon's head to Polydectes. So he flew to Seriphos.

When he came to Seriphos, he put off his winged shoes and walked to the town. But he could not find his mother. The fact was, King Polydectes had persecuted her, and told her she must be his wife, whether she liked it or not. He knew only that Perseus had gone, but he did not know how, and he felt sure he would never come back. Then Perseus found his mother in the temple, where she had fled for refuge, and with her the kind man who had brought him up, who was the King's brother.

When Danaë saw Perseus, she cried, "Oh my son! You have come back, and I thought you were dead!"

"What are you doing here?" he asked.

She said, "The King was so violent and threatening that I have fled to this temple for refuge. But I am afraid even here, for he says he will come and fetch me out. And there he is!"

Indeed, there he was, with his bodyguard of soldiers, come to drag Danaë from the temple.

"Come out!" he cried. "My patience is at an end—but who is this? Never [1] Perseus, returned from his journey? Welcome, dear boy!" for he began to be afraid now.

Then Perseus said, "Do not call me dear boy, when you want to lay violent hands on my mother."

[1] *never:* not.

"Nonsense," he answered; "but tell me about your journey. Did you get the Gorgon's head?"

"Oh yes," said Perseus, "would you like to see it?"

"Indeed I should," said the King.

Then Perseus whispered to his mother, "Turn your head away," and as she turned away, he drew out the Gorgon's head from the bag, and turned it towards Polydectes.

As Polydectes looked at it, a shiver ran through him, and in a moment he was a statue of stone with the smile still on his false lips. His men also turned into stone, as many as looked upon the Gorgon's head, but those who were behind turned and ran out of the temple.

Perseus put the head back, and led his mother to her home. The kind man who had helped them became King, and all was well.

The three deities appeared once more to Perseus. Athena said, "I see you have got the head of Medusa and come back safe. I am very glad to see it, and now you must return to us what we lent you."

Perseus thanked them all for their help. Then he gave the bag and the shield to Athena, and the cap to Hades, and to Hermes the sickle and winged shoes; but the head of Medusa he gave to Athena, and Athena fixed it upon her shield. Ever after she bore the shield with the Gorgon's head; and if she showed it to her enemies, they turned into stone.

Perseus sent for his bride, and they lived a happy life. I need not tell you all that happened to him, but I have one thing more to tell.

There used to be games in the island of Seriphos, as you know; and once Acrisius came to attend them. Perseus had to throw a quoit in the games, and it went a little to one side where Acrisius was craning his head forward to look on. The quoit caught his head and killed him; and so the prophecy was fulfilled, which had made him so cruel to Danaë. This was quite an accident, for Perseus had been very kind to Acrisius; he even restored him to the throne when an enemy had turned him out.

Chapter 38 PEGASUS AND BELLEROPHON

You have heard how Pegasus, the winged horse, sprang up from the drops of blood that fell from the neck of Medusa. But why should a horse spring up from Medusa's blood? Because Medusa was the daughter of Phorcys, the old god of the sea, brother of old Mother Earth. When Zeus and his family came into power, the ancient deities were put out of power. The sea was taken by Poseidon, but old Phorcys lived there still, in the depths.

Now the sea is full of horses, as I told you before. If you look over the sea when there is a fresh breeze, you will behold the horses of the sea, with their white manes, leaping to the top of the waves, and sinking again. Poseidon gave the horse to mankind; and so this winged horse, Pegasus, sprang up from the blood of Medusa, daughter of old Phorcys.

He was a beauty, the noblest horse man ever saw, a glossy bay color, and besides his four legs, he had wings on the shoulders. When he was made, he shook off the water from his wings and mane and neighed loudly and flew up to the house of Olympus. There Zeus kept him in the immortal stables; and he used to fly to earth and get the thunderbolts from the Cyclopes and bring them to Zeus when he wanted a new stock.

Once when he came to earth, he stamped on the rock with one foot, and a fountain of clear water gushed out, which ever afterward flowed in plenty. This was on the rock of Corinth, and the fountain was called after him the Horse's Fountain, or Hippocrene.

I will leave Pegasus awhile in the immortal stables of Zeus, and you will soon see why I have told you about him. For I have now to tell you the story of another hero, named Bellerophon. Do you remember Sisyphus, who had to roll the stone up the hill in the dark house of Hades? Bellerophon was his grandson.

Bellerophon was an unlucky man. He happened by accident to kill another man; and therefore he was obliged to run away from Corinth, where his father was king, and take refuge in another country. He found refuge with a king named Proetus. This king had also been unlucky; for he was the brother of Acrisius, whom you remember in the story of Danaë, the brother that he was always fighting with. Acrisius turned him out, and he took refuge with King Iobates in Lycia. He married the daughter of Iobates, and Iobates helped him to make head [1] against Acrisius, so that at last he had a kingdom of his own close by. Acrisius was King of Argos, and Proetus King of Tiryns. You have heard all these names before, so they ought not to puzzle you very much.

As I said, the unlucky Bellerophon took refuge with the unlucky Proetus, who had become lucky again, and Bellerophon hoped that he might become lucky too; and so he was, for a good long time, and he became a great man at last.

But now his bad luck had a turn. For the King's wife was a bad wife; and when she saw Bellerophon every day, doing brave deeds, and as handsome as a god, she fell in love with him. Worse than that, she did not keep it to herself, but prayed Bellerophon to betray her husband, and to carry her off somewhere away from him. Bellerophon was ashamed to hear such a proposal and would have nothing to do with it. Then the wife did the worst thing of all: for she complained to her husband that Bellerophon had insulted her. In fact, she told her husband that Bellerophon had done the very thing she had done herself, and wrongfully accused an innocent man.

Proetus believed his wife. It is hard for a man to think that his wife is a liar and a traitor, and it was natural that Proetus should take the word of his wife as true. But he was afraid to do anything openly against Bellerophon, because all the people admired him; and he made a cunning plan to destroy him. He wrote a letter to Iobates.

You remember how Cadmus taught the alphabet to the Greeks; he brought it from Asia with him, and Iobates, who lived in Asia, knew it too. No doubt he had taught Proetus his ABC when he lived in his court; and Proetus wrote a letter in these strange signs which nobody knew but himself, to Iobates, and this was the letter: "Kill the bearer of this as soon as you can." Then he folded up the tablets, on which the message was written, and gave the letter to Bellerophon as an introduction to King Iobates. "For," he said, "I have something I wish you to do, and Iobates will tell you about it when you get there." Then Beller-

[1] *make head:* to advance.

ophon took his leave and departed and the Queen looked on, gloating over her coming revenge.

Bellerophon arrived safely at the court of King Iobates, and the King received him with rich hospitality, as was the way of men in those days.

But as Bellerophon entered the hall of feasting, he had a great shock. For among those who stood round the King, he saw the wicked Queen, the wife of Proetus.

Or at least so he thought. The Queen was a most beautiful woman, and this woman was exactly like her, in figure, in coloring, and hair; but when he examined closer, she had a very different look on her face. The Queen was bold, she was modest; the Queen was hard, she was gentle: in fact, she looked as good as she was beautiful. In a moment, Bellerophon fell in love with the beautiful girl, and she with him.

"This," the King said, "is my daughter"—and so the two really were sisters, and that was why they were so much alike.

After the feasting was over, the King asked his errand. Bellerophon said, "Sir, King Proetus has sent a letter by me, written in strange signs which he said you would understand," and he presented the tablets which he had brought. The King took them, and put them aside until he had time to puzzle them out, for he did not read as easily as you or I do. I daresay he had never had a letter before.

When in the evening he did read the letter, he was horrified to find that all it said was, "Kill the bearer of this as soon as you can." If you are surprised that Proetus could ask such a thing without any reason, you must know that once Proetus had saved the life of Iobates; and then Iobates had promised, under oath, that he would do whatever Proetus might ask, if he were ever in need. So he was in perplexity: either he must break his oath, which was a terrible crime, or he must kill a man without any reason, and perhaps an innocent man. It was like the oath of Herod, which he kept by cutting off the head of John the Baptist. Of course you know that it was wrong to make such an oath, and therefore it was right not to keep it; but this king did not understand that.

But what was he to do? At last a way occurred to him, by which he thought he might keep his oath, and yet not hurt his conscience. You must wait a minute before I tell you what this way was.

For a long time past, the country had been ravaged by a hideous monster called the Chimaera. The word means "goat," but we have borrowed it in English in the form "chimera," to signify a tale of nonsense. But this was no tale of nonsense to the people whose cattle and sheep were carried off or killed by its fiery breath and their crops set in a blaze by a puff from its mouth. They said it was a huge monster, with a lion's head and a goat's body and a long snake instead of a tail. It left a horrible stench behind it, and all the land was laid waste, and the people ruined, or even killed.

Now then, the King thought that if he sent Bellerophon to destroy this monster, he would be sure to be killed, and thus he might keep his oath without wrong, for it was a worthy enterprise to attack a monster like that, such a thing as Hercules and Theseus were glad to do.

Accordingly, next day he said to Bellerophon, "King Proetus tells me how brave a warrior you are, and how you have fought for him. Will you do something for me?"

"Yes, if I can," said Bellerophon.

Then King Iobates told him about the Chimaera and what havoc had been made in the countryside; and Bellerophon was sorry for the country people, and so he said without really thinking about it, "I will destroy this monster."

"And if you do," said Iobates, "I will give you my daughter to wife, if you wish it."

Imagine whether Bellerophon wished it! That was the one thing he did wish; and it made him all the more eager to destroy the monster.

Bellerophon went about the country to ask what the monster was like. He saw burned houses and burned crops and dead bodies lying about, and at last he found a countryman, crawling along and looking more dead than alive. He said:

"My good man, can you tell me about this monster?"

"Ah, sir," he said, "it is an awful tale! There was a meeting; all the neighbors came in to a wedding and they sang and danced and made merry. I was working on the farm not far off. Suddenly I heard a harsh sound in the air, like a corn crake,[1] but very loud

[1] *corn crake* (kôrn krāk): a bird.

like a dry rattle, very loud, and the sky looked a sort of green color, full of smoky mist. They were all singing happily when I heard a shriek and saw a great ugly shape come down among them. They scattered this way and that, all shrieking now, until in a short time all was silent. I hid until it seemed to have gone away, and then I escaped."

"What was it like?" asked Bellerophon.

"Well," said the man, "I can hardly tell, I was so frightened. But it looked as big as a mountain! like a lion too, and a snake whipping about it, but I was too much frightened to see clear."

This was the monster he had to fight. He did not know what to do, so he prayed to the gods for help.

That night he had a dream. A figure appeared to him, and said, "You must return to Corinth, and bring back the winged horse Pegasus. For Pegasus often comes down from heaven to drink of the sweet water of the Horse's Fountain, which he made by a blow of his foot."

Bellerophon took this to be an answer to his prayer, as indeed it was; so he prepared to set out. He had to go in disguise, for you remember he was a banished man; and he went alone, that no one might guess who he was.

In due time he arrived in Corinth, and for many nights he watched at the Horse's Fountain and saw nothing. But at last he saw the winged horse sailing through the sky and shining in the moonlight. Down it came to the fountain, and drank. In a moment Bellerophon's hand was upon it, clutching at the mane; but the horse Pegasus shook him off with a flap of his wings, and soared away into the sky.

Indeed, it was foolish to think that he could catch an immortal horse as easily as all that. Bellerophon saw that it was foolish, and very sad he was, as he lay down to sleep in Athena's temple, with his head upon the altar steps.

But in the middle of the night, he was awakened to see a great light in the temple; the light shone from the figure of the goddess Athena herself, who stood before him in full armor, holding something in her hand. She said, smiling, "Are you asleep, Bellerophon? So you could not catch Pegasus?"

"No, my Queen," he said, "it was foolish to expect it."

"But not foolish if I help you," she said. "See here: this is a charm for horses, a golden master for mouth and mind. Take it, and when you have succeeded, give thanks to the Lord of the Allmastering Sea, your father's father."

What she gave him was a twisted bar of gold, with two long streamers running from each end and a curved golden ribbon rounded over the top. He could not make it out. He had never seen anything like it before, but he resolved to try what it could do; and as Athena said it was to be a master for mind and mouth, he decided to put it into the mouth of Pegasus.

The next night, Pegasus came again, and Bellerophon walked up to him quietly, this time, and patted him gently and stroked him and talked to him as men do to their horses. Then suddenly he popped the golden bar into his mouth, and he saw to his surprise that the round part fitted over the head, behind the ears. For as you have guessed already, no doubt, it was a bit and bridle. This was Athena's own invention; for there was none on earth before: men used to pull the horse's mane this way and that, and hope he would go too, or at best they tied a rope round his neck. But they never thought of his mouth.

Pegasus did not seem to mind this new thing in his mouth, but he chewed it contentedly; and suddenly Bellerophon vaulted upon his back, holding the two streamers in his hand. The horse was perfectly quiet. When Bellerophon dug his knees into his flanks, Pegasus spread his wings and flew up into the sky; and the rider found that he could make him go any way he liked by pulling the rein in that direction. And so, before long, he was soaring over the sea, and before long he was landing in Lycia. He put the horse in a convenient stable and went to report himself to the King.

Now the King had missed him, for he had not told the King of his dream; and even now he did not tell him about Pegasus, but he only said that he meant to set out soon, and hoped to destroy the monster. The King hardly knew whether he wanted him to succeed, or not.

Then Bellerophon mounted the winged horse, and the horse whinnied with pleasure and pranced about, and at a touch of knees and rein, he rose up into the air. Bellerophon guided him over the wasted country until he saw a dark shape below him which appeared to be gnawing some mangled creature upon the ground. Down he swooped, and it was the monster! Then the monster left his prey and looked up: his lion's head croaked and rattled, his snaky tail hissed and spat poison, and he rose up to receive his foe.

Bellerophon felt very sick at the smell of the monster and the green smoke that came from its mouth, but he circled round and round until he got a chance—then swooped down and pierced its side with his spear. The monster leaped, Pegasus swerved, and green blood ran from the monster's side. Again and again Bellerophon pierced it with his spear; its struggles grew less, and at last it lay still upon the ground, dead. And as it lay there, the body gradually smoldered away, until there was nothing left but a heap of grey ashes.

What rejoicings there were when the news went abroad that the Chimaera was dead! What honors were paid to Bellerophon when he returned! I need not tell you all his later adventures. There were others, for Iobates still tried to compass his death; but in the end, he was obliged to desist. He gave his daughter to Bellerophon, and now you might think the man's bad luck was ended. But no! A man's bad luck is generally in himself, one way or another; and Bellerophon, after these triumphs, thought himself equal to the gods.

So he mounted on Pegasus once more and rode him straight up to Olympus. When Pegasus once more saw the divine stables which he loved, he neighed loudly and threw off Bellerophon from his back. Down fell Bellerophon to the earth! Even a fall like that could not always kill a hero, and it did not kill Bellerophon; but it maimed him and made him a wretched man. For the rest of his life, he wandered about and kept far from mankind. So pride goeth before a fall, as Solomon said; and presumptuous pride was the one thing the Greek gods could not abide.

Chapter 39 IAMUS

Hercules and Theseus were heroes who helped to explore the world and to clear it of monsters, like those of our own day who have shown how to destroy the little insects which cause yellow fever and malaria.

But I am now to tell you of a hero who left his mark in a different way. There were many like him, for you remember that the souls of the heroes who died in the early ages watched over mankind and helped good men or punished bad men. My hero today is Iamus.

Iamus was doubly a hero; for his mother's father was Poseidon, and his own father was Apollo. His mother, Euadne, had long dark hair, like the purple of a pansy. She was brought up in the glens of Arcadia, and there she was seen and loved by Apollo, and bore him a son.

She laid the baby down in a thicket; and when the servants found him, he lay in a bed of pansies, purple and golden, and the sunlight shone upon them so that the light itself seemed to be purple and golden. They found two large serpents, with bright eyes, which the gods had sent to feed him; and the serpents fed him with drops of honey from a honeycomb. The voice of Apollo declared, "This child shall be a great prophet, notable above all mankind, and his family shall never fail."

When he grew up, he went down at dead of night into the river Alpheus, which flowed through Arcadia by his home, and called aloud upon Poseidon his grandfather and Apollo his father, and said, "Grant me a people to rule in the world." And his father spoke and said, "Arise, my boy, and follow the sound of my voice." They went along the river, down to a plain through which it flowed to the sea, the place where in future days the city of Olympia was to stand. There Apollo said, "I give you a double treasure of prophecy. At this time, you shall hear the voice which cannot lie; and later, when Hercules shall come here to found the great games of Olympia, he will establish an oracle of Zeus; and your family shall be always priests of the oracle." And so it befell. Iamus' clan became great and happy, and held their holy place at Olympia, declaring the true mind of Zeus to men.

Chapter 40 THE GOLDEN APPLE OF DISCORD

You remember how long ago I told you of Peleus and Thetis, and how Peleus held her fast while she changed into all sorts of shapes. There was a grand wedding feast, you remember, and among the guests were the sea nymphs and the gods themselves; but something happened at that feast which I did not tell you. When the invitations were sent, one of the nymphs was left out, and with good reason; for she was Eris, the lady of Discord, as her name denotes, and they did not want discord and quarrels at the wedding feast. But Discord had something to say to that, as you will hear.

Next day two of the sea-nymphs were talking about it. Their names were Allspy and Calm.

ALLSPY. My dear, did you see what Eris did yesterday at the feast in Thessaly, because she was not invited?

CALM. No, I was not there; I had to keep the sea calm, you know.

ALLSPY. Peleus and Thetis had just retired, when Eris crept in unseen and sent an apple rolling along the floor, a lovely apple, my dear, all of gold! And it had a sentence graven upon it: *For the pretty one!* It rolled where three goddesses were sitting, Hera and Athena and Aphrodite. Hera picked up the apple and read the words, *For the pretty one!* "That's mine!" said Hera. "No, mine!" said Athena. "No, no, mine, of course!" said Aphrodite. And there was a pretty quarrel! They wanted Zeus to decide, but he said, "No, thank you; whichever I give it to, the others will plague my life out. Take it to young Paris of Troy; he is a good judge of beauty."

CALM. And what then?

ALLSPY. Then the three goddesses went as fast as they could to Troy. I wish I knew what was happening there!

Meanwhile Zeus gave the apple to Hermes and told him to conduct the goddesses to Mount Ida, where Paris kept his flocks. But first he made the three of them promise to play fair and to be content with the sentence of the judge. So away they flew. On the way, Aphrodite whispered to Hermes:

APHRODITE. Is he married?

HERMES. Not quite, but he has a sort of wife with him. What made you ask?

APHRODITE. Oh, nothing.

ATHENA. That's not fair; you are whispering to Hermes.

HERMES. She only asked if Paris were married.

ATHENA. What's the reason?

HERMES. Oh, nothing, she says.

ATHENA (to HERMES). I wonder if he is ambitious, and wants to be a great warrior.

APHRODITE. Who's whispering now? I do not complain, you see.

HERMES. There is Mount Ida, and there's the man.

HERA. Where? I can't see anything.

HERMES. There, look along my finger. Do you see those little cows?

HERA. Yes, I see now; I thank you, if that's the man.

HERMES. Yes, that is the man. Let us go down here, and walk up to him, or he will be frightened.—Good day, young man.

PARIS. Good day to you, sir. Who are these gentlewomen?

HERMES. They are not women, my dear Paris, but Hera and Athena and Aphrodite. They want you to decide who shall have this apple.

PARIS. Let me see it. *For the pretty one.* How on earth can a mortal like me decide between goddesses? They are all splendid. When I look at one, I think she is the best, and then if I look at another, I think she is the best.

HERMES. Well, you must do it, for it is the command of Zeus.

PARIS. Well, pray them not to be angry with me.

HERMES. They have all promised that.

PARIS. Very well, I will do my best; no one can do more. Pray let me see them one at a time, for they dazzle me all together.

HERMES. Quite right. Go away, you two, and let Hera stay.

HERA. Now, young man, look at my grandeur; and let me tell you, if you vote for me, you shall be king of Asia.

PARIS. No bribes for me. Please retire, for I have seen enough now. Athena next, please.

ATHENA. Here I am. If you vote for me, you shall be a great warrior, always victorious.

PARIS. I want no wars and fighting. Peace is what I want.

But you shall be none the worse, even if I do not accept your gift. Aphrodite now, please.

APHRODITE. She is here. I see you are young and handsome, too good to waste in this wilderness. You ought to have a beautiful wife, like Helen.

PARIS. Who is Helen?

APHRODITE. A daughter of Zeus himself, and all the noblest young men in the world wooed her, but she chose Menelaus, King of Sparta. Vote for me, and you shall have Helen.

PARIS. What! When she has a husband already!

APHRODITE. You are simple, indeed. You do not know how these things are managed. All you have to do is to pay them a visit; leave the rest to me.

PARIS. I am in love with Helen already! I want to be off.

APHRODITE. Wait, no hurry; let me do my part first.

PARIS. And if I give you the apple, you will forget all about me.

APHRODITE. No, I promise you; I will swear an oath if you like.

PARIS. Your promise is enough for me. Here is the apple.

So the other two had to make the best of it. And all fell out, as Aphrodite had said. Paris paid a visit to Sparta; Helen fell in love with him at once, for she had been maddened by Aphrodite; and Helen left her husband, and followed Paris to Troy.

Then King Menelaus of Sparta and King Agamemnon, his brother, made a league of all the cities in Greece; and a great fleet sailed to Troy, and a great army laid siege to it. For ten years the siege lasted, and then Troy was taken and burned and razed to the ground. There lay the ruins for three thousand years, until quite a short time ago an explorer dug them up, and now you can see for yourself the marks of the fire upon the old stones. And how many thousands of men lost their lives, and how much misery was caused by the golden apple of Discord! Some of the stories of this great siege you shall hear before long.

Chapter 41 THE ARMS OF ACHILLES

But now we are coming into the history of men, rather than gods. By this time, the gods are well established, and manage the world regularly enough; but the stories are more about men, and the gods come in occasionally.

The apple of Discord, as I told you, was the cause of a dreadful war; and one of the great men in this war was Achilles, whom you remember as a baby in the arms of Chiron's wife. Achilles was a magnificent warrior and a generous man, but he had his faults, like the rest of us. One of them was a fierce pride which would not put up with the smallest slight, if he thought it touched his honor. And King Agamemnon had insulted him. We cannot go into the whole story now; but the upshot was that Achilles retired to his tent and said, "Very well, you may fight your battles yourself. I did not come here to be insulted, and I hope you will be well beaten."

You see they had both lost their temper. I do not make any excuse for either of them; I am just telling the story.

When Achilles the champion would not fight, the Trojans took heart, and really did beat off the Greeks; indeed, they got as far as the Greek ships by the shore, and set a number of them on fire. Achilles was deeply distressed at this, for he did not really want the Trojans to win. But he would not make friends again and say that he had gone too far. "I said I would not fight," he told them, "and I will not fight. But I will lend my armor to my friend Patroclus, and when the Trojans see it, they will think he is Achilles, and run away."

So Patroclus put on the armor of Achilles. Then there was a great fight; but in the end Patroclus was himself killed by Hector of Troy, and Hector carried off the armor of Achilles.

This was too much for Achilles. He loved Patroclus more than he hated Agamemnon, so he determined to avenge him. But where was his armor? In the enemy's hands. He poured dust on his head and cried aloud: and his mother heard it in the depths of the sea; Thetis his mother, the sea nymph. She cried to her friends around her, the other nymphs of the sea, "I hear my son's voice, and I know he will die! Did I not tell him that he would die, if he came to this cruel war? Be happy at home, I said, and live long; for if you go to the war, your life shall be glorious, but your days shall be few. And he chose glory and few days! I will go and see what troubles him."

She left her cave and came to the shore and called aloud, "My son, why do you weep? Tell me, and hide it not. If the Greeks are defeated, that is what you prayed for."

He answered, "I did so, but what do I care for that? My dear friend is dead, whom I loved as my own life. Hector killed him! Hector has my beautiful armor! I do not wish to live, if I may not kill Hector with my own hands!"

She said, "Ah, my boy, when Hector dies, your death must soon follow."

He said, "I care not, I wish I could die now."

She said, "Well, if you must fight, I will go and bring back new armor for you, from Hephaestus himself."

Then Thetis made her way to Olympus, and came to the house of Hephaestus. He was busy in the forge, but his wife said, "What brings you here, Thetis, my dear friend? You do not often pay us a visit."

She led her to a seat and called out, "Husband, come this way. Thetis has something to ask you."

Hephaestus said, "Indeed she is one whom I respect, and I am grateful to her because she took care of me when I was thrown out of heaven. What pretty things I used to make for her in those days! Brooches and necklaces and all sorts of gewgaws, in the cave under the sea, and nobody knew where I was!"

He put down his tools and wiped his face and chest with a sponge and put on a clean vest and hobbled in; and two waiting women attended upon him, made by himself; they were made all of gold, but they could speak, and they could understand what he said to them. He clasped Thetis by the hand and said, "What brings you here, Thetis my dear friend? You do not often pay us a visit. Say what you want, and it shall be done, if I can do it."

She said, "Hephaestus, is there any one of the Olympians whom Zeus has treated so badly as me? He gave me a mortal husband, who is now old and useless in his palace; I did not want him. I had a lovely son, and I had to let him go to the war at Troy. I shall never see him at home again, never find him a wife! And now his friend has been killed, and his armor is lost.

That is what brings me here. I beg you to make him shield and helmet and breastplate and greaves,[1] for those which were lost along with his friend."

"Set your mind at rest," said the smith. "You shall have them, and a fine sight they shall be!"

And a fine sight they were when Thetis presented them to her son. He was amazed, and all his men were amazed. And he put on the armor and went out to the fight. He met, and he conquered, his great enemy Hector, and the Greeks once more prevailed.

But as his mother foretold, his death followed soon after. He was killed by an arrow shot by Paris, which hit him in the heel. That is the place where his mother held him, if you remember, when she bathed him in the Styx to make him invulnerable. We often use the words, "the heel of Achilles," to mean a weak spot in anyone, which comes from this story.

Chapter 42 ARES IN BATTLE

In the siege of Troy, the gods took sides and often quarreled about it. Aphrodite, of course, was on the side of Paris, and so was her lover, Ares; Hera and Athena, of course, were against Paris. Zeus kept them in order as well as he could and tried to be fair, but they would keep on meddling. And sometimes the gods became so excited that they joined in themselves. One of these times I am going to tell you about.

Athena had a great favorite among the Greeks, named Diomedes, and she encouraged him to go into battle. "Fight, and fear not," she said, "I will be near you. But keep clear of the gods, if you see any on the field. Only Aphrodite you may wound a little, if you happen to meet her; leave the others alone."

So Diomedes went into the fray. Before long, he had a fight with Aeneas, the man who was to escape from Troy and after-

[1] *greaves:* leg armor.

wards to found the Roman people. Diomedes wounded Aeneas and would have killed him, but his mother saved him; Aphrodite herself was his mother, and she laid her arms round him, and he was carried to his chariot.

Then Diomedes went straight for Aphrodite, since he knew that she was no fighter, and wounded her on the hand. The gods have not blood, like men, but they have something instead in their veins, and that something ran out, and she gave a shriek. Diomedes shouted out:

"Away from the battle, daughter of Zeus! Is it not enough that you are a plague to women? Leave war alone, or you shall shiver when you hear the word!"

Aphrodite ran out of the battle to the place where Ares was sitting and looking on. She cried out, "Dear brother, save me, and lend me your horses to go home! I have a dreadful wound which a mortal man has dealt me!"

Ares helped her into his car, and Iris took the reins and drove her up to Olympus. And Aphrodite ran to her mother and fell upon her lap. Her mother threw her arms round her and said, "Who has done this to you, dear child?" She answered, "I was wounded by a man, Diomedes, when I was saving my son. These Greeks are not content with fighting Trojans, you see, they fight with us too!"

"Bear up, my child!" her mother said. "We all have our troubles from these troublesome men. Think how Ares was shut up in a brazen jar for thirteen months. Think how Hera was hit by Hercules with an arrow. Think how the same Hercules shot Hades himself with another. As for Diomedes, he shall soon be sorry he attacked one of the immortals!" And she wiped the wound clean and cured the pain.

But Athena and Hera made fun of her and said, "Look, father Zeus, see Aphrodite has been with her friends, the Trojan women, and scratched her finger on someone's brooch!"

Meanwhile the battle went on furiously; for Ares himself was ranging about and urging on the Trojans to fight. Hera complained to Zeus that this was not fair; so Zeus said:

"Very well, go down and tell him to stop."

Then Hera and Athena drove down to the field. Athena found Diomedes wounded and said, "What, not fighting? I see you are not the man your father was."

"I did fight," he said, "and I wounded Aphrodite; but I came away when I found that Ares was taking a hand because you told me to leave the gods alone, except Aphrodite. And now I am wounded too."

"Fear nothing," said Athena, "not even Ares himself. Go in again, and I will be with you. Go, and strike that false traitor himself! He promised us to fight against the Trojans, and now he is helping them." So saying, she drove him in his car to the battlefield. She put on her head the cap of Hades, that she might become invisible.

When Ares saw Diomedes, he threw his spear at him, but Athena caught it and guided it harmless away. Then Diomedes lunged with his spear at Ares; and Athena guided it straight, so that it pierced his flank and came out at the back. Diomedes pulled out the spear, and Ares roared as loud as nine or ten thousand men roaring together.

Almost before they could look, Ares was gone. Like a black whirlwind of dust he shot through the air, and in a moment he was beside the throne of Zeus, and pointing to the immortal blood that flowed from his wound. He said in a complaining tone:

"Father Zeus, do not you mind seeing crimes like this? We gods are always suffering horrors, all for the sake of men. It is the fault of that crazy girl of yours, Athena, curse her. The rest of us obey you, but she does just what she likes, and you take no notice. Now she has made that overbearing young Diomedes attack the immortal gods. He wounded Aphrodite first, and now look at me! If I had not a quick pair of feet, I should be lying amid a heap of corpses."

Zeus frowned at him and said, "Do not come whimpering here to me, you facing-both-ways! I hate you worse than any god in Olympus. All you care for is battle and sudden death. You have your mother's hard temper, unendurable. I will not put up with it. If you were not my own son, you should have been long ago the lowest of the immortals."

Then he left Ares to get his wound cured and to be petted by his mother, Hera.

I cannot help thinking that the poet who told this tale was poking fun at the gods a little. But they were a kindly race and could all take a joke against themselves except perhaps Artemis. One of them at least, Dionysus, had a theater in later days, where comic plays were acted; and these often made fun of the god himself, with the high priest sitting in the chief chair of honor and laughing with the rest. But the god took it all in good part.

What they could not abide was pride and presumptuousness, for men were always becoming puffed up and pretending to be equal with the gods; and there was some excuse when so many of them were sons of the gods. One man, the brother of Sisyphus, claimed to have sacrifices paid to himself and imitated the thunder and lightning of Zeus; but Zeus visited him with the real lightning. Even the gentle Leto, gentlest of all the immortals, was roused to anger by Niobe. Niobe was the daughter of Tantalus, whom you saw in the dark house of Hades, standing in a lake. She had six fine sons and six lovely daughters, and she boasted that she was superior to Leto, who had only twins. Nor was she inferior in birth, for Tantalus was the son of Zeus. This infuriated the gentle Leto, who complained to her twins, Apollo and Artemis. They shot all the sons and daughters of Niobe with their arrows. Niobe wept for her children until she herself was turned into stone. You may see her figure still, in the mountains near Smyrna, with the tears ever running down her cheeks, as the dew and the rain distill upon her head.

Chapter 43 ODYSSEUS

At last the Trojan war was over. It is a long story, well worth your hearing, but I cannot tell it all now. I must tell you, however, of the adventures of one of the men who went home.

This was Odysseus of Ithaca. Now Ithaca is a small and rocky island, which lies in the sea west of Greece, not far south of Corfu. All the islands in this group once belonged to England, only we gave them back to the King of Greece after the Greeks made themselves free of the Turks. It is a lovely island, full of flowers, and the people are kind and still very proud of their great man, Odysseus, after three thousand years.

Odyssesus had left behind him his wife, named Penelope, whom he loved so much that all he wanted was to go home again and be at peace. When he bade good-by to her and his baby son Telemachus, he said, "My wife, I may be killed in the war. If I die, bring up our son to be a good man, and when he is old enough to manage the house, I hope you will marry again and be happy." But she said, "My husband, I want no one but you." He was away for twenty years: the siege lasted for ten years, and he took ten years to get home, but when he arrived, he found her waiting for him. And this is the story.

Odysseus set sail from Troy with his countrymen of Ithaca and the islands round about, twelve ships in all. They were blown far away to the west of the Mediterranean Sea, and when the wind fell, they came to land in a lovely country. The people welcomed those who went on shore, and gave them to eat of the fruit of the country, the lotus, which they lived on, sweet as honey. Anyone who ate of it wished never to come away, but only to go on forever eating the sweet lotus. It seemed to be always afternoon, and nobody wanted to do any more work forever and ever. But Odysseus would not have that. He carried off the lazy men and tied them down under the benches until the ships were well away.

By and by the wind took them to a little wild island, and Odysseus went off with one ship to explore. As he came near the mainland, he saw an enclosure upon the hillside, full of sheep and goats; so he took a few men with him and climbed up to the place. They found a great cave within the walls of the enclosure. There were pens for lambs and pens for kids; rows and rows of cheeses, pans and jars full of whey or milk. They helped themselves to milk and cheese, and roasted a lamb, and enjoyed themselves.

By and by, a horrible monster approached, big and hairy, and they ran and hid in the cave. He milked all the sheep and goats, and curdled the milk; then he lit a fire and saw the men.

"Who are you, stranger?" he asked.

Odysseus said, "Sir, we are strangers from Troy; have pity on us, for Zeus is the god of strangers."

"Pooh, pooh!" he said—"Zeus! we care nothing for Zeus, or any gods; we are stronger than they are."

He stretched out his hands and caught two of the men and

dashed them like puppies on the ground, so that their brains ran out. Then he carved them limb from limb and ate them for his supper and slept.

This monster was a Cyclops, named Polyphemus. You remember that dreadful brood of creatures, and the three who were guardians of fire in the early days.

Next morning, the Cyclops killed and ate two more men, and went about his work. But he rolled a huge stone in front of the cave so that no one could get out.

But Odysseus was never at a loss for a plan. He picked up a sapling of olive wood which lay in the cave and smoothed it and made it ready; and he chose out four good men to help him, when the night should come.

In the evening, the Cyclops drove in all his rams, and rolled the great stone in front of the door; next, as before, he killed and ate two more men for supper. Then Odysseus came up to him, bearing a skin of wine which he had brought from the ship, and he said, "Cyclops, here, have a drink after your supper!"

He drank it, and it pleased him so much that he said "Another, please!" Odysseus gave him another, and another still, and he said, "Indeed, this is fine stuff, better than our wine! I must give you a stranger's gift for this. What is your name?"

"My name," said Odysseus, "is Noman."

"Very well, Noman, your gift shall be that I will eat you last of all."

Then he lay down and went to sleep, grunting and growling.

There was Odysseus, and there were his men, shut up in the cave, and they could not get out; for the stone was too heavy for them to move. But Odysseus had his plan ready.

He took the olive sapling and buried it under the ashes; and when it was red hot, he made his four men hold it straight, while he pushed the point hard into the eye of the Cyclops; for he has only one eye, as you remember, in the middle of his forehead, with a thick bushy eyebrow running right across his face. The red-hot point burned the eyeball, which sizzled like fat in the fire.

The Cyclops roared aloud and pulled out the stake and threw it from him, and the men ran off and hid in the corners of the cave. The Cyclops made such a noise that all the other

Cyclopes came running up to the cave and called out, "Why are you making all that noise? Is anyone killing you?" Polyphemus replied, "Noman is killing me!" Then they said, "If no man is killing you, you must just pray to the gods. What is the use of waking us all out of our sleep?" And they went away, but Odysseus laughed to himself at the success of his trick.

Then he caught up the long withies that lay on the floor in a heap and tied his men each under one of the fleecy rams, with another ram tied to this ram on each side. He picked the biggest ram of all for himself and waited for morning.

In the morning, the Cyclops rolled back the stone from the door of the cave and let his rams out, holding out his hands and feeling their backs; but he did not feel underneath, so the men all got safely out, fastened together in threes. Odysseus came last, hanging on underneath the biggest ram of all. And so they escaped from the Cyclops. But this Cyclops was a son of Poseidon, and ever afterwards Poseidon hated Odysseus and did his best to destroy him.

They all sailed away, until they reached the island of Aeolus, the steward of the winds. Aeolus wished to help Odysseus on his way, so he bottled up all the winds in a leather bag, except the West Wind which was to blow them home. They went bowling along for nine days, until they actually came in sight of Ithaca, their home; and then Odysseus, tired out, fell asleep.

While he was asleep, the sailors eyed this bag, and one said to another, "I wonder what Aeolus gave him. Gold and silver, to be sure! Let us see." So they opened the mouth of the bag, and all the winds poured out and began to blow together, north, south, east, and west, and blew them far away. They had many adventures, which I cannot tell of now, but after a long time they came to land in a pleasant island, and Odysseus sent some of his men to explore.

They found a fine house among the trees; and as they came near, what should they see but all sorts of animals, lions and tigers, leopards and wild boars, which did them no harm; they just ran up, wagging their tails and barking in a friendly way. The men all went in, except one, who remained to watch.

Within the hall was a woman, singing sweetly as she plied the loom. She gave them welcome and provided a good feast; and when they had eaten, she tapped each with her stick and said,

"Away to the sty with you!" At once their hair changed into bristles, and they turned into pigs and ran away into the sty.

The watcher reported to Odysseus that the others had all disappeared; and Odysseus himself went to explore. On the way, he met the god Hermes, who gave him a magic root which would protect him against enchantments. So when he came to the house of Circe—that was the witch's name—she had no power over him, and he compelled her to change his men back to their proper shape.

Circe was a good friend to them after this and helped them with advice and gave them all they wanted. Odysseus had to visit the dark Kingdom of Hades where he received directions for his homeward voyage. And on the way back he had many other dangers to face.

He had to pass by the island of the Sirens. These were witches who looked like birds; they sang so sweetly that everyone who heard them felt obliged to land. There they sat in a meadow, singing, and all round them were the shriveled bodies of the men who had come to hear and sat down and listened, until they died. Odysseus was warned of this by Circe; and before he came to the island, he plugged up all the ears of all his men with wax so that they should not hear. But he wanted to hear himself, yet not to be hurt; so he told his men to tie him to the mast, and not to let him loose, whatever happened.

Then they rowed on. Soon the lovely song of the Sirens was heard, and Odysseus struggled to get free and shouted to his men to let him loose; but they rowed on until they were safe out of hearing.

Next they had to pass between Scylla and Charybdis. On one side of a strait was Charybdis, where a whirlpool three times a day sucked up the water and spouted it out again: no ship could live in that whirlpool. On the other side was a rock, and on this rock in a cave lived a monster, Scylla, with twelve legs and six long necks with heads like dogs; and if a ship passed by, she curled down her six necks and caught up a sailor with each head. This is what she did to Odysseus and his crew.

After this, all his ships were destroyed in a frightful storm, but Odysseus himself was saved and washed up on another island. On this island lived another witch, Calypso, who saved him and kept him there for seven long years. She wanted him for a husband, and she offered to make him immortal; but he refused, because all he wanted was to return to his beloved wife, Penelope. And he did return and found his wife waiting for him, although he had to fight a terrible battle with his enemies before he won her again. But after all his troubles, he spent with his wife a peaceful and quiet old age.

Chapter 44 CUPID AND PSYCHE

You remember Cupid, the mischievous and disobedient boy who shot his arrows at Medea, and how he was ready to shoot anyone for a toy, or just for fun. Cupid by and by began to grow up, and then fell in love himself! Here is the story.

The King and Queen of a certain place, whose name I do not know, had three daughters. The two elder daughters were nothing in particular; but the youngest was the most beautiful creature ever born. She was so beautiful that people thought she must be Aphrodite herself come to earth. They came to look at her in crowds, and showered flowers upon her as she passed by. The worshipers no longer frequented the temples of Aphrodite, but turned to this new goddess. Her name was Psyche, which means "the soul."

Aphrodite saw that her temples were deserted, and no sacrifices were paid to her; and she became jealous and angry. She called her boy Cupid, and said to him, "Do you see how your mother is neglected? insulted? pushed aside for a mortal? Go and shoot one of your arrows at her, so that she may fall in love with the ugliest and meanest man in the world!"

Cupid was still not too old for mischief, so he only said, "All right, mother!" and off he flew.

Meanwhile the King, Psyche's father, was in trouble, and did not know what to do. His two elder daughters were soon married, but no one wanted to marry Psyche. She was too high for them;

they only scattered flowers and offered prayers. So he inquired of the oracle of Apollo; and Aphrodite had already persuaded Apollo to help her. The god replied, "It is her fate to be married to a dragon. You must lay her out on a bier, as if she were dead, and place her on the hill which overlooks a deep valley near your town."

While this was preparing, Cupid flew by and saw her. He needed no arrow, and he shot none, but he fell head over ears in love at first sight. Then he laid his plans.

When the funeral procession was ready, Psyche was carried out, and laid on the hilltop; and the people returned home lamenting sadly. But when they were gone, the South Wind blew strong and gentle, and lifted up Psyche from the bier and carried her to the bottom of the valley, where he left her sleeping peacefully on a bed of flowers.

Psyche woke up, and could not make out where she was. Then she rose and wandered about, until she found a beautiful house, full of gold and marble, but not a soul to be seen. She saw a table, covered with all sorts of food, and sat down by it. Then a voice was heard from the air, "Fear nothing, my lady; all you see is yours, and we are your servants to wait upon you." Whatever she wanted, the unseen servants read her thought, and the viands [1] seemed to come of themselves to her hands. In the evening there was beautiful music and singing, but still no one to be seen. Then she went to bed and slept.

In the middle of the night, she awoke and felt someone by her side. "I suppose this is the dragon!" she thought, and shuddered. But when she plucked up courage to put out her hand, she felt a soft face and soft flowing hair, and a voice said, "I am your husband, Psyche, do not be afraid. I am yours, and this place is yours; only one thing I must ask you—never try to see me, or great trouble will follow." They talked pleasantly for a long time, and Psyche told him all her strange adventures. Then she fell asleep; and in the morning, there was no one there.

But naturally enough she was dull with no one to talk to, and no one to see her lovely house. So one night she begged her husband to let her sisters pay her a visit. He did not want to agree; but at last he said, "Very well, if you must have them, I will bring them to you; but be careful to tell them nothing about me."

[1] *viands* (vī′ăndz): food.

Then he sent the South Wind, and the wind caught up her sisters, and wafted them softly down to her door. Imagine their astonishment to see this grand house, and Psyche ready to welcome them! They went round, and looked at everything, and asked all sorts of questions. In particular, they wanted to know where her husband was.

She said first, "He is hunting," and then in her excitement she forgot all about that, and said, "Oh, he has some weighty business to do." The sisters were jealous and suspicious, and at last one said, "I don't believe you have a husband at all! I believe he is that old dragon, and you are ashamed to show him!"

This made Psyche angry, but she blurted out the truth, how he came only at night, and she never saw him, but he was certainly no dragon.

"How do you know," said the elder sister, "if you have never seen him? I'll tell you what. Put a lamp in your cupboard, and a sharp knife. When he is asleep, just take a look, and if he is the dragon, cut off his head, and you will be safe."

Psyche was a simple soul, and agreed; and the South Wind wafted the sisters home again.

So that night Psyche hid a lamp in the cupboard, with a sharp knife; and in the middle of the night, when her husband was asleep, she got up softly, and opened the cupboard, and took the knife in her right hand and the lamp in her left, and turned to look at her husband. What did she see but a beautiful boy, with flowing hair, and most wonderful of all, a pair of wings, green and gold, folded over his shoulders! For of course you have guessed long ago that he was no other than Cupid. She was so much amazed that she let a drop of hot oil drop from the lamp upon Cupid's arm, and it burned him, and he awoke. Then he saw his beloved Psyche, with a sharp knife in her hand!

"You wicked thing!" he cried, "do you want to murder me in my sleep?"

"Oh, no, no," she said, as the tears ran from her eyes. "I only wanted to see that you had not turned into a dragon."

"Do I look like a dragon?" said Cupid. "Did I feel like a dragon, when I put my arms round you and kissed you? Well, I told you that you must not see me, and you promised, and now you have broken your promise I must fly away, and I do not suppose you will see me again."

With these words, he spread his wings and flew out of the open window.

Now Psyche was in despair. She had done wrong, and she knew it, and all her happy life was at an end. However, as life was nothing to her without her husband, she set out to tramp all over the world and find him, or at least to die and have no more trouble.

So she tramped over hill and dale; she tore her clothes in the brambles and wounded her feet on the stones, but no trace could she find of Cupid.

Now Aphrodite knew quite well what was going on, and she thought she would like to enjoy the sight of Psyche, humbled and sorry. So she sent out Hermes, the crier of the gods who cried all over the country, "Oyez, oyez, oyez! Lost, stolen, or strayed, one slave-girl of our lady Aphrodite, answers to the name of Psyche. Reward for finding, one kiss to the finder!" Everybody was agog to win such a prize; and in the end, some one found Psyche, wandering about, and brought her to Aphrodite's door.

When she was taken before Aphrodite, the goddess said, "So here is the proud girl who set up to be my rival. She does not look much now, but as she is my slave, let us see if she can do any work. You there, get the job ready," and she signaled to some of her servants.

They went into the next room, and there they brought baskets of seed and grains: wheat, oats, and barley; millet and mustard; thistledown and all the seeds of all the weeds in the garden. They poured them all onto the ground and mixed them up, and there was a great heap of everything so that you could not tell what was what. Then Psyche was brought in, and Aphrodite said, "Sort them out, and let them be ready by sunset."

There was a task! Was ever anyone set to do a task like that? Psyche knew she could not do it; so she sat down in the corner and covered up her head with her robe and waited for whatever might happen.

But there was an ant in the corner, who heard and saw all that was done. He was delighted at the sight of these heaps of corn and seed, but he was a kind ant, and he felt very sorry for poor Psyche. "Look here, wife," said he, "let us sort them out for the young lady. Hullo, you fellows!" he shouted to the other ants, "here's a treasure for us! We have to sort them all out, and then we may take whatever we like." Out came the ants in swarms, from every hole, till the heap of seeds was black with them. They made quick work of it. Long before sunset, the seeds were all sorted into heaps, and the army of ants went away, with as much as they could carry for their own store.

And when Psyche looked up, there were all the seeds in little heaps: wheat, and barley, and oats, and mustard, and thistledown, each in its own heap.

Aphrodite was not at all pleased to find her task done; but she had nothing to say, so she gave Psyche a crust of bread and told her there would be other work on the morrow.

Indeed, she set Psyche many strange tasks, which somehow or other she always managed to do; and at the last she said, "Well, you are a better workwoman than I thought. I have only one thing more, and if you can do that, I will set you free. Take this casket; and go down to the dark world of Hades and give it to Queen Persephone and ask her to send me an ounce of her beauty; for I have lost a lot of mine, through nursing my poor son Cupid, who is ill with a bad burn on his arm."

Psyche took the casket. She went into the dark cavern, and through the dark tunnel where Orpheus had passed, and into the dark house of Hades. She gave the casket to Persephone and received a jar from her; and set out on her last journey homeward. Through the dark tunnel she came, and out of the dark cavern; and as she came into the light of day, she felt weary and lay down to rest.

"What is in this jar?" she thought. "An ounce of beauty? Perhaps she might spare some for me, then I might be more beautiful in my husband's eyes, if I were to see him again." She opened the jar. And what was in the jar? I suppose Aphrodite had put some message in the casket; for there was no ounce of beauty in the jar. Out of it came a stream of smoky mist, and it got into Psyche's lungs and choked her, and she fell back unconscious.

But what was Cupid doing all this time? He was ill in bed with the burn on his arm, which had come from Psyche's hot oil; and Aphrodite his mother, who was nursing him, kept him locked up in his room, that he might not get into any more mischief. But she forgot the window. Now Cupid's wound was well, and he got up, and he thought he would try his wings, to see if they were stiff after lying there so long. So he flew out of the window.

Cupid found his wings were all right. He flew about until he spied a bundle lying at the mouth of the dark cave. He was a little curious to know what this bundle was, and flew closer. What was his surprise to see his own Psyche, unconscious and pale as death!

One puff of immortal breath from his lips, and the misty fog dispersed, and Psyche opened her eyes and saw Cupid.

Then indeed there was rejoicing. Psyche told Cupid all her adventures, and this last one, and then remembering, she said, "And I opened the bottle! But I must finish my errand and deliver it to the Lady Aphrodite."

"Very well," says Cupid, "I will go with you." And they went together to his mother, and Psyche gave her the jar but said nothing about opening it.

Aphrodite was not at all pleased, but she could not hold out any longer when Cupid said, "Mother, this is my wife." She answered, "That is all very well, but if you care nothing for your mother, you cannot marry without the consent of Father Zeus." "Then we'll get it!" said Cupid and caught Psyche in his arms and spread his wings and flew up to the throne of Zeus.

He told Zeus the whole story: how he had been sent to shoot an arrow at Psyche, and had fallen in love himself; about the plan he made to win her, before the dragon could find her; what terrible hardships Psyche had gone through; what tasks she had done; and how Cupid had found her again. Zeus was rather pleased at the story, and said, "You are a young rogue, but if you really want to marry and settle down into a respectable member of Olympus, I will not make any objection." So there was a fine wedding feast; all the gods were happy, and even Aphrodite was made a friend when, for a wedding present, Zeus gave Psyche the gift of immortality.

Chapter 45 GREAT PAN IS DEAD

I daresay you will wonder why I tell you nothing of our own ancestors or the French or Germans or Russians. The reason is that they were of no account; they were just savages, and their gods were monsters who have perished off the earth and left hardly a trace behind; only their names remain in the names Tuesday, Wednesday, Thursday, and Friday. They were not worthy of the notice of the Greek gods, so the gods took no wives from them. These nations were preparing for their parts in the history of the world, but the time was not yet come. The Indians, it is true, had a large family of gods who were distantly related to the Greeks, but it is too long a story to tell of them now. I must pass on to the end of the Greek gods, for their end was approaching.

In a far-off corner of the world there was a small nation, unnoticed or despised, who had a special God of their own; a terrible God, and quite different from the Greeks, for he could tolerate no other god. Clouds and darkness were round about him, righteousness and judgment were the habitation of his seat; a fire went out before him and burned up his enemies round about. And after many hundreds of years, there came one from him who was called Jesus Christ, a God of goodwill and a Prince of peace. This religion, which seemed to the Greeks foolish and contemptible, spread all over the world where the Greek gods ruled, and it took their power from them. The temples of the old gods were taken to be churches for the new God, and named after his holy saints. For the priests of the new God were wise men. They only changed what was bad in the old religion and took over many of its feasts, such as Christmas and Easter, which they joined with the Christian feasts. They chose the patron saints of the churches so as to remind the Greek of their old gods, in order that they might feel at home with them. Thus at Athens, the great temple of Athena, the maiden goddess, became the church of the Virgin Mary; the temple of Theseus became the church of St. George. St. Elias, that is Elijah the prophet, took over the temples of Helios, the Sun-god, because the names were alike. The temples of Helios were on the tops of the hills, and there you may see now the chapels of St. Elias. St. Demetrius took the place of Demeter.

And there was a group of three very ancient gods, which had shrines in Delos and Athens and elsewhere; they were called the Three Fathers, and their shrines now became sacred to the Holy Trinity. The sick people, who used to worship Asclepius, now turned to those saints who cared for healing; and they made the same offerings of gratitude in the churches as they used to do. You may still see in the churches silver models of arms, legs, and teeth, made by people who have had them cured.

One evening, when this great change was taking place, a traveler set sail from Greece to Italy. The wind fell, and the ship was becalmed while it was making its way through the crowd of little islands off the west coast; and it drifted close to the island of Paxos. The passengers had all dined, and they were lounging about on deck, when from the island a loud voice was heard crying out—"Thamus!" This did amaze them, for Thamus was the name of the steersman. He did not answer, and a second cry came —"Thamus!" and a third—"Thamus!"

Then the steersman did answer, "Ahoy! what is it?" and the voice rejoined, "When you come over against Palodes, tell them that Great Pan is dead!"

This caused much excitement, and they all debated whether to go there or not. At last the steersman said, "If there is a wind, I will sail straight on; but if we drift near the place, I will give the news."

The wind came not; they drifted on. And by and by the ship was over against the place. The steersman went into the bows of the ship and called in a loud voice toward the land, "Great Pan is dead!"

Immediately they heard a loud noise on shore, weeping and wailing and lamentation; and a wind sprang up, and they sailed away on their voyage.

Great Pan really was dead, and so were all the Olympian gods. They were not immortal, as they thought. They played their part in the world's history and passed away. Of all that mighty company, two only are left. One we will no longer call Cupid, for he has grown up, and he has turned out to be no other than that strange and wonderful Eros, or Love, who appeared at the very first out of Chaos—no one knew how—and still remains as the spirit of the new religion. The other is Psyche, or the soul of man, who has been taken up into heaven and made immortal.

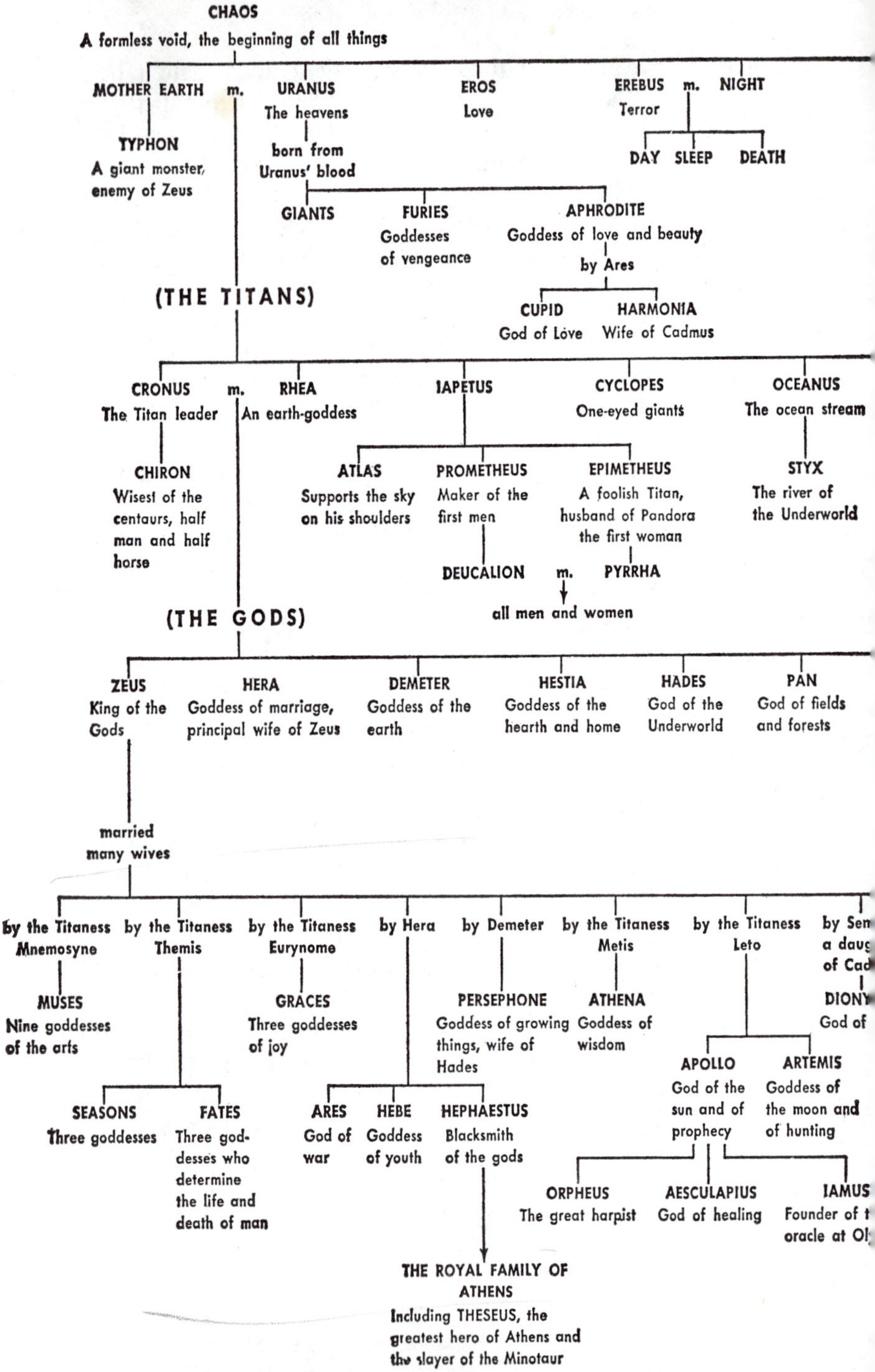

CHAOS
A formless void, the beginning of all things
MOTHER EARTH m. URANUS
The heavens
EROS
Love
EREBUS m. NIGHT
Terror
TYPHON
A giant monster, enemy of Zeus
born from Uranus' blood
DAY
SLEEP
DEATH
GIANTS
FURIES
Goddesses of vengeance
APHRODITE
Goddess of love and beauty
by Ares
CUPID
God of Love
HARMONIA
Wife of Cadmus
(THE TITANS)
CRONUS m. RHEA
The Titan leader
An earth-goddess
IAPETUS
CYCLOPES
One-eyed giants
OCEANUS
The ocean stream
CHIRON
Wisest of the centaurs, half man and half horse
ATLAS
Supports the sky on his shoulders
PROMETHEUS
Maker of the first men
EPIMETHEUS
A foolish Titan, husband of Pandora the first woman
STYX
The river of the Underworld
DEUCALION m. PYRRHA
all men and women
(THE GODS)
ZEUS
King of the Gods
HERA
Goddess of marriage, principal wife of Zeus
DEMETER
Goddess of the earth
HESTIA
Goddess of the hearth and home
HADES
God of the Underworld
PAN
God of fields and forests
married many wives
by the Titaness Mnemosyne
by the Titaness Themis
by the Titaness Eurynome
by Hera
by Demeter
by the Titaness Metis
by the Titaness Leto
by Sem
a daug
of Cad
MUSES
Nine goddesses of the arts
GRACES
Three goddesses of joy
PERSEPHONE
Goddess of growing things, wife of Hades
ATHENA
Goddess of wisdom
DIONY
God of
APOLLO
God of the sun and of prophecy
ARTEMIS
Goddess of the moon and of hunting
SEASONS
Three goddesses
FATES
Three goddesses who determine the life and death of man
ARES
God of war
HEBE
Goddess of youth
HEPHAESTUS
Blacksmith of the gods
ORPHEUS
The great harpist
AESCULAPIUS
God of healing
IAMUS
Founder of t
oracle at Ol
THE ROYAL FAMILY OF ATHENS
Including THESEUS, the greatest hero of Athens and the slayer of the Minotaur

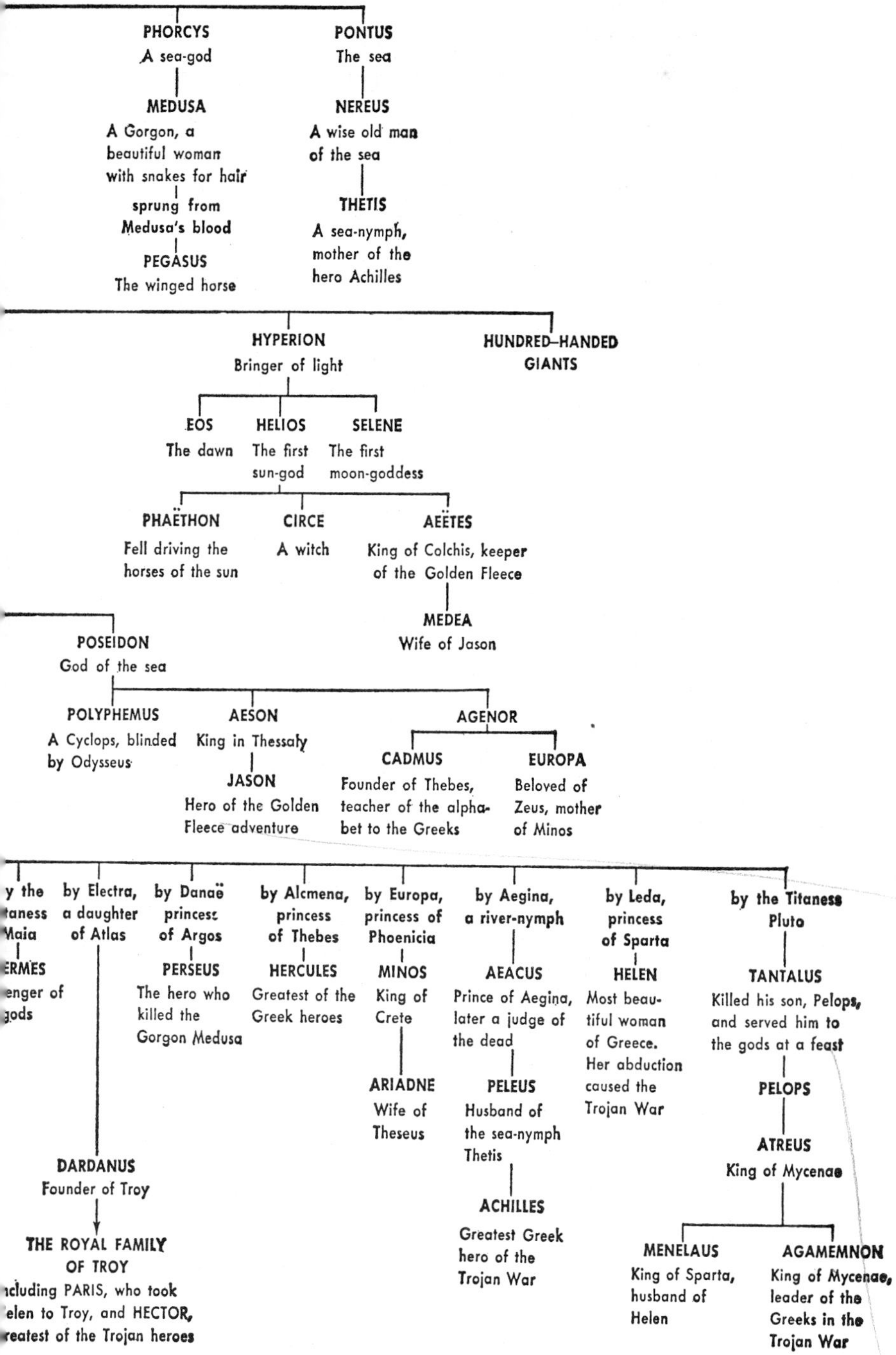
PHORCYS
A sea-god
MEDUSA
A Gorgon, a beautiful woman with snakes for hair
sprung from Medusa's blood
PEGASUS
The winged horse
PONTUS
The sea
NEREUS
A wise old man of the sea
THETIS
A sea-nymph, mother of the hero Achilles
HYPERION
Bringer of light
HUNDRED–HANDED GIANTS
EOS
The dawn
HELIOS
The first sun-god
SELENE
The first moon-goddess
PHAËTHON
Fell driving the horses of the sun
CIRCE
A witch
AEËTES
King of Colchis, keeper of the Golden Fleece
MEDEA
Wife of Jason
POSEIDON
God of the sea
POLYPHEMUS
A Cyclops, blinded by Odysseus
AESON
King in Thessaly
JASON
Hero of the Golden Fleece adventure
AGENOR
CADMUS
Founder of Thebes, teacher of the alphabet to the Greeks
EUROPA
Beloved of Zeus, mother of Minos
y the
taness
Maia
ERMES
enger of
gods
by Electra, a daughter of Atlas
DARDANUS
Founder of Troy
THE ROYAL FAMILY OF TROY
ncluding PARIS, who took
elen to Troy, and HECTOR,
reatest of the Trojan heroes
by Danaë princess of Argos
PERSEUS
The hero who killed the Gorgon Medusa
by Alcmena, princess of Thebes
HERCULES
Greatest of the Greek heroes
by Europa, princess of Phoenicia
MINOS
King of Crete
ARIADNE
Wife of Theseus
by Aegina, a river-nymph
AEACUS
Prince of Aegina, later a judge of the dead
PELEUS
Husband of the sea-nymph Thetis
ACHILLES
Greatest Greek hero of the Trojan War
by Leda, princess of Sparta
HELEN
Most beautiful woman of Greece. Her abduction caused the Trojan War
by the Titaness Pluto
TANTALUS
Killed his son, Pelops, and served him to the gods at a feast
PELOPS
ATREUS
King of Mycenae
MENELAUS
King of Sparta, husband of Helen
AGAMEMNON
King of Mycenae, leader of the Greeks in the Trojan War

PRONOUNCING LIST

In the following list, the pronunciation is given in parentheses. If there is a major Roman god or goddess who corresponds to the Greek one, the name is printed in heavy type.

Absyrtus (ab·sûr′tŭs)
Achelous (ăk′ĕ·lō′ŭs)
Achilles (ȧ·kĭl′ēz)
Acrisius (ȧ·krĭs′ĭ·ŭs)
Actaeon (ăk·tē′ŏn)
Admetus (ăd·mē′tŭs)
Aeacus (ē′ȧ·kŭs)
Aeëtes (ē·ē′tēz)
Aegeus (ē′jūs)
Aegina (ē̇·jī′nȧ)
Aegyptus (ē̇·jĭp′tŭs)
Aeneas (ē̇·nē′ăs)
Aeolus (ē′ô·lŭs)
Aeson (ē′sŭn)
Aether (ē′thẽr)
Aethra (ē′thrȧ)
Agamemnon (ăg′ȧ·mĕm′nŏn)
Alcestis (ăl·sĕs′tĭs)
Alcmena (ălk·mē′nē̇)
Alpheus (ăl·fē′ŭs)
Althaea (ăl·thē′ȧ)
Amazon (ăm′ȧ·zŏn)
Amphitrite (ăm′fĭ·trī′tē̇)
Amphitryon (ăm·fĭt′rĭ·ŏn)
Andromeda (ăn·drŏm′ē̇·dȧ)
Aphrodite (ăf′rô·dī′tē̇) **Venus**
Apollo (ȧ·pŏl′ō)
Arcadia (är·kā′dĭ·ȧ)
Areopagus (ăr′ē̇·ŏp′ȧ·gŭs)
Ares (ā′rēz) **Mars**
Argo (är′gō)
Argonaut (är′gô·nôt)
Argus (är′gŭs)
Ariadne (ăr′ĭ·ăd′nē̇)
Artemis (är′tē̇·mĭs) **Diana**
Asclepius (ăs·klē′pĭ·ŭs) **Aesculapius**
Atalanta (ăt′ȧ·lăn′tȧ)
Athena (ȧ·thē′nȧ) **Minerva**
Athos (ăth′ŏs)
Atlas (ăt′lăs)
Augeas (ô·jē′ăs)

Bellerophon (bĕ·lĕr′ô·fŏn)
Bendis (bĕn′dĭs)
Boeotia (bē̇·ō′shȧ)
Bosporus (bŏs′pô·rŭs)
Briareus (brī·âr′ē̇·ŭs)
Britomartis (brĭt′ô·mär′tĭs)

Cadmus (kăd′mŭs)
Calais (kăl′â·ĭs)
Calydon (kăl′ĭ·dŏn)
Calypso (kȧ·lĭp′sō)
Castor (kȧs′tẽr)
Caucasus (kô′kȧ·sŭs)
Celeus (sĕ′lĕ·ŭs)
Centaur (sĕn′tôr)
Cerberus (sûr′bẽr·ŭs)
Cercopes (sûr·kō′pēz)
Chaos (kā′ŏs)
Charybdis (kȧ·rĭb′dĭs)
Chimaera (kī·mēr′ȧ)
Chiron (kī′rŏn)
Circe (sûr′sē̇)
Cithaeron (sĭ·thē′rŏn)
Coeus (sē′ŭs)
Colchis (kŏl′kĭs)
Corybant (kŏr′ĭ·bănt)
Cottus (kŏt′ŭs)
Creon (krē′ŏn)
Crete (krēt)
Creus (krē′ŭs)
Crissa (krī′sȧ)

Cronus (krō′nŭs) **Saturn**
Cyclopes (sī′klō′pēz)

Daedalus (dĕd′ȧ·lŭs)
Danaë (dăn′â·ē)
Danaïdes (dȧ·nā′ĭ·dēz)
Danaüs (dăn′â·ŭs)
Deianira (dē′yȧ·nī′rȧ)
Delos (dē′lŏs)
Delphi (dĕl′fī)
Demeter (dê·mē′tẽr) **Ceres**
Demetrius (dê·mē′trĭ·ŭs)
Deucalion (dû·kā′lĭ·ŏn)
Dicte (dĭk′tē)
Dictynna (dĭk·tĭn′ȧ)
Diomedes (dī′ô·mē′dēz)
Dionysus (dī′ô·nī′sŭs) **Bacchus**
Dodona (dô·dō′nȧ)

Echo (ĕk′ō)
Eileithyia (ī′lī·thī′yȧ)
Eleusis (ê·lū′sĭs)
Elis (ē′lĭs)
Endymion (ĕn·dĭm′ĭ·ŏn)
Eos (ē′ŏs) **Aurora**
Ephialtes (ĕf′ĭ·ăl′tēz)
Epimetheus (ĕp′ĭ·mē′thūs)
Erebus (ĕr′ê·bŭs)
Eridanus (ê·rĭd′ȧ·nŭs)
Eris (ē′rĭs)
Eros (ē̦r′ŏs) **Cupid**
Europa (û·rō′pȧ)
Eurydice (û·rĭd′ĭ·sē)
Eurystheus (û·rĭs′thūs)

Gaea (jē′ȧ)
Ganymede (găn′ĭ·mēd)
Geryon (jē′rĭ·ŏn)
Gorgons (gôr′gŭnz)
Gyges (jī′jēz)

Hades (hā′dēz)
Harmonia (här·mō′nĭ·ȧ)

Hebe (hē′bê)
Hebrus (hē′brŭs)
Hecate (hĕk′ȧ·tê)
Hector (hĕk′tẽr)
Helios (hē′lĭ·ŏs) **Sol**
Helle (hĕl′ē)
Hellespont (hĕl′ĕs·pŏnt)
Hephaestus (hê·fĕs′tŭs) **Vulcan**
Hera (Hē′rȧ) **Juno**
Hercules (hûr′kû·lēz)
Hermes (hûr′mēz) **Mercury**
Hesperides (hĕs·pĕr′ĭ·dēz)
Hestia (hĕs′tĭ·ȧ) **Vesta**
Hippocrene (hĭp′·ô·krē′nē)
Hippolyte (hĭ·pŏl′ĭ·tē)
Horae (hō′rē)
Hydra (hī′drȧ)
Hygeia (hī·jē′ȧ)
Hylas (hī′lȧs)
Hyperion (hī·pē̦r′ĭ·ŏn)
Hypermnestra (hī′pẽrm·nĕs′trȧ)

Iapetus (ī·ăp′ê·tŭs)
Icarus (ĭk′ȧ·rŭs)
Ida (ī′dȧ)
Ino (ī′nō)
Io (ī′ō)
Iobates (ī·ob′ȧ·tēs)
Iolaus (ī′ô·lā′ŭs)
Iris (ī′rĭs)
Ithaca (ĭth′ȧ·kȧ)
Ixion (ĭks·ī′ŏn)

Jason (jā′sŭn)

Lemnos (lĕm′nŏs)
Lerna (lĕr′nȧ)
Lesbos (lĕz′bŏs)
Leto (lē′tō) **Latona**
Lindos (lĭn′dŏs)
Lycaon (lī·kā′ŏn)
Lycia (lĭsh′ĭ·ȧ)
Lynceus (lĭn′sūs)

Maia (mā′yȧ)
Marathon (măr′ȧ·thŏn)
Medea (mē̇·dē′ȧ)
Medusa (mē̇·dū′sȧ)
Megara (mĕg′ȧ·rȧ)
Meleager (mĕl′ē̇·ā′jẽr)
Menelaus (mĕn′ĕ·lā′ŭs)
Metis (mē′tĭs)
Midas (mī′dăs)
Milanion (mī·lăn′ĭ·ŏn)
Minos (mī′nŏs)
Minotaur (mĭn′ō̇·tôr)
Mnemosyne (mē̇·mŏs′ĭ·nē)
Mopsus (mŏp′sŭs)
Mycenae (mī·sē′nē)

Nemean (nē̇·mē′ăn)
Nephele (nĕf′ĕ·lē)
Nereid (nē̦r′ē̇·ĭd)
Nereus (nē̦r′ūs)
Nessus (nĕs′ŭs)
Niobe (nī′ō̇·bē̇)

Oceanus (ō̇·sē′ȧ·nŭs)
Odysseus (ō̇·dĭs′ūs) **Ulysses**
Olympus (ō̇·lĭm′pŭs)
Omphale (ŏm′fȧ·lē)
Orion (ō̇·rī′ŏn)
Orpheus (ôr′fūs; -fē̇·ŭs)
Ossa (ŏs′ȧ)
Otus (ō′tŭs)

Pan (păn) **Faunus**
Panacea (păn′ȧ·sē′ȧ)
Pandora (păn·dō′rȧ)
Parnassus (pär·năs′ŭs)
Patroclus (pȧ·trō′klŭs)
Paxos (păk′sŏs)
Pegasus (pĕg′ȧ·sŭs)
Pirithoüs (pī·rĭth′ō̇·ŭs)
Peleus (pē′lūs)
Pelias (pē′lĭ·ăs)
Pelion (pē′lĭ·ŏn)
Pelops (pē′lŏps)
Penelope (pē̇·nĕl′ō̇·pē̇)
Persephone (pẽr·sĕf′ō̇·nē̇)
Perseus (pûr′sūs)
Phaëthon (fā′ĕ·thŏn)
Phasis (fā′sĭs)
Phineus (fī′nūs)
Phoebe (fē′bē̇)
Phoenicia (fē̇·nĭsh′ĭ·ȧ)
Pholus (fō′lŭs)
Phorcus (fôr′kŭs)
Phrygia (frĭj′ĭ·ȧ)
Phrixus (frĭk′sŭs)
Pleiades (plē′yȧ·dēz)
Polydectes (pŏl′ĭ·dĕk·tēz)
Polydeuces (pŏl′ĭ·dū′sēz)
Polyphemus (pŏl′ĭ·fē′mŭs)
Pontus (pŏn′tŭs)
Poseidon (pō̇·sī′dŏn) **Neptune**
Priam (prī′ăm)
Procrustes (prō̇·krŭs′tēz)
Proetus (prē′tŭs)
Prometheus (prō̇·mē′thūs; -thē̇·ŭs)
Propontis (prō̇·pŏn′tĭs)
Psyche (sī′kē̇)
Pyrrha (pĭr′ȧ)
Python (pī′thŏn)

Rhadamanthus (răd′ȧ·măn′thŭs)
Rhea (rē′ȧ)
Rhodus (rō′dŭs)

Salamis (săl′ȧ·mĭs)
Satyr (săt′ẽr)
Sciron (skī′rŏn)
Scylla (sĭl′ȧ)
Silenus (sī·lē′nŭs)
Selene (sē̇·lē′nē)
Semele (sĕm′ĕ·lē)
Seriphos (sĕ·rī·fŏs)
Sisyphus (sĭs′ĭ·fŭs)
Stymphalis (stĭm·fā′lĭs)

Styx (stĭks)
Syrinx (sĭr′ĭngks)

Taínaron (tâ′nä·rôn)
Tantalus (tăn′tȧ·lŭs)
Tartarus (tär′tȧ·rŭs)
Teiresias (tī·rē′sĭ·ăs)
Telemachus (tê·lĕm′ȧ·kŭs)
Telephus (tĕl′ê·fŭs)
Tethys (tē′thĭs)
Thamus (thā′mŭs)
Thebes (thēbz)
Thea (thē′yȧ)
Themis (thē′mĭs)
Theseus (thē′sūs)

Thetis (thē′tĭs)
Tiresias (tī·rē′sĭ·ăs)
Tiryns (tī′rĭnz)
Titan (tī′tăn)
Triptolemus (trĭp·tŏl′ê·mŭs)
Triton (trī′tŏn)
Troezen (trĕ′zĕn)
Typhon (tī′fŏn)

Uranus (ū′rȧ·nŭs)

Zetes (zē′tēz)
Zeus (zūs) **Jupiter**
Zodiac (zō′dĭ·ăk)

AFTERWORD

The world of the Greek myths was a little world. Look at a map of our modern world and find the Mediterranean Sea. (Mediterranean means "at the middle of the world.") That sea and its shores together with the Black Sea and its shores is really all there was to that world. But it was a wonderful world.

The ancient Greeks found parts of their world as strange and as frightening and as exciting as our own great universe. The Greeks made up these stories which we call myths in order to try to explain what they could not understand.

It is hard to say when these stories were first told. It is even harder to think about them the way the ancient Greeks did. This is because all of these myths have been used for more than three thousand years, first by the Greeks themselves, later by the Romans, and still later by most of the people in Europe and America. They have been used in many different ways and for many different purposes. Whenever people want to explain how they feel, what they think, and what they are afraid of, they have used these myths. And because so many people know them, they provide a kind of common language. When someone has gotten into a lot of trouble we sometimes say, "He has opened Pandora's jar." When someone has a very hard job to do we say, "That's a Herculean task." Sometimes we use a Roman name for one of the Greek gods or heroes. We use the name *Mercury* (Hermes) or the word *mercurial* when we talk about speed or someone lively or changeable. In fact most of the names of the gods and heroes and monsters in these myths have been put into modern languages as words for ordinary things and happenings. Mr. Rouse has mentioned some of them: panic, chimera, typhoon, hygiene, panacea. You will find it very interesting and useful to keep a notebook of these names and the words that have been made from them.

Which was the first myth? It is really impossible to tell which myth is the oldest. The way Mr. Rouse tells these stories makes sense. He begins with the creation of the world, just as the Old Testament of the Bible does. But we can be sure that this myth is not the first one. This is because even to think about such a big idea as the creation of the world, you must already have thought of the simpler things of everyday life, such as sleep and dreams, the weather and the seasons, day and night, joy and sadness. The list you could make would be very long. It is important to realize that people have to reach a pretty high level of civilization before they can even make myths about the big questions. Today we have great scholars who spend their whole lives trying to understand how these myths developed.

We do know, however, that when these myths were finally written down, they were already very old. Homer was probably the first man to collect these stories in any form. We are not absolutely sure when he lived or even who he was, but we believe that he lived in Greece about one thousand years before Christ. He put these myths into his great poems, called the *Iliad* and the *Odyssey*. These tell the stories about the Trojan War and the wanderings of Odysseus (whom the Romans called Ulysses). Most of you have read stories from these poems or have seen movies that were based upon parts of them.

We do know that a Greek farmer named Hesiod wrote down the myths in about the form we have them in Mr. Rouse's collection. He did this sometime in the ninth century B.C. His book is called the *Theogony* which means "the birth of the gods."

What was the use of these myths? This is really a very practical question. Of course they were entertaining. They were also frightening in a safe sort of way, which is another meaning for "entertaining." But these myths also tell what happens to people who do wrong. They tell a great deal about the meaning of love and loyalty. They explain how and why hard work can be good. (Remember when Hercules realizes he has to learn how to control himself?) They show the way in which people learn to understand each other. Stories that can do all these things can be used in a special way. It is easy to guess what this was. These myths became the first schoolbooks! Not only did the Greek boys (and girls too, sometimes) learn to read and write from them, they learned good manners and morality. You can be sure the teacher had to point out that some of the things the gods did were wrong and even stupid. Think of the tricks they played on each other—Apollo, Hermes, and Zeus himself.

In addition to all this, the Greek school children learned something very much like history from their myths. They learned their language, probably the way we learn English in school today. Their Greek teacher, like your English teacher, probably gave them homework assignments, too, and complained about misspellings and sloppy handwriting.

As the title of the book tells you, these Greek myths deal with gods, heroes, and men. In many ways, as you have already seen, the gods and heroes were very much alike. In fact, the important difference between them is that the gods were immortal. The heroes were men, but they did things, sometimes with the help of the gods and sometimes in spite of them, that ordinary men could never do. At least it seems that way when we read about them today.

This is one of the tricks that myths play upon us: when people remember what a great man did, they tend to exaggerate his deeds. In fact many people who have adventures do the same thing today. Sometimes they tell tall tales to their friends and are believed. For instance, a man who had to swim for an hour before being rescued from a shipwreck during the war, might say at first that it seemed as if he were in the water all day. As the years go by, and he tells of his experiences again and again, he forgets the facts and only remembers his feelings. Soon he believes that he swam for days through shark-infested waters, catching and killing fish with his bare hands. And when his friends and his children tell these stories they *improve* on them even more—don't we all do things like that sometimes?

Travelers who go to strange places, where none of their countrymen have ever been, come home with weird and wonderful tales. The travelers who went from Europe to Asia and Africa during the Middle Ages did this. You can still read their exaggerated, unrealistic descriptions of elephants, ostriches, and camels. Such creatures as they described never could have lived. Neither could the Sphinx or the Cyclopes or the Centaurs or the Gorgons. But they do represent ideas, and the wonder men felt before strange events and the power of nature.

Memory plays strange tricks on us too. Three thousand years ago Hesiod wrote of a time long before he lived, which he called the Golden Age. He said everything was much better then. Men lived like gods and were always happy. Hesiod himself was a very unhappy person and probably not a very good farmer. He was doing something many of us do today. We remember only the good times we have had. And when people write history, they often record only the high points and the great deeds, otherwise it would be a boring story. So, when we remember our own early life, even last year, we sometimes see only what was fun or exciting, and we do not remember what was dull and painful and confusing.

As historians and archeologists learn more and more about the ancient Greeks they find that daily life was generally pretty ordinary. The great walled city of Troy was really a rather small town. The gates of Hercules is the Strait of Gibraltar. Scylla and Charybdis is the extremely rough tidal current in the Strait of Messina between Italy and Sicily. This is not to say that the Greeks were liars—although they insisted that all Cretans were—it only means that memory and exaggeration work together to make things bigger and even stranger than they were.

The biggest question anyone can ask is: "How did the world begin?" There are other questions that may be more important, such as "What is Truth? or Goodness? or Beauty?" but these have to do with people. There are many answers to that big question. You will find some in the Bible. Different scientists give different answers. But all of these questions start with an idea that there *was* a beginning. This is where our myths start. "In the beginning there was Chaos . . ." Today the word *chaos* means "disorder," but for the ancient Greeks it was the name for "formlessness." Out of this formlessness, this void (which means emptiness), a being came. This being is not described in any way. It is only given a name. We are told that this was "Eros, or Love, who came no one knows how, and was quite different from all the others; he outlived them all, and still lives, the most mighty of all divine powers."

Eros came before the Titans and the gods. In later times he is called the god of love and is given the name of Cupid. But by that time he is in charge of only the simplest kind of love, the feeling of one person for another. The Greeks were trying to express what the Christians today mean by love which includes all humanity. It includes in its great meaning all the other meanings, such as charity, care, faithfulness, responsibility. One can say, as the Greeks said and as the modern Christian would say, that we must use our lives in finding and practicing these meanings of love.

After Eros, came the Titans. At the beginning we are told that they were all monsters with more heads and arms than they needed. Some had only a single eye, like the Cyclopes. They all had special jobs, like Oceanus who ran the great ocean-river which the Greeks at one time thought surrounded the world; or Hyperion, who took charge of the light of night and day.

Most of the Titans were horrible creatures who hated and feared each other and were always at war. Some of the Titans gave birth to the Giants and the Furies who were also monstrous creatures. But one of them, Cronus, the worst Titan of all, gave birth to the gods.

So you see, from the beginning of the beginning, this is a mixed-up story. This is because the Greeks kept telling the oldest myths while the newer ones were being invented. We must not worry about this. It is only natural, in trying to explain what is hard to understand, that explanations get mixed up. And in trying to straighten things out, we always learn something.

One of the last of the Titans was Prometheus. He was more god-like than most of the gods. He was not a monster at all, but like the gods who came after him he was shaped like a man, or rather, Prometheus shaped man out of clay and gave him the form the gods had. In fact, and here the mix-up gets more complicated, one way of reading the myths seems to show that the gods and men came into existence at about the same time—that is, if Time had been invented by then!

Prometheus was wise and practical and kind. Remember at the beginning of the war in heaven he was on the side of Cronus; after all they were both Titans. He told Cronus to free the other Titans, but

> When Prometheus found that Cronus was too stupid to take good advice, he went over to the side of Zeus. To Zeus he gave the name advice; and although Zeus was not very wise, he was wise enough to take this advice. So he set free the three Cyclopes named Thunderer, Lightener, and Shiner; and they were so grateful that they gave Zeus a gift each—the thunder and the lightning and the thunderbolt. They also gave Hades a cap which made him invisible when he put it on; and they gave Poseidon a trident, or three-pronged spear. . . . In the end, they conquered Cronus and bound him in chains and shut him in dark Tartarus.

We are also told that Prometheus was an inventor and an artist. He made all the animals including Man.

> . . . and into him he put a speck of all the creatures on earth which he had already made, to see what would come of the mixture. There was a speck of a lion and of the deer, a speck of the cow and of the serpent, a speck of the dog and of the fox, of the monkey and of the owl, the dove and the vulture. It was, indeed, a strange mixture, and so are we still, are not we? Sometimes brave and sometimes timid, now calm and now spiteful, truthful or cunning, mischievous or solemn, gentle or greedy!

This is a way of saying that Prometheus made it possible for man to behave in almost any way. He could be good or bad, wise or foolish, true or false, loyal or treacherous—in fact, man can behave in many of these ways at the same time. He could act almost like a god or just like an animal—and he still can.

It is very hard to keep the family trees of the Titans and the gods straight. But Prometheus, whose name means "Forethought," was the cleverest of them all. Finally he even sacrificed himself so that man could have fire. Today, we often use the name Prometheus when we try to describe something that is at once grand, noble, and marvelously creative. We speak of the control of atomic energy as a Promethean experiment and of the plans for space flight as a Promethean adventure. The name Prometheus stands for all that is daringly noble in man's hopes and ideas. Perhaps this is what the old myths have tried to say.

The behavior of the gods and goddesses was very much like that of men. They were not always good or kind. They often did foolish things. They could sulk when they did not get what they wanted. They could be embarrassed. They could be fooled. They often held a grudge for a very long time. And they could also be friendly and helpful to each other and to men. But when it was very important, they could act like the gods they were, with dignity, honesty, and wisdom.

Sometimes Zeus behaves like a father who has worked hard all day. When he comes home, he wants a little peace and quiet. If the children are noisy, he shouts and scolds. After a while he forgives them and everyone is happy again. But when he had made a decision, that was that! "When Zeus bowed his head, all must obey."

Each god or goddess had one special responsibility. Zeus was the king of the gods. He kept order in the heavens and throughout the world. This was not always easy. Sometimes it was also boring. When it was, Zeus acted like a human being. He went in search of fun or a fight or an adventure. He usually found all three.

Demeter, the Earth Goddess, was in charge of the crops, but when Hades stole her daughter Persephone, she went on strike. When she finally got her daughter back it was only for two thirds of the year. This is the way the Greeks explained the seasons. When Persephone is with Hades, we have winter.

Helios was in charge of the Sun, and though the other gods sometimes envied him his job, they left him alone because they knew how difficult it was. However, he had a son Phaëthon, who was probably the first boy in his teens who wanted to ride high and fast. He took the golden chariot of the sun and very nearly burned up the world before Zeus put an end to the game. You know what kind of moral you can draw from that! You see, these myths can still be useful. You must remember another young fellow who did not take his father's advice, Icarus. Unlike Phaëthon and Helios, Daedalus and Icarus were merely men. But Daedalus was a great engineer and inventor. The myth tells how he planned an escape from Crete, the island ruled by Minos, by air, with wings. Icarus did not listen to his father's warning and flew too high. He had a sea named after him, because he drowned in its waters.

So, you can see, even today these myths can still talk to us and tell us tales. Aside from the grand adventures and the strange and frightening monsters, most of the stories tell about people or gods or heroes who learn things, or lose their way, who are good or bad in very much the same manner as human beings. Although we cannot believe some of the explanations of what happened and why, we can understand the feelings of the characters in the stories and appreciate the problems and the pleasures they had.

As you grow older, you will read about these myths in many different forms. You will learn more about Greek history and understand more about what was noble and what was mean in all they did and thought. You will learn, too, what it was that made them lose one of the greatest civilizations in the world, possibly the very greatest. But, perhaps most important of all, you will someday understand how the ideas of love and brotherhood and human dignity that the Greeks have taught us not only still shine in the best of their myths, but also in our own lives.

STUDY QUESTIONS

1. What did the ancient Greeks mean by *chaos?* What does it mean to us?
2. Compare the beginning of the world as described in Greek stories with that told in the Book of Genesis in the Bible. Are there any similarities?
3. How did the Greeks explain the origin of man? Can you see any similarity between the Greek explanation and that of modern science?
4. How did Greek mythology explain natural events like the rising and setting of the sun and moon? thunder and lightning? the seasons? Try to pretend that you have no modern scientific knowledge and tell whether or not you think that the Greek explanations of natural events are at all believable.
5. How did the Greeks explain the fact that man seems to be a complex mixture of good and bad, boldness and cowardice, wisdom and foolishness?
6. Who were the Titans? What do we mean when we say that something is *titanic* or that a person is a *titan?*
7. How were the Titans overthrown? Who took their place as rulers of the heavens?
8. What actually is Mount Olympus? If you do not know, look it up in an encyclopedia or dictionary. What has Mount Olympus to do with the story of the Greek gods? If today we call a person or a thing *Olympian,* what do we mean?
9. There are some very vivid scenes in Greek mythology: for instance, the battle between Zeus and

Cronus (page 331) or the prison of Cronus (page 332). Some of these scenes are fun to draw. They also make very good reading aloud. Select four or five scenes that you find especially memorable, find them in the book, and prepare to read them aloud to the class. If you wish, illustrate some of them and show your pictures while you are reading.

10. The Greek gods intervened in spectacular ways in the affairs of men. Find several examples of such intervention. In your opinion, do these interventions of the gods make the stories more exciting, or less?

11. Who was Hermes? (You may look him up in Chapter 9.) What was his Roman name? What were his main characteristics? his duties? Can you think of any present-day uses of his Greek and Roman names?

12. Who was Hercules? How many of his twelve labors can you remember? (Look them up in Chapter 13.) When we speak of a *Herculean* task, what do we mean? In addition to his great labors, what momentous task did Hercules have that we all have to some degree?

13. Who was Apollo? (You may look him up in Chapter 7.) When we say of a young man: "He is a regular Apollo," what do we mean?

14. What is a labyrinth? What was it in Greek mythology? Explain the connection of each of the following with the labyrinth: Minos, the Minotaur, Theseus, Daedalus, Ariadne, Aphrodite, Aegeus.

15. One of the most appealing stories of the Greeks is that of Icarus. What moral for teen-agers might you draw from it?

16. W. H. D. Rouse tells us that he used his imagination for the dialogues in these stories. He justifies this by explaining that the Greek writers of the stories did the same. Find examples of dialogue that you think were made up by Rouse—and probably not by any Greek.

17. How did the Greek gods die in the end? Which two did not die?

18. How does our idea of God differ from the Greeks' idea of their gods? What are some of the traits of character of the Greek gods?

19. What do we mean today when we say a person is "between Scylla and Charybdis"? What do we mean when we call a woman an Amazon? a harpy? a siren? Why is a book of maps called an atlas? Can you think of other present-day words and expressions that have their origin in Greek mythology?

20. Be alert during the next day or two to note and jot down every reference to Greek mythology that you see or hear. You will find advertising and brand names sources of reference. You may also find references in books, conversations, the movies, and television.

Treasure Island

by Robert Louis Stevenson

SOMETIME or other before he is very old, every boy draws a map of an island. Sometimes when a grown man daydreams, he too draws a map of a Magic Island, a Desert Island, or a Treasure Island. This is what Robert Louis Stevenson did one afternoon in 1883.

He was thirty-three years old and already a very well-known writer of stories, essays, and poetry, but he had never published a novel. He had written several of them in earlier years; in fact, Stevenson wrote his first novel, which he called *Rathillett,* when he was not yet fifteen.

This is the way *Treasure Island* came to be written: Stevenson had gone to Kinnaird in Scotland to stay with his father. A young college boy was also a guest in the house. This fellow thought he might become an artist and so spent his days painting and drawing in one of the rooms. Stevenson visited him there and one day he took a piece of paper and started to doodle with both a pen and water colors. Suddenly Stevenson realized that he had made something very interesting. This is what he wrote about the event later:

> I made a map of an island . . . the shape of it took my fancy beyond expression; it contained harbors that pleased me like sonnets; and with an unconsciousness of the predestined, I ticketed my performance, "Treasure Island."

Now, as he looked at this map of his imaginary island, he knew that he must write a novel. He said, "It was to be a novel for boys." It was to be about a boy. "Women were excluded."

He gave names to the harbors, the hills, the rivers, and the forest lands. Then he started to think of characters and their adventures. The ideas he got came from tales he had heard, stories he had read, and people he had known. There was Edgar Allan Poe's tale "The Gold Bug"; there was Daniel Defoe's *Robinson Crusoe;* there were Washington Irving's *Tales of a Traveller* and Captain Frederick Marryat's *Masterman Ready*. Stevenson says all of these stories helped him as he planned his novel.

For Long John Silver, Stevenson used a very good friend of his as a model. He took this friend's character and, as he says, deprived him of "all his finer qualities and higher graces of temperament to leave him with nothing but his strength, his courage, his quickness, his magnificent geniality." What was left was the black-hearted but somehow lovable one-legged pirate. This man became the Sea Cook in the story. Stevenson even called the book the *Sea Cook* at first, but his publisher changed the title to *Treasure Island*. And so it became one of the greatest book treasures of all time.

To
S. L. O.,
AN AMERICAN GENTLEMAN,
IN ACCORDANCE WITH WHOSE CLASSIC TASTE
THE FOLLOWING NARRATIVE HAS BEEN DESIGNED,
IT IS NOW, IN RETURN FOR NUMEROUS DELIGHTFUL HOURS,
AND WITH THE KINDEST WISHES,
DEDICATED
BY HIS AFFECTIONATE FRIEND,

THE AUTHOR

PART ONE—The Old Buccaneer

Chapter 1

THE OLD SEA DOG AT THE "ADMIRAL BENBOW"

Squire [1] Trelawney, Dr. Livesey, and the rest of these gentlemen having asked me to write down the whole particulars about Treasure Island from the beginning to the end, keeping nothing back but the bearings of the island, and that only because there is still treasure not yet lifted, I take up my pen in the year of grace 17–, and go back to the time when my father kept the "Admiral Benbow" inn, and the brown old seaman with the saber cut first took up his lodging under our roof.

I remember him as if it were yesterday, as he came plodding to the inn door, his sea chest following behind him in a handbarrow; a tall, strong, heavy, nut-brown man; his tarry pigtail falling over the shoulders of his soiled blue coat; his hands ragged and scarred, with black, broken nails; and the saber cut across one cheek, a dirty, livid [2] white. I remember him looking round the cove and whistling to himself as he did so and then breaking out in that old sea song that he sang so often afterwards:

> Fifteen men on the Dead Man's Chest—
> Yo-ho-ho, and a bottle of rum!

in the high, old tottering voice that seemed to have been tuned and broken at the capstan bars. Then he rapped on the door with a bit of stick like a handspike that he carried and when my father

[1] *squire* (skwīr): land owner, country gentleman. [2] *livid* (lĭv′ĭd): discolored.

appeared, called roughly for a glass of rum. This, when it was brought to him, he drank slowly, like a connoisseur,[1] lingering on the taste and still looking about him at the cliffs and up at our signboard.

"This is a handy cove," says he, at length; "and a pleasant sittyated grog shop. Much company, mate?"

My father told him no, very little company, the more was the pity.

"Well, then," said he, "this is the berth for me. Here you, matey," he cried to the man who trundled the barrow; "bring up alongside and help up my chest. I'll stay here a bit," he continued. "I'm a plain man; rum and bacon and eggs is what I want, and that head [2] up there for to watch ships off. What you mought call me? You mought call me captain. Oh, I see what you're at—there"; and he threw down three or four gold pieces on the threshold. "You can tell me when I've worked through that," says he, looking as fierce as a commander.

And, indeed, bad as his clothes were, and coarsely as he spoke, he had none of the appearance of a man who sailed before the mast; [3] but seemed, like a mate or skipper, accustomed to be obeyed or to strike. The man who came with the barrow told us the mail [4] had set him down the morning before at the "Royal George"; that he had inquired what inns there were along the coast and hearing ours well spoken of, I suppose, and described as lonely, had chosen it from the others for his place of residence. And that was all we could learn of our guest.

He was a very silent man by custom. All day he hung round the cove or upon the cliffs, with a brass telescope; all evening he sat in a corner of the parlor next the fire and drank rum and water very strong. Mostly he would not speak when spoken to; only look up sudden and fierce and blow through his nose like a foghorn; and we and the people who came about our house soon learned to let him be. Every day, when he came back from his stroll, he would ask if any seafaring men had gone by along the road. At first we thought it was the want of company of his own kind that made him ask this question; but at last we began to see

[1] *connoisseur* (kŏn′ĭ·sûr′): an expert judge. [2] *head:* a high point of land. [3] *a man . . . before the mast:* a crew member, so called because the crew's quarters were in the forward part of the ship. [4] *mail:* the carriage bringing the mail.

he was desirous to avoid them. When a seaman put up at the "Admiral Benbow" (as now and then some did, making by the coast road for Bristol), he would look in at him through the curtained door before he entered the parlor; and he was always sure to be as silent as a mouse when any such was present. For me, at least, there was no secret about the matter; for I was, in a way, a sharer in his alarms. He had taken me aside one day and promised me a silver fourpenny on the first of every month if I would only keep my "weather-eye open for a seafaring man with one leg" and let him know the moment he appeared. Often enough, when the first of the month came round and I applied to him for my wage, he would only blow through his nose at me and stare me down; but before the week was out he was sure to think better of it, bring me my fourpenny piece, and repeat his orders to look out for "the seafaring man with one leg."

How that personage haunted my dreams, I need scarcely tell you. On stormy nights, when the wind shook the four corners of the house, and the surf roared along the cove and up the cliffs, I would see him in a thousand forms, and with a thousand diabolical [1] expressions. Now the leg would be cut off at the knee, now at the hip; now he was a monstrous kind of creature who had never had but the one leg, and that in the middle of his body. To see him leap and run and pursue me over hedge and ditch was the worst of nightmares. And altogether I paid pretty dear for my monthly fourpenny piece, in the shape of these abominable fancies.

But though I was so terrified by the idea of the seafaring man with one leg, I was far less afraid of the captain himself than anybody else who knew him. There were nights when he took a deal more rum and water than his head would carry; and then he would sometimes sit and sing his wicked, old, wild sea songs, minding nobody; but sometimes he would call for glasses round and force all the trembling company to listen to his stories or bear a chorus to his singing. Often I have heard the house shaking with "Yo-ho-ho, and a bottle of rum"; all the neighbors joining in for dear life, with the fear of death upon them, and each singing louder than the other to avoid remark. For in these fits he was the most over-riding companion ever known; he would slap his hand on the table for silence all round; he would fly up in a passion of

[1] *diabolical* (dī′ȧ·bŏl′ĭ·kăl): devil-like.

anger at a question, or sometimes because none was put, and so he judged the company was not following his story. Nor would he allow anyone to leave the inn till he had drunk himself sleepy and reeled off to bed.

His stories were what frightened people worst of all. Dreadful stories they were; about hanging, and walking the plank, and storms at sea, and the Dry Tortugas,[1] and wild deeds, and places on the Spanish Main.[2] By his own account he must have lived his life among some of the wickedest men that God ever allowed upon the sea; and the language in which he told these stories shocked our plain country people almost as much as the crimes that he described. My father was always saying the inn would be ruined, for people would soon cease coming there to be tyrannized over and put down, and sent shivering to their beds; but I really believe his presence did us good. People were frightened at the time, but on looking back they rather liked it; it was a fine excitement in a quiet country life; and there was even a party of the younger men who pretended to admire him, calling him a "true sea-dog," and a "real old salt," and such like names, and saying there was the sort of man that made England terrible [3] at sea.

In one way, indeed, he bade fair to ruin us; for he kept on staying week after week, and at last month after month, so that all the money had been long exhausted, and still my father never plucked up the heart to insist on having more. If ever he mentioned it, the captain blew through his nose so loudly that you might say he roared and stared my poor father out of the room. I have seen him wringing his hands after such a rebuff, and I am sure the annoyance and the terror he lived in must have greatly hastened his early and unhappy death.

All the time he lived with us the captain made no change whatever in his dress but to buy some stockings from a hawker. One of the cocks of his hat having fallen down, he let it hang from that day forth, though it was a great annoyance when it blew. I remember the appearance of his coat, which he patched himself upstairs in his room, and which, before the end, was nothing but patches. He never wrote or received a letter, and he never spoke with any but the neighbors, and with these, for the most

[1] *Dry Tortugas* (tôr·too̅′gȧs): small islands in the West Indies. [2] *Spanish Main:* the part of the Caribbean Sea near the north coast of South America. [3] *terrible:* a cause of terror.

part, only when drunk on rum. The great sea chest none of us had ever seen open.

He was only once crossed, and that was towards the end, when my poor father was far gone in a decline that took him off. Dr. Livesey came late one afternoon to see the patient, took a bit of dinner from my mother, and went into the parlor to smoke a pipe until his horse should come down from the hamlet, for we had no stabling at the old "Benbow." I followed him in, and I remember observing the contrast the neat, bright doctor, with his powder as white as snow, and his bright, black eyes and pleasant manners made with the coltish [1] country folk, and above all with that filthy, heavy, bleared scarecrow of a pirate of ours, sitting far gone in rum, with his arms on the table. Suddenly he—the captain, that is—began to pipe up his eternal song:

Fifteen men on the Dead Man's Chest—
  Yo-ho-ho, and a bottle of rum!
Drink and the devil had done for the rest—
  Yo-ho-ho, and a bottle of rum!

At first I had supposed "the dead man's chest" to be that identical big box of his upstairs in the front room, and the thought had been mingled in my nightmares with that of the one-legged seafaring man. But by this time we had all long ceased to pay any particular notice to the song; it was new that night to nobody but Dr. Livesey, and on him I observed it did not produce an agreeable effect, for he looked up for a moment quite angrily before he went on with his talk to old Taylor, the gardener, on a new cure for the rheumatics. In the meantime, the captain gradually brightened up at his own music and at last flapped his hand upon the table before him in a way we all knew to mean—silence. The voices stopped at once, all but Dr. Livesey's; he went on as before, speaking clear and kind, and drawing briskly at his pipe between every word or two. The captain glared at him for a while, flapped his hand again, glared still harder, and at last broke out with a villainous, low oath: "Silence, there, between decks!"

"Were you addressing me, sir?" says the doctor; and when the ruffian had told him, with another oath, that this was so, "I have only one thing to say to you, sir," replies the doctor, "that if you keep on drinking rum, the world will soon be quit of a very dirty scoundrel!"

[1] *coltish* (kōlt′ĭsh): inexperienced.

The old fellow's fury was awful. He sprang to his feet, drew and opened a sailor's clasp-knife, and balancing it open on the palm of his hand, threatened to pin the doctor to the wall.

The doctor never so much as moved. He spoke to him, as before, over his shoulder, and in the same tone of voice; rather high, so that all the room might hear, but perfectly calm and steady:

"If you do not put that knife this instant in your pocket, I promise, upon my honor, you shall hang at the next assizes." [1]

Then followed a battle of looks between them; but the captain soon knuckled under, put up his weapon, and resumed his seat, grumbling like a beaten dog.

"And now, sir," continued the doctor, "since I now know there's such a fellow in my district, you may count I'll have an eye upon you day and night. I'm not a doctor only; I'm a magistrate; [2] and if I catch a breath of complaint against you, if it's only for a piece of incivility like tonight's, I'll take effectual means to have you hunted down and routed out of this. Let that suffice."

Soon after, Dr. Livesey's horse came to the door and he rode away; but the captain held his peace that evening, and for many evenings to come.

Chapter 2

BLACK DOG APPEARS AND DISAPPEARS

It was not very long after this that there occurred the first of the mysterious events that rid us at last of the captain, though not, as you will see, of his affairs. It was a bitter cold winter, with long, hard frosts and heavy gales; and it was plain from the first that my poor father was little likely to see the spring. He sank daily, and my mother and I had all the inn upon our hands and

[1] *assizes* (ă·sīz′ĕz): the time when judges hold court. [2] *magistrate* (măj′ĭs·trāt): a public official.

were kept busy enough without paying much regard to our unpleasant guest.

It was one January morning, very early—a pinching frosty morning—the cove all gray with hoar-frost, the ripple lapping softly on the stones, the sun still low and only touching the hilltops and shining far to seaward. The captain had risen earlier than usual and set out down the beach, his cutlass swinging under the broad skirts of the old blue coat, his brass telescope under his arm, his hat tilted back upon his head. I remember his breath hanging like smoke in his wake as he strode off, and the last sound I heard of him, as he turned the big rock, was a loud snort of indignation, as though his mind was still running upon Dr. Livesey.

Well, mother was upstairs with father; and I was laying the breakfast table against the captain's return, when the parlor door opened, and a man stepped in on whom I had never set my eyes before. He was a pale, tallowy creature, wanting two fingers of the left hand; and, though he wore a cutlass, he did not look much like a fighter. I had always my eye open for seafaring men, with one leg or two, and I remember this one puzzled me. He was not sailorly, and yet he had a smack of the sea about him too.

I asked him what was for his service, and he said he would take rum; but as I was going out of the room to fetch it he sat down upon a table and motioned me to draw near. I paused where I was with my napkin in my hand.

"Come here, sonny," says he. "Come nearer here."

I took a step nearer.

"Is this here table for my mate, Bill?" he asked, with a kind of leer.

I told him I did not know his mate Bill; and this was for a person who stayed in our house, whom we called the captain.

"Well," said he, "my mate Bill would be called the captain, as like as not. He has a cut on one cheek, and a mighty pleasant way with him, particularly in drink, has my mate, Bill. We'll put it, for argument like, that your captain has a cut on one cheek—and we'll put it, if you like, that that cheek's the right one. Ah, well! I told you. Now, is my mate Bill in this here house?"

I told him he was out walking.

"Which way, sonny? Which way is he gone?"

And when I had pointed out the rock and told him how the

captain was likely to return, and how soon, and answered a few other questions, "Ah," said he, "this'll be as good as drink to my mate Bill."

The expression of his face as he said these words was not at all pleasant, and I had my own reasons for thinking that the stranger was mistaken, even supposing he meant what he said. But it was no affair of mine, I thought; and besides, it was difficult to know what to do. The stranger kept hanging about just inside the inn door, peering round the corner like a cat waiting for a mouse. Once I stepped out myself into the road, but he immediately called me back, and as I did not obey quick enough for his fancy, a most horrible change came over his tallowy face, and he ordered me in, with an oath that made me jump. As soon as I was back again he returned to his former manner, half fawning,[1] half sneering, patted me on the shoulder, told me I was a good boy, and he had taken quite a fancy to me. "I have a son of my own," said he, "as like you as two blocks, and he's all the pride of my 'art. But the great thing for boys is discipline, sonny—discipline. Now, if you had sailed along of Bill, you wouldn't have stood there to be spoke to twice—not you. That was never Bill's way, nor the way of sich as sailed with him. And here, sure enough, is my mate Bill, with a spy-glass under his arm, bless his old 'art, to be sure. You and me'll just go back into the parlor, sonny, and get behind the door, and we'll give Bill a little surprise—bless his 'art, I say again."

So saying, the stranger backed along with me into the parlor and put me behind him in the corner, so that we were both hidden by the open door. I was very uneasy and alarmed, as you may fancy, and it rather added to my fears to observe that the stranger was certainly frightened himself. He cleared the hilt of his cutlass and loosened the blade in the sheath; and all the time we were waiting there he kept swallowing as if he felt what we used to call a lump in the throat.

At last in strode the captain, slammed the door behind him, without looking to the right or left, and marched straight across the room to where his breakfast awaited him.

"Bill," said the stranger, in a voice that I thought he had tried to make bold and big.

The captain spun round on his heel and fronted us; all the

[1] *fawning* (fôn′ĭng): trying to win affection or approval.

brown had gone out of his face, and even his nose was blue; he had the look of a man who sees a ghost, or the evil one, or something worse, if anything can be; and upon my word, I felt sorry to see him, all in a moment, turn so old and sick.

"Come, Bill, you know me; you know an old shipmate, Bill, surely," said the stranger.

The captain made a sort of gasp.

"Black Dog!" said he.

"And who else?" returned the other, getting more at his ease. "Black Dog as ever was, come for to see his old shipmate Billy, at the 'Admiral Benbow' inn. Ah, Bill, Bill, we have seen a sight of times, us two, since I lost them two talons," holding up his mutilated hand.

"Now, look here," said the captain; "you've run me down; here I am; well, then, speak up: what is it?"

"That's you, Bill," returned Black Dog, "you're in the right of it, Billy. I'll have a glass of rum from this dear child here, as I've took such a liking to; and we'll sit down, if you please, and talk square, like old shipmates."

When I returned with the rum, they were already seated on either side of the captain's breakfast table—Black Dog next to the door and sitting sideways, so as to have one eye on his old shipmate, and one, as I thought, on his retreat.

He bade me go and leave the door wide open. "None of your keyholes for me, sonny," he said; and I left them together and retired into the bar.

For a long time, though I certainly did my best to listen, I could hear nothing but a low gabbling; but at last the voices began to grow higher, and I could pick up a word or two, mostly oaths, from the captain.

"No, no, no, no: and an end of it!" he cried once. And again, "If it comes to swinging,[1] swing all, say I."

Then all of a sudden there was a tremendous explosion of oaths and other noises—the chair and table went over in a lump, a clash of steel followed, and then a cry of pain, and the next instant I saw Black Dog in full flight, and the captain hotly pursuing, both with drawn cutlasses, and the former streaming blood from the left shoulder. Just at the door the captain aimed at the fugitive one last tremendous cut, which would certainly have split

[1] *swinging:* hanging (for a crime).

him to the chine had it not been intercepted by our big signboard of Admiral Benbow. You may see the notch on the lower side of the frame to this day.

That blow was the last of the battle. Once out upon the road, Black Dog, in spite of his wound, showed a wonderful clean pair of heels and disappeared over the edge of the hill in half a minute. The captain, for his part, stood staring at the signboard like a bewildered man. Then he passed his hand over his eyes several times and at last turned back into the house.

"Jim," says he, "rum"; and as he spoke he reeled a little and caught himself with one hand against the wall.

"Are you hurt?" cried I.

"Rum," he repeated. "I must get away from here. Rum! rum!"

I ran to fetch it; but I was quite unsteadied by all that had fallen out, and I broke one glass and fouled the tap, and while I was still getting in my own way, I heard a loud fall in the parlor, and running in, beheld the captain lying full length upon the floor. At the same instant my mother, alarmed by the cries and fighting, came running downstairs to help me. Between us we raised his head. He was breathing very loud and hard; but his eyes were closed, and his face a horrible color.

"Dear, deary me," cried my mother, "what a disgrace upon the house! And your poor father sick!"

In the meantime, we had no idea what to do to help the captain, nor any other thought but that he had got his death-hurt in the scuffle with the stranger. I got the rum, to be sure, and tried to put it down his throat; but his teeth were tightly shut, and his jaws as strong as iron. It was a happy relief for us when the door opened and Doctor Livesey came in, on his visit to my father.

"Oh, doctor," we cried, "what shall we do? Where is he wounded?"

"Wounded? A fiddle-stick's end!" said the doctor. "No more wounded than you or I. The man has had a stroke, as I warned him. Now, Mrs. Hawkins, just you run upstairs to your husband and tell him, if possible, nothing about it. For my part, I must do my best to save this fellow's trebly worthless life; and Jim, you get me a basin."

When I got back with the basin, the doctor had already ripped up the captain's sleeve and exposed his great sinewy arm.

It was tattooed in several places. "Here's luck," "A fair wind," and "Billy Bones his fancy," were very neatly and clearly executed on the forearm; and up near the shoulder there was a sketch of a gallows and a man hanging from it—done, as I thought, with great spirit.

"Prophetic," [1] said the doctor, touching this picture with his finger. "And now, Master Billy Bones, if that be your name, we'll have a look at the color of your blood. Jim," he said, "are you afraid of blood?"

"No, sir," said I.

"Well, then," said he, "you hold the basin"; and with that he took his lancet and opened a vein.

A great deal of blood was taken before the captain opened his eyes and looked mistily about him. First he recognized the doctor with an unmistakable frown; then his glance fell upon me, and he looked relieved. But suddenly his color changed, and he tried to raise himself, crying:

"Where's Black Dog?"

"There is no Black Dog here," said the doctor, "except what you have on your own back. You have been drinking rum; you have had a stroke, precisely as I told you; and I have just, very much against my own will, dragged you headforemost out of the grave. Now, Mr. Bones——"

"That's not my name," he interrupted.

"Much I care," returned the doctor. "It's the name of a buccaneer of my acquaintance; and I call you by it for the sake of shortness, and what I have to say to you is this: one glass of rum won't kill you, but if you take one you'll take another and another, and I stake my wig if you don't break off short, you'll die—do you understand that?—die and go to your own place, like the man in the Bible. Come, now, make an effort. I'll help you to your bed for once."

Between us, with much trouble, we managed to hoist him upstairs and laid him on his bed, where his head fell back on the pillow as if he were almost fainting.

"Now, mind you," said the doctor, "I clear my conscience—the name of rum for you is death."

And with that he went off to see my father, taking me with him by the arm.

[1] *prophetic* (prô·fĕt′ĭk): foretelling the future.

"This is nothing," he said, as soon as he had closed the door. "I have drawn blood enough to keep him quiet a while; he should lie for a week where he is—that is the best thing for him and you; but another stroke would settle him."

Chapter 3 THE BLACK SPOT

About noon I stopped at the captain's door with some cooling drinks and medicines. He was lying very much as we had left him, only a little higher, and he seemed both weak and excited.

"Jim," he said, "you're the only one here that's worth anything; and you know I've been always good to you. Never a month but I've given you a silver fourpenny for yourself. And now you see, mate, I'm pretty low, and deserted by all; and Jim, you'll bring me one noggin of rum, now, won't you, matey?"

"The doctor——" I began.

But he broke in cursing the doctor, in a feeble voice, but heartily. "Doctors is all swabs," he said; "and that doctor there, why, what do he know about seafaring men? I been in places hot as pitch, and mates dropping round with Yellow Jack, and the blessed land a-heaving like the sea with earthquakes—what do the doctor know of lands like that?—and I lived on rum, I tell you. It's been meat and drink, and man and wife, to me; and if I'm not to have my rum now I'm a poor old hulk on a lee shore, my blood 'll be on you,[1] Jim, and that doctor swab"; and he ran on again for a while with curses. "Look, Jim, how my fingers fidges," he continued, in the pleading tone. "I can't keep 'em still, not I. I haven't had a drop this blessed day. That doctor's a fool, I tell you. If I don't have a drain o' rum, Jim, I'll have the horrors; I seen some on 'em already. I seen old Flint in the corner there, behind you; as plain as print, I seen him; and if I get the horrors,

[1] *my blood 'll be on you:* you'll be responsible for my death.

I'm a man that has lived rough, and I'll raise Cain. Your doctor hisself said one glass wouldn't hurt me. I'll give you a golden guinea for a noggin, Jim."

He was growing more and more excited, and this alarmed me for my father, who was very low that day and needed quiet; besides, I was reassured by the doctor's words now quoted to me and rather offended by the offer of a bribe.

"I want none of your money," said I, "but what you owe my father. I'll get you one glass, and no more."

When I brought it to him, he seized it greedily, and drank it out.

"Aye, aye," said he, "that's some better, sure enough. And now, matey, did that doctor say how long I was to lie here in this old berth?"

"A week at least," said I.

"Thunder!" he cried. "A week! I can't do that; they'd have the black spot on me by then. The lubbers [1] is going about to get the wind of me this blessed moment; lubbers as couldn't keep what they got, and want to nail what is another's. Is that seamanly behavior, now, I want to know? But I'm a saving soul. I never wasted good money of mine, nor lost it neither; and I'll trick 'em again. I'm not afraid on 'em. I'll shake out another reef, matey, and dabble 'em again." [2]

As he was thus speaking, he had risen from bed with great difficulty, holding to my shoulder with a grip that almost made me cry out, and moving his legs like so much dead weight. His words, spirited as they were in meaning, contrasted sadly with the weakness of the voice in which they were uttered. He paused when he had got into a sitting position on the edge.

"That doctor's done me," he murmured. "My ears is singing. Lay me back."

Before I could do much to help him he had fallen back again to his former place, where he lay for a while silent.

"Jim," he said, at length, "you saw that seafaring man today?"

"Black Dog?" I asked.

"Ah! Black Dog," says he. "*He's* a bad 'un; but there's worse that put him on. Now, if I can't get away nohow, and they tip me

[1] *lubber* (lŭb′ĕr): a clumsy person. [2] *I'll shake out another reef, matey, and dabble 'em again:* I'll move on and fool them again.

the black spot, mind you, it's my old sea chest they're after; you get on a horse—you can, can't you? Well, then, you get on a horse, and go to—well, yes, I will!—to that eternal doctor swab and tell him to pipe all hands [1]—magistrates and sich—and he'll lay 'em aboard at the 'Admiral Benbow'—all old Flint's crew, man and boy, all on 'em that's left. I was first mate, I was, old Flint's first mate, and I'm the on'y one as knows the place. He gave it me at Savannah, when he lay a-dying, like as if I was to now, you see. But you won't peach [2] unless they get the black spot on me, or unless you see that Black Dog again, or a seafaring man with one leg, Jim—him above all."

"But what is the black spot, Captain?" I asked.

"That's a summons,[3] mate. I'll tell you if they get that. But you keep your weather-eye open, Jim, and I'll share with you equals, upon my honor."

He wandered a little longer, his voice growing weaker; but soon after I had given him his medicine, which he took like a child, with the remark, "If ever a seaman wanted drugs, it's me," he fell at last into a heavy, swoonlike sleep, in which I left him. What I should have done had all gone well I do not know. Probably I should have told the whole story to the doctor; for I was in mortal fear lest the captain should repent of his confessions and make an end of me. But as things fell out, my poor father died quite suddenly that evening, which put all other matters on one side. Our natural distress, the visits of the neighbors, the arranging of the funeral, and all the work of the inn to be carried on in the meanwhile kept me so busy that I had scarcely time to think of the captain, far less to be afraid of him.

He got downstairs next morning, to be sure, and had his meals as usual, though he ate little and had more, I am afraid, than his usual supply of rum, for he helped himself out of the bar, scowling and blowing through his nose, and no one dared to cross him. On the night before the funeral he was as drunk as ever; and it was shocking, in that house of mourning, to hear him singing away at his ugly old sea song; but, weak as he was, we were all in fear of death for him, and the doctor was suddenly taken up with a case many miles away and was never near the house after my father's death. I have said the captain was weak; and indeed he

[1] *pipe all hands:* to call all the crew together. [2] *peach:* to tell a secret.
[3] *summons* (sŭm′ŭnz): a call or signal.

seemed rather to grow weaker than regain his strength. He clambered up and downstairs, and went from the parlor to the bar and back again, and sometimes put his nose out of doors to smell the sea, holding on to the walls as he went for support, and breathing hard and fast like a man on a steep mountain. He never particularly addressed me, and it is my belief he had as good as forgotten his confidences; but his temper was more flighty, and allowing for his bodily weakness, more violent than ever. He had an alarming way now when he was drunk of drawing his cutlass and laying it bare before him on the table. But, with all that, he minded people less and seemed shut up in his own thoughts and rather wandering. Once, for instance, to our extreme wonder, he piped up to a different air, a kind of country love song, that he must have learned in his youth before he had begun to follow the sea.

So things passed until, the day after the funeral, and about three o'clock of a bitter, foggy, frosty afternoon, I was standing at the door for a moment, full of sad thoughts about my father, when I saw someone drawing slowly near along the road. He was plainly blind, for he tapped before him with a stick and wore a great green shade over his eyes and nose; and he was hunched, as if with age or weakness, and wore a huge old tattered sea-cloak with a hood, that made him appear positively deformed. I never saw in my life a more dreadful looking figure. He stopped a little from the inn and, raising his voice in an odd singsong, addressed the air in front of him:

"Will any kind friend inform a poor blind man, who has lost the precious sight of his eyes in the gracious defense of his native country, England, and God bless King George!—where or in what part of this country he may now be?"

"You are at the 'Admiral Benbow,' Black Hill Cove, my good man," said I.

"I hear a voice," said he—"a young voice. Will you give me your hand, my kind, young friend, and lead me in?"

I held out my hand, and the horrible, soft-spoken, eyeless creature gripped it in a moment like a vice. I was so much startled that I struggled to withdraw; but the blind man pulled me close up to him with a single action of his arm.

"Now, boy," he said, "take me in to the captain."

"Sir," said I, "upon my word I dare not."

"Oh," he sneered, "that's it! Take me in straight, or I'll break your arm."

And he gave it, as he spoke, a wrench that made me cry out.

"Sir," said I, "it is for yourself I mean. The captain is not what he used to be. He sits with a drawn cutlass. Another gentleman——"

"Come, now, march," interrupted he; and I never heard a voice so cruel, and cold, and ugly as that blind man's. It cowed me more than the pain; and I began to obey him at once, walking straight in at the door and towards the parlor, where our sick old buccaneer was sitting, dazed with rum. The blind man clung close to me, holding me in one iron fist and leaning almost more of his weight on me than I could carry. "Lead me straight up to him, and when I'm in view, cry out, 'Here's a friend for you, Bill.' If you don't I'll do this"; and with that he gave me a twitch that I thought would have made me faint. Between this and that, I was so utterly terrified of the blind beggar that I forgot my terror of the captain, and as I opened the parlor door, cried out the words he had ordered, in a trembling voice.

The poor captain raised his eyes, and at one look the rum went out of him and left him staring sober. The expression of his face was not so much of terror as of mortal sickness. He made a movement to rise, but I do not believe he had enough force left in his body.

"Now, Bill, sit where you are," said the beggar. "If I can't see, I can hear a finger stirring. Business is business. Hold out your left hand. Boy, take his left hand by the wrist and bring it near to my right."

We both obeyed him to the letter, and I saw him pass something from the hollow of the hand that held his stick into the palm of the captain's, which closed upon it instantly.

"And now that's done," said the blind man; and at the words he suddenly left hold of me and, with incredible accuracy and nimbleness, skipped out of the parlor and into the road, where, as I still stood motionless, I could hear his stick go tap-tap-tapping into the distance.

It was some time before either I or the captain seemed to gather our senses; but at length, and about at the same moment, I released his wrist, which I was still holding, and he drew in his hand and looked sharply into the palm.

"Ten o'clock!" he cried. "Six hours. We'll do them yet"; and he sprang to his feet.

Even as he did so, he reeled, put his hand to his throat, stood swaying for a moment, and then, with a peculiar sound, fell from his whole height face foremost to the floor.

I ran to him at once, calling to my mother. But haste was all in vain. The captain had been struck dead by thundering apoplexy.[1] It is a curious thing to understand, for I had certainly never liked the man, though of late I had begun to pity him, but as soon as I saw that he was dead, I burst into a flood of tears. It was the second death I had known, and the sorrow of the first was still fresh in my heart.

Chapter 4 THE SEA CHEST

I lost no time, of course, in telling my mother all that I knew and perhaps should have told her long before, and we saw ourselves at once in a difficult and dangerous position. Some of the man's money—if he had any—was certainly due to us; but it was not likely that our captain's shipmates, above all the two specimens seen by me, Black Dog and the blind beggar, would be inclined to give up their booty in payment of the dead man's debts. The captain's order to mount at once and ride for Doctor Livesey would have left my mother alone and unprotected, which was not to be thought of. Indeed, it seemed impossible for either of us to remain much longer in the house: the fall of coals in the kitchen grate, the very ticking of the clock filled us with alarms. The neighborhood, to our ears, seemed haunted by approaching footsteps; and what between the dead body of the captain on the parlor floor, and the thought of that detestable blind beggar hovering near at hand, and ready to return, there were moments when, as the saying goes, I jumped in my skin for terror. Something must

[1] *apoplexy* (ăp'ô·plĕk'sĭ): sudden paralysis, a stroke.

speedily be resolved upon; and it occurred to us at last to go forth together and seek help in the neighboring hamlet.[1] No sooner said than done. Bare-headed as we were, we ran out at once in the gathering evening and the frosty fog.

The hamlet lay not many hundred yards away though out of view, on the other side of the next cove; and what greatly encouraged me, it was in an opposite direction from that whence the blind man had made his appearance and whither he had presumably returned. We were not many minutes on the road, though we sometimes stopped to lay hold of each other and hearken. But there was no unusual sound—nothing but the low wash of the ripple and the croaking of the inmates of the wood.

It was already candlelight when we reached the hamlet, and I shall never forget how much I was cheered to see the yellow shine in doors and windows; but that, as it proved, was the best of the help we were likely to get in that quarter. For—you would have thought men would have been ashamed of themselves—no soul would consent to return with us to the "Admiral Benbow." The more we told of our troubles, the more—man, woman, and child—they clung to the shelter of their houses. The name of Captain Flint, though it was strange to me, was well enough known to some there and carried a great weight of terror. Some of the men who had been to field-work on the far side of the "Admiral Benbow" remembered, besides, to have seen several strangers on the road, and taking them to be smugglers, to have bolted away; and one at least had seen a little lugger [2] in what we called Kitt's Hole. For that matter, anyone who was a comrade of the captain's was enough to frighten them to death. And the short and long of the matter was that while we could get several who were willing enough to ride to Dr. Livesey's, which lay in another direction, not one would help us to defend the inn.

They say cowardice is infectious; but then argument is, on the other hand, a great emboldener; and so when each had said his say, my mother made them a speech. She would not, she declared, lose money that belonged to her fatherless boy; "if none of the rest of you dare," she said, "Jim and I dare. Back we will go, the way we came, and small thanks to you big, hulking, chick-

[1] *hamlet* (hăm′lĕt): a small country village. [2] *lugger* (lŭg′ĕr): a ship carrying lugsails, or four-sided sails.

en-hearted men. We'll have that chest open, if we die for it. And I'll thank you for that bag, Mrs. Crossley, to bring back our lawful money in."

Of course I said I would go with my mother; and of course they all cried out at our foolhardiness; but even then not a man would go along with us. All they would do was to give me a loaded pistol, lest we were attacked; and to promise to have horses ready saddled, in case we were pursued on our return; while one lad was to ride forward to the doctor's in search of armed assistance.

My heart was beating finely when we two set forth in the cold night upon this dangerous venture. A full moon was beginning to rise and peered redly through the upper edges of the fog, and this increased our haste, for it was plain, before we came forth again, that all would be as bright as day, and our departure exposed to the eyes of any watchers. We slipped along the hedges, noiseless and swift, nor did we see or hear anything to increase our terrors, till, to our relief, the door of the "Admiral Benbow" had closed behind us.

I slipped the bolt at once, and we stood and panted for a moment in the dark, alone in the house with the dead captain's body. Then my mother got a candle in the bar, and holding each other's hands, we advanced into the parlor. He lay as we had left him, on his back, with his eyes open, and one arm stretched out.

"Draw down the blind, Jim," whispered my mother; "they might come and watch outside. And now," said she, when I had done so, "we have to get the key off *that;* and who's to touch it, I should like to know!" and she gave a kind of sob as she said the words.

I went down on my knees at once. On the floor close to his hand there was a little round of paper, blackened on the one side. I could not doubt that this was the *black spot;* and taking it up, I found written on the other side, in a very good, clear hand, this short message: "You have till ten tonight."

"He had till ten, mother," said I; and just as I said it our old clock began striking. This sudden noise startled us shockingly; but the news was good, for it was only six.

"Now, Jim," she said, "that key."

I felt in his pockets, one after another. A few small coins, a thimble, and some thread and big needles, a piece of pigtail tobacco bitten away at the end, his gully [1] with the crooked handle, a pocket compass, and a tinder box were all that they contained, and I began to despair.

"Perhaps it's round his neck," suggested my mother.

Overcoming a strong repugnance, I tore open his shirt at the neck, and there, sure enough, hanging to a bit of tarry string, which I cut with his own gully, we found the key. At this triumph we were filled with hope and hurried upstairs, without delay, to the little room where he had slept so long, and where his box had stood since the day of his arrival.

It was like any other seaman's chest on the outside, the initial "B." burned on the top of it with a hot iron, and the corners somewhat smashed and broken as by long, rough usage.

"Give me the key," said my mother; and though the lock was very stiff, she had turned it and thrown back the lid in a twinkling.

A strong smell of tobacco and tar rose from the interior, but nothing was to be seen on the top except a suit of very good clothes, carefully brushed and folded. They had never been worn, my mother said. Under that the miscellany began—a quadrant,[2] a tin cannikin, several sticks of tobacco, two brace of very handsome pistols, a piece of bar silver, an old Spanish watch and some other trinkets of little value and mostly of foreign make, a pair of compasses mounted with brass, and five or six curious West Indian shells. I have often wondered since why he should have carried about these shells with him in his wandering, guilty, and hunted life.

In the meantime, we had found nothing of any value but the silver and the trinkets, and neither of these were in our way.[3] Underneath there was an old boat cloak, whitened with sea salt on many a harbor bar. My mother pulled it up with impatience, and there lay before us the last things in the chest, a bundle tied up in oilcloth and looking like papers, and a canvas bag that gave forth, at a touch, the jingle of gold.

"I'll show these rogues that I'm an honest woman," said my mother. "I'll have my dues, and not a farthing over. Hold Mrs. Crossley's bag." And she began to count over the amount of the

[1] *gully* (gŭl'ĭ): a large knife. [2] *quadrant* (kwŏd'rănt): a device for measuring altitude. [3] *in our way:* in our line of business.

captain's score from the sailor's bag into the one that I was holding.

It was a long, difficult business, for the coins were of all countries and sizes—doubloons,[1] and louis d'ors,[2] and guineas,[3] and pieces of eight,[4] and I know not what besides, all shaken together at random. The guineas, too, were about the scarcest, and it was with these that my mother knew how to make her count.

When we were about halfway through, I suddenly put my hand upon her arm; for I had heard in the silent, frosty air a sound that brought my heart into my mouth—the tap-tapping of the blind man's stick upon the frozen road. It drew nearer and nearer, while we sat holding our breath. Then it struck sharp on the inn door, and then we could hear the handle being turned and the bolt rattling as the wretched being tried to enter; and then there was a long time of silence both within and without. At last the tapping recommenced and, to our indescribable joy and gratitude, died slowly away again until it ceased to be heard.

"Mother," said I, "take the whole and let's be going"; for I was sure the bolted door must have seemed suspicious and would bring the whole hornet's nest about our ears; though how thankful I was that I had bolted it, none could tell who had never met that terrible blind man.

But my mother, frightened as she was, would not consent to take a fraction more than was due to her and was obstinately unwilling to be content with less. It was not yet seven, she said, by a long way; she knew her rights and she would have them; and she was still arguing with me, when a little low whistle sounded a good way off upon the hill. That was enough, and more than enough, for both of us.

"I'll take what I have," she said, jumping to her feet.

"And I'll take this to square the count," said I, picking up the oilskin packet.

Next moment we were both groping downstairs, leaving the candle by the empty chest; and the next we had opened the door and were in full retreat. We had not started a moment too soon. The fog was rapidly dispersing; already the moon shone quite clear on the high ground on either side; and it was only in the ex-

[1] *doubloon* (dŭb·lo͞on′): a Spanish gold coin. [2] *louis d'or* (lo͞o′ĭ dôr′): a French gold coin. [3] *guinea* (gĭn′ĭ): an English gold coin. [4] *piece of eight:* a Spanish dollar.

act bottom of the dell and round the tavern door that a thin veil still hung unbroken to conceal the first steps of our escape. Far less than halfway to the hamlet, very little beyond the bottom of the hill, we must come forth into the moonlight. Nor was this all; for the sound of several footsteps running came already to our ears, and as we looked back in their direction, a light tossing to and fro and still rapidly advancing showed that one of the new-comers carried a lantern.

"My dear," said my mother suddenly, "take the money and run on. I am going to faint."

This was certainly the end for both of us, I thought. How I cursed the cowardice of the neighbors; how I blamed my poor mother for her honesty and her greed, for her past foolhardiness and present weakness! We were just at the little bridge, by good fortune; and I helped her, tottering as she was, to the edge of the bank, where, sure enough, she gave a sigh and fell on my shoulder. I do not know how I found the strength to do it at all, and I am afraid it was roughly done; but I managed to drag her down the bank and a little way under the arch. Farther I could not move her, for the bridge was too low to let me do more than crawl below it. So there we had to stay—my mother almost entirely exposed, and both of us within earshot of the inn.

Chapter 5 THE LAST OF THE BLIND MAN

My curiosity, in a sense, was stronger than my fear; for I could not remain where I was but crept back to the bank again, whence, sheltering my head behind a bush of broom, I might command the road before our door. I was scarcely in position ere my enemies began to arrive, seven or eight of them, running hard, their feet beating out of time along the road, and the man with the lantern some paces in front. Three men ran together, hand in hand; and I made out, even through the mist, that the middle man of this trio was the blind beggar. The next moment his voice showed me that I was right.

"Down with the door!" he cried.

"Aye, aye, sir!" answered two or three; and a rush was made upon the "Admiral Benbow," the lantern-bearer following; and then I could see them pause and hear speeches passed in a lower key, as if they were surprised to find the door open. But the pause was brief, for the blind man again issued his commands. His voice sounded louder and higher, as if he were afire with eagerness and rage.

"In, in, in!" he shouted, and cursed them for their delay.

Four or five of them obeyed at once, two remaining on the road with the formidable beggar. There was a pause, then a cry of surprise, and then a voice shouting from the house:

"Bill's dead!"

But the blind man swore at them again for their delay.

"Search him, some of you shirking lubbers, and the rest of you aloft and get the chest," he cried.

I could hear their feet rattling up our old stairs, so that the house must have shook with it. Promptly afterwards, fresh sounds of astonishment arose; the window of the Captain's room was thrown open with a slam and a jingle of broken glass; and a man leaned out into the moonlight, head and shoulders, and addressed the blind beggar on the road below him.

"Pew," he cried, "they've been before us. Someone's turned the chest out alow and aloft." [1]

"It is there?" roared Pew.

"The money's there."

The blind man cursed the money.

"Flint's fist, I mean," he cried.

"We don't see it here nohow," returned the man.

"Here, you below there, is it on Bill?" cried the blind man again.

At that, another fellow, probably him who had remained below to search the captain's body, came to the door of the inn. "Bill's been overhauled [2] a'ready," said he, "nothin' left."

"It's these people of the inn—it's that boy. I wish I had put

[1] *alow and aloft:* from top to bottom. [2] *overhauled:* searched.

his eyes out!" cried the blind man Pew. "They were here no time ago—they had the door bolted when I tried it. Scatter, lads, and find 'em."

"Sure enough, they left their glim [1] here," said the fellow from the window.

"Scatter and find 'em! Rout the house out!" reiterated Pew, striking with his stick upon the road.

Then there followed a great to-do through all our old inn, heavy feet pounding to and fro, furniture thrown over, doors kicked in, until the very rocks re-echoed, and the men came out again, one after another, on the road, and declared that we were nowhere to be found. And just then the same whistle that had alarmed my mother and myself over the dead captain's money was once more clearly audible through the night, but this time twice repeated. I had thought it to be the blind man's trumpet, so to speak, summoning his crew to the assault; but I now found that it was a signal from the hillside towards the hamlet, and from its effect upon the buccaneers, a signal to warn them of approaching danger.

"There's Dirk again," said one. "Twice! We'll have to budge, mates."

"Budge, you skulk!" cried Pew. "Dirk was a fool and a coward from the first—you wouldn't mind him. They must be close by; they can't be far; you have your hands on it. Scatter and look for them, dogs! Oh, shiver my soul," he cried, "if I had eyes!"

This appeal seemed to produce some effect, for two of the fellows began to look here and there among the lumber, but half-heartedly, I thought, and with half an eye to their own danger all the time, while the rest stood irresolute [2] on the road.

"You have your hands on thousands, you fools, and you hang a leg! You'd be rich as kings if you could find it, and you know it's here, and you stand there skulking. There wasn't one of you dared face Bill, and I did it—a blind man! And I'm to lose my chance for you! I'm to be a poor, crawling beggar, sponging for rum, when I might be rolling in a coach! If you had the pluck [3] of a weevil [4] in a biscuit you would catch them still."

"Hang it, Pew, we've got the doubloons!" grumbled one.

"They might have hid the blessed thing," said another.

[1] *glim* (glĭm): a light (slang). [2] *irresolute* (ĭ·rĕz′ō·lūt): undecided. [3] *pluck* (plŭk): courage. [4] *weevil* (wē′v'l): a beetle.

"Take the Georges,[1] Pew, and don't stand there squalling."[2]

Squalling was the word for it, Pew's anger rose so high at these objections; till at last, his passion completely taking the upper hand, he struck at them right and left in his blindness, and his stick sounded heavily on more than one.

These, in their turn, cursed back at the blind miscreant,[3] threatened him in horrid terms, and tried in vain to catch the stick and wrest it from his grasp.

This quarrel was the saving of us; for while it was still raging, another sound came from the top of the hill on the side of the hamlet—the tramp of horses galloping. Almost at the same time a pistol-shot, flash, and report, came from the hedge side. And that was plainly the last signal of danger; for the buccaneers[4] turned at once and ran, separating in every direction, one seaward along the cove, one slant across the hill, and so on, so that in half a minute not a sign of them remained but Pew. Him they had deserted, whether in sheer panic or out of revenge for his ill words and blows, I know not; but there he remained behind, tapping up and down the road in a frenzy, and groping and calling for his comrades. Finally he took the wrong turn and ran a few steps past me, towards the hamlet, crying:

"Johnny, Black Dog, Dirk," and other names, "you won't leave old Pew, mates—not old Pew!"

Just then the noise of horses topped the rise, and four or five riders came in sight in the moonlight and swept at full gallop down the slope.

At this Pew saw his error, turned with a scream, and ran straight for the ditch, into which he rolled. But he was on his feet again in a second and made another dash, now utterly bewildered, right under the nearest of the coming horses.

The rider tried to save him, but in vain. Down went Pew with a cry that rang high into the night; and the four hoofs trampled and spurned him and passed by. He fell on his side, then gently collapsed upon his face and moved no more.

I leaped to my feet and hailed the riders. They were pulling up, at any rate, horrified at the accident; and I soon saw what they were. One, tailing out behind the rest, was a lad that had gone from the hamlet to Dr. Livesey's; the rest were revenue offi-

[1] *Georges:* coins (slang). [2] *squall* (skwôl): to scream. [3] *miscreant* (mĭs′krē̇·ănt): a villain. [4] *buccaneer* (bŭk′ȧ·nēr′): a pirate.

cers, whom he had met by the way, and with whom he had had the intelligence to return at once. Some news of the lugger in Kitt's Hole had found its way to Supervisor Dance and set him forth that night in our direction, and to that circumstance my mother and I owed our preservation from death.

Pew was dead, stone dead. As for my mother, when we had carried her up to the hamlet, a little cold water and salts and that soon brought her back again, and she was none the worse for her terror, though she still continued to deplore the balance of the money.[1] In the meantime, the supervisor rode on as fast as he could to Kitt's Hole; but his men had to dismount and grope down the dingle,[2] leading, and sometimes supporting, their horses, and in continual fear of ambushes; so it was no great matter for surprise that when they got down to the Hole, the lugger was already under way, though still close in. He hailed her. A voice replied, telling him to keep out of the moonlight, or he would get some lead in him, and at the same time a bullet whistled close by his arm. Soon after, the lugger doubled the point and disappeared. Mr. Dance stood there, as he said, "like a fish out of water," and all he could do was to despatch a man to B—— to warn the cutter. "And that," said he, "is just about as good as nothing. They've got off clean, and there's an end. Only," he added, "I'm glad I trod on Master Pew's corns"; for by this time he had heard my story.

I went back with him to the "Admiral Benbow," and you cannot imagine a house in such a state of smash; the very clock had been thrown down by these fellows in their furious hunt after my mother and myself; and though nothing had actually been taken away except the captain's moneybag and a little silver from the till, I could see at once that we were ruined. Mr. Dance could make nothing of the scene.

"They got the money, you say? Well, then, Hawkins, what in fortune were they after? More money, I suppose?"

"No, sir; not money, I think," replied I. "In fact, sir, I believe I have the thing in my breast pocket; and, to tell you the truth, I should like to get it put in safety."

"To be sure, boy; quite right," said he. "I'll take it, if you like."

[1] *deplore the balance of the money:* to regret not having been paid in full. [2] *dingle* (dĭng′g'l): a wooded valley.

"I thought, perhaps, Dr. Livesey——" I began.

"Perfectly right," he interrupted, very cheerily, "perfectly right—a gentleman and a magistrate. And, now I come to think of it, I might as well ride round there myself and report to him or squire. Master Pew's dead, when all's done; not that I regret it, but he's dead, you see, and people will make it out against an officer of his Majesty's revenue, if make it out they can. Now, I'll tell you, Hawkins: if you like, I'll take you along."

I thanked him heartily for the offer, and we walked back to the hamlet where the horses were. By the time I had told mother of my purpose they were all in the saddle.

"Dogger," said Mr. Dance, "you have a good horse; take up this lad behind you."

As soon as I was mounted, holding on to Dogger's belt, the supervisor gave the word, and the party struck out at a bouncing trot on the road to Dr. Livesey's house.

Chapter 6 THE CAPTAIN'S PAPERS

We rode hard all the way, till we drew up before Dr. Livesey's door. The house was all dark to the front.

Mr. Dance told me to jump down and knock, and Dogger gave me a stirrup to descend by. The door was opened almost at once by the maid.

"Is Dr. Livesey in?" I asked.

No, she said; he had come home in the afternoon, but had gone up to the Hall to dine and pass the evening with the squire.

This time, as the distance was short, I did not mount, but ran with Dogger's stirrup-leather to the lodge gates, and up the long, leafless, moonlit avenue to where the white line of the Hall buildings looked on either hand on great old gardens. Here Mr. Dance dismounted, and, taking me along with him, was admitted at a word into the house.

The servant led us down a matted passage and showed us at the end into a great library, all lined with bookcases and busts upon the top of them, where the squire and Dr. Livesey sat, pipe in hand, on either side of a bright fire.

I had never seen the squire so near at hand. He was a tall man, over six feet high, and broad in proportion, and he had a bluff, rough-and-ready face, all roughened and reddened and lined in his long travels. His eyebrows were very black and moved readily, and this gave him a look of some temper, not bad, you would say, but quick and high.

"Come in, Mr. Dance," says he, very stately and condescending.

"Good evening, Dance," says the doctor, with a nod. "And good evening to you, friend Jim. What good wind brings you here?"

The supervisor stood up straight and stiff and told his story like a lesson; and you should have seen how the two gentlemen leaned forward and looked at each other, and forgot to smoke in their surprise and interest. When they heard how my mother went back to the inn, Dr. Livesey fairly slapped his thigh, and the squire cried "Bravo!" and broke his long pipe against the grate. Long before it was done, Mr. Trelawney (that, you will remember, was the squire's name) had got up from his seat, and was striding about the room, and the doctor, as if to hear the better, had taken off his powdered wig, and sat there, looking very strange indeed with his own close-cropped, black poll.

At last Mr. Dance finished the story.

"Mr. Dance," said the squire, "you are a very noble fellow. And as for riding down that black, atrocious miscreant, I regard it as an act of virtue, sir, like stamping on a cockroach. This lad Hawkins is a trump, I perceive. Hawkins, will you ring that bell? Mr. Dance must have some ale."

"And so, Jim," said the doctor, "you have the thing that they were after, have you?"

"Here it is, sir," said I, and gave him the oilskin packet.

The doctor looked it all over, as if his fingers were itching to open it; but, instead of doing that, he put it quietly in the pocket of his coat.

"Squire," said he, "when Dance has had his ale he must, of course, be off on his Majesty's service; but I mean to keep Jim

Hawkins here to sleep at my house, and, with your permission, I propose we should have up the cold pie, and let him sup."

"As you will, Livesey," said the squire; "Hawkins has earned better than cold pie."

So a big pigeon pie was brought in and put on a side-table, and I made a hearty supper, for I was as hungry as a hawk, while Mr. Dance was further complimented and at last dismissed.

"And now, squire," said the doctor.

"And now, Livesey," said the squire, in the same breath.

"One at a time, one at a time," laughed Dr. Livesey. "You have heard of this Flint, I suppose?"

"Heard of him!" cried the squire. "Heard of him, you say! He was the bloodthirstiest buccaneer that sailed. Blackbeard was a child to Flint. The Spaniards were so prodigiously afraid of him that, I tell you, sir, I was sometimes proud he was an Englishman. I've seen his topsails with these eyes, off Trinidad, and the cowardly son of a rumpuncheon [1] that I sailed with put back—put back, sir, into Port of Spain."

"Well, I've heard of him myself, in England," said the doctor. "But the point is, had he money?"

"Money!" cried the squire. "Have you heard the story? What were these villains after but money? What do they care for but money? For what would they risk their rascal carcasses but money?"

"That we shall soon know," replied the doctor. "But you are so confoundedly hot-headed and exclamatory that I cannot get a word in. What I want to know is this: Supposing that I have here in my pocket some clue to where Flint buried his treasure, will that treasure amount to much?"

"Amount, sir!" cried the squire. "It will amount to this: if we have the clue you talk about, I fit out a ship in Bristol dock and take you and Hawkins here along, and I'll have that treasure if I search a year."

"Very well," said the doctor. "Now, then, if Jim is agreeable, we'll open the packet"; and he laid it before him on the table.

The bundle was sewn together, and the doctor had to get out his instrument case and cut the stitches with his medical scissors. It contained two things—a book and a sealed paper.

[1] *rumpuncheon* (rŭm·pŭn′chŭn): a cask of rum.

"First of all we'll try the book," observed the doctor.

The squire and I were both peering over his shoulder as he opened it, for Dr. Livesey had kindly motioned me to come round from the side-table, where I had been eating, to enjoy the sport of the search. On the first page there were only some scraps of writing, such as a man with a pen in his hand might make for idleness or practice. One was the same as the tattoo mark, "Billy Bones his fancy"; then there was "Mr. W. Bones, mate." "No more rum." "Off Palm Key he got itt"; and some other snatches, mostly single words and unintelligible. I could not help wondering who it was that had "got itt," and what "itt" was that he got. A knife in his back as like as not.

"Not much instruction there," said Dr. Livesey as he passed on.

The next ten or twelve pages were filled with a curious series of entries. There was a date at one end of the line and at the other a sum of money, as in common account books; but instead of explanatory writing, only a varying number of crosses between the two. On the 12th of June, 1745, for instance, a sum of seventy pounds had plainly become due to some one, and there was nothing but six crosses to explain the cause. In a few cases, to be sure, the name of a place would be added, as "Offe Caraccas"; or a mere entry of latitude and longitude,[1] as "62° 17′ 20″, 19° 2′ 40″."

The record lasted over nearly twenty years, the amount of the separate entries growing larger as time went on, and at the end a grand total had been made out, after five or six wrong additions, and these words appended, "Bones, his pile."

"I can't make head or tail of this," said Dr. Livesey.

"The thing is as clear as noonday," cried the squire. "This is the black-hearted hound's account book. These crosses stand for the names of ships or towns that they sank or plundered. The sums are the scoundrel's share, and where he feared an ambiguity,[2] you see, he added something clearer. 'Offe Caraccas,' now; you see, here was some unhappy vessel boarded off that coast. God help the poor souls that manned her—coral [3] long ago."

[1] *latitude and longitude* (lăt′ĭ·tūd; lŏn′jĭ·tūd): lines on a map indicating distance north-south and east-west; used to find a position. [2] *ambiguity* (ăm′bĭ·gū′ĭ·tĭ): uncertainty. [3] *coral:* He means "turned to coral"—dead.

"Right!" said the doctor. "See what it is to be a traveler. Right! And the amounts increase, you see, as he rose in rank."

There was little else in the volume but a few bearings of places noted in the blank leaves towards the end, and a table for reducing French, English, and Spanish moneys to a common value.

"Thrifty man!" cried the doctor. "He wasn't the one to be cheated."

"And now," said the squire, "for the other."

The paper had been sealed in several places with a thimble by way of seal; the very thimble, perhaps, that I had found in the captain's pocket. The doctor opened the seals with great care, and there fell out the map of an island, with latitude and longitude, soundings,[1] names of hills, and bays and inlets, and every particular that would be needed to bring a ship to a safe anchorage upon its shores. It was about nine miles long and five across, shaped, you might say, like a fat dragon standing up, and had two fine land-locked harbors, and a hill in the center part marked "The Spy-glass." There were several additions of a later date; but, above all, three crosses of red ink—two on the north part of the island, one in the southwest, and, beside this last, in the same red ink, and in a small, neat hand, very different from the captain's tottery characters, these words: "Bulk of treasure here."

Over on the back the same hand had written this further information:

> Tall tree, Spy-glass shoulder, bearing point to the N. of N.N.E.
> Skeleton Island E.S.E. and by E.
> Ten feet.
> The bar silver is in the north cache;[2] you can find it by the trend of the east hummock, ten fathoms south of the black crag with the face on it.
> The arms are easy found, in the sand hill N. point of north inlet cape, bearing E. and a quarter N. J. F.

That was all; but brief as it was, and, to me, incomprehensible, it filled the squire and Dr. Livesey with delight.

"Livesey," said the squire, "you will give up this wretched practice at once. Tomorrow I start for Bristol. In three weeks' time—three weeks!—two weeks—ten days—we'll have the best ship, sir, and the choicest crew in England. Hawkins shall come

[1] *soundings:* measures of depth of water. [2] *cache* (kăsh): a hiding place.

as cabin boy. You'll make a famous cabin boy, Hawkins. You, Livesey, are ship's doctor; I am admiral. We'll take Redruth, Joyce, and Hunter. We'll have favorable winds, a quick passage, and not the least difficulty in finding the spot, and money to eat—to roll in—to play duck and drake with ever after."

"Trelawney," said the doctor, "I'll go with you; and, I'll go bail for it, so will Jim, and be a credit to the undertaking. There's only one man I'm afraid of."

"And who's that?" cried the squire. "Name the dog, sir!"

"You," replied the doctor; "for you cannot hold your tongue. We are not the only men who know of this paper. These fellows who attacked the inn tonight—bold, desperate blades, for sure—and the rest who stayed aboard that lugger, and more, I dare say, not far off, are, one and all, through thick and thin, bound that they'll get that money. We must none of us go alone till we get to sea. Jim and I shall stick together in the meanwhile; you'll take Joyce and Hunter when you ride to Bristol, and, from first to last, not one of us must breathe a word of what we've found."

"Livesey," returned the squire, "you are always in the right of it. I'll be as silent as the grave."

PART TWO—The Sea Cook

Chapter 7 I GO TO BRISTOL

It was longer than the squire imagined ere we were ready for the sea, and none of our first plans—not even Dr. Livesey's, of keeping me beside him—could be carried out as we intended. The doctor had to go to London for a physician to take charge of his practice; the squire was hard at work at Bristol; and I lived on at the Hall under the charge of old Redruth, the gamekeeper, almost a prisoner, but full of sea dreams and the most charming anticipations of strange islands and adventures. I brooded by the hour together over the map, all the details of which I well remembered. Sitting by the fire in the housekeeper's room, I approached that island in my fancy from every possible direction; I explored every acre of its surface; I climbed a thousand times to that tall hill they call the Spy-glass and from the top enjoyed the most wonderful and changing prospects. Sometimes the isle was thick with savages, with whom we fought; sometimes full of dangerous animals that hunted us; but in all my fancies nothing occurred to me so strange and tragic as our actual adventures.

So the weeks passed on, till one fine day there came a letter addressed to Dr. Livesey, with this addition, "To be opened, in the case of his absence, by Tom Redruth or young Hawkins." Obeying this order, we found, or rather, I found—for the gamekeeper was a poor hand at reading anything but print—the following important news:

Old Anchor Inn, Bristol, March 1, 17—.

Dear Livesey,

As I do not know whether you are at the Hall or still in London, I send this in double to both places.

The ship is bought and fitted. She lies at anchor, ready for sea. You never imagined a sweeter schooner—a child might sail her—two hundred tons; name *Hispaniola.*

I got her through my old friend Blandly, who has proved himself throughout the most surprising trump. The admirable fellow literally slaved in my interest, and so, I may say, did every one in Bristol as soon as they got wind of the port we sailed for—treasure, I mean.

"Redruth," said I, interrupting the letter, "Doctor Livesey will not like that. The squire has been talking, after all."

"Well, who's a better right?" growled the gamekeeper. "A pretty rum go if squire ain't to talk for [1] Doctor Livesey, I should think."

At that I gave up all attempt at commentary, and read straight on:

Blandly himself found the *Hispaniola,* and by the most admirable management got her for the merest trifle. There is a class of men in Bristol monstrously prejudiced against Blandly. They go the length of declaring that this honest creature would do anything for money, that the *Hispaniola* belonged to him, and that he sold it me absurdly high

[1] *for:* because of.

—the most transparent calumnies. None of them dare, however, to deny the merits of the ship.

So far there was not a hitch. The workpeople, to be sure—riggers and what not—were most annoyingly slow; but time cured that. It was the crew that troubled me.

I wished a round score of men—in case of natives, buccaneers, or the odious French—and I had the worry of the deuce itself to find so much as half a dozen, till the most remarkable stroke of fortune brought me the very man that I required.

I was standing on the dock, when, by the merest accident, I fell in talk with him. I found he was an old sailor, kept a public-house, knew all the seafaring men in Bristol, had lost his health ashore, and wanted a good berth as cook to get to sea again. He had hobbled down there that morning, he said, to get a smell of the salt.

I was monstrously touched—so would you have been—and, out of pure pity, I engaged him on the spot to be the ship's cook. Long John Silver, he is called, and has lost a leg; but that I regarded as a recommendation, since he lost it in his country's service, under the immortal Hawke.[1] He has no pension, Livesey. Imagine the abominable age we live in!

Well, sir, I thought I had only found a cook, but it was a crew I had discovered. Between Silver and myself we got together in a few days a company of the toughest old salts imaginable—not pretty to look at, but fellows, by their faces, of the most indomitable spirit. I declare we could fight a frigate.

Long John even got rid of two out of the six or seven I had already engaged. He showed me in a moment that they were just the sort of fresh water swabs we had to fear in an adventure of importance.

I am in the most magnificent health and spirits, eating like a bull, sleeping like a tree, yet I shall not enjoy a moment till I hear my old tarpaulins tramping round the capstan. Seaward ho! Hang the treasure! It's the glory of the sea that has turned my head. So now, Livesey, come post; do not lose an hour, if you respect me.

Let young Hawkins go at once to see his mother, with Redruth for a guard; and then both come full speed to Bristol.

JOHN TRELAWNEY.

Postscript—I did not tell you that Blandly, who, by the way, is to send a consort after us if we don't turn up by the end of August, had found an admirable fellow for sailing master—a stiff man, which I regret, but, in all other respects, a treasure. Long John Silver unearthed a very competent man for a mate, a man named Arrow. I have a boatswain [2] who pipes, Livesey; so things shall go man-o'-war fashion on board the good ship *Hispaniola*.

I forgot to tell you that Silver is a man of substance; I know of my

[1] *Hawke:* a famous British admiral. [2] *boatswain* (bō′s'n): the seaman in charge of anchors, rigging, etc.

own knowledge that he has a banker's account which has never been overdrawn. He leaves his wife to manage the inn; and as she is a woman of color, a pair of old bachelors like you and I may be excused for guessing that it is the wife, quite as much as the health, that sends him back to roving. J. T.

P.P.S.—Hawkins may stay one night with his mother.

J. T.

You can fancy the excitement into which that letter put me. I was half beside myself with glee; and if ever I despised a man, it was old Tom Redruth, who could do nothing but grumble and lament. Any of the under-gamekeepers would gladly have changed places with him; but such was not the squire's pleasure, and the squire's pleasure was like law among them all. Nobody but old Redruth would have dared so much as even to grumble.

The next morning he and I set out on foot for the "Admiral Benbow," and there I found my mother in good health and spirits. The captain, who had so long been a cause of so much discomfort, was gone where the wicked cease from troubling. The squire had had everything repaired, and the public rooms and the sign repainted, and had added some furniture—above all a beautiful armchair for mother in the bar. He had found her a boy as an apprentice also, so that she should not want [1] help while I was gone.

It was on seeing that boy that I understood, for the first time, my situation. I had thought up to that moment of the adventures before me, not at all of the home that I was leaving; and now, at sight of this clumsy stranger, who was to stay here in my place beside my mother, I had my first attack of tears. I am afraid I led that boy a dog's life; for as he was new to the work, I had a hundred opportunities of setting him right and putting him down, and I was not slow to profit by them.

The night passed, and the next day, after dinner, Redruth and I were afoot again, and on the road. I said good-by to mother, and the cove where I had lived since I was born, and the dear old "Admiral Benbow"—since he was repainted, no longer quite so dear. One of my last thoughts was of the captain, who had so often strode along the beach with his cocked hat, his saber-cut cheek, and his old brass telescope. Next moment we had turned the corner, and my home was out of sight.

[1] *want:* to need.

The mail picked us up about dusk at the "Royal George" on the heath. I was wedged in between Redruth and a stout old gentleman, and in spite of the swift motion and the cold night air, I must have dozed a great deal from the very first, and then slept like a log up hill and down dale through stage after stage; for when I was awakened, at last, it was by a punch in the ribs, and I opened my eyes to find that we were standing still before a large building in a city street, and that the day had already broken a long time.

"Where are we?" I asked.

"Bristol," said Tom. "Get down."

Mr. Trelawney had taken up his residence at an inn far down the docks to superintend the work upon the schooner. Thither we had now to walk, and our way, to my great delight, lay along the quays [1] and beside the great multitude of ships of all sizes, and rigs, and nations. In one, sailors were singing at their work; in another, there were men aloft, high over my head, hanging to threads that seemed no thicker than a spider's. Though I had lived by the shore all my life, I seemed never to have been near the sea till then. The smell of tar and salt was something new. I saw the most wonderful figureheads, that had all been far over the ocean. I saw, besides, many old sailors, with rings in their ears, and whiskers curled in ringlets, and tarry pigtails, and their swaggering, clumsy sea walk; and if I had seen as many kings or archbishops I could not have been more delighted.

And I was going to sea myself; to sea in a schooner, with a piping boatswain, and pigtailed singing seamen; to sea, bound for an unknown island, and to seek for buried treasure!

While I was still in this delightful dream, we came suddenly in front of a large inn and met Squire Trelawney, all dressed out like a sea-officer, in stout blue cloth, coming out of the door with a smile on his face, and a capital imitation of a sailor's walk.

"Here you are," he cried, "and the doctor came last night from London. Bravo! the ship's company complete!"

"Oh, sir," cried I, "when do we sail?"

"Sail!" says he. "We sail tomorrow!"

[1] *quay* (kē): a dock.

Chapter 8

AT THE SIGN OF THE "SPY-GLASS"

When I had done breakfasting, the squire gave me a note addressed to John Silver, at the sign of the "Spy-glass," and told me I should easily find the place by following the line of the docks and keeping a bright lookout for a little tavern with a large brass telescope for sign. I set off, overjoyed at this opportunity to see some more of the ships and seamen, and picked my way among a great crowd of people and carts and bales, for the dock was now at its busiest, until I found the tavern in question.

It was a bright enough little place of entertainment. The sign was newly painted; the windows had neat red curtains; the floor was cleanly sanded. There was a street on each side and an open door on both, which made the large, low room pretty clear to see in, in spite of clouds of tobacco smoke.

The customers were mostly seafaring men; and they talked so loudly that I hung at the door, almost afraid to enter.

As I was waiting, a man came out of a side room, and, at a glance, I was sure he must be Long John. His left leg was cut off close by the hip, and under the left shoulder he carried a crutch, which he managed with wonderful dexterity, hopping about upon it like a bird. He was very tall and strong, with a face as big as a ham—plain and pale, but intelligent and smiling. Indeed, he seemed in the most cheerful spirits, whistling as he moved about among the tables, with a merry word or a slap on the shoulder for the more favored of his guests.

Now, to tell you the truth, from the very first mention of Long John in Squire Trelawney's letter, I had taken a fear in my mind that he might prove to be the very one-legged sailor whom I had watched for so long at the old "Benbow." But one look at the man before me was enough. I had seen the captain, and Black Dog, and the blind man Pew, and I thought I knew what a buccaneer was like—a very different creature, according to me, from this clean and pleasant-tempered landlord.

I plucked up courage at once, crossed the threshold, and

walked right up to the man where he stood, propped on his crutch, talking to a customer.

"Mr. Silver, sir?" I asked, holding out the note.

"Yes, my lad," said he; "such is my name, to be sure. And who may you be?" And when he saw the squire's letter, he seemed to me to give something almost like a start.

"Oh!" said he, quite loud, and offering his hand. "I see. You are our new cabin boy; pleased I am to see you."

And he took my hand in his large firm grasp.

Just then one of the customers at the far side rose suddenly and made for the door. It was close by him, and he was out in the street in a moment. But his hurry had attracted my notice, and I recognized him at a glance. It was the tallow-faced man, wanting two fingers, who had come first to the "Admiral Benbow."

"Oh," I cried, "stop him! it's Black Dog!"

"I don't care two coppers who he is," cried Silver. "But he hasn't paid his score.[1] Harry, run and catch him."

One of the others who was nearest the door leaped up and started in pursuit.

"If he were Admiral Hawke he shall pay his score," cried Silver; and then, relinquishing my hand—"who did you say he was?" he asked. "Black what?"

"Dog, sir," said I. "Has Mr. Trelawney not told you of the buccaneers? He was one of them."

"So?" cried Silver. "In my house! Ben, run and help Harry. One of those swabs, was he? Was that you drinking with him, Morgan? Step up here."

The man whom he called Morgan—an old, gray-haired, mahogany-faced sailor—came forward pretty sheepishly, rolling his quid.

"Now, Morgan," said Long John, very sternly; "you never clapped your eyes on that Black—Black Dog before, did you, now?"

"Not I, sir," said Morgan, with a salute.

"You didn't know his name, did you?"

"No, sir."

"By the powers, Tom Morgan, it's as good for you!" exclaimed the landlord. "If you had been mixed up with the like

[1] *score:* the bill.

of that, you would never have put another foot in my house, you may lay to that. And what was he saying to you?"

"I don't rightly know, sir," answered Morgan.

"Do you call that a head on your shoulders or a blessed dead-eye?" cried Long John. "Don't rightly know, don't you! Perhaps you don't happen to rightly know who you was speaking to, perhaps? Come, now, what was he jawing—v'yages, cap'ns, ships? Pipe up! What was it?"

"We was a-talkin' of keel-hauling,[1] " answered Morgan.

"Keel-hauling, was you? and a mighty suitable thing, too, and you may lay to that. Get back to your place for a lubber, Tom."

And then, as Morgan rolled back to his seat, Silver added to me in a confidential whisper, that was very flattering, as I thought:

"He's quite an honest man, Tom Morgan, on'y stupid. And now," he ran on again, aloud, "let's see—Black Dog? No, I don't know the name, not I. Yet I kind of think I've—yes, I've seen the swab. He used to come here with a blind beggar, he used."

"That he did, you may be sure," said I. "I knew that blind man, too. His name was Pew."

"It was!" cried Silver, now quite excited. "Pew! That were his name for certain. Ah, he looked a shark, he did! If we run down this Black Dog, now, there'll be news for Cap'n Trelawney! Ben's a good runner; few seamen run better than Ben. He should run him down, hand over hand, by the powers! He talked o' keel-hauling, did he? *I'll* keel-haul him!"

All the time he was jerking out these phrases, he was stumping up and down the tavern on his crutch, slapping tables with his hand, and giving such a show of excitement as would have convinced an Old Bailey judge or a Bow Street runner. My suspicions had been thoroughly reawakened on finding Black Dog at the "Spy-glass," and I watched the cook narrowly. But he was too deep, and too ready, and too clever for me, and by the time the two men had come back out of breath, and confessed that they had lost the track in a crowd, and been scolded like thieves, I would have gone bail for the innocence of Long John Silver.

"See here, now, Hawkins," said he, "here's a blessed hard

[1] *keel-haul* (kēl′-hôl′): to punish by hauling under the keel of a ship.

thing on a man like me, now, ain't it? There's Cap'n Trelawney—what's he to think? Here I have this confounded son of a Dutchman sitting in my own house, drinking of my own rum! Here you comes and tells me of it plain; and here I let him give us all the slip before my blessed deadlights! [1] Now, Hawkins, you do me justice with the cap'n. You're a lad, you are, but you're smart as paint. I see that when you first came in. Now, here it is: What could I do, with this old timber I hobble on? When I was an A B master mariner I'd have come up alongside of him, hand over hand, and broached him to in a brace of old shakes,[2] I would; but now——"

And then, all of a sudden, he stopped, and his jaw dropped as though he had remembered something.

"The score!" he burst out. "Three goes o' rum! Why, shiver my timbers, if I hadn't forgotten my score!"

And falling on a bench, he laughed until the tears ran down his cheeks. I could not help joining; and we laughed together, peal after peal, until the tavern rang again.

"Why, what a precious old sea calf I am!" he said at last, wiping his cheeks. "You and me should get on well, Hawkins, for I'll take my davy I should be rated ship's boy. But, come, now, stand by to go about. This don't do. Dooty is dooty, messmates. I'll put on my old cocked hat, and step along of you to Cap'n Trelawney, and report this here affair. For, mind you, it's serious, young Hawkins; and neither you nor me's come out of it with what I should make so bold as to call credit. Nor you neither, says you; not smart—none of the pair of us smart. But dash my buttons; that was a good 'un about my score."

And he began to laugh again, and that so heartily that though I did not see the joke as he did, I was again obliged to join him in his mirth.

On our little walk along the quays he made himself the most interesting companion, telling me about the different ships that we passed by, their rig, tonnage, and nationality, explaining the work that was going forward—how one was discharging, another taking in cargo, and a third making ready for sea; and every now and then telling me some little anecdote of ships or seamen, or repeating a nautical phrase till I had learned it per-

[1] *deadlights:* eyes (slang). [2] *broached him to in a brace of old shakes:* captured him in a moment.

fectly. I began to see that here was one of the best of possible shipmates.

When we got to the inn, the squire and Dr. Livesey were seated together, finishing a quart of ale with a toast in it before they should go aboard the schooner on a visit of inspection.

Long John told the story from first to last, with a great deal of spirit and the most perfect truth. "That was how it were, now, weren't it, Hawkins?" he would say, now and again, and I could always bear him entirely out.

The two gentlemen regretted that Black Dog had got away; but we all agreed there was nothing to be done, and after he had been complimented, Long John took up his crutch and departed.

"All hands aboard by four this afternoon," shouted the squire after him.

"Aye, aye, sir," cried the cook, in the passage.

"Well, squire," said Dr. Livesey, "I don't put much faith in your discoveries, as a general thing; but I will say this, John Silver suits me."

"The man's a perfect trump," declared the squire.

"And now," added the doctor, "Jim may come on board with us, may he not?"

"To be sure he may," says squire. "Take your hat, Hawkins, and we'll see the ship."

Chapter 9 POWDER AND ARMS

The *Hispaniola* lay some way out, and we went under the figureheads and round the sterns of many other ships, and their cables sometimes grated underneath our keel, and sometimes swung above us. At last, however, we got alongside, and were met and saluted as we stepped aboard by the mate, Mr. Arrow, a brown old sailor, with earrings in his ears and a squint. He and the squire were very thick and friendly, but I soon observed that things were not the same between Mr. Trelawney and the captain.

This last was a sharp-looking man, who seemed angry with everything on board, and was soon to tell us why, for we had hardly got down into the cabin, when a sailor followed us.

"Captain Smollett, sir, axing to speak with you," said he.

"I am always at the captain's orders. Show him in," said the squire.

The captain, who was close behind his messenger, entered at once and shut the door behind him.

"Well, Captain Smollett, what have you to say? All well, I hope; all shipshape and seaworthy?"

"Well, sir," said the captain, "better speak plain, I believe, even at the risk of offense. I don't like this cruise; I don't like the men; and I don't like my officer.[1] That's short and sweet."

"Perhaps, sir, you don't like the ship?" inquired the squire, very angry, as I could see.

"I can't speak as to that, sir, not having seen her tried," said the captain. "She seems a clever craft; more I can't say."

"Possibly, sir, you may not like your employer either?" says the squire.

But here Dr. Livesey cut in.

"Stay a bit," said he, "stay a bit. No use of such questions as that but to produce ill-feeling. The captain has said too much or he has said too little, and I'm bound to say that I require an explanation of his words. You don't, you say, like this cruise. Now, why?"

"I was engaged, sir, on what we call sealed orders, to sail this ship for that gentleman where he should bid me," said the captain. "So far so good. But now I find that every man before the mast knows more than I do. I don't call that fair, now, do you?"

"No," said Dr. Livesey, "I don't."

"Next," said the captain, "I learn we are going after treasure—hear it from my own hands, mind you. Now, treasure is ticklish work; I don't like treasure voyages on any account; and I don't like them, above all, when they are secret, and when (begging your pardon, Mr. Trelawney) the secret has been told to the parrot."

"Silver's parrot?" asked the squire.

[1] *officer:* the mate or the first officer below the captain.

"It's a way of speaking," said the captain. "Blabbed, I mean. It's my belief neither of you gentlemen know what you are about; but I'll tell you my way of it—life or death, and a close run."

"That is all clear and, I daresay, true enough," replied Dr. Livesey. "We take the risk; but we are not so ignorant as you believe us. Next, you say you don't like the crew. Are they not good seamen?"

"I don't like them, sir," returned Captain Smollett. "And I think I should have had the choosing of my own hands, if you go to that."

"Perhaps you should," replied the doctor. "My friend should, perhaps, have taken you along with him; but the slight, if there be one, was unintentional. And you don't like Mr. Arrow?"

"I don't, sir. I believe he's a good seaman; but he's too free with the crew to be a good officer. A mate should keep himself to himself—shouldn't drink with the men before the mast!"

"Do you mean he drinks?" cried the squire.

"No, sir," replied the captain; "only that he's too familiar."

"Well, now, and the short and long of it, captain?" asked the doctor. "Tell us what you want."

"Well, gentlemen, are you determined to go on this cruise?"

"Like iron," answered the squire.

"Very good," said the captain. "Then, as you've heard me very patiently, saying things that I could not prove, hear me a few words more. They are putting the powder and the arms in the forehold. Now, you have a good place under the cabin; why not put them there?—first point. Then you are bringing four of your own people with you, and they tell me some of them are to be berthed forward. Why not give them the berths here beside the cabin?—second point."

"Any more?" asked Mr. Trelawney.

"One more," said the captain. "There's been too much blabbing already."

"Far too much," agreed the doctor.

"I'll tell you what I've heard myself," continued Captain Smollett: "that you have a map of an island; that there's crosses on the map to show where treasure is; and that the island lies——" And then he named the latitude and longitude exactly.

"I never told that," cried the squire, "to a soul!"

"The hands know it, sir," returned the captain.

"Livesey, that must have been you or Hawkins," cried the squire.

"It doesn't much matter who it was," replied the doctor. And I could see that neither he nor the captain paid much regard to Mr. Trelawney's protestations. Neither did I, to be sure, he was so loose a talker; yet in this case I believe he was really right, and that nobody had told the situation of the island.

"Well, gentlemen," continued the captain, "I don't know who has this map; but I make it a point, it shall be kept secret even from me and Mr. Arrow. Otherwise I would ask you to let me resign."

"I see," said the doctor. "You wish us to keep this matter dark, and to make a garrison of the stern part of the ship, manned with my friend's own people and provided with all the arms and powder on board. In other words, you fear a mutiny." [1]

"Sir," said Captain Smollett, "with no intention to take offense, I deny your right to put words into my mouth. No captain, sir, would be justified in going to sea at all if he had ground enough to say that. As for Mr. Arrow, I believe him thoroughly honest; some of the men are the same; all may be for what I know. But I am responsible for the ship's safety and the life of every man Jack aboard of her. I see things going, as I think, not quite right. And I ask you to take certain precautions or let me resign my berth. And that's all."

"Captain Smollett," began the doctor, with a smile, "did ever you hear the fable of the mountain and the mouse? You'll excuse me, I daresay, but you remind me of that fable. When you came in here I'll stake my wig you meant more than this."

"Doctor," said the captain, "you are smart. When I came in here, I meant to get discharged. I had no thought that Mr. Trelawney would hear a word."

"No more I would," cried the squire. "Had Livesey not been here I should have seen you to the deuce. As it is, I have heard you. I will do as you desire; but I think the worse of you."

"That's as you please, sir," said the captain. "You'll find I do my duty."

And with that he took his leave.

"Trelawney," said the doctor, "contrary to all my notions, I

[1] *mutiny* (mū′tĭ·nĭ): an uprising against the captain.

believe you have managed to get two honest men on board with you—that man and John Silver."

"Silver, if you like," cried the squire; "but as for that intolerable humbug, I declare I think his conduct unmanly, unsailorly, and downright un-English."

"Well," says the doctor, "we shall see."

When we came on deck, the men had begun already to take out the arms and powder, yo-ho-ing at their work, while the captain and Mr. Arrow stood by superintending.

The new arrangement was quite to my liking. The whole schooner had been overhauled; six berths had been made astern out of what had been the after-part of the main hold; and this set of cabins was only joined to the galley [1] and forecastle [2] by a sparred passage on the port [3] side. It had been originally meant that the captain, Mr. Arrow, Hunter, Joyce, the doctor, and the squire were to occupy these six berths. Now, Redruth and I were to get two of them, and Mr. Arrow and the captain were to sleep on deck in the companion,[4] which had been enlarged on each side till you might almost have called it a round-house. Very low it was still, of course; but there was room to swing two hammocks, and even the mate seemed pleased with the arrangement. Even he, perhaps, had been doubtful as to the crew, but that is only guess; for, as you shall hear, we had not long the benefit of his opinion.

We were all hard at work, changing the powder and the berths, when the last man or two, and Long John along with them, came off in a shore boat.

The cook came up the side like a monkey for cleverness, and, as soon as he saw what was doing, "So ho, mates!" says he, "what's this?"

"We're a-changing of the powder, Jack," answers one.

"Why, by the powers," cried Long John, "if we do, we'll miss the morning tide!"

"My orders!" said the captain shortly. "You may go below, my man. Hands will want supper."

[1] *galley* (găl′ĭ): a ship's kitchen. [2] *forecastle* (fōk′s'l): the upper forward part of a ship, where the crew live. [3] *port:* the left side of a ship looking forward; starboard is the right side. [4] *companion:* the space occupied by a step leading down to the cabin.

"Aye, aye, sir," answered the cook; and, touching his forelock, he disappeared at once in the direction of his galley.

"That's a good man, captain," said the doctor.

"Very likely, sir," replied Captain Smollett. "Easy with that, men—easy," he ran on to the fellows who were shifting the powder; and then suddenly observing me examining the swivel we carried amidships, a long brass nine—"Here, you, ship's boy," he cried, "out o' that! Off with you to the cook and get some work."

And then as I was hurrying off, I heard him say, quite loudly, to the doctor:

"I'll have no favorites on my ship."

I assure you I was quite of the squire's way of thinking and hated the captain deeply.

Chapter 10 THE VOYAGE

All that night we were in a great bustle getting things stowed in their place, and boatfuls of the squire's friends, Mr. Blandly and the like, coming off to wish him a good voyage and a safe return. We never had a night at the "Admiral Benbow" when I had half the work; and I was dog-tired when, a little before dawn, the boatswain sounded his pipe, and the crew began to man the capstan bars.[1] I might have been twice as weary, yet I would not have left the deck; all was so new and interesting to me—the brief commands, the shrill note of the whistle, the men bustling to their places in the glimmer of the ship's lanterns.

"Now, Barbecue, tip us a stave,[2] " cried one voice.

"The old one," cried another.

"Aye, aye, mates," said Long John, who was standing by,

[1] *capstan bar* (kăp′stăn): a bar to turn the drum to raise anchor. [2] *tip us a stave:* start a song for us.

with his crutch under his arm, and at once broke out in the air and words I knew so well:

Fifteen men on the Dead Man's Chest.

And then the whole crew bore chorus:

Yo-ho-ho, and a bottle of rum!

And at the third "ho!" drove the bars before them with a will.

Even at that exciting moment it carried me back to the old "Admiral Benbow" in a second; and I seemed to hear the voice of the captain piping in the chorus. But soon the anchor was short up; soon it was hanging dripping at the bows; soon the sails began to draw, and the land and shipping to flit by on either side; and before I could lie down to snatch an hour of slumber, the *Hispaniola* had begun her voyage to the Isle of Treasure.

I am not going to relate that voyage in detail. It was fairly prosperous. The ship proved to be a good ship, the crew were capable seamen, and the captain thoroughly understood his business. But before we came the length of Treasure Island, two or three things had happened which require to be known.

Mr. Arrow, first of all, turned out even worse than the captain had feared. He had no command among the men, and people did what they pleased with him. But that was by no means the worst of it; for after a day or two at sea he began to appear on deck with hazy eye, red cheeks, stuttering tongue, and other marks of drunkenness. Time after time he was ordered below in disgrace. Sometimes he fell and cut himself; sometimes he lay all day long in his little bunk at one side of the companion; sometimes for a day or two he would be almost sober and attend to his work at least passably.

In the meantime, we could never make out where he got the drink. That was the ship's mystery. Watch him as we pleased, we could do nothing to solve it; and when we asked him to his face, he would only laugh, if he were drunk, and if he were sober, deny solemnly that he ever tasted anything but water.

He was not only useless as an officer and a bad influence amongst the men, but it was plain that at this rate he must soon kill himself outright; so nobody was much surprised, nor very sorry, when one dark night, with a hard sea, he disappeared entirely and was seen no more.

"Overboard!" said the captain. "Well, gentlemen, that saves the trouble of putting him in irons."

But there we were, without a mate; and it was necessary, of course, to advance one of the men. The boatswain, Job Anderson, was the likeliest man aboard, and, though he kept his old title, he served in a way as mate. Mr. Trelawney had followed the sea, and his knowledge made him very useful, for he often took a watch himself in easy weather. And the coxswain,[1] Israel Hands, was a careful, wily, old, experienced seaman, who could be trusted at a pinch with almost anything.

He was a great confidant of Long John Silver, and so the mention of his name leads me on to speak of our ship's cook, Barbecue, as the men called him.

Aboard ship he carried his crutch by a lanyard [2] round his neck, to have both hands as free as possible. It was something to see him wedge the foot of the crutch against a bulkhead [3] and propped against it, yielding to every movement of the ship, get on with his cooking like someone safe ashore. Still more strange was it to see him in the heaviest of weather cross the deck. He had a line or two rigged up to help him across the widest spaces—Long John's earrings they were called; and he would hand himself from one place to another, now using the crutch, now trailing it alongside by the lanyard, as quickly as another man could walk. Yet some of the men who had sailed with him before expressed their pity to see him so reduced.

"He's no common man, Barbecue," said the coxswain to me. "He had good schooling in his young days and can speak like a book when so minded; and brave—a lion's nothing alongside of Long John! I seen him grapple four, and knocked their heads together—him unarmed."

All the crew respected and even obeyed him. He had a way of talking to each and doing everybody some particular service. To me he was unweariedly kind and always glad to see me in the galley, which he kept as clean as a new pin, the dishes hanging up burnished, and his parrot in a cage in one corner.

"Come away, Hawkins," he would say; "come and have a

[1] *coxswain* (kŏk′s'n): the seaman who steers the ship's small boat. [2] *lanyard* (lăn′yĕrd): a cord. [3] *bulkhead* (bŭlk′hĕd): a wall or partition in a ship.

yarn with John. Nobody more welcome than yourself, my son. Sit you down and hear the news. Here's Cap'n Flint—I calls my parrot Cap'n Flint, after the famous buccaneer—here's Cap'n Flint predicting success to our v'yage. Wasn't you, cap'n?"

And the parrot would say, with great rapidity, "Pieces of eight! pieces of eight! pieces of eight!" till you wondered that it was not out of breath or till John threw his handkerchief over the cage.

"Now, that bird," he would say, "is, maybe, two hundred years old, Hawkins—they lives forever mostly; and if anybody's seen more wickedness it must be the devil himself. She's sailed with England, the great Cap'n England, the pirate. She's been at Madagascar, and at Malabar, and Surinam, and Providence, and Portobello. She was at the fishing up of the wrecked plate ships.[1] It's there she learned 'Pieces of eight,' and little wonder; three hundred and fifty thousand of 'em, Hawkins! She was at the boarding of the Viceroy of the Indies out of Goa, she was; and to look at her you would think she was a babby. But you smelt powder—didn't you, cap'n?"

"Stand by to go about," the parrot would scream.

"Ah, she's a handsome craft, she is," the cook would say, and give her sugar from his pocket, and then the bird would peck at the bars and swear straight on, passing belief for wickedness. "There," John would add, "you can't touch pitch and not be mucked, lad. Here's this poor old innocent bird o' mine swearing blue fire, and none the wiser, you may lay to that. She would swear the same, in a manner of speaking, before chaplain." And John would touch his forelock with a solemn way he had that made me think he was the best of men.

In the meantime, the squire and Captain Smollett were still on pretty distant terms with one another. The squire made no bones about the matter; he despised the captain. The captain, on his part, never spoke but when he was spoken to, and then sharp and short and dry, and not a word wasted. He owned,[2] when driven into a corner, that he seemed to have been wrong about the crew, that some of them were as brisk as he wanted to see, and all had behaved fairly well. As for the ship, he had taken a downright fancy to her. "She'll lie a point nearer the wind than

[1] *plate ships:* ships carrying silver. [2] *owned:* admitted.

a man has a right to expect of his own married wife, sir. But," he would add, "all I say is we're not home again, and I don't like the cruise."

The squire, at this, would turn away and march up and down the deck, chin in air.

"A trifle more of that man," he would say, "and I shall explode."

We had some heavy weather, which only proved the qualities of the *Hispaniola*. Every man on board seemed well content, and they must have been hard to please if they had been otherwise; for it is my belief there was never a ship's company so spoiled since Noah put to sea. Double grog [1] was going on the least excuse; there was duff [2] on odd days, as, for instance, if the squire heard it was any man's birthday; and always a barrel of apples standing broached [3] in the waist, for anyone to help himself that had a fancy.

"Never knew good come of it yet," the captain said to Dr. Livesey. "Spoil fo'c'sle hands, make devils. That's my belief."

But good did come of the apple barrel, as you shall hear; for if it had not been for that, we should have had no note of warning, and might all have perished by the hand of treachery.

This was how it came about.

We had run up the trades to get the wind of the island we were after—I am not allowed to be more plain—and now we were running down for it [4] with a bright lookout day and night. It was about the last day of our outward voyage, by the largest computation; some time that night, or, at latest, before noon of the morrow, we should sight the Treasure Island. We were heading S.S.W. and had a steady breeze abeam and a quiet sea. The *Hispaniola* rolled steadily, dipping her bowsprit now and then with a whiff of spray. All was drawing [5] alow and aloft; everyone was in the bravest spirits, because we were now so near an end of the first part of our adventure.

Now, just after sundown, when all my work was over, and I was on my way to my berth, it occurred to me that I should like an apple. I ran on deck. The watch was all forward looking out for the island. The man at the helm was watching the luff of the

[1] *double grog:* double rations of rum. [2] *duff:* pudding. [3] *broach* (brōch): to open. [4] *running down for it:* sailing toward it. [5] *all was drawing:* all sails were filled with wind.

sail and whistling away gently to himself; and that was the only sound excepting the swish of the sea against the bows and around the sides of the ship.

In I got bodily into the apple barrel and found there was scarce an apple left; but, sitting down there in the dark, what with the sound of the waters and the rocking movement of the ship, I had either fallen asleep or was on the point of doing so, when a heavy man sat down with rather a clash close by. The barrel shook as he leaned his shoulders against it, and I was about to jump up when the man began to speak. It was Silver's voice, and, before I had heard a dozen words, I would not have shown myself for all the world, but lay there, trembling and listening, in the extreme of fear and curiosity; for from these dozen words I understood that the lives of all the honest men aboard depended upon me alone.

Chapter 11

WHAT I HEARD IN THE APPLE BARREL

"No, not I," said Silver. "Flint was cap'n; I was quartermaster,[1] along of my timber leg. The same broadside I lost my leg, old Pew lost his deadlights. It was a master surgeon, him that ampytated me—out of college and all—Latin by the bucket, and what not; but he was hanged like a dog and sun-dried like the rest, at Corso Castle. That was Roberts' men, that was, and comed of changing names to their ships—*Royal Fortune* and so on. Now, what a ship was christened, so let her stay, I says. So it was with the *Cassandra,* as brought us all safe home from Malabar, after England took the Viceroy of the Indies; so it was with the old *Walrus,* Flint's old ship, as I've seen a-muck with the red blood and fit to sink with gold."

[1] *quartermaster:* an officer.

"Ah!" cried another voice, that of the youngest hand on board, and evidently full of admiration, "he was the flower of the flock, was Flint!"

"Davis was a man, too, by all accounts," said Silver. "I never sailed along of him; first with England, then with Flint, that's my story; and now here on my own account, in a manner of speaking. I laid by nine hundred safe, from England, and two thousand after Flint. That ain't bad for a man before the mast—all safe in bank. 'Tain't earning now, it's saving does it, you may lay to that. Where's all England's men now? I dunno. Where's Flint's? Why, most on 'em aboard here, and glad to get the duff—been begging before that, some on 'em. Old Pew, as has lost his sight and might have thought shame, spends twelve hundred pound in a year, like a lord in Parliament. Where is he now? Well, he's dead now and under hatches; but for two years before that, shiver my timbers! the man was starving. He begged, and he stole, and he cut throats, and starved at that, by the powers!"

"Well, it ain't much use, after all," said the young seaman.

" 'Tain't much use for fools, you may lay to it—that, nor nothing," cried Silver. "But now, you look here; you're young, you are, but you're as smart as paint. I see that when I set my eyes on you, and I'll talk to you like a man."

You may imagine how I felt when I heard this abominable old rogue addressing another in the very same words of flattery as he had used to myself. I think, if I had been able, that I would have killed him through the barrel. Meantime, he ran on, little supposing he was overheard.

"Here it is about gentlemen of fortune. They lives rough, and they risk swinging, but they eat and drink like fighting cocks, and when a cruise is done, why, it's hundreds of pounds instead of hundreds of farthings in their pockets. Now, the most goes for rum and a good fling, and to sea again in their shirts. But that's not the course I lay. I puts it all away, some here, some there, and none too much anywheres, by reason of suspicion. I'm fifty, mark you; once back from this cruise, I set up gentleman in earnest. Time enough, too, says you. Ah, but I've lived easy in the meantime; never denied myself o' nothing heart desires, and slep' soft and ate dainty all my days, but when at sea. And how did I begin? Before the mast, like you!"

"Well," said the other, "but all the other money's gone now, ain't it? You daren't show face in Bristol after this."

"Why, where might you suppose it was?" asked Silver, derisively.

"At Bristol, in banks and places," answered his companion.

"It were," said the cook; "it were when we weighed anchor. But my old missis has it all by now. And the 'Spy-glass' is sold, lease and goodwill and rigging; and the old girl's off to meet me. I would tell you where, for I trust you; but it 'ud make jealousy among the mates."

"And can you trust your missis?" asked the other.

"Gentlemen of fortune," returned the cook, "usually trusts little among themselves, and right they are, you may lay to it. But I have a way with me, I have. When a mate brings a slip on his cable—one as knows me, I mean—it won't be in the same world with old John. There was some that was feared of Pew, and some that was feared of Flint; but Flint his own self was feared of me. Feared he was, and proud. They was the roughest crew afloat, was Flint's; the devil himself would have been feared to go to sea with them. Well, now, I tell you, I'm not a boasting man, and you seen yourself how easy I keep company; but when I was quartermaster, *lambs* wasn't the word for Flint's old buccaneers. Ah, you may be sure of yourself in old John's ship."

"Well, I tell you now," replied the lad, "I didn't half a quarter like the job till I had this talk with you, John; but there's my hand on it now."

"And a brave lad you were, and smart, too," answered Silver, shaking hands so heartily that all the barrel shook, "and a finer figurehead for a gentleman of fortune I never clapped my eyes on."

By this time I had begun to understand the meaning of their terms. By a "gentleman of fortune" they plainly meant neither more nor less than a common pirate, and the little scene that I had overheard was the last act in the corruption of one of the honest hands—perhaps of the last one left aboard. But on this point I was soon to be relieved, for Silver giving a little whistle, a third man strolled up and sat down by the party.

"Dick's square," said Silver.

"Oh, I know'd Dick was square," returned the voice of the coxswain, Israel Hands. "He's no fool, is Dick." And he turned his quid and spat. "But, look here," he went on, "here's what I want to know, Barbecue: how long are we a-going to stand off and on like a blessed bumboat? [1] I've had a'most enough o' Captain Smollet; he's hazed me long enough, by thunder! I want to go into that cabin, I do. I want their pickles and wines, and that."

"Israel," said Silver, "your head ain't much account, nor ever was. But you're able to hear, I reckon; leastways, your ears is big enough. Now, here's what I say: you'll berth forward, and you'll live hard, and you'll speak soft, and you'll keep sober, till I give the word; and you may lay to that, my son."

"Well, I don't say no, do I?" growled the coxswain. "What I say is, when? That's what I say."

"When! by the powers!" cried Silver. "Well, now, if you want to know, I'll tell you when. The last moment I can manage; and that's when. Here's a first-rate seaman, Cap'n Smollett, sails the blessed ship for us. Here's this squire and doctor with a map and such—I don't know where it is, do I? No more do you, says you. Well, then, I mean this squire and doctor shall find the stuff, and help us to get it aboard, by the powers. Then we'll see. If I was sure of you all, sons of double Dutchmen, I'd have Cap'n Smollett navigate us halfway back again before I struck."

"Why, we're all seamen aboard here, I should think," said the lad Dick.

"We're all fo'c'sle hands, you mean," snapped Silver. "We can steer a course, but who's to set one? That's what all you gentlemen split on, first and last. If I had my way, I'd have Cap'n Smollett work us back into the trades at least; then we'd have no blessed miscalculations and a spoonful of water a day. But I know the sort you are. I'll finish with 'em at the island, as soon's the blunt's on board, and a pity it is. But you're never happy till you're drunk. Split my sides, I've a sick heart to sail with the likes of you!"

"Easy all, Long John," cried Israel. "Who's a-crossin' of you?"

"Why, how many tall ships, think ye, now, have I seen laid aboard? and how many brisk lads drying in the sun at Execution Dock?" cried Silver, "and all for this same hurry and hurry and

[1] *bumboat* (bŭm′bōt′): a boat that brings articles for sale to ships in port or offshore.

hurry. You hear me? I seen a thing or two at sea, I have. If you would on'y lay your course, and a p'int to windward, you would ride in carriages, you would. But not you! I know you. You'll have your mouthful of rum tomorrow, and go hang."

"Everybody know'd you was a kind of a chapling, John; but there's others as could hand and steer as well as you," said Israel. "They liked a bit o' fun, they did. They wasn't so high and dry, nohow, but took their fling like jolly companions every one."

"So?" says Silver. "Well, and where are they now? Pew was that sort, and he died a beggarman. Flint was, and he died of rum at Savannah. Ah, they was a sweet crew, they was! on'y, where are they?"

"But," asked Dick, "when we do lay 'em athwart,[1] what are we to do with 'em, anyhow?"

"There's the man for me!" cried the cook, admiringly. "That's what I call business. Well, what would you think? Put 'em ashore like maroons? [2] That would have been England's way. Or cut 'em down like that much pork? That would have been Flint's or Billy Bones's."

"Billy was the man for that," said Israel. " 'Dead men don't bite,' says he. Well, he's dead now hisself; he know the long and short on it now; and if ever a rough hand come to port, it was Billy."

"Right you are," said Silver, "rough and ready. But mark you here: I'm an easy man—I'm quite the gentleman, says you; but this time it's serious. Dooty is dooty, mates. I give my vote—death. When I'm in Parlyment and riding in my coach, I don't want none of these sea lawyers in the cabin a-coming home, unlooked for, like the devil at prayers. Wait is what I say; but when the time comes, why let her rip!"

"John," cried the coxswain, "you're a man!"

"You'll say so, Israel, when you see," said Silver. "Only one thing I claim—I claim Trelawney. I'll wring his calf's head off his body with these hands, Dick!" he added, breaking off, "you just jump up, like a sweet lad, and get me an apple, to wet my pipe like."

You may fancy the terror I was in! I should have leaped out and run for it, if I had found the strength; but my limbs and heart

[1] *lay 'em athwart* (ȧ·thwôrt′): to capture them. [2] *maroon* (mȧ·rōōn′): a person left behind helpless.

alike misgave me. I heard Dick begin to rise, and then someone seemingly stopped him, and the voice of Hands exclaimed:

"Oh, stow that! Don't you get sucking of that bilge, John. Let's have a go of the rum."

"Dick," said Silver, "I trust you. I've a gauge on the keg, mind. There's the key; you fill a pannikin [1] and bring it up."

Terrified as I was, I could not help thinking to myself that this must have been how Mr. Arrow got the strong waters that destroyed him.

Dick was gone but a little while, and during his absence Israel spoke straight on in the cook's ear. It was but a word or two that I could catch, and yet I gathered some important news; for, besides other scraps that tended to the same purpose, this whole clause was audible: "Not another man of them 'll jine." Hence there were still faithful men on board.

When Dick returned, one after another of the trio took the pannikin and drank—one "To luck"; another with a "Here's to old Flint"; and Silver himself saying, in a kind of song, "Here's to ourselves, and hold your luff, plenty of prizes and plenty of duff."

Just then a sort of brightness fell upon me in the barrel, and, looking up, I found the moon had risen and was silvering the mizzen top and shining white on the luff of the foresail; and almost at the same time the voice of the lookout shouted, "Land ho!"

Chapter 12 COUNCIL OF WAR

There was a great rush of feet across the deck. I could hear people tumbling up from the cabin and the foc's'le, and, slipping in an instant outside my barrel, I dived behind the foresail, made a double towards the stern, and came out upon the open deck in

[1] *pannikin* (păn'ĭ·kĭn): a cup.

time to join Hunter and Dr. Livesey in the rush for the weather bow.

There all hands were already congregated. A belt of fog had lifted almost simultaneously with the appearance of the moon. Away to the southwest of us we saw two low hills, about a couple of miles apart, and rising behind one of them, a third and higher hill, whose peak was still buried in the fog. All three seemed sharp and conical in figure.

So much I saw, almost in a dream, for I had not yet recovered from my horrid fear of a minute or two before. And then I heard the voice of Captain Smollett issuing orders. The *Hispaniola* was laid a couple of points nearer the wind and now sailed a course that would just clear the island on the east.

"And now, men," said the captain, when all was sheeted home, "has anyone of you ever seen that land ahead?"

"I have, sir," said Silver. "I've watered there with a trader I was cook in."

"The anchorage is on the south, behind an islet, I fancy?" asked the captain.

"Yes, sir; Skeleton Island they calls it. It were a main place for pirates once, and a hand we had on board knowed all their names for it. That hill to the nor'ard they calls the Fore-mast Hill; there are three hills in a row running south'ard—fore, main, and mizzen, sir. But the main—that's the big 'un, with the cloud on it—they usually calls the Spy-glass, by reason of a lookout they kept when they was in the anchorage cleaning; for it's there they cleaned their ships, sir, asking your pardon."

"I have a chart here," says Captain Smollett. "See if that's the place."

Long John's eyes burned in his head as he took the chart; but, by the fresh look of the paper, I knew he was doomed to disappointment. This was not the map we found in Billy Bones's chest, but an accurate copy, complete in all things—names and heights and soundings—with the single exception of the red crosses and the written notes. Sharp as must have been his annoyance, Silver had the strength of mind to hide it.

"Yes, sir," said he, "this is the spot, to be sure; and very prettily drawed out. Who might have done that, I wonder? The pirates were too ignorant, I reckon. Aye, here it is: 'Capt. Kidd's Anchorage'—just the name my shipmate called it. There's a strong current runs along the south and then away nor'ard up the west coast. Right you was, sir," says he, "to haul your wind and keep the weather of the island. Leastways, if such was your intention as to enter and careen,[1] and there ain't no better place for that in these waters."

"Thank you, my man," says Captain Smollett. "I'll ask you, later on, to give us a help. You may go."

I was surprised at the coolness with which John avowed his knowledge of the island; and I own I was half-frightened when I saw him drawing nearer to myself. He did not know, to be sure, that I had overheard his council from the apple barrel, and yet I had, by this time, taken such a horror of his cruelty, duplicity,[2] and power, that I could scarce conceal a shudder when he laid his hand upon my arm.

"Ah," says he, "this here is a sweet spot, this island—a sweet spot for a lad to get ashore on. You'll bathe, and you'll climb trees, and you'll hunt goats, you will; and you'll get aloft on them hills like a goat yourself. Why, it makes me young again. I was going to forget my timber leg, I was. It's a pleasant thing to be young, and have ten toes, and you may lay to that. When you want to go a bit of exploring, you just ask old John, and he'll put up a snack for you to take along."

And clapping me in the friendliest way upon the shoulder, he hobbled off forward, and went below.

Captain Smollett, the squire, and Dr. Livesey were talking together on the quarter-deck, and, anxious as I was to tell them my story, I durst not interrupt them openly. While I was still casting about in my thoughts to find some probable excuse, Dr. Livesey called me to his side. He had left his pipe below and being a slave to tobacco, had meant that I should fetch it; but as soon as I was near enough to speak and not be overheard, I broke out immediately: "Doctor, let me speak. Get the captain and squire down to the cabin and then make some pretense to send for me. I have terrible news."

The doctor changed countenance a little, but next moment he was master of himself.

"Thank you, Jim," said he, quite loudly, "that was all I wanted to know," as if he had asked me a question.

[1] *careen* (kȧ·rēn′): to lean a ship over for repairs. [2] *duplicity* (dů·plĭs′ĭ·tĭ): double-dealing.

And with that he turned on his heel and rejoined the other two. They spoke together for a little, and though none of them started, or raised his voice, or so much as whistled, it was plain enough that Dr. Livesey had communicated my request; for the next thing that I heard was the captain giving an order to Job Anderson, and all hands were piped on deck.

"My lads," said Captain Smollett, "I've a word to say to you. This land that we have sighted is the place we have been sailing for. Mr. Trelawney, being a very open-handed gentleman, as we all know, has just asked me a word or two, and as I was able to tell him that every man on board had done his duty, alow and aloft, as I never ask to see it done better, why, he and I and the doctor are going below to the cabin to drink *your* health and luck, and you'll have grog served out for you to drink *our* health and luck. I'll tell you what I think of this: I think it handsome. And if you think as I do, you'll give a good sea cheer for the gentleman that does it."

The cheer followed—that was a matter of course; but it rang out so full and hearty that I confess I could hardly believe these same men were plotting for our blood.

"One more cheer for Cap'n Smollett," cried Long John, when the first had subsided.

And this also was given with a will.

On the top of that the three gentlemen went below, and, not long after, word was sent forward that Jim Hawkins was wanted in the cabin.

I found them all three seated round the table, a bottle of Spanish wine and some raisins before them, and the doctor smoking away, with his wig on his lap, and that, I knew, was a sign that he was agitated. The stern window was open, for it was a warm night, and you could see the moon shining behind on the ship's wake.

"Now, Hawkins," said the squire, "you have something to say. Speak up."

I did as I was bid, and as short as I could make it, told the whole details of Silver's conversation. Nobody interrupted me till I was done, nor did any one of the three of them make so much as a movement, but they kept their eyes upon my face from first to last.

"Jim," said Dr. Livesey, "take a seat."

And they made me sit down at table beside them, poured me out a glass of wine, filled my hands with raisins, and all three, one after the other, and each with a bow, drank my good health and their service to me, for my luck and courage.

"Now, captain," said the squire, "you were right, and I was wrong. I own myself an ass, and I await your orders."

"No more an ass than I, sir," returned the captain. "I never heard of a crew that meant to mutiny but what showed signs before, for any man that had an eye in his head to see the mischief and take steps according. But this crew," he added, "beats me."

"Captain," said the doctor, "with your permission, that's Silver. A very remarkable man."

"He'd look remarkably well from a yardarm,[1] sir," returned the captain. "But this is talk; this don't lead to anything. I see three or four points, and, with Mr. Trelawney's permission, I'll name them."

"You, sir, are the captain. It is for you to speak," says Mr. Trelawney grandly.

"First point," began Mr. Smollett. "We must go on, because we can't turn back. If I give the word to go about, they would rise at once. Second point, we have time before us—at least until this treasure's found. Third point, there are faithful hands. Now, sir, it's got to come to blows sooner or later; and what I propose is to take time by the forelocks, as the saying is, and come to blows some fine day when they least expect it. We can count, I take it, on your own home servants, Mr. Trelawney?"

"As upon myself," declared the squire.

"Three," reckoned the captain, "ourselves make seven, counting Hawkins here. Now, about the honest hands?"

"Most likely Trelawney's own men," said the doctor; "those he picked up for himself, before he lit on Silver."

"Nay," replied the squire, "Hands was one of mine."

"I did think I could have trusted Hands," added the captain.

"And to think that they're all Englishmen!" broke out the squire. "Sir, I could find it in my heart to blow the ship up."

"Well, gentlemen," said the captain, "the best that I can say is not much. We must lay to,[2] if you please, and keep a bright lookout. It's trying on a man, I know. It would be pleasanter to

[1] *yardarm:* a long piece of wood supporting a sail. (The captain means that Silver should be hung.) [2] *lay to:* stop the ship.

come to blows. But there's no help for it till we know our men. Lay to, and whistle for a wind, that's my view."

"Jim here," said the doctor, "can help us more than anyone. The men are not shy with him, and Jim is a noticing lad."

"Hawkins, I put prodigious faith in you," added the squire.

I began to feel pretty desperate at this, for I felt altogether helpless; and yet, by an odd train of circumstances, it was indeed through me that safety came. In the meantime, talk as we pleased, there were only seven out of the twenty-six on whom we could rely; and out of these seven one was a boy, so that the grown men on our side were six to their nineteen.

PART THREE—My Shore Adventure

Chapter 13

HOW MY SHORE ADVENTURE BEGAN

The appearance of the island when I came on deck next morning was altogether changed. Although the breeze had now utterly ceased, we had made a great deal of way during the night and were now lying becalmed about half a mile to the southeast of the low eastern coast. Gray-colored woods covered a large part of the surface. This even tint was indeed broken up by streaks of yellow sandbreak in the lower lands, and by many tall trees of the pine family, out-topping the others—some singly, some in clumps; but the general coloring was uniform and sad. The hills ran up clear above the vegetation in spires of naked rock. All were strangely shaped, and the Spy-glass, which was by three or four hundred feet the tallest on the island, was likewise the strangest in configuration, running up sheer from almost every side, and then suddenly cut off at the top like a pedestal to put a statue on.

The *Hispaniola* was rolling scuppers [1] under in the ocean

[1] *scupper* (skŭp′ẽr): the drain on the edge of a deck.

swell. The booms were tearing at the blocks, the rudder was banging to and fro, and the whole ship creaking, groaning, and jumping like a manufactory. I had to cling tight to the backstay, and the world turned giddily before my eyes; for though I was a good enough sailor when there was way on,[1] this standing still and being rolled about like a bottle was a thing I never learned to stand without a qualm or so, above all in the morning, on an empty stomach.

Perhaps it was this—perhaps it was the look of the island with its gray, melancholy woods, and wild stone spires, and the surf that we could both see and hear foaming and thundering on the steep beach—at least, although the sun shone bright and hot, and the shore birds were fishing and crying all around us, and you would have thought anyone would have been glad to get to land after being so long at sea, my heart sank, as the saying is, into my boots; and from that first look onward, I hated the very thought of Treasure Island.

We had a dreary morning's work before us, for there was no sign of any wind, and the boats had to be got out and manned, and the ship warped [2] three or four miles round the corner of the island and up the narrow passage to the haven behind Skeleton Island. I volunteered for one of the boats, where I had, of course, no business. The heat was sweltering, and the men grumbled fiercely over their work. Anderson was in command of my boat, and instead of keeping the crew in order, he grumbled as loud as the worst.

"Well," he said, with an oath, "it's not forever."

I thought this was a very bad sign; for, up to that day, the men had gone briskly and willingly about their business; but the very sight of the island had relaxed the cords of discipline.

All the way in, Long John stood by the steersman and conned [3] the ship. He knew the passage like the palm of his hand; and though the man in the chains [4] got everywhere more water than was down in the chart, John never hesitated once.

"There's a strong scour with the ebb," [5] he said, "and this

[1] *there was way on:* the ship was sailing. [2] *warp* (wôrp): to pull by rope. [3] *conn:* to direct the steering of a ship. [4] *chains:* a bar or plate on the hull support the rigging where a man stands to determine the depth of the water. [5] *scour with the ebb* (skour) (ĕb): a current in an outgoing tide which digs out the bottom.

here passage has been dug out, in a manner of speaking, with a spade."

We brought up just where the anchor was in the chart, about a third of a mile from each shore, the mainland on one side, and Skeleton Island on the other. The bottom was clean sand. The plunge of our anchor sent up clouds of birds wheeling and crying over the woods; but in less than a minute they were down again, and all was once more silent.

The place was entirely land-locked, buried in woods, the trees coming right down to high-water mark, the shores mostly flat, and the hilltops standing round at a distance in a sort of amphitheater, one here, one there. Two little rivers, or rather, two swamps, emptied out into this pond, as you might call it; and the foliage round that part of the shore had a kind of poisonous brightness. From the ship we could see nothing of the house or stockade,[1] for they were quite buried among trees; and if it had not been for the chart on the companion, we might have been the first that had ever anchored there since the island arose out of the seas.

There was not a breath of air moving, nor a sound but that of the surf booming half a mile away along the beaches and against the rocks outside. A peculiar stagnant smell hung over the anchorage—a smell of sodden leaves and rotting tree trunks. I observed the doctor sniffing and sniffing, like someone tasting a bad egg.

"I don't know about treasure," he said, "but I'll stake my wig there's fever here."

If the conduct of the men had been alarming in the boat, it became truly threatening when they had come aboard. They lay about the deck, growling together in talk. The slightest order was received with a black look, and grudgingly and carelessly obeyed. Even the honest hands must have caught the infection, for there was not one man aboard to mend another. Mutiny, it was plain, hung over us like a thundercloud.

And it was not only we of the cabin party who perceived the danger. Long John was hard at work going from group to group, spending himself in good advice, and as for example, no man could have shown a better. He fairly outstripped himself in willingness and civility; he was all smiles to everyone. If an order

[1] *stockade* (stŏk·ād′): an enclosure made with stakes.

were given, John would be on his crutch in an instant, with the cheeriest "Aye, aye, sir!" in the world; and when there was nothing else to do, he kept up one song after another, as if to conceal the discontent of the rest.

Of all the gloomy features of that gloomy afternoon, this obvious anxiety on the part of Long John appeared the worst.

We held a council in the cabin.

"Sir," said the captain, "if I risk another order, the whole ship 'll come about our ears by the run. You see, sir, here it is. I get a rough answer, do I not? Well, if I speak back, pikes [1] will be going in two shakes; if I don't, Silver will see there's something under that, and the game's up. Now, we've only one man to rely on."

"And who is that?" asked the squire.

"Silver, sir," returned the captain; "he's as anxious as you and I to smother things up. This is a tiff; [2] he'd soon talk 'em out of it if he had the chance, and what I propose to do is to give him the chance. Let's allow the men an afternoon ashore. If they all go, why, we'll fight the ship. If they none of them go, well, then, we hold the cabin, and God defend the right. If some go, you mark my words, sir, Silver 'll bring 'em aboard again as mild as lambs."

It was so decided; loaded pistols were served out to all the sure men; Hunter, Joyce, and Redruth were taken into our confidence and received the news with less surprise and a better spirit than we had looked for, and then the captain went on deck and addressed the crew.

"My lads," said he, "we've had a hot day, and are all tired and out of sorts. A turn ashore 'll hurt nobody—the boats are still in the water; you can take the gigs,[3] and as many as please may go ashore for the afternoon. I'll fire a gun half an hour before sundown."

I believe the silly fellows must have thought they would break their shins over treasure as soon as they were landed; for they all came out of their sulks in a moment, and gave a cheer that started the echo in a far-away hill and sent the birds once more flying and squalling round the anchorage.

The captain was too bright to be in the way. He whipped

[1] *pike:* a wooden spear with a metal point. [2] *tiff:* a small quarrel.
[3] *gig:* a ship's small rowing boat.

out of sight in a moment, leaving Silver to arrange the party; and I fancy it was well he did so. Had he been on deck, he could no longer so much as have pretended not to understand the situation. It was as plain as day. Silver was the captain, and a mighty rebellious crew he had of it. The honest hands—and I was soon to see it proved that there were such on board—must have been very stupid fellows. Or rather, I suppose the truth was this, that all hands were disaffected by the example of the ringleaders—only some more, some less; and a few, being good fellows in the main, could neither be led nor driven any further. It is one thing to be idle and skulk, and quite another to take a ship and murder a number of innocent men.

At last, however, the party was made up. Six fellows were to stay on board, and the remaining thirteen, including Silver, began to embark.

Then it was that there came into my head the first of the mad notions that contributed so much to save our lives. If six men were left by Silver, it was plain our party could not take and fight the ship; and since only six were left, it was equally plain that the cabin party had no present need of my assistance. It occurred to me at once to go ashore. In a jiffy I had slipped over the side and curled up in the foresheets of the nearest boat, and almost at the same moment she shoved off.

No one took notice of me, only the bow oar saying, "Is that you, Jim? Keep your head down." But Silver, from the other boat, looked sharply over and called out to know if that were me; and from that moment I began to regret what I had done.

The crews raced for the beach; but the boat I was in, having some start, and being at once the lighter and the better-manned, shot far ahead of her consort, and the bow had struck among the shoreside trees, and I had caught a branch and swung myself out, and plunged into the nearest thicket, while Silver and the rest were still a hundred yards behind.

"Jim, Jim!" I heard him shouting.

But you may suppose I paid no heed; jumping, ducking, and breaking through, I ran straight before my nose, till I could run no longer.

Chapter 14 THE FIRST BLOW

I was so pleased at having given the slip to Long John that I began to enjoy myself and look around me with some interest on the strange land that I was in.

I had crossed a marshy tract full of willows, bulrushes, and odd, outlandish, swampy trees; and I had now come out upon the skirts of an open piece of undulating, sandy country, about a mile long, dotted with a few pines and a great number of contorted trees, not unlike the oak in growth, but pale in the foliage, like willows. On the far side of the open stood one of the hills, with two quaint, craggy peaks, shining vividly in the sun.

I now felt for the first time the joy of exploration. The isle was uninhabited; my shipmates I had left behind, and nothing lived in front of me but dumb brutes and fowls. I turned hither and thither among the trees. Here and there were flowering plants, unknown to me; here and there I saw snakes, and one raised his head from a ledge of rock and hissed at me with a noise not unlike the spinning of a top. Little did I suppose that he was a deadly enemy, and that the noise was the famous rattle.

Then I came to a long thicket of these oak-like trees—live, or evergreen, oaks, I heard afterwards they should be called—which grew low along the sand like brambles, the boughs curiously twisted, the foliage compact, like thatch. The thicket stretched down from the top of one of the sandy knolls, spreading and growing taller as it went, until it reached the margin of the broad, reedy fen [1] through which the nearest of the little rivers soaked its way into the anchorage. The marsh was steaming in the strong sun, and the outline of the Spy-glass trembled through the haze.

All at once there began to go a sort of bustle among the bulrushes; a wild duck flew up with a quack, another followed, and soon over the whole surface of the marsh a great cloud of birds hung screaming and circling in the air. I judged at once that some of my shipmates must be drawing near along the borders of the fen. Nor was I deceived; for soon I heard the very distant and low tones of a human voice, which, as I continued to give ear, grew steadily louder and nearer.

[1] *fen:* a marsh.

This put me in a great fear, and I crawled under cover of the nearest live oak and squatted there, hearkening, as silent as a mouse.

Another's voice answered; and then the first voice, which I now recognized to be Silver's, once more took up the story and ran on for a long while in a stream, only now and again interrupted by the other. By the sound they must have been talking earnestly, and almost fiercely; but no distinct word came to my hearing.

At last the speakers seemed to have paused and perhaps to have sat down; for not only did they cease to draw any nearer, but the birds themselves began to grow more quiet and to settle again to their places in the swamp.

And now I began to feel that I was neglecting my business; that since I had been so foolhardy as to come ashore with these desperadoes, the least I could do was to overhear them at their councils; and that my plain and obvious duty was to draw as close as I could manage, under the favorable ambush of the crouching trees.

I could tell the direction of the speakers pretty exactly, not only by the sound of their voices, but by the behavior of the few birds that still hung in alarm above the heads of the intruders.

Crawling on all fours, I made steadily but slowly towards them; till at last, raising my head to an aperture among the leaves, I could see clear down into a little green dell beside the marsh and closely set about with trees, where Long John Silver and another of the crew stood face to face in conversation.

The sun beat full upon them. Silver had thrown his hat beside him on the ground, and his great, smooth, bland face, all shining with heat, was lifted to the other man's in a kind of appeal.

"Mate," he was saying, "it's because I thinks gold dust of you—gold dust, and you may lay to that! If I hadn't took to you like pitch, do you think I'd have been here a-warning of you? All's up—you can't make nor mend; it's to save your neck that I'm a-speaking, and if one of the wild 'uns knew it, where 'ud I be, Tom—now, tell me, where 'ud I be?"

"Silver," said the other man—and I observed he was not only red in the face, but spoke as hoarse as a crow, and his voice shook too, like a taut rope—"Silver," says he, "you're old, and you're honest, or has the name for it; and you've money too, which lots of poor sailors hasn't; and you're brave or I'm mistook. And will you tell me you'll let yourself be led away with that kind of a mess of swabs? not you! As sure as God sees me, I'd sooner lose my hand. If I turn agin my dooty——"

And then all of a sudden he was interrupted by a noise. I had found one of the honest hands—well, here, at that same moment, came news of another. Far away out in the marsh there arose, all of a sudden, a sound like the cry of anger, then another on the back of it; and then one horrid, long-drawn scream. The rocks of the Spy-glass re-echoed it a score of times; the whole troop of marsh birds rose again, darkening heaven, with a simultaneous whirr; and long after that death yell was still ringing in my brain, silence had re-established its empire, and only the rustle of the redescending birds and the boom of the distant surges disturbed the languor of the afternoon.

Tom had leaped at the sound, like a horse at the spur; but Silver had not winked an eye. He stood where he was, resting lightly on his crutch, watching his companion like a snake about to spring.

"John!" said the sailor, stretching out his hand.

"Hands off!" cried Silver, leaping back a yard, as it seemed to me, with the speed and security of a trained gymnast.

"Hands off, if you like, John Silver," said the other. "It's a black conscience that can make you feard of me. But, in Heaven's name, tell me what was that?"

"That?" returned Silver, smiling away, but warier than ever, his eye a mere pin point in his big face, but gleaming like a crumb of glass. "That? Oh, I reckon that'll be Alan."

And at this poor Tom flashed out like a hero.

"Alan!" he cried. "Then rest his soul for a true seaman! And as for you, John Silver, long you've been a mate of mine, but you're mate of mine no more. If I die like a dog, I'll die in my dooty. You've killed Alan, have you? Kill me, too, if you can. But I defies you."

And with that, this brave fellow turned his back directly on the cook and set off walking for the beach. But he was not destined to go far. With a cry, John seized the branch of a tree, whipped the crutch out of his armpit, and sent that uncouth missile hurtling through the air. It struck poor Tom, point foremost, and with stunning violence, right between the shoulders in the middle of his back. His hands flew up, he gave a sort of a gasp, and fell.

Whether he were injured much or little, none could ever tell. Like enough, to judge from the sound, his back was broken on the spot. But he had no time given him to recover. Silver, agile as a monkey, even without leg or crutch, was on the top of him next moment, and had twice buried his knife up to the hilt in that defenseless body. From my place of ambush, I could hear him pant aloud as he struck the blows.

I do not know what it rightly is to faint, but I do know that for the next little while the whole world swam away from before me in a whirling mist; Silver and the birds and the tall Spy-glass hilltop going round and round and topsy-turvy before my eyes, and all manner of bells ringing and distant voices shouting in my ear.

When I came again to myself, the monster had pulled himself together, his crutch under his arm, his hat upon his head. Just before him Tom lay motionless upon the sward; but the murderer minded him not a whit, cleansing his blood-stained knife the while upon a wisp of grass. Everything else was unchanged, the sun still shining mercilessly on the steaming marsh and the tall pinnacle of the mountain, and I could scarce persuade myself that murder had been actually done and a human life cruelly cut short a moment since, before my eyes.

But now John put his hand into his pocket, brought out a whistle, and blew upon it several modulated blasts, that rang far across the heated air. I could not tell, of course, the meaning of the signal; but it instantly awoke my fears. More men would be coming. I might be discovered. They had already slain two of the honest people; after Tom and Alan, might not I come next?

Instantly I began to extricate myself and crawl back again, with what speed and silence I could manage, to the more open portion of the wood. As I did so, I could hear hails coming and going between the old buccaneer and his comrades, and this sound of danger lent me wings. As soon as I was clear of the thicket, I ran as I never ran before, scarce minding the direction of my flight, so long as it led me from the murderers; and as I ran, fear grew and grew upon me, until it turned into a kind of frenzy.

Indeed, could anyone be more entirely lost than I? When

the gun fired, how should I dare to go down to the boats among those fiends, still smoking from their crime? Would not the first of them who saw me wring my neck like a snipe's? Would not my absence itself be an evidence to them of my alarm and therefore of my fatal knowledge? It was all over, I thought. Good-by to the *Hispaniola;* good-by to the squire, the doctor, and the captain! There was nothing left for me but death by starvation or death by the hands of the mutineers.

All this while, as I say, I was still running, and, without taking any notice, I had drawn near to the foot of the little hill with the two peaks, and had got into a part of the island where the live oaks grew more widely apart and seemed more like forest trees in their bearing and dimensions. Mingled with these were a few scattered pines, some fifty, some nearer seventy, feet high. The air, too, smelt more freshly than down beside the marsh.

And here a fresh alarm brought me to a standstill with a thumping heart.

Chapter 15 THE MAN OF THE ISLAND

From the side of the hill, which was here steep and stony, a spout of gravel was dislodged and fell rattling and bounding through the trees. My eyes turned instinctively in that direction, and I saw a figure leap with great rapidity behind the trunk of a pine. What it was, whether bear or man or monkey, I could in no wise tell. It seemed dark and shaggy; more I know not. But the terror of this new apparition brought me to a stand.

I was now, it seemed, cut off upon both sides; behind me the murderers, before me this lurking nondescript.[1] And immediately I began to prefer the dangers that I knew to those I knew not. Silver himself appeared less terrible in contrast with this creature of the woods, and I turned on my heel and looking

[1] *nondescript* (nŏn′dê·skrĭpt): something that cannot be described.

sharply behind me over my shoulder, began to retrace my steps in the direction of the boats.

Instantly the figure reappeared and making a wide circuit, began to head me off. I was tired, at any rate; but had I been as fresh as when I rose, I could see it was in vain for me to contend in speed with such an adversary. From trunk to trunk the creature flitted like a deer, running manlike on two legs, but unlike any man that I had ever seen, stooping almost double as it ran. Yet a man it was, I could no longer be in doubt about that.

I began to recall what I had heard of cannibals. I was within an ace of calling for help. But the mere fact that he was a man, however wild, had somewhat reassured me, and my fear of Silver began to revive in proportion. I stood still, therefore, and cast about for some method of escape; and as I was so thinking, the recollection of my pistol flashed into my mind. As soon as I remembered I was not defenseless, courage glowed again in my heart; and I set my face resolutely for this man of the island and walked briskly towards him.

He was concealed by this time, behind another tree trunk; but he must have been watching me closely, for as soon as I began to move in his direction he reappeared and took a step to meet me. Then he hesitated, drew back, came forward again, and at last, to my wonder and confusion, threw himself on his knees and held out his clasped hands in supplication.

At that I once more stopped.

"Who are you?" I asked.

"Ben Gunn," he answered, and his voice sounded hoarse and awkward, like a rusty lock. "I'm poor Ben Gunn, I am; and I haven't spoke with a Christian these three years."

I could now see that he was a white man like myself, and that his features were even pleasing. His skin, wherever it was exposed, was burnt by the sun; even his lips were black, and his fair eyes looked quite startling in so dark a face. Of all the beggarmen that I had seen or fancied, he was the chief for raggedness. He was clothed with tatters of old ship's canvas and old sea cloth; and this extraordinary patchwork was all held together by a system of the most various and incongruous fastenings, brass buttons, bits of stick, and loops of tarry gaskin. About his waist he wore an old brass-buckled leather belt, which was the one thing solid in his whole accoutrement.

"Three years!" I cried. "Were you shipwrecked?"

"Nay, mate," said he—"marooned."

I had heard the word, and I knew it stood for a horrible kind of punishment, common enough among the buccaneers, in which the offender is put ashore with a little powder and shot and left behind on some desolate and distant island.

"Marooned three years agone," he continued, "and lived on goats since then, and berries, and oysters. Wherever a man is, says I, a man can do for himself. But, mate, my heart is sore for Christian diet. You mightn't happen to have a piece of cheese about you, now? No? Well, many's the long night I've dreamed of cheese—toasted, mostly—and woke up again, and here I were."

"If ever I can get aboard again," said I, "you shall have cheese by the stone."

All this time he had been feeling the stuff of my jacket, smoothing my hands, looking at my boots, and generally, in the intervals of his speech, showing a childish pleasure in the presence of a fellow creature. But at my last words he perked up into a kind of startled slyness.

"If ever you can get aboard again, says you?" he repeated. "Why, now, who's to hinder you?"

"Not you, I know," was my reply.

"And right you was," he cried. "Now you—what do you call yourself, mate?"

"Jim," I told him.

"Jim, Jim," says he, quite pleased apparently. "Well, now, Jim, I've lived that rough as you'd be ashamed to hear of. Now, for instance, you wouldn't think I had had a pious [1] mother—to look at me?" he asked.

"Why, no, not in particular," I answered.

"Ah, well," said he, "but I had—remarkable pious. And I was a civil, pious boy and could rattle off my catechism that fast, as you couldn't tell one word from another. And here's what it come to, Jim, and it begun with chuck-farthen [2] on the blessed gravestones! That's what it begun with, but it went further'n that; and so my mother told me, and predicked the whole, she did, the pious woman! But it were Providence that put me here. I've thought it all out in this here lonely island, and I'm back on piety.

[1] *pious* (pī′ŭs): religious. [2] *chuck-farthen* (chŭk′-fär′th̶n): a game played by throwing coins.

You don't catch me tasting rum so much; but just a thimbleful for luck, of course, the first chance I have. I'm bound I'll be good, and I see the way to. And, Jim"—looking all round him, and lowering his voice to a whisper—"I'm rich."

I now felt sure that the poor fellow had gone crazy in his solitude, and I suppose I must have shown the feeling in my face; for he repeated the statement hotly:

"Rich! rich! I says. And I'll tell you what: I'll make a man of you, Jim. Ah, Jim, you'll bless your stars, you will, you was the first that found me!"

And at this there came suddenly a lowering shadow over his face, and he tightened his grasp upon my hand and raised a forefinger threateningly before my eyes.

"Now, Jim, you tell me true: that ain't Flint's ship?" he asked.

At this I had a happy inspiration. I began to believe that I had found an ally, and I answered him at once.

"It's not Flint's ship, and Flint is dead; but I'll tell you true, as you ask me—there are some of Flint's hands aboard; worse luck for the rest of us."

"Not a man—with one—leg?" he gasped.

"Silver?" I asked.

"Ah, Silver!" says he; "that were his name."

"He's the cook, and the ringleader too."

He was still holding me by the wrist, and at that he gave it quite a wring.

"If you was sent by Long John," he said, "I'm as good as pork, and I know it. But where was you, do you suppose?"

I had made my mind up in a moment, and by way of answer told him the whole story of our voyage and the predicament in which we found ourselves. He heard me with the keenest interest, and when I had done, he patted me on the head.

"You're a good lad, Jim," he said; "and you're all in a clove hitch,[1] ain't you? Well, you just put your trust in Ben Gunn—Ben Gunn's the man to do it. Would you think it likely, now, that your squire would prove a liberal-minded one in case of help—him being in a clove hitch, as you remark?"

I told him the squire was the most liberal of men.

[1] *clove hitch:* literally, a knot; Gunn means that Jim has a knotty problem.

"Aye, but you see," returned Ben Gunn, "I didn't mean giving me a gate to keep, and a shuit of livery clothes, and such; that's not my mark, Jim. What I mean is, would he be likely to come down to the toon of, say one thousand pounds out of money that's as good as a man's own already?"

"I am sure he would," said I. "As it was, all hands were to share."

"*And* a passage home?" he added, with a look of great shrewdness.

"Why," I cried, "the squire's a gentleman. And, besides, if we got rid of the others, we should want you to help work the vessel home."

"Ah," said he, "so you would." And he seemed very much relieved.

"Now, I'll tell you what," he went on. "So much I'll tell you, and no more. I were in Flint's ship when he buried the treasure; he and six along—six strong seamen. They was ashore nigh on a week, and us standing off and on in the old *Walrus*. One fine day up went the signal, and here comes Flint by himself in a little boat, and his head done up in a blue scarf. The sun was getting up, and mortal white he looked about the cutwater.[1] But there he was, you mind, and the six all dead—dead and buried. How he done it, not a man aboard us could make out. It was battle, murder, and sudden death, leastways—him against six. Billy Bones was the mate; Long John, he was quartermaster; and they asked him where the treasure was. 'Ah,' says he, 'you can go ashore, if you like, and stay,' he says; 'but as for the ship, she'll beat up for more, by thunder!' That's what he said.

"Well, I was in another ship three years back, and we sighted this island. 'Boys,' said I, 'here's Flint's treasure; let's land and find it.' The cap'n was displeased at that; but my messmates were all of a mind and landed. Twelve days they looked for it, and every day they had the worse word for me, until one fine morning all hands went aboard. 'As for you, Benjamin Gunn,' says they, 'here's a musket,' they says, 'and a spade, and pickax. You can stay here and find Flint's money for yourself,' they says.

"Well, Jim, three years have I been here, and not a bite of Christian diet from that day to this. But now, you look here; look

[1] *cutwater:* the foremost part of a ship.

at me. Do I look like a man before the mast? No, says you. Nor I weren't, neither, I says."

And with that he winked and pinched me hard.

"Just you mention them words to your squire, Jim"—he went on: "Nor he weren't, neither—that's the words. Three years he were the man of this island, light and dark, fair and rain; and sometimes he would, maybe, think upon a prayer (says you), and sometimes he would, maybe, think of his old mother, so be as she's alive (you'll say); but the most part of Gunn's time (this is what you'll say)—the most part of his time was took up with another matter. And then you'll give him a nip, like I do."

And he pinched me again in the most confidential manner.

"Then," he continued; "then you'll up, and you'll say this: Gunn is a good man (you'll say), and he puts a precious sight more confidence—a precious sight, mind that—in a gen'leman born than in these gen'lemen of fortune, having been one hisself."

"Well," I said, "I don't understand one word that you've been saying. But that's neither here nor there; for how am I to get on board?"

"Ah," said he, "that's the hitch, for sure. Well, there's my boat, that I made with my two hands. I keep her under the white rock. If the worst come to the worst, we might try that after dark. Hi!" he broke out, "what's that?"

For just then, although the sun had still an hour or two to run, all the echoes of the island awoke and bellowed to the thunder of a cannon.

"They have begun to fight!" I cried. "Follow me."

And I began to run towards the anchorage, my terrors all forgotten; while, close at my side, the marooned man in his goatskins trotted easily and lightly.

"Left, left," says he; "keep to your left hand, mate Jim! Under the trees with you! Theer's where I killed my first goat. They don't come down here now; they're all mastheaded on them mountings for the fear of Benjamin Gunn. Ah! and there's the cetemery"—cemetery, he must have meant. "You see the mounds? I come here and prayed, nows and thens, when I thought maybe a Sunday would be about doo. It weren't quite a chapel, but it seemed more solemn like; and then, says you, Ben Gunn was shorthanded—no chapling, nor so much as a Bible and a flag, you says."

So he kept talking as I ran, neither expecting nor receiving any answer.

The cannon shot was followed, after a considerable interval, by a volley of small arms.

Another pause, and then, not a quarter of a mile in front of me, I beheld the Union Jack [1] flutter in the air above a wood.

PART FOUR—The Stockade

Chapter 16

NARRATIVE CONTINUED BY THE DOCTOR: HOW THE SHIP WAS ABANDONED

It was about half-past one—three bells in the sea phrase—that the two boats went ashore from the *Hispaniola*. The captain, the squire, and I were talking matters over in the cabin. Had there been a breath of wind, we should have fallen on the six mutineers who were left aboard with us, slipped our cable, and away to sea. But the wind was wanting; and, to complete our helplessness, down came Hunter with the news that Jim Hawkins had slipped into a boat and was gone ashore with the rest.

It never occurred to us to doubt Jim Hawkins; but we were alarmed for his safety. With the men in the temper they were in, it seemed an even chance if we should see the lad again. We ran on deck. The pitch was bubbling in the seams; the nasty stench of the place turned me sick; if ever a man smelt fever and dysentery, it was in that abominable anchorage. The six scoundrels

[1] *Union Jack:* the British flag.

were sitting grumbling under a sail in the forecastle; ashore we could see the gigs made fast and a man sitting in each, hard by where the river runs in. One of them was whistling "Lillibullero."

Waiting was a strain; and it was decided that Hunter and I should go ashore with the jolly boat,[1] in quest of information.

The gigs had leaned to their right; but Hunter and I pulled straight in, in the direction of the stockade upon the chart. The two who were left guarding their boats seemed in a bustle at our appearance; "Lillibullero" stopped off, and I could see the pair discussing what they ought to do. Had they gone and told Silver, all might have turned out differently; but they had their orders, I suppose, and decided to sit quietly where they were and hark back again to "Lillibullero."

There was a slight bend in the coast, and I steered so as to put it between us; even before we landed, we had thus lost sight of the gigs. I jumped out and came as near running as I durst, with a big silk handkerchief under my hat for coolness' sake and a brace of pistols ready primed for safety.

I had not gone a hundred yards when I reached the stockade.

This was how it was: a spring of clear water rose almost at the top of a knoll. Well on the knoll, and enclosing the spring, they had clapped a stout log house, fit to hold two score of people on a pinch, and loopholed for musketry on every side. All round this they had cleared a wide space, and then the thing was completed by a paling[2] six feet high, without door or opening, too strong to pull down without time and labor, and too open to shelter the besiegers. The people in the log house had them[3] in every way; they stood quiet in shelter and shot the others like partridges. All they wanted was a good watch and food, for, short of a complete surprise, they might have held the place against a regiment.

What particularly took my fancy was the spring. For, though we had a good enough place of it in the cabin of the *Hispaniola,* with plenty of arms and ammunition, and things to eat, and excellent wines, there had been one thing overlooked—we had no water. I was thinking this over, when there came ringing over the island the cry of a man at the point of death. I was not new to violent death—I have served his Royal Highness the Duke of

[1] *jolly boat:* a medium sized ship's boat. [2] *paling* (pāl′ĭng): a fence made of stakes. [3] *had them:* had the advantage over any attackers.

Cumberland, and got a wound myself at Fontenoy—but I know my pulse went dot and carry one. "Jim Hawkins is gone," was my first thought.

It is something to have been an old soldier, but more still to have been a doctor. There is no time to dilly-dally in our work. And so now I made up my mind instantly and with no time lost, returned to the shore and jumped on board the jolly boat.

By good fortune Hunter pulled a good oar. We made the water fly; and the boat was soon alongside, and I aboard the schooner.

I found them all shaken, as was natural. The squire was sitting down, as white as a sheet, thinking of the harm he had led us to, the good soul; and one of the six forecastle hands was little better.

"There's a man," says Captain Smollett, nodding towards him, "new to this work. He came nigh-hand fainting, doctor, when he heard the cry. Another touch of the rudder and that man would join us."

I told my plan to the captain, and between us we settled on the details of its accomplishment.

We put old Redruth in the gallery between the cabin and the forecastle, with three or four loaded muskets and a mattress for protection. Hunter brought the boat round under the stern port, and Joyce and I set to work loading her with powder tins, muskets, bags of biscuits, kegs of pork, a cask of cognac, and my invaluable medicine chest.

In the meantime, the squire and the captain stayed on deck, and the latter hailed the coxswain, who was the principal man aboard.

"Mr. Hands," he said, "here are two of us with a brace of pistols each. If any one of you six make a signal of any description, that man's dead."

They were a good deal taken aback; and, after a little consultation, one and all tumbled down the fore companion, thinking, no doubt, to take us on the rear. But when they saw Redruth waiting for them in the sparred gallery, they went about ship at once, and a head popped out again on deck.

"Down, dog!" cries the captain.

And the head popped back again; and we heard no more, for the time, of these six very fainthearted seamen.

By this time, tumbling things in as they came, we had the jolly boat loaded as much as we dared. Joyce and I got out through the stern port, and we made for shore again, as fast as the oars could take us.

This second trip fairly aroused the watchers along shore. "Lillibullero" was dropped again; and just before we lost sight of them behind the little point, one of them whipped ashore and disappeared. I had half a mind to change my plan and destroy their boats, but I feared that Silver and the others might be close at hand, and all might very well be lost by trying for too much.

We had soon touched land in the same place as before and set to provision the blockhouse. All three made the first journey, heavily laden, and tossed our stores over the palisade. Then, leaving Joyce to guard them—one man, to be sure, but with half a dozen muskets—Hunter and I returned to the jolly boat and loaded ourselves once more. So we proceeded, without pausing to take breath, till the whole cargo was bestowed, when the two servants took up their position in the blockhouse, and I, with all my power, sculled [1] back to the *Hispaniola.*

That we should have risked a second boat load seems more daring than it really was. They had the advantage of numbers, of course, but we had the advantage of arms. Not one of the men ashore had a musket, and before they could get within range for pistol shooting, we flattered ourselves we should be able to give a good account of a half-dozen at least.

The squire was waiting for me at the stern window, all his faintness gone from him. He caught the painter and made it fast, and we fell to loading the boat for our very lives. Pork, powder, and biscuit was the cargo, with only a musket and a cutlass apiece for the squire and me and Redruth and the captain. The rest of the arms and powder we dropped overboard in two fathoms and a half of water, so that we could see the bright steel shining far below us in the sun, on the clean, sandy bottom.

By this time the tide was beginning to ebb, and the ship was swinging round to her anchor. Voices were heard faintly halloaing in the direction of the two gigs; and though this reassured us for Joyce and Hunter, who were well to the eastward, it warned our party to be off.

Redruth retreated from his place in the gallery and dropped

[1] *sculled:* rowed.

into the boat, which we then brought round to the ship's counter, to be handier for Captain Smollett.

"Now, men," said he, "do you hear me?"

There was no answer from the forecastle.

"It's to you, Abraham Gray—it's to you I am speaking."

Still no reply.

"Gray," resumed Mr. Smollett, a little louder, "I am leaving this ship, and I order you to follow your captain. I know you are a good man at bottom, and I daresay not one of the lot of you's as bad as he makes out. I have my watch here in my hand; I give you thirty seconds to join me in."

There was a pause.

"Come, my fine fellow," continued the captain, "don't hang so long in stays. I'm risking my life and the lives of these good gentlemen every second."

There was a sudden scuffle, a sound of blows, and out burst Abraham Gray, with a knife-cut on the side of the cheek, and came running to the captain, like a dog to the whistle.

"I'm with you, sir," said he.

And the next moment he and the captain had dropped aboard of us, and we had shoved off and given way.

We were clear out of the ship, but not yet ashore in our stockade.

Chapter 17

NARRATIVE CONTINUED BY THE DOCTOR: THE JOLLY BOAT'S LAST TRIP

This fifth trip was quite different from any of the others. In the first place, the little gallipot of a boat that we were in was gravely overloaded. Five grown men, and three of them—Trelawney, Redruth, and the captain—over six feet high, was already more than she was meant to carry. Add to that the powder, pork, and bread-bags. The gunwale was lipping astern. Several times we shipped a little water, and my breeches and the tails of my coat were all soaking wet before we had gone a hundred yards.

The captain made us trim the boat, and we got her to lie a little more evenly. All the same we were afraid to breathe.

In the second place, the ebb was now making [1]—a strong rippling current running westward through the basin, and then south'ard and seaward down by the straits by which we had entered in the morning. Even the ripples were a danger to our overloaded craft; but the worst of it was that we were swept out of our true course and away from our proper landing place behind the point. If we let the current have its way we should come ashore beside the gigs, where the pirates might appear at any moment.

"I cannot keep her head for the stockade, sir," said I to the captain. I was steering, while he and Redruth, two fresh men, were at the oars. "The tide keeps washing her down. Could you pull a little stronger?"

"Not without swamping the boat," said he. "You must bear up, sir, if you please—bear up until you see you're gaining."

I tried and found by experiment that the tide kept sweeping us westward until I had laid her head due east, or just about right angles to the way we ought to go.

"We'll never get ashore at this rate," said I.

"If it's the only course that we can lie, sir, we must even lie it," returned the captain. "We must keep upstream. You see, sir," he went on, "if once we dropped to leeward of the landing place, it's hard to say where we should get ashore, besides the chance of being boarded by the gigs; whereas, the way we go the current must slacken, and then we can dodge back along the shore."

"The current's less a'ready, sir," said the man Gray, who was sitting in the fore sheets; "you can ease her off a bit."

"Thank you, my man," said I, quite as if nothing had happened; for we had all quietly made up our minds to treat him like one of ourselves.

Suddenly the captain spoke up again, and I thought his voice was a little changed.

"The gun!" said he.

[1] *the ebb was now making:* the tide was going out.

"I have thought of that," said I, for I made sure he was thinking of a bombardment of the fort. "They could never get the gun ashore, and if they did, they could never haul it through the woods."

"Look astern, doctor," replied the captain.

We had entirely forgotten the long nine; [1] and there, to our horror, were the five rogues busy about her, getting off her jacket, as they called the stout tarpaulin cover under which she sailed. Not only that, but it flashed into my mind at the same moment that the round shot and the powder for the gun had been left behind, and a stroke with an ax would put it all into the possession of the evil ones aboard.

"Israel was Flint's gunner," said Gray hoarsely.

At any risk, we put the boat's head direct for the landing place. By this time we had got so far out of the run of the current that we kept steerage way even at our necessarily gentle rate of rowing, and I could keep her steady for the goal. But the worst of it was that, with the course I now held, we turned our broadside instead of our stern to the *Hispaniola* and offered a target like a barn door.

I could hear, as well as see, that brandy-faced rascal, Israel Hands, plumping down a round shot on the deck.

"Who's the best shot?" asked the captain.

"Mr. Trelawney, out and away," said I.

"Mr. Trelawney, will you please pick me off one of these men, sir? Hands, if possible," said the captain.

Trelawney was as cool as steel. He looked to the priming of his gun.

"Now," cried the captain, "easy with that gun, sir, or you'll swamp the boat. All hands stand by to trim her when he aims."

The squire raised his gun, the rowing ceased, and we leaned over the other side to keep the balance, and all was so nicely contrived that we did not ship a drop.

They had the gun, by this time, slewed round upon the swivel, and Hands, who was at the muzzle with the rammer, was, in consequence, the most exposed. However, we had no luck; for just as Trelawney fired, down he stooped, the ball whistled over him, and it was one of the other four who fell.

The cry he gave was echoed, not only by his companions

[1] *long nine:* a long-barreled ship's gun firing a nine-pound shot.

on board, but by a great number of voices from the shore, and looking in that direction I saw the other pirates trooping out from among the trees and tumbling into their places in the boats.

"Here come the gigs, sir," said I.

"Give way then," cried the captain. "We mustn't mind if we swamp her now. If we can't get ashore, all's up."

"Only one of the gigs is being manned, sir," I added, "the crew of the other most likely going round by shore to cut us off."

"They'll have a hot run, sir," returned the captain. "Jack ashore, you know. It's not them I mind; it's the round shot. Carpet bowls! My lady's maid couldn't miss. Tell us, squire, when you see the match, and we'll hold water." [1]

In the meanwhile we had been making headway at a good pace for a boat so overloaded, and we had shipped but little water in the process. We were now close in; thirty or forty strokes and we should beach her; for the ebb had already disclosed a narrow belt of sand below the clustering trees. The gig was no longer to be feared; the little point had already concealed it from our eyes. The ebb tide, which had so cruelly delayed us, was now making reparation and delaying our assailants. The one source of danger was the gun.

"If I durst," said the captain, "I'd stop and pick off another man."

But it was plain that they meant nothing should delay their shot. They had never so much as looked at their fallen comrade, though he was not dead, and I could see him trying to crawl away.

"Ready!" cried the squire.

"Hold!" cried the captain, quick as an echo.

And he and Redruth backed with a great heave that sent her stern bodily under water. The report fell in at the same instant of time. This was the first that Jim heard, the sound of the squire's shot not having reached him. Where the ball passed, not one of us precisely knew; but I fancy it must have been over our heads, and that the wind of it may have contributed to our disaster.

At any rate, the boat sank by the stern, quite gently, in three feet of water, leaving the captain and myself, facing each other, on our feet. The other three took complete headers, and came up again, drenched and bubbling.

[1] *when you see the match, and we'll hold water:* when you see them ignite the powder, and we'll stop rowing.

So far there was no great harm. No lives were lost, and we could wade ashore in safety. But there were all our stores at the bottom, and, to make things worse, only two guns out of five remained in a state for service. Mine I had snatched from my knees and held over my head, by a sort of instinct. As for the captain, he had carried his over his shoulder by a bandoleer,[1] and, like a wise man, lock uppermost. The other three had gone down with the boat.

To add to our concern, we heard voices already drawing near us in the woods along shore; and we had not only the danger of being cut off from the stockade in our half-crippled state, but the fear before us whether, if Hunter and Joyce were attacked by half a dozen, they would have the sense and conduct to stand firm. Hunter was steady, that we knew; Joyce was a doubtful case—a pleasant, polite man for a valet, and to brush one's clothes, but not entirely fitted for a man of war.

With all this in our minds, we waded ashore as fast as we could, leaving behind us the poor jolly boat, and a good half of all our powder and provisions.

Chapter 18

NARRATIVE CONTINUED BY THE DOCTOR: END OF THE FIRST DAY'S FIGHTING

We made our best speed across the strip of wood that now divided us from the stockade; and at every step we took, the voices of the buccaneers rang nearer. Soon we could hear their footfalls as they ran, and the cracking of the branches as they breasted across a bit of thicket.

I began to see we should have a brush for it in earnest and looked to my priming.

[1] *bandoleer* (băn′dȯ·lēr′): a shoulder strap.

"Captain," said I, "Trelawney is the dead shot. Give him your gun; his own is useless."

They exchanged guns, and Trelawney, silent and cool as he had been since the beginning of the bustle, hung a moment on his heel to see that all was fit for service. At the same time, observing Gray to be unarmed, I handed him my cutlass. It did all our hearts good to see him spit in his hand, knit his brows, and make the blade sing through the air. It was plain from every line of his body that our new hand was worth his salt.

Forty paces farther we came to the edge of the wood and saw the stockade in front of us. We struck the enclosure about the middle of the south side, and almost at the same time, seven mutineers—Job Anderson, the boatswain, at their head—appeared in full cry at the southwestern corner.

They paused, as if taken aback; and before they recovered, not only the squire and I, but Hunter and Joyce from the blockhouse, had time to fire. The four shots came in rather a scattering volley; but they did the business: one of the enemy actually fell, and the rest, without hesitation, turned and plunged into the trees.

After reloading, we walked down the outside of the palisade to see the fallen enemy. He was stone dead—shot through the heart.

We began to rejoice over our good success, when just at that moment a pistol cracked in the bush, a ball whistled close past my ear, and poor Tom Redruth stumbled and fell his length on the ground. Both the squire and I returned the shot; but as we had nothing to aim at, it is probable we only wasted powder. Then we reloaded and turned our attention to poor Tom. The captain and Gray were already examining him; and I saw with half an eye that all was over.

I believe the readiness of our return volley had scattered the mutineers once more, for we were suffered without further molestation to get the poor old gamekeeper hoisted over the stockade and carried, groaning and bleeding, into the log house.

Poor old fellow, he had not uttered one word of surprise, complaint, fear, or even acquiescence, from the very beginning of our troubles till now, when we had laid him down in the log house to die. He had lain like a Trojan behind his mattress in the gallery; he had followed every order silently, doggedly, and well; he was the oldest of our party by a score of years; and now, sullen, old, serviceable servant, it was he that was to die.

The squire dropped down beside him on his knees and kissed his hand, crying like a child.

"Be I going, doctor?" he asked.

"Tom, my man," said I, "you're going home."

"I wish I had had a lick at them with the gun first," he replied.

"Tom," said the squire, "say you forgive me, won't you?"

"Would that be respectful like, from me to you, squire?" was the answer. "Howsoever, so be it, amen!"

After a little while of silence, he said he thought somebody might read a prayer. "It's the custom, sir," he added apologetically. And not long after, without another word, he passed away.

In the meantime the captain, whom I had observed to be wonderfully swollen about the chest and pockets, had turned out a great many various stores—the British colors, a Bible, a coil of stoutish rope, pen, ink, the logbook, and pounds of tobacco. He had found a longish fir tree lying felled and trimmed in the enclosure, and, with the help of Hunter, he had set it up at the corner of the log house where the trunks crossed and made an angle. Then, climbing on the roof, he had with his own hand bent and run up the colors.[1]

This seemed mightily to relieve him. He re-entered the log house and set about counting up the stores, as if nothing else existed. But he had an eye on Tom's passage for all that and as soon as all was over, came forward with another flag and reverently spread it on the body.

"Don't you take on, sir," he said, shaking the squire's hand. "All's well with him; no fear for a hand that's been shot down in his duty to captain and owner. It mayn't be good divinity, but it's a fact."

Then he pulled me aside.

"Dr. Livesey," he said, "in how many weeks do you and squire expect the consort?"[2]

I told him it was a question, not of weeks, but of months; that if we were not back by the end of August, Blandly was to

[1] *run up the colors:* to raise the flag. [2] *consort* (kŏn′sôrt): the ship that was to follow if they did not return.

send to find us; but neither sooner nor later. "You can calculate for yourself," I said.

"Why, yes," returned the captain, scratching his head, "and making a large allowance, sir, for all the gifts of Providence, I should say we were pretty close hauled."

"How do you mean?" I asked.

"It's a pity, sir, we lost that second load. That's what I mean," replied the captain. "As for powder and shot, we'll do. But the rations are short, very short—so short, Doctor Livesey, that we're perhaps as well without that extra mouth."

And he pointed to the dead body under the flag.

Just then, with a roar and a whistle, a round shot passed high above the roof of the log house and plumped far beyond us in the wood.

"Oho!" said the captain. "Blaze away! You've little enough powder already, my lads."

At the second trial the aim was better, and the ball descended inside the stockade, scattering a cloud of sand, but doing no further damage.

"Captain," said the squire, "the house is quite invisible from the ship. It must be the flag they are aiming at. Would it not be wiser to take it in?"

"Strike my colors!" cried the captain. "No, sir, not I"; and as soon as he had said the words, I think we all agreed with him. For it was not only a piece of stout, seamanly good feeling; it was good policy besides, and showed our enemies that we despised their cannonade.

All through the evening they kept thundering away. Ball after ball flew over or fell short or kicked up the sand in the enclosure; but they had to fire so high that the shot fell dead and buried itself in the soft sand. We had no ricochet to fear; and though one popped in through the roof of the log house and out again through the floor, we soon got used to that sort of horse-play and minded it not more than cricket.

"There is one thing good about all this," observed the captain: "the wood in front of us is likely clear. The ebb has made a good while; our stores should be uncovered. Volunteers to go and bring in pork."

Gray and Hunter were the first to come forward. Well armed, they stole out of the stockade; but it proved a useless mission. The mutineers were bolder than we fancied, or they put more trust in Israel's gunnery. For four or five of them were busy carrying off our stores and wading out with them to one of the gigs that lay close by, pulling an oar or so to hold her steady against the current. Silver was in the stern sheets in command; and every man of them was now provided with a musket from some secret magazine of their own.

The captain sat down to his log, and here is the beginning of the entry:

"Alexander Smollett, master; David Livesey, ship's doctor; Abraham Gray, carpenter's mate; John Trelawney, owner; John Hunter and Richard Joyce, owner's servants, landsmen—being all that is left faithful of the ship's company—with stores for ten days at short rations, came ashore this day and flew British colors on the log house in Treasure Island. Thomas Redruth, owner's servant, landsman, shot by the mutineers; James Hawkins, cabin boy——"

And at the same time I was wondering over poor Jim Hawkins's fate.

A hail on the land side.

"Somebody hailing us," said Hunter, who was on guard.

"Doctor! squire! captain! Hullo, Hunter, is that you?" came the cries.

And I ran to the door in time to see Jim Hawkins, safe and sound, come climbing over the stockade.

Chapter 19

NARRATIVE RESUMED BY JIM HAWKINS: THE GARRISON IN THE STOCKADE

As soon as Ben Gunn saw the colors, he came to a halt, stopped me by the arm, and sat down.

"Now," said he, "there's your friends, sure enough."

"Far more likely it's the mutineers," I answered.

"That!" he cried. "Why, in a place like this, where nobody puts in but gen'lemen of fortune, Silver would fly the Jolly Roger,[1] you don't make no doubt of that. No; that's your friends. There's been blows, too, and I reckon your friends has had the best of it; and here they are ashore in the old stockade, as was made years and years ago by Flint. Ah, he was the man to have a headpiece, was Flint! Barring rum, his match were never seen. He were afraid of none, not he; on'y Silver—Silver was that genteel."

"Well," said I, "that may be so, and so be it; all the more reason that I should hurry on and join my friends."

"Nay, mate," returned Ben, "not you. You're a good boy, or I'm mistook; but you're on'y a boy, all told. Now, Ben Gunn is fly. Rum wouldn't bring me there, where you're going—not rum wouldn't, till I see your born gen'leman and gets it on his word of honor. And you won't forget my words: 'A precious sight (that's what you'll say), a precious sight more confidence'—and then nips him."

And he pinched me the third time with the same air of cleverness.

"And when Ben Gunn is wanted, you know where to find him, Jim. Just wheer you found him today. And him that comes is to have a white thing in his hand; and he's to come alone. Oh! and you'll say this: 'Ben Gunn,' says you, 'has reasons of his own.' "

"Well," said I, "I believe I understand. You have something to propose, and you wish to see the squire or the doctor; and you're to be found where I found you. Is that all?"

"And when? says you," he added. "Why, from about noon observation to about six bells." [2]

"Good," said I, "and now may I go?"

"You won't forget?" he inquired anxiously. "Precious sight, and reasons of his own, says you. Reasons of his own; that's the mainstay; as between man and man. Well, then"—still holding me—"I reckon you can go, Jim. And, Jim, if you was to see Silver, you wouldn't go to sell Ben Gunn? wild horses wouldn't draw it from you? No, says you. And if them pirates camp ashore, Jim, what would you say but there'd be widders in the morning?"

Here he was interrupted by a loud report, and a cannon ball

[1] *Jolly Roger:* a pirate flag; skull and crossbones on a black ground.
[2] *about noon . . . six bells:* from noon till three o'clock.

came tearing through the trees and pitched in the sand, not a hundred yards from where we two were talking. The next moment each of us had taken to his heels in a different direction.

For a good hour to come frequent reports shook the island, and balls kept crashing through the woods. I moved from hiding place to hiding place, always pursued, or so it seemed to me, by these terrifying missiles. But towards the end of the bombardment, though still I durst not venture in the direction of the stockade, where the balls fell oftenest, I had begun, in a manner, to pluck up my heart again; and after a long detour to the east, crept down among the shoreside trees.

The sun had just set, the sea breeze was rustling and tumbling in the woods, and ruffling the gray surface of the anchorage; the tide, too, was far out, and great tracts of sand lay uncovered; the air, after the heat of the day, chilled me through my jacket.

The *Hispaniola* still lay where she had anchored; but, sure enough, there was the Jolly Roger—the black flag of piracy—flying from her peak. Even as I looked, there came another red flash and another report, that sent the echoes clattering, and one more round shot whistled through the air. It was the last of the cannonade.

I lay for some time, watching the bustle which succeeded the attack. Men were demolishing something with axes on the beach near the stockade; the poor jolly boat, I afterwards discovered. Away, near the mouth of the river, a great fire was glowing among the trees, and between that point and the ship, one of the gigs kept coming and going, the men, whom I had seen so gloomy, shouting at the oars like children. But there was a sound in their voices which suggested rum.

At length I thought I might return towards the stockade. I was pretty far down on the low, sandy spit that incloses the anchorage to the east and is joined at half-water to Skeleton Island; and now, as I rose to my feet, I saw, some distance further down the spit and rising from among low bushes, an isolated rock, pretty high, and peculiarly white in color. It occurred to me that this might be the white rock of which Ben Gunn had spoken, and that some day or other a boat might be wanted, and I should know where to look for one.

Then I skirted among the woods until I had regained the

rear, or shoreward side, of the stockade, and was soon warmly welcomed by the faithful party.

I had soon told my story, and began to look about me. The log house was made of unsquared trunks of pine—roof, walls, and floor. The latter stood in several places as much as a foot or a foot and a half above the surface of the sand. There was a porch at the door, and under this porch the little spring welled up into an artificial basin of a rather odd kind—no other than a great ship's kettle of iron, with the bottom knocked out, and sunk "to her bearings," as the captain said, among the sand.

Little had been left beside the framework of the house; but in one corner there was a stone slab laid down by way of hearth, and an old rusty iron basket to contain the fire.

The slopes of the knoll and all the inside of the stockade had been cleared of timber to build the house, and we could see by the stumps what a fine and lofty grove had been destroyed. Most of the soil had been washed away or buried in drift after the removal of the trees; only where the streamlet ran down from the kettle a thick bed of moss and some ferns and little creeping bushes were still green among the sand. Very close around the stockade—too close for defense, they said—the wood still flourished high and dense, all of fir on the land side, but towards the sea with a large admixture of live oaks.

The cold evening breeze, of which I have spoken, whistled through every chink of the rude building and sprinkled the floor with a continual rain of fine sand. There was sand in our eyes, sand in our teeth, sand in our suppers, sand dancing in the spring at the bottom of the kettle, for all the world like porridge beginning to boil. Our chimney was a square hole in the roof; it was but a little part of the smoke that found its way out, and the rest eddied about the house, and kept us coughing and piping the eye.

Add to this that Gray, the new man, had his face tied up in a bandage for a cut he had got in breaking away from the mutineers; and that poor old Tom Redruth, still unburied, lay along the wall, stiff and stark, under the Union Jack.

If we had been allowed to sit idle, we should all have fallen in the blues, but Captain Smollett was never the man for that. All hands were called up before him, and he divided us into watches. The doctor, and Gray, and I, for one; the squire, Hunter, and Joyce, upon the other. Tired though we all were, two were sent out for firewood; two more were set to dig a grave for Redruth; the doctor was named cook; I was put sentry at the door; and the captain himself went from one to another keeping up our spirits and lending a hand wherever it was wanted.

From time to time the doctor came to the door for a little air and to rest his eyes, which were almost smoked out of his head; and whenever he did so, he had a word for me.

"That man Smollett," he said once, "is a better man than I am. And when I say that it means a deal, Jim."

Another time he came and was silent for a while. Then he put his head on one side and looked at me.

"Is this Ben Gunn a man?" he asked.

"I do not know, sir," said I. "I am not very sure whether he's sane."

"If there's any doubt about the matter, he is," returned the doctor. "A man who has been three years biting his nails on a desert island, Jim, can't expect to appear as sane as you or me. It doesn't lie in human nature. Was it cheese you said he had a fancy for?"

"Yes, sir, cheese," I answered.

"Well, Jim," says he, "just see the good that comes of being dainty in your food. You've seen my snuff box, haven't you? And you never saw me take snuff; the reason being that in my snuff box I carry a piece of Parmesan cheese—a cheese made in Italy, very nutritious. Well, that's for Ben Gunn!"

Before supper was eaten, we buried old Tom in the sand and stood round him for a while, bare-headed in the breeze. A good deal of firewood had been got in, but not enough for the captain's fancy; and he shook his head over it and told us we "must get back to this tomorrow rather livelier." Then, when we had eaten our pork and each had a good stiff glass of brandy grog, the three chiefs got together in a corner to discuss our prospects.

It appears they were at their wit's end what to do, the stores being so low that we must have been starved into surrender long before help came. But our best hope, it was decided, was to kill off the buccaneers until they either hauled down their flag or ran away with the *Hispaniola*. From nineteen they were already reduced to fifteen, two others were wounded, and one, at least—the man shot beside the gun—severely wounded, if he were not dead. Every time we had a crack at them, we were to take it, saving our own lives, with the extremest care. And, besides that, we had two able allies—rum and the climate.

As for the first, though we were about half a mile away, we could hear them roaring and singing late into the night; and as for the second, the doctor staked his wig that, camped where they were in the marsh, and unprovided with remedies, the half of them would be on their backs before a week.

"So," he added," if we are not all shot down first they'll be glad to be packing in the schooner. It's always a ship, and they can get to buccaneering again, I suppose."

"First ship that ever I lost," said Captain Smollett.

I was dead tired, as you may fancy; and when I got to sleep, which was not till after a great deal of tossing, I slept like a log of wood.

The rest had long been up, and had already breakfasted and increased the pile of firewood by about half as much again, when I was wakened by a bustle and the sound of voices.

"Flag of truce!" I heard someone say; and then, immediately after, with a cry of surprise, "Silver himself!"

And at that, up I jumped and, rubbing my eyes, ran to a loophole in the wall.

Chapter 20 SILVER'S EMBASSY

Sure enough, there were two men just outside the stockade, one of them waving a white cloth; the other, no less a person than Silver himself, standing placidly by.

It was still quite early, and the coldest morning that I think I ever was abroad in; a chill that pierced into the marrow. The sky was bright and cloudless overhead, and the tops of the trees shone rosily in the sun. But where Silver stood with his lieutenant all was still in shadow, and they waded knee deep in a low, white vapor that had crawled during the night out of the morass. The chill and the vapor taken together told a poor tale of the island. It was plainly a damp, feverish, unhealthy spot.

"Keep indoors, men," said the captain. "Ten to one this is a trick."

Then he hailed the buccaneer.

"Who goes? Stand, or we fire."

"Flag of truce," cried Silver.

The captain was in the porch, keeping himself carefully out of the way of a treacherous shot, should any be intended. He turned and spoke to us:

"Doctor's watch on the lookout. Dr. Livesey take the north side, if you please; Jim, the east; Gray, west. The watch below, all hands to load muskets. Lively, men, and careful."

And then he turned again to the mutineers.

"And what do you want with your flag of truce?" he cried.

This time it was the other man who replied.

"Cap'n Silver, sir, to come on board and make terms," he shouted.

"Cap'n Silver! Don't know him. Who's he?" cried the captain. And we could hear him adding to himself: "Cap'n, is it? My heart, and here's promotion!"

Long John answered for himself.

"Me, sir. These poor lads have chosen me cap'n, after your desertion, sir"—laying a particular emphasis upon the word "desertion." "We're willing to submit, if we can come to terms, and no bones about it. All I ask is your word, Cap'n Smollett, to let me safe and sound out of this here stockade, and one minute to get out o' shot before a gun is fired."

"My man," said Captain Smollett, "I have not the slightest desire to talk to you. If you wish to talk to me, you can come, that's all. If there's any treachery, it'll be on your side, and the Lord help you."

"That's enough, cap'n," shouted Long John, cheerily. "A word from you's enough. I know a gentleman, and you may lay to that."

We could see the man who carried the flag of truce attempting to hold Silver back. Nor was that wonderful, seeing how cavalier had been the captain's answer. But Silver laughed at him aloud and slapped him on the back, as if the idea of alarm had been absurd. Then he advanced to the stockade, threw over his crutch, got a leg up, and with great vigor and skill succeeded in surmounting the fence and dropping safely to the other side.

I will confess that I was far too much taken up with what was going on to be of the slightest use as sentry; indeed, I had already deserted my eastern loophole and crept up behind the captain, who had now seated himself on the threshold, with his elbows on his knees, his head in his hands, and his eyes fixed on the water, as it bubbled out of the old iron kettle in the sand. He was whistling to himself, "Come, Lasses and Lads."

Silver had terrible hard work getting up the knoll. What with the steepness of the incline, the thick tree stumps, and the soft sand, he and his crutch were as helpless as a ship in stays. But he stuck to it like a man, in silence, and at last arrived before the captain, whom he saluted in the handsomest style. He was tricked out in his best; an immense blue coat, thick with brass buttons, hung as low as to his knees, and a fine laced hat was set on the back of his head.

"Here you are, my man," said the captain, raising his head. "You had better sit down."

"You ain't a-going to let me inside, cap'n?" complained Long John. "It's a main cold morning, to be sure, sir, to sit outside upon the sand."

"Why, Silver," said the captain, "if you had pleased to be an honest man, you might have been sitting in your galley. It's your own doing. You're either my ship's cook—and then you were treated handsome—or Cap'n Silver, a common mutineer and pirate, and then you can go hang!"

"Well, well, cap'n," returned the sea cook, sitting down as he was bidden on the sand, "you'll have to give me a hand up again, that's all. A sweet pretty place you have of it here. Ah, there's Jim! The top of the morning to you, Jim. Doctor, here's my service. Why, there you all are together, like a happy family, in a manner of speaking."

"If you have anything to say, my man, better say it," said the captain.

"Right you were, Cap'n Smollett," replied Silver. "Dooty is dooty, to be sure. Well, now, you look here, that was a good lay of yours last night. I don't deny it was a good lay. Some of you pretty handy with a handspike [1] end. And I'll not deny neither

[1] *handspike:* an iron bar.

but what some of my people was shook—maybe all was shook; maybe I was shook myself; maybe that's why I'm here for terms. But you mark me, cap'n, it won't do twice, by thunder! We'll have to do sentry-go, and ease off a point or so on the rum. Maybe you think we were all a sheet in the wind's eye.[1] But I'll tell you I was sober; I was on'y dog tired; and if I'd awoke a second sooner, I'd a' caught you at the act, I would. He wasn't dead when I got round to him, not he."

"Well?" says Captain Smollett, as cool as can be.

All that Silver said was a riddle to him, but you would never have guessed it from his tone. As for me, I began to have an inkling. Ben Gunn's last words came back to my mind. I began to suppose that he had paid the buccaneers a visit while they all lay drunk together round their fire, and I reckoned up with glee that we had only fourteen enemies to deal with.

"Well, here it is," said Silver. "We want that treasure, and we'll have it—that's our point! You would just as soon save your lives, I reckon; and that's yours. You have a chart, haven't you?"

"That's as may be," replied the captain.

"Oh, well, you have, I know that," returned Long John. "You needn't be so husky with a man; there ain't a particle of service in that, and you may lay to it. What I mean is, we want your chart. Now, I never meant you no harm myself."

"That won't do with me, my man," interrupted the captain. "We know exactly what you meant to do, and we don't care; for now, you see, you can't do it."

And the captain looked at him calmly and proceeded to fill a pipe.

"If Abe Gray——" Silver broke out.

"Avast there!" cried Mr. Smollett. "Gray told me nothing, and I asked him nothing; and what's more I would see you and him and this whole island blown clean out of the water into blazes first. So there's my mind for you, my man, on that."

This little whiff of temper seemed to cool Silver down. He had been growing nettled before, but now he pulled himself together.

"Like enough," said he. "I would set no limits to what gentlemen might consider shipshape, or might not, as the case were.

[1] *a sheet in the wind's eye:* drunk.

And, seein' as how you are about to take a pipe, cap'n, I'll make so free as do likewise."

And he filled a pipe and lighted it; and the two men sat silently smoking for quite a while, now looking each other in the face, now stopping their tobacco, now leaning forward to spit. It was as good as the play to see them.

"Now," resumed Silver, "here it is. You give us the chart to get the treasure by, and drop shooting poor seamen and stoving of their heads in while asleep. You do that, and we'll offer you a choice. Either you come aboard along of us, once the treasure shipped, and then I'll give you my affy-davy, upon my word of honor, to clap you somewhere safe ashore. Or, if that ain't to your fancy, some of my hands being rough and having old scores, on account of hazing, then you can stay here, you can. We'll divide stores with you, man for man; and I'll give my affy-davy, as before, to speak the first ship I sight and send 'em here to pick you up. Now, you'll own that's talking. Handsomer you couldn't look to get, not you. And I hope"—raising his voice—"that all hands in this here blockhouse will overhaul my words, for what is spoke to one is spoke to all."

Captain Smollett rose from his seat and knocked out the ashes of his pipe in the palm of his left hand.

"Is that all?" he asked.

"Every last word, by thunder!" answered John. "Refuse that and you've seen the last of me but musket balls."

"Very good," said the captain. "Now you'll hear me. If you'll come up one by one, unarmed, I'll engage to clap you all in irons and take you home to a fair trial in England. If you won't, my name is Alexander Smollett, I've flown my sovereign's colors, and I'll see you all to Davy Jones. You can't find the treasure. You can't sail the ship—there's not a man among you fit to sail the ship. You can't fight us—Gray, there, got away from five of you. Your ship's in irons,[1] Master Silver; you're on a lee shore, and so you'll find. I stand here and tell you so; and they're the last good words you'll get from me; for, in the name of heaven, I'll put a bullet in your back when next I meet you. Tramp, my lad. Bundle out of this, please, hand over hand, and double quick."

[1] *in irons:* unable to turn around so that the sails will move the ship.

Silver's face was a picture; his eyes started in his head with wrath. He shook the fire out of his pipe.

"Give me a hand up!" he cried.

"Not I," returned the captain.

"Who'll give me a hand up?" he roared.

Not a man among us moved. Growling the foulest imprecations,[1] he crawled along the sand till he got hold of the porch and could hoist himself again upon his crutch. Then he spat into the spring.

"There!" he cried, "that's what I think of ye. Before an hour's out, I'll stove in your old blockhouse like a rumpuncheon. Laugh, by thunder, laugh! Before an hour's out, ye'll laugh upon the other side. Them that die 'll be the lucky ones."

And with a dreadful oath he stumbled off, plowed down the sand, was helped across the stockade, after four or five failures, by the man with the flag of truce, and disappeared in an instant afterwards among the trees.

Chapter 21 THE ATTACK

As soon as Silver disappeared, the captain, who had been closely watching him, turned towards the interior of the house and found not a man of us at his post but Gray. It was the first time we had ever seen him angry.

"Quarters!" he roared. And then, as we all slunk back to our places, "Gray," he said, "I'll put your name in the log; you've stood by your duty like a seaman. Mr. Trelawney, I'm surprised at you, sir. Doctor, I thought you had worn the king's coat! If that was how you served at Fontenoy, sir, you'd have been better in your berth."

The doctor's watch were all back at their loopholes; the rest were busy loading the spare muskets, and every one with a red

[1] *imprecation* (ĭm′prē·kā′shŭn) : a curse.

face, you may be certain, and a flea in his ear, as the saying is.

The captain looked on for a while in silence. Then he spoke.

"My lads," said he, "I've given Silver a broadside. I pitched it in red-hot on purpose; and before the hour's out, as he said, we shall be boarded. We're outnumbered, I needn't tell you that, but we fight in shelter; and, a minute ago, I should have said we fought with discipline. I've no manner of doubt that we can drub them if you choose."

Then he went the rounds and saw, as he said, that all was clear.

On the two shore sides of the house, east and west, there were only two loopholes; on the south side where the porch was, two again; and on the north side, five. There was a round score of muskets for the seven of us; the firewood had been built into four piles—tables, you might say—one about the middle of each side, and on each of these tables some ammunition and four loaded muskets were laid ready to the hand of the defenders. In the middle, the cutlasses lay ranged.

"Toss out the fire," said the captain; "the chill is past, and we mustn't have smoke in our eyes."

The iron fire basket was carried bodily out by Mr. Trelawney, and the embers smothered among sand.

"Hawkins hasn't had his breakfast. Hawkins, help yourself, and back to your post to eat it," continued Captain Smollett. "Lively, now, my lad; you'll want it before you've done. Hunter, serve out a round of brandy to all hands."

And while this was going on, the captain completed, in his own mind, the plan of the defense.

"Doctor, you will take the door," he resumed. "See, and don't expose yourself; keep within and fire through the porch. Hunter, take the east side, there. Joyce, you stand by the west, my man. Mr. Trelawney, you are the best shot—you and Gray will take this long north side, with the five loopholes; it's there the danger is. If they can get up to it and fire in upon us through our own ports, things would begin to look dirty. Hawkins, neither you nor I are much account at the shooting; we'll stand by to load and bear a hand."

As the captain had said, the chill was past. As soon as the sun had climbed above our girdle of trees, it fell with all its force upon the clearing and drank up the vapors at a draught. Soon the sand was baking, and the resin melting in the logs of the blockhouse. Jackets and coats were flung aside; shirts thrown open at the neck and rolled up to the shoulders; and we stood there, each at his post, in a fever of heat and anxiety.

An hour passed away.

"Hang them!" said the captain. "This is as dull as the doldrums. Gray, whistle for a wind."

And just at that moment came the first news of the attack.

"If you please, sir," said Joyce, "if I see anyone am I to fire?"

"I told you so!" cried the captain.

"Thank you, sir," returned Joyce, with the same quiet civility.

Nothing followed for a time; but the remark had set us all on the alert, straining ears and eyes—the musketeers with their pieces balanced in their hands, the captain out in the middle of the blockhouse, with his mouth very tight and a frown on his face.

So some seconds passed, till suddenly Joyce whipped up his musket and fired. The report had scarcely died away ere it was repeated, and repeated from without in a scattering volley, shot behind shot, like a string of geese, from every side of the enclosure. Several bullets struck the log house, but not one entered; and, as the smoke cleared away and vanished, the stockade and the woods around it looked as quiet and empty as before. Not a bough waved, not the gleam of a musket-barrel betrayed the presence of our foes.

"Did you hit your man?" asked the captain.

"No, sir," replied Joyce. "I believe not, sir."

"Next best thing to tell the truth," muttered Captain Smollett. "Load his gun, Hawkins. How many should you say there were on your side, doctor?"

"I know precisely," said Dr. Livesey. "Three shots were fired on this side. I saw the three flashes—two close together—one farther to the west."

"Three!" repeated the captain. "And how many on yours, Mr. Trelawney?"

But this was not so easily answered. There had come many from the north—seven, by the squire's computation; eight or nine, according to Gray. From the east and west only a single shot had been fired. It was plain, therefore, that the attack would be developed from the north, and that on the other three sides we were only to be annoyed by a show of hostilities. But Captain Smollett made no change in his arrangements. If the mutineers succeeded in crossing the stockade, he argued, they would take possession of any unprotected loophole and shoot us down like rats in our own stronghold.

Nor had we much time left to us for thought. Suddenly, with a loud huzza, a little cloud of pirates leaped from the woods on the north side and ran straight on the stockade. At the same moment, the fire was once more opened from the woods, and a rifle ball sang through the doorway and knocked the doctor's musket into bits.

The boarders swarmed over the fence like monkeys. Squire and Gray fired again and yet again; three men fell, one forwards into the enclosure, two back on the outside. But of these, one was evidently more frightened than hurt, for he was on his feet again in a crack and instantly disappeared among the trees.

Two had bit the dust, one had fled, four had made good their footing inside our defenses; while from the shelter of the woods seven or eight men, each evidently supplied with several muskets, kept up a hot though useless fire on the log house.

The four who had boarded made straight before them for the building, shouting as they ran, and the men among the trees shouted back to encourage them. Several shots were fired; but, such was the hurry of the marksmen that not one appears to have taken effect. In a moment, the four pirates had swarmed up the mound and were upon us.

The head of Job Anderson, the boatswain, appeared at the middle loophole.

"At 'em, all hands—all hands!" he roared in a voice of thunder.

At the same moment, another pirate grasped Hunter's musket by the muzzle, wrenched it from his hands, plucked it through the loophole, and, with one stunning blow, laid the poor fellow senseless on the floor. Meanwhile a third, running unharmed all round the house, appeared suddenly in the doorway and fell with his cutlass on the doctor.

Our position was utterly reversed. A moment since, we were firing, under cover, at an exposed enemy; now it was we who lay uncovered and could not return a blow.

The log house was full of smoke, to which we owed our comparative safety. Cries and confusion, the flashes and reports of pistol shots, and one loud groan rang in my ears.

"Out, lads, out, and fight 'em in the open! Cutlasses!" cried the captain.

I snatched a cutlass from the pile, and someone, at the same time snatching another, gave me a cut across the knuckles which I hardly felt. I dashed out of the door into the clear sunlight. Someone was close behind, I knew not whom. Right in front, the doctor was pursuing his assailant down the hill, and, just as my eyes fell upon him, beat down his guard and sent him sprawling on his back, with a great slash across the face.

"Round the house, lads! round the house!" cried the captain; and even in the hurly-burly I perceived a change in his voice.

Mechanically, I obeyed, turned eastwards and with my cutlass raised, ran round the corner of the house. Next moment I was face to face with Anderson. He roared aloud, and his hanger went up above his head, flashing in the sunlight. I had not time to be afraid, but, as the blow still hung impending, leaped in a trice upon one side and missing my foot in the soft sand, rolled headlong down the slope.

When I had first sallied from the door, the other mutineers had been already swarming up the palisade to make an end of us. One man, in a red nightcap, with his cutlass in his mouth, had even got upon the top and thrown a leg across. Well, so short had been the interval that when I found my feet again all was in the same posture, the fellow with the red nightcap still halfway over, another still just showing his head above the top of the stockade. And yet, in this breath of time, the fight was over, and the victory was ours.

Gray, following close behind me, had cut down the big boatswain ere he had time to recover from his lost blow. Another had been shot at a loophole in the very act of firing into the house and now lay in agony, the pistol still smoking in his hand. A third, as I had seen, the doctor had disposed of at a blow. Of the four who had scaled the palisade, one only remained unaccounted for, and he, having left his cutlass on the field, was now clambering out again with the fear of death upon him.

"Fire—fire from the house!" cried the doctor. "And you, lads, back into cover."

But his words were unheeded, no shot was fired, and the last boarder made good his escape and disappeared with the rest into the wood. In three seconds nothing remained of the attacking party but the five who had fallen, four on the inside, and one on the outside, of the palisade.

The doctor and Gray and I ran full speed for shelter. The survivors would soon be back where they had left their muskets, and at any moment the fire might recommence.

The house was by this time somewhat cleared of smoke, and we saw at a glance the price we had paid for victory. Hunter lay beside his loophole, stunned; Joyce by his, shot through the head, never to move again; while right in the center, the squire was supporting the captain, one as pale as the other.

"The captain's wounded," said Mr. Trelawney.

"Have they run?" asked Mr. Smollett.

"All that could, you may be bound," returned the doctor; "but there's five of them will never run again."

"Five!" cried the captain. "Come, that's better. Five against three leaves us four to nine. That's better odds than we had at starting. We were seven to nineteen then, or thought we were, and that's as bad to bear." *

PART FIVE—My Sea Adventure

Chapter 22 HOW MY SEA ADVENTURE BEGAN

There was no return of the mutineers—not so much as another shot out of the woods. They had "got their rations for that day," as the captain put it, and we had the place to ourselves and a quiet time to overhaul the wounded and get dinner. Squire and

* The mutineers were soon only eight in number, for the man shot by Mr. Trelawney on board the schooner died that same evening of his wound. But this was, of course, not known till after by the faithful party.

I cooked outside in spite of the danger, and even outside we could hardly tell what we were at for horror of the loud groans that reached us from the doctor's patients.

Out of the eight men who had fallen in the action, only three still breathed—that one of the pirates who had been shot at the loophole, Hunter, and Captain Smollett; and of these the first two were as good as dead; the mutineer, indeed, died under the doctor's knife, and Hunter, do what we could, never recovered consciousness in this world. He lingered all day, breathing loudly, like the old buccaneer at home in his apoplectic fit; but the bones of his chest had been crushed by the blow and his skull fractured in falling, and some time in the following night, without sign or sound, he went to his Maker.

As for the captain, his wounds were grievous indeed, but not dangerous. No organ was fatally injured. Anderson's ball—for it was Job that shot him first—had broken his shoulder blade and touched the lung, not badly; the second had only torn and displaced some muscles in the calf. He was sure to recover, the doctor said, but, in the meantime and for weeks to come, he must not walk nor move his arm nor so much as speak when he could help it.

My own accidental cut across the knuckles was a fleabite. Doctor Livesey patched it up with plaster and pulled my ears for me into the bargain.

After dinner, the squire and the doctor sat by the captain's side a while in consultation; and when they had talked to their heart's content, it being then a little past noon, the doctor took up his hat and pistols, girt on a cutlass, put the chart in his pocket, and with a musket over his shoulder, crossed the palisade on the north side and set off briskly through the trees.

Gray and I were sitting together at the far end of the blockhouse to be out of earshot of our officers consulting; and Gray took his pipe out of his mouth and fairly forgot to put it back again, so thunderstruck he was at this occurrence.

"Why, in the name of Davy Jones," said he, "is Dr. Livesey mad?"

"Why, no," says I. "He's about the last of this crew for that, I take it."

"Well, shipmate," said Gray, "mad he may not be; but if *he's* not, you mark my words, *I* am."

"I take it," replied I, "the doctor has his idea; and if I am right, he's going now to see Ben Gunn."

I was right, as appeared later; but, in the meantime, the house being stifling hot, and the little patch of sand inside the palisade ablaze with midday sun, I began to get another thought into my head, which was not by any means so right. What I began to do was to envy the doctor, walking in the cool shadow of the woods, with the birds about him and the pleasant smell of the pines, while I sat grilling, with my clothes stuck to the hot resin, and so much blood about me, and so many poor dead bodies lying all around that I took a disgust of the place that was almost as strong as fear.

All the time I was washing out the blockhouse and then washing up the things from dinner, this disgust and envy kept growing stronger and stronger, till at last, being near a bread bag and no one then observing me, I took the first step towards my escapade and filled both pockets of my coat with biscuit.

I was a fool, if you like, and certainly I was going to do a foolish, overbold act; but I was determined to do it with all the precautions in my power. These biscuits, should anything befall me, would keep me, at least, from starving till far on in the next day.

The next thing I laid hold of was a brace of pistols, and as I already had a powder horn and bullets, I felt myself well supplied with arms.

As for the scheme I had in my head, it was not a bad one in itself. I was to go down the sandy spit that divides the anchorage on the east from the open sea, find the white rock I had observed last evening, and ascertain whether it was there or not that Ben Gunn had hidden his boat; a thing quite worth doing, as I still believe. But as I was certain I should not be allowed to leave the enclosure, my only plan was to take French leave and slip out when nobody was watching; and that was so bad a way of doing it as made the thing itself wrong. But I was only a boy, and I had made my mind up.

Well, as things at last fell out, I found an admirable opportunity. The squire and Gray were busy helping the captain with his bandages; the coast was clear; I made a bolt for it over the stockade and into the thickest of the trees, and before my absence was observed, I was out of cry of my companions.

This was my second folly, far worse than the first, as I left but two sound men to guard the house; but like the first, it was a help towards saving all of us.

I took my way straight for the east coast of the island, for I was determined to go down the sea side of the spit to avoid all chance of observation from the anchorage. It was already late in the afternoon, although still warm and sunny. As I continued to thread the tall woods, I could hear from far before me not only the continuous thunder of the surf, but a certain tossing of foliage and grinding of boughs which showed me the sea breeze had set in higher than usual. Soon cool drafts of air began to reach me; and a few steps farther I came forth into the open borders of the grove and saw the sea lying blue and sunny to the horizon, and the surf tumbling and tossing its foam along the beach.

I have never seen the sea quiet round Treasure Island. The sun might blaze overhead, the air be without a breath, the surface smooth and blue, but still these great rollers would be running along all the external coast, thundering and thundering by day and night; and I scarce believe there is one spot in the island where a man would be out of earshot of their noise.

I walked along beside the surf with great enjoyment, till, thinking I was now got far enough to the south, I took the cover of some thick bushes and crept warily up to the ridge of the spit.

Behind me was the sea, in front the anchorage. The sea breeze, as though it had the sooner blown itself out by its unusual violence, was already at an end; it had been succeeded by light, variable airs from the south and southeast, carrying great banks of fog; and the anchorage, under lee of Skeleton Island, lay still and leaden as when first we entered it. The *Hispaniola,* in that unbroken mirror, was exactly portrayed from the truck [1] to the water line, the Jolly Roger hanging from her peak.

Alongside lay one of the gigs, Silver in the stern sheets—him I could always recognize—while a couple of men were leaning over the stern bulwarks, one of them with a red cap—the very rogue that I had seen some hours before, stride-legs upon the palisade. Apparently they were talking and laughing, though at that distance—upwards of a mile—I could, of course, hear no word of what was said. All at once, there began the most horrid, unearthly screaming, which at first startled me badly, though I had

[1] *truck:* the top of the mast.

soon remembered the voice of Captain Flint and even thought I could make out the bird by her bright plumage, as she sat perched upon her master's wrist.

Soon after, the jolly boat shoved off and pulled for shore, and the man with the red cap and his comrade went below by the cabin companion.

Just about the same time, the sun had gone down behind the Spy-glass, and as the fog was collecting rapidly, it began to grow dark in earnest. I saw I must lose no time if I were to find the boat that evening.

The white rock, visible enough above the brush, was still some eighth of a mile further down the spit, and it took me a goodish while to get up with it, crawling, often on all fours, among the scrub. Night had almost come when I laid my hand on its rough sides. Right below it there was an exceedingly small hollow of green turf, hidden by banks and a thick underwood about knee-deep, that grew there very plentifully; and in the center of the dell, sure enough, a little tent of goatskins, like what the gypsies carry about with them in England.

I dropped into the hollow, lifted the side of the tent, and there was Ben Gunn's boat—homemade if ever anything was homemade: a rude, lop-sided framework of tough wood, and stretched upon that, a covering of goatskin, with the hair inside. The thing was extremely small, even for me, and I can hardly imagine that it could have floated with a full-sized man. There was one thwart, set as low as possible, a kind of stretcher in the bows, and a double paddle for propulsion.

I had not then seen a coracle, such as the ancient Britons made, but I have seen one since, and I can give you no fairer idea of Ben Gunn's boat than by saying it was like the first and the worst coracle ever made by man. But the great advantage of the coracle it certainly possessed, for it was exceedingly light and portable.

Well, now that I had found the boat, you would have thought I had had enough of truantry for once; but, in the meantime, I had taken another notion and become so obstinately fond of it that I would have carried it out, I believe, in the teeth of Captain Smollett himself. This was to slip out under cover of the night, cut the *Hispaniola* adrift, and let her go ashore where she fancied. I had quite made up my mind that the mutineers, after their repulse of the morning, had nothing nearer their hearts than to up anchor and away to sea; this, I thought, it would be a fine thing to prevent, and now that I had seen how they left their watchmen unprovided with a boat, I thought it might be done with little risk.

Down I sat to wait for darkness and made a hearty meal of biscuit. It was a night of ten thousand for my purpose. The fog had now buried all heaven. As the last rays of daylight dwindled and disappeared, absolute blackness settled down on Treasure Island. And when at last I shouldered the coracle and groped my way stumblingly out of the hollow where I had supped, there were but two points visible on the whole anchorage.

One was the great fire on shore by which the defeated pirates lay carousing in the swamp. The other, a mere blur of light upon the darkness, indicated the position of the anchored ship. She had swung round to the ebb—her bow was now towards me—the only lights on board were in the cabin; and what I saw was merely a reflection on the fog of the strong rays that flowed from the stern window.

The ebb had already run some time, and I had to wade through a long belt of swampy sand, where I sank several times above the ankle before I came to the edge of the retreating water, and wading a little way in, with some strength and dexterity, set my coracle, keel downwards, on the surface.

Chapter 23 THE EBB TIDE RUNS

The coracle—as I had ample reason to know before I was done with her—was a very safe boat for a person of my height and weight, both buoyant and clever in a seaway; but she was the most cross-grained lop-sided craft to manage. Do as you pleased, she always made more leeway [1] than anything else, and turning

[1] *leeway* (lē′wā′): movement sideways.

round and round was the maneuver she was best at. Even Ben Gunn himself has admitted that she was "queer to handle till you knew her way."

Certainly I did not know her way. She turned in every direction but the one I was bound to go; the most part of the time we were broadside on, and I am very sure I never should have made the ship at all but for the tide. By good fortune, paddle as I pleased, the tide was still sweeping me down; and there lay the *Hispaniola* right in the fair way, hardly to be missed.

First she loomed before me like a blot of something yet blacker than darkness, then her spars and hull began to take shape, and the next moment, as it seemed (for the further I went, the brisker grew the current of the ebb), I was alongside of her hawser [1] and had laid hold.

The hawser was as taut as a bowstring, and the current so strong she pulled upon her anchor. All round the hull, in the blackness, the rippling current bubbled and chattered like a little mountain stream. One cut with my sea-gully and the *Hispaniola* would go humming down the tide.

So far so good; but it next occurred to my recollection that a taut hawser, suddenly cut, is a thing as dangerous as a kicking horse. Ten to one, if I were so foolhardy as to cut the *Hispaniola* from her anchor, I and the coracle would be knocked clean out of the water.

This brought me to a full stop, and if fortune had not again particularly favored me, I should have had to abandon my design. But the light airs which had begun blowing from the southeast and south had hauled round after nightfall into the southwest. Just while I was meditating, a puff came, caught the *Hispaniola,* and forced her up into the current; and to my great joy, I felt the hawser slacken in my grasp and the hand by which I held it dip for a second under water.

With that I made my mind up, took out my gully, opened it with my teeth, and cut one strand after another, till the vessel swung only by two. Then I lay quiet, waiting to sever these last when the strain should be once more lightened by a breath of wind.

All this time I had heard the sound of loud voices from the cabin; but, to say truth, my mind had been so entirely taken up

[1] *hawser* (hô′zẽr): a large rope for mooring a ship.

with other thoughts that I had scarcely given ear. Now, however, when I had nothing else to do, I began to pay more heed.

One I recognized for the coxswain, Israel Hands, that had been Flint's gunner in former days. The other was, of course, my friend of the red nightcap. Both men were plainly the worse of drink, and they were still drinking; for, even while I was listening, one of them, with a drunken cry, opened the stern window and threw out something which I divined to be an empty bottle. But they were not only tipsy; it was plain that they were furiously angry. Oaths flew like hailstones, and every now and then there came forth such an explosion as I thought was sure to end in blows. But each time the quarrel passed off, and the voices grumbled lower for a while, until the next crisis came, and, in its turn, passed away without result.

On shore, I could see the glow of the great campfire burning warmly through the shoreside trees. Someone was singing, a dull, old, droning sailor's song, with a droop and a quaver at the end of every verse, and seemingly no end to it at all but the patience of the singer. I had heard it on the voyage more than once and remembered these words:

But one man of her crew alive,
What put to sea with seventy-five.

And I thought it was a ditty rather too dolefully appropriate for a company that had met such cruel losses in the morning. But, indeed, from what I saw, all these buccaneers were as callous [1] as the sea they sailed on.

At last the breeze came; the schooner sidled and drew nearer in the dark; I felt the hawser slacken once more, and with a good, tough effort, cut the last fibers through.

The breeze had but little action on the coracle, and I was almost instantly swept against the bows of the *Hispaniola.* At the same time, the schooner began to turn upon her heel, spinning slowly, end for end, across the current.

I wrought like a fiend, for I expected every moment to be swamped; and since I found I could not push the coracle directly off, I now shoved straight astern. At length I was clear of my dangerous neighbor; and just as I gave the last impulsion, my

[1] *callous* (kăl′ŭs): insensitive.

hands came across a light cord that was trailing overboard across the stern bulwarks. Instantly I grasped it.

Why I should have done so I can hardly say. It was at first mere instinct; but once I had it in my hands and found it fast, curiosity began to get the upper hand, and I determined I should have one look through the cabin window.

I pulled in hand over hand on the cord, and, when I judged myself near enough, rose at infinite risk to about half my height and thus commanded the roof and a slice of the interior of the cabin.

By this time the schooner and her little consort were gliding pretty swiftly through the water; indeed, we had already fetched up level with the campfire. The ship was talking, as sailors say, loudly, treading the innumerable ripples with an incessant weltering splash; and until I got my eye above the window sill, I could not comprehend why the watchmen had taken no alarm. One glance, however, was sufficient; and it was only one glance that I durst take from that unsteady skiff. It showed me Hands and his companion locked together in deadly wrestle, each with a hand upon the other's throat.

I dropped upon the thwart again, none too soon, for I was near overboard. I could see nothing for the moment but these two furious, encrimsoned faces, swaying together under the smoky lamp; and I shut my eyes to let them grow once more familiar with the darkness.

The endless ballad had come to an end at last, and the whole diminished company about the campfire had broken into the chorus I had heard so often:

Fifteen men on the Dead Man's Chest—
  Yo-ho-ho, and a bottle of rum!
Drink and the devil had done for the rest—
  Yo-ho-ho, and a bottle of rum!

I was just thinking how busy drink and the devil were at that very moment in the cabin of the *Hispaniola,* when I was surprised by a sudden lurch of the coracle. At the same moment she yawed [1] sharply and seemed to change her course. The speed in the meantime had strangely increased.

[1] *yaw* (yô): to shift course suddenly.

I opened my eyes at once. All round me were little ripples, combing over with a sharp, bristling sound and slightly phosphorescent. The *Hispaniola* herself, a few yards in whose wake I was still being whirled along, seemed to stagger in her course, and I saw her spars toss a little against the blackness of the night; nay, as I looked longer, I made sure she also was wheeling to the southward.

I glanced over my shoulder, and my heart jumped against my ribs. There, right behind me, was the glow of the campfire. The current had turned at right angles, sweeping round along with it the tall schooner and the little dancing coracle; ever quickening, ever bubbling higher, ever muttering louder, it went spinning through the narrows for the open sea.

Suddenly the schooner in front of me gave a violent yaw, turning perhaps through twenty degrees; and almost at the same moment, one shout followed another from on board; I could hear feet pounding on the companion ladder; and I knew that the two drunkards had at last been interrupted in their quarrel and awakened to a sense of their disaster.

I lay down flat in the bottom of that wretched skiff and devoutly recommended my spirit to its Maker. At the end of the straits I made sure we must fall into some bar of raging breakers, where all my troubles would be ended speedily; and though I could, perhaps, bear to die, I could not bear to look upon my fate as it approached.

So I must have lain for hours, continually beaten to and fro upon the billows, now and again wetted with flying sprays, and never ceasing to expect death at the next plunge. Gradually weariness grew upon me; a numbness, an occasional stupor, fell upon my mind even in the midst of my terrors; until sleep at last supervened, and in my sea-tossed coracle I lay and dreamed of home and the old "Admiral Benbow."

Chapter 24 THE CRUISE OF THE CORACLE

It was broad day when I awoke and found myself tossing at the southwest end of Treasure Island. The sun was up, but was still hid from me behind the great bulk of the Spy-glass, which on this side descended almost to the sea in formidable cliffs.

Haulbowline Head and Mizzenmast Hill were at my elbow; the hill bare and dark, the head bound with cliffs forty or fifty feet high and fringed with great masses of fallen rock. I was scarce a quarter of a mile to seaward, and it was my first thought to paddle in and land.

That notion was soon given over. Among the fallen rocks the breakers spouted and bellowed; loud reverberations, heavy sprays flying and falling, succeeded one another from second to second; and I saw myself, if I ventured nearer, dashed to death upon the rough shore or spending my strength in vain to scale the beetling crags.

Nor was that all; for crawling together on flat tables of rock, or letting themselves drop into the sea with loud reports, I beheld huge slimy monsters—soft snails, as it were, of incredible bigness—two or three score of them together, making the rocks to echo with their barkings.

I have understood since that they were sea lions and entirely harmless. But the look of them, added to the difficulty of the shore and the high running of the surf, was more than enough to disgust me of that landing place. I felt willing rather to starve at sea than to confront such perils.

In the meantime I had a better chance, as I supposed, before me. North of Haulbowline Head the land runs in a long way, leaving, at low tide, a long stretch of yellow sand. To the north of that again there comes another cape—Cape of the Woods, as it was marked upon the chart—buried in tall green pines, which descended to the margin of the sea.

I remembered what Silver had said about the current that sets northward along the whole west coast of Treasure Island; and seeing from my position that I was already under its influence, I preferred to leave Haulbowline Head behind me and reserve my strength for an attempt to land upon the kindlier-looking Cape of the Woods.

There was a great, smooth swell upon the sea. The wind blowing steady and gentle from the south, there was no contrariety between that and the current, and the billows rose and fell unbroken.

Had it been otherwise, I must long ago have perished; but as it was, it is surprising how easily and securely my little and light boat could ride. Often, as I still lay at the bottom and kept no more than an eye above the gunwale, I would see a big blue summit heaving close above me; yet the coracle would but bounce a little, dance as if on springs, and subside on the other side into the trough as lightly as a bird.

I began, after a little, to grow very bold and sat up to try my skill at paddling. But even a small change in the disposition of the weight will produce violent changes in the behavior of a coracle. And I had hardly moved, before the boat, giving up at once her gentle dancing movement, ran straight down a slope of water so steep that it made me giddy, and struck her nose, with a spout of spray, deep into the side of the next wave.

I was drenched and terrified and fell instantly back into my old position, whereupon the coracle seemed to find her head again and led me as softly as before among the billows. It was plain she was not to be interfered with, and at that rate, since I could in no way influence her course, what hope had I left of reaching land?

I began to be horribly frightened, but I kept my head, for all that. First, moving with all care, I gradually baled out the coracle with my sea cap; then getting my eye once more above the gunwale, I set myself to study how it was she managed to slip so quietly through the rollers.

I found each wave, instead of the big, smooth glossy mountain it looks from shore, or from a vessel's deck, was for all the world like any range of hills on the dry land, full of peaks and smooth places and valleys. The coracle, left to herself, turning from side to side, threaded, so to speak, her way through these lower parts and avoided the steep slopes and higher, toppling summits of the wave.

"Well, now," thought I to myself, "it is plain I must lie where I am and not disturb the balance; but it is plain, also, that I can put the paddle over the side and from time to time, in smooth places, give her a shove or two towards land." No sooner thought upon than done. There I lay on my elbows, in the most trying attitude, and every now and again gave a weak stroke or two to turn her head to shore.

It was very tiring and slow work, yet I did visibly gain ground; and, as we drew near the Cape of the Woods, though I saw I must infallibly miss that point, I had still made some hundred yards of easting. I was, indeed, close in. I could see the cool, green treetops swaying together in the breeze, and I felt sure I should make the next promontory without fail.

It was high time, for I now began to be tortured with thirst. The glow of the sun from above, its thousandfold reflection from the waves, the sea water that fell and dried upon me, caking my very lips with salt, combined to make my throat burn and my brain ache. The sight of the trees so near at hand had almost made me sick with longing; but the current had soon carried me past the point; and, as the next reach of sea opened out, I beheld a sight that changed the nature of my thoughts.

Right in front of me, not half a mile away, I beheld the *Hispaniola* under sail. I made sure, of course, that I should be taken; but I was so distressed for want of water, that I scarce knew whether to be glad or sorry at the thought; and, long before I had come to a conclusion, surprise had taken entire possession of my mind, and I could do nothing but stare and wonder.

The *Hispaniola* was under her mainsail and two jibs, and the beautiful white canvas shone in the sun like snow or silver. When I first sighted her, all her sails were drawing; she was lying a course about northwest; and I presumed the men on board were going round the island on their way back to the anchorage. Presently she began to fetch more and more to the westward, so that I thought they had sighted me and were going about in chase. At last, however, she fell right into the wind's eye, was taken dead aback, and stood there a while helpless, with her sails shivering.

"Clumsy fellows," said I; "they must still be drunk as owls." And I thought how Captain Smollett would have set them skipping.

Meanwhile, the schooner gradually fell off and filled again upon another tack, sailed swiftly for a minute or so, and brought up once more dead in the wind's eye. Again and again was this repeated. To and fro, up and down, north, south, east, and west the *Hispaniola* sailed by swoops and dashes, and at each repetition ended as she had begun, with idly flapping canvas. It became plain to me that nobody was steering. And, if so, where were the men? Either they were dead drunk or had deserted her, I thought, and perhaps if I could get on board, I might return the vessel to her captain.

The current was bearing coracle and schooner southward at an equal rate. As for the latter's sailing, it was so wild and intermittent, and she hung each time so long in irons, that she certainly gained nothing, if she did not even lose. If only I dared to sit up and paddle, I made sure that I could overhaul her. The scheme had an air of adventure that inspired me, and the thought of the water breaker beside the fore companion doubled my growing courage.

Up I got, was welcomed almost instantly by another cloud of spray, but this time stuck to my purpose and set myself, with all my strength and caution, to paddle after the unsteered *Hispaniola.* Once I shipped a sea so heavy that I had to stop and bail, with my heart fluttering like a bird; but gradually I got into the way of the thing, and guided my coracle among the waves, with only now and then a blow upon her bows and a dash of foam in my face.

I was now gaining rapidly on the schooner; I could see the brass glisten on the tiller [1] as it banged about; and still no soul appeared upon her decks. I could not choose but suppose she was deserted. If not, the men were lying drunk below, where I might batten them down, perhaps, and do what I chose with the ship.

For some time she had been doing the worst thing possible for me—standing still. She headed nearly due south, yawing, of course, all the time. Each time she fell off, her sails partly filled, and these brought her, in a moment, right to the wind again. I have said this was the worst thing possible for me; for helpless as she looked in this situation, with the canvas cracking like cannon, and the blocks trundling and banging on the deck, she still continued to run away from me, not only with the speed of the current, but by the whole amount of her leeway, which was naturally great.

But now, at last, I had my chance. The breeze fell, for some seconds, very low, and the current gradually turning her, the *His-*

[1] *tiller:* the rudder handle.

paniola revolved slowly round her center and at last presented me her stern, with the cabin window still gaping open, and the lamp over the table still burning on into the day. The mainsail hung drooped like a banner. She was stock-still, but for the current.

For the last little while I had even lost; but now, redoubling my efforts, I began once more to overhaul the chase.

I was not a hundred yards from her when the wind came again in a clap; she filled on the port tack and was off again, stooping and skimming like a swallow.

My first impulse was one of despair, but my second was towards joy. Round she came, till she was broadside on to me—round still, till she had covered a half, and then two-thirds, and then three-quarters of the distance that separated us. I could see the waves boiling white under her forefoot. Immensely tall she looked to me from my low station in the coracle.

And then, of a sudden, I began to comprehend. I had scarce time to think—scarce time to act and save myself. I was on the summit of one swell when the schooner came stooping over the next. The bowsprit was over my head. I sprang to my feet and leaped, stamping the coracle under water. With one hand I caught the jib-boom,[1] while my foot was lodged between the stay and the brace; and as I still clung there panting, a dull blow told me that the schooner had charged down upon and struck the coracle, and that I was left without retreat on the *Hispaniola*.

Chapter 25 I STRIKE[2] THE JOLLY ROGER

I had scarce gained a position on the bowsprit, when the flying jib flapped and filled upon the other tack, with a report like a gun. The schooner trembled to her keel under the reverse; but

[1] *jib-boom:* the pole supporting the jib sail in the front of a ship.
[2] *strike:* to haul down.

next moment, the other sails still drawing, the jib flapped back again and hung idle.

This had nearly tossed me off into the sea; and now I lost no time, crawled back along the bowsprit, and tumbled head foremost on the deck.

I was on the lee side of the forecastle, and the mainsail, which was still drawing, concealed from me a certain portion of the afterdeck. Not a soul was to be seen. The planks, which had not been swabbed since the mutiny, bore the print of many feet; and an empty bottle, broken by the neck, tumbled to and fro like a live thing in the scuppers.

Suddenly the *Hispaniola* came right into the wind. The jibs behind me cracked aloud; the rudder slammed to; the whole ship gave a sickening heave and shudder, and at the same moment the main boom swung inboard, the sheet groaning in the blocks, and showed me the lee afterdeck.

There were the two watchmen, sure enough: red-cap on his back, as stiff as a handspike, with his arms stretched out like those of a crucifix and his teeth showing through his open lips; Israel Hands propped against the bulwarks, his chin on his chest, his hands lying open before him on the deck, his face as white, under its tan, as a tallow candle.

For a while the ship kept bucking and sidling like a vicious horse, the sails filling, now on one tack, now on another, and the boom swinging to and fro till the mast groaned aloud under the strain. Now and again, too, there would come a cloud of light sprays over the bulwark and a heavy blow of the ship's bows against the swell: so much heavier weather was made of it by this great rigged ship than by my homemade, lop-sided coracle, now gone to the bottom of the sea.

At every jump of the schooner, red-cap slipped to and fro; but—what was ghastly to behold—neither his attitude nor his fixed teeth-disclosing grin was anyway disturbed by this rough usage. At every jump, too, Hands appeared still more to sink into himself and settle down upon the deck, his feet sliding ever the farther out, and the whole body canting towards the stern, so that his face became, little by little, hid from me; and at last I could see nothing beyond his ear and the frayed ringlet of one whisker.

At the same time, I observed, around both of them, splashes

of dark blood upon the planks and began to feel sure that they had killed each other in their drunken wrath.

While I was thus looking and wondering, in a calm moment, when the ship was still, Israel Hands turned partly round and with a low moan, writhed himself back to the position in which I had seen him first. The moan, which told of pain and deadly weakness, and the way in which his jaw hung open went right to my heart. But when I remembered the talk I had overheard from the apple barrel, all pity left me.

I walked aft until I reached the mainmast.

"Come aboard, Mr. Hands," I said, ironically.

He rolled his eyes round heavily; but he was too far gone to express surprise. All he could do was to utter one word, "Brandy."

It occurred to me there was no time to lose; and, dodging the boom as it once more lurched across the deck, I slipped aft and down the companion stairs into the cabin.

It was such a scene of confusion as you can hardly fancy. All the lockfast places had been broken open in quest of the chart. The floor was thick with mud where ruffians had sat down to drink or consult after wading in the marshes round their camp. The bulkheads, all painted in clear white and beaded round with gilt, bore a pattern of dirty hands. Dozens of empty bottles clinked together in corners to the rolling of the ship. One of the doctor's medical books lay open on the table, half of the leaves gutted out, I suppose, for pipelights. In the midst of all this the lamp still cast a smoky glow, obscure and brown as umber.

I went into the cellar; all the barrels were gone, and of the bottles a most surprising number had been drunk out and thrown away. Certainly, since the mutiny began, not a man of them could ever have been sober.

Foraging about, I found a bottle with some brandy left, for Hands; and for myself I routed out some biscuit, some pickled fruits, a great bunch of raisins, and a piece of cheese. With these I came on deck, put down my own stock behind the rudder head and well out of the coxswain's reach, went forward to the water breaker, and had a good, deep drink of water, and then, and not till then, gave Hands the brandy.

He must have drunk a gill before he took the bottle from his mouth.

"Aye," said he, "by thunder, but I wanted some o' that!"

I had sat down already in my own corner and begun to eat.

"Much hurt?" I asked him.

He grunted, or, rather, I might say, he barked.

"If that doctor was aboard," he said. "I'd be right enough in a couple of turns; but I don't have no manner of luck, you see, and that's what's the matter with me. As for that swab, he's good and dead, he is," he added, indicating the man with the red cap. "He warn't no seaman, anyhow. And where mought you have come from?"

"Well," said I, "I've come aboard to take possession of this ship, Mr. Hands; and you'll please regard me as your captain until further notice."

He looked at me sourly enough, but said nothing. Some of the color had come back into his cheeks, though he still looked very sick and still continued to slip out and settle down as the ship banked about.

"By-the-by," I continued, "I can't have these colors, Mr. Hands; and by your leave, I'll strike 'em. Better none than these."

And, again dodging the boom, I ran to the color lines, handed down their cursed black flag, and chucked it overboard.

"God save the king!" said I, waving my cap; "and there's an end to Captain Silver!"

He watched me keenly and slyly, his chin all the while on his breast.

"I reckon," he said at last—"I reckon, Cap'n Hawkins, you'll kind of want to get ashore now. S'pose we talks."

"Why, yes," says I, "with all my heart, Mr. Hands. Say on." And I went back to my meal with a good appetite.

"This man," he began, nodding feebly at the corpse—"O'Brien were his name—a rank Irelander—this man and me got the canvas on her, meaning for to sail her back. Well, *he's* dead now, he is—as dead as bilge; and who's to sail this ship, I don't see. Without I gives you a hint, you ain't that man, as far's I can tell. Now, look here, you gives me food and drink, and a old scarf or ankecher to tie my wound up, you do; and I'll tell you how to sail her; and that's about square all round, I take it."

"I'll tell you one thing," says I: "I'm not going back to Captain Kidd's anchorage. I mean to get into North Inlet, and beach her quietly there."

"To be sure you did," he cried. "Why, I ain't sich an infernal lubber, after all. I can see, can't I? I've tried my fling, I have, and I've lost, and it's you has the wind of me. North Inlet? Why, I haven't no ch'ice, not I! I'd help you sail her up to Execution Dock, by thunder! so I would."

Well, as it seemed to me, there was some sense in this. We struck our bargain on the spot. In three minutes I had the *Hispaniola* sailing easily before the wind along the coast of Treasure Island, with good hopes of turning the northern point ere noon, and beating down again as far as North Inlet before high water, when we might beach her safely and wait till the subsiding tide permitted us to land.

Then I lashed the tiller and went below to my own chest, where I got a soft silk handkerchief of my mother's. With this, and with my aid, Hands bound up the great bleeding stab he had received in the thigh, and after he had eaten a little and had a swallow or two more of the brandy, he began to pick up visibly, sat straighter up, spoke louder and clearer, and looked in every way another man.

The breeze served us admirably. We skimmed before it like a bird, the coast of the island flashing by, and the view changing every minute. Soon we were past the high lands and bowling beside low, sandy country, sparsely dotted with dwarf pines, and soon we were beyond that again and had turned the corner of the rocky hill that ends the island on the north.

I was greatly elated with my new command and pleased with the bright, sunshiny weather and these different prospects of the coast. I had now plenty of water and good things to eat, and my conscience, which had smitten me hard for my desertion, was quieted by the great conquest I had made. I should, I think, have had nothing left me to desire but for the eyes of the coxswain as they followed me derisively about the deck, and the odd smile that appeared continually on his face. It was a smile that had in it something both of pain and weakness—a haggard, old man's smile; but there was, besides that, a grain of derision, a shadow of treachery in his expression as he craftily watched, and watched, and watched me at my work.

Chapter 26 ISRAEL HANDS

The wind, serving us to a desire, now hauled into the west. We could run so much the easier from the northeast corner of the island to the mouth of the North Inlet. Only, as we had no power to anchor, and dared not beach her till the tide had flowed a good deal farther, time hung on our hands. The coxswain told me how to lay the ship to;[1] after a good many trials I succeeded, and we both sat in silence over another meal.

"Cap'n," said he at length, with that same uncomfortable smile, "here's my old shipmate, O'Brien; s'pose you was to heave him overboard. I ain't partic'lar as a rule, and I don't take no blame for settling his hash; but I don't reckon him ornamental, now, do you?"

"I'm not strong enough, and I don't like the job; and there he lies, for me," said I.

"This here's an unlucky ship—this *Hispaniola,* Jim," he went on, blinking. "There's a power of men been killed in this *Hispaniola*—a sight o' poor seamen dead and gone since you and me took ship to Bristol. I never seen sich dirty luck, not I. There was this here O'Brien, now—he's dead, ain't he? Well, now, I'm no scholar, and you're a lad as can read and figure; and, to put it straight, do you take it as a dead man is dead for good, or do he come alive again?"

"You can kill the body, Mr. Hands, but not the spirit; you must know that already," I replied. "O'Brien there is in another world and maybe watching us."

"Ah!" says he. "Well, that's unfort'nate—appears as if killing parties was a waste of time. Howsomever, sperrits don't reckon for much, by what I've seen. I'll chance it with the sperrits, Jim. And now, you've spoke up free, and I'll take it kind if you'd step down into that there cabin and get me a—well, a—shiver my timbers! I can't hit the name on 't; well, you get me a bottle of wine, Jim—this here brandy's too strong for my head."

Now, the coxswain's hesitation seemed to be unnatural; and as for the notion of his preferring wine to brandy, I entirely disbelieved it. The whole story was a pretext. He wanted me to leave

[1] *lay to:* to stop.

the deck—so much was plain; but with what purpose I could in no way imagine. His eyes never met mine; they kept wandering to and fro, up and down, now with a look to the sky, now with a flitting glance upon the dead O'Brien. All the time he kept smiling and putting his tongue out in the most guilty, embarrassed manner, so that a child could have told that he was bent on some deception. I was prompt with my answer, however, for I saw where my advantage lay; and that with a fellow so densely stupid I could easily conceal my suspicions to the end.

"Some wine?" I said. "Far better. Will you have white or red?"

"Well, I reckon it's about the blessed same to me, shipmate," he replied; "so it's strong and plenty of it, what's the odds?"

"All right," I answered. "I'll bring you port, Mr. Hands. But I'll have to dig for it."

With that I scuttled down the companion with all the noise I could, slipped off my shoes, ran quietly along the sparred gallery, mounted the forecastle ladder, and popped my head out of the fore companion. I knew he would not expect to see me there; yet I took every precaution possible; and certainly the worst of my suspicions proved too true.

He had risen from his position to his hands and knees; and, though his leg obviously hurt him pretty sharply when he moved—for I could hear him stifle a groan—yet it was at a good, rattling rate that he trailed himself across the deck. In half a minute he had reached the port scuppers and picked, out of a coil of rope, a long knife, or rather a short dirk, discolored to the hilt with blood. He looked upon it for a moment, thrusting forth his under jaw, tried the point upon his hand, and then, hastily concealing it in the bosom of his jacket, trundled back again into his old place against the bulwark.

This was all that I required to know. Israel could move about; he was now armed; and if he had been at so much trouble to get rid of me, it was plain that I was meant to be the victim. What he would do afterwards—whether he would try to crawl right across the island from North Inlet to the camp among the swamps, or whether he would fire Long Tom, trusting that his own comrades might come first to help him, was, of course, more than I could say.

Yet I felt sure that I could trust him in one point, since in that our interests jumped together, and that was in the disposition of the schooner. We both desired to have her stranded safe enough, in a sheltered place, and so that, when the time came, she could be got off again with as little labor and danger as might be; and until that was done, I considered that my life would certainly be spared.

While I was thus turning the business over in my mind, I had not been idle with my body. I had stolen back to the cabin, slipped once more into my shoes, and laid my hand at random on a bottle of wine, and now, with this for an excuse, I made my reappearance on the deck.

Hands lay as I had left him, all fallen together in a bundle, and with his eyelids lowered, as though he were too weak to bear the light. He looked up, however, at my coming, knocked the neck off the bottle, like a man who had done the same thing often, and took a good swig, with his favorite toast of "Here's luck!" Then he lay quiet for a little, and then, pulling out a stick of tobacco, begged me to cut him a quid.

"Cut me a junk o' that," says he, "for I haven't no knife, and hardly strength enough, so be as I had. Ah, Jim, Jim, I reckon I've missed stays! Cut me a quid, as 'll likely be the last, lad; for I'm for my long home,[1] and no mistake."

"Well," said I, "I'll cut you some tobacco; but if I was you and thought myself so badly, I would go to my prayers, like a Christian man."

"Why?" said he. "Now, you tell me why."

"Why?" I cried. "You were asking me just now about the dead. You've broken your trust; you've lived in sin and lies and blood; there's a man you killed lying at your feet this moment; and you ask me why! For God's mercy, Mr. Hands, that's why."

I spoke with a little heat, thinking of the bloody dirk he had hidden in his pocket and designed, in his ill thoughts, to end me with. He, for his part, took a great draught of the wine and spoke with the most unusual solemnity.

"For thirty years," he said, "I've sailed the seas and seen good and bad, better and worse, fair weather and foul, provisions running out, knives going, and what not. Well, now I tell you, I never seen good come o' goodness yet. Him as strikes first is my

[1] *I'm for my long home:* I'm going to die.

fancy, dead men don't bite; them's my views—amen, so be it. And now, you look here," he added, suddenly changing his tone, "we've had about enough of this foolery. The tide's made good enough by now. You just take my orders, Cap'n Hawkins, and we'll sail slap in and be done with it."

All told, we had scarce two miles to run; but the navigation was delicate, the entrance to this northern anchorage was not only narrow and shoal, but lay east and west, so that the schooner must be nicely handled to be got in. I think I was a good, prompt subaltern, and I am very sure that Hands was an excellent pilot; for we went about and about, and dodged in, shaving the banks, with a certainty and a neatness that were a pleasure to behold.

Scarcely had we passed the heads, before the land closed around us. The shores of North Inlet were as thickly wooded as those of the southern anchorage; but the space was longer and narrower, and more like, what in truth it was, the estuary [1] of a river. Right before us, at the southern end, we saw the wreck of a ship in the last stages of dilapidation. It had been a great vessel of three masts, but had lain so long exposed to the injuries of the weather that it was hung about with great webs of dripping sea-weed, and on the deck of it shore bushes had taken root and now flourished thick with flowers. It was a sad sight, but it showed us that the anchorage was calm.

"Now," said Hands, "look there; there's a pet bit for to beach a ship in. Fine flat sand, never a catspaw,[2] trees all around of it, and flowers a-blowing like a garding on that old ship."

"And once beached," I inquired, "how shall we get her off again?"

"Why, so," he replied: "you take a line ashore there on the other side at low water: take a turn about one o' them big pines; bring it back, take a turn round the capstan, and lie-to for the tide. Come high water, all hands take a pull upon the line, and off she comes as sweet as natur'. And now, boy, you stand by. We're near the bit now, and she's too much way on her. Starboard a little—so—steady—starboard—larboard a little—steady—steady!"

So he issued his commands, which I breathlessly obeyed; till, all of a sudden, he cried, "Now, my hearty, luff!" And I put the

[1] *estuary* (ĕs′tů·ĕr′ĭ): the narrow place where a river meets the sea.
[2] *catspaw:* a breeze that ripples the water.

helm hard up, and the *Hispaniola* swung round rapidly and ran stem [1] on for the low wooded shore.

The excitement of these last maneuvers had somewhat interfered with the watch I had kept hitherto, sharply enough, upon the coxswain. Even then I was still so much interested, waiting for the ship to touch, that I had quite forgot the peril that hung over my head, and stood craning over the starboard bulwarks and watching the ripples spreading wide before the bows. I might have fallen without a struggle for my life, had not a sudden disquietude seized upon me and made me turn my head. Perhaps I had heard a creak or seen his shadow moving with the tail of my eye; perhaps it was an instinct like a cat's; but, sure enough, when I looked round, there was Hands, already halfway towards me, with the dirk in his right hand.

We must both have cried out aloud when our eyes met; but while mine was the shrill cry of terror, his was a roar of fury, like a charging bull's. At the same instant he threw himself forward, and I leapt sideways towards the bows. As I did so, I let go of the tiller, which sprang sharp to leeward; and I think this saved my life, for it struck Hands across the chest and stopped him, for the moment, dead.

Before he could recover, I was safe out of the corner where he had me trapped, with all the deck to dodge about. Just forward of the mainmast I stopped, drew a pistol from my pocket, took cool aim, though he had already turned and was once more coming directly after me, and drew the trigger. The hammer fell, but there followed neither flash nor sound; the priming was useless with sea water. I cursed myself for my neglect. Why had not I, long before, reprimed and reloaded my only weapons? Then I should not have been as now, a mere fleeing sheep before this butcher.

Wounded as he was, it was wonderful how fast he could move, his grizzled hair tumbling over his face, and his face itself as red as a red ensign with his haste and fury. I had no time to try my other pistol, nor, indeed, much inclination, for I was sure it would be useless. One thing I saw plainly: I must not simply retreat before him, or he would speedily hold me boxed into the bows, as a moment since he had so nearly boxed me in the stern. Once so caught, and nine or ten inches of the blood-stained dirk

[1] *stem:* the bow or front of a boat.

would be my last experience on this side of eternity. I placed my palms against the mainmast, which was of a goodish bigness, and waited, every nerve upon the stretch.

Seeing that I meant to dodge, he also paused; and a moment or two passed in feints [1] on his part and corresponding movements upon mine. It was such a game as I had often played at home about the rocks of Black Hill Cove; but never before, you may be sure, with such a wildly beating heart as now. Still, as I say, it was a boy's game, and I thought I could hold my own at it, against an elderly seaman with a wounded thigh. Indeed, my courage had begun to rise so high that I allowed myself a few darting thoughts on what would be the end of the affair; and while I saw certainly that I could spin it out for long, I saw no hope of any ultimate escape.

Well, while things stood thus, suddenly the *Hispaniola* struck, staggered, ground for an instant in the sand, and then, swift as a blow, canted over to the port side, till the deck stood at an angle of forty-five degrees, and about a puncheon of water splashed into the scupper holes and lay in a pool between the deck and bulwark.

We were both of us capsized in a second, and both of us rolled, almost together, into the scuppers; the dead red-cap, with his arms still spread out, tumbling stiffly after us. So near were we, indeed, that my head came against the coxswain's foot with a crack that made my teeth rattle. Blow and all, I was the first afoot again; for Hands had got involved with the dead body. The sudden canting [2] of the ship had made the deck no place for running on; I had to find some new way of escape and that upon the instant, for my foe was almost touching me. Quick as thought, I sprang into the mizzen shrouds,[3] rattled up hand over hand, and did not draw a breath till I was seated on the crosstrees.

I had been saved by being prompt; the dirk had struck not half a foot below me, as I pursued my upward flight; and there stood Israel Hands, with his mouth open and his face upturned to mine, a perfect statue of surprise and disappointment.

Now that I had a moment to myself, I lost no time in changing the priming of my pistol, and then, having one ready for service, and to make assurance doubly sure, I proceeded to draw

[1] *feint* (fānt): a mock attack. [2] *canting:* tipping. [3] *mizzen shrouds* (mĭz′n shroudz): the ropes supporting the mizzen, or rear-most mast.

the load of the other and recharge it afresh from the beginning.

My new employment struck Hands all of a heap; he began to see the dice going against him; and after an obvious hesitation, he also hauled himself heavily into the shrouds and with the dirk in his teeth, began slowly and painfully to mount. It cost him no end of time and groans to haul his wounded leg behind him; and I had quietly finished my arrangements before he was much more than a third of the way up. Then, with a pistol in either hand, I addressed him.

"One more step, Mr. Hands," said I, "and I'll blow your brains out! Dead men don't bite, you know," I added, with a chuckle.

He stopped instantly. I could see by the working of his face that he was trying to think, and the process was so slow and laborious that, in my new-found security, I laughed aloud. At last, with a swallow or two, he spoke, his face still wearing the same expression of extreme perplexity. In order to speak he had to take the dagger from his mouth, but, in all else, he remained unmoved.

"Jim," says he, "I reckon we're fouled, you and me, and we'll have to sign articles.[1] I'd have had you but for that there lurch: but I don't have no luck, not I; and I reckon I'll have to strike, which comes hard, you see, for a master mariner to a ship's younker [2] like you, Jim."

I was drinking in his words and smiling away, as conceited as a cock upon a wall, when, all in a breath, back went his right hand over his shoulder. Something sang like an arrow through the air; I felt a blow and then a sharp pang, and there I was pinned by the shoulder to the mast. In the horrid pain and surprise of the moment—I scarce can say it was my own volition, and I am sure it was without a conscious aim—both my pistols went off, and both escaped out of my hands. They did not fall alone; with a choked cry, the coxswain loosed his grasp upon the shrouds and plunged head first into the water.

[1] *sign articles:* to make an agreement. [2] *younker* (yŭng′kẽr): a youngster.

Chapter 27 "PIECES OF EIGHT"

Owing to the cant of the vessel, the masts hung far out over the water, and from my perch on the crosstrees, I had nothing below me but the surface of the bay. Hands, who was not so far up, was, in consequence, nearer to the ship and fell between me and the bulwarks. He rose once to the surface in a lather of foam and blood, and then sank again for good. As the water settled, I could see him lying huddled together on the clean, bright sand in the shadow of the vessel's side. A fish or two whipped past his body. Sometimes, by the quivering of the water, he appeared to move a little, as if he were trying to rise. But he was dead enough, for all that, being both shot and drowned, and was food for fish in the very place where he had designed my slaughter.

I was no sooner certain of this than I began to feel sick, faint, and terrified. The hot blood was running over my back and chest. The dirk, where it had pinned my shoulder to the mast, seemed to burn like a hot iron; yet it was not so much these real sufferings that distressed me, for these, it seemed to me, I could bear without a murmur; it was the horror I had upon my mind of falling from the crosstrees into that still green water, beside the body of the coxswain.

I clung with both hands till my nails ached, and I shut my eyes as if to cover up the peril. Gradually my mind came back again, my pulses quieted down to a more natural time, and I was once more in possession of myself.

It was my first thought to pluck forth the dirk; but either it stuck too hard or my nerve failed me; and I desisted with a violent shudder. Oddly enough, that very shudder did the business. The knife, in fact, had come the nearest in the world to missing me altogether; it held me by a mere pinch of skin, and this the shudder tore away. The blood ran down the faster, to be sure; but I was my own master again and only tacked to the mast by my coat and shirt.

These last I broke through with a sudden jerk and then regained the deck by the starboard shrouds. For nothing in the world would I have again ventured, shaken as I was, upon the overhanging port shrouds, from which Israel had so lately fallen.

I went below and did what I could for my wound; it pained me a good deal and still bled freely; but it was neither deep nor dangerous, nor did it greatly gall me when I used my arm. Then I looked around me, and as the ship was now, in a sense, my own, I began to think of clearing it from its last passenger—the dead man, O'Brien.

He had pitched, as I have said, against the bulwarks, where he lay like some horrible, ungainly sort of puppet; life-size, indeed, but how different from life's color or life's comeliness! In that position, I could easily have my way with him; and as the habit of tragical adventures had worn off almost all my terror for the dead, I took him by the waist as if he had been a sack of bran, and, with one good heave, tumbled him overboard. He went in with a sounding plunge; the red cap came off and remained floating on the surface; and as soon as the splash subsided, I could see him and Israel lying side by side, both wavering with the tremulous movement of the water. O'Brien, though still quite a young man, was very bald. There he lay, with that bald head across the knees of the man who had killed him, and the quick fishes steering to and fro over both.

I was now alone upon the ship; the tide had just turned. The sun was within so few degrees of setting that already the shadow of the pines upon the western shore began to reach right across the anchorage and fall in patterns on the deck. The evening breeze had sprung up, and though it was well warded off by the hill with the two peaks upon the east, the cordage [1] had begun to sing a little softly to itself and the idle sails to rattle to and fro.

I began to see a danger to the ship. The jibs I speedily doused [2] and brought tumbling to the deck; but the mainsail was a harder matter. Of course, when the schooner canted over, the boom had swung outboard, and the cap of it and a foot or two of sail hung even under water. I thought this made it still more dangerous; yet the strain was so heavy that I half feared to meddle. At last I got my knife and cut the halyards.[3] The peak dropped instantly, a great belly of loose canvas floated broad upon the water; and since, pull as I liked, I could not budge the downhaul, that was the extent of what I could accomplish. For the rest, the *Hispaniola* must trust to luck, like myself.

[1] *cordage* (kôr′dĭj): the ropes of a ship. [2] *douse* (dous): to lower. [3] *halyard* (hăl′yĕrd): a rope for hoisting and lowering the sails.

By this time the whole anchorage had fallen into shadow—the last rays, I remember, falling through a glade of the wood and shining bright as jewels on the flowery mantle of the wreck. It began to be chill; the tide was rapidly fleeting seaward, the schooner settling more and more on her beam-ends.[1]

I scrambled forward and looked over. It seemed shallow enough, and holding the cut hawser in both hands for a last security, I let myself drop softly overboard. The water scarcely reached my waist; the sand was firm and covered with ripple marks, and I waded ashore in great spirits, leaving the *Hispaniola* on her side, with her mainsail trailing wide upon the surface of the bay. About the same time the sun went fairly down, and the breeze whistled low in the dusk among the tossing pines.

At least, and at last, I was off the sea, nor had I returned thence empty handed. There lay the schooner, clear at last from buccaneers and ready for our own men to board and get to sea again. I had nothing nearer my fancy than to get home to the stockade and boast of my achievements. Possibly I might be blamed a bit for my truantry, but the recapture of the *Hispaniola* was a clenching answer, and I hoped that even Captain Smollett would confess I had not lost my time.

So thinking, and in famous spirits, I began to set my face homeward for the blockhouse and my companions. I remembered that the most easterly of the rivers which drain into Captain Kidd's anchorage ran from the two-peaked hill upon my left; and I bent my course in that direction that I might pass the stream while it was small. The wood was pretty open, and keeping along the lower spurs, I had soon turned the corner of that hill and not long after waded to the mid-calf across the water-course.

This brought me near to where I had encountered Ben Gunn, the maroon; and I walked more circumspectly,[2] keeping an eye on every side. The dusk had come nigh hand completely, and, as I opened out the cleft between the two peaks, I became aware of a wavering glow against the sky, where, as I judged, the man of the island was cooking his supper before a roaring fire. And yet I wondered, in my heart, that he should show himself so careless. For if I could see this radiance, might it not reach the eyes of Silver himself where he camped upon the shore among the marshes?

[1] *beam-ends:* side. [2] *circumspectly* (sûr′kŭm·spĕkt·lĭ): cautiously.

Gradually the night fell blacker; it was all I could do to guide myself even roughly towards my destination; the double hill behind me and the Spy-glass on my right hand loomed faint and fainter; the stars were few and pale; and in the low ground where I wandered I kept tripping among bushes and rolling into sandy pits.

Suddenly a kind of brightness fell about me. I looked up; a pale glimmer of moonbeams had alighted on the summit of the Spy-glass, and soon after I saw something broad and silvery moving low down behind the trees and knew the moon had risen.

With this to help me, I passed rapidly over what remained to me of my journey; and, sometimes walking, sometimes running, impatiently drew near to the stockade. Yet, as I began to thread the grove that lies before it, I was not so thoughtless but that I slacked my pace and went a trifle warily. It would have been a poor end of my adventures to get shot down by my own party in mistake.

The moon was climbing higher and higher; its light began to fall here and there in masses through the more open districts of the wood; and right in front of me a glow of a different color appeared among the trees. It was red and hot, and now and again it was a little darkened—as it were the embers of a bonfire smoldering.

For the life of me, I could not think what it might be.

At last I came right down upon the borders of the clearing. The western end was already steeped in moonshine; the rest, and the blockhouse itself, still lay in a black shadow, checkered with long, silvery streaks of light. On the other side of the house an immense fire had burned itself into clear embers and shed a steady red reverberation, contrasted strongly with the mellow paleness of the moon. There was not a soul stirring, nor a sound beside the noises of the breeze.

I stopped, with much wonder in my heart, and perhaps a little terror also. It had not been our way to build great fires; we were, indeed, by the captain's orders, somewhat niggardly of firewood; and I began to fear that something had gone wrong while I was absent.

I stole around by the eastern end, keeping close in shadow, and at a convenient place, where the darkness was thickest, crossed the palisade.

To make assurance surer, I got upon my hands and knees and crawled, without a sound, towards the corner of the house. As I drew nearer, my heart was suddenly and greatly lightened. It is not a pleasant noise in itself, and I have often complained of it at other times; but just then it was like music to hear my friends snoring together so loud and peaceful in their sleep. The sea cry of the watch, that beautiful "All's well," never fell more reassuringly on my ear.

In the meantime, there was no doubt of one thing; they kept an infamous bad watch. If it had been Silver and his lads that were now creeping in on them, not a soul would have seen day-break. That was what it was, thought I, to have the captain wounded; and again I blamed myself sharply for leaving them in that danger with so few to mount guard.

By this time I had got to the door and stood up. All was dark within, so that I could distinguish nothing by the eye. As for sounds, there was the steady drone of the snorers and a small occasional noise, a flickering or pecking that I could in no way account for.

With my arms before me I walked steadily in. I should lie down in my own place (I thought, with a silent chuckle) and en-joy their faces when they found me in the morning.

My foot struck something yielding—it was a sleeper's leg; and he turned and groaned, but without awaking.

And then, all of a sudden, a shrill voice broke forth out of the darkness:

"Pieces of eight! pieces of eight! pieces of eight! pieces of eight! pieces of eight!" and so forth, without pause or change, like the clacking of a tiny mill.

Silver's green parrot, Captain Flint! It was she whom I had heard pecking at a piece of bark; it was she, keeping better watch than any human being, who thus announced my arrival with her wearisome refrain.

I had no time left me to recover. At the sharp, clipping tone of the parrot, the sleepers awoke and sprang up; and with a mighty oath, the voice of Silver cried:

"Who goes?"

I turned to run, struck violently against one person, recoiled, and ran full into the arms of a second, who, for his part, closed upon and held me tight.

"Bring a torch, Dick," said Silver, when my capture was thus assured.

And one of the men left the log house and presently returned with a lighted brand.

PART SIX—Captain Silver

Chapter 28 IN THE ENEMY'S CAMP

The red glare of the torch, lighting up the interior of the blockhouse, showed me the worst of my apprehensions realized. The pirates were in possession of the house and stores: there was the cask of cognac, there were the pork and bread, as before; and, what tenfold increased my horror, not a sign of any prisoner. I could only judge that all had perished, and my heart smote me sorely that I had not been there to perish with them.

There were six of the buccaneers, all told; not another man was left alive. Five of them were on their feet, flushed and swollen, suddenly called out of the first sleep of drunkenness. The sixth had only risen upon his elbow: he was deadly pale, and the blood-stained bandage round his head told that he had recently been wounded, and still more recently dressed. I remembered the man who had been shot and had run back among the woods in the great attack, and doubted not that this was he.

The parrot sat, preening her plumage, on Long John's shoulder. He himself, I thought, looked somewhat paler and more stern than I was used to. He still wore the fine broadcloth suit in which he had fulfilled his mission, but it was bitterly the worse for wear, daubed with clay and torn with the sharp briers of the wood.

"So," said he, "here's Jim Hawkins, shiver my timbers! dropped in, like eh? Well, come, I take that friendly."

And thereupon he sat down across the brandy cask and began to fill a pipe.

"Give me a loan of the link, Dick," said he; and then, when he had a good light, "That'll do, lad," he added; "stick the glim in the wood heap; and you, gentlemen, bring yourselves to!—you needn't stand up for Mr. Hawkins; *he'll* excuse you, you may lay to that. And so, Jim"—stopping the tobacco—"here you were, and quite a pleasant surprise for poor old John. I see you were smart when first I set my eyes on you; but this here gets away from me clean, it do."

To all this, as may be well supposed, I made no answer. They had set me with my back against the wall; and I stood there looking Silver in the face, pluckily enough, I hope, to all outward appearance, but with black despair in my heart.

Silver took a whiff or two of his pipe with great composure and then ran on again.

"Now, you see, Jim, so be as you *are* here," says he, "I'll give you a piece of my mind. I've always liked you, I have, for a lad of spirit and the picter of my own self when I was young and handsome. I always wanted you to jine and take your share, and die a gentleman, and now, my cock, you've got to. Cap'n Smollett's a fine seaman, as I'll own up to any day, but stiff on discipline. 'Dooty is dooty,' says he, and right he is. Just you keep clear of the cap'n. The doctor himself is gone dead again you—'ungrateful scamp' was what he said; and the short and the long of the whole story is about here: you can't go back to your own lot, for they won't have you; and, without you start a third ship's company all by yourself, which might be lonely, you'll have to jine with Cap'n Silver."

So far so good. My friends, then, were still alive, and though I partly believed the truth of Silver's statement, that the cabin party were incensed at me for my desertion, I was more relieved than distressed by what I heard.

"I don't say nothing as to your being in our hands," continued Silver, "though there you are, and you may lay to it. I'm all for argyment; I never seen good come out o' threatening. If you like the service, well, you'll jine; and if you don't, Jim, why, you're free to answer no—free and welcome, shipmate; and if fairer can be said by mortal seaman, shiver my sides!"

"Am I to answer then?" I asked, with a very tremulous voice.

Through all this sneering talk I was made to feel the threat of death that overhung me, and my cheeks burned and my heart beat painfully in my breast.

"Lad," said Silver, "no one's a-pressing of you. Take your bearings. None of us won't hurry you, mate; time goes so pleasant in your company, you see."

"Well," says I, growing a bit bolder, "if I'm to choose, I declare I have a right to know what's what, and why you're here, and where my friends are."

"Wot's wot?" repeated one of the buccaneers, in a deep growl. "Ah, he'd be a lucky one as knowed that!"

"You'll perhaps batten down your hatches [1] till you're spoke to, my friend," cried Silver truculently to this speaker. And then, in his first gracious tones, he replied to me: "Yesterday morning, Mr. Hawkins," said he, "in the dog-watch, down came Doctor Livesey with a flag of truce. Says he, 'Cap'n Silver, you're sold out. Ship's gone.' Well, maybe we'd been taking a glass and a song to help it round. I won't say no. Leastways, none of us had looked out. We looked out, and, by thunder! the old ship was gone. I never seen a pack o' fools look fishier; and you may lay to that, if I tells you that looked the fishiest. 'Well,' says the doctor, 'let's bargain.' We bargained, him and I, and here we are: stores, brandy, blockhouse, the firewood you was thoughtful enough to cut, and, in a manner of speaking, the whole blessed boat, from crosstrees to kelson. As for them, they've tramped; I don't know where's they are."

He drew again quietly at his pipe.

"And lest you should take it into that head of yours," he went on, "that you was included in the treaty, here's the last word that he said: 'How many are you,' says I, 'to leave?' 'Four,' says he—'four, and one of us wounded. As for that boy, I don't know where is he, confound him,' says he, 'nor I don't much care. We're about sick of him.' These was his words."

"Is that all?" I asked.

"Well, it's all that you're to hear, my son," returned Silver.

"And now I am to choose?"

"And now you are to choose, and you may lay to that," said Silver.

"Well," said I, "I am not such a fool but I know pretty well

[1] *batten down your hatches:* be quiet (slang).

what I have to look for. Let the worst come to the worst, it's little I care. I've seen too many die since I fell in with you. But there's a thing or two I have to tell you," I said, and by this time I was quite excited; "and the first is this: here you are, in a bad way: ship lost, treasure lost, men lost; your whole business gone to wreck; and if you want to know who did it—it was I! I was in the apple barrel the night we sighted land, and I heard you, John, and you, Dick Johnson, and Hands, who is now at the bottom of the sea, and told every word you said before the hour was out. And as for the schooner, it was I who cut her cable, and it was I that killed the men you had aboard of her, and it was I who brought her where you'll never see her more, not one of you. The laugh's on my side; I've had the top of this business from the first; I no more fear you than I fear a fly. Kill me, if you please, or spare me. But one thing I'll say, and no more; if you spare me, bygones are bygones, and when you fellows are in court for piracy, I'll save you all I can. It is for you to choose. Kill another and do yourselves no good, or spare me and keep a witness to save you from the gallows."

I stopped, for, I tell you, I was out of breath, and, to my wonder, not a man of them moved, but all sat staring at me like as many sheep. And while they were still staring, I broke out again:

"And now, Mr. Silver," I said, "I believe you're the best man here, and if things go to the worst, I'll take it kind of you to let the doctor know the way I took it."

"I'll bear it in mind," said Silver, with an accent so curious that I could not, for the life of me, decide whether he were laughing at my request or had been favorably affected by my courage.

"I'll put one to that," cried the old mahogany-faced seaman—Morgan by name—whom I had seen in Long John's public house upon the quays of Bristol. "It was him that knowed Black Dog."

"Well, and see here," added the sea cook. "I'll put another again to that, by thunder! for it was this same boy that faked the chart from Billy Bones. First and last, we've split upon Jim Hawkins!"

"Then here goes!" said Morgan, with an oath.

And he sprang up, drawing his knife as if he had been twenty.

"Avast, there!" cried Silver. "Who are you, Tom Morgan? Maybe you thought you was cap'n here, perhaps. By the powers, but I'll teach you better! Cross me and you'll go where many a good man's gone before you, first and last, these thirty year back —some to the yardarm, shiver my timbers! and some by the board, and all to feed the fishes. There's never a man looked me between the eyes and seen a good day a'terwards, Tom Morgan, you may lay to that."

Morgan paused; but a hoarse murmur rose from the others.

"Tom's right," said one.

"I stood hazing[1] long enough from one," added another. "I'll be hanged if I'll be hazed by you, John Silver."

"Did any of you gentlemen want to have it out with *me?"* roared Silver, bending far forward from his position on the keg, with his pipe still glowing in his right hand. "Put a name on what you're at; you ain't dumb, I reckon. Him that wants shall get it. Have I lived this many years, and a son of a rumpuncheon cock his hat athwart my hawse at the latter end of it? You know the way; you're all gentlemen o' fortune, by your account. Well, I'm ready. Take a cutlass, him that dares, and I'll see the color of his inside, crutch and all, before that pipe's empty."

Not a man stirred; not a man answered.

"That's your sort, is it?" he added, returning his pipe to his mouth. "Well, you're a gay lot to look at, anyway. Not much worth to fight, you ain't. P'r'aps you can understand King George's English. I'm cap'n here by 'lection. I'm cap'n here because I'm the best man by a long sea mile. You won't fight, as gentlemen o' fortune should; then, by thunder, you'll obey, and you may lay to it! I like that boy, now; I never seen a better boy than that. He's more a man than any pair of rats of you in this here house, and what I say is this: let me see him that'll lay a hand on him—that's what I say, and you may lay to it."

There was a long pause after this. I stood straight up against the wall, my heart still going like a sledge hammer, but with a ray of hope now shining in my bosom. Silver leant back against the wall, his arms crossed, his pipe in the corner of his mouth, as calm as though he had been in church; yet his eye kept wandering furtively, and he kept the tail of it on his unruly followers. They, on their part, drew gradually together towards the far end of the

[1] *haze:* to force to do hard work; to humiliate.

blockhouse, and the low hiss of their whispering sounded in my ear continuously, like a stream. One after another, they would look up, and the red light of the torch would fall for a second on their nervous faces; but it was not towards me, it was towards Silver that they turned their eyes.

"You seem to have a lot to say," remarked Silver, spitting far into the air. "Pipe up and let me hear it, or lay to."

"Ax your pardon, sir," returned one of the men, "you're pretty free with some of the rules; maybe you'll kindly keep an eye upon the rest. This crew's dissatisfied; this crew don't vally bullying a marlin-spike; this crew has its rights like other crews, I'll make so free as that; and by your own rules, I take it we can talk together. I ax your pardon, sir, acknowledging you for to be capting at this present; but I claim my right and steps outside for a council."

And with an elaborate sea-salute, this fellow, a long, ill-looking, yellow-eyed man of five and thirty, stepped coolly towards the door and disappeared out of the house. One after another, the rest followed his example; each making a salute as he passed; each adding some apology.

"According to rules," said one.

"Fo'c'sle council," [1] said Morgan.

And so with one remark or another, all marched out, and left Silver and me alone with the torch.

The sea cook instantly removed his pipe.

"Now, look you here, Jim Hawkins," he said, in a steady whisper, that was no more than audible, "you're within half a plank of death, and, what's a long sight worse, of torture. They're going to throw me off. But, you mark, I stand by you through thick and thin. I didn't mean to; no, not till you spoke up. I was about desperate to lose that much blunt [2] and be hanged into the bargain. But I see you was the right sort. I says to myself: You stand by Hawkins, John, and Hawkins 'll stand by you. You're his last card, and, by the living thunder, John, he's yours! Back to back, says I. You will save your witness, and he'll save your neck!"

I began dimly to understand.

"You mean all's lost?" I asked.

[1] *fo'c'sle council:* a consultation among the men, without officers.
[2] *blunt:* money (slang).

"Aye, by gum, I do!" he answered. "Ship gone, neck gone—that's the size of it. Once I looked into that bay, Jim Hawkins, and seen no schooner—well, I'm tough, but I gave out. As for that lot and their council, mark me, they're outright fools and cowards. I'll save your life—if so be as I can—from them. But see here, Jim—tit for tat—you save Long John from swinging."

I was bewildered; it seemed a thing so hopeless he was asking—he, the old buccaneer, the ringleader throughout.

"What I can do, that I'll do," I said.

"It's a bargain!" cried Long John. "You speak up plucky, and by thunder! I've a chance."

He hobbled to the torch where it stood propped among the firewood and took a fresh light to his pipe.

"Understand me, Jim," he said, returning. "I've a head on my shoulders, I have. I'm on the squire's side now. I know you've got that ship safe somewheres. How you done it, I don't know, but safe it is. I guess Hands and O'Brien turned soft. I never much believed in neither of *them*. Now you mark me. I ask no questions, nor I won't let others. I know when a game's up, I do; and I know a lad that's staunch. Ah, you that's young—you and me might have done a power of good together!"

He drew some cognac from the cask into a tin cannikin.

"Will you taste, messmate?" he asked; and when I had refused: "Well, I'll take a drain myself, Jim," said he. "I need a caulker, for there's trouble on hand. And, talking o' trouble, why did that doctor give me the chart, Jim?"

My face expressed a wonder so unaffected that he saw the needlessness of further questions.

"Ah, well, he did, though," said he. "And there's something under that, no doubt—something, surely, under that, Jim, bad or good."

And he took another swallow of the brandy, shaking his great fair head like a man who looks forward to the worst.

Chapter 29 THE BLACK SPOT AGAIN

The council of the buccaneers had lasted some time when one of them re-entered the house and, with a repetition of the same salute, which had in my eyes an ironical air, begged for a moment's loan of the torch. Silver briefly agreed; and this emissary retired again, leaving us together in the dark.

"There's a breeze coming, Jim," said Silver, who had, by this time, adopted quite a friendly and familiar tone.

I turned to the loophole nearest me and looked out. The embers of the great fire had so far burned themselves out, and now glowed so low and duskily, that I understood why these conspirators desired a torch. About halfway down the slope to the stockade they were collected in a group; one held the light; another was on his knees in their midst, and I saw the blade of an open knife shine in his hand with varying colors in the moon and torchlight. The rest were all somewhat stooping, as though watching the maneuvers of this last. I could just make out that he had a book as well as a knife in his hand and was still wondering how anything so incongruous had come in their possession, when the kneeling figure rose once more to his feet, and the whole party began to move together towards the house.

"Here they come," said I; and I returned to my former position, for it seemed beneath my dignity that they should find me watching them.

"Well, let 'em come, lad—let 'em come," said Silver cheerily. "I've still a shot in my locker."

The door opened, and the five men, standing huddled together just inside, pushed one of the number forward. In any other circumstances it would have been comical to see his slow advance, hesitating as he set down each foot, but holding his closed right hand in front of him.

"Step up, lad," cried Silver. "I won't eat you. Hand it over, lubber. I know the rules, I do; I won't hurt a depytation." [1]

Thus encouraged, the buccaneer stepped forth more briskly,

[1] *depytation;* he means **deputation** (dĕp′ū·tā′shŭn): an official bargaining group.

and having passed something to Silver, from nand to hand, slipped yet more smartly back again to his companions.

The sea cook looked at what had been given him.

"The black spot! I thought so," he observed. "Where might you have got the paper? Why, hillo! look here, now: this ain't lucky! You've gone and cut this out of a Bible. What fool's cut a Bible?"

"Ah, there!" said Morgan—"there! Wot did I say? No good'll come o' that, I said."

"Well, you've about fixed it now, among you," continued Silver. "You'll all swing now, I reckon. What soft-headed lubber had a Bible?"

"It was Dick," said one.

"Dick, was it? Then Dick can get to prayers," said Silver. "He's seen his slice of luck, has Dick, and you may lay to that."

But here the long man with the yellow eyes struck in.

"Belay that talk, John Silver," he said. "This crew has tipped you the black spot in full council, as in dooty bound; just you turn it over, as in dooty bound, and see what's wrote there. Then you can talk."

"Thanky, George," replied the sea cook. "You always was brisk for business, and has the rules by heart, George, as I'm pleased to see. Well, what is it, anyway? Ah! 'Deposed'—that's it, is it? Very pretty wrote, to be sure; like print, I swear. Your hand o' write, George? Why, you was gettin' quite a leadin' man in this here crew. You'll be cap'n next, I shouldn't wonder. Just oblige me with that torch again, will you? this pipe don't draw."

"Come, now," said George, "you don't fool this crew no more. You're a funny man, by your account; but you're over now, and you'll maybe step down off that barrel and help vote."

"I thought you said you knowed the rules," returned Silver contemptuously. "Leastways, if you don't, I do; and I wait here—and I'm still your cap'n, mind—till you outs with your grievances, and I reply; in the meantime, your black spot ain't worth a biscuit. After that, we'll see."

"Oh," replied George, "you don't be under no kind of apprehension; *we're* all square, we are. First, you've made a hash of this cruise—you'll be a bold man to say no to that. Second, you let the enemy out o' this here trap for nothing. Why did they want out? I dunno; but it's pretty plain they wanted it. Third, you wouldn't let us go at them upon the march. Oh, we see through you, John Silver; you want to play booty, that's what's wrong with you. And then, fourth, there's this here boy."

"Is that all?" asked Silver quietly.

"Enough, too," retorted George. "We'll all swing and sun dry for your bungling."

"Well, now, look here, I'll answer these four p'ints; one after another I'll answer 'em. I made a hash o' this cruise, did I? Well, now you all know what I wanted; and you all know, if that had been done, that we'd 'a' been aboard the *Hispaniola* this night as ever was, every man of us alive, and fit, and full of good plum duff, and the treasure in the hold of her, by thunder! Well, who crossed me? Who forced my hand, as was the lawful cap'n? Who tipped me the black spot the day we landed and began this dance? Ah, it's a fine dance—I'm with you there—and looks mighty like a hornpipe in a rope's end at Execution Dock by London town, it does. But who done it? Why, it was Anderson, and Hands, and you, George Merry! And you're the last above board of that same meddling crew; and you have the Davy Jones's insolence to up and stand for cap'n over me—you, that sank the lot of us! By the powers! but this tops the stiffest yarn to nothing."

Silver paused, and I could see by the faces of George and his late comrades that these words had not been said in vain.

"That's for number one," cried the accused, wiping the sweat from his brow, for he had been talking with a vehemence that shook the house. "Why, I give you my word, I'm sick to speak to you. You've neither sense nor memory, and I leave it to fancy where your mothers was that let you come to sea. Sea! Gentlemen o' fortune! I reckon tailors is your trade."

"Go on, John," said Morgan. "Speak up to the others."

"Ah, the others!" returned John. "They're a nice lot, ain't they? You say this cruise is bungled. Ah; by gum, if you could understand how bad it's bungled, you would see! We're that near the gibbet [1] that my neck's stiff with thinking on it. You've seen 'em, maybe, hanged in chains, birds about 'em, seamen p'inting 'em out as they go down with the tide. 'Who's that?' says one. 'That! Why that's John Silver. I knowed him well,' says another. And you can hear the chains a-jangle as you go about and reach for the other buoy. Now, that's about where we are, every mother's

[1] *gibbet* (jĭb′ĕt): gallows for hanging criminals in chains.

son of us, thanks to him, and Hands, and Anderson, and other ruination fools of you. And if you want to know about number four, and that boy, why, shiver my timbers! isn't he a hostage? [1] Are we a-going to waste a hostage? No, not us; he might be our last chance, and I shouldn't wonder. Kill that boy? not me, mates! And number three? Ah, well, there's a deal to say to number three. Maybe you don't count it nothing to have a real college doctor come to see you every day—you, John, with your head broke—or you, George Merry, that had the ague shakes upon you not six hours agone, and has your eyes the color of lemon peel to this same moment on the clock? And may be, perhaps, you didn't know there was a consort coming, either? But there is; and not so long till then; and we'll see who'll be glad to have a hostage when it comes to that. And as for number two, and why I made a bargain—well, you came crawling on your knees to me to make it—on your knees you came, you was that down-hearted—and you'd have starved, too, if I hadn't—but that's a trifle! you look there—that's why!"

And he cast down upon the floor a paper that I instantly recognized—none other than the chart on yellow paper, with the three red crosses, that I had found in the oilcloth at the bottom of the captain's chest. Why the doctor had given it to him was more than I could fancy.

But if it were inexplicable to me, the appearance of the chart was incredible to the surviving mutineers. They leaped upon it like cats upon a mouse. It went from hand to hand, one tearing it from another; and by the oaths and the cries and the childish laughter with which they accompanied their examination, you would have thought not only they were fingering the very gold, but were at sea with it, besides, in safety.

"Yes," said one, "that's Flint, sure enough. J. F. and a score below, with a clove hitch to it; so he done ever."

"Mighty pretty," said George. "But how are we to get away with it, and us no ship?"

Silver suddenly sprang up, and supporting himself with a hand against the wall: "Now I give you warning, George," he cried. "One more word of your sauce, and I'll call you down and fight you. How? Why, how do I know? You had ought to tell me

[1] *hostage* (hŏs′tĭj): a person held by one side in a conflict to make sure the other side keeps its promises.

that—you and the rest, that lost me my schooner with your interference, burn you! But not you, you can't; you hain't got the invention of a cockroach. But civil you can speak, and shall, George Merry, you may lay to that."

"That's fair enow," said the old man Morgan.

"Fair! I reckon so," said the sea cook. "You lost the ship; I found the treasure. Who's the better man at that? And now I resign, by thunder! Elect whom you please to be your cap'n now; I'm done with it."

"Silver!" they cried. "Barbecue forever! Barbecue for cap'n!"

"So that's the toon, is it?" cried the cook. "George, I reckon you'll have to wait another turn, friend; and lucky for you as I'm not a revengeful man. But that was never my way. And now, shipmates, this black spot? 'Tain't much good now, is it? Dick's crossed his luck and spoiled his Bible, and that's about all."

"It'll do to kiss the book on still, won't it?" growled Dick, who was evidently uneasy at the curse he had brought upon himself.

"A Bible with a bit cut out!" returned Silver derisively. "Not it. It don't bind no more'n a ballad book."

"Don't it, though?" cried Dick, with a sort of joy. "Well, I reckon that's worth having too."

"Here, Jim—here's a cur'osity for you," said Silver; and he tossed me the paper.

It was a round about the size of a crown piece. One side was blank, for it had been the last leaf; the other contained a verse or two of Revelation—these words among the rest, which struck sharply home upon my mind: "Without are dogs and murderers." The printed side had been blackened with wood ash, which already began to come off and soil my fingers; on the blank side had been written with the same material the one word "Depposed." I have that curiosity beside me at this moment; but not a trace of writing now remains beyond a single scratch, such as a man might make with his thumb nail.

That was the end of the night's business. Soon after, with a drink all round, we lay down to sleep, and the outside of Silver's vengeance was to put George Merry up for sentinel and threaten him with death if he should prove unfaithful.

It was long ere I could close an eye, and Heaven knows I had matter enough for thought in the man whom I had slain that afternoon, in my own most perilous position, and, above all, in the remarkable game that I saw Silver now engaged upon—keeping the mutineers together with one hand and grasping, with the other, after every means, possible and impossible, to make his peace and save his miserable life. He himself slept peacefully and snored aloud; yet my heart was sore for him, wicked as he was, to think on the dark perils that environed and the shameful gibbet that awaited him.

Chapter 30 ON PAROLE

I was wakened—indeed, we were all wakened, for I could see even the sentinel shake himself together from where he had fallen against the doorpost—by a clear, hearty voice hailing us from the margin of the wood:

"Blockhouse, ahoy!" it cried. "Here's the doctor."

And the doctor it was. Although I was glad to hear the sound, yet my gladness was not without admixture. I remembered with confusion my insubordinate and stealthy conduct; and when I saw where it had brought me—among what companions and surrounded by what dangers—I felt ashamed to look him in the face.

He must have risen in the dark, for the day had hardly come; and when I ran to a loophole and looked out, I saw him standing, like Silver once before, up to the mid-leg in creeping vapor.

"You, doctor! Top o' the morning to you, sir!" cried Silver, broad awake and beaming with good nature in a moment. "Bright and early, to be sure; and it's the early bird, as the saying goes, that gets the rations. George, shake up your timbers, son, and help Dr. Livesey over the ship's side. All a-doin' well, your patients was—all well and merry."

So he pattered on, standing on the hilltop, with his crutch under his elbow and one hand upon the side of the log house—quite the old John in voice, manner, and expression.

"We've quite a surprise for you too, sir," he continued. "We've a little stranger here—he! he! A noo boarder and lodger, sir, and looking fit and taut as a fiddle; slep' like a supercargo, he did, right alongside of John—stem to stem we was, all night."

Dr. Livesey was by this time across the stockade and pretty near the cook; and I could hear the alteration in his voice as he said:

"Not Jim?"

"The very same Jim as ever was," says Silver.

The doctor stopped outright, although he did not speak, and it was some seconds before he seemed able to move on.

"Well, well," he said, at last, "duty first and pleasure afterwards, as you might have said yourself, Silver. Let us overhaul these patients of yours."

A moment afterwards he had entered the blockhouse and with one grim nod to me, proceeded with his work among the sick. He seemed under no apprehension, though he must have known that his life, among these treacherous demons, depended on a hair; and he rattled on to his patients as if he were paying an ordinary professional visit in a quiet English family. His manner, I suppose, reacted on the men; for they behaved to him as if nothing had occurred—as if he were still ship's doctor, and they still faithful hands before the mast.

"You're doing well, my friend," he said to the fellow with the bandaged head, "and if ever any person had a close shave, it was you; your head must be as hard as iron. Well, George, how goes it? You're a pretty color, certainly; why your liver, man, is upside down. Did you take that medicine? Did he take that medicine, men?"

"Aye, aye, sir, he took it, sure enough," returned Morgan.

"Because, you see, since I am mutineers' doctor, or prison doctor, as I prefer to call it," says Doctor Livesey, in his pleasantest way, "I make it a point of honor not to lose a man for King George (God bless him!) and the gallows."

The rogues looked at each other, but swallowed the home-thrust in silence.

"Dick don't feel well, sir," said one.

"Don't he?" replied the doctor. "Well, step up here, Dick, and let me see your tongue. No, I should be surprised if he did! the man's tongue is fit to frighten the French. Another fever."

"Ah, there," said Morgan, "that comed of sp'iling Bibles."

"That comed—as you call it—of being arrant[1] asses," retorted the doctor, "and not having sense enough to know honest air from poison, and the dry land from a vile, pestiferous slough. I think it most probable—though, of course, it's only an opinion—that you'll all have the deuce to pay before you get that malaria out of your systems. Camp in a bog, would you? Silver, I'm surprised at you. You're less of a fool than many, take you all round; but you don't appear to me to have the rudiments of a notion of the rules of health.

"Well," he added, after he had dosed them round, and they had taken his prescriptions, with really laughable humility, more like charity school children than blood-guilty mutineers and pirates—"well, that's done for today. And now I should wish to have a talk with that boy, please."

And he nodded his head in my direction carelessly.

George Merry was at the door, spitting and spluttering over some bad tasted medicine; but at the first word of the doctor's proposal, he swung round with a deep flush and cried "No!" and swore.

Silver struck the barrel with his open hand.

"Si-lence!" he roared and looked about him positively like a lion. "Doctor," he went on, in his usual tones, "I was a-thinking of that, knowing as how you had a fancy for the boy. We're all humbly grateful for your kindness and, as you see, puts faith in you and takes the drugs down like that much grog. And I take it I've found a way as 'll suit all. Hawkins, will you give me your word of honor as a young gentleman—for a young gentleman you are, although poor born—your word of honor not to slip your cable?"

I readily gave the pledge required.

"Then, doctor," said Silver, "you just step outside o' that stockade, and once you're there, I'll bring the boy down on the inside, and I reckon you can yarn through the spars. Good day to you, sir, and all our dooties to the squire and Cap'n Smollett."

The explosion of disapproval, which nothing but Silver's black looks had restrained, broke out immediately the doctor had left the house. Silver was roundly accused of playing double—of trying to make a separate peace for himself—of sacrificing

[1] *arrant* (ăr′ănt): utter; thoroughgoing.

the interests of his accomplices and victims; and, in one word, of the identical, exact thing that he was doing. It seemed to me so obvious, in this case, that I could not imagine how he was to turn their anger. But he was twice the man the rest were; and his last night's victory had given him a huge preponderance [1] on their minds. He called them all the fools and dolts you can imagine, said it was necessary I should talk to the doctor, fluttered the chart in their faces, asked them if they could afford to break the treaty the very day they were bound a-treasure hunting.

"No, by thunder!" he cried, "it's us must break the treaty when the time comes; and till then I'll gammon [2] that doctor, if I have to ile his boots with brandy."

And then he bade them get the fire lit and stalked out upon his crutch, with his hand on my shoulder, leaving them in a disarray [3] and silenced by his volubility [4] rather than convinced.

"Slow, lad, slow," he said. "They might round upon us in a twinkle of an eye, if we was seen to hurry."

Very deliberately, then, did we advance across the sand to where the doctor awaited us on the other side of the stockade, and as soon as we were within easy speaking distance, Silver stopped.

"You'll make a note of this here also, doctor," says he, "and the boy'll tell you how I saved his life and were deposed for it too, and you may lay to that. Doctor, when a man's steering as near the wind as me—playing chuck-farthing [5] with the last breath in his body, like—you wouldn't think it too much, mayhap, to give him one good word? You'll please bear in mind it's not my life only now—it's that boy's into the bargain; and you'll speak me fair, doctor, and give me a bit o' hope to go on, for the sake of mercy."

Silver was a changed man once he was out there and had his back to his friends and the blockhouse; his cheeks seemed to have fallen in, his voice trembled; never was a soul more dead in earnest.

"Why, John, you're not afraid?" asked Doctor Livesey.

"Doctor, I'm no coward; no, not I—not *so* much!" and he snapped his fingers. "If I was I wouldn't say it. But I'll own up

[1] *preponderance* (prē·pŏn′dẽr·ăns): a superior influence. [2] *gammon* (găm′ŭn): to fool or deceive. [3] *disarray* (dĭs·ă·rā′): confusion. [4] *volubility* (vŏl′ū·bĭl′ĭ·tĭ): smooth talk. [5] *playing chuck-farthing:* gambling.

fairly, I've the shakes upon me for the gallows. You're a good man and a true; I never seen a better man! And you'll not forget what I done good, not any more than you'll forget the bad, I know. And I step aside—see here—and leave you and Jim alone. And you'll put that down for me too, for it's a long stretch, is that!"

So saying, he stepped back a little way, till he was out of earshot, and there sat down upon a tree stump and began to whistle; spinning round now and again upon his seat so as to command a sight, sometimes of me and the doctor, and sometimes of his unruly ruffians as they went to and fro in the sand, between the fire—which they were busy rekindling—and the house, from which they brought forth pork and bread to make the breakfast.

"So, Jim," said the doctor sadly, "here you are. As you have brewed, so shall you drink, my boy. Heaven knows, I cannot find it in my heart to blame you; but this much I will say, be it kind or unkind; when Captain Smollett was well, you dared not have gone off; and when he was ill and couldn't help it, by George, it was downright cowardly!"

I will own that I here began to weep. "Doctor," I said, "you might spare me. I have blamed myself enough; my life's forfeit anyway, and I should have been dead by now, if Silver hadn't stood for me; and doctor, believe this, I can die—and I daresay I deserve it—but what I fear is torture. If they come to torture me——"

"Jim," the doctor interrupted, and his voice was quite changed, "Jim, I can't have this. Whip over, and we'll run for it."

"Doctor," said I, "I passed my word."

"I know, I know," he cried. "We can't help that, Jim, now. I'll take it on my shoulders, holus, bolus, blame, and shame, my boy; but stay here, I cannot let you. Jump! One jump, and you're out, and we'll run for it like antelopes."

"No," I replied, "you know right well you wouldn't do the thing yourself; neither you, nor squire, nor captain; and no more will I. Silver trusted me; I passed my word, and back I go. But, doctor, you did not let me finish. If they come to torture me, I might let slip a word of where the ship is; for I got the ship, part by luck and part by risking, and she lies in North Inlet, on the southern beach, and just below high water. At half tide she must be high and dry."

"The ship!" exclaimed the doctor.

Rapidly I described to him my adventures, and he heard me out in silence.

"There is a kind of fate in this," he observed, when I had done. "Every step, it's you that saves our lives; and do you suppose by any chance that we are going to let you lose yours? That would be a poor return, my boy. You found out the plot; you found Ben Gunn—the best deed that ever you did, or will do, though you live to ninety. Oh, by Jupiter, and talking of Ben Gunn! why, this is the mischief in person. Silver!" he cried, "Silver! I'll give you a piece of advice," he continued, as the cook drew near again, "don't you be in any great hurry after that treasure."

"Why, sir, I do my possible, which that ain't," said Silver. "I can only, asking your pardon, save my life and the boy's by seeking for that treasure; and you may lay to that."

"Well, Silver," replied the doctor, "if that is so, I'll go one step further: look out for squalls [1] when you find it."

"Sir," said Silver, "as between man and man, that's too much and too little. What you're after, why you left the blockhouse, why you given me that there chart, I don't know, now, do I? and yet I done your bidding with my eyes shut and never a word of hope! But no, this here's too much. If you won't tell me what you mean plain out, just say so, and I'll leave the helm."

"No," said the doctor, musingly, "I've no right to say more; it's not my secret, you see, Silver, or, I give you my word, I'd tell it you. But I'll go as far with you as I dare go, and a step beyond; for I'll have my wig sorted by the captain or I'm mistaken! And, first, I'll give you a bit of hope: Silver, if we both get alive out of this wolf trap, I'll do my best to save you, short of perjury."

Silver's face was radiant. "You couldn't say more, I'm sure, sir, not if you was my mother," he cried.

"Well, that's my first concession," added the doctor. "My second is a piece of advice: Keep the boy close beside you, and when you need help, halloo. I'm off to seek it for you, and that itself will show you if I speak at random. Good-by, Jim."

And Dr. Livesey shook hands with me through the stockade, nodded to Silver, and set off at a brisk pace into the wood.

[1] *squall* (skwôl): a sudden gust of wind (Livesey means "look out for trouble").

Chapter 31

THE TREASURE HUNT—FLINT'S POINTER

"Jim," said Silver when we were alone, "if I saved your life, you saved mine; and I'll not forget it. I seen the doctor waving you to run for it—with the tail of my eye, I did; and I seen you say no, as plain as hearing. Jim, that's one to you. This is the first glint of hope I had since the attack failed, and I owe it you. And now, Jim, we're to go in for this here treasure hunting, with sealed orders too, and I don't like it; and you and me must stick close, back to back like, and we'll save our necks in spite o' fate and fortune."

Just then a man hailed us from the fire that breakfast was ready, and we were soon seated here and there about the sand over biscuit and fried junk.[1] They had lit a fire fit to roast an ox; and it was now grown so hot that they could only approach it from the windward, and even there not without precaution. In the same wasteful spirit they had cooked, I suppose, three times more than we could eat; and one of them, with an empty laugh, threw what was left into the fire, which blazed and roared again over this unusual fuel. I never in my life saw men so careless of the morrow; hand to mouth is the only word that can describe their way of doing; and what with wasted food and sleeping sentries, though they were bold enough for a brush [2] and be done with it, I could see their entire unfitness for anything like a prolonged campaign.

Even Silver, eating away, with Captain Flint upon his shoulder, had not a word of blame for their recklessness. And this the more surprised me, for I thought he had never shown himself so cunning as he did then.

"Aye, mates," said he, "it's lucky you have Barbecue to think for you with this here head. I got what I wanted, I did. Sure enough, they have the ship. Where they have it, I don't know yet; but once we hit the treasure, we'll have to jump about and find out. And then, mates, us that has the boats, I reckon, has the upper hand."

[1] *junk* (jŭngk): salted beef. [2] *brush:* a fight.

Thus he kept running on, with his mouth full of the hot bacon: thus he restored their hope and confidence, and, I more than suspect, repaired his own at the same time.

"As for hostage," he continued, "that's his last talk, I guess, with them he loves so dear. I've got my piece o' news, and thanky to him for that; but it's over and done. I'll take him in a line when we go treasure hunting, for we'll keep him like so much gold, in case of accidents, you mark, and in the meantime. Once we got the ship and treasure both, and off to sea like jolly companions, why, then, we'll talk Mr. Hawkins over, we will, and we'll give him his share, to be sure, for all his kindness."

It was no wonder the men were in a good humor now. For my part, I was horribly cast down. Should the scheme he had now sketched prove feasible, Silver, already doubly a traitor, would not hesitate to adopt it. He had still a foot in either camp, and there was no doubt he would prefer wealth and freedom with the pirates to a bare escape from hanging, which was the best he had to hope on our side.

Nay, and even if things so fell out that he was forced to keep his faith with Dr. Livesey, even then what danger lay before us! What a moment that would be when the suspicions of his followers turned to certainty, and he and I should have to fight for dear life—he, a cripple, and I, a boy—against five strong and active seamen!

Add to this double apprehension the mystery that still hung over the behavior of my friends; their unexplained desertion of the stockade; their inexplicable cession of the chart; or, harder still to understand, the doctor's last warning to Silver, "Look out for squalls when you find it"; and you will readily believe how little taste I found in my breakfast and with how uneasy a heart I set forth behind my captors on the quest for treasure.

We made a curious figure, had anyone been there to see us; all in soiled sailor clothes and all but me armed to the teeth. Silver had two guns slung about him—one before and one behind—besides the great cutlass at his waist and a pistol in each pocket of his square-tailed coat. To complete his strange appearance, Captain Flint sat perched upon his shoulder and gabbling odds and ends of purposeless sea talk. I had a line about my waist and followed obediently after the sea cook, who held the loose end of the rope, now in his free hand, now between his powerful teeth. For all the world, I was led like a dancing bear.

The other men were variously burthened; some carrying picks and shovels—for that had been the very first necessary they brought ashore from the *Hispaniola*—others laden with pork, bread, and brandy for the midday meal. All the stores, I observed, came from our stock; and I could see the truth of Silver's words the night before. Had he not struck a bargain with the doctor, he and his mutineers, deserted by the ship, must have been driven to subsist on clear water and the proceeds of their hunting. Water would have been little to their taste; a sailor is not usually a good shot; and, besides all that, when they were so short of eatables, it was not likely they would be very flush [1] of powder.

Well, thus equipped, we all set out—even the fellow with the broken head, who should certainly have kept in shadow—and straggled, one after another, to the beach, where the two gigs awaited us. Even these bore trace of the drunken folly of the pirates, one in a broken thwart and both in their muddy and unbailed condition. Both were to be carried along with us, for the sake of safety; and so, with our numbers divided between them, we set forth upon the bosom of the anchorage.

As we pulled over, there was some discussion on the chart. The red cross was, of course, far too large to be a guide; and the terms of the note on the back, as you will hear, admitted of some ambiguity. They ran, the reader may remember, thus:

> Tall tree, Spy-glass shoulder, bearing point to the N. of N.N.E.
> Skeleton Island E.S.E. and by E.
> Ten feet.

A tall tree was thus the principal mark. Now, right before us, the anchorage was bounded by a plateau from two to three hundred feet high, adjoining on the north the sloping southern shoulder of the Spy-glass, and rising again towards the south into the rough, cliffy eminence called the Mizzenmast Hill. The top of the plateau was dotted thickly with pine trees of varying height. Every here and there one of a different species rose forty or fifty feet clear above its neighbors, and which of these was the particular "tall tree" of Captain Flint could only be decided on the spot and by the readings of the compass.

[1] *flush:* well-supplied.

Yet, although that was the case, every man on board the boats had picked a favorite of his own ere we were halfway over, Long John alone shrugging his shoulders and bidding them wait till they were there.

We pulled easily, by Silver's directions, not to weary the hands prematurely; and, after quite a long passage, landed at the mouth of the second river—that which runs down a woody cleft of the Spy-glass. Thence, bending to our left, we began to ascend the slope towards the plateau.

At the first outset, heavy, miry ground and a matted, marish vegetation greatly delayed our progress; but, by little and little, the hill began to steepen and become stony underfoot, and the wood to change its character and to grow in a more open order. It was, indeed, a most pleasant portion of the island that we were now approaching. A heavy-scented broom and many flowering shrubs had almost taken the place of grass. Thickets of green nutmeg trees were dotted here and there with the red columns and the broad shadow of the pines; and the first mingled their spice with the aroma of the others. The air, besides, was fresh and stirring, and this, under the sheer sunbeams, was a wonderful refreshment to our senses.

The party spread itself abroad, in a fan shape, shouting and leaping to and fro. About the center, and a good way behind the rest, Silver and I followed—I tethered by my rope, he plowing, with deep pants, among the sliding gravel. From time to time, indeed, I had to lend him a hand or he must have missed his footing and fallen backward down the hill.

We had thus proceeded for about half a mile, and were approaching the brow of the plateau, when the man upon the farthest left began to cry aloud, as if in terror. Shout after shout came from him, and the others began to run in his direction.

"He can't 'a' found the treasure," said old Morgan, hurrying past us from the right, "for that's clean a-top."

Indeed, as we found when we also reached the spot, it was something very different. At the foot of a pretty big pine, and involved in a green creeper, which had even partly lifted some of the smaller bones, a human skeleton lay, with a few shreds of clothing, on the ground. I believe a chill struck for a moment to every heart.

"He was a seaman," said George Merry, who, bolder than

the rest, had gone up close, and was examining the rags of clothing. "Leastways, this is good sea cloth."

"Aye, aye," said Silver, "like enough; you wouldn't look to find a bishop here, I reckon. But what sort of a way is that for bones to lie? 'Tain't in natur'."

Indeed, on a second glance, it seemed impossible to fancy that the body was in a natural position. But for some disarray (the work, perhaps, of the birds that had fed upon him or of the slow-growing creeper that had gradually enveloped his remains) the man lay perfectly straight—his feet pointing in one direction, his hand, raised above his head like a diver's, pointing directly in the opposite.

"I've taken a notion into my old numskull," observed Silver. "Here's the compass; there's the tiptop p'int o' Skeleton Island, stickin' out like a tooth. Just take a bearing, will you, along the line of them bones."

It was done. The body pointed straight in the direction of the island, and the compass read duly E.S.E. and by E.

"I thought so," cried the cook; "this here is a p'inter. Right up there is our line for the Pole Star and the jolly dollars. But, by thunder! if it don't make me cold inside to think of Flint. This is one of *his* jokes, and no mistake. Him and these six was alone here; he killed 'em, every man; and this one he hauled here and laid down by compass, shiver my timbers! They're long bones, and the hair's been yellow. Aye, that would be Allardyce. You mind Allardyce, Tom Morgan?"

"Aye, aye," returned Morgan, "I mind him; he owed me money, he did, and took my knife ashore with him."

"Speaking of knives," said another, "why don't we find his'n lying round? Flint warn't the man to pick a seaman's pocket; and the birds, I guess, would leave it be."

"By the powers, and that's true!" cried Silver.

"There ain't a thing left here," said Merry, still feeling round among the bones, "not a copper doit nor a baccy box. It don't look nat'ral to me."

"No, by gum, it don't," agreed Silver; "not nat'ral, nor not nice, says you. Great guns! messmates, but if Flint was living, this would be a hot spot for you and me. Six they were, and six are we; and bones is what they are now."

"I saw him dead with these here deadlights," said Morgan.

"Billy took me in. There he laid, with penny pieces on his eyes."

"Dead—aye, sure enough he's dead and gone below," said the fellow with the bandage; "but if ever sperrit walked, it would be Flint's. Dear heart, but he died bad, did Flint!"

"Aye, that he did," observed another; "now he raged, and now he hollered for the rum, and now he sang. 'Fifteen Men' were his only song, mates; and I tell you true, I never rightly liked to hear it since. It was main hot, and the windy was open, and I hear that old song comin' out as clear as clear—and the death-haul on the man already."

"Come, come," said Silver, "stow this talk. He's dead, and he don't walk, that I know; leastways, he won't walk by day, and you may lay to that. Care killed a cat. Fetch ahead for the doubloons."

We started, certainly; but in spite of the hot sun and the staring daylight, the pirates no longer ran separate and shouting through the wood, but kept side by side and spoke with bated breath. The terror of the dead buccaneer had fallen on their spirits.

Chapter 32

THE TREASURE HUNT— THE VOICE AMONG THE TREES

Partly from the damping influence of this alarm, partly to rest Silver and the sick folk, the whole party sat down as soon as they had gained the brow of the ascent.

The plateau being somewhat tilted towards the west, this spot on which we had paused commanded a wide prospect on either hand. Before us, over the treetops, we beheld the Cape of the Woods, fringed with surf; behind, we not only looked down upon the anchorage and Skeleton Island, but saw—clear across the spit and the eastern lowlands—a great field of open sea upon the east. Sheer above us rose the Spy-glass, here dotted with single pines, there black with precipices. There was no sound but that of the distant breakers, mounting from all round, and the chirp of countless insects in the brush. Not a man, not a sail upon the sea; the very largeness of the view increased the sense of solitude.

Silver, as he sat, took certain bearings with his compass.

"There are three 'tall trees,' " said he, "about in the right line from Skeleton Island. 'Spy-glass Shoulder,' I take it, means that lower p'int there. It's child's play to find the stuff now. I've half a mind to dine first."

"I don't feel sharp," growled Morgan. "Thinkin' o' Flint—I think it were—'as done me."

"Ah, well, my son, you praise your stars he's dead," said Silver.

"He were an ugly devil," cried a third pirate, with a shudder; "that blue in the face, too!"

"That was how the rum took him," added Merry. "Blue! well, I reckon he was blue. That's a true word."

Ever since they had found the skeleton and got upon this train of thought, they had spoken lower and lower, and they had almost got to whispering by now, so that the sound of their talk hardly interrupted the silence of the wood. All of a sudden, out of the middle of the trees in front of us, a thin, high, trembling voice struck up the well-known air and words:

Fifteen men on the Dead Man's Chest—
Yo-ho-ho, and a bottle of rum!

I never have seen men more dreadfully affected than the pirates. The color went from their six faces like enchantment; some leaped to their feet, some clawed hold of others; Morgan groveled on the ground.

"It's Flint, by——!" cried Merry.

The song had stopped as suddenly as it began—broken off, you would have said, in the middle of a note, as though someone had laid his hand upon the singer's mouth. Coming so far through the clear, sunny atmosphere, among the green treetops, I thought it had sounded airily and sweetly; and the effect on my companions was the stranger.

"Come," said Silver, struggling with his ashen lips to get

the word out, "this won't do. Stand by to go about. This is a rum start, and I can't name the voice; but it's someone skylarking —someone that's flesh and blood, and you may lay to that."

His courage had come back as he spoke, and some of the color to his face along with it. Already the others had begun to lend an ear to this encouragement, and were coming a little to themselves, when the same voice broke out again—not this time singing, but in a faint distant hail, that echoed yet fainter among the clefts of the Spy-glass.

"Darby M'Graw," it wailed—for that is the word that best describes the sound—"Darby M'Graw! Darby M'Graw!" again and again and again; and then rising a little higher, and with an oath that I leave out, "Fetch aft the rum, Darby!"

The buccaneers remained rooted to the ground, their eyes starting from their heads. Long after the voice had died away, they still stared in silence, dreadfully, before them.

"That fixes it!" gasped one. "Let's go."

"They was his last words," moaned Morgan, "his last words above board."

Dick had his Bible out and was praying volubly. He had been well brought up, had Dick, before he came to sea and fell among bad companions.

Still, Silver was unconquered. I could hear his teeth rattle in his head; but he had not yet surrendered.

"Nobody in this here island ever heard of Darby," he muttered; "not one but us that's here." And then, making a great effort, "Shipmates," he cried, "I'm here to get that stuff, and I'll not be beat by man nor devil. I never was feared of Flint in his life, and, by the powers, I'll face him dead. There's seven hundred thousand pound not a quarter of a mile from here. When did ever a gentleman o' fortune show his stern to that much dollars for a boosy old seaman with a blue mug—and him dead, too?"

But there was no sign of reawakening courage in his followers; rather, indeed, of growing terror at the irreverence of his words.

"Belay [1] there, John!" said Merry. "Don't you cross a sperrit."

And the rest were all too terrified to reply. They would have

[1] *belay* (bē·lā′): stop.

run away severally had they dared; but fear kept them together and kept them close by John, as if his daring helped them. He, on his part, had pretty well fought his weakness down.

"Sperrit? Well, maybe," he said. "But there's one thing not clear to me. There was an echo. Now, no man ever seen a sperrit with a shadow; well, then, what's he doing with an echo to him, I should like to know? That ain't in natur', surely?"

This argument seemed weak enough to me. But you can never tell what will affect the superstitious, and, to my wonder, George Merry was greatly relieved.

"Well, that's so," he said. "You've a head upon your shoulders, John, and no mistake. 'Bout ship, mates! This here crew is on a wrong tack, I do believe. And come to think on it, it was like Flint's voice, I grant you, but not just so clear-away like it, after all. It was liker somebody else's voice now—it was liker———"

"By the powers, Ben Gunn!" roared Silver.

"Aye, and so it were," cried Morgan, springing on his knees. "Ben Gunn it were!"

"It don't make much odds, do it, now?" asked Dick. "Ben Gunn's not here in the body, any more'n Flint."

But the older hands greeted this remark with scorn.

"Why, nobody minds Ben Gunn," cried Merry; "dead or alive, nobody minds him."

It was extraordinary how their spirits had returned and how the natural color had revived in their faces. Soon they were chatting together, with intervals of listening; and not long after, hearing no further sound, they shouldered the tools and set forth again, Merry walking first with Silver's compass to keep them on the right line with Skeleton Island. He had said the truth: dead or alive, nobody minded Ben Gunn.

Dick alone still held his Bible and looked around him as he went, with fearful glances; but he found no sympathy, and Silver even joked him on his precautions.

"I told you," said he—"I told you, you had sp'iled your Bible. If it ain't no good to swear by, what do you suppose a sperrit would give for it? Not that!" and he snapped his big fingers, halting a moment on his crutch.

But Dick was not to be comforted; indeed, it was soon plain to me that the lad was falling sick; hastened by heat, exhaustion, and the shock of his alarm, the fever predicted by Doctor Livesey was evidently growing swiftly higher.

It was fine open walking here, upon the summit; our way lay a little downhill, for as I have said, the plateau tilted towards the west. The pines, great and small, grew wide apart; and even between the clumps of nutmeg and azalea wide open spaces baked in the hot sunshine. Striking, as we did, pretty near northwest across the island, we drew, on the one hand, ever nearer under the shoulders of the Spy-glass and on the other, looked ever wider over that western bay where I had once tossed and trembled in the coracle.

The first of the tall trees was reached, and by the bearing,[1] proved the wrong one. So with the second. The third rose nearly two hundred feet into the air above a clump of underwood; a giant of a vegetable, with a red column as big as a cottage and a wide shadow around in which a company could have maneuvered. It was conspicuous far to sea both on the east and west, and might have been entered as a sailing mark upon the chart.

But it was not its size that now impressed my companions; it was the knowledge that seven hundred thousand pounds in gold lay somewhere buried below its spreading shadow. The thought of the money, as they drew nearer, swallowed up their previous terrors. Their eyes burned in their heads; their feet grew speedier and lighter; their whole soul was bound up in that fortune, that whole lifetime of extravagance and pleasure that lay waiting there for each of them.

Silver hobbled, grunting, on his crutch; his nostrils stood out and quivered; he cursed like a madman when the flies settled on his hot and shiny countenance; he plucked furiously at the line that held me to him and, from time to time, turned his eyes upon me with a deadly look. Certainly he took no pains to hide his thoughts; and certainly I read them like print. In the immediate nearness of the gold, all else had been forgotten; his promise and the doctor's warning were both things of the past; and I could not doubt that he hoped to seize upon the treasure, find and board the *Hispaniola* under cover of night, cut every honest throat about that island, and sail away as he had at first intended, laden with crimes and riches.

Shaken as I was with these alarms, it was hard for me to

[1] *by the bearing:* by the direction on the compass.

keep up with the rapid pace of the treasure hunters. Now and again I stumbled; and it was then that Silver plucked so roughly at the rope and launched at me his murderous glances. Dick, who had dropped behind us and now brought up the rear, was babbling to himself both prayers and curses as his fever kept rising. This also added to my wretchedness, and, to crown all, I was haunted by the thought of the tragedy that had once been acted on that plateau, when that ungodly buccaneer with the blue face —he who died at Savannah, singing and shouting for drink—had there, with his own hand, cut down his six accomplices. This grove, that was now so peaceful, must then have rung with cries, I thought; and even with the thought I could believe I heard it ringing still.

We were now at the margin of the thicket.

"Huzza, mates, all together!" shouted Merry; and the foremost broke into a run.

And suddenly, not ten yards further, we beheld them stop. A low cry arose. Silver doubled his pace, digging away with the foot of his crutch like one possessed; and next moment he and I had come also to a dead halt.

Before us was a great excavation, not very recent, for the sides had fallen in and grass had sprouted on the bottom. In this were the shaft of a pick broken in two and the boards of several packing-cases strewn around. On one of these boards I saw, branded with a hot iron, the name *Walrus*—the name of Flint's ship.

All was clear to probation. The *cache* had been found and rifled; the seven hundred thousand pounds were gone!

Chapter 33 THE FALL OF A CHIEFTAIN

There never was such an overturn in this world. Each of these six men was as though he had been struck. But with Silver the blow passed almost instantly. Every thought of his soul had been set full-stretch, like a racer, on that money; well, he was brought up in a single second, dead; and he kept his head, found his temper, and changed his plan before the others had had time to realize the disappointment.

"Jim," he whispered, "take that and stand by for trouble."

And he passed me a double-barreled pistol.

At the same time he began quietly moving northward, and in a few steps had put the hollow between us two and the other five. Then he looked at me and nodded, as much as to say, "Here is a narrow corner," as, indeed, I thought it was. His looks were now quite friendly; and I was so revolted at these constant changes that I could not forbear whispering, "So you've changed sides again."

There was no time left for him to answer in. The buccaneers, with oaths and cries, began to leap, one after another, into the pit and to dig with their fingers, throwing the boards aside as they did so. Morgan found a piece of gold. He held it up with a perfect spout of oaths. It was a two-guinea piece, and it went from hand to hand among them for a quarter of a minute.

"Two guineas!" roared Merry, shaking it at Silver. "That's your seven hundred thousand pounds, is it? You're the man for bargains, ain't you? You're him that never bungled nothing, you wooden-headed lubber!"

"Dig away, boys," said Silver, with the coolest insolence; "you'll find some pig nuts and I shouldn't wonder."

"Pig nuts!" repeated Merry, in a scream. "Mates, do you hear that? I tell you, now, that man there knew it all along. Look in the face of him, and you'll see it wrote there."

"Ah, Merry," remarked Silver, "standing for cap'n again? You're a pushing lad, to be sure."

But this time everyone was entirely in Merry's favor. They began to scramble out of the excavation, darting furious glances behind them. One thing I observed, which looked well for us: they all got out upon the opposite side from Silver.

Well, there we stood, two on one side, five on the other, the pit between us, and nobody screwed up high enough to offer the first blow. Silver never moved; he watched them, very upright on his crutch, and looked as cool as ever I saw him. He was brave, and no mistake.

At last, Merry seemed to think a speech might help matters.

"Mates," says he, "there's two of them alone there; one's

the old cripple that brought us all here and blundered us down to this; the other's that cub that I mean to have the heart of. Now mates——"

He was raising his arm and his voice and plainly meant to lead a charge. But just then—crack! crack! crack!—three musket shots flashed out of the thicket. Merry tumbled head foremost into the excavation; the man with the bandage spun round like a teetotum and fell all his length upon his side, where he lay dead, but still twitching; and the other three turned and ran for it with all their might.

Before you could wink, Long John had fired two barrels of a pistol into the struggling Merry; and as the man rolled up his eyes at him in the last agony, "George," said he, "I reckon I settled you."

At the same moment the doctor, Gray, and Ben Gunn joined us, with smoking muskets, from among the nutmeg trees.

"Forward!" cried the doctor. "Double quick, my lads. We must head 'em off the boats."

And we set off at a great pace, sometimes plunging through the bushes, to the chest.

I tell you, but Silver was anxious to keep up with us. The work that man went through, leaping on his crutch till the muscles of his chest were fit to burst, was work no sound man ever equaled; and so thinks the doctor. As it was, he was already thirty yards behind us and on the verge of strangling when we reached the brow of the slope.

"Doctor," he hailed, "see there! no hurry!"

Sure enough there was no hurry. In a more open part of the plateau, we could see the three survivors still running in the same direction as they had started, right for Mizzenmast Hill. We were already between them and the boats; and so we four sat down to breathe, while Long John, mopping his face, came slowly up with us.

"Thank ye kindly, doctor," says he. "You came in in about the nick, I guess, for me and Hawkins. And so it's you, Ben Gunn!" he added. "Well, you're a nice one, to be sure."

"I'm Ben Gunn, I am," replied the maroon, wriggling like an eel in his embarrassment. "And," he added, after a long pause, "how do, Mr. Silver? Pretty well, I thank ye, says you."

"Ben, Ben," murmured Silver, "to think as you've done me!"

The doctor sent back Gray for one of the pickaxes deserted, in their flight, by the mutineers; and then as we proceeded leisurely downhill to where the boats were lying, related, in a few words, what had taken place. It was a story that profoundly interested Silver; and Ben Gunn, the half-idiot maroon, was the hero from beginning to end.

Ben, in his long, lonely wanderings about the island, had found the skeleton—it was he that had rifled [1] it; he had found the treasure; he had dug it up (it was the haft of his pickax that lay broken in the excavation); he had carried it on his back, in many weary journeys, from the foot of the tall pine to a cave he had on the two-pointed hill at the northeast angle of the island, and there it had lain stored in safety since two months before the arrival of the *Hispaniola.*

When the doctor had wormed this secret from him, on the afternoon of the attack, and when, next morning, he saw the anchorage deserted, he had gone to Silver, given him the chart, which was now useless—given him the stores, for Ben Gunn's cave was well supplied with goats' meat salted by himself—given anything and everything to get a chance of moving in safety from the stockade to the two-pointed hill, there to be clear of malaria and keep a guard upon the money.

"As for you, Jim," he said, "it went against my heart, but I did what I thought best for those who had stood by their duty; and if you were not one of these, whose fault was it?"

That morning, finding that I was to be involved in the horrid disappointment he had prepared for the mutineers, he had run all the way to the cave and leaving the squire to guard the captain, had taken Gray and the maroon and started, making the diagonal across the island, to be at hand beside the pine. Soon, however, he saw that our party had the start of him; and Ben Gunn, being fleet of foot, had been despatched in front to do his best alone. Then it had occurred to him to work upon the superstitions of his former shipmates; and he was so far successful that Gray and the doctor had come up and were already ambushed [2] before the arrival of the treasure hunters.

[1] *rifle* (rī′f'l): to steal from. [2] *ambushed* (ăm′bo͝oshd): hidden so as to attack by surprise.

"Ah," said Silver, "it were fortunate for me that I had Hawkins here. You would have let old John be cut to bits and never given it a thought, Doctor."

"Not a thought," replied Doctor Livesey cheerily.

And by this time we had reached the gigs. The doctor, with the pickax, demolished one of them, and then we all got aboard the other and set out to go round by sea for North Inlet.

This was a run of eight or nine miles. Silver, though he was almost killed already with fatigue, was set to an oar, like the rest of us, and we were soon skimming swiftly over a smooth sea. Soon we passed out of the straits and doubled the southeast corner of the island, round which, four days ago, we had towed the *Hispaniola.*

As we passed the two-pointed hill, we could see the black mouth of Ben Gunn's cave and a figure standing by it, leaning on a musket. It was the squire; and we waved a handkerchief and gave him three cheers, in which the voice of Silver joined as heartily as any.

Three miles farther, just inside the mouth of North Inlet, what should we meet but the *Hispaniola,* cruising by herself? The last flood had lifted her; and had there been much wind, or a strong tide current, as in the southern anchorage, we should never have found her more or found her stranded beyond help. As it was, there was little amiss, beyond the wreck of the mainsail. Another anchor was got ready and dropped in a fathom and a half of water. We all pulled round again to Rum Cove, the nearest point for Ben Gunn's treasure house; and then Gray, singlehanded, returned with the gig to the *Hispaniola,* where he was to pass the night on guard.

A gentle slope ran up from the beach to the entrance of the cave. At the top, the squire met us. To me he was cordial and kind, saying nothing of my escapade, either in the way of blame or praise. At Silver's polite salute he somewhat flushed.

"John Silver," he said, "you're a prodigious villain and imposter—a monstrous imposter, sir. I am told I am not to prosecute you. Well, then, I will not. But the dead men, sir, hang about your neck like millstones."

"Thank you kindly, sir," replied Long John, again saluting.

"I dare you to thank me!" cried the squire. "It is a gross dereliction of my duty. Stand back."

And thereupon we all entered the cave. It was a large, airy place, with a little spring and a pool of clear water overhung with ferns. The floor was sand. Before a big fire lay Captain Smollett; and in a far corner, only duskily flickered over by the blaze, I beheld great heaps of coin and quadrilaterals built of bars of gold. That was Flint's treasure that we had come so far to seek and that had cost already the lives of seventeen men from the *Hispaniola.* How many it had cost in the amassing, what blood and sorrow, what good ships scuttled on the deep, what brave men walking the plank blindfold, what shot of cannon, what shame and lies and cruelty, perhaps no man alive could tell. Yet there were still three upon that island—Silver, and old Morgan, and Ben Gunn—who had each taken his share in these crimes, as each had hoped in vain to share in the reward.

"Come in, Jim," said the captain. "You're a good boy in your line, Jim; but I don't think you and me'll go to sea again. You're too much of the born favorite for me. Is that you, John Silver? What brings you here, man?"

"Come back to my dooty, sir," returned Silver.

"Ah!" said the captain; and that was all he said.

What a supper I had of it that night, with all my friends around me; and what a meal it was, with Ben Gunn's salted goat, and some delicacies and a bottle of old wine from the *Hispaniola.* Never, I am sure, were people gayer or happier. And there was Silver, sitting back almost out of the firelight, but eating heartily, prompt to spring forward when anything was wanted, even joining quietly in our laughter—the same bland, polite, obsequious [1] seaman of the voyage out.

[1] *obsequious* (ŏb·sē′kwĭ·ŭs): slavishly seeking to please.

Chapter 34 AND LAST

The next morning we fell early to work, for the transportation of this great mass of gold near a mile by land to the beach and thence three miles by boat to the *Hispaniola* was a considerable task for so small a number of workmen. The three fellows still abroad upon the Island did not greatly trouble us; a single sentry on the shoulder of the hill was sufficient to insure us against any sudden onslaught, and we thought, besides, they had had more than enough of fighting.

Therefore the work was pushed on briskly. Gray and Ben Gunn came and went with the boat, while the rest, during their absences, piled treasure on the beach. Two of the bars, slung in a rope's end, made a good load for a grown man—one that he was glad to walk slowly with. For my part, as I was not much use at carrying, I was kept busy all day in the cave, packing the minted money into breadbags.

It was a strange collection, like Billy Bones's hoard for the diversity of coinage, but so much larger and so much more varied that I think I never had more pleasure than in sorting them. English, French, Spanish, Portuguese, Georges, and Louises, doubloons and double guineas and moidores and sequins, the pictures of all the kings of Europe for the last hundred years, strange Oriental pieces stamped with what looked like wisps of string or bits of spider's web, round pieces and square pieces, and pieces bored through the middle, as if to wear them round your neck—nearly every variety of money in the world must, I think, have found a place in that collection; and for number, I am sure they were like autumn leaves, so that my back ached with stooping and my fingers with sorting them out.

Day after day this work went on; by every evening a fortune had been stowed aboard, but there was another fortune waiting for the morrow; and all this time we heard nothing of the three surviving mutineers.

At last—I think it was on the third night—the doctor and I were strolling on the shoulder of the hill where it overlooks the lowlands of the isle, when, from out the thick darkness below, the wind brought us a noise between shrieking and singing. It was only a snatch that reached our ears, followed by the former silence.

"Heaven forgive them," said the doctor, " 'tis the mutineers!"

"All drunk, sir," struck in the voice of Silver from behind us.

Silver, I should say, was allowed his entire liberty, and, in spite of daily rebuffs, seemed to regard himself once more as quite a privileged and friendly dependent. Indeed, it was remarkable how well he bore these slights and with what unwearying politeness he kept on trying to ingratiate himself with all.

Yet, I think, none treated him better than a dog; unless it was Ben Gunn, who was still terribly afraid of his old quartermaster, or myself, who had really something to thank him for; although for that matter, I suppose, I had reason to think even worse of him than anybody else, for I had seen him meditating a fresh treachery upon the plateau. Accordingly, it was pretty gruffly that the doctor answered him.

"Drunk or raving," said he.

"Right you were, sir," replied Silver; "and precious little odds which, to you and me."

"I suppose you would hardly ask me to call you a humane man," returned the doctor, with a sneer, "and so my feelings may surprise you, Master Silver. But if I were sure they were raving—as I am morally certain one, at least, of them is down with fever—I should leave this camp and, at whatever risk to my own carcass, take them the assistance of my skill."

"Ask your pardon, sir, you would be very wrong," quoth Silver. "You would lose your precious life, and you may lay to that. I'm on your side now, hand and glove; and I shouldn't wish for to see the party weakened, let alone yourself, seeing as I know what I owes you. But these men down there, they couldn't keep their word—no, not supposing they wished to; and what's more, they couldn't believe as you could."

"No," said the doctor. "You're the man to keep your word, we know that."

Well, that was about the last news we had of the three pirates. Only once we heard a gunshot a great way off and supposed them to be hunting. A council was held, and it was decided that we must desert them on the island—to the huge glee, I must say, of Ben Gunn, and with the strong approval of Gray. We left a good stock of powder and shot, the bulk of the salt goat, a few medicines, and some other necessaries, tools, clothing, a spare sail, a fathom or two of rope, and, by the particular desire of the doctor, a handsome present of tobacco.

That was about our last doing on the island. Before that we had got the treasure stowed, and had shipped enough water and the remainder of the goat meat, in case of any distress; and at last, one fine morning, we weighed anchor, which was about all that we could manage, and stood out of North Inlet, the same colors flying that the captain had flown and fought under at the palisade.

The three fellows must have been watching us closer than we thought, as we soon proved. For, coming through the narrows, we had to lie very near the southern point, and there we saw all three of them kneeling together on a spit of sand, with their arms raised in supplication.[1] It went to all our hearts, I think, to leave them in that wretched state; but we could not risk another mutiny; and to take them home for the gibbet would have been a cruel sort of kindness. The doctor hailed them and told them of the stores we had left, and where they were to find them. But they continued to call us by name and appeal to us, for God's sake, to be merciful and not leave them to die in such a place.

At last, seeing the ship still bore on her course and was now swiftly drawing out of earshot, one of them—I know not which it was—leapt to his feet with a hoarse cry, whipped his musket to his shoulder, and sent a shot whistling over Silver's head and through the mainsail.

After that, we kept under cover of the bulwarks, and when next I looked out, they had disappeared from the spit, and the spit itself had almost melted out of sight in the growing distance. That was, at least, the end of that; and before noon, to my inexpressible joy, the highest rock of Treasure Island had sunk into the blue round of sea.

We were so short of men that everyone on board had to bear a hand—only the captain lying on a mattress in the stern and giving his orders; for, though greatly recovered, he was still in want of quiet. We laid her head for the nearest port in Spanish America, for we could not risk the voyage home without fresh hands; and as it was, what with baffling winds and a couple of fresh gales, we were all worn out before we reached it.

[1] *supplication* (sŭp′lĭ·kā′shŭn): a humble plea.

It was just at sundown when we cast anchor in a most beautiful land-locked gulf and were immediately surrounded by shore boats full of negroes, and Mexican Indians, and half-bloods, selling fruits and vegetables, and offering to dive for bits of money. The sight of so many good-humored faces (especially the blacks), the taste of the tropical fruits, and above all, the lights that began to shine in the town, made a most charming contrast to our dark and bloody sojourn on the island; and the doctor and the squire, taking me along with them, went ashore to pass the early part of the night. Here they met the captain of an English man-of-war, fell in talk with him, went on board his ship, and, in short, had so agreeable a time that day was breaking when we came alongside the *Hispaniola.*

Ben Gunn was on deck alone, and, as soon as we came on board, he began, with wonderful contortions, to make us a confession. Silver was gone. The maroon had connived at his escape in a shore boat some hours ago, and he now assured us he had only done so to preserve our lives, which would certainly have been forfeit if "that man with the one leg had stayed aboard." But this was not all. The sea cook had not gone empty-handed. He had cut through a bulkhead unobserved and had removed one of the sacks of coin, worth perhaps three or four hundred guineas, to help him on his further wanderings.

I think we were all pleased to be so cheaply quit of him.

Well, to make a long story short, we got a few hands on board, made a good cruise home, and the *Hispaniola* reached Bristol just as Mr. Blandly was beginning to think of fitting out her consort. Five men only of those who had sailed returned with her. "Drink and the devil had done for the rest," with a vengeance; although, to be sure, we were not quite in so bad a case as that other ship they sang about:

> With one man of her crew alive,
> What put to sea with seventy-five.

All of us had an ample share of the treasure and used it wisely or foolishly, according to our natures. Captain Smollett is now retired from the sea. Gray not only saved his money, but, being suddenly smit with the desire to rise, also studied his profession; and he is now mate and part owner of a fine full-rigged ship; married besides, and the father of a family. As for Ben Gunn, he got a thousand pounds, which he spent or lost in three weeks, or, to be more exact, in nineteen days, for he was back begging on the twentieth. Then he was given a lodge to keep, exactly as he had feared upon the island; and he still lives, a great favorite, though something of a butt,[1] with the country boys, and a notable singer in church on Sundays and saints' days.

Of Silver we have heard no more. That formidable seafaring man with one leg has at last gone clean out of my life; but I daresay he met his old wife and perhaps still lives in comfort with her and Captain Flint. It is to be hoped so, I suppose, for his chances of comfort in another world are very small.

The bar silver and the arms still lie, for all that I know, where Flint buried them; and certainly they shall lie there for me. Oxen and wain-ropes would not bring me back again to that accursed island; and the worst dreams that ever I have are when I hear the surf booming about its coasts or start upright in bed, with the sharp voice of Captain Flint still ringing in my ears: "Pieces of eight! pieces of eight!"

AFTERWORD

The natives of Samoa, an island in the South Pacific where Robert Louis Stevenson spent his last years, called him *Tusitala.* In their language this means "teller of tales." In any language this is what he must be called.

See how he begins the story of *Treasure Island.* He asks you to believe that what you are about to read really happened.

> Squire Trelawney, Dr. Livesey, and the rest of these gentlemen . . . asked me to write down the whole particulars about Treasure Island from the beginning to the end, keeping nothing back but the bearings of the island, and that only because there is still treasure not yet lifted. . . .

Almost everything that will happen in this story is hinted at right in the beginning. Besides this, the storyteller in this novel is someone like yourself. Today, Jim Hawkins would probably be in a school like yours.

Billy Bones, "the brown old seaman with the saber cut" appears on the very first page. He strides up to the old inn door whistling the

[1] *butt:* a person to play jokes on.

pirate song that echoes throughout the book, "Fifteen men on the Dead Man's Chest . . ."

You find out immediately what kind of a man he is. This is still the day of the pirates. And even if Jim Hawkins doesn't know it yet, the reader can guess that this old sailor must have been a pirate: he has a sea chest; he drinks rum; he has a saber cut on his face; he chooses an inn on the seacoast. And he pays Jim to warn him if "a seafaring man with one leg" should ever appear. He tells wild stories of sea fights and pirates and places with strange and exciting names like Dry Tortugas and other places on the Spanish Main.

Treasure Island is a *romance* in the old and wonderful meaning of that word. Webster's dictionary says that a *romance* is ". . . any fictitious and wonderful tale . . . a sort of novel whose interest lies . . . in adventure, surprising incident, or the like." *Treasure Island* is all of this, especially "the like." It is about adventure and danger; about treachery and daring; about courage and cunning; about honest fools and wise villains. But best of all, romance is filled with action: the bustle of the docks where the ships are being loaded; the schooner *Hispaniola* (a wonderful romantic name) rolling, hull-down, through tropical seas; the gun fights; the clash of sabers—and most of all, the dead men. There are twenty corpses and a skeleton in *Treasure Island.*

Yet all of this excitement is romantic in another way. It is never really violent. And it is never violently real. Read again the chapter in which Jim Hawkins fights with Israel Hands for the possession of the schooner. Jim shoots the knife-throwing pirate dead almost by accident. But even though this is a very exciting scene, it is neither gory nor frightening. It is just a wonderful story.

You can read a novel (or a short story or a poem) in many different ways. You can read to learn what happens, and that can be great fun. You can read to find out more about the way people behave. This requires more thinking. It can bring you more satisfaction than just learning what the story is about. By understanding why the characters behave the way they do, you can learn much about the world they live in.

The main characters are seen very clearly in *Treasure Island*—Jim, the doctor, the squire, the captain, and most of all, Long John Silver. The rest are really there for the scenery. They are part of the background even when, like Job Anderson, they are leading a charge. This does not mean that we cannot see who they are. Stevenson is a genius when it comes to describing a man or an island. He has a way of letting us come to know his characters by the way they talk and what they do. In the case of Jim and the doctor, he even lets you know how and what they think. He can do this because Jim and the doctor tell the actual story in their own words.

Let us think about Long John Silver for a moment. Remember that Stevenson said he used a friend of his as a model for the pirate. There is a shadow of Long John in the very first chapter when Billy Bones pays Jim to be on the lookout for "a seafaring man with one leg." When we first hear about the pirate, it is in the squire's letter to the doctor. Remember what he writes?

> . . . he lost it [his leg] in his country's service, under the immortal Hawke. He has no pension . . . [He] is a man of substance . . . he has a banker's account which has never been overdrawn.

Everything we learn about Long John in the first part of the novel is about his good qualities. He has good qualities, it is true, even though from the very beginning we suspect the worst from him. When Jim visits him at the Spy-glass he finds that "It was a bright enough little place of entertainment. The sign was newly painted; the windows had neat red curtains; the floor was cleanly sanded." All these words—*bright, newly painted, neat, cleanly sanded* almost force us to think of Silver as the opposite of what a pirate should be.

Jim admits to himself that when he first heard what the squire had written in the letter, he immediately feared that Silver might be the "one-legged seafaring" man Billy Bones had had him watch for, but, says Jim,

> . . . one look at the man before me was enough . . . I thought I knew what a buccaneer was like—a very different creature, according to me, from this clean and pleasant-tempered landlord.

Long John Silver acts honestly—and the reader can see that it is just an act—but can we be sure? Aboard ship he keeps his cook's galley spic and span. Everything about him is neat. That word is used over and over again in descriptions of the man. Even the doctor, who seems to be the most sensible man aboard ship, says to the bumbling squire,

> Trelawney . . . contrary to all my notions, I believe you have managed to get two honest men on board with you—that man [the captain] and John Silver.

We can see from the very beginning of the story that the squire is not a very good judge of men or of situations. He is brave, generous, loud-mouthed, and almost stupid. He can do what has to be done if he is told to do it, as when he is ordered to fire from the gig at the gunner aboard the schooner. On his own, he is a blabber-mouth who hired a pirate crew and believed them honest.

To return to Silver—as the *Hispaniola* is being loaded, we learn a bit more about the man. Israel Hands, the coxswain, says,

> He's no common man, Barbecue [Long John]. . . . He had good schooling in his young days and can speak like a book when so minded; and brave—a lion's nothing alongside of Long John! I seen him grapple four, and knocked their heads together—him unarmed.

Jim tells us that

> All the crew respected and even obeyed him. He had a way of talking to each and doing everybody some particular service. To me he was unweariedly kind and always glad to see me in the galley, which he kept as clean as a new pin. . . .

Even in the fateful scene of the apple barrel, in which Jim learns of the pirate's plot, we learn something interesting about Long John, the man. After talking about pirates and their ways, how they spend what they steal as quickly as they get it, he says,

> . . . I puts it all away, some here, some there, and none too much anywheres, by reason of suspicion. I'm fifty, mark you; once back from this cruise, I set up gentleman in earnest. . . .

He tells how he has arranged to have his wife take all his savings and meet him at the end of the voyage.

Long John is a very special kind of pirate. He is looking out for a comfortable and "honorable" old age. As one of his mates says, "Everybody know'd you was a kind of a chapling, John." He is forever saying "Dooty is dooty." He even seems to mean it. He may be evil, but he is not a hypocrite.

It is interesting that the one act of violence we actually see him commit is done in a dreamlike way. Jim watches from his hiding place and reports that, except for the dead body,

> Everything else was unchanged, the sun still shining mercilessly on the steaming marsh and the tall pinnacle of the mountain, and I could scarce persuade myself that murder had been actually done. . . .

When John next appears, at the stockade, with the flag of truce, he is almost an object of pity as he struggles alone over the stockade. But he is dignified too, as he sits and bargains with the captain. His reasoning is very good even though it is about things that are wrong.

If *Tusitala* was really a great storyteller, we should know a great deal about all of the other major characters in *Treasure Island*. We can use Captain Smollett as a test. He really only appears a few times in the story. There is the big scene when we first meet him, and he tells the squire what he thinks of the crew and the voyage plans; there is the escape from the schooner to the stockade; and finally there is the fight for the stockade. Through the rest of the story he is almost always in the background.

Stevenson tells us just what kind of a man the captain is, how he talks, how he thinks, and how brave he is. We know how different he is from the doctor and the squire. In fact, we know enough about this man so that we can imagine what he is doing and saying, even when he does not appear in the story.

Remember the first time we see him. We are told that he was "a sharp-looking man, who seemed angry with everything on board, and was soon to tell us why . . ." He follows the adventure party into the cabin and asks permission to speak. He says to the squire,

> . . . better speak plain, I believe, even at the risk of offense. I don't like this cruise; I don't like the men; and I don't like my officer. That's short and sweet. . . .

He complains that nothing is really shipshape and that even Silver's parrot knows more about the plans for the voyage than he does.

The captain tells them that this is obviously a voyage of adventure, and adventure means danger. But there should be no more chance-taking than is absolutely necessary. He says that the men are putting the powder and arms in the forward hold.

> . . . Now, you have a good place under the cabin; why not put them there?—first point. Then you are bringing four of your own people with you, and they tell me some of them are to be berthed forward. Why not give them the berths here beside the cabin?—second point.

When the squire asks him if he has anything more to say, he adds ". . . There's been too much blabbing already." He says he has learned at second hand that there is a treasure map with the information about the island. He had learned from the crew (remember they are Long John's men) just where the island was.

> "Well, gentlemen," continued the captain, "I don't know who has this map; but I make it a point, it shall be kept secret even from me and Mr. Arrow. Otherwise I would ask you to let me resign."

He makes it very clear that unless he is allowed to run the ship, they had better find another captain.

The doctor believes that the captain is honest. (He also believes that Long John Silver is honest.) The squire says that he thinks the captain is an ". . . intolerable humbug, I declare I think his conduct unmanly, unsailorly, and downright un-English." The squire is like so many characters in English stories. He is honest, bungling, not very intelligent, but in a pinch, brave and loyal to the very end.

You can see that none of the characters in *Treasure Island* is all good or all bad. The captain is honest, but he is also short-tempered and stubborn. The squire is generous and brave. He is also too trusting and he talks too much. Even the doctor, who seems to be the most sensible man in the story, has some weaknesses. He tries to be a doctor and a fighting man at the same time. He believes that people are what they say they are. These are fine traits in a gentleman. They are dangerous ones in an adventurer.

What is important and wonderful in the way Stevenson draws his characters is that they are believable as human beings. They are not merely *types,* such as the "good guys and bad guys" in most television adventure stories.

Jim Hawkins is a brave and intelligent boy. But as most boys his age would do, he makes his part in a story really stand out. It is true enough that without him, the pirates would have won. But even when he admits that he has done something dangerous and foolish, he explains this all away by showing that everything turned out well in the end. Now, most of us are not able to get away with this kind of reasoning. Recall how he tells of the beginning of his "Shore Adventure." Most of the pirates have deliberately been allowed to go ashore on the island after Jim has told the captain, the doctor, and the squire about the plot he had overheard from the apple barrel.

> Then it was that there came into my head the first of the mad notions that contributed so much to save our lives. If six men were left [aboard ship] by Silver, it was plain our party could not take and fight the ship; and since only six were left, it was equally plain that the cabin party had no present need of my assistance. It occurred to me at once to go ashore. In a jiffy I had slipped over the side and curled up in the foresheets of the nearest boat, and almost at the same moment she shoved off.

That phrase, *"It occurred to me at once . . ."* is almost Jim's motto. It occurs to him at once: to go to the island—to find Ben Gunn's coracle—to cut the *Hispaniola* loose from her mooring—to board the schooner. It is true that these "mad notions" saved their lives. But Jim seems to have had much more than his share of luck. In addition to this, Jim *seems* really to like Long John in spite of the plot, the murder of Tom, and everything else this "big, bland-faced, one-legged pirate" was guilty of. But then, perhaps Jim is not to blame for this. Stevenson liked Long John, and probably most of the readers of *Treasure Island* have always like him also.

Finally, when the tale of *Treasure Island* is almost done, and Long John sits back of the fire in Ben Gunn's cave, he is, as Jim says, "the same bland, polite, obsequious seaman of the voyage out." And when the *Hispaniola* anchors in a tropical port to take on a new crew and provisions for the long voyage home, Ben Gunn helps his old shipmate to escape and we are told that

> The sea cook had not gone empty-handed. He had cut through a bulkhead unobserved and had removed one of the sacks of coin, worth perhaps three or four hundred guineas, to help him on his further wanderings.

"Further wanderings"—there is the key to a real romance. It never really ends. We can imagine the resourceful Long John Silver getting another pirate crew, with another tale of hidden treasure and high adventure.

You can call *Treasure Island* Jim Hawkins' story about Long John Silver. Jim is the hero and he knows it. The way he tells the tale, it is about the struggle between him and his men (the captain, doctor, and squire) and Long John and his men. Even though the captain is honest, brave, and resourceful, he is out of most of the action. Even though the doctor is the most intelligent and experienced man of them all, he does not take the risks Jim takes. He is too cautious and practical to take the boy's wild chances. About all that can be said for the squire is that he paid the bills. He seems never to understand what is happening or why it is happening. Finally, Ben Gunn seems almost to be made up of ideas left over from *Robinson Crusoe*. He is funny and pathetic, and in some ways he is a bit like the squire. In the end, he spends his share of the treasure "in nineteen days" and is "back begging on the twentieth."

Jim tells most of the story of *Treasure Island*. The part told by the doctor is almost like a report. He tells of the escape from the ship and the first fight at the stockade. It is well told and exciting, but his story has a very different quality from Jim's. There is more seriousness about it. At the battle of the stockade, the doctor tells the wounded captain ". . . Trelawney is the dead shot. Give him your gun; his own is useless."

> They exchanged guns, and Trelawney, silent and cool as he had been since the beginning of the bustle, hung a moment on his heel to see that all was fit for service. At the same time, observing Gray to be unarmed, I handed him my cutlass. It did all our hearts good to see him spit in his hand, knit his brows, and make the blade sing through the air. It was plain from every line of his body that our new hand was worth his salt.

Notice the difference when Jim recounts a scene: he and Long John are in the stockade. The other pirates have rebelled against the old sea cook. He says to Jim:

> "But see here, Jim—tit for tat—you save Long John from swinging."
>
> I was bewildered; it seemed a thing so hopeless he was asking—he, the old buccaneer, the ringleader throughout.

"What I can do, that I'll do," I said.

"It's a bargain!" cried Long John. "You speak up plucky, and by thunder I've a chance."

He hobbled to the torch where it stood propped among the firewood and took a fresh light to his pipe.

"Understand me, Jim," he said, returning. "I've a head on my shoulders, I have. I'm on squire's side now. I know you've got that ship safe somewheres. How you done it, I don't know, but safe it is . . ."

The difference that you notice in these two scenes is, of course, what Stevenson intended you to see. The first is a full-grown man's sober and clear report. The second has all the excitement of a boy's remembering what he was mixed up in.

So there it is: *Treasure Island* tells one great story from beginning to end. But remember, we called it a "romance." Like ripples on a pond, other stories spread out from it and circle within it. Ben Gunn tells a little about old Captain Flint's fight to the death with the six other pirates who helped him to bury the treasure. You would need a whole book to tell that story. Billy Bones, who was one of the toughest of all the pirates, died in an inn singing a "country love song." His life story would be very interesting. And those three pirates left on the island, did they die? Were they rescued? Did they find the rest of the treasure and save themselves?

At the end of the story, Jim tells what some of the others did with their shares of the treasure. But what about himself? He says nothing about the squire or the doctor. Could either of these gentlemen go back to the quiet life they had led? And finally, what really happened to Long John Silver? Each of us can answer these questions in his own way. But we would all probably agree that the one-legged pirate did not end his days sitting under a palm tree with his ancient parrot, telling wild sea tales to little children. Of course he would do that too because he was fond of young people, but in the back of his mind he must have always said, "there are other treasure islands waiting for me."

STUDY QUESTIONS

1. In life, most people are mixtures of strength and weakness, good and bad. Is this true of the characters in *Treasure Island?* Consider Jim Hawkins, Squire Trelawney, Long John Silver, Captain Smollett, Ben Gunn, Dr. Livesey, Israel Hands.

2. Jim Hawkins was a brave but rash boy. Can you remember situations in which he did not use his head or showed poor judgment?

What were the effects of his rashness on the fortunes of his friends?

3. Perhaps the most complex character in *Treasure Island* is Long John Silver. What is there about him that is admirable? What is there that causes you to dislike him?

4. Long John Silver might be called a cool customer. He almost always seems to have himself well under control. However, once or twice he loses control. Do you recall these instances? How do you explain them?

5. Pew, the blind man, is an interesting minor character. How does he manage to dominate Jim and others despite his blindness? How does he meet his end?

6. Billy Bones is a crude, loudmouthed braggart. What is his reaction when he comes up against a really calm and courageous man? Who is this man?

7. "There is honor among thieves," said Sir Walter Scott. What evidence is there that Stevenson believed this? Can you cite instances where the thieves in *Treasure Island* are honorable in their dealings with each other?

8. Stevenson paints the pirates as a superstitious lot. What specific evidence do you recall that, despite their roughness, they are frightened by things which would probably not frighten you?

9. What evidence is there that despite their courage and occasional cleverness the pirates probably could never make a real success of anything? What weaknesses do they have as a group?

10. Long John Silver is always able to maintain his leadership over the pirates. How is he able to do this? At one point he is "deposed." How does he win back his leadership?

11. Just after the *Hispaniola* anchors off Treasure Island, Jim sneaks ashore with the pirates. What happens during his brief stay ashore that sets the stage for the final defeat of the pirates?

12. When Long John Silver bargains with Captain Smollett in the stockade, why is it that Smollett scornfully refuses Silver's guarantee of safety in exchange for the treasure map?

13. Why does Jim set the *Hispaniola* adrift? What are the consequences of this action?

14. In his encounter with Israel Hands aboard the *Hispaniola,* Jim reveals that he is quite an immature person. How? What is it that finally enables him to defeat Hands?

15. When Jim returns to the stockade after killing Israel Hands, what does he find there? How does his mood suddenly change?

16. From the time Jim is captured by the pirates in the stockade, Long John Silver plays a dangerous double game. What is this double game? What are the possible outcomes that the sea cook hopes for?

17. At the end of Chapter 29, Jim exhibits a rather strange attitude toward the man he knows had vowed to kill him and his friends. Why does he sympathize with Long John Silver? What does this show about the boy? Do you think Long John Silver deserves the sympathy?

18. In Chapter 30, Dr. Livesey visits the sick and wounded among the pirates. Why is he willing to do this? Why do the pirates allow him to return safely? When Livesey is allowed to speak to Jim privately,

how does Jim show his bravery, even through his tears?

19. Many traits of character are exhibited in the book: courage, cunning, honesty, stubbornness, cruelty, kindness, cool-headedness. Perhaps you can think of others. Can you think of an incident or two to illustrate each of these?

20. One of the most influential people in the story never appears. Who is he? How does he influence the people and events of the story?

21. What impression do you have of the state of mind of the villagers who live near the "Admiral Benbow"? Do you admire these people?

22. What are the advantages of having Jim Hawkins narrate the story himself, that is, in the first person?

23. Why does Stevenson have Dr. Livesey narrate Chapters 16, 17, and 18?

24. Why does Dr. Livesey give the treasure map to Long John Silver? How does the sea cook attempt to influence Jim by his possession of the map?

25. When the pirates find the treasure missing from the place where it was buried (Chapter 33), what sudden change occurs in Long John Silver?

26. There are some wonderful names in *Treasure Island.* List several names of men or places in the book which appeal to you. How do the names add to the sense of excitement of the book?

27. There are a number of scenes in the book where Stevenson shows his mastery of the storyteller's craft by building suspense to a very high point. Can you recall some of these scenes? Find two or three of them in the book, note the page numbers, and prepare to read aloud to the class the five or ten lines in each scene where you found the suspense to be the greatest.

28. In addition, there are some superb action sequences. Which ones do you remember best? Choose a paragraph or two of vigorous action and prepare to read the passage aloud to the class.

29. Stevenson created the setting and the plot for *Treasure Island* from his imagination. Do you think he did a convincing job of it? Could the story actually have happened? If you do not think so, what is there about the story that you find unconvincing? If you find the story convincing and realistic, what details make it seem especially authentic?

30. If you were to write a sequel to *Treasure Island,* or if you could ask Stevenson to do so, what would be the most interesting parts of the story to carry on? What matters are left in suspense or incomplete?

31. What other stories of treasure hunts and mysterious islands have you read or seen in the movies or on television?

I Remember Mama

by John Van Druten

USUALLY plays are written to be acted. No matter how much a writer of a play puts on paper, the play only comes alive on the stage. The playwright can say what kind of person he wants for each part; he can describe in great detail what the set should look like; he can give stage directions telling what his characters do, how they look at each other, and how they should speak. But when the acting begins, the play becomes something much more than the words on the page.

A play is almost all dialogue; that is, words spoken by one person to one or more other persons. There are some sentences of instruction telling what the writer wants his actors, scene designer, and director to do. Because of this you have to read a play in a special way. In your imagination you have to do all of the things that the people who work on the staging of the play must do. First, you must tell yourself how each character looks; then, you must imagine what the place in which they are acting looks like. Finally, you must even imagine how the people sound when they talk. In fact, it is a very good idea to read some of the dialogue aloud.

Now you have done many of these things ever since you learned how to read well. You surely have done this with the other stories in this book. But here, with *I Remember Mama* you must do them deliberately. The more attention you pay to this part of play-reading, the more pleasure you will have and the better you will appreciate what you are reading.

A book or a story or a poem is published. A play is produced. It is true of course that almost all plays are published, too, but what you read on the printed page is only part of the play. The actors, the director, the set designer, the costume designer, the lighting expert, the stage manager, the producer, and the theater itself, complete with the stage and the audience, are all needed for the play to come "alive."

And yet it is probably true that many more people read plays than see them acted, or rather this was once true. Today, with television and the movies, almost everyone has seen some kind of play. But—and this is very important—there is a great difference between *looking* at a movie or a television screen and *attending* a play. Live actors make that difference. Even if the actors are just your own classmates, they add something that cannot be gotten from the screen or the printed page. That "something" is what goes on between the actor and the audience. People try to describe this "something" in many ways. They call it "sympathy" or "a response" or even "love." Whatever it is, it brings life to the words that have been written. It gives extra meaning to the actions that are described. It is a wonderful kind of magic. There is a saying among theater people: "When the curtain goes up, a miracle happens."

You and your classmates will probably want to try out some of the scenes from *I Remember Mama.* This is to be expected. A play almost says, "Act me out!"

Kathryn Forbes wrote a story called "Mama's Bank Account" from which John Van Druten made this play. You may want to read this story later and compare it to what you are about to read now.

Characters

KATRIN	AUNT JENNY	A NURSE
MAMA	AUNT SIGRID	ANOTHER NURSE
PAPA	UNCLE CHRIS	SODA CLERK
DAGMAR	A WOMAN	MADELINE
CHRISTINE	MR. THORKELSON	DOROTHY SCHILLER
NELS	DR. JOHNSON	FLORENCE DANA MOORHEAD
MR. HYDE	ARNE	BELLBOY
AUNT TRINA	Scrub woman, nurses, doctors, and hotel guests.	

The action passes in and around San Francisco some years ago.

ACT I

The period of the play is around 1910.

On either side of the stage, down[1] *front, are two small turntables, left and right, on which the shorter front scenes are played against very simplified backgrounds. As each scene finishes the lights dim and the table revolves out, leaving an unobstructed view of the main stage. The main stage is raised by two steps, above which traveler curtains open and close.*

When the curtain rises, KATRIN, *in a spotlight, is seated at a desk on the right turntable, facing the audience. She is writing.* KATRIN *is somewhere in her early twenties. She should be played by an actress who is small in stature, and capable of looking sufficiently like a child not to break the illusion in subsequent scenes. She is a blonde. Her hair, when we see her first, is in a modern "up" style, capable of being easily loosened to fall to shoulder length for the childhood scenes. She wears a very short dress, the skirt of which is concealed for the prologue by the desk behind which she is seated.*

KATRIN *writes in silence for a few moments, then puts down*

[1] *Downstage* is toward the audience; *upstage* is away from the audience. The directions *left* and *right* are from the actor's point of view.

her pen, takes up her manuscript, and begins to read aloud what she has written.

KATRIN (*reading*). "For as long as I could remember, the house on Steiner Street had been home. Papa and Mama had both been born in Norway, but they came to San Francisco because Mama's sisters were here. All of us were born here. Nels, the oldest and the only boy—my sister Christine—and the littlest sister, Dagmar." (*She puts down her manuscript and looks out front.*) It's funny, but when I look back, I always see Nels and Christine and myself looking almost as we do today. I guess that's because the people you see all the time stay the same age in your head. Dagmar's different. She was always the baby—so I see her as a baby. Even Mama—it's funny, but I always see Mama as around forty. She couldn't *always* have been forty. (*She picks up her manuscript and starts to read again.*) "Besides us, there was our boarder, Mr. Hyde. Mr. Hyde was an Englishman who had once been an actor, and Mama was very impressed by his flowery talk and courtly manners. He used to read aloud to us in the evenings. But first and foremost, I remember Mama."

[*The light dims down, leaving* KATRIN *only faintly visible. Lights come up on the main stage, revealing the house on Steiner Street—a kitchen room. It has a back flat, with a dresser C.,*[1] *holding china. On either side of the dresser is a door; the one to the R. leads to the pantry; the one to the L. to the rest of the house. The L. wall is a short one. It is the wall of the house, and contains a door upstage leading into the street, being presumably the back door of the house, but the one most commonly used as the entry door. Beyond it the street is visible, with a single lamppost L., just outside the house. Behind the room rises the house itself with upper windows lighted, and behind it a painted backdrop of the San Francisco hills, houses, and telegraph posts.*

The furniture of the kitchen is simple. A table C., with two chairs above it, armchairs at either end, and a low bench below it. Against the R. wall upstage, a large stove; below it another armchair. The window is below the door in the L. wall and has a low Norwegian chest under it.]

[1] *C.* = Center; *R.* = Right; *L.* = Left.

KATRIN'S VOICE (*continuing in the half-dark, as the scene is revealed*). "I remember that every Saturday night Mama would sit down by the kitchen table and count out the money Papa had brought home in the little envelope."

[*By now the tableau is revealed in full, and the light on* KATRIN *dwindles further. The picture is as she described.* MAMA*—looking around forty—is in the armchair R. of the table, emptying the envelope of its silver dollars and smaller coins.* PAPA*—looking a little older than* MAMA*—stands above her. His English throughout is better than hers, with less accent.*]

MAMA. You call the children, Lars. Is good they should know about money.

PAPA (*goes to door back L., and calls*). Children! Nels—Christine—Katrin!

CHILDREN'S VOICES (*off, answering*). Coming, Papa!

MAMA. You call loud for Katrin. She is in her study, maybe.

PAPA. She is where?

MAMA. Katrin make the old attic under the roof into a study.

PAPA (*amused*). So? (*Shouting*) Katrin! Katrin!

KATRIN (*still at her desk, down front*). Yes, Papa. I heard.

PAPA (*returning to the room*). A study now, huh? What does Katrin study?

MAMA. I think Katrin wants to be author.

PAPA. Author?

MAMA. Stories she will write. For the magazines. And books, too, maybe, one day.

PAPA (*taking out his pipe*). Is good pay to be author?

MAMA. I don't know. For magazines, I think maybe yes. For books, I think no.

PAPA. Then she become writer for magazines.

MAMA. Maybe. But I like she writes books. Like the ones Mr. Hyde reads us.

[DAGMAR *enters from the pantry. She is a plump child of about eight and carries an alley cat in her arms.*]

Dagmar, you bring that cat in again?

DAGMAR. Sure, she's my Elizabeth—my beautiful Elizabeth!

[*She crosses to the chest under the window, and sits, nursing the cat.*]

PAPA. Poor Elizabeth looks as if she had been in fight again.

DAGMAR. Not poor Elizabeth. *Brave* Elizabeth. Elizabeth's a Viking cat. She fights for her honor!

PAPA (*exchanging an amused glance with* MAMA). And just what is a cat's honor, little one?

DAGMAR. The honor of being the bravest cat in San Francisco.

[CHRISTINE *comes in back L. She, like* KATRIN, *should be played by a small young actress, but not a child. Her hair is to her shoulders—her dress short—her age indeterminate. Actually, she is about 13 at this time. She is the cool, aloof, matter-of-fact one of the family.*]

Aren't you, Elizabeth?

CHRISTINE (*sitting above the table*). That disgusting cat!

DAGMAR. She's not disgusting. She's beautiful. Beautiful as the dawn!

CHRISTINE. And when have *you* ever seen the dawn?

DAGMAR. I haven't seen it, but Mr. Hyde read to us about it.

[MR. HYDE *comes in from door back L. He is a slightly seedy, long-haired man in his fifties. Rather of the old-fashioned English "laddie" actor type. He wears a very shabby long overcoat, with a deplorable fur collar, and carries his hat. His accent is English.*]

Didn't you, Mr. Hyde? Didn't you read to us about the dawn?

MR. HYDE. I did, my child of joy. The dawn, the rosy-finger-tipped Aurora . . .

DAGMAR. When can I get to *see* the dawn, Mama?

MAMA. Any morning you get up early.

DAGMAR. Is there a dawn every morning?

MAMA. Sure.

DAGMAR (*incredulous* [1]). It's all that beautiful, and it happens every *morning?* Why didn't anyone *tell* me?

MR. HYDE. My child, that is what the poets are for. To tell you of *all* the beautiful things that are happening every day, and that no one sees until they tell them.

[1] *incredulous* (ĭn·krĕd′ů·lŭs): finding it hard to believe.

[*He starts for the door L.*]

MAMA. You go out, Mr. Hyde?

MR. HYDE. For a few moments only, dear madam. To buy myself a modicum [1] of that tawny weed, tobacco, that I lust after, as Ben Jonson says. I shall be back in time for our nightly reading.

[*He goes out and disappears down the street, into the wings, off L.*]

MAMA (*who has gone to the door back L., calls with a good deal of sharpness and firmness*). Nels! Katrin! You do not hear Papa call you?

NELS (*from off, upstairs*). Coming, Mama!

KATRIN (*at her desk*). Yes, Mama. I'm coming.

[*She rises. In her few moments in the dark, she has loosened her hair to her shoulders, and we see that her skirt is short as she walks from her desk, and up the steps into the set. As soon as she has left it, the turntable revolves out. Immediately after her,* NELS *comes in back L. He is a tall, strapping young fellow old enough to look 18 or 19, or 15 or 16, according to his dress, or demeanor. Now, he is about 15.*]

PAPA. So now all are here.

MAMA. Come, then.

[CHRISTINE, NELS, *and* KATRIN *gather around the table.* DAGMAR *remains crooning to* ELIZABETH. MAMA *is sorting coins.*]

First, for the landlord.

[*She makes a pile of silver dollars. It gets pushed down the table from one member of the family to the next, each speaking as he passes it.* PAPA *comes last.*]

NELS (*passing it on*). For the landlord.

KATRIN (*doing likewise*). For the landlord.

CHRISTINE (*passing it to* PAPA). The landlord.

PAPA. For the landlord.

[*He dumps the pile at his end of the table, writing on a piece of paper, which he wraps around the pile.*]

[1] *modicum* (mŏd′ĭ·kŭm): a small quantity.

MAMA (*who has been sorting*). For the grocer.

[*The business is repeated. During this repeat,* DAGMAR'S *crooning to the cat becomes audible, contrapuntally*[1] *to the repetitions of "For the grocer."*]

DAGMAR (*in a crescendo*[2]). In all the United States no cat was as brave as Elizabeth. (*Fortissimo.*[3]) In all the *world* no cat was as brave as Elizabeth!

MAMA (*gently*)..Hush, Dagmar. Quietly. You put Elizabeth back into the pantry.

DAGMAR (*in a loud stage whisper as she crosses to pantry*). In Heaven or HELL no cat was as brave as Elizabeth!

[*She goes out with the cat.*]

MAMA. For Katrin's shoes to be half-soled. (*She passes a half dollar.*)

NELS. Katrin's shoes.

KATRIN (*proudly*). *My* shoes!

CHRISTINE (*contemptuously*). Katrin's old shoes.

PAPA. Katrin's shoes.

CHRISTINE. Mama, Teacher says this week I'll need a new notebook.

MAMA. How much it will be?

CHRISTINE. A dime.

MAMA (*giving her a dime*). For the notebook. You don't lose it.

CHRISTINE. I won't lose it. (*She wraps it in her handkerchief.*)

MAMA. You take care when you blow your nose.

CHRISTINE. I'll take care.

PAPA. Is all, Mama?

MAMA. Is all for this week. Is good. We do not have to go to the Bank.

[*She starts to gather up the few remaining coins.* KATRIN *leaves the group, comes and sits on steps, front.*]

NELS. Mama . . .

[1] *contrapuntally* (kŏn′trȧ·pŭn′tăl·ĭ): like two different melodies sung at the same time. [2] *crescendo* (krĕ·shĕn′dō): increasing in volume. [3] *fortissimo* (fôr·tĭs′ĭ·mō): very loud.

[*She looks up, catching an urgency in his tone.* PAPA *suspends smoking for a moment.*]

Mama, I'll be graduating from grammar school next month. Could I . . . could I go on to High, do you think?

MAMA (*pleased*). You want to go to High School?

NELS. I'd like to . . . if you think I could.

MAMA. Is good.

[PAPA *nods approvingly.*]

NELS (*awkwardly*). It . . . it'll cost a little money. I've got it all written down. (*Producing a piece of paper from his pocket*) Carfare, clothes, notebooks, things I'll really need. I figured it out with Cy Nichols. He went to High last year.

[MAMA *and* PAPA *come closer together, to look at the paper he puts before them.*]

MAMA. Get the *Little* Bank, Christine.

[CHRISTINE *gets a small box from the dresser.*]

KATRIN (*from the steps—herself again, in the present—looking out front*). The Little Bank! That was the most important thing in the whole house. It was a box we used to keep for emergencies—like the time when Dagmar had croup and Papa had to go and get medicine to put in a steam kettle. I can *smell* that medicine now! The things that came out of the Little Bank! Mama was always going to buy herself a warm coat out of it, when there was enough, only there never was.

[*Meanwhile,* MAMA *has been counting the contents.*]

NELS (*anxiously*). Is there enough, Mama?

MAMA (*shaking her head*). Is not much in the Little Bank right now. We give to the dentist, you remember? And for your roller skates?

NELS (*his face falling*). I know. And there's your warm coat you've been saving for.

MAMA. The coat I can get another time. But even so . . . (*She shakes her head.*)

CHRISTINE. You mean Nels can't go to High?

MAMA. Is not enough here. We do not want to have to go to the Bank, do we?

NELS. No, Mama, no. I'll work in Dillon's grocery after school.

[MAMA *writes a figure on the paper and starts to count on her fingers.* PAPA *looks over, and does the sum in his head.*]

PAPA. Is not enough.

MAMA (*finishing on her fingers against her collarbone*). No, is not enough.

PAPA (*taking his pipe out of his mouth and looking at it a long time*). I give up tobacco.

[MAMA *looks at him, almost speaks, then just touches his sleeve, writes another figure and starts on her fingers again.*]

CHRISTINE. I'll mind the Maxwell children Friday nights. Katrin can help me.

[MAMA *writes another figure.* PAPA *looks it over—calculates again, nods with satisfaction.*]

MAMA (*triumphantly*). Is good! Is enough!

NELS. Gee!

MAMA. We do not have to go to the Bank.

[DAGMAR *returns, without the cat.*]

DAGMAR (*hearing the last line*). Where is the Bank?

CHRISTINE. Downtown.

DAGMAR. What's it look like?

CHRISTINE. Just a building.

DAGMAR. Like a prison?

CHRISTINE (*sharply*). No, nothing like a prison.

DAGMAR. Well, then, why does Mama always say, "We don't want to go to the Bank"?

CHRISTINE. Because . . . well, because no one ever wants to go to the Bank.

DAGMAR. Why not?

CHRISTINE. Because if we went to the Bank all the time, there'd be no money left there. And then if we couldn't pay our rent, they'd turn us out like Mrs. Jensen down the street.

DAGMAR. You mean it's like saving some of your candy for tomorrow?

MAMA. Yes, my Dagmar. Is exactly like saving your candy.

DAGMAR. But if . . . if all the other people go to the Bank, then there won't be any money left for us, either.

NELS (*kindly*). It isn't like that, Dagmar. Everyone can only get so much.

DAGMAR. How much?

NELS. However much you've got there . . . put away. You see, it's *our* money that we put there, to keep safe.

DAGMAR. When did we put it there?

NELS. I . . . I don't know when. A long time back, I guess. Wasn't it, Mama?

MAMA. Is enough about the Bank.

DAGMAR. How much money have we got in the Bank?

NELS. I don't know. How much, Mama?

MAMA. Enough.

[*During the last speeches* AUNT TRINA *appears from the wings down front L. She is a timid, mouselike little woman of about forty, with some prettiness about her. She wears her hat and coat, and a pathetic feather boa.*[1] *She comes up the street and knocks on the house door.*]

MAMA (*hearing the knock*). Was the door?

CHRISTINE (*quickly*). If it's the Aunts, I'm going to my boodwar.

KATRIN (*rising, entering the scene*). And I'm going to my study.

MAMA (*stopping them*). You cannot run away. We must be polite to the Aunts. (PAPA *has opened the door.*) Why, is Trina!

PAPA. Trina, and all by herself!

MAMA. Say good evening to Aunt Trina, children.

CHILDREN (*together*). Good evening, Aunt Trina.

TRINA. Good evening, children. How well they all look.

MAMA. You have a feather boa. Is new. (*Inspecting it*) Beautiful.

TRINA (*simpering a little*). It was a present.

MAMA (*smiling*). A present! Look, Lars. Trina has a present.

PAPA (*feeling it*). Is fine.

[*He puts Trina's hat, coat, and boa on the chest under the window.*]

[1] *boa* (bō′ȧ): a scarf.

MAMA. Jenny and Sigrid don't come with you, Trina?

TRINA (*embarrassed*). No, I . . . I didn't tell them I was coming. I want to talk to you, Marta.

MAMA (*smiling*). So? Sit then, and we talk.

TRINA (*nervously agitated*). Could we talk alone?

MAMA. Alone?

TRINA. If you wouldn't mind.

MAMA (*going to the stove*). Children, you leave us alone a little. I call you. Dagmar, you go with Katrin.

KATRIN (*protesting*). Oh, but, Mama . . .

MAMA (*firmly*). Katrin, you take Dagmar!

KATRIN. Yes, Mama. (*Pushing* DAGMAR, *resentfully*) Come on.

[*The* CHILDREN *go out back L.*]

MAMA. Now—what is it, Trina?

TRINA (*looking down, embarrassed*). Marta . . .

MAMA (*helpfully*). Yes?

TRINA. Oh, no, I can't say it.

MAMA (*anxiously*). Trina, what is it?

TRINA. It's . . . something very personal.

MAMA. You want Lars should go outside?

TRINA. Would you mind, Lars? Just for a minute?

PAPA (*good-humoredly*). No, I go. I know what women's secrets are. (*Teasing*) As your Uncle Chris say—"Vomen! Pff!"

MAMA. You have your pipe, Lars? Is fine night. (PAPA *takes out his pipe—then lays it down.*) What is it?

PAPA. I forget. I give up tobacco.

MAMA. Is still some tobacco in your pouch? (PAPA *nods.*) Then you do not give up tobacco till you have finish. You give up *more* tobacco—not the tobacco you already have.

PAPA. Is not right, Marta.

[*He pats her, takes his pipe, and goes out L., standing outside the house, under the lamppost, and looking up at the stars, smoking.*]

MAMA. So, Trina. Now. What is it?

TRINA. Marta . . . I want to get married.

MAMA. You mean . . . you want to get married, or there is someone you want to marry?

TRINA. There's someone I want to marry.

MAMA. Does *he* want to marry *you?*

TRINA. He says he does.

MAMA (*delighted*). Trina! Is wonderful!

TRINA (*crying a little*). *I* think it is.

MAMA. Who is?

TRINA. Mr. Thorkelson.

MAMA. From the Funeral Parlor?

[TRINA *nods.* MAMA *nods, speculatively, but with less enthusiasm.*]

TRINA. I know he isn't very handsome or . . . or tall. I know it isn't what most people would think a very nice profession, but . . .

MAMA. You love him, Trina?

[TRINA *nods ecstatically.*]

Then is good. (*She pats* TRINA'S *hand.*)

TRINA. Marta, will you . . . will you help me tell the others?

MAMA. Oh . . . Jenny and Sigrid . . . they do not know?

TRINA. No. I was afraid they'd laugh at me. But if *you* tell them . . .

MAMA. Jenny will not like you tell me first.

TRINA (*desperately*). I can't help that. You've got to tell them not to laugh at me. If they laugh at me, I'll . . . I'll kill myself.

MAMA (*with decision*). Jenny and Sigrid will not laugh. I promise you, Trina.

TRINA. Oh, thank you, Marta. And . . . Uncle Chris?

MAMA (*with some seriousness*). Ah!

TRINA. Will you talk to him?

MAMA. It is Mr. Thorkelson who must talk to Uncle Chris. Always it is the husband who must talk to the head of the family.

TRINA. Yes. I know, but . . . well, Uncle Chris is so very frightening. He's so big and black, and he shouts so. And Mr. Thorkelson is . . . well, kind of timid, really.

MAMA (*gently*). But, Trina, if he is to be your husband, he must learn not to be timid. You do not want husband should be timid. *You* are timid. Is not good when *both* are timid. (*Then firmly*) No! Jenny and Sigrid I speak to, but Mr. Thorkelson must go to Uncle Chris.

PAPA (*re-entering the house*). Marta, Trina, I do not want to interrupt your talk, but Jenny and Sigrid are coming.

TRINA (*alarmed*). Oh, dear!

PAPA. I see them get off the cable car. They come up the hill.

TRINA (*in a flurry*). I'd better go to your room for a minute.

[*She starts for the door, turns back, gets her things from the chest, and runs out, carrying them, back L. Meanwhile,* MAMA *has been whispering the news to* PAPA.]

MAMA. The coffee is ready—I get more cups.

[*During the above,* AUNTS JENNY *and* SIGRID *have entered from the wings L., front.* JENNY *is a domineering woman in her fifties;* SIGRID, *whining and complaining.*]

SIGRID (*in the street*). Wait, Jenny, I must get my breath. This hill kills me every time I climb it.

JENNY. You climbed bigger hills than that in the old country.

SIGRID. I was a *girl* in the old country.

[*They march to the door and knock*—SIGRID *following* JENNY.]

MAMA (*opening the door to them*). Jenny. Sigrid. Is surprise. (*To* SIGRID) Where's Ole?

SIGRID. Working. He's always working. I never see anything of him at all.

MAMA (*crossing to the stove for coffeepot*). Is good to work.

SIGRID. It's good to see your husband once in a while, too.

JENNY (*no nonsense about her*). Has Trina been here?

MAMA. Trina?

JENNY. She's gone somewhere. And she doesn't know anyone but *you*. . . .

MAMA. That is what *you* think.

JENNY. What do you mean by that?

MAMA. Give Lars your coat. I give you some coffee. Then we talk about Trina.

SIGRID (*as* PAPA *helps with coats*). She *has* been here?

MAMA. Yes, she has been here. (*Pouring coffee and passing cups*)

JENNY. What did Trina want?

MAMA. She want to talk to me.

JENNY. What about?

MAMA. Marriage.

SIGRID. What?

MAMA (*pouring calmly*). Marriage. (*Passing Sigrid's cup*) Trina wants to get married.

JENNY. That's no news. Of course she wants to get married. Every old maid wants to get married.

MAMA. There is someone who wants to marry Trina.

JENNY. Who'd want to marry Trina?

MAMA. Mr. Thorkelson.

SIGRID. Peter Thorkelson? Little Peter? (*She gestures a midget.*)

MAMA. He is not so little.

SIGRID. He's hardly bigger than my Arne—and Arne is not ten yet.

MAMA. So he is hardly bigger than your Arne. Does every husband have to be big man?

JENNY. Trina's making it up. That happens with old maids, when they get to Trina's age.

MAMA (*firmly*). No, Jenny—it is true. Mr. Thorkelson wants to marry Trina.

JENNY (*changing her tactics slightly*). Mr. Thorkelson. She'd be the laughing stock. (*She laughs.*)

MAMA (*moving to her*). Jenny, Trina is here. She will come in in a minute. This is serious for her. You will not laugh at her.

JENNY. I shall do what I please.

MAMA. No, Jenny, you will not.

JENNY. And why won't I?

MAMA. Because I will not let you.

JENNY. And how will you stop me?

MAMA. If you laugh at Trina, I will tell her of the time before your wedding when your husband try to run away.

SIGRID. What is that?

JENNY. Who told you that?

MAMA. I know.

SIGRID (*intrigued*). Erik . . . tried to run away?

JENNY. It's not true.

MAMA. Then you do not mind if I tell Trina.

JENNY. Uncle Chris told you.

SIGRID (*tenaciously*[1]). Tried to run away?

MAMA. It does not matter, Sigrid. Jenny will not laugh at Trina now. Nor will you! For if *you* laugh at her, I will tell of your

[1] *tenaciously* (tê·nā′shŭs·lĭ): refusing to let go.

wedding night with Ole, when you cry all the time, and he bring you home to Mother.

PAPA (*with sudden enjoyment*). This I do *not* know!

MAMA (*reprovingly*). Is no need you should know. I do not tell these stories for spite—only so they do not laugh at Trina. Call her, Lars. You like more coffee, Jenny? Sigrid?

[PAPA *goes to the door back L., calls, "Trina."* MAMA *pours coffee for* JENNY. MR. HYDE *reappears down front L., and lets himself into the house.*]

MR. HYDE (*seeing company*). Oh, I beg your pardon. I was not aware . . .

MAMA. Mr. Hyde, these are my sisters.

MR. HYDE. Enchanted, ladies. Madame. Madame. The Three Graces.

[*He bows.* SIGRID *giggles coyly. He goes to the door back L.*]

You will excuse me?

MAMA. Sure, Mr. Hyde.

MR. HYDE. I shall be in my room.

[*He goes out.*]

JENNY. So *that's* your famous boarder. Has he paid you his rent yet? Three months he's been here, hasn't he?

MAMA. Is hard to ask. Surely he will pay soon.

JENNY (*with a snort*). Surely he won't! If I ran my boarding-house the way you run this place . . .

PAPA. Maybe your boarders wouldn't always leave you.

JENNY. If Marta thinks she's going to get the warm coat she's always talking about out of *that* one . . .

MAMA. Jenny, Mr. Hyde is a gentleman. He reads to us aloud. Wonderful books . . . Longfellow, and Charles Dickens, and Fenimore Kipling.

[TRINA *steals back.*]

MAMA (*seeing her hesitant in the doorway*). Come in, Trina. The coffee is getting cold. (*She pours a cup. There is a silence.*) I tell them.

JENNY. Why did you come to Marta first?

PAPA. She thought Marta would understand.

JENNY. Aren't Sigrid and I married women, too?

PAPA. You have been married longer than Marta. She think maybe you forget.

JENNY. What sort of a living does Mr. Thorkelson make?

TRINA. I . . . I haven't asked.

SIGRID. Can he keep you?

TRINA. I don't think he would have asked me to marry him if he couldn't.

JENNY. Maybe he thinks you are going to keep *him.*

MAMA (*warningly*). Jenny!

SIGRID. Maybe he thinks Trina will have a dowry [1] like the girls at home.

TRINA. Well, why shouldn't I? You all had dowries. . . .

JENNY. We were married in Norway. And our parents were alive. Where would your dowry come from, I'd like to know?

TRINA. Uncle Chris. He's head of the family.

JENNY. And who will ask him?

TRINA. He won't need asking. When Mr. Thorkelson goes to see him . . .

JENNY. Uncle Chris will eat him!

SIGRID (*giggling maliciously*). Little Peter and Uncle Chris!

MAMA (*with meaning*). Maybe Uncle Chris will tell him some family stories. He knows many, does Uncle Chris.

[*The* AUNTS *put down their cups, discomfited.*[2]]

JENNY (*to change the subject*). Where are the children? Aren't we going to see them before we go?

PAPA. Of course, I'll call them. (*He goes to the door and does so, shouting.*) Children! Your Aunts are *leaving!*

CHILDREN'S VOICES (*eagerly*). Coming, Papa!

JENNY. You come with us, Trina?

MAMA. I think maybe Trina like to stay here and listen to Mr. Hyde read to us. You like, Trina?

TRINA. Well, if I wouldn't be in the way. I asked Mr. Thorkelson to call for me here. He'll see me home. I'll help you with the coffee things.

[1] *dowry* (dou′rĭ): money or property brought by a bride to her husband as a part of the marriage agreement. [2] *discomfited* (dĭs·kŭm′fĭt·ĕd): embarrassed.

[*She takes the tray of coffee cups and goes into the pantry.* KATRIN *returns, back L. She carries her diary,* DAGMAR *follows her, and behind them,* CHRISTINE.]

KATRIN *and* DAGMAR (*curtsying*). Good evening, Aunt Sigrid. Good evening, Aunt Jenny.

[CHRISTINE *sketches a perfunctory curtsy without speaking.*]

JENNY. Where have *you* all been hiding yourselves?

DAGMAR (*going into the pantry*). We've been in Christine's boodwar.

JENNY. Her *what?*

MAMA. Christine makes the little closet into a boudoir. I give her those bead portieres,[1] Jenny, that you lend us when we come from the old country.

SIGRID. And what does she do there?

CHRISTINE (*impertinently*). What people usually do in boudoirs.

MAMA. Christine, that is rude. It is her little place to herself.

[NELS *enters, back L.*]

NELS. Hello, Aunt Sigrid. Hello, Aunt Jenny.

SIGRID (*shaking hands*). Good evening, Nels. My, how tall he is getting!

MAMA (*proudly*). Yes, is almost as tall as his Papa.

SIGRID. He looks to me as if he was outgrowing his strength. Dagmar was looking pale, too.

[DAGMAR *returns now, carrying the cat again.*]

SIGRID (*jumping*). Goodness, what a horrid-looking cat.

DAGMAR. She's not. She's beautiful.

PAPA. Is her new friend. She goes with Dagmar everywhere.

CHRISTINE. She does. First thing you know, she'll have the cat sleeping with her.

DAGMAR (*eagerly*). Oh, Mama, can I? Can I, Mama?

JENNY. Certainly not. Don't you know a cat draws breath from a sleeping child? You wouldn't want to wake up some morning *smothered,* would you?

DAGMAR. I wouldn't care. Elizabeth can have *all* my breath! (*She blows into the cat's face.*) There!

[1] *portiere* (pōr·tyâr′): a curtain to hang across a doorway.

JENNY (*putting on gloves*). Elizabeth—what a very silly name for a cat.

NELS. It's a very silly name for *that* cat. It's a Tom. So you'd better think up another name for him.

DAGMAR. I won't. He's Elizabeth. And he's going to *stay* Elizabeth.

PAPA. We could call him *Uncle* Elizabeth!

DAGMAR (*laughing delightedly*). Uncle Elizabeth! Do you hear, Elizabeth? You're called *Uncle* Elizabeth now!

JENNY. Such foolishness! Well, good-by, all. Marta. Lars.

[*Good-bys are exchanged all around, the* CHILDREN *curtsying formally*.]

MAMA. Good-by, Jenny. Good-by, Sigrid. Nels, you go tell Mr. Hyde we are ready for the reading.

[NELS *goes off, back L. The* AUNTS *leave and walk down L.* MAMA *stands in the doorway, waving good-by*.]

SIGRID (*as they go*). Well, I never thought we'd live to see Trina get married.

JENNY. She's not married yet. She's got Uncle Chris to deal with first.

[*They disappear into wings L*.]

MAMA (*returning to the room and calling into the pantry*). Trina, they have gone. Dagmar, you put Elizabeth out for the night now.

DAGMAR (*correcting her*). *Uncle* Elizabeth!

MAMA. *Uncle* Elizabeth!!

[DAGMAR *goes out into the pantry with the cat.* TRINA *comes in as* MR. HYDE *and* NELS *return back L*.]

Mr. Hyde, this is my sister Trina.

MR. HYDE (*bowing*). Enchanted!

MAMA (*seating herself R. of the table*). Mr. Hyde reads to us "The Tales From Two Cities." Is a beautiful story. But sad.

TRINA (*brightly*). I like sad stories. (*She gets out her handkerchief*.)

[*The whole family group themselves around the table,* DAGMAR *returning and seating herself on the floor below* MAMA. MR.

HYDE *takes the armchair L. of table.* KATRIN *is on the steps R. front.*]

MR. HYDE. Tonight, I would like to finish it.

MAMA. Is good.

MR. HYDE. Are you ready?

CHILDREN. Yes, please, Mr. Hyde.

MR. HYDE. I will go on from where we left off. (*He starts to read.*) "In the black prison of the Conciergerie, the doomed of the day awaited their fate. They were in number as the weeks of the year. Fifty-two were to roll that afternoon on the life-tide of the City to the boundless, everlasting sea. . . ."

[*The lights dim down slowly, leaving spots on* KATRIN *and* MR. HYDE *only.*]

KATRIN. I don't think I shall ever forget that night. It was almost midnight when he came to the end, and none of us had noticed.

MR. HYDE (*reading from the last page*). "It is a far, far better thing that I do than I have ever done; it is a far, far better rest that I go to than I have ever known." (*He closes the book.*) "The End."

[*The R. turntable revolves in again.* KATRIN *rises from the step, and crosses to her desk on the turntable.*]

KATRIN. I wrote in my diary that night before I went to bed. (*She reads aloud from it.*) "Tonight Mr. Hyde finished *The Tale of Two Cities*. The closing chapters are indeed superb. How beautiful a thing is self-sacrifice. I wish there were someone *I* could die for." (*She sits looking out front.*) Mr. Hyde read us all kinds of books. He thrilled us with *Treasure Island,* and terrified us with *The Hound of the Baskervilles.* I can still remember the horror in his voice as he read . . .

MR. HYDE (*still on the main stage in his spot, reading*). "Dr. Mortimer looked strangely at us for an instant, and his voice sank almost to a whisper as he answered: 'Mr. Holmes, they were the footprints of a gigantic *hound!*' " (*He closes the book.*) We will continue tomorrow night. If you are interested.

KATRIN (*looking out front*). If we were interested! You couldn't have kept us from it. It meant a lot to Mama, too, because Nels stopped going nights to the street corner to hang about with the neighborhood boys. The night they got into trouble for breaking into Mr. Dillon's store, Nels was home with us. And sometimes Mr. Hyde read us poetry. "The Lady of the Lake" . . . and "The Rime of the Ancient Mariner."

MR. HYDE (*reading*).

"About, about, in reel and rout
The death fires danced at night.
The water, like a witch's oils,
Burnt green and blue and white."

[*His spot goes out, and the traveler curtains close on the kitchen scene.*]

KATRIN. There were many nights I couldn't sleep for the way he had set my imagination dancing. (*Reading from her diary again*) "What a wonderful thing is literature, transporting us to realms unknown." (*To herself*) And all the time my schoolteacher kept telling me that I ought to write about things I knew. I did write a piece for her once about Uncle Chris, and she said it wasn't nice to write like that about a member of one's own family. Papa called Mama's Uncle Chris a black Norwegian, because of his dark hair and fierce mustache, but there were others in the family who claimed that he was black in a different way. The Aunts, for example.

[*Spot goes up on L. front turntable, representing Jenny's kitchen.* JENNY *and* TRINA *are discovered.* JENNY *is rolling pastry.* TRINA *is crocheting.*]

JENNY. Black! I'll say he's black. Black in his heart. Cursing and swearing . . .

TRINA. Marta says that's only because it hurts him to walk.

JENNY. Rubbish. I know all about his limp and the accident back in the old country—but has anyone ever heard him complain? Marta's always making excuses for him.

TRINA. I know . . . but he *is* good to the children. All those oranges he's always sending them . . .

JENNY. Oranges! What good is oranges? Turn 'em yellow. They're the only things he's ever been known to give away, anyway. He's got other uses for his money.

TRINA. What you mean?

JENNY. Bottles! And that woman he lives with!

TRINA. He *says* she's his housekeeper.

JENNY. Well, he couldn't very well come right out and call her what she is, could he? Though *I* will one of these days. And to his face, too.

[SIGRID *comes through the curtains C. She crosses to* JENNY *and* TRINA.]

SIGRID. Jenny. Trina. What do you think? What do you think Uncle Chris has done now?

TRINA. What?

JENNY. Tell us.

SIGRID. You know my little Arne's knee—that fall he had two months ago? The man at the drugstore said it was only a bruise, but today it was hurting him again, so I left him home when I went to do the marketing. I asked Mrs. Schultz next door to keep an eye on him, and who should turn up, not ten minutes after I'd gone, but Uncle Chris. And what do you think?

JENNY. Well, tell us, if you're going to. Don't keep *asking* us.

SIGRID. He took one look at Arne's knee, bundled him into that rattletrap old automobile of his, and rushed him straight off to the hospital. I've just come from there . . . and what do you think? They've operated! They've got him in plaster of Paris!

JENNY. Without consulting you?

SIGRID. It seems the doctor is a friend of his . . . that's why he did it. No, this time he's gone too far. To put a child of Arne's age through all that pain! They wouldn't even let me *see* Arne. I'm going to tell Uncle Chris exactly what I think of him. . . .

JENNY. That's right.

SIGRID. I'm going to tell him right now. (*Weakening a little*) Come with me, Jenny.

JENNY. Well, I . . . No, I can't leave my baking.

SIGRID. You must, Jenny. We must stand together. You come, too, Trina, and ask about your dowry. *Make* him give it to you.

TRINA. Oh, but . . . Marta said Mr. Thorkelson should do that. . . .

JENNY. Well, then, go and get Mr. Thorkelson. Go down to the mortuary and get him now. Sigrid's quite right. We girls have got to stand together!

[*Blackout. Turntable revolves out.*]

KATRIN (*at her desk*). Nobody knew where Uncle Chris lived. That was part of the mystery about him. He used to roam up and down the state buying up farms and ranches that had gone to pieces, and bullying them back into prosperity. Then he'd sell at a profit and move on again. Two or three times a year he'd descend on the city in his automobile and come roaring and stamping into our house.

[*Her light dims. The sound of a very old and noisy Ford car changing gears is heard off L. A grinding and screaming as it comes to a standstill. Then* UNCLE CHRIS'S VOICE, *shouting.*]

UNCLE CHRIS'S VOICE. Marta! Lars! Children—vere are you?

[*The curtains part on the kitchen again. Outside in the street is Uncle Chris's car—an antique model. A woman is seated beside the empty driver's seat.* UNCLE CHRIS *is knocking on the house door. He is an elderly, powerful, swarthy man with a limp. In the kitchen,* NELS *and* CHRISTINE *are cowering.*]

UNCLE CHRIS. Marta! Lars!

CHRISTINE (*scared*). It's Uncle Chris.

NELS (*equally so*). I know.

CHRISTINE. What'll we do?

UNCLE CHRIS. Is nobody home? Hey, there—is nobody home? (*Banging on the door*) Hey—someone—answer the door.

[*He tries the door handle; it opens and he strides, limpingly, in. He has a strong accent and uses the Norwegian pronunciation of the children's names.*]

So, vat is—you do not answer the door? You do not hear me calling? (*The* CHILDREN *cower silently.*) I say, you do not hear me calling? I do not call loud enough?

CHRISTINE. Y-yes, Uncle Chris.

UNCLE CHRIS. Which yes? Yes, you do not hear me—or yes I do not call loud enough?

NELS. We heard you, Uncle Chris.

UNCLE CHRIS. Then why you do not come?

NELS. We . . . we were just going to.

[KATRIN *has left her desk and has come up the steps.*]

UNCLE CHRIS. Let me look at you. You too, Katrinë, do not stand there—come and let me look at you.

[*They line up as though for inspection. He thumps* NELS *between the shoulder blades.*]

Stand tall! (*They all straighten up.*) Um-hum. By the dresser, where the marks are.

[NELS *goes to the wall by the dresser.* UNCLE CHRIS *compares his mark with the previous one—and makes a new one on the wall, writing by it.*]

Two inches. Two inches in . . . (*examining the date*) six months. Is good. Christinë. (CHRISTINE *replaces* NELS.) Show me your teeth. (*She does so.*) You brush them goot? (*She nods.*) Nils, there is a box of oranges in the automobile. You fetch them in.

[NELS *goes out L.* UNCLE CHRIS *measures* CHRISTINE.]

Where is the little von? Dagmar?

KATRIN. She's sick, Uncle Chris.

UNCLE CHRIS (*arrested*). Sick? What is the matter with her?

KATRIN. It's her ear. She's had an earache for two days. Bad earache. Mama sent for the doctor.

UNCLE CHRIS. Goot doctor? What he say?

KATRIN. He's in there now.

[*She points off, back L. Meanwhile* CHRISTINE *has remained standing by the wall, afraid to move.*]

UNCLE CHRIS. I go in.

[*He starts to the door back L., but* MAMA *and* DR. JOHNSON *come into the room as he does so. During this* NELS *has gone to the car, and with nervous smiles at the woman seated by the driver's seat, has heaved out a huge box of oranges. He returns with the oranges during the ensuing scene.*]

MAMA (*greeting him*). Uncle Chris.

UNCLE CHRIS. How is with Dagmar?

MAMA. Is bad. Doctor, this is my uncle, Mr. Halvorsen.

DOCTOR. How do you do, sir?

UNCLE CHRIS. What is with the child?

DOCTOR. We must get her to a hospital. At once. We'll have to operate.

MAMA. Operate?

DOCTOR. I'm afraid so.

MAMA. Can wait? Until my husband comes home from work?

DOCTOR. I'm afraid not. Her best chance is for us to operate immediately.

MAMA (*after a second*). We go. (*She goes to the dresser for the Little Bank.*)

UNCLE CHRIS (*who has watched her decision with approval, turns to the doctor*). What is with the child?

DOCTOR. I'm afraid it's a mastoid.[1]

UNCLE CHRIS. Ah . . . then you operate immediately.

DOCTOR (*resenting this*). That's what I said.

UNCLE CHRIS. Immediately!

MAMA (*who has poured the contents of the Little Bank onto the table*). Doctor . . . is enough?

DOCTOR. I was thinking of the County Hospital.

MAMA. No. No. We pay. Is enough?

KATRIN. If there isn't we can go to the Bank.

CHRISTINE. We've got a Bank Account.

MAMA. Is enough without we go to the Bank, Doctor? My husband is carpenter. Make good money.

UNCLE CHRIS. If there is need of money, *I* pay.

DOCTOR (*mainly in dislike of Uncle Chris*). It'll be all right. We'll take her to the Clinic. You pay what you can afford.

UNCLE CHRIS. Goot. Goot. I have a patient there already. My nephew, Arne. They operate this morning on his knee.

DOCTOR. Are you a physician, sir?

UNCLE CHRIS. I am better physician than most doctors. Nils, there, my other nephew, he become doctor when he grow up.

[NELS *looks up, surprised.*]

DOCTOR (*chillily*). Oh, indeed . . . very interesting. Well, now, if you will have the child at the Clinic in . . . shall we say an hour's time . . .

[1] *mastoid* (măs′toid): a bone just behind the ear. The doctor means that it is infected.

UNCLE CHRIS. The child will be at the Clinic in *ten minutes'* time. I haf my automobile.

DOCTOR. I can hardly make arrangements in ten minutes.

UNCLE CHRIS. *I* make arrangements. I know doctors.

MAMA. Uncle Chris, Dr. Johnson arrange. He is good doctor.

DOCTOR (*ironically*). Thank you, madam.

MAMA. You go, Doctor. We come.

DOCTOR. Very well, in an hour, then. And Dagmar will be well taken care of, I promise you. I will do the operation myself.

UNCLE CHRIS. I watch.

DOCTOR. You will do no such thing, sir.

UNCLE CHRIS. Always I watch operations. I am head of family.

DOCTOR. I allow no one to attend my operations.

UNCLE CHRIS. Are so bad?

DOCTOR (*to* MAMA). Mrs. Hanson, if I am to undertake this operation and the care of your child, it must be on the strict understanding that this gentleman does not come near either me or my patient.

MAMA. Yes, Doctor, I talk to him. . . . You go to hospital now, please.

DOCTOR. Very well. But you understand . . . nowhere near me, or I withdraw from the case.

[*He goes.*]

UNCLE CHRIS. I go see Dagmar.

MAMA. Wait. Uncle Chris, is kind of you, but Dagmar is sick. You frighten her.

UNCLE CHRIS. I frighten her?

MAMA. Yes, Uncle Chris. You frighten everyone. . . .

UNCLE CHRIS (*amazed*). I??

MAMA. Everyone but me. Even the girls . . . Jenny, Sigrid, Trina . . . they are frightened of you.

UNCLE CHRIS. The girls! Vomen! Pff!

MAMA. And the children, too. So Nels and I get Dagmar. You drive us to hospital in your automobile, but you do not frighten Dagmar. And you leave Doctor alone. Dr. Johnson is *fine* doctor. You come with me, Nels. You carry Dagmar.

[NELS *and* MAMA *go out back L.* UNCLE CHRIS *stands in amazement and puzzlement. The* TWO GIRLS *watch him, hardly daring to move.*]

UNCLE CHRIS. Is true? I frighten you? Christinë . . . Katrin . . . you are frightened of me? Come, I ask you. Tell me the truth. You are frightened of me?

KATRIN (*tremulously*). A . . . a little, Uncle Chris.

UNCLE CHRIS. No? And you, Christinë?

CHRISTINE. Y . . . yes, Uncle Chris.

UNCLE CHRIS. But Nils . . . Nils is a boy . . . he is not frightened?

CHRISTINE. Not . . . not as much as we are. . . .

UNCLE CHRIS. But he is frightened?

CHRISTINE. Yes, Uncle Chris.

UNCLE CHRIS. But, why? What is there to be frightened of? I am your Uncle Chris . . . why do I frighten you?

CHRISTINE. I don't know.

UNCLE CHRIS. But that is bad. Very bad. The Aunts, yes, I like to frighten them. (THE GIRLS *giggle.*) That makes you laugh. You do not like the Aunts? Come, tell me. You do not like the Aunts? Say!

KATRIN. Not . . . very much, Uncle Chris.

UNCLE CHRIS. And which do you not like the most? Jenny . . . Sigrid . . . Trina. . . . Tell me—huh?

KATRIN. I think I like Aunt Jenny least. She's so . . . so bossy.

CHRISTINE. I can't stand Aunt Sigrid. Always whining and complaining.

UNCLE CHRIS (*with a great roar of laughter*). Is good. Jenny, bossy. Sigrid, whining. Is true! But your Mama, she is different. And she cook goot. The Aunts, they cannot cook at all. Only you do not tell your Mama we have talked of them so. It is a secret, for us. Then you cannot be frightened of me any more . . . when we have secret. I tell you my secret, too. *I* do not like the Aunts. And so that they do not bother me, I frighten them and shout at them. You I do not shout at if you are goot children, and clean your teeth goot, and eat your oranges. (*He takes out a snuffbox and partakes of its contents.*)

[*On the cue "You I do not shout at," the posse of* AUNTS *appears, in outdoor clothes, accompanied by* MR. THORKELSON, *a terrified little man. They come in down L. and start up to the house.*]

SIGRID (*stopping in the street*). Jenny. Do you see what I see? A woman, in his automobile.

JENNY. How shameful!

SIGRID. Ought we to bow?

JENNY. Bow? To a woman like that? We cut her. That's what we do. I'll show you.

[*She strides to the front door, ignoring the woman in the car, and enters the house. The others follow.*]

JENNY (*entering*). Uncle Chris, Sigrid has something to say to you.

SIGRID (*with false bravery*). Uncle Chris, you took Arne to the hospital. . . .

UNCLE CHRIS. Yes, I take Arne to the hospital. And now we take Dagmar to the hospital, so you do not clutter up the place.

JENNY. What's the matter with Dagmar?

CHRISTINE. It's her ear. Dr. Johnson's going to operate.

SIGRID (*catching her favorite word*). Operate? This is some more of Uncle Chris's doings. Did you hear what he did to Arne?

UNCLE CHRIS (*turning on her*). Sigrid, you are a whining old fool, and you get out of here. . . .

SIGRID (*deflating*). We'd better go, Jenny. . . .

JENNY (*stoutly*). No . . . there has been enough of these highhanded goings on. . . .

UNCLE CHRIS. And you, Jenny . . . you are a bossy old fool, and you get out of here, too, and we take Dagmar to hospital.

[NELS *enters, carrying* DAGMAR *in his arms, wrapped in a blanket.*]

You got her goot, Nils?

NELS. Sure, Uncle Chris.

UNCLE CHRIS. We go.

JENNY (*getting between them and the door*). No! You are going to hear me out. (*Weakening*) That is, you are going to hear *Sigrid* out. . . .

UNCLE CHRIS. If you do not get out of the way of the door before I count three, I trow you out. And Sigrid, too, as big as she is. Von . . . (SIGRID *moves.*) Two . . .

[JENNY *moves. He looks back at the* CHILDREN *with a wink and a smile.*]

Is goot! You put her in back of the car, Nils.

[NELS *goes out, carrying* DAGMAR, *and lifts her into the car.* UNCLE CHRIS *follows and starts cranking.*]

TRINA (*running to the door after him, with* MR. THORKELSON). But, Uncle Chris, I want to introduce Mr. Thorkelson. . . .

[*But* UNCLE CHRIS *ignores her, continuing to crank. She returns crestfallen into the room with* MR. THORKELSON. MAMA *re-enters back L., wearing a hat and coat and carrying a cheap little overnight case.*]

MAMA. Jenny . . . Trina, we go to hospital. (*She goes to* KATRIN *and* CHRISTINE.) You will be good children until Mama comes home?

THE GIRLS. Sure, Mama.

UNCLE CHRIS (*calling from the car*). Marta, we go!

MAMA (*calling back*). I come! (*She turns to the* CHILDREN *again.*) There is milk in the cooler, and fruit and cookies for your lunch.

CHRISTINE. We'll be all right, Mama. Don't worry.

MAMA. I go now.

[*She starts for the door.*]

SIGRID (*stopping her*). Marta!

MAMA. What is it?

SIGRID. You *can't* go in his automobile.

MAMA. Why not?

UNCLE CHRIS (*calling again*). Marta, we go!

MAMA. I come!

SIGRID. Because . . . because *she's* in it. The . . . the woman!

MAMA. So it will kill me, or Dagmar, if we sit in the automobile with her? I have see her. She looks nice woman. (*Calling off, as she goes*) I come!

UNCLE CHRIS. We go!

[*She climbs into the rear of the car, which backs noisily off during the next speeches.*]

MR. THORKELSON (*in a low whisper to* TRINA). Is that woman his wife?

TRINA (*nervously*). Yes. . . .

MR. THORKELSON. Yes?

TRINA (*whispering back, loudly*). No!

JENNY (*to* THE GIRLS). Don't stand there gaping like that, girls. (*She shoos them into the pantry.*) Go away! Go away!

[THE GIRLS *go.* JENNY *turns and sees the disappearing car through the open door.*]

Oh! They've gone! We go after them! Sigrid, you lead the way!

[*She gives* SIGRID *a push and the four go out, with* JENNY *dragging* MR. THORKELSON, *and* TRINA *following. Blackout. The curtains close.*

Spot on R. turntable, representing a kind of closet room. Roller skates hanging on the wall. KATRIN *and* CHRISTINE *are seated on a small kitchen stepladder with glasses of milk, and cookies on plates.*]

KATRIN. How long have they been gone now?

CHRISTINE. About three hours. And I wish you wouldn't keep asking that.

KATRIN. How long do operations take? I heard Aunt Sigrid telling about Mrs. Bergman who was five hours on the table.

CHRISTINE. Aunt Sigrid's friends always have everything worse than anyone else. And it gets worse each time she tells it, too.

[KATRIN *smiles—drinks some milk and eats a cookie.*]

KATRIN (*with a certain melancholy enjoyment*). The house feels lonesome, doesn't it—without Mama? It's like in a book. "The sisters sat huddled in the empty house, waiting for the verdict that was to spell life or death to the little family."

CHRISTINE. Oh, don't talk such nonsense.

KATRIN. It's not nonsense.

CHRISTINE. It is, too. In the first place, we're not a little family. We're a big one. And who said anything about life or death, anyway? Always trying to make everything so dramatic!

KATRIN. Well, it *is* dramatic.

CHRISTINE. It's not. It's just . . . well, worrying. But you don't have to make a tragedy out of it. (*Pause.*)

KATRIN. You're not eating anything.

CHRISTINE. I know that.

KATRIN. You're not drinking your milk, either. Aren't you hungry?

CHRISTINE. No. And you wouldn't be, either, if you'd any feeling for Mama and Dagmar, instead of just heartlessly sitting there eating and enjoying making a story out of it.

KATRIN. Oh, Chris, I'm not heartless. I do have feeling for them. I can't help it if it goes into words like that. Everything always does with me. But it doesn't mean I don't feel it. And I think we *ought* to eat. I think Mama would want us to.

[*Pause.* CHRISTINE *hesitates a moment, then takes a bite of a cookie. They both eat in silence. The light dims on them, and the turntable revolves out.*

The curtains part on the hospital corridor. A main back flat representing the wall, running diagonally up from the front of the main stage L. toward the back. Down front L. is a bench, on which MAMA *and* NELS *are sitting, holding hands, looking off. Below the bench is the elevator, and above the bench, set back a little, is a closet for brooms and mops, etc. The reception desk, at which a nurse is sitting, is R.C., toward the front. The wall goes up into darkness, and behind the nurse's desk is darkness.*

As the curtains open, there is a hubbub down front by the nurse's desk, where the AUNTS *are haranguing* UNCLE CHRIS. MR. THORKELSON *stands slightly in back of them.*]

SIGRID. But, Uncle Chris, I tell you I must see him!

UNCLE CHRIS (*storming*). You don't understand English? No visitors for twenty-four hours.

SIGRID. But *you've* seen him.

UNCLE CHRIS. I am not visitor. I am exception.

SIGRID. Well, then, his mother should be an exception, too. I'll see the doctor.

UNCLE CHRIS. *I* have seen doctor. I have told him you are not goot for Arne.

SIGRID. Not good for my own son. . . .

UNCLE CHRIS. Not goot at all. You cry over him. I go now. (*He starts to do so, but* JENNY *pushes* TRINA *forward.*)

TRINA (*with desperate courage*). Uncle Chris . . . Uncle Chris . . . I *must* speak to you.

UNCLE CHRIS. I have business.

TRINA. But, Uncle Chris. . . . I want to get married.

UNCLE CHRIS. Well, then, *get* married.

[*He starts off again.*]

TRINA. No, wait, I . . . I want to marry Mr. Thorkelson. Here. (*She produces him from behind her.*) Peter, this is Uncle Chris. Uncle Chris, this is Mr. Thorkelson.

UNCLE CHRIS (*staring at him*). So?

MR. THORKELSON. How are you, sir?

UNCLE CHRIS. Busy. (*He turns again.*)

TRINA. Please, Uncle Chris . . .

UNCLE CHRIS. What is? You want to marry him? All right, marry him. I have other things to think about.

TRINA (*eagerly*). Then . . . then you give your permission?

UNCLE CHRIS. Yes, I give my permission. If you want to be a fool, I cannot stop you.

TRINA (*gratefully*). Oh, thank you, Uncle Chris.

UNCLE CHRIS. So. Is all?

TRINA (*anxious to escape*). Yes, I think is all.

JENNY (*firmly*). No!!

UNCLE CHRIS. No?

[MR. THORKELSON *is pushed forward again.*]

MR. THORKELSON. Well, there . . . there was a little something else. You see, Trina mentioned . . . well, in the old country it was always usual . . . and after all, we do all come from the old country. . . .

UNCLE CHRIS. What is it? What you want?

MR. THORKELSON. Well, it's a question of Trina's . . . well, not to mince matters . . . her dowry.

UNCLE CHRIS (*shouting*). Her what?

MR. THORKELSON (*very faintly*). Her dowry . . .

UNCLE CHRIS. Ah. Her dowry. Trina wants a dowry. She is forty-two years old . . .

TRINA (*interrupting*). No, Uncle Chris. . . .

UNCLE CHRIS (*without pausing*). And it is not enough she gets husband. She must have dowry.

NURSE (*who has been trying to interrupt, now bangs on her desk*). PLEASE! Would you mind going and discussing your family matters somewhere else? This is a hospital, not a marriage bureau!

UNCLE CHRIS (*after glaring at the* NURSE, *turns to* MR. THORKELSON). You come into waiting room. I talk to you about dowry.

[*He strides off into the darkness behind the nurse's desk.* MR. THORKELSON, *with an appealing look back at* TRINA, *follows him. The* AUNTS *now remember* MAMA, *sitting on the bench, and cross to her.*]

JENNY. Did you hear that, Marta?

MAMA (*out of a trance*). What?

JENNY. Uncle Chris.

MAMA. No, I do not hear. I wait for doctor. Is two hours since they take Dagmar to operating room. More.

SIGRID. Two hours? That's nothing! When Mrs. Bergman had her gallbladder removed she was *six* hours on the table.

MAMA. Sigrid, I do not want to hear about Mrs. Bergman. I do not want to hear about anything. I wait for doctor. Please, you go away now. You come this evening.

TRINA. But, Marta, you can't stay here all by yourself.

MAMA. I have Nels. Please, Trina . . . I wait for doctor . . . you go now.

JENNY. We go.

TRINA. Oh, but I must wait for Peter and Uncle Chris. . . .

JENNY. We'll go next door and have some coffee. Sigrid, do you have money?

SIGRID. Yes, I . . . I have a little.

JENNY. Good. Then I treat you. We'll be next door if you want us, Marta.

[MAMA *nods without looking at them, her eyes still fixed on the elevator door. The* AUNTS *leave, going down the steps from the stage as though they were the hospital steps, and off L.*

For a moment, the stage is quiet. Then a SCRUB WOMAN *enters from down R. carrying a mop and pail which she puts into the closet, and then leaves. The elevator door opens and a doctor in white coat comes out, followed by an orderly, carrying a tray of dressings. They disappear up R. behind the desk.* MAMA *rises, agitatedly, looking after them. Then* DR. JOHNSON *returns from R. front, carrying his hat and bag. He sees* MAMA *and crosses to her, C.*]

DOCTOR. Oh, Mrs. Hanson . . .

MAMA. Doctor . . .

DOCTOR. Well, Dagmar's fine. She came through it beautifully. She's back in bed now, sleeping off the anesthetic.

MAMA. Thank you, Doctor. (*She shakes hands with him.*)

DOCTOR. You're very welcome.

MAMA. Is good of you, Doctor. (*She shakes hands with him again.*) Where is she? I go to her now.

DOCTOR. Oh, I'm sorry, but I'm afraid that's against the rules. You shall see her tomorrow.

MAMA. Tomorrow? But, Doctor, she is so little. When she wakes she will be frightened.

DOCTOR. The nurses will take care of her. Excellent care. You needn't worry. You see, for the first twenty-four hours, clinic patients aren't allowed to see visitors. The wards must be kept quiet.

MAMA. I will not make a sound.

DOCTOR. I'm very sorry. Tomorrow. And now . . . (*He glances at his watch.*) Good afternoon.

[*He puts on his hat and goes out L., down the steps and off.* MAMA *stands still a moment, looking after him.*]

MAMA. Come, Nels. We go find Dagmar.

NELS. But, Mama, the doctor said . . .

MAMA. We find Dagmar.

[*She looks vaguely around her. Then goes to the nurse's desk.*]

You tell me, please, where I can find my daughter?

NURSE. What name?

MAMA. Dagmar.

NELS. Dagmar Hanson.

NURSE (*looking at her record book*). Hanson, Ward A. Along there. (*She points upstage.* MAMA *starts to go up.*) Oh, just a moment. (MAMA *returns.*) When did she come in?

MAMA. This morning. They just finish operation.

NURSE. Oh, well, then I'm afraid you can't see her today. No visitors for the first twenty-four hours.

MAMA. Am not visitor. I am her Mama.

NURSE. I'm sorry, but it's against the rules.

MAMA. Just for one minute. Please.

NURSE. I'm sorry. It's against the rules.

[MAMA *stands staring.* NELS *touches her arm. She looks at him, nods, trying to smile, then turns and walks with him to L. and down the steps.*]

MAMA. We must think of some way.

NELS. Mama, they'll let you see her tomorrow. They said so.

MAMA. If I don't see her today how will I know that all is well with her? What can I tell Papa when he comes home from work?

NELS. The nurses will look after her, Mama. Would you like to come next door for some coffee?

MAMA (*shaking her head*). We go home. We have coffee at home. But I must see Dagmar today.

[*She plods off L. with* NELS. *The curtains close.*

Spot goes up on R. turntable. UNCLE CHRIS *and* MR. THORKELSON *are seated on a bench and chair, as in a waiting room. A table with a potted plant is between them. A clock on the wall points to 2:30* P.M.]

UNCLE CHRIS. Well, it comes then to this. You love my niece, Trina? (MR. THORKELSON, *very scared, gulps and nods.*) You want to marry her? (MR. THORKELSON *nods again.*) You are in position to support her? (MR. THORKELSON *nods again.*) Why, then, you want dowry? (*No answer. He shouts.*) What for you want dowry?

MR. THORKELSON. Well . . . well, it would be a nice help. And it is customary.

UNCLE CHRIS. Is not customary. Who gives dowries? Parents. Why? Because they are so glad they will not have to support their daughters any more, they pay money. I do not support Trina. I do not care if Trina gets married. Why then should I pay to have her married?

MR. THORKELSON. I never thought of it like that.

UNCLE CHRIS. Is insult to girl to pay dowry. If I do not give dowry, will you still marry Trina?

MR. THORKELSON. I . . . I don't know.

UNCLE CHRIS. You don't know? You don't know?? You think I let Trina marry a man who will not take her without dowry?

MR. THORKELSON. No, I suppose you wouldn't.

UNCLE CHRIS. What kind of man would that be? I ask you, what kind of man would that be?

MR. THORKELSON (*fascinated—helpless*). Well, not a very nice kind of man.

UNCLE CHRIS. And are you that kind of man?

MR. THORKELSON. I . . . I don't think so.

UNCLE CHRIS (*conclusively*). Then you don't want dowry!!

MR. THORKELSON (*giving up*). No, I . . . I guess I don't.

UNCLE CHRIS (*slapping his back*). Goot. Goot. You are goot man. I like you. I give you my blessing. And I send you vedding present. I send you box of oranges!

[*While he is boisterously shaking Mr. Thorkelson's hand, blackout. Turntable revolves out.*

The curtains open on the kitchen. It is empty. MAMA *and* NELS *come up the hill from the L. and let themselves into the house. There is silence as they take off their hats and coats.*]

MAMA (*after a moment*). Where are the girls?

NELS. I guess they're upstairs. (*Goes to door back L. and calls.*) Chris! Katrin!

GIRLS' VOICES. Coming!

NELS. Shall I make you some coffee? (MAMA *shakes her head.*) You said you'd have coffee when you got home.

MAMA. Later. First I must think.

NELS. Mama, please don't worry like that. Dagmar's all right. You know she's all right.

[THE GIRLS *come in back L.*]

CHRISTINE (*trying to be casual*). Well, Mama, everything all right?

MAMA (*nodding*). Is all right. You have eaten?

KATRIN. Yes, Mama.

MAMA. You drink your milk?

CHRISTINE. Yes, Mama.

MAMA. Is good.

CHRISTINE (*seeing her face*). Mama, something's the matter.

KATRIN (*overdramatically*). Mama, Dagmar's not—? Mama! She isn't—?

MAMA. No, Dagmar is fine. The doctor say she is fine. (*She rises.*) What is time?

NELS. It's three o'clock.

MAMA. Three hours till Papa come.

[*She looks around and then goes slowly into the pantry, back R.*]

KATRIN. Nels, what is it? There *is* something the matter.

NELS. They wouldn't let Mama see Dagmar. It's a rule of the hospital.

CHRISTINE. But Dagmar's all right?

NELS. Oh, yes, she's all right.

CHRISTINE (*impatiently*). Well, then . . . !

NELS. But Mama's very upset. She started talking to me in Norwegian in the streetcar.

KATRIN (*emotionally*). What can we do?

CHRISTINE (*coldly*). You can't do anything. When will they let her see Dagmar?

NELS. Tomorrow.

CHRISTINE. Well, then, we'll just have to wait till tomorrow.

KATRIN. Chris, how can you be so callous? Can't you see that Mama's heart is breaking?

CHRISTINE. No, I can't. And you can't, either. People's hearts don't break.

KATRIN. They do, too.

CHRISTINE. Only in books.

[MAMA *comes back; she wears an apron, and carries a scrub brush and a bucket of hot water.*]

Why, Mama, what are you going to do?

MAMA. I scrub the floor. (*She gets down on her knees.*)

CHRISTINE. But you scrubbed it yesterday.

MAMA. I scrub it again. (*She starts to do so.*)

KATRIN. But, Mama . . .

MAMA (*bending low*). Comes a time when you've got to get down on your knees.

KATRIN (*to* CHRISTINE). Now do you believe me?

[CHRISTINE, *suddenly unendurably moved, turns and rushes from the room.*]

NELS. Mama, don't. Please don't. You must be tired.

KATRIN (*strangely*). Let her alone, Nels.

[*They stand in silence watching* MAMA *scrub. Suddenly she stops.*]

What is it, Mama? What is it?

MAMA (*sitting back on her haunches*). I think of something! (*Slowly*) I think I think of something!

[*The lights dim and the curtains close on the kitchen.*
From down front L. UNCLE CHRIS'S VOICE *singing. The lights slowly come up on the L. turntable, showing* ARNE (*a child of about eight*) *in a hospital bed, with* UNCLE CHRIS *beside him.*]

UNCLE CHRIS (*singing*).

"Ten t'ousand Svedes vent t'rough de veeds
At de battle of Coppen-hagen.
Ten t'ousand Svedes vent t'rough de veeds
Chasing von Nor-ve-gan!

ARNE. Uncle Chris!

UNCLE CHRIS. Yes, Arne?

ARNE. Uncle Chris, does it *have* to hurt like this?

UNCLE CHRIS. If you vant it to be vell, and not to valk always like Uncle Chris, it does . . . for a little. Is very bad?

ARNE. It is . . . kinda. . . . Oo—oo . . . !

UNCLE CHRIS. Arne, don't you know any svear vords?

ARNE. W-what?

UNCLE CHRIS. Don't you know any svear vords?

ARNE. N-no, Uncle Chris. Not real ones.

UNCLE CHRIS. Then I tell you von fine von to use when pain is bad. Is "Damn." You say it?

ARNE. N-now?

UNCLE CHRIS. No, not now. When pain comes again. You say it then. They help plenty. I know. I haf pain, too. I say them all the time. And if pain is *very* bad, you say, "Damittohell." But only if is *very* bad. Is bad now?

ARNE. No, it's . . . it's a little better.

UNCLE CHRIS. You sleep some now, maybe?

ARNE. I'll try. Will . . . will you stay here, Uncle Chris?

UNCLE CHRIS. Sure. Sure. I stay here. You are not frightened of Uncle Chris?

ARNE. No. Not any more.

UNCLE CHRIS. Goot. Goot. You like I sing some more?

ARNE. If you wouldn't mind. But maybe something a little . . . well, quieter.

UNCLE CHRIS (*tenderly*). Sure. Sure.

[*He begins quietly to sing a Norwegian lullaby; in the midst,* ARNE *cries out.*]

ARNE. Oo—oo . . . Oh, *damn.* Damn. Damittohell!

UNCLE CHRIS (*delighted*). Goot! It helps—eh?

ARNE (*with pleased surprise*). Yes—yes.

UNCLE CHRIS. Then you sleep some!

[*He fixes Arne's pillows for him, and resumes the lullaby, seated on his chair beside the bed. After another verse, he leans over, assuring himself that the child is asleep, and then very quietly, without interrupting his singing, takes a flask from his pocket and lifts it to his lips, as the light dims. The table revolves out. The curtains part on the hospital corridor again. There is a different* NURSE *now at the reception desk, talking on the telephone as* MAMA *and* KATRIN *come in from L. and up the steps.*]

MAMA (*as they come up, in an undertone*). Is not the same nurse. Katrin, you take my hat and coat.

[*She takes them off, revealing that she still wears her apron.*]

KATRIN. But, Mama, won't they . . .

MAMA (*interrupting, finger to lips*). Ssh! You let me go ahead. You wait on bench for me.

[*She goes to the closet door above the bench and opens it.* KATRIN *stares after her in trepidation.*[1] MAMA *takes out a damp mop and pail, and gets down on her knees in front of the nurse's desk, starting to clean the floor. The* NURSE *looks up.* MAMA *catches her eye.*]

MAMA (*brightly*). Very dirty floors.

NURSE. Yes, I'm glad they've finally decided to clean them. Aren't you working late?

MAMA (*quickly, lowering her head*). Floors need cleaning.

[*She pushes her way, crawling on hands and knees, up behind the desk, and disappears up the corridor, still scrubbing.* KATRIN

[1] *trepidation* (trĕp′ĭ·dā′shŭn): fear.

steals to the bench, where she sits, still clutching Mama's hat and coat, looking interestedly around her. The light dims, leaving her in a single spot, as she starts to talk to herself.]

KATRIN (*to herself*). "The Hospital" . . . A poem by Katrin Hanson. (*She starts to improvise.*)

"She waited fearful, in the hall,
And held her bated breath."

Breath—yes, that'll rhyme with death. (*She repeats the first two lines.*)

"She waited fearful in the hall
And held her bated breath.
She trembled at the least footfall,
And kept her mind on death."

[*She gets a piece of paper and pencil from her pocket and begins to scribble, as a* NURSE *comes out of the elevator, carrying some charts, which she takes to the desk, and then goes out down R.* KATRIN *goes on with her poem.*]

"Ah, God, 'twas agony to wait.
To wait and watch and wonder . . ."

Wonder—under—bunder—funder—sunder. Sunder! (*Nods to herself and goes on again.*)

"To wait and watch and wonder,
About her infant sister's fate,
If Death life's bonds would sunder."

(*Then to herself again, looking front*) That's beautiful. Yes, but it isn't true. Dagmar isn't dying. It's funny—I don't want her to die—and yet when Mama said she was all right, I was almost—well, almost disappointed. It wasn't exciting any more. Maybe Christine's right, and I haven't any heart. How awful! "The girl without a heart." That'd be a nice title for a story. "The girl without a heart sat in the hospital corridor. . . ."

[*The lights comes up again as* UNCLE CHRIS *appears, up R. behind the desk. He wears his hat and is more than a little drunk. He sees* KATRIN.]

UNCLE CHRIS. Katrin! What you do here? (*He sits on the bench beside her.*)

KATRIN (*nervously*). I'm waiting for Mama.

UNCLE CHRIS. Where is she?

KATRIN (*scared*). I . . . I don't know.

UNCLE CHRIS. What you mean . . . you don't know?

KATRIN (*whispering*). I think . . . I think she's seeing Dagmar.

UNCLE CHRIS (*shaking his head*). Is first day. They do not allow visitors first day.

KATRIN (*trying to make him aware of the* NURSE). I know. But I think that's where she is.

UNCLE CHRIS. Where *is* Dagmar?

KATRIN. I don't know.

[UNCLE CHRIS *rises and goes to the* NURSE *at the desk.*]

UNCLE CHRIS. In what room is my great-niece, Dagmar Hanson?

NURSE (*looking at her book*). Hanson . . . Hanson . . . when did she come in?

UNCLE CHRIS. This morning.

NURSE. Oh, yes. Were you wanting to see her?

UNCLE CHRIS. What room is she in?

NURSE. I asked were you wanting to see her.

UNCLE CHRIS. And *I* ask what room she is in.

NURSE. We don't allow visitors the first day.

UNCLE CHRIS. Have I said I vant to visit her? I ask what room she is in.

NURSE. Are you by any chance, Mr. . . . (*looking at her book*) Halvorsen?

UNCLE CHRIS (*proudly, and correcting her pronunciation*). Christopher Halvorsen.

NURSE. Did you say you were her uncle?

UNCLE CHRIS. Her great-uncle.

NURSE. Well, then, I'm afraid I can't tell you anything about her.

UNCLE CHRIS. Why not?

NURSE. Orders.

UNCLE CHRIS. Whose orders?

NURSE. Dr. Johnson's. There's a special note here. Patient's uncle, Mr. Halvorsen, not to be admitted or given information under any circumstances.

UNCLE CHRIS (*after a moment's angry stupefaction*[1]). Damittohell!

[*He strides away down L., taking out his flask, and shaking it, only to find it empty.* MAMA *returns from up R., carrying the mop and pail, walking now and smiling triumphantly.*]

MAMA (*to the* NURSE). Thank you.

[*She replaces the mop and pail in the closet, and then sees* UNCLE CHRIS.]

Uncle Chris, Dagmar is fine!

UNCLE CHRIS (*coming back to her, amazed*). You see her?

MAMA. Sure, Uncle Chris, I see her.

UNCLE CHRIS (*reiterating, incredulous*). You see Dagmar?

MAMA. Sure. (*She takes her hat from* KATRIN *and starts to put it on.*) Is fine hospital. But such floors! A mop is never good. Floors should be scrubbed with a brush. We go home. Uncle Chris, you come with us? I make coffee.

UNCLE CHRIS. Pah! Vot good is coffee? I go get drink.

MAMA (*reprovingly*). Uncle Chris!

UNCLE CHRIS. Marta, you are fine voman. Fine. But I go get drink. I get drunk.

MAMA (*quickly aside to* KATRIN). His leg hurts him.

UNCLE CHRIS. And you do not make excuses for me! I get drunk because I like it.

MAMA (*conciliating him*). Sure, Uncle Chris.

UNCLE CHRIS (*shouting*). I like it! (*Then, with a change*) No, is not true. You know is not true. I do not like to get drunk at all. But I do not like to come home with you, either. (*Growing slightly maudlin*[2]) You have family. Is fine thing. You do not know how fine. Katrin, one day when you grow up, maybe you know what a fine thing family is. I haf no family.

KATRIN. But, Uncle Chris, Mama's always said you were the *head* of the family.

UNCLE CHRIS. Sure. Sure. I am head of the family, but I haf no family. So I go get drunk. You understand, Marta?

MAMA. Sure, Uncle Chris. You go get drunk. (*Sharply*) But don't you feel sorry for yourself!

[1] *stupefaction* (stū·pē·făk′shŭn): bewilderment or astonishment.
[2] *maudlin* (môd′lĭn): tearful or sentimental.

[UNCLE CHRIS *glares at her a moment, then strides off R., boisterously singing his song of "Ten Thousand Swedes."* MAMA *watches him go, then takes her coat from* KATRIN.]

Is fine man. Has fine ideas about family. (KATRIN *helps her on with her coat.*) I can tell Papa now that Dagmar is fine. She wake while I am with her. I explain rules to her. She will not expect us now until tomorrow afternoon.

KATRIN. You won't try and see her again before that?

MAMA (*gravely*). No. That would be against the rules! Come. We go home.

[*They go off L.*]

CURTAIN

ACT II

SCENE. *Opening, exactly as in Act I.* KATRIN *at her desk.*

KATRIN (*reading*). "It wasn't very often that I could get Mama to talk—about herself, or her life in the old country, or what she felt about things. You had to catch her unawares, or when she had nothing to do, which was very, very seldom. I don't think I can ever remember seeing Mama unoccupied." (*Laying down the manuscript and looking out front*) I do remember one occasion, though. It was the day before Dagmar came home from the hospital. And as we left, Mama suggested treating me to an ice-cream soda.

[*She rises, gets her hat from beside her—a schoolgirl hat—puts it on and crosses C. while she speaks the next lines.*]

She had never done such a thing before, and I remember how proud it made me feel—just to sit and talk to her quietly like a grown-up person. It was a kind of special *treat*-moment in my life that I'll always remember—quite apart from the soda, which was *wonderful.*

[*She has reached C. stage now.* MAMA *has come from between the curtains, and starts down the steps.*]

MAMA. Katrin, you like we go next door, and I treat you to an ice-cream soda?

KATRIN (*young now, and overcome*). Mama—do you mean it?

MAMA. Sure. We celebrate. We celebrate that Dagmar is well, and coming home again.

[*They cross to the L., where the turntable represents a drugstore, with a table and two chairs at which they seat themselves.*]

What you like to have, Katrin?

KATRIN. I think a chocolate . . . no, a strawberry . . . no, a chocolate soda.

MAMA (*smiling*). You are sure?

KATRIN (*gravely*). I think so. But, Mama, can we *afford* it?

MAMA. I think this once we can afford it.

[*The* SODA CLERK *appears from L.*]

SODA CLERK. What's it going to be, ladies?

MAMA. A chocolate ice-cream soda, please—and a cup of coffee.

[*The* SODA CLERK *goes.*]

KATRIN. Mama, he called us "ladies"! (MAMA *smiles.*) Why aren't you having a soda, too?

MAMA. Better I like coffee.

KATRIN. When can I drink coffee?

MAMA. When you are grown up.

KATRIN. When I'm eighteen?

MAMA. Maybe before that.

KATRIN. When I graduate?

MAMA. Maybe. I don't know. Comes the day you are grown up, Papa and I will know.

KATRIN. Is coffee really nicer than a soda?

MAMA. When you are grown up, it is.

KATRIN. Did you used to like sodas better . . . before you were grown up?

MAMA. We didn't have sodas before I was grown up. It was in the old country.

KATRIN (*incredulous*). You mean they don't have sodas in Norway?

MAMA. Now, maybe. Now I think they have many things from America. But not when I was little girl.

[*The* SODA CLERK *brings the soda and the coffee.*]

SODA CLERK. There you are, folks. (*He sets them and departs.*)

KATRIN (*after a good pull at the soda*). Mama, do you ever want to go back to the old country?

MAMA. I like to go back once to look, maybe. To see the mountains and the fjords.[1] I like to show them once to you all. When Dagmar is big, maybe we all go back once . . . one summer . . . like tourists. But that is how it would be. I would be tourist there now. There is no one I would know any more. And maybe we see the little house where Papa and I live when we first marry. And . . . (*Her eyes grow misty and reminiscent.*) Something else I would look at.

KATRIN. What is that? (MAMA *does not answer.*) What would you look at, Mama?

MAMA. Katrin, you do not know you have brother? Besides Nels?

KATRIN. No! A brother? In Norway? Mama . . .

MAMA. He is my first baby. I am eighteen when he is born.

KATRIN. Is he there now?

MAMA (*simply*). He is dead.

KATRIN (*disappointed*). Oh. I thought you meant . . . I thought you meant a real brother. A long-lost one, like in stories. When did he die?

MAMA. When he is two years old. It is his grave I would like to see again.

[*She is suddenly near tears, biting her lip and stirring her coffee violently, spilling a few drops on her suit. She gets her handkerchief from her pocketbook, dabs at her skirt, then briefly at her nose, then she returns the handkerchief and turns to* KATRIN *again.*]

(*Matter-of-factly*) Is good, your ice-cream soda?

KATRIN (*more interested now in* MAMA *than in it*). Yes. Mama . . . have you had a very *hard* life?

MAMA (*surprised*). Hard? No. No life is easy all the time. It is not meant to be.

KATRIN. But . . . rich people . . . aren't *their* lives easy?

[1] *fjords* (fyôrdz): narrow inlets of the sea between steep hills or mountains.

MAMA. I don't know, Katrin. I have never known rich people. But I see them sometimes in stores and in the streets, and they do not *look* as if they were easy.

KATRIN. Wouldn't you like to be rich?

MAMA. I would like to be rich the way I would like to be ten feet high. Would be good for some things—bad for others.

KATRIN. But didn't you come to America to *get* rich?

MAMA (*shocked*). No. We come to America because they are all here—all the others. Is good for families to be together.

KATRIN. And did you like it right away?

MAMA. Right away. When we get off the ferry boat and I see San Francisco and all the family, I say: "Is like Norway," only it is better than Norway. And then you are all born here, and I become American citizen. But not to get rich.

KATRIN. *I* want to be rich. Rich and famous. I'd buy you your warm coat. When are you going to get that coat, Mama?

MAMA. Soon now, maybe—when we pay doctor, and Mr. Hyde pay his rent. I think now I *must* ask him. I ask him tomorrow, after Dagmar comes home.

KATRIN. When I'm rich and famous, I'll buy you lovely clothes. White satin gowns with long trains to them. And jewelry. I'll buy you a pearl necklace.

MAMA. We talk too much! (*She signs to the* SODA CLERK.) Come, finish your soda. We must go home.

[*The* SODA CLERK *comes.*]

How much it is, please?

SODA CLERK. Fifteen cents.

MAMA. Here are two dimes. You keep the nickel. And thank you. Was good coffee.

[*They start out and up the steps toward the curtains C.*]

Tomorrow Dagmar will be home again. And, Katrin, you see Uncle Elizabeth is there. This afternoon again she was asking for him. You keep Uncle Elizabeth in the house all day until she comes home.

[*They disappear behind the curtains. After a second, the howls of a cat in pain are heard from behind the curtains—low at first, then rising to a heart-rending volume, and then diminishing again as the curtains part on the kitchen once more.* MAMA, PAPA, *and* DAGMAR *are entering the house.*]

DAGMAR (*standing on threshold, transfixed*). It's Uncle Elizabeth, welcoming me home! That's his song of welcome. Where is he, Mama? (*She looks around for the source of the howls.*)

MAMA. He is in the pantry . . . (*As* DAGMAR *starts to rush thither*) But wait . . . wait a minute, Dagmar. I must tell you. Uncle Elizabeth is . . . sick.

DAGMAR. Sick? What's the matter with him?

PAPA. He has been in fight. Last night. He come home this morning very sick indeed.

[DAGMAR *starts for the pantry door, back R., as* NELS *comes out.*]

MAMA. Nels, how is Uncle Elizabeth? Nels has been doctoring him.

NELS. He's pretty bad, Mama. I've dressed all his wounds again with boric acid, but . . . (*as* DAGMAR *tries to get past him*) I wouldn't go and see him now, baby.

DAGMAR. I've got to. He's *my* cat. I haven't seen him in a whole month. More.

[*She runs into the pantry and disappears.*]

MAMA. Nels, what you think?

NELS. I think we ought to have had him put away before she came home.

MAMA. But she would have been so unhappy if he was not here *at all.*

NELS. She'll be unhappier still if he dies.

[*Another howl is heard from the pantry, and then* DAGMAR *comes rushing back.*]

DAGMAR. Mama, what happened to him? What happened to him? Oh, Mama . . . when I tried to pick him up, his bandage slipped over his eye. It was bleeding. Oh, Mama, it looked awful. Oh . . . (*She starts to cry.*)

MAMA (*fondling her*). He look like that all over. Nels, you go see to his eye again.

[*Wearily,* NELS *returns to the pantry.*]

Listen, Dagmar . . . *Lille Ven* [1] . . . would it not be better for the poor thing to go quietly to sleep?

DAGMAR. You mean—go to sleep and never wake up again? (MAMA *nods gently.*) No.

PAPA. I think he die, anyway. Nels try to make him well. But I do not think he can.

DAGMAR. Mama can. Mama can do everything. (*Another howl from offstage. She clutches* MAMA *agonizedly.*) Make him live, Mama. Make him well again. *Please!*

MAMA. We see. Let us see how he gets through the night. And now, Dagmar, you must go to bed. I bring you your supper.

DAGMAR. But you will fix Uncle Elizabeth? You promise, Mama?

MAMA. I promise I try. Go now.

[DAGMAR *goes out, back L.*]

I must fix her supper.

[*She starts for the pantry. Howls again. She and* PAPA *stand and look at each other.* NELS *comes out.*]

NELS. Mama, it's just cruelty, keeping that cat alive.

MAMA. I know.

PAPA (*as another howl, the loudest yet, emerges*). You say we see how the cat get through the night. I ask you how do *we* get through the night? Is no use, Marta. We must put the cat to sleep. Nels, you go to the drugstore, and get something. Some chloroform [2] maybe. (*He gives him a coin.*)

NELS. How much shall I get?

PAPA. You ask the man. You tell him it is for a cat. He knows.

[NELS *goes out L. and down the street into the wings.*]

(*Looking at* MAMA'S *face*) Is best. Is the only thing.

MAMA. I know. But poor Dagmar. It is sad homecoming for her. And she has been so good in hospital. Never once she cry. (*She pulls herself together.*) I get her supper. (*Another howl*

[1] *Lille Ven:* Norwegian for "little pretty one." [2] *chloroform* (klō′rō-fôrm): a colorless liquid with a strong odor used to lessen pain which, in large doses, can kill small animals.

from offstage) And I take the cat outside. Right outside, where we . . . where *Dagmar* cannot hear him.

[*She goes into the pantry.* PAPA *takes a folded newspaper from his pocket, puts on his glasses and starts to read. The door, back L., opens gently and* MR. HYDE *peeps out. He wears his hat and coat and carries his suitcase and a letter.* PAPA *has his back to him.* MR. HYDE *lays the letter on the dresser and then starts to tiptoe across to the door. Then* PAPA *sees him.*]

PAPA. You go out, Mr. Hyde?

MR. HYDE (*pretending surprise*). Oh . . . Oh, I did not see you, Mr. Hanson. (*He puts down the suitcase.*) I did not know you were back. As a matter of fact, I . . . I was about to leave this letter for you. (*He fetches it.*) The fact is . . . I . . . I have been called away.

PAPA. So?

MR. HYDE. A letter I received this morning necessitates my departure. My immediate departure.

PAPA. I am sorry.

[MAMA *returns with a tray, on which are milk, bread, butter, and jelly.*]

Mama, Mr. Hyde says he goes away.

MAMA (*coming to the table with the tray*). Is true?

MR. HYDE. Alas, dear madam, yes. " 'Tis true, 'tis pity. And pity 'tis, 'tis true." [1] You will find here . . . (*He presents the letter.*) my check for all I owe you, and a note expressing my profoundest thanks for all your most kind hospitality. You will say good-by to the children for me? (*He bows, as* MAMA *takes the letter.*)

MAMA (*distressed*). Sure. Sure.

MR. HYDE (*bowing again*). Madam, my deepest gratitude.

[*He kisses her hand.* MAMA *looks astonished. He bows to* PAPA.]

Sir—my sincerest admiration! (*He opens the street door.*) It has been a privilege. Ave atque vale! Hail and farewell! (*He makes a gesture and goes.*)

[1] Mr. Hyde is quoting from Shakespeare's *Hamlet,* a speech of Polonius, Act II, scene 2.

MAMA. Was wonderful man! Is too bad. (*She opens the letter, takes out the check.*)

PAPA. How much is the check for?

MAMA. Hundred ten dollar! Is four months.

PAPA. Good. Good.

MAMA. Is wonderful. Now we pay doctor everything.

PAPA. And you buy your warm coat. With fur now, maybe.

MAMA (*sadly*). But there will be no more reading. You take the check, Lars. You get the money?

PAPA (*taking it*). Sure, I get it. What does he say in his letter?

MAMA. You read it while I fix supper for Dagmar.

[*She starts to butter the bread, and spread jelly, while* PAPA *reads.*]

PAPA (*reading*). "Dear Friends, I find myself compelled to take a somewhat hasty departure from this house of happiness. . . ."

MAMA. Is beautiful letter.

PAPA (*continuing*). "I am leaving you my library for the children. . . ."

MAMA. He leaves his books?

PAPA. He says so.

MAMA. But is wonderful. Go see, Lars. See if they are in his room.

[PAPA *lays down the letter and goes out back L.* NELS *and* CHRISTINE *appear down L., coming up to the house.* CHRISTINE *carries schoolbooks.*]

CHRISTINE. I'm sure it was him, Nels. Carrying his suitcase, and getting on the cable car. I'm sure he's going away.

NELS. Well, I hope he's paid Mama. (*They open the street door.*)

CHRISTINE (*bursting in*). Mama, I saw Mr. Hyde getting on the cable car.

MAMA. I know. He leave.

CHRISTINE. Did he pay you?

MAMA. Sure, he pay me. Hundred ten dollar . . .

NELS. Gee . . .

MAMA (*smiling*). Is good.

CHRISTINE. Are you going to put it in the Bank?

MAMA. We need it right away. (PAPA *returns, staggering under an armload of books.*) Mr. Hyde leaves his books, too. For you.

NELS. Say!

[PAPA *stacks them on the table.* NELS *and* CHRISTINE *rush to them, reading the titles.*]

The Pickwick Papers, The Complete Shakespeare . . .

CHRISTINE. *Alice in Wonderland, The Oxford Book of Verse . . .*

NELS. *The Last of the Mohicans, Ivanhoe . . .*

CHRISTINE. We were right in the middle of that.

MAMA. Nels can finish it. He can read to us now in the evenings. He has fine voice, too, like Mr. Hyde. (NELS *flushes with pleasure.*) Is wonderful. So much we can learn. (*She finishes the supper-making.*) Christine, you take the butter back to the cooler for me, and the yelly, too. (CHRISTINE *does so.*) I go up to Dagmar now. (*She lifts the tray, then pauses.*) You get it, Nels?

NELS. What? . . . Oh. . . . (*Taking a druggist's small bottle from his pocket*) Here.

MAMA. You put it down. After I come back, we do it. You know how?

NELS. Why, no, Mama, I . . .

MAMA. You do not ask?

NELS. No, I . . . I thought Papa . . .

MAMA. You know, Lars?

PAPA. No, I don't *know* . . . but it cannot be difficult. If you *hold* the cat . . .

MAMA. And watch him die? No! I think better you get rags . . . and a big sponge, to soak up the chloroform. You put it in the box with him, and cover him over. You get them ready out there.

NELS. Sure, Mama.

MAMA. I bring some blankets.

[NELS *goes off to the pantry, as* CHRISTINE *comes back. Again* MAMA *lifts the tray and starts for the door back L. But there is a knock on the street door from* AUNT JENNY, *who has come to the house from down L. in a state of some excitement.*]

MAMA (*agitated*). So much goes on! See who it is, Christine.

CHRISTINE (*peeping*). It's Aunt Jenny. (*She opens the door.*)

MAMA. Jenny . . .

JENNY (*breathless*). Marta . . . has he gone?

MAMA. Who?

JENNY. Your boarder . . . Mr. Hyde . . .

MAMA. Yes, he has gone. Why?

JENNY. Did he pay you?

MAMA. Sure he pay me.

JENNY. How?

MAMA. He give me a check. Lars has it right there.

JENNY (*with meaning*). A check!

MAMA. Jenny, what is it? Christine, you give Dagmar her supper. I come soon. (CHRISTINE *takes the tray from her and goes out back L.*) What is it, Jenny? How do you know that Mr. Hyde has gone?

JENNY. I was at Mr. Kruper's down the street . . . you know, the restaurant and bakery . . . and he told me Mr. Hyde was there today having his lunch, and when he left he asked if he would cash a check for him. For fifty dollars. (*She pauses.*)

PAPA. Well, go on.

JENNY. Your fine Mr. Hyde didn't expect Mr. Kruper to take it to the bank until tomorrow, but he did. And what do you think? Mr. Hyde hasn't even an *account* at that bank!

[NELS *returns and stands in the pantry doorway.*]

MAMA. I don't understand.

PAPA (*taking the check from his pocket*). You mean the check is no good?

JENNY. No good at all. (*Triumphantly*) Your Mr. Hyde was a crook, just as I always thought he was, for all his reading and fine ways. Mr. Kruper said he'd been cashing them all over the neighborhood. (MAMA *stands quite still, without answering.*) How much did he owe you? Plenty, I'll bet. (*Still no answer*) Eh? Marta, I said I bet he owed you plenty. Didn't he?

MAMA (*looks around, first at* NELS *and then down at the books on the table. She touches them.*) No. No, he owed us nothing. (*She takes the check from* PAPA, *tearing it.*) Nothing.

JENNY (*persistently*). How much was that check for? (*She reaches her hand for it.*)

MAMA (*evading her*). It does not matter. He pay with better things than money.

[*She goes to the stove, where she throws the check, watching it burn.*]

JENNY. I told you right in the beginning that you shouldn't trust him. But you were so sure . . . just like you always are. Mr. Hyde was a gentleman. A gentleman! I bet it must have been a hundred dollars that he rooked you of. Wasn't it?

MAMA (*returning*). Jenny, I cannot talk now. Maybe you don't have things to do. I have.

JENNY (*sneeringly*). What? What have *you* got to do that's so important?

MAMA (*taking up the medicine bottle*). I have to chloroform a cat!

[JENNY *steps back in momentary alarm, almost as though* MAMA *were referring to her, as she goes out into the pantry with the medicine bottle, not so very unlike Lady Macbeth with the daggers.*[1]

Blackout and curtains close.

After a moment, the curtains part again on the kitchen, the next morning. The books have been taken off the table, and MAMA *is setting the breakfast dishes, with* PAPA *helping her.* DAGMAR *comes bursting into the room, back L.*]

DAGMAR. Good morning, Mama. 'Morning, Papa. Is Uncle Elizabeth all better?

MAMA. Dagmar, there is something I must tell you.

DAGMAR. I want to see Uncle Elizabeth first.

[*She runs into the pantry.* MAMA *turns helplessly to* PAPA.]

MAMA. Do something! Tell her!

PAPA. If we just let her think the cat die . . . by itself. . . .

MAMA. No. We cannot tell her lies. (PAPA *goes to the pantry door, opening it.*)

DAGMAR (*heard in pantry, off*). What a funny, funny smell. Good morning, my darling, my darling Elizabeth.

[MAMA *and* PAPA *stand stricken.* DAGMAR *comes in, carrying the cat, wrapped in an old shirt, with its head covered.*]

[1] In Act II, Scene 2 of Shakespeare's *Macbeth,* Lady Macbeth takes the daggers with which her husband has murdered King Duncan to place them beside his sleeping servants.

My goodness, you put enough blankets on him! Did you think he'd catch cold?

MAMA (*horror-stricken*). Dagmar, you must not. . . .

[*She stops at the sight of the cat, whose tail is twitching, quite obviously alive.*]

Dagmar, let me see . . . Let me see the cat! (*She goes over to her, and uncovers its head.*)

DAGMAR (*overjoyed*). He's well. Oh, Mama, I *knew* you'd fix him.

MAMA (*appalled*). But, Dagmar, I didn't. I . . .

DAGMAR (*ignoring her*). I'm going to take him right up and show him to Nels. (*She runs off back L., calling*) Nels! Nels! Uncle Elizabeth's well again!

MAMA (*turning to* PAPA). Is a miracle!

PAPA (*shrugging*). You cannot have used enough chloroform. You just give him good sleep, and that cures him. We rechristen the cat, Lazarus! [1]

MAMA. But, Lars, we must tell her. Is not *good* to let her grow up believing I can fix *everything!*

PAPA. Is best thing in the world for her to believe. (*He chuckles.*) Besides, I know *exactly* how she feels. (*He lays his hand on hers.*)

MAMA (*turning with embarrassment from his demonstrativeness*). We finish getting breakfast.

[*She turns back to the table. The curtains close.*

Lights up down front R. KATRIN *and* CHRISTINE *enter from the wings, in school clothes, wearing hats.* CHRISTINE *carries schoolbooks in a strap.* KATRIN *is reciting.*]

KATRIN.

"The quality of mercy is not strained,
It droppeth as the gentle rain from heaven
Upon the place beneath: it is twice blest;
It blesseth him that gives and him that takes. . . ."

(*She dries up.*)

". . . him that takes. It blesseth him that gives and him that

[1] *Lazarus* (lăz′ȧ·rŭs): a man whom Jesus raised from the dead.

takes. . . ."[1] (*She turns to* CHRISTINE.) What comes after that?

CHRISTINE. I don't know. And I don't care.

KATRIN. Why, Chris!

CHRISTINE. I don't. It's all I've heard for weeks. The school play, and your graduation, and going on to High. And never a thought of what's happening at home.

KATRIN. What do you mean?

CHRISTINE. You see—you don't even know!

KATRIN. Oh, you mean the strike?

CHRISTINE. Yes, I mean the strike. Papa hasn't worked for four whole weeks, and a lot you care. Why, I don't believe you even know what they're striking *for*. Do you? All you and your friends can talk about is the presents you're going to get. You make me ashamed of being a girl.

[*Two girls,* MADELINE *and* DOROTHY, *come through the curtains, C., talking.*]

MADELINE (*to* DOROTHY). Thyra Walsh's family's going to add seven pearls to the necklace they started for her when she was a baby. Oh, hello, Katrin! Did you hear about Thyra's graduation present?

KATRIN (*not very happily*). Yes, I heard.

MADELINE. I'm getting an onyx ring, with a diamond in it.

KATRIN. A real diamond?

MADELINE. Yes, of course. A *small* diamond.

DOROTHY. What are *you* getting?

KATRIN. Well . . . well, they haven't actually told me, but I think . . . I think I'm going to get that pink celluloid dresser set in your father's drugstore.

DOROTHY. You mean that one in the window?

KATRIN (*to* MADELINE). It's got a brush and comb and mirror . . . and a hair receiver. It's genuine celluloid!

DOROTHY. I wanted Father to give it to me, out of stock, but he said it was too expensive. Father's an awful tightwad. They're giving me a bangle.[2]

MADELINE. Oh, there's the streetcar. We've got to fly. 'By, Katrin. 'By, Christine. See you tomorrow. Come on, Dorothy.

[1] She recites Portia's lines in Act IV, Scene 1 of Shakespeare's *The Merchant of Venice*. [2] *bangle* (băng′g'l): a bracelet.

[*The* TWO GIRLS *rush off L.*]

CHRISTINE. Who said you were going to get the dresser set?

KATRIN. Nobody's said so . . . for certain. But I've sort of hinted, and . . .

CHRISTINE. Well, you're not going to get it.

KATRIN. How do you know?

CHRISTINE. Because I know what you *are* getting. I heard Mama tell Aunt Jenny. Aunt Jenny said you were too young to appreciate it.

KATRIN. What is it?

CHRISTINE. Mama's giving you her brooch.[1] Her *solje*.

KATRIN. You mean that old silver thing she wears that belonged to Grandmother? What would I want an old thing like that for?

CHRISTINE. It's an heirloom. Mama thinks a lot of it.

KATRIN. Well, then, she ought to keep it. You don't really mean that's *all* they're going to give me?

CHRISTINE. What more do you want?

KATRIN. I want the dresser set. My goodness, if Mama doesn't realize what's a suitable present . . . why, it's practically the most important time in a girl's life, when she graduates.

CHRISTINE. And you say you're not selfish!

KATRIN. It's not selfishness.

CHRISTINE. Well, I don't know what else you'd call it. With Papa not working, we need every penny we can lay our hands on. Even the Little Bank's empty. But you'll devil Mama into giving you the dresser set somehow. So why talk about it? I'm going home.

[*She turns and goes up the steps and through the curtains.* KATRIN *stands alone with a set and stubborn mouth, and then sits on the steps.*]

KATRIN. Christine was right. I got the dresser set. They gave it to me just before supper on graduation night. Papa could not attend the exercises because there was a strike meeting to decide about going back to work. I was so excited that night, I could hardly eat, and the present took the last remnants of my appetite clean away.

[1] *brooch* (brōch): an ornamental pin with clasp.

[*The curtains part on the kitchen.* PAPA, MAMA, *and* DAGMAR *at table, with coffee.* CHRISTINE *is clearing dishes.*]

CHRISTINE. I'll just stack the dishes now, Mama. We'll wash them when we come home. (*She carries them into the pantry.*)

PAPA (*holding up a cube of sugar*). Who wants coffee-sugar? (*He dips it in his coffee.*) Dagmar? (*He hands it to her.*) Katrin? (*She rises from the step, coming into the scene for the sugar.*)

MAMA. You get your coat, Katrin; you need it.

[KATRIN *goes out back L.*]

DAGMAR. Aunt Jenny says if we drank black coffee like you do at our age, it would turn our complexions dark. I'd like to be a black Norwegian. Like Uncle Chris. Can I, Papa?

PAPA. I like you better blonde. Like Mama.

DAGMAR. When do you get old enough for your complexion *not* to turn dark? When can we drink coffee?

PAPA. One day, when you are grown up.

[JENNY *and* TRINA *have come to the street door L.* JENNY *knocks.*]

MAMA. There are Jenny and Trina. (*She goes to the door.*) Is good. We can start now. (*She opens the door.* JENNY *and* TRINA *come in.*)

JENNY. Well, are you all ready? Is Katrin very excited?

PAPA (*nodding*). She ate no supper.

[MAMA *has started to put on her hat, and to put on Dagmar's hat and coat for her.* CHRISTINE *comes back from the pantry.* PAPA *gives her a dipped cube of sugar.*]

JENNY. Is that *black* coffee you dipped that sugar in? Lars, you shouldn't. It's not good for them. It'll . . .

PAPA (*finishing for her*). Turn their complexions black. I know. Well, maybe it is all right if we have *one* dark Norwegian.

JENNY. Lars, really!

[KATRIN *returns with her coat.*]

KATRIN. Aunt Jenny, did you see my graduation present?

[*She gets it from a chair.* CHRISTINE *gives her a disgusted look, and goes out back L.* KATRIN *displays the dresser set.*]

Look! It's got a hair receiver.

JENNY. But I thought . . . Marta, I thought you were going to give her . . .

MAMA. No, you were right, Jenny. She is too young to appreciate that. She like something more gay . . . more modern.

JENNY. H'm. Well, it's very pretty, I suppose, but . . . (*She looks up as* MAMA *puts on her coat.*) You're not wearing your *solje!*

MAMA (*quickly*). No. I do not wear it tonight. Come Trina, we shall be late.

TRINA. Oh, but Peter isn't here yet.

MAMA. Katrin has her costume to put on. He can follow. Or do you like to wait for Peter?

TRINA. I think . . . if you don't mind . . .

MAMA. You can stay with Lars. He does not have to go yet.

JENNY. I hope Katrin knows her part.

PAPA. Sure she knows it. *I* know it, too.

TRINA. It's too bad he can't see Katrin's debut as an actress.

MAMA. You will be back before us, Lars?

PAPA (*nodding*). I think the meeting will not last long.

MAMA. Is good. We go now.

[*She goes out with* JENNY *and* DAGMAR. CHRISTINE *and* NELS *return from back L., and follow, waiting outside for* KATRIN, *while the others go ahead.* KATRIN *puts on her hat and coat and picks up the dresser set.*]

PAPA (*to* TRINA). You like we play a game of checkers while we wait?

TRINA. Oh, I haven't played checkers in years.

PAPA. Then I beat you. (*He rises to get the checker set.* KATRIN *kisses him.*)

KATRIN. Good-by, Papa.

PAPA. Good-by, daughter. I think of you.

KATRIN. I'll see you there, Aunt Trina.

TRINA. Good luck!

PAPA. I get the checkers.

[KATRIN *goes out L.,* PAPA *gets the checker set from a cupboard under the dresser, brings it to the table and sets it up during the ensuing scene, which is played outside in the street.*]

CHRISTINE (*contemptuously*). Oh, bringing your cheap trash with you to show off?

KATRIN. It's not trash. It's beautiful. You're just jealous.

CHRISTINE. I told you you'd devil Mama into giving it to you.

KATRIN. I didn't. I didn't devil her at all. I just showed it to her in Mr. Schiller's window.

CHRISTINE. And made her go and sell her brooch that her very own mother gave her.

KATRIN. What?

NELS. Chris . . . you weren't supposed to tell that!

CHRISTINE. I don't care. I think she ought to know.

KATRIN. Is that true? Did Mama—Nels—?

NELS. Well, yes, as a matter of fact, she did. Now, come on.

KATRIN. No, no, I don't believe it. I'm going to ask Papa.

NELS. You haven't time.

KATRIN. I don't care.

[*She rushes back to the house and dashes into the kitchen.* CHRISTINE *goes off down L.,* NELS *follows her.*]

Papa—Papa—Christine says—Papa, did Mama sell her brooch to give me this?

PAPA. Christine should not have told you that.

KATRIN. It's true, then?

PAPA. She did not sell it. She traded it to Mr. Schiller for your present.

KATRIN (*near tears*). Oh, but she shouldn't. . . . I never meant . . .

PAPA. Look, Katrin. You wanted the present. Mama wanted your happiness; she wanted it more than she wanted the brooch.

KATRIN. But I never meant her to do *that*. (*Crying*) She *loved* it so. It was all she had of Grandmother's.

PAPA. She always meant it for you, Katrin. And you must not cry. You have your play to act.

KATRIN (*sobbing*). I don't want to act in it now.

PAPA. But you must. Your audience is waiting.

KATRIN (*as before*). I don't care.

PAPA. But you must care. Tonight you are not Katrin any longer. You are an actress. And an actress must act, whatever she is feeling. There is a saying—what is it—

TRINA (*brightly*). The mails must go through!

PAPA. No, no. The show must go on. So you stop crying, and go and act your play. We talk of this later. Afterwards.

KATRIN (*pulling herself together*). All right. I'll go.

[*Sniffing a good deal, she picks up the dresser set and goes back to the street and off down L.* PAPA *and* TRINA *exchange glances, and then settle down to their checkers.*]

PAPA. Now we play.

[*The lights fade and the curtains close. Spot up on stage R. turntable. The two girls from the earlier scene are dressing in costumes for* The Merchant of Venice *before a plank dressing table.*]

DOROTHY. I'm getting worried about Katrin. If anything's happened to her . . .

MADELINE (*pulling up her tights*). I'll forget my lines. I know I will. I'll look out and see Miss Forrester sitting there, and forget every single line.

[KATRIN *rushes in from the L. She carries the dresser set, places it on the dressing table.*]

We thought you'd had an accident, or something. . . .

KATRIN. Dorothy, is your father here tonight?

DOROTHY. He's going to be. Why?

KATRIN. I want to speak to him. (*As she pulls off her hat and coat*) Will you tell him . . . please . . . not to go away without speaking to me? After. After the exercises.

DOROTHY. What on earth do you want to speak to Father for?

KATRIN. I've got something to say to him. Something to ask him. It's important. *Very* important.

MADELINE. Is that the dresser set? (*Picking it up*) Can I look at it a minute?

KATRIN (*snatching it from her, violently*). No!

MADELINE. Why, what's the matter? I only wanted to look at it.

KATRIN (*emotionally*). You can't. You're not to touch it. Dorothy, you take it and put it where I can't see it. (*She thrusts it at her.*) Go on. . . . Take it! Take it! Take it!

[*Blackout.*

Curtains part on the kitchen. MAMA *and* PAPA *in conclave* [1] *at the table with cups of coffee.*]

MAMA. I am worried about her, Lars. When it was over, I see her talking with Mr. Schiller—and then she goes to take off her costume and Nels tells me that he will bring her home. But it is long time, and is late for her to be out. And in the play, Lars, she was not good. I have heard her practice it here, and she was good, but tonight, no. It was as if . . . as if she was thinking of something else all the time.

PAPA. I think maybe she was.

MAMA. But what? What can be worrying her?

PAPA. Marta . . . tonight, after you leave, Katrin found out about your brooch.

MAMA. My brooch? But how? Who told her?

PAPA. Christine.

MAMA (*angry*). Why?

PAPA. I do not know.

MAMA (*rising with a sternness we have not seen before, and calling*). Christine! Christine!

CHRISTINE (*emerging from the pantry, wiping a dish*). Were you calling me, Mama?

MAMA. Yes. Christine, did you tell Katrin tonight about my brooch?

CHRISTINE (*frightened, but firm*). Yes.

MAMA. Why did you?

CHRISTINE. Because I hated the smug way she was acting over that dresser set.

MAMA. Is no excuse. You make her unhappy. You make her not good in the play.

CHRISTINE. Well, she made *you* unhappy, giving up your brooch for her selfishness.

MAMA. Is not your business. I choose to give my brooch. Is not for you to judge. And you know I do not want you to tell. I am angry with you, Christine.

CHRISTINE. I'm sorry. But I'm not sorry I told. (*She goes back to the pantry with a set, obstinate face.*)

PAPA. Christine is the stubborn one.

[1] *conclave* (kŏn′klāv): a private meeting.

[NELS *and* KATRIN *have approached the house outside L. They stop and look at each other in the lamplight.* KATRIN *looks scared. Then* NELS *pats her, and she goes in,* NELS *following.* MAMA *looks up inquiringly and searchingly into Katrin's face.* KATRIN *turns away, taking off her hat and coat, and taking something from her pocket.*]

NELS. What happened at the meeting, Papa?

PAPA. We go back to work tomorrow.

NELS. Gee, that's bully. Isn't it, Mama?

MAMA (*absently*). Yes, is good.

KATRIN (*coming to* MAMA). Mama . . . here's your brooch. (*She gives it to her.*) I'm sorry I was so bad in the play. I'll go and help Christine with the dishes. (*She turns and goes into the pantry.*)

MAMA (*unwrapping the brooch from tissue paper*). Mr. Schiller give it back to her?

NELS. We went to his house to get it. He didn't want to. He was planning to give it to his wife for her birthday. But Katrin begged and begged him. She even offered to go and work in his store during her vacation if he'd give it back.

PAPA (*impressed*). So? So!

MAMA. And what did Mr. Schiller say?

NELS. He said that wasn't necessary. But he gave her a job all the same. She's going to work for him, afternoons, for three dollars a week.

MAMA. And the dresser set—she gave that back?

NELS. Yes. She was awful upset, Mama. It was kinda hard for her to do. She's a good kid. Well, I'll say good night. I've got to be up early.

PAPA. Good night, Nels.

NELS. Good night, Papa.

[*He goes out back L.*]

MAMA. Good night, Nels.

PAPA. Nels is the kind one.

[*He starts to refill Mama's coffee cup. She stops him, putting her hand over her cup.*]

No?

MAMA (*rising, crossing R. and calling*). Katrin! Katrin!

KATRIN (*coming to the pantry door*). Yes, Mama?

MAMA. Come here. (KATRIN *comes to her.* MAMA *holds out the brooch.*) You put this on.

KATRIN. No . . . it's yours.

MAMA. It is your graduation present. I put it on for you. (*She pins the brooch on Katrin's dress.*)

KATRIN (*near tears*). I'll wear it always. I'll keep it forever.

MAMA. Christine should not have told you.

KATRIN. I'm glad she did. Now.

PAPA. And I am glad, too. (*He dips a lump of sugar and holds it out to her.*) Katrin?

KATRIN (*tearful again, shakes her head*). I'm sorry, Papa. I . . . I don't feel like it.

[*She moves away and sits on the chest under the window, with her back to the room.*]

PAPA. So? So? (*He goes to the dresser.*)

MAMA. What you want, Lars?

[*He does not answer, but takes a cup and saucer, comes to the table and pours a cup of coffee, indicating* KATRIN *with his head.* MAMA *nods, pleased, then checks his pouring and fills up the cup from the cream pitcher which she empties in so doing.* PAPA *puts in sugar, and moves to* KATRIN.]

PAPA. Katrin. (*She turns. He holds out the cup.*)

KATRIN (*incredulous*). For me?

PAPA. For our grown-up daughter.

[MAMA *nods.* KATRIN *takes the cup, lifts it—then her emotion overcomes her. She thrusts it at* PAPA *and rushes from the room.*]

PAPA. Katrin is the dramatic one! Is too bad. Her first cup of coffee, and she does not drink it.

MAMA. It would not have been good for her, so late at night.

PAPA (*smiling*). And you, Marta, you are the practical one.

MAMA. You drink the coffee, Lars. We do not want to waste it. (*She pushes it across to him.*)

[*Lights dim. Curtains close.*
Lights up on L. turntable, representing the parlor of Jenny's

house. A telephone is on a table, at which TRINA *is discovered, talking.*]

TRINA (*into phone*). Yes, Peter. Yes, Peter. I know, Peter, but we don't know where he is. It's so long since we heard from him. He's sure to turn up soon. Yes, I know, Peter. I know, but . . . (*Subsiding obediently*) Yes, Peter. Yes, Peter. (*Sentimentally*) Oh, Peter, you know I do. Good-by, Peter.

[*She hangs up, and turns, to see* JENNY, *who has come in behind her, eating a piece of toast and jam.*]

JENNY. What was all that about?

TRINA. Peter says we shouldn't wait any longer to hear from Uncle Chris. He says we should send the wedding invitations out right away. He was quite insistent about it. Peter can be very masterful, sometimes . . . when he's alone with *me!*

[*The telephone rings again.* JENNY *answers it, putting down the toast, which* TRINA *takes up and nibbles at during the scene.*]

JENNY. This is Mrs. Stenborg's boardinghouse. Mrs. Stenborg speaking. Oh, yes, Marta . . . what is it? (*She listens.*)

[*Spot up on R. turntable, disclosing* MAMA *standing at a wall telephone booth. She wears a hat and coat, and has an opened telegram in her hand.*]

MAMA. Jenny, is Uncle Chris. I have a telegram. It says if we want to see him again we should come without delay.

JENNY. Where is he?

MAMA (*consulting the telegram*). It comes from a place called Ukiah. Nels says it is up north from San Francisco.

JENNY. Who is the telegram from?

MAMA. It does not say.

JENNY. That . . . woman?

MAMA. I don't know, Jenny. I think maybe.

JENNY. I won't go.

[SIGRID *comes in through the curtains C., dressed in a hat and coat, carrying string marketing bags, full of vegetables.* JENNY *speaks to her, whisperingly, aside.*]

It's Uncle Chris. Marta say he's dying. (*Then, back into phone*) Why was the telegram sent to *you?* I'm the eldest.

MAMA. Jenny, is not the time to think of who is eldest. Uncle Chris is dying.

JENNY. I don't believe it. He's too mean to die. Ever.

[NELS *comes to booth from wings, R., and hands* MAMA *a slip of paper.*]

I'm not going.

MAMA. Jenny, I cannot stop to argue. There is a train at eleven o'clock. It takes four hours. You call Sigrid.

JENNY. Sigrid is here now.

MAMA. Good. Then you tell her.

JENNY. What do you say the name of the place is?

MAMA. Ukiah. (*Spelling in Norwegian*) U.K.I.A.H.

JENNY. I won't go.

MAMA. That *you* decide. (*She hangs up. Her spot goes out.*)

SIGRID. Uncle Chris dying!

JENNY. The wages of sin.

TRINA. Oh, he's old. Maybe it is time for him to go.

JENNY. Four hours by train, and maybe have to stay all night. All that expense to watch a wicked old man die of the D.T.'s.

SIGRID. I know, but . . . there is his will. . . .

JENNY. Huh, even supposing he's anything to leave—you know who he'd leave it *to,* don't you?

SIGRID. Yes. But all the same, he's dying now, and blood is thicker than water. Especially when it's Norwegian. I'm going. I shall take Arne with me. Uncle Chris was always fond of children.

TRINA. I agree with Sigrid. I think we *should* go.

JENNY. Well, *you* can't go, anyway.

TRINA. Why not?

JENNY. Because of that woman. You can't meet a woman like that.

TRINA. Why not? If you two can . . .

SIGRID. We're married women.

TRINA. I'm engaged!

JENNY. That's not the same thing.

SIGRID. Not the same thing at all!

TRINA. Nonsense. I've never met a woman like that. Maybe I'll never get another chance. Besides, if he's going to change his will, there's still my dowry, remember. Do you think we should take Peter?

JENNY. Peter Thorkelson? Whatever for?

TRINA. Well, after all, I mean . . . I mean, his profession . . .

JENNY. Trina, you always were a fool. Anyone would know the last person a dying man wants to see is an undertaker!

[*Blackout. Turntable revolves out. Spot up on* KATRIN, *standing down front, R.C. She wears her schoolgirl hat.*]

KATRIN. When Mama said I was to go with her, I was excited and I was frightened. It was exciting to take sandwiches for the train, almost as though we were going on a picnic. But I was scared at the idea of seeing death, though I told myself that if I was going to be a writer I had to experience everything. But all the same, I hoped it would be all over when we got there. (*She starts to walk toward C. and up the steps.*)

It was afternoon when we arrived. We asked at the station for the Halvorsen ranch, and it seemed to me that the man looked at us strangely. Uncle Chris was obviously considered an odd character. The ranch was about three miles from the town; a derelict, rambling old place. There was long grass, and tall trees, and a smell of honeysuckle. We made quite a cavalcade, walking up from the gate.

[*The procession comes in from the R., behind* KATRIN. MAMA, JENNY, TRINA, SIGRID, *and* ARNE.]

The woman came out on the steps to meet us.

[*The procession starts toward the C., moving upward. The* WOMAN *comes through the curtains, down one step. The* AUNTS *freeze in their tracks.* MAMA *goes forward to her.*]

MAMA. How is he? Is he—?

WOMAN (*with grave self-possession*). Come in, won't you?

[*She holds the curtains slightly aside.* MAMA *goes in.* KATRIN *follows, looking curiously at the* WOMAN. *The* AUNTS *walk stiffly past her,* SIGRID *clutching* ARNE *and shielding him from contact with the* WOMAN. *They disappear behind the curtains. The* WOMAN *stands a moment, looking off into the distance. Then she goes in behind the curtains, too.*

The curtains draw apart, revealing Uncle Chris's bedroom. It is simple, and shabby. The door to the room is at the back, L. In the L. wall is a window, with curtains, drawn aside now. In front of it, a washstand. The afternoon sunlight comes through the window, falling onto the big double bed, in which UNCLE CHRIS *is propped up on pillows. Beside him, R., on a small table is a pitcher of water. He has a glass in his hand.* MAMA *stands to the R. of him:* JENNY *to the L. The others are ranged below the window. The* WOMAN *is not present.*]

UNCLE CHRIS (*handing* MAMA *the empty glass*). I want more. You give me more. Is still some in the bottle.

MAMA. Uncle Chris, that will not help now.

UNCLE CHRIS. It always help. (*With a glance at* JENNY) Now especially.

JENNY (*firmly*). Uncle Chris, I don't think you realize . . .

UNCLE CHRIS. What I don't realize? That I am dying? Why else do I think you come here? Why else do I think you stand there, watching me? (*He sits upright.*) Get out. Get out. I don't want you here. Get out!

JENNY. Oh, very well. Very well. We'll be outside on the porch, if you want us. (*She starts toward the door.*)

UNCLE CHRIS. That is where I want you—on the porch!

[JENNY *goes out.* TRINA *follows.* SIGRID *is about to go, too, when* UNCLE CHRIS *stops her.*]

Wait. That is Arne. Come here, Arne. (ARNE, *propelled by* SIGRID, *advances toward the bed.*) How is your knee?

ARNE. It's fine, Uncle Chris.

UNCLE CHRIS. Not hurt any more? You don't use svear vords any more?

ARNE. N-no, Uncle Chris.

UNCLE CHRIS. You walk goot? Quite goot? Let me see you walk. Walk around the room. (ARNE *does so.*) Fast. Fast. Run! Run! (ARNE *does so.*) Is goot.

SIGRID (*encouraged and advancing*). Uncle Chris, Arne has always been so fond of you. . . .

UNCLE CHRIS (*shouting*). I tell you all to get out. Except Marta. (*As* KATRIN *edges with the* AUNTS *to the door*) And Katrin. Katrin and I haf secret. You remember, Katrin?

KATRIN. Yes, Uncle Chris.

MAMA. Uncle Chris, you must lie down again.

UNCLE CHRIS. Then you give me drink.

MAMA. No, Uncle Chris.

UNCLE CHRIS. We cannot waste what is left in the bottle. You do not drink it . . . who will drink it when I am gone? What harm can it do . . . now? I die, anyway. . . . You give it to me.

[MAMA *goes to the washstand, pours him a drink of whisky and water, and takes it to him, sitting on the bed beside him. He drinks, then turns to her, leaning back against her arm and the pillows.*]

Marta, I haf never made a will. Was never enough money. But you sell this ranch. It will not bring moch. I have not had it long enough. And there is mortgage. Big mortgage. But it leave a little. Maybe two, t'ree hundred dollars. You give to Yessie.

MAMA. Yessie?

UNCLE CHRIS. Yessie Brown. My housekeeper. No, why I call her that to you? You understand. She is my voman. Twelve years she has been my wife. She was trained nurse, but she get sick and I bring her to the country to get well again. There will be no money for *you,* Marta. Always I wanted there should be money to make Nils doctor. But there were other things . . . quick things. And now there is no time to make more. There is no money, but you make Nils doctor, all the same. You like?

MAMA. Sure, Uncle Chris. It is what Lars and I have always wanted for him. To help people who suffer . . .

UNCLE CHRIS. Is the greatest thing in the world. It is to have a little of God in you. Always I wanted to be doctor myself. Is the only thing I have ever wanted. Nils must do it for me.

MAMA. He will, Uncle Chris.

UNCLE CHRIS. Is goot. (*He strokes her hand.*) You are the goot one. I am glad you come, *Lille Ven.* (*He moves his head restlessly.*) Where is Yessie?

MAMA. I think she wait outside.

UNCLE CHRIS. You call her. I like you both be here.

[MAMA *goes, with a quick glance at* KATRIN. UNCLE CHRIS *signs to* KATRIN *to come closer. She sits on the chair beside the bed.*]

Katrin, your Mama write me you drink coffee now? (*She nods. He looks at her affectionately.*) Katrin, who will be writer. . . . You are not frightened of me now?

KATRIN. No, Uncle Chris.

UNCLE CHRIS. One day maybe you write story about Uncle Chris. If you remember.

KATRIN (*whispering*). I'll remember.

[MAMA *returns with the* WOMAN. *They come to the side of his bed.*]

UNCLE CHRIS (*obviously exhausted and in pain*). I like you both stay with me . . . now. I think best now maybe Katrin go away. Good-by, Katrin. (*Then he repeats it in Norwegian.*) Farvell, Katrin.

KATRIN. Good-by, Uncle Chris.

UNCLE CHRIS. You say it in Norwegian, like I do.

KATRIN (*in Norwegian*). Farvell, Onkel Chris. (*She slips out, in tears.*)

UNCLE CHRIS. Yessie! Maybe I should introduce you to each other. Yessie, this is my niece, Marta. The only von of my nieces I can stand. Marta, this is Yessie, who have give me much happiness. . . . (*The* TWO WOMEN *shake hands.*)

MAMA. I am very glad to meet you.

JESSIE. I am, too.

UNCLE CHRIS (*as they shake*). Is goot. And now you give me von more drink. You have drink with me . . . both of you. That way we finish the bottle. Yes? (JESSIE *and* MAMA *look at each other.*)

MAMA. Sure, Uncle Chris.

UNCLE CHRIS. Goot. Yessie, you get best glasses. (*With a chuckle to* MAMA) Yessie does not like to drink, but this is special occasion. (JESSIE *gets three glasses from a wall shelf.*) What is the time?

MAMA. It is about half past four, Uncle Chris.

UNCLE CHRIS. The sun come around this side the house in afternoon. You draw the curtain a little maybe. Is strong for my eyes.

[MAMA *goes over and draws the curtain over the window. The stage darkens.* JESSIE *pours three drinks, filling two of the glasses with water. She is about to put water in the third when* UNCLE CHRIS *stops her.*]

No, no, I take it now without water. Always the last drink without water. Is Norwegian custom. (*To* MAMA, *with a smile*) True?

[JESSIE *sits on the bed beside him, about to feed his drink to him, but he pushes her aside.*]

No. No. I do not need you feed it to me. I can drink myself. (*He takes the glass from her.*) Give Marta her glass.

[JESSIE *hands a glass to* MAMA. *The two women stand on either side of the bed, holding their glasses.*]

So. . . . Skoal!

JESSIE (*clinking glasses with him*). Skoal.

MAMA (*doing likewise*). Skoal.

[*They all three drink. Slow dim to blackout. Curtains close.*
Spot up on R. turntable. A porch with a bench, and a chair, on which the three AUNTS *are sitting.* JENNY *is dozing.*]

SIGRID (*flicking her handkerchief*). These gnats are awful. I'm being simply eaten alive.

TRINA. Gnats are always worse around sunset. (*She catches one.*)

JENNY (*rousing herself*). I should never have let you talk me into coming. To be insulted like that . . . turned out of his room . . . and then expected to sit here hour after hour without as much as a cup of coffee. . . .

SIGRID. I'd make coffee if I knew where the kitchen was.

JENNY. *Her* kitchen? It would poison me. (*Rising*) No, I'm going home. Are you coming, Trina?

TRINA. Oh, I think we ought to wait a little longer. After all, you can't *hurry* these things. . . . I mean . . . (*She breaks off in confusion at what she has said.*)

JENNY (*to* SIGRID). And all your talk about his will. A lot of chance we got to say a word!

TRINA. Maybe Marta's been talking to him.

[MAMA *comes from between the curtains C.*]

JENNY. Well?

MAMA. Uncle Chris has . . . gone.

[*There is a silence.*]

JENNY (*more gently than is her wont*). Did he . . . say anything about a will?

MAMA. There is no will.

JENNY. Well, then, that means . . . we're his nearest relatives. . . .

MAMA. There is no money, either.

SIGRID. How do you know?

MAMA. He told me. (*She brings out a small notebook that she is carrying.*)

JENNY. What's that?

MAMA. Is an account of how he spent the money.

JENNY. Bills from a liquor store.

MAMA. No, Jenny. No. I read it to you. (JENNY *sits again.*) You know how Uncle Chris was lame . . . how he walked always with limp. It was his one thought . . . lame people. He would have liked to be doctor and help them. Instead, he help them other ways. I read you the last page. . . . (*She reads from the notebook.*) "Joseph Spinelli. Four years old. Tubercular left leg. Three hundred thirty-seven dollars, eighteen cents." (*Pause.*) "Walks now. Esta Jensen. Nine years. Clubfoot. Two hundred seventeen dollars, fifty cents. Walks now." (*Then reading very slowly*) "*Arne* Solfeldt. . . ."

SIGRID (*startled*). *My* Arne?

MAMA (*reading on*). "Nine years. Fractured kneecap. Four hundred forty-two dollars, sixteen cents."

[KATRIN *and* ARNE *come running in from the L. across the stage.*]

ARNE (*calling as he comes running across*). Mother . . . Mother . . . Are we going to eat soon?

[*He stops, awed by the solemnity of the group, and by* MAMA, *who puts out her hand gently, to silence him.*]

What is it? Is Uncle Chris . . . ?

MAMA (*to the* AUNTS). It does not tell the end about Arne. I like to write "Walks now." Yes?

SIGRID (*very subdued*). Yes.

MAMA (*taking a pencil from the book*). Maybe even . . . "runs"?

[SIGRID *nods, moist-eyed.* TRINA *is crying.* MAMA *writes in the book, and then closes it.*]

So. Is finished. Is all. (*She touches* JENNY *on the shoulder.*) It was good.

JENNY (*after a gulping moment*). I go and make some coffee.

[*The woman,* JESSIE, *appears from between the curtains on the steps.*]

JESSIE. You can go in and see him now if you want.

[JENNY *looks back, half hesitant at the others. Then she nods and goes in.* TRINA *follows her, mopping her eyes.* SIGRID *puts her arm suddenly around* ARNE *in a spasm of maternal affection, and they, too, go in.* MAMA, KATRIN, *and* JESSIE *are left alone.*]

I'm moving down to the hotel for tonight . . . so that you can all stay. (*She is about to go back, when* MAMA *stops her.*)

MAMA. Wait. What will you do now . . . after he is buried? You have money? (JESSIE *shakes her head.*) Where you live?

JESSIE. I'll find a room somewhere. I'll probably go back to nursing.

MAMA. You like to come to San Francisco for a little? To our house? We have room. Plenty room.

JESSIE (*touched, moving to* MAMA). That's very kind of you, but . . .

MAMA. I like to have you. You come for a little as our guest. When you get work you can be our boarder.

JESSIE (*awkwardly grateful*). I don't know why you should bother. . . .

MAMA (*touching her*). You were good to Uncle Chris.

[JESSIE *grasps her hand, deeply moved, then turns and goes quickly back through the curtains.* MAMA *turns to* KATRIN.]

Katrin, you come and see him?

KATRIN (*scared*). See him? You mean . . .

MAMA. I like you see him. You need not be frightened. He looks . . . happy and at peace. I like you to know what death looks like. Then you are not frightened of it, ever.

KATRIN. Will you come with me?

MAMA. Sure.

[*She stretches out her hand, puts her arm around her, and then leads her gently in through the curtains.*
Spot up on L. turntable, representing a park bench against a hedge. TRINA, *and* MR. THORKELSON, *in outdoor clothes, are seated together.* TRINA *is cooing over a baby carriage.*]

TRINA. Who's the most beautiful Norwegian baby in San Francisco? Who's going to be three months old tomorrow? Little Christopher Thorkelson! (*To* MR. THORKELSON) Do you know, Peter, I think he's even beginning to *look* a little like Uncle Chris! Quite apart from his black curls—and those, of course, he gets from *you*. (*To baby again*) He's going to grow up to be a black Norwegian, isn't he, just like his daddy and his Uncle Chris? (*Settling down beside* MR. THORKELSON) I think there's something about his mouth . . . a sort of . . . well . . . *firmness*. Of course, it's *your* mouth, too. But then I've always thought you had quite a lot of Uncle Chris about you. (*She looks back at the baby.*) Look—he's asleep!

MR. THORKELSON. Trina, do you know what next Thursday is?

TRINA (*nodding, smiling*). Our anniversary.

MR. THORKELSON. What would you think of our giving a little party?

TRINA. A party?

MR. THORKELSON. Oh, quite a modest one. Nothing showy or ostentatious—but, after all, we have been married a year, and with your having been in mourning and the baby coming so soon and everything, we've not been able to entertain. I think it's time you . . . took your place in society.

TRINA (*scared*). What . . . sort of a party?

MR. THORKELSON. An evening party. (*Proudly*) A soiree! [1] I should say about ten people . . . some of the Norwegian colony . . . and Lars and Marta, of course. . . .

TRINA (*beginning to count on her fingers*). And Jenny and Sigrid. . . .

MR. THORKELSON. Oh . . . I . . . I hadn't thought of asking Jenny and Sigrid.

TRINA. Oh, we'd have to. We couldn't leave them out.

MR. THORKELSON. Trina, I hope you won't be offended if I say that I have never really felt . . . well, altogether com-

[1] *soiree* (swä·rā′): an evening party.

fortable with Jenny and Sigrid. They have always made me feel that they didn't think I was . . . well . . . *worthy* of you. Of course, I know I'm not, but . . . well . . . one doesn't like to be reminded of it . . . *all* the time.

TRINA (*taking his hand*). Oh, Peter.

MR. THORKELSON. But you're quite right. We must ask them. Now, as to the matter of refreshments . . . what would you suggest?

TRINA (*flustered*). Oh, I don't know. I . . . what would you say to . . . ice cream and cookies for the ladies . . . and coffee, of course . . . and . . . perhaps port wine for the gentlemen?

MR. THORKELSON (*anxiously*). Port wine?

TRINA. Just a little. You could bring it in already poured out, in *little* glasses. Jenny and Sigrid can help me serve the ice cream.

MR. THORKELSON (*firmly*). No. If Jenny and Sigrid come, they come as guests, like everyone else. You shall have someone in to help you in the kitchen.

TRINA. You mean a waitress? (MR. THORKELSON *nods, beaming.*) Oh, but none of us have *ever* . . . do you really think . . . I mean . . . you did say we shouldn't be ostentatious. . . .

MR. THORKELSON (*nervously*). Trina, there's something I would like to say. I've never been very good at expressing myself or my . . . well . . . *deeper* feelings—but I want you to know that I'm not only very fond of you, but very . . . well . . . very *proud* of you as well, and I want you to have the best of everything, as far as it's in my power to give it to you. (*As a climax*) I want you to have a waitress!

TRINA (*overcome*). Yes, Peter. (*They hold hands.*)

[*The lights fade and the turntable revolves out.*
Curtains part on kitchen, slightly changed, smartened and refurnished now. MAMA *and* PAPA *seated as ususal.* DAGMAR, *looking a little older, is seated on the chest, reading a solid-looking book.* NELS *enters from back L. door, carrying a newspaper. He wears long trousers now, and looks about seventeen.*]

NELS. Hello! Here's your evening paper, Papa.

[PAPA *puts down the morning paper he is reading, and takes the evening one from* NELS.]

PAPA. Is there any news?

NELS. No.

[*He takes out a package of cigarettes with elaborate unconcern.* MAMA *watches with disapproval. Then, as he is about to light his cigarette, he stops, remembering something.*]

Oh, I forgot. There's a letter for Katrin. I picked it up on the mat as I came in. (*Going to door back L., and calling*) Katrin! Katrin! There's a letter for you.

KATRIN (*answering from off stage*). Coming!

MAMA. Nels, you know who the letter is from?

NELS. Why, no Mama. (*Hands it to her*) It looks like her own handwriting.

MAMA (*gravely inspecting it*). Is bad.

PAPA. Why is bad?

MAMA. She get too many like that. I think they are stories she send to the magazines.

DAGMAR (*closing her book loudly, rising*). Well, I'll go and see if I have any puppies yet. Mama, I've just decided something.

MAMA. What have you decided?

DAGMAR. If Nels is going to be a doctor, when I grow up, I'm going to be a—(*looking at the book title, and stumbling over the word*) vet-vet-veterinarian.

MAMA. And what is that?

DAGMAR. A doctor for animals.

MAMA. Is good. Is good.

DAGMAR. There are far more animals in the world than there are human beings, and far more human·doctors than animal ones. It isn't fair. (*She goes to the pantry door.*) I suppose we couldn't have a horse, could we?

[*This only produces a concerted laugh from the family. She turns, sadly.*]

No. . . . I was afraid we couldn't.

[*She goes into the pantry.* KATRIN *comes in, back L. She wears a slightly more adult dress than before. Her hair is up and she looks about eighteen.*]

KATRIN. Where's the letter?

MAMA (*handing it to her*). Here.

[KATRIN *takes it, nervously. She looks at the envelope, and her face falls. She opens it, pulls out a manuscript and a rejection slip, looks at it a moment, and then replaces both in the envelope. The others watch her covertly. Then she looks up, with determination.*]

KATRIN. Mama . . . Papa . . . I want to say something.

PAPA. What is it?

KATRIN. I'm not going to go to college.

PAPA. Why not?

KATRIN. Because it would be a waste of time and money. The only point in my going to college was to be a writer. Well, I'm not going to be one, so . . .

MAMA. Katrin, is it your letter that makes you say this? It is a story come back again?

KATRIN. Again is right. This is the tenth time. I made this one a test. It's the best I've ever written, or ever shall write. I know that. Well, it's no good.

NELS. What kind of a story is it?

KATRIN. Oh . . . it's a story about a painter, who's a genius, and he goes blind.

NELS. Sounds like *The Light That Failed.*[1]

KATRIN. Well, what's wrong with that?

NELS (*quickly*). Nothing. Nothing!

KATRIN. Besides, it's not like that. My painter gets better. He has an operation and recovers his sight, and paints better than ever before.

MAMA. Is good.

KATRIN (*bitterly unhappy*). No, it isn't. It's rotten. But it's the best I can do.

MAMA. You have asked your teachers about this?

KATRIN. Teachers don't know anything about writing. They just know about literature.

MAMA. If there was someone we could ask . . . for advice . . . to tell us . . . tell us if your stories are good.

KATRIN. Yes. Well, there isn't. And they're *not.*

PAPA (*looking at the evening paper*). There is something here in the paper about a lady writer. I just noticed the headline. Wait.

[1] *The Light That Failed:* a novel by Rudyard Kipling.

(*He looks back for it and reads.*) "Woman writer tells key to literary success."

KATRIN. Who?

PAPA. A lady called Florence Dana Moorhead. It gives her picture. A fat lady. You have heard of her?

KATRIN. Yes, of course. Everyone has. She's terribly successful. She's here on a lecture tour.

MAMA. What does she say is the secret?

PAPA. You read it, Katrin. (*He hands her the paper.*)

KATRIN (*gabbling the first part*). "Florence Dana Moorhead, celebrated novelist and short-story writer . . . blah-blah-blah . . . interviewed today in her suite at the Fairmont . . . blah-blah-blah . . . pronounced sincerity the one essential quality for success as a writer." (*Throwing aside the paper*) A lot of help that is.

MAMA. Katrin, this lady . . . maybe if you sent her your stories, *she* could tell you what is wrong with them?

KATRIN (*wearily*). Oh, Mama, don't be silly.

MAMA. Why is silly?

KATRIN. Well, in the first place because she's a very important person . . . a celebrity . . . and she'd never read them. And in the second, because . . . you seem to think writing's like . . . well, like cooking, or something. That all you have to have is the recipe. It takes a lot more than that. You have to have a gift for it.

MAMA. You have to have a gift for cooking, too. But there are things you can learn, if you have the gift.

KATRIN. Well, that's the whole point. I haven't. I *know* . . . now. So, if you've finished with the morning paper, Papa, I'll take the want ad section, and see if I can find myself a job.

[*She takes the morning paper and goes out R.*]

MAMA. Is bad. Nels, what you think?

NELS. I don't know, Mama. Her stories seem all right to me, but I don't know.

MAMA. It would be good to know. Nels, this lady in the paper . . . what else does she say?

NELS (*taking up the paper*). Not much. The rest seems to be about *her* and her home. Let's see. . . . (*He reads.*) "Apart from literature, Mrs. Moorhead's main interest in life is gastronomy."

MAMA. The stars?

NELS. No—eating. "A brilliant cook herself, she says that she would as soon turn out a good soufflé as a short story, or find a new recipe as she would a first edition."

MAMA (*reaching for the paper*). I see her picture? (*She looks at it.*) Is kind face. (*Pause while she reads a moment. Then she looks up and asks*) What is first edition?

[*Blackout. Lights up on L. turntable, representing the lobby of the Fairmont hotel. A couch against a column with a palm behind it. An orchestra plays softly in the background.* MAMA *is discovered seated on the couch, waiting patiently. She wears a hat and a suit, and clutches a newspaper and a bundle of manuscripts. A couple of guests come through the curtains and cross, disappearing into the wings L.* MAMA *watches them. Then* FLORENCE DANA MOORHEAD *enters through the curtains. She is a stout, dressy, good-natured, middle-aged woman. A* BELLBOY *comes from the R., paging her.*]

BELLBOY. Miss Moorhead?

F. D. MOORHEAD. Yes?

BELLBOY. Telegram.

F. D. MOORHEAD. Oh. . . . Thank you.

[*She tips him, and he goes.* MAMA *rises and moves toward her.*]

MAMA. Please . . . Please . . . Miss Moorhead . . . Miss Moorhead.

F. D. MOORHEAD. (*Looking up from her telegram, on the steps*). Were you calling me?

MAMA. Yes. You are . . . Miss Florence Dana Moorhead?

F. D. MOORHEAD. Yes.

MAMA. Please . . . might I speak to you for a moment?

F. D. MOORHEAD. Yes—what's it about?

MAMA. I read in the paper what you say about writing.

F. D. MOORHEAD (*with a vague social smile*). Oh, yes?

MAMA. My daughter, Katrin, wants to be writer.

F. D. MOORHEAD (*who has heard that one before*). Oh, really? (*She glances at her watch on her bosom.*)

MAMA. I bring her stories.

F. D. MOORHEAD. Look, I'm afraid I'm in rather a hurry. I'm leaving San Francisco this evening. . . .

MAMA. I wait two hours here for you to come in. Please, if I may talk to you for one, two minutes. That is all.

F. D. MOORHEAD (*kindly*). Of course, but I think I'd better tell you that if you want me to read your daughter's stories, it's no use. I'm very sorry, but I've had to make it a rule never to read anyone's unpublished material.

MAMA (*nods—then after a pause*). It said in the paper you like to collect recipes . . . for eating.

F. D. MOORHEAD. Yes, I do. I've written several books on cooking.

MAMA. I, too, am interested in gastronomy. I am good cook. Norwegian. I make good Norwegian dishes. Lutefisk.[1] And Kjödboller. That is meat balls with sauce.

F. D. MOORHEAD. Yes, I know, I've eaten them in Christiania.[2]

MAMA. I have a special recipe for Kjödboller . . . my mother give me. She was best cook I ever knew. Never have I told this recipe, not even to my own sisters, because they are not good cooks.

F. D. MOORHEAD (*amused*). Oh?

MAMA. But . . . if you let me talk to you . . . I give it to you. I promise it is good recipe.

F. D. MOORHEAD (*vastly tickled now*). Well, that seems fair enough. Let's sit down. (*They move to the couch and sit.*) Now, your daughter wants to write, you say? How old is she?

MAMA. She is eighteen. Just.

F. D. MOORHEAD. *Does* she write, or does she just . . . *want* to write?

MAMA. Oh, she writes all the time. Maybe she should not be author, but it is hard to give up something that has meant so much.

F. D. MOORHEAD. I agree, but . . .

MAMA. I bring her stories. I bring twelve.

F. D. MOORHEAD (*aghast*). Twelve!

MAMA. But if you could read maybe just one . . . To know if someone is good cook, you do not need to eat a whole dinner.

F. D. MOORHEAD. You're very persuasive. How is it your daughter did not come herself?

[1] *Lutefisk:* specially treated codfish. [2] *Christiania:* the former name of Oslo, capital of Norway.

MAMA. She was too unhappy. And too scared . . . of you. Because you are celebrity. But I see your picture in the paper. . . .

F. D. MOORHEAD. That frightful picture!

MAMA. Is the picture of woman who like to eat good. . . .

F. D. MOORHEAD (*with a rueful smile*). It certainly is. Now, tell me about the Kjödboller.

MAMA. When you make the meat balls you drop them in boiling stock. Not water. That is one of the secrets.

F. D. MOORHEAD. Ah!

MAMA. And the cream sauce. That is another secret. It is half *sour* cream, added at the last.

F. D. MOORHEAD. That sounds marvelous.

MAMA. You must grind the meat six times. I could write it out for you. And . . . (*tentatively*) while I write, you could read?

F. D. MOORHEAD (*with a laugh*). All right. You win. Come upstairs to my apartment. (*She rises.*)

MAMA. Is kind of you. (*They start out L.*) Maybe if you read *two* stories, I could write the recipe for Lutefisk as well. You know Lutefisk . . . ?

[*They have disappeared into the wings, and the turntable revolves out.*
Spot up, R. turntable. KATRIN *at her desk.*]

KATRIN. When Mama came back, I was sitting with my diary, which I called my Journal now, writing a Tragic Farewell to my Art. It was very seldom that Mama came to the attic, thinking that a writer needed privacy, and I was surprised to see her standing in the doorway. (*She looks up.* MAMA *is standing on the steps, C.*) Mama!

MAMA. You are busy, Katrin?

KATRIN (*jumping up*). No, of course not. Come in.

MAMA (*coming down*). I like to talk to you.

KATRIN. Yes, of course.

MAMA (*seating herself at the desk*). You are writing?

KATRIN. No. I told you, that's all over.

MAMA. That is what I want to talk to you about.

KATRIN. It's all right, Mama. Really, it's all right. I was planning to tear up all my stories this afternoon, only I couldn't find half of them.

MAMA. They are here.

KATRIN. Did *you* take them? What for?

MAMA. Katrin, I have been to see Miss Moorhead.

KATRIN. Who's Miss . . . ? You don't mean Florence Dana Moorhead? (MAMA *nods.*) You don't mean . . . Mama, you don't mean you took her my stories?

MAMA. She read five of them. I was two hours with her. We have glass of sherry. Two glass of sherry.

KATRIN. What . . . what did she say about them?

MAMA (*quietly*). She say they are not good.

KATRIN (*turning away*). Well, I knew that. It was hardly worth your going to all that trouble just to be told that.

MAMA. She say more. Will you listen, Katrin?

KATRIN (*trying to be gracious*). Sure. Sure. I'll listen.

MAMA. I will try and remember. She say you write now only because of what you have read in other books, and that no one can write good until they have felt what they write about. That for years she write bad stories about people in the olden times, until one day she remember something that happen in her own town . . . something that only she could know and understand . . . and she feels she must tell it . . . and that is how she write her first good story. She say you must write more of things you know. . . .

KATRIN. That's what my teacher always told me at school.

MAMA. Maybe your teacher was right. I do not know if I explain good what Miss Moorhead means, but while she talks I think I understand. Your story about the painter who is blind . . . that is because . . . forgive me if I speak plain, my Katrin, but it is important to you . . . because you are the dramatic one, as Papa has said . . . and you think it would feel good to be a painter and be blind and not complain. But never have you imagined how it would really be. Is true?

KATRIN (*subdued*). Yes, I . . . I guess it's true.

MAMA. But she say you are to go on writing. That you have the gift. (KATRIN *turns back to her, suddenly aglow.*) And that when you have written story that is real and true . . . then you send it to someone whose name she give me. (*She fumbles for a piece of paper.*) It is her . . . agent . . . and say she recommend you. Here. No, that is recipe she give me for goulash as her grandmother make it . . . here . . . (*She hands over the paper.*) It helps, Katrin, what I told you?

KATRIN (*subdued again*). Yes, I . . . I guess it helps. Some. But what have *I* got to write about? I haven't seen anything, or been anywhere.

MAMA. Could you write about San Francisco, maybe? Is fine city. Miss Moorhead write about her home town.

KATRIN. Yes, I know. But you've got to have a central character or something. She writes about her grandfather . . . he was a wonderful old man.

MAMA. Could you maybe write about Papa?

KATRIN. Papa?

MAMA. Papa is fine man. Is wonderful man.

KATRIN. Yes, I know, but . . .

MAMA (*rising*). I must go fix supper. Is late. Papa will be home. (*She goes up the steps to the curtains, and then turns back.*) I like you should write about Papa. (*She goes inside.*)

KATRIN (*going back to her seat behind the desk*). Papa. Yes, but what's he ever done? What's ever happened to him? What's ever happened to *any* of us? Except always being poor and having illnesses, like the time when Dagmar went to the hospital and Mama . . . (*The idea hits her like a flash.*) Oh. . . . Oh. . . . (*Pause—then she becomes the* KATRIN *of today.*)

And that was how it was born . . . suddenly in a flash . . . the story of "Mama and the Hospital" . . . the first of all the stories. I wrote it . . . oh, quite soon after that. I didn't tell Mama or any of them. But I sent it to Miss Moorhead's agent. It was a long time before I heard anything . . . and then one evening the letter came. (*She takes an envelope from the desk in front of her.*) For a moment I couldn't believe it. Then I went rushing into the kitchen, shouting. . . .

[*She rises from the desk, taking some papers with her, and rushes upstage, crying, "Mama, Mama." The curtains have parted on the kitchen—and the family tableau—*MAMA, PAPA, CHRISTINE, *and* NELS. DAGMAR *is not present.* KATRIN *comes rushing in, up the steps. The R. turntable revolves out as soon as she has left it.*]

Mama . . . Mama . . . I've sold a story!

MAMA. A story?

KATRIN. Yes, I've got a letter from the agent . . . with a check for . . . (*gasping*) five hundred dollars!

NELS. No kidding?

MAMA. Katrin . . . is true?

KATRIN. Here it is. Here's the letter. Maybe I haven't read it right. (*She hands them the letter.* PAPA *and* MAMA *huddle and gloat over it.*)

CHRISTINE. What will you *do* with five hundred dollars?

KATRIN. I don't know. I'll buy Mama her warm coat, I know that.

CHRISTINE. Coats don't cost five hundred dollars.

KATRIN. I know. We'll put the rest in the Bank.

NELS (*kidding*). Quick. Before they change their mind, and stop the check.

KATRIN. Will you, Mama? Will you take it to the Bank downtown tomorrow? (MAMA *looks vague.*) What is it?

MAMA. I do not know how.

NELS. Just give it to the man and tell him to put it in your account, like you always do. (MAMA *looks up at* PAPA.)

PAPA. You tell them . . . now.

CHRISTINE. Tell us what?

MAMA (*desperately*). Is no Bank Account! Never in my life have I been inside a bank.

CHRISTINE. But you always told us . . .

KATRIN. Mama, you've always said . . .

MAMA. I know. But was not true. I tell a lie.

KATRIN. But why, Mama? Why did you pretend?

MAMA. Is not good for little ones to be afraid . . . to not feel secure. But now . . . with five hundred dollar . . . I think I can tell.

KATRIN (*going to her, emotionally*). Mama!

MAMA (*stopping her, quickly*). You read us the story. You have it there?

KATRIN. Yes.

MAMA. Then read.

KATRIN. Now?

MAMA. Yes. No—Wait. Dagmar must hear. (*She opens pantry door and calls.*) Dagmar.

DAGMAR (*off*). Yes, Mama?

MAMA (*calling*). Come here, I want you.

DAGMAR (*off*). What is it?

MAMA. I want you. No, you leave the rabbits! (*She comes back.*) What is it called . . . the story?

KATRIN (*seating herself in the chair that Mr. Hyde took in the opening scene*). It's called "Mama and the Hospital."

PAPA (*delighted*). You write about Mama?

KATRIN. Yes.

MAMA. But I thought . . . I thought you say . . . I tell you . . . (*She gestures at* PAPA, *behind his back.*)

KATRIN. I know, Mama, but . . . well, that's how it came out.

[DAGMAR *comes in.*]

DAGMAR. What is it? What do you want?

MAMA. Katrin write story for magazine. They pay her five hundred dollar to print it.

DAGMAR (*completely uninterested*). Oh. (*She starts back for the pantry.*)

MAMA (*stopping her*). She read it to us. I want you should listen. You are ready, Katrin?

KATRIN. Sure.

MAMA. Then read.

[*The group around the table is now a duplicate of the grouping around* MR. HYDE *in the first scene, with* KATRIN *in his place.*]

KATRIN (*reading*). "For as long as I could remember, the house on Steiner Street had been home. All of us were born there. Nels, the oldest and the only boy . . ." (NELS *looks up, astonished to be in a story.*) "my sister Christine . . ." (CHRISTINE *does likewise.*) "and the littlest sister, Dagmar. . . ."

DAGMAR. Am I in the story?

MAMA. Hush, Dagmar. We are all in the story.

KATRIN. "But first and foremost, I remember Mama."

[*The lights begin to dim and the curtain slowly to fall. As it descends, we hear her voice continuing.*]

"I remember that every Saturday night Mama would sit down by the kitchen table and count out the money Papa had brought home in the little envelope. . . ."

[*By now, the curtain is down.*]

THE END

AFTERWORD

Any kind of storytelling asks the reader to believe that what is being told is really true. A good writer can make you believe even if you try not to. In real life things do not usually happen in the neat and orderly way that they do in stories and plays. In between short periods of excitement there are usually long periods that are ordinary and even boring. When any of us tells about our experiences we leave things out. If we do not our listeners will tell us to "hurry up and get on with the story."

I Remember Mama covers a period of more than a year in the life of the Hanson family who lived in San Francisco about fifty years ago. The play begins and ends with Katrin reading the beginning of a story she has written. In this way the playwright lets you know several things:

First, this is a story about a girl's growing up.

Secondly, it shows that part of the business of growing up has to do with her choosing and staying with a career as a writer.

Thirdly, and just as important, it is the story of family life that is just the same today as it was fifty years ago.

Finally, through the story we meet several people, some of them are likable and some are not, but they are all real people, perhaps like our own neighbors and relatives.

I Remember Mama is not an adventure story in the same way that *The White Company* or *Treasure Island* is. But it does show that ordinary people are sometimes wonderful. It shows that everyday family life and everyday family problems can be just as important as great adventures. Lastly, this play shows that there is often something very special about ordinary people.

We hear a great deal about Uncle Chris before he comes on stage. When he does appear he behaves just as we expect him to. He is loud, almost a bully. The children are afraid of him, but we learn immediately that he is as kind and practical as Mama herself. But Uncle Chris is mysterious. No one knows just where he lives. His relatives all think he has lots of money. The Aunts, Sigrid and Jenny, do not like him or his Woman, as they call his wife. He is the head of the family, that is, of all the relatives because he is the oldest man. He makes all the big decisions, but he is still an outsider.

He is a strange man. He drinks too much, but we learn this is because he has a lame leg that hurts him very much. He is loud and bossy and he has a darker complexion than most Norwegians. Yet we know almost immediately that he is a good man. Near the end of the play, after he has died, we learn that he has spent all of his money helping children who have had trouble with their legs. This is why he knows so much about doctors and hospitals. He brought so many sick children to them. Remember how Mama reads from his little notebook the names of the children he has helped and how much he paid for their medical care? After each name were the words "walks now."

Uncle Chris, in his own odd way, was trying to make the world a better and a happier place to live in. When Peter Thorkelson finally gets up enough courage to speak to him about Trina's dowry, Uncle Chris shows him that this old country way is not right. Peter must love Trina for herself and not for the money she might bring him. But Peter probably would never have even thought of the dowry if Sigrid and Jenny had not suggested it to him.

It is Mama, of course, who holds the family together. It is her character that really makes the play. We see her actively helping the children to grow up as independent and fair-minded people. She keeps the family and the relatives together even more than Uncle Chris does. In fact, she seems to be the only one he really respects. She helps anyone who asks for or needs help. But, most important, she helps each child and adult to become what each wants most to be.

You can see this most clearly in what happens to Katrin. She wants to write stories for magazines. Her teachers tell her that she has talent. Like many girls she tends to be "dramatic." Although her teachers tell her that she ought to write about what she knows best, she wants to write stories about strange people in other times and places. The ideas she likes best seem to come out of books and not out of her own experience.

When Katrin is discouraged because no magazine will buy her stories, Mama takes them to Miss Florence Dana Moorhead. This professional writer reads the stories when Mama offers her some prize recipes. Mama is told what the teachers had told Katrin. She can write good stories, but she should write about the things she knows best. Katrin is able to take this advice because she had really begun to grow up. And perhaps it is easier because the advice came from someone who was doing what she hoped to do herself someday.

It is interesting to see what the playwright has done with Katrin's problem. It takes most of the play for her to solve it—with Mama's help, of course. And then there is Nels's problem. He wants to go to high school. Fifty years ago this was not automatic. Not everyone could go to high school and it cost quite a bit of money too. Although the whole family was willing to make sacrifices to send him, he realizes that it is his problem mainly. He gets a part-time job.

There are other problems. Some of them simple and even silly. Dagmar wants to keep the alley cat. Some of the problems are very serious. Trina wants to get married. Dagmar has to have an operation. And, of course, the family always needs more money. In fact, money difficulties are in the background of the whole play. We see this in the first scene where Mama is dividing Papa's wages to pay the family debts. We see this again when she takes the "Little Bank" from the dresser to see if there is enough money to allow Nels to go to high school. We see this each time Mama speaks about *the* Bank. This seems to be a mysterious place downtown where people can go when they need financial help.

It is important to remember that Mama's bank account is an imaginary one. It was really a kind of myth. Perhaps it was Mama's way of saying that she believed that problems can always be solved if you understand what causes them and if you think hard enough and plan carefully enough to solve them.

We see Mr. Hyde only twice and for a very short time. He is a likable man even though he is not very honest. When he leaves the Hanson's house after giving Papa a bad check, Aunt Jenny is happy because she feels that she has been proven to be right. She says, "Your Mr. Hyde was a crook, just as I always thought he was, for all his reading and fine ways." But Mama has a different opinion of him. It does not matter about the check, she says, "He pay with better things than money." And of course he did. He brought pleasure to the whole family. We can be pretty sure that it was his reading that inspired Katrin to want to become a writer. The list of books he left for the children was another kind of "bank account." *The Pickwick Papers* and *A Tale of Two Cities, Treasure Island, Alice In Wonderland, The Last of the Mohicans, Ivanhoe, The Oxford Book of Verse,* and Shakespeare—all this is a great treasure. You must understand that this happened long before the days of radio, the movies, and television. Books were almost the only means of having entertainment in the home. Yes, Mr. Hyde paid his room rent in something more valuable than money. On the stage his part is played by a man with a very fine voice.

The part of Papa is not a very big part, but it is important. Even though he is in the background most of the time, we always know that he is a strong, firm, honest, and responsible father. Mama may be the great problem-solver, but Papa is the quiet and steady head of his family.

Sometimes a writer will take a simple happening and make it mean something very important. Mama chloroforms the poor battered cat to put it out of its misery. The next morning she and Papa expect to find a dead cat. They are upset when Dagmar rushes behind the curtain and comes out with the animal. They are amazed to find it alive and wriggling.

Dagmar thinks that Mama has done something wonderful again, as she always seems to be doing. Mama wants to tell her the truth because, as she tells Papa, "Is not good to let her grow up believing I can fix everything."

Now in this scene the playwright is doing more than just telling a good story. By showing that the cat can recover from a terrible hurt, he is saying that the family can recover from its troubles too. In fact, if you read carefully, you can sometimes find these extra meanings that writers put into their plays and stories.

Think about these scenes; they have more than one meaning:

Old Uncle Chris dies. We learn that he was a very good and kind man. A little while later a baby is born to Peter and Trina. We learn that Peter is a good and strong man too. He was a meek and timid man who has learned how to be brave and forceful.

Katrin is discouraged. Mama visits Miss Moorhead. She comes back home and tells Katrin what she has learned. The young girl suddenly learns what it means to begin to grow up.

Earlier, Mama had dressed up like a scrub woman and had gone to the hospital. She is able to get into Dagmar's room for a minute. She knows that in times like that a little girl is frightened and needs to know her mother is close by. Mama breaks a hospital rule, but she too "pays in something better than money." We can be sure that she cleaned the hospital floors better than they had ever been cleaned.

Now, you can argue about what other meanings these scenes have, but they do make you think about more than just the story itself. After all, things like this can happen in the life of almost any family during a year. Yet, when this kind of a story is put on a stage, these events are seen more clearly than they would be in real life. In fact we can use a word from the theater to describe what happens to them. They are *highlighted*. They stand out. They are given additional meaning.

Both Mr. Van Druten and Miss Forbes use this story of a family in order to say something important about life itself. Notice that the first and last words of the play are exactly the same. The first time we hear them (or read them) they mean only and exactly what they say. When you hear them again at the end of the play, what do these words do to your imagination? Do you think again of the whole play? Do you think that some things in life seem to happen again and again? Do you wonder how Katrin actually wrote her story? Do you try to think of reasons why the playwright put those words just where he did?

You may think any and all of these things. You will probably have other ideas as well. What is important is that besides enjoying the play, you will be searching for more meaning and for a better understanding of what you have read and experienced. After all, our own experiences are always limited to what can happen to one person. And the younger we are, the less experience we have. Through reading we can share wider experiences than we could otherwise have. We can learn a great deal about people and about life and we can learn this in a safe and comfortable way. This is what makes all reading more enjoyable.

STUDY QUESTIONS

1. Seeing a play and reading a play are quite different experiences. Explain the differences. Can you think of any advantages that reading a play has over seeing it?

2. In order to get the most out of reading a play, what should the reader try to do as he reads?

3. It is clear that Mama is the outstanding person in both her immediate family and the larger family of relatives. What qualities did she have that made everyone respect her, love her, and need her?

4. *I Remember Mama* is about family life. What was it that made the life of the Hansons a good and mainly a happy one?

5. Much of the interest and suspense of the play arises from the question of how different problems are to be solved. What were the main problems faced by the Hanson family? Can you mention at least one problem for each character in the play? What are some problems that are faced by many families that the Hansons did not have?

6. What is a hero? Are there any heroes or heroines in this play? Explain.

7. Mr. Hyde is unsuccessful and dishonest. Yet you like him. How do you explain this?

8. What does Mama mean when she says, "I would like to be rich the way I would like to be ten feet high. Would be good for some things—bad for others"? What did the richness of the Hanson family consist of?

9. You remember the episode of the graduation gift. How does Katrin show herself to be selfish and immature during this episode? Why does Papa allow her to have a cup of coffee at the end of the episode?

10. Uncle Chris is a strange and difficult man. He frightens both adults and children. How do you know that he is a good man? When do you first begin to feel that he's more good than bad?

11. How does Uncle Chris persuade Mr. Thorkelson not to insist on a dowry before marrying Aunt Trina?

12. Why do you think Dr. Johnson gave orders that under no circumstances was Uncle Chris to be given information about Dagmar in the hospital?

13. How do Christine and Katrin react after Dagmar is taken to the hospital? What does this show about the kind of girl each of them is? Do you think one of them felt more deeply than the other?

14. Who is the most self-righteous character in the play? Does this person have any reason for feeling self-righteous? Do you find anything likable about this person?

15. What ruse does Mama use to get in to visit Dagmar in the hospital? Do you think what she did was dishonest? When Mama says on page 734, "Comes a time when you've got to get down on your knees," what does she mean? Do the words have more than one meaning?

16. What do you think of the poem which Katrin writes while waiting in the hospital? Why do you think Kathryn Forbes put it in her book?

17. What advice about writing does Florence Dana Moorhead give to Katrin by way of her mother? Did the advice work for Katrin? Do you think it's good advice for yourself when you have to write? Why?

18. How does Mama persuade Florence Dana Moorhead to read Katrin's stories?

19. Why does Mama ask Katrin to look at Uncle Chris after he has died?

20. What was Mama's Bank Account? Why did she let the children think the family had money in the bank? *Mama's Bank Account* is the title of the original book. Does this show you anything about what Miss Forbes thought was important about the story?

21. This play, and the original book, *Mama's Bank Account,* are based on real events, and yet undoubtedly the events in real life did not occur just as they are portrayed in the play. Tell which events in the play seem to you to be absolutely real and which you think were probably invented. What are some differences between real life and the sort of life shown here on the stage?

22. What device does John Van Druten use to begin the play and to end it? Why does he use exactly the same lines at the start and at the finish? Do the lines impress you differently the first time and the second time they are used? Explain.

23. The play is a mixture of humor and sadness. Can you find places where, on a single page, the reader—or the audience—might laugh and then cry, almost at the same moment? Do you think the author did well to mix humor and sadness?

24. The play moves so fast and smoothly that you may not realize that it is divided into several scenes in each act. How many scenes are there in Act I? in Act II?